D0397128

ARCHER AT LARGE

Three Exciting Novels

THE GALTON CASE

THE CHILL

BLACK MONEY

ЛЛЛЛЛ

ARCHER

AT LARGE

by Ross Macdonald

With a Foreword by the Author

NEW YORK: *Alfred • A • Knopf*

Contents

FOREWORD

PEOPLE often ask me when and how I became a professional writer. I think I can say when. How, and possibly why, may emerge in the telling.

In early June of 1939, in Toronto, I was a student teacher with no money and a very pregnant wife. I left Margaret at home one afternoon in order to hear Lord Tweedsmuir deliver a high school graduation address. Lord Tweedsmuir was the Governor-General of Canada at that time, but the reason I went to hear him was that he was also John Buchan, the author of *The Thirty-nine Steps*.

He turned out to be a small, bright-eyed Scot who wore the mantle of empire easily. At the climax of his speech he told the graduating seniors the old story of the race between the hare and the tortoise. But he told it with a difference. The hare fooled around a good deal while the slow dependable tortoise stuck to the course and never even looked up. Still the hare won easily. Lord Tweedsmuir drew the moral that the race is not always to the slow.

About this time I won a typewriter on a radio quiz show and started immediately to write for publication. I like to think that the Governor-General inspired me; but like most other would-be writers I drew on more mundane sources of inspiration. Though I had a teaching job waiting in the fall at my old high school in Kitchener, Margaret and I had nothing to live on between June and September. My wife's approaching confinement and the prospective hospital bill made the situation urgent.

If I had been a genuine hare, I'd have dashed off a detective novel in about three weeks, sent it to the biggest publisher in New York, and got an immediate acceptance by telegram. (A year or so later Margaret did just that.) I aimed lower, at tortoise level, writing a flock of short stories and sketches for quickly available Toronto markets, most of which were so-called Sunday School papers paying a cent a word. I made over a hundred dollars the first few weeks, and with this blessed wad of cash ransomed my wife and infant daughter out of the Women's College Hospital. I was a pro.

Our lives changed rapidly in the next five years. Margaret became a full-fledged novelist. I left high school teaching to accept a fellowship at the University of Michigan, and moved my family to the United States, where I was born. In June 1944, when my first novel was published (*The Dark Tunnel*, a novel of espionage suggested by my own experiences in Nazi Germany but showing the influence of John Buchan) I was an ensign in the U.S. Naval Reserve. When I was released from service, as I recorded in the introduction to *Archer in Hollywood*, I settled down in my native state, in Santa Barbara, and became a California crime novelist.

Ten years and ten novels later, seismic disturbances occurred in my life. My half-suppressed Canadian years, my whole childhood and youth, rose like a corpse from the bottom of the sea to confront me. Margaret and I moved to the Bay area for a year, settling not many miles from my birthplace in Los Gatos. There I went through belated mental growing pains, trying to understand the peculiar shape of my life.

The inner shape of a man's life, if he is a man of action, plots the curve of his movements. If he is a writer, it is what he writes from and about. But it remains as personal and hidden as his skeleton, just as intricate, almost as unchangeable.

Since I couldn't change the shape of my life, I decided to make the best of it. In the summer of 1957 Margaret and I returned to Santa Barbara and rented a house on a cliff which overlooked the sea. A further advantage of the neighborhood was that the English poet Donald Davie was living nearby. We became friends, and I learned that Davie was working on the epic theme of a lost father. After my year's immersion in memories of my own past, a similar theme was growing in my mind.

The theme developed through the fall and winter. (It's fall on the California coast when migrating sea birds move in dark skeins across the blue water; we call it winter when it rains a bit.) As I sat in my study looking out over the sea, I was conscious that a few hundred yards away along the cliff, Davie was writing his epic poem. His working presence nerved me to commit a legend of my own to paper, and I wrote what I considered a breakthrough novel, *The Galton Case*.

What did it break through into? My early years in Canada, for one thing. I hardly knew my father. My mother and I lived, when we were lucky, on the charity of her mother and her sister. They were good women (Aunt Adeline, who paid for my education, was a Stoic saint) but in their puritanical household I felt both surrounded and displaced. I was my wandering father's son, after all, and my mother's female relatives could hardly help discerning on my brow the mark of the paternal curse.

One of the things that supported me through my long Canadian childhood was the knowledge, which my mother insisted on, that I was an American citizen by birth. But for good or ill my early days made a Canadian out of me as well. I ended up split along emotional and political lines which neatly corresponded. My sense of self and my sense of territory were both askew.

The Galton Case goes into some of these matters. It doesn't tell the naked truth, of course. It broke free of my actual life and my rather murky feelings, into the clearer and more ordered world where fiction lays out its concentrated, terrifying versions of the truth. Fiction, when it is working well, lifts out of the writer's life patterns which tend toward the legendary. But the patterns are disrupted and authenticated by bits and pieces of the original life-stuff—names and places, scraps of conversation, old feelings and forces like spawning salmon working their way back up the stream of time.

A central figure in *The Galton Case* is a nameless boy who has taken the name of John (my father's name). When this fictional John made his way to Ann Arbor and entered the University of Michigan, he was following in my footsteps. John and I had other things in common. We shared a sense of displacement, a feeling that, no matter where we were, we were on the alien side of some border. We felt like dubious claimants to a lost inheritance.

Still, any novel worth writing has a strong positive aspect, conforming to and filling out the shape of the novelist's life. Writing is an action as well as a passion. In writing *The Galton Case* and mastering its materials, I felt an exhilaration which I hope the book communicates to its readers. For me, in its indirect way, it stated and made good the right to my inheritance as an American citizen and writer, while bringing into unsparing view the poverty and brokenness of my worst days.

I was a real pro now—a writer who would do anything within his power to make his stories true in essence, and his own.

If my idea of fiction seems too personal and special, let me adjust it. In the red Spiral notebook where I made my original jottings for *The Galton Case*, I can still find this short note: "Oedipus angry vs. parents for sending him away into a foreign country." The reader will remember that when the legendary Oedipus was born, it was foretold that he would kill his father; so his parents sent him away to be raised by peasants. My novel was shaped not in imitation exactly, but in awareness of such early Greek models.

The Chill, which continued my modern Oedipean legend, was written five years later. Margaret and I had bought a house in a canyon and moved inland. The air was warm and dry there. The narrow sky was laced with trees and interlaced with swallows. I went through an illness and felt like a lucky survivor, ready to shake hands with any skeleton or look any Medusa in the eye.

But *The Chill*, that basilisk of a book, was not easy to write. The opening two or three chapters took several months and went through seven or eight versions. I had my central idea, perhaps one of the stronger single plot ideas that ever came to me. But I found that I had to imagine the whole development of the book before I could write an assured opening chapter. Gradually, as my pen moved uncertainly across the lined pages of my notebooks, memory and invention wove a fabric of related lives which stretched from California (where Archer always begins) to Reno and Illinois.

The Chill is too recent for me to play the critic with. And if I were to write about it in any detail it would tend to pad the jolt which I am told the book delivers.

As I look over such later books as *The Chill* and *Black Money*, I'm struck by obvious changes in my work. When I took up the hardboiled novel, beginning in 1946 with *Blue City*, I was writing in reaction against a number of things, among them my strict academic background. The world of gamblers and gunmen and crooked politicians and their floozies seemed realer somehow, more central to experience, than the cool university life I knew.

In these later books, the academic life keeps creeping back in. Its privileged upper world, like the sub-world of professional crime, does have of course its plots and counterplots, its knifings and its bloodless assassinations, its politicians and players for high stakes, its guilty lover. And the campus, which seemed in my prewar youth to have a seductive lingering medieval unreality, has become where it is at.

In *Black Money*, the corruptions of the world invade a college campus and make themselves at home there. Perhaps because its binocular view includes in a single pattern the pits of Las Vegas and the groves of academe, some academic reviewers have considered *Black Money* anti-academic. I'm afraid on the other hand it betrays how persistently academic my mind has remained through twenty-six years of detective-story writing. In either case, as university people become central figures in our society, they merit unsheltered treatment in fiction as in life. The lords of the military-industrial-academic complex may be as subject to tragic flaws as Shakespeare's kings.

The reader who comes to *Black Money* fresh from *The Galton Case* will notice similarities in structure, and in the central characters. The boy from Canada and the boy from Panama were intended to match and balance each other. But the world, or my vision of it, darkened in the seven years that elapsed between the two novels; and the Panamanian boy comes to a worse end.

I spent a short week in Panama in the spring of 1946, when my carrier was on its way to Boston to be mothballed. The visit left a deep impression on my mind. The life of Panama seemed to be angry and oppressed, under the shadow of imperial power.

The Canadian provinces lived in similar case when I was a boy, though we were almost unconscious of our condition. The imperial shadow on us was gray and fading, like an aging woman's influence. Our anger was muted and turned against ourselves. If we were not British subjects, what could we become?

The question is moot. The power of empire, becoming steadily more generous as it failed, has failed completely since the day I went to hear the Governor-General speak. The bright boys he encouraged are middle-aged. Tweedsmuir himself is long since dead, and he is mainly remembered under his other name, as the author of some good books. I hope the same thing will be true of me.

Ross Macdonald
Santa Barbara
September, 1969

THE
GALTON
CASE

1

THE law offices of Wellesley and Sable were over a savings bank on the main street of Santa Teresa. Their private elevator lifted you from a bare little lobby into an atmosphere of elegant simplicity. It created the impression that after years of struggle you were rising effortlessly to your natural level, one of the chosen.

Facing the elevator, a woman with carefully dyed red hair was toying with the keyboard of an electric typewriter. A bowl full of floating begonias sat on the desk in front of her. Audubon prints picked up the colors and tossed them discreetly around the oak walls. A Harvard chair stood casually in one corner.

I sat down on it, in the interests of self-improvement, and picked up a fresh copy of the *Wall Street Journal*. Apparently this was the right thing to do. The red-headed secretary stopped typing and condescended to notice me.

"Do you wish to see anyone?"

"I have an appointment with Mr. Sable."

"Would you be Mr. Archer?"

"Yes."

She relaxed her formal manner: I wasn't one of the chosen after all. "I'm Mrs. Haines. Mr. Sable didn't come into the office today, but he asked me to give you a message when you got here. Would you mind going out to his house?"

"I guess not." I got up out of the Harvard chair. It was like being expelled.

"I realize it's a nuisance," she said sympathetically. "Do you know how to reach his place?"

"Is he still in his beach cottage?"

"No, he gave that up when he got married. They built a house in the country."

"I didn't know he was married."

"Mr. Sable's been married for nearly two years now. Very much so."

The feline note in her voice made me wonder if she was married.

Though she called herself Mrs. Haines, she had the air of a woman who had lost her husband to death or divorce and was looking for a successor. She leaned toward me in sudden intimacy:

"You're the detective, aren't you?"

I acknowledged that I was.

"Is Mr. Sable hiring you personally, on his own hook? I mean, the reason I asked, he didn't say anything to me about it."

The reason for that was obvious. "Me, either," I said. "How do I get to his house?"

"It's out in Arroyo Park. Maybe I better show you on the map."

We had a brief session of map-reading. "You turn off the highway just before you get to the wye," she said, "and then you turn right here at the Arroyo Country Day School. You curve around the lake for about a half a mile, and you'll see the Sables' mailbox."

I found the mailbox twenty minutes later. It stood under an oak tree at the foot of a private road. The road climbed a wooded hill and ended at a house with many windows set under the overhang of a flat green gravel roof.

The front door opened before I got to it. A man with streaked gray hair growing low on his forehead came across the lawn to meet me. He wore the white jacket of domestic service, but even with this protective coloration he didn't fit into the expensive suburb. He carried his heavy shoulders jauntily, as if he was taking his body for a well-deserved walk.

"Looking for somebody, mister?"

"Mr. Sable sent for me."

"What for?"

"If he didn't tell you," I said, "the chances are that he doesn't want you to know."

The houseman came up closer to me and smiled. His smile was wide and raw, like a dog's grin, and meaningless, except that it meant trouble. His face was seamed with the marks of the trouble-prone. He invited violence, as certain other people invite friendship.

Gordon Sable called from the doorway: "It's all right, Peter. I'm expecting this chap." He trotted down the flagstone path and gave me his hand. "Good to see you, Lew. It's been several years, hasn't it?"

"Four."

Sable didn't look any older. The contrast of his tanned face with his wavy white hair somehow supported an illusion of youth. He had on a Madras shirt cinched in by formfitting English flannels which called attention to his tennis-player's waistline.

"I hear you got married," I said.

"Yes. I took the plunge." His happy expression seemed a little forced. He turned to the houseman, who was standing there listening: "You'd better see if Mrs. Sable needs anything. And then come out to my study. Mr. Archer's had a long drive, and he'll be wanting a drink."

"Yaas, massuh," the houseman said broadly.

Sable pretended not to notice. He led me into the house, along a black-and-white terrazzo corridor, across an enclosed court crowded with tropical plants whose massed colors were broken up and reflected by an oval pool in the center. Our destination was a sun-filled room remote from the rest of the house and further insulated by the hundreds of books lining its walls.

Sable offered me a leather chair facing the desk and the windows. He adjusted the drapes to shut off some of the light.

"Peter should be along in a minute. I'm afraid I must apologize for his manners, or lack of them. It's hard to get the right sort of help these days."

"I have the same trouble. The squares want security, and the hipsters want a chance to push people around at fifty dollars a day. Neither of which I can give them. So I still do most of my own work."

"I'm glad to hear that." Sable sat on the edge of the desk and leaned toward me confidentially: "The matter that I'm thinking of entrusting to you is a rather delicate one. It's essential, for reasons that will emerge, that there should be no publicity. Anything you find out, if you do find anything out, you report to me. Orally. I don't want anything in writing. Is that understood?"

"You make it very clear. Is this your personal business, or for a client?"

"For a client, of course. Didn't I say so on the telephone? She's saddled me with a rather difficult assignment. Frankly, I see very little chance of satisfying her hopes."

"What does she hope for?"

Sable lifted his eyes to the bleached beams of the ceiling. "The impossible, I'm afraid. When a man's dropped out of sight for over twenty years, we have to assume that he's dead and buried. Or, at the very least, that he doesn't want to be found."

"This is a missing-persons case, then?"

"A rather hopeless one, as I've tried to tell my client. On the other hand, I can't refuse to make an attempt to carry out her wishes. She's old, and ill, and used to having her own way."

"And rich?"

Sable frowned at my levity. He specialized in estate work, and moved in circles where money was seen but not heard.

"The lady's husband left her excellently provided for." He added, to put me in my place: "You'll be well paid for your work, no matter how it turns out."

The houseman came in behind me. I knew he was there by the change in the lighting. He wore old yachting sneakers, and moved without sound.

"You took your time," Sable said.

"Martinis take time to mix."

"I didn't order Martinis."

"The Mrs. did."

"You shouldn't be serving her Martinis before lunch, or any other time."

"Tell her that."

"I intend to. At the moment I'm telling you."

"Yaas, massuh."

Sable reddened under his tan. "That dialect bit isn't funny, you know."

The houseman made no reply. His green eyes were bold and restless. He looked down at me, as if for applause.

"Quite a servant problem you have," I said, by way of supporting Sable.

"Oh, Peter means well, don't you, old boy?" As if to foreclose an answer, he looked at me with a grin pasted on over his embarrassment. "What will you drink, Lew? I'm going to have a tonic."

"That will do for me."

The houseman retreated.

"What about this disappearance?" I said.

"Perhaps disappearance isn't exactly the right word. My client's son walked out on his family deliberately. They made no attempt to follow him up or bring him back, at least not for many years."

"Why not?"

"I gather they were just as dissatisfied with him as he was with them. They disapproved of the girl he'd married. 'Disapproved' is putting it mildly, and there were other bones of contention. You can see how serious the rift was from the fact that he sacrificed his right to inherit a large estate."

"Does he have a name, or do we call him Mr. X?"

Sable looked pained. It hurt him physically to divulge information. "The family's name is Galton. The son's name is, or was, Anthony Galton. He dropped out of sight in 1936. He was twenty-two at the time, just out of Stanford."

"That's a long time ago." From where I sat, it was like a previous century.

"I told you this thing was very nearly hopeless. However, Mrs. Galton wants her son looked for. She's going to die any day herself, and she feels the need for some sort of reconciliation with the past."

"Who says she's going to die?"

"Her doctor. Dr. Howell says it could happen at any time."

The houseman loped into the room with a clinking tray. He made a show of serviceability as he passed us our gin-and-tonics. I noticed the blue anchor tattoo on the back of his hand, and wondered if he was a sailor. Nobody would mistake him for a trained servant. A half-moon of old lipstick clung to the rim of the glass he handed me.

When he went away again, I said:

"Young Galton got married before he left?"

"Indeed he did. His wife was the immediate cause of the trouble in the family. She was going to have a child."

"And all three of them dropped out of sight?"

"As if the earth had opened and swallowed them," Sable said dramatically.

"Were there any indications of foul play?"

"Not so far as I know. I wasn't associated with the Galton family at the time. I'm going to ask Mrs. Galton herself to tell you about the circumstances of her son's departure. I don't know exactly how much of it she wants aired."

"Is there more to it?"

"I believe so. Well, cheers," he said cheerlessly. He gulped his drink standing. "Before I take you to see her, I'd like some assurance that you can give us your full time for as long as necessary."

"I have no commitments. How much of an effort does she want?"

"The best you can give, naturally."

"You might do better with one of the big organizations."

"I think not. I know you, and I trust you to handle this affair with some degree of urbanity. I can't have Mrs. Galton's last days darkened by scandal. My overriding concern in this affair is the protection of the family name."

Sable's voice throbbed with emotion, but I doubted that it was related to any deep feeling he had for the Galton family. He kept looking past me or through me, anxiously, as if his real concerns lay somewhere else.

I got some hint of what they were when we were on our way out. A pretty blond woman about half his age emerged from behind a banana tree in the court. She was wearing jeans and an open-necked white shirt. She moved with a kind of clumsy stealth, like somebody stepping out of ambush.

"Hello, Gordon," she said in a brittle voice. "Fancy meeting you here."

"I live here, don't I?"

"That was supposed to be the theory."

Sable spoke carefully to her, as if he was editing his sentences in his head: "Alice, this is no time to go into all of it again. Why do you think I stayed home this morning?"

"A lot of good it did me. Where do you think you're going now?"

"Out."

"Out where?"

"You have no right to cross-examine me, you know."

"Oh yes I have a right."

She stood squarely in front of him in a deliberately ugly posture, one hip out, her breasts thrust forward under the white shirt, at the same time sharp and tender. She didn't seem to be drunk, but there was a hot moist glitter in her eyes. Her eyes were large and violet, and should have been beautiful. With dark circles under them, and heavy eyeshadow on the upper lids, they were like two spreading bruises.

"Where are you taking my husband?" she said to me.

"Mr. Sable is doing the taking. It's a business matter."

"What sort of business, eh? Whose business?"

"Certainly not yours, dear." Sable put his arm around her. "Come to your room now. Mr. Archer is a private detective working on a case for me—nothing to do with you."

"I bet not." She jerked away from him, and swung back to me. "What do you want from me? There's nothing to find out. I sit in this morgue of a house, with nobody to talk to, nothing to do. I wish I was back in Chicago. People in Chicago *like* me."

"People here like you, too." Sable was watching her patiently, waiting for her bout of emotion to wear itself out.

"People here hate me. I can't even order drinks in my own house."

"Not in the morning, and this is why."

"You don't love me at all." Her anger was dissolving into self-pity. A shift of internal pressure forced tears from her eyes. "You don't care a thing about me."

"I care very much. Which is why I hate to see you fling yourself around the landscape. Come on, dear, let's go in."

He touched her waist, and this time she didn't resist. With one arm holding her, he escorted her around the pool to a door which opened on the court. When he closed the door behind them, she was leaning heavily on him.

I found my own way out.

2

SABLE kept me waiting for half an hour. From where I sat in my car, I could see Santa Teresa laid out like a contour map, distinct in the noon light. It was an old and settled city, as such things go in California. Its buildings seemed to belong to its hills, to lean with some security on the past. In contrast with them, Sable's house was a living-machine, so new it hardly existed.

When he came out, he was wearing a brown suit with a wicked little red pin stripe in it, and carrying a cordovan dispatch case. His manner had changed to match his change in costume. He was businesslike, brisk, and remote.

Following his instructions and his black Imperial, I drove into the city and across it to an older residential section. Massive traditional houses stood far back from the street, behind high masonry walls or topiary hedges.

Arroyo Park was an economic battleground where managers and professional people matched wits and incomes. The people on Mrs. Galton's street didn't know there had been a war. Their grandfathers or great-grandfathers had won it for them; death and taxes were all they had to cope with.

Sable made a signal for a left turn. I followed him between stone gateposts in which the name Galton was cut. The majestic iron gates gave a portcullis effect. A serf who was cutting the lawn with a power-mower paused to tug at his forelock as we went by. The lawn was the color of the ink they use to print the serial numbers on banknotes, and it stretched in unbroken smoothness for a couple of hundred yards. The white façade of a pre-Mizener Spanish mansion glared in the green distance.

The driveway curved around to the side of the house, and through a porte-cochere. I parked behind a Chevrolet coupé displaying a doctor's caduceus. Further back, in the shade of a great oak, two girls in shorts were playing badminton. The bird flew back and forth between them in flashing repartee. When the dark-headed girl with her back to us missed, she said:

"Oh, damn it!"

"Temper," Gordon Sable said.

She pivoted like a dancer. I saw that she wasn't a girl, but a woman with a girl's body. A slow blush spread over her face. She covered her discomfiture with an exaggerated pout which made the most of her girlishness:

"I'm off my form. Sheila *never* beats me."

"I do so!" cried the girl on the other side of the net. "I beat you three times in the last week. Today is the fourth time."

"The set isn't over yet."

"No, but I'm going to beat you." Sheila's voice had an intensity which didn't seem to go with her appearance. She was very young, no more than eighteen. She had a peaches-and-cream complexion and soft doe eyes.

The woman scooped up the bird and tossed it over the net. They went on playing, all out, as if a great deal depended on the game.

A Negro maid in a white cap let us into a reception room. Wrought-iron chandeliers hung like giant black bunches of withered grapes from the high ceiling. Ancient black furniture stood in museum arrangements around the walls under old dark pictures. The windows were narrow and deep in the thick walls, like the windows of a medieval castle.

"Is Dr. Howell with her?" Sable asked the maid.

"Yes, sir, but he ought to be leaving any time now. He's been here for quite a while."

"She didn't have an attack?"

"No, sir. It's just the doctor's regular visit."

"Would you tell him I'd like to see him before he leaves?"

"Yes, sir."

She whisked away. Sable said in a neutral tone, without looking at me: "I won't apologize for my wife. You know how women are."

"Uh-huh." I didn't really want his confidences.

If I had, he wouldn't have given them to me. "There are certain South American tribes that segregate women one week out of the month. Shut them up in a hut by themselves and let them rip. There's quite a lot to be said for the system."

"I can see that."

"Are you married, Archer?"

"I have been."

"Then you know what it's like. They want you with them all the time. I've given up yachting. I've given up golf. I've practically given up living. And still she isn't satisfied. What do you do with a woman like that?"

I'd given up offering advice. Even when people asked for it, they resented getting it. "You're the lawyer."

I strolled around the room and looked at the pictures on the walls. They were mostly ancestor-worship art: portraits of Spanish dons, ladies in hoop skirts with bare monolithic bosoms, a Civil War officer in blue, and several gentlemen in nineteenth-century suits with sour nineteenth-century pusses between their whiskers. The one I liked best depicted a group of top-hatted tycoons watching a bulldog-faced tycoon hammer a gold spike into a railroad tie. There was a buffalo in the background, looking sullen.

The maid returned with a man in Harris tweeds. Sable introduced him as Dr. Howell. He was a big man in his fifties, who carried himself with unconscious authority.

"Mr. Archer is a private investigator," Sable said. "Did Mrs. Galton mention what she has in mind?"

"Indeed she did." The doctor ran his fingers through his gray crewcut. The lines in his forehead deepened. "I thought that whole business of Tony was finished and forgotten years ago. Who persuaded her to drag it back into the light?"

"Nobody did, so far as I know. It was her own idea. How is she, Doctor?"

"As well as can be expected. Maria is in her seventies. She has a heart. She has asthma. It's an unpredictable combination."

"But there's no immediate danger?"

"I wouldn't think so. I can't say what will happen if she's subjected to shock or distress. Asthma is one of those things."

"Psychosomatic, you mean?"

"Somatopsychic, whatever you want to call it. In any case it's a disease that's affected by the emotions. Which is why I hate to see Maria getting all stirred up again about that wretched son of hers. What does she hope to gain?"

"Emotional satisfaction, I suppose. She feels she treated him badly, and wants to make up for it."

"But isn't he dead? I thought he was found to be legally dead."

"He could have been. We had an official search made some years ago. He'd already been missing for fourteen years, which is twice the time required by the law to establish presumption of death. Mrs. Galton wouldn't let me make the petition, however. I think she's always dreamed of Anthony coming back to claim his inheritance and all that. In the last few weeks it's become an obsession with her."

"I wouldn't go that far," the doctor said. "I still think somebody put a bee in her bonnet, and I can't help wondering why."

"Who do you have in mind?"

"Cassie Hildreth, perhaps. She has a lot of influence on Maria. And speaking of dreams, she had a few of her own when she was a kid. She used to follow Tony around as if he was the light of the world. Which he was far from being, as you know." Howell's smile was one-sided and saturnine.

"This is news to me. I'll talk to Miss Hildreth."

"It's pure speculation on my part, don't misunderstand me. I do think this business should be played down as much as possible."

"I've been trying to play it down. On the other hand I can't downright refuse to lift a finger."

"No, but it would be all to the good if you could just keep it going along, without any definite results, until she gets interested in something different." The doctor included me in his shrewd glance. "You understand me?"

"I understand you all right," I said. "Go through the motions but don't do any real investigating. Isn't that pretty expensive therapy?"

"She can afford it, if that's what worries you. Maria has more coming in every month than she spends every year." He regarded me in silence for a moment, stroking his prow of a nose. "I don't mean you shouldn't do your job. I wouldn't ask any man to lie down on a job he's paid to do. But if you find out anything that might upset Mrs. Galton—"

Sable put in quickly: "I've already taken that up with Archer. He'll report to me. I think you know you can rely on my discretion."

"I think I know I can."

Sable's face changed subtly. His eyelids flickered as though he had been threatened with a blow, and remained heavy over his watchful eyes. For a man of his age and financial weight, he was very easily hurt.

I said to the doctor: "Did you know Anthony Galton?"

"Somewhat."

"What kind of person was he?"

Howell glanced toward the maid, who was still waiting in the doorway. She caught his look and withdrew out of sight. Howell lowered his voice:

"Tony was a sport. I mean that in the biological sense, as well as the sociological. He didn't inherit the Galton characteristics. He had utter contempt for business of any kind. Tony used to say he wanted to be a writer, but I never saw any evidence of talent. What he was really good at was boozing and fornicating. I gather he ran with a very rough crowd in San Francisco. I've always believed myself that one of them killed him for the money in his pockets and threw him in the Bay."

"Was there any indication of that sort of thing?"

"Not to my certain knowledge. But San Francisco in the thirties was a dangerous place for a boy to play around in. He must have dredged pretty deep to turn up the girl he married."

"You knew her, did you?" Sable said.

"I examined her. His mother sent her to me, and I examined her."

"Was she here in town?" I said.

"Briefly. Tony brought her home the week he married her. I don't believe he had any notion the family would accept her. It was more a case of flinging her in their faces. If that was his idea, it succeeded very well."

"What was the matter with the girl?"

"The obvious thing, and it was obvious—she was seven months' pregnant."

"And you say they'd just been married?"

"That's correct. She hooked him. I talked with her a little, and I'd wager he picked her up, hot off the streets. She was a pretty enough little thing, in spite of her big belly, but she'd had a hard life. There were scars on her thighs and buttocks. She wouldn't explain them to me, but it was evident that she'd been beaten, more than once." The cruel memory raised faint traces of scarlet on the doctor's cheekbones.

The doe-eyed girl from the badminton court appeared in the doorway behind him. Her body was like ripening fruit, only partly concealed by her sleeveless jersey and rolled shorts. She glowed with healthy beauty, but her mouth was impatient:

"Daddy? How much longer?"

The color on his cheekbones heightened when he saw her. "Roll down your pants, Sheila."

"They're not pants."

"Whatever they are, roll them down."

"Why should I?"

"Because I'm telling you to."

"You could at least tell me in private. How much longer do I have to wait?"

"I thought you were going to read to your Aunt Maria."

"Well, I'm not."

"You promised."

"You were the one who promised for me. I played badminton with Cassie, and that's my good turn for the day."

She moved away, deliberately exaggerating the swing of her hips. Howell glared at the chronometer on his wrist, as if it was the source of all his troubles. "I must be getting along. I have other calls to make."

"Can you give me the wife's description?" I said. "Or her name?"

"I don't recall her name. As for appearance, she was a little blue-eyed brunette, rather thin in spite of her condition. Mrs. Galton—no, on second thought I wouldn't ask her about the girl unless she brings the matter up herself."

The doctor turned to go, but Sable detained him: "Is it all right for Mr. Archer to question her? I mean, it won't affect her heart or bring on an asthmatic attack?"

"I can't guarantee it. If Maria insists on having an attack, there's nothing I can do to prevent it. Seriously, though, if Tony's on her mind she might as well talk about him. It's better than sitting and brooding. Good-by, Mr. Archer, nice to meet you. Good day, Sable."

3
.

THE maid took Sable and me to a sitting-room on the second floor where Mrs. Galton was waiting. The room smelled of medicine, and had a hushed hospital atmosphere. The heavy drapes were partly drawn over the windows. Mrs. Galton was resting in semi-twilight on a chaise longue, with a robe over her knees.

She was fully dressed, with something white and frilly at her withered throat; and she held her gray head ramrod straight. Her voice was reedy, but surprisingly resonant. It seemed to carry all the remaining force of her personality:

"You've kept me waiting, Gordon. It's nearly time for my lunch. I expected you before Dr. Howell came."

"I'm awfully sorry, Mrs. Galton. I was delayed at home."

"Don't apologize. I detest apologies, they're really just further demands on one's patience." She cocked a bright eye at him. "Has that wife of yours been giving you trouble again?"

"Oh, no, nothing of that sort."

"Good. You know my thoughts on the subject of divorce. On the other hand, you should have taken my advice and not married her. A man who waits until he's nearly fifty to get married should give up the idea entirely. Mr. Galton was in his late forties when we were married. As a direct consequence, I've had to endure nearly twenty years of widowhood."

"It's been hard, I know," Sable said with unction.

The maid had started out of the room. Mrs. Galton called her back: "Wait a minute. I want you to tell Miss Hildreth to bring me my lunch herself. She can bring up a sandwich and eat it with me if she likes. You tell Miss Hildreth that."

"Yes, Mrs. Galton."

The old lady waved us into chairs, one on each side of her, and turned her eye on me. It was bright and alert but somehow inhuman, like a bird's eye. It looked at me as if I belonged to an entirely different species:

"Is this the man who is going to find my prodigal son for me?"

"Yes, this is Mr. Archer."

"I'm going to give it a try," I said, remembering the doctor's advice. "I can't promise any definite results. Your son has been missing for a very long time."

"I'm better aware of that than you, young man. I last set eyes on Anthony on the eleventh day of October 1936. We parted in bitter anger and hatred. I've lived ever since with that anger and hatred corroding my heart. But I can't die with it inside of me. I want to see Anthony again, and talk to him. I want to forgive him. I want him to forgive me."

Deep feeling sounded in her voice. I had no doubt that the feeling was partly sincere. Still, there was something unreal about it. I suspected that she'd been playing tricks with her emotions for a long time, until none of them was quite valid.

"Forgive you?" I said.

"For treating him as I did. He was a young fool, and he made some disastrous mistakes, but none of them really justified Mr. Galton's action, and mine, in casting him off. It was a shameful action, and if it's not too late I intend to rectify it. If he still has his little wife, I'm willing to accept her. I authorize you to tell him that. I want to see my grandchild before I die."

I looked at Sable. He shook his head slightly, deprecatingly. His client was just a little out of context, but she had quick insight, at least into other people:

"I know what you're both thinking. You're thinking that Anthony is dead. If he were dead, I'd know it here." Her hand strayed over the flat silk surface of her breast. "He's my only son. He must be alive, and he must be somewhere. Nothing is lost in the universe."

Except human beings, I thought. "I'll do my best, Mrs. Galton. There are one or two things you can do to help me. Give me a list of his friends at the time of his disappearance."

"I never knew his friends."

"He must have had friends in college. Wasn't he attending Stanford?"

"He'd left there the previous spring. He didn't even wait to graduate. Anyway, none of his schoolmates knew what happened to him. His father canvassed them thoroughly at the time."

"Where was your son living after he left college?"

"In a flat in the slums of San Francisco. With that woman."

"Do you have the address?"

"I believe I may have it somewhere. I'll have Miss Hildreth look for it."

"That will be a start, anyway. When he left here with his wife, did they plan to go back to San Francisco?"

"I haven't any idea. I didn't see them before they left."

"I understood they came to visit you."

"Yes, but they didn't even stay the night."

"What might help most," I said carefully, "would be if you could tell me the exact circumstances of their visit, and their departure. Anything your son said about his plans, anything the girl said, anything you remember about her. Do you remember her name?"

"He called her Teddy. I have no idea if that was her name or not. We had very little conversation. I can't recall what was said. The atmosphere was unpleasant, and it left a bad taste in my mouth. *She* left a bad taste in my mouth. It was so evident that she was a cheap little gold-digger."

"How do you know?"

"I have eyes. I have ears." Anger had begun to whine in the undertones of her voice. "She was dressed and painted like a woman of the streets, and when she opened her mouth—well, she spoke the language of the streets. She made coarse jokes about the child in her womb, and how"—her voice faded almost out—"it got there. She had no respect for herself as a woman, no moral standards. That girl destroyed my son."

She'd forgotten all about her hope of reconciliation. The angry wheezing in the passages of her head sounded like a ghost in a ruined house. Sable was looking at her anxiously, but he held his tongue.

"Destroyed him?" I said.

"Morally, she destroyed him. She possessed him like an evil spirit. My son would never have taken the money if it hadn't been for the spell she cast on him. I know that with utter certitude."

Sable leaned forward in his chair. "What money are you referring to?"

"The money Anthony stole from his father. Haven't I told you about it, Gordon? No, I don't believe I have. I've told no one, I've always been so ashamed." She lifted her hands and dropped them in her robed lap. "But now I can forgive him for that, too."

"How much money was involved?" I said.

"I don't know exactly how much, to the penny. Several thousand dollars, anyway. Ever since the day the banks closed, Mr. Galton had had a habit of keeping a certain amount of cash for current expenses."

"Where did he keep it?"

"In his private safe, in the study. The combination was on a piece of paper pasted to the inside of his desk drawer. Anthony must have found it there, and used it to open the safe. He took everything in it, all the money, and even some of my jewels which I kept there."

"Are you sure he took it?"

"Unfortunately, yes. It disappeared at the same time he did. It's why he hid himself away, and never came back to us."

Sable's glum look deepened. Probably he was thinking the same thing I was: that several thousand dollars in cash, in the slums of San Francisco, in the depths of the depression, were a very likely passport to oblivion.

But we couldn't say it out loud. With her money, and her asthma, and her heart, Mrs. Galton was living at several removes from reality. Apparently that was how it had to be.

"Do you have a picture of your son, taken not too long before his disappearance?"

"I believe I have. I'll ask Cassie to have a look. She should be coming soon."

"In the meantime, can you give me any other information? Particularly about where your son might have gone, who or where he might have visited."

"I know nothing of his life after he left the university. He cut himself off from all decent society. He was perversely bound to sink in the social scale, to declass himself. I'm afraid my son had a *nostalgie de la boue*—a nostalgia for the gutter. He tried to cover it over with fancy talk about re-establishing contact with the earth, becoming a poet of the people, and such nonsense. His real interest was dirt for dirt's own sake. I brought him up to be pure in thought and desire,

but somehow—somehow he became fascinated with the pitch that de-
fileth. And the pitch defiled him."

Her breathing was noisy. She had begun to shake, and scratch with
waxy fingers at the robe that covered her knees.

Sable leaned toward her solicitously. "You mustn't excite yourself,
Mrs. Galton. It was all over long ago."

"It's not all over. I want Anthony back. I have nobody. I have nothing. He was stolen away from me."

"We'll get him back if it's humanly possible."

"Yes, I know you will, Gordon." Her mood had changed like a fitful
wind. Her head inclined toward Sable's shoulder as though to rest
against it. She spoke like a little girl betrayed by time and loss, by fading
hair and wrinkles and the fear of death: "I'm a foolish angry old
woman. You're always so good to me. Anthony will be good to me, too,
won't he, when he comes? In spite of all I've said against him, he was
a darling boy. He was always good to his poor mother, and he will be
again."

She was chanting in a ritual of hope. If she said it often enough,
it would have to come true.

"I'm sure he will, Mrs. Galton."

Sable rose and pressed her hand. I was always a little suspicious of
men who put themselves out too much for rich old ladies, or even poor
ones. But then it was part of his job.

"I'm hungry," she said. "I want my lunch. What's going on downstairs?"

She lunged half out of her long chair and got hold of a wired bellpush on the table beside it. She kept her finger pressed on the button
until her lunch arrived. That was a tense five minutes.

4

IT CAME on a covered platter carried by the woman I'd seen on the
badminton court. She had changed her shorts for a plain linen dress

which managed to conceal her figure, if not her fine brown legs. Her blue eyes were watchful.

"You kept me waiting, Cassie," the old woman said. "What on earth were you doing?"

"Preparing your food. Before that I played some badminton with Sheila Howell."

"I might have known you two would be enjoying yourselves while I sit up here starving."

"Oh come, it's not as bad as all that."

"It's not for you to say. You're not my doctor. Ask August Howell, and he'll tell you how important it is that I have my nourishment."

"I'm sorry, Aunt Maria. I thought you wouldn't want to be disturbed while you were in conference."

She stood just inside the doorway, still holding the tray like a shield in front of her. She wasn't young: close up, I could see the fortyish lines in her face and the knowledge in her blue eyes. But she held herself with adolescent awkwardness, immobilized by feelings she couldn't express.

"Well, you needn't stand there like a dummy."

Cassie moved suddenly. She set the tray on the table and uncovered the food. There was a good deal of food. Mrs. Galton began to fork salad into her mouth. The movements of her hands and jaws were rapid and mechanical. She was oblivious to the three of us watching her.

Sable and I retreated into the hallway and along it to the head of the stairs which curved in a baronial sweep down to the entrance hall. He leaned on the iron balustrade and lit a cigarette.

"Well, Lew, what do you think?"

I lit a cigarette of my own before I replied. "I think it's a waste of time and money."

"I told you that."

"But you want me to go ahead with it anyway?"

"I can't see any other way to handle it, or handle her. Mrs. Galton takes a good deal of handling."

"Can you trust her memory? She seems to be reliving the past. Sometimes old people get mixed up about what actually happened. That story about the money he stole, for example. Do you believe it?"

"I've never known her to lie. And I really doubt that she's as confused as she sounds. She likes to dramatize herself. It's the only excitement she has left."

"How old is she?"

"Seventy-three, I believe."

"That isn't so old. What about her son?"

"He'll be about forty-four, if he's still extant."

"She doesn't seem to realize that. She talks about him as if he was still a boy. How long has she been sitting in that room?"

"Ever since I've known her, anyway. Ten years. Occasionally, when she has a good day, she lets Miss Hildreth take her for a drive. It doesn't do much to bring her up to date, though. It's usually just a quick trip to the cemetery where her husband is buried. He died soon after Anthony took off. According to Mrs. Galton, that was what killed him. Miss Hildreth says he died of a coronary."

"Is Miss Hildreth a relative?"

"A distant one, second or third cousin. Cassie's known the family all her life, and lived with Mrs. Galton since before the war. I'm hoping she can give you something more definite to go on."

"I can use it."

A telephone shrilled somewhere, like a cricket in the wall. Cassie Hildreth came out of Mrs. Galton's room and moved briskly toward us:

"You're wanted on the telephone. It's Mrs. Sable."

"What does she want?"

"She didn't say, but she seems upset about something."

"She always is."

"You can take it downstairs if you like. There's an extension under the stairs."

"I know. I'll do that." Sable treated her brusquely, like a servant. "This is Mr. Archer, by the way. He wants to ask you some questions."

"Right now?"

"If you can spare the time," I said. "Mrs. Galton thought you could give me some pictures, perhaps some information."

"Pictures of Tony?"

"If you have them."

"I keep them for Mrs. Galton. She likes to look at them when the mood is on her."

"You work for her, do you?"

"If you can call it work. I'm a paid companion."

"I call it work."

Our eyes met. Hers were dark ocean blue. Discontent flicked a fin in their depths, but she said dutifully: "She isn't so bad. She's not at her best today. It's hard on her to rake up the past like this."

"Why is she doing it?"

"She had a serious scare not long ago. Her heart almost failed. They had to put her in an oxygen tent. She wants to make amends to Tony before she dies. She treated him badly, you know."

"Badly in what way?"

"She didn't want him to live his own life, as they say. She tried to keep him all to herself, like a—a belonging. But you'd better not get me started on that."

Cassie Hildreth bit her lip. I recalled what the doctor had said about her feeling for Tony. The whole household seemed to revolve around the missing man, as if he'd left only the day before.

Quick footsteps crossed the hallway below the stairs. I leaned over the balustrade and saw Sable wrench the front door open. It slammed behind him.

"Where's he off to?"

"Probably home. That wife of his—" She hesitated, editing the end of the sentence: "She lives on emergencies. If you'd like to see those pictures, they're in my room."

Her door was next to Mrs. Galton's sitting-room. She unlocked it with a Yale key. Apart from its size and shape, its lofty ceiling, the room bore no relation to the rest of the house. The furniture was modern. There were Paul Klee reproductions on the walls, new novels on the bookshelves. The ugly windows were masked with monks-cloth drapes. A narrow bed stood behind a woven wood screen in one corner.

Cassie Hildreth went into the closet and emerged with a sheaf of photographs in her hand.

"Show me the best likeness first."

She shuffled through them, her face intent and peaked, and handed me a posed studio portrait. Anthony Galton had been a handsome boy. I stood and let his features sink into my mind: light eyes set wide apart and arched over by intelligent brows, short straight nose, small mouth with rather full lips, a round girlish chin. The missing feature was character or personality, the meaning that should have held the features together. The only trace of this was in the one-sided smile. It seemed to say: to hell with you. Or maybe, to hell with me.

"This was his graduation picture," Cassie Hildreth said softly.

"I thought he never graduated from college."

"He didn't. This was made before he dropped out."

"Why didn't he graduate?"

"He wouldn't give his father the satisfaction. Or his mother. They forced him to study mechanical engineering, which was the last thing Tony was interested in. He stuck it out for four years, but he finally refused to take his degree in it."

"Did he flunk out?"

"Heavens, no. Tony was very bright. Some of his professors thought he was brilliant."

"But not in engineering?"

"There wasn't anything he couldn't do, if he wanted to. His real interests were literary. He wanted to be a writer."

"I take it you knew him well."

"Of course. I wasn't living with the Galtons then, but I used to visit here, often, when Tony was on vacation. He used to talk to me. He was a wonderful conversationalist."

"Describe him, will you?"

"But you've just seen his picture. And here are others."

"I'll look at them in a minute. Right now I want you to tell me about him."

"If you insist, I'll try." She closed her eyes. Her face smoothed out, as if years were being erased: "He was a lovely man. His body was finely proportioned, lean and strong. His head was beautifully balanced on his neck, and he had close fair curls." She opened her eyes. "Did you ever see the Praxiteles Hermes?"

I felt a little embarrassed, not only because I hadn't. Her description of Tony had the force of a passionate avowal. I hadn't expected anything like it. Cassie's emotion was like spontaneous combustion in an old hope chest.

"No," I said. "What color were his eyes?"

"Gray. A lovely soft gray. He had the eyes of a poet."

"I see. Were you in love with him?"

She gave me a startled look. "Surely you don't expect me to answer that."

"You just did. You say he used to talk to you. Did he ever discuss his plans for the future?"

"Just in general terms. He wanted to go away and write."

"Go away where?"

"Somewhere quiet and peaceful, I suppose."

"Out of the country?"

"I doubt it. Tony disapproved of expatriates. He always said he wanted to get *closer* to America. This was in the depression, remember. He was very strong for the rights of the working class."

"Radical?"

"I guess you'd call him that. But he wasn't a Communist, if that's what you mean. He did feel that having money cut him off from life. Tony hated social snobbery—which was one reason he was so unhappy at college. He often said he wanted to live like ordinary people, lose himself in the mass."

"It looks as if he succeeded in doing just that. Did he ever talk to you about his wife?"

"Never. I didn't even know he was married, or intended to get married." She was very self-conscious. Not knowing what to do with her face, she tried to smile. The teeth between her parted lips were like white bone showing in a wound.

As if to divert my attention from her, she thrust the other pictures into my hands. Most of them were candid shots of Tony Galton doing various things: riding a horse, sitting on a rock in swimming trunks, holding a tennis racket with a winner's fixed grin on his face. From the pictures, and from what the people said, I got the impression of a boy going through the motions. He made the gestures of enjoyment but kept himself hidden, even from the camera. I began to have some glimmering of the psychology that made him want to lose himself.

"What did he like doing?"

"Writing. Reading and writing."

"Besides that. Tennis? Swimming?"

"Not really. Tony despised sports. He used to jeer at me for going in for them."

"What about wine and women? Dr. Howell said he was quite a playboy."

"Dr. Howell never understood him," she said. "Tony did have relations with women, and I suppose he drank, but he did it on principle."

"Is that what he told you?"

"Yes, and it's true. He was practicing Rimbaud's theory of the violation of the senses. He thought that having all sorts of remarkable experiences would make him a good poet, like Rimbaud." She saw my uncomprehending look, and added: "Arthur Rimbaud was a French poet. He and Charles Baudelaire were Tony's great idols."

"I see." We were getting off the track into territory where I felt lost. "Did you ever meet any of his women?"

"Oh, no." She seemed shocked at the idea. "He never brought any of them here."

"He brought his wife home."

"Yes, I know. I was away at school when it happened."

"When what happened?"

"The big explosion," she said. "Mr. Galton told him never to darken his door again. It was all very Victorian and heavy-father. And Tony never did darken his door again."

"Let's see, that was in October 1936. Did you ever see Tony after that?"

"Never. I was at school in the east."

"Ever hear from him?"

Her mouth started to shape the word "no," then tightened. "I had a little note from him, some time in the course of the winter. It must have been before Christmas, because I got it at school, and I didn't go back after Christmas. I think it was in the early part of December that it came."

"What did it say?"

"Nothing very definite. Simply that he was doing well, and had broken into print. He'd had a poem accepted by a little magazine in San Francisco. He sent it to me under separate cover. I've kept it, if you'd like to look at it."

She kept it in a manila envelope on the top shelf of her bookcase. The magazine was a thin little publication smudgily printed on pulp paper; its name was *Chisel*. She opened it to a middle page, and handed it to me. I read:

"*LUNA*, by John Brown

"*White her breast*
As the white foam
Where the gulls rest
Yet find no home.

"*Green her eyes*
As the green deep
Where the tides rise
And the storms sleep.

"*And fearful am I*
As a mariner
When the sea and the sky
Begin to stir.

"*For wild is her heart*
As the sea's leaping:
She will rise and depart
While I lie sleeping."

"Did Tony Galton write this? It's signed 'John Brown.'"

"It was the name he used. Tony wouldn't use the family name. 'John Brown' had a special meaning for him, besides. He had a theory that the country was going through another civil war—a war between the rich people and the poor people. He thought of the poor people as white Negroes, and he wanted to do for them what John Brown did for the slaves. Lead them out of bondage—in the spiritual sense, of course. Tony didn't believe in violence."

"I see," I said, though it all sounded strange to me. "Where did he send this from?"

"The magazine was published in San Francisco, and Tony sent it from there."

"This was the only time you ever heard from him?"

"The only time."

"May I keep these pictures, and the magazine? I'll try to bring them back."

"If they'll help you to find Tony."

"I understand he went to live in San Francisco. Do you have his last address?"

"I had it, but there's no use going there."

"Why not?"

"Because I did, the year after he went away. It was a wretched old tenement, and it had been condemned. They were tearing it down."

"Did you make any further attempt to find him?"

"I wanted to, but I was afraid. I was only seventeen."

"Why didn't you go back to school, Cassie?"

"I didn't especially want to. Mr. Galton wasn't well, and Aunt Maria asked me to stay with her. She was the one sending me to school, so that I couldn't very well refuse."

"And you've been here ever since?"

"Yes." The word came out with pressure behind it.

As if on cue, Mrs. Galton raised her voice on the other side of the wall: "Cassie! Cassie? Are you in there? What are you doing in there?"

"I'd better go," Cassie said.

She locked the door of her sanctuary, and went, with her head down.

After twenty-odd years of that, I'd have been crawling.

5
.

I MET the doctor's daughter on the stairs. She gave me a tentative smile. "Are you the detective?"

"I'm the detective. My name is Archer."

"Mine's Sheila Howell. Do you think you can find him for her?"

"I can try, Miss Howell."

"That doesn't sound too hopeful."

"It wasn't meant to."

"But you will do your best, won't you?"

"Is it important to you? You're too young to have known Anthony Galton."

"It's important to Aunt Maria." She added in a rush of feeling: "She needs somebody to love her. I try, honestly, but I just can't do it."

"Is she a relative of yours?"

"Not exactly. She's my godmother. I call her aunt because she likes me to. But I've never succeeded in feeling like a niece to her."

"I imagine she makes it hard."

"She doesn't mean to, but she simply doesn't know how to treat *people*. She's had her own way for so long." The girl colored, and compressed her lips. "I don't mean to be *critical*. You must think I'm an awful person, talking about her to a stranger like this. I really do wish her well, in spite of what Dad thinks. And if she wants me to read *Pendennis* to her, I will."

"Good for you. I was on my way to make a phone call. Is there a telephone handy?"

She showed me the telephone under the stairs. It was an ancient wall telephone which nobody had ever bothered to change for a modern one. The Santa Teresa directory lay on a table under it. I looked up Sable's number.

He was a long time answering. Finally, I heard the receiver being lifted at the other end of the line. After another wait, I heard his voice. I hardly recognized it. It had a blurred quality, almost as if Sable had been crying:

"This is Gordon Sable."

"Archer speaking. You took off before we could make definite arrangements. On a case like this I need an advance, and expense money, at least three hundred."

There was a click, and then a whirring on the wire. Someone was dialing. A woman's voice said: "Operator! I want the police."

"Get off the line," Sable said.

"I'm calling the police." It was his wife's voice, shrill with hysteria.

"I've already called them. Now get off the line. It's in use."

A receiver was fumbled into place. I said: "You still there, Sable?"

"Yes. There's been an accident, as you must have gathered." He paused. I could hear his breathing.

"To Mrs. Sable?"

"No, though she's badly upset. My houseman, Peter, has been stabbed. I'm afraid he's dead."

"Who stabbed him?"

"It isn't clear. I can't get much out of my wife. Apparently some goon came to the door. When Peter opened it, he was knifed."

"You want me to come out?"

"If you think it will do any good. Peter is past help."

"I'll be there in a few minutes."

But it took me longer than that. The Arroyo Park suburb was new to me. I took a wrong turning and got lost in its system of winding roads. The roads all looked alike, with flat-roofed houses, white and gray and adobe, scattered along the terraced hillsides.

I went around in circles for a while, and came out on top of the wrong hill. The road dwindled into a pair of ruts in a field where nothing stood but a water tower. I turned, and stopped to get my bearings.

On a hilltop a mile or more to my left, I could make out a flat pale green roof which looked like the Arizona gravel roof of Sable's house. On my right, far below, a narrow asphalt road ran like a dark stream along the floor of the valley. Between the road and a clump of scrub oaks an orange rag of flame came and went. Black smoke trickled up from it into the still blue air. When I moved I caught a flash of sunlight on metal. It was a car, nose down in the ditch, and burning.

I drove down the long grade and turned right along the asphalt road. A fire siren was ululating in the distance. The smoke above the burning car was twisting higher and spreading like a slow stain over the trees. Watching it, I almost ran down a man.

He was walking toward me with his head bent, as if in meditation, a thick young man with shoulders like a bull. I honked at him and applied the brakes. He came on doggedly. One of his arms swung slack, dripping red from the fingers. The other arm was cradled in the front of his sharp flannel jacket.

He came up to the door on my side and leaned against it. "Can you gimme a lift?" Oily black curls tumbled over his hot black eyes. The bright blood on his mouth gave him an obscene look, like a painted girl.

"Smash up your car?"

He grunted.

"Come around to the other side if you can make it."

"Negative. This side."

I caught the glint of larceny in his eyes, and something worse. I reached for my car keys. He was ahead of me. The short blue gun in his right hand peered at the corner of the open window:

"Leave the keys where they are. Open the door and get out."

Curlyhead talked and acted like a pro, or at least a gifted amateur with a vocation. I opened the door and got out.

He waved me away from the car. "Start walking."

I hesitated, weighing my chances of taking him.

He used his gun to point toward the city. "Get going, Bud. You don't want a calldown with me."

I started walking. The engine of my car roared behind me. I got off the road. But Curlyhead turned in a driveway, and drove off in the other direction, away from the sirens.

The fire was out when I got to it. The county firemen were coiling their hose, replacing it on the side of the long red truck. I went up to the cab and asked the man at the wheel:

"Do you have two-way radio?"

"What's it to you?"

"My car was stolen. I think the character who took it was driving the one in the ditch there. The Highway Patrol should be notified."

"Give me the details, I'll shoot them in."

I gave him the license number and description of my car, and a thumbnail sketch of Curlyhead. He started feeding them into his mike. I climbed down the bank to look at the car I'd traded mine in on. It was a black Jaguar sedan, about five years old. It had slewed off the road, gouging deep tracks in the dirt, and crumpled its nose against a boulder. One of the front tires had blown out. The windshield was starred, and the finish blistered by fire. Both doors were sprung.

I made a note of the license number, and moved up closer to look at the steering-post. The registration was missing. I got in and opened the dash compartment. It was clean.

In the road above, another car shrieked to a halt. Two sheriff's men got out on opposite sides and came down the bank in a double cloud of dust. They had guns in their hands, no-nonsense looks on their brown faces.

"This your car?" the first one snapped at me.

"No."

I started to tell him what had happened to mine, but he didn't want to hear about it:

"Out of there! Keep your hands in sight, shoulder-high."

I got out, feeling that all this had happened before. The first deputy held his gun on me while the second deputy shook me down. He was very thorough. He even investigated the fuzz in my pockets. I commented on this.

"This is no joke. What's your name?"

The firemen had begun to gather around us. I was angry and sweating. I opened my mouth and put both feet in, all the way up to the knee.

"I'm Captain Nemo," I said. "I just came ashore from a hostile submarine. Curiously enough, we fuel our subs with seaweed. The hull itself is formed from highly compressed seaweed. So take me to your wisest man. There is no time to be lost."

"He's a hophead," the first deputy said. "I kind of figured the slasher was a hophead. You heard me say so, Barney."

"Yeah." Barney was reading the contents of my wallet. "He's got a driver's license made out to somebody name of Archer, West Hollywood. And a statewide private-eye ducat, same name. But it's probably a phony."

"It's no phony." Vaudeville had got me nowhere except into deeper trouble. "My name is Archer. I'm a private investigator, employed by Mr. Sable, the lawyer."

"Sable, he says." The deputies exchanged significant looks. "Give him his wallet, Barney."

Barney held it out to me. I reached for it. The cuffs clinked snug on my wrist.

"Other wrist now," he said in a soothing voice. I was a hophead. "Let's have the other wrist now."

I hesitated. But rough stuff not only wouldn't work. It would put me in the wrong. I wanted them to be in the wrong, falling on their faces with foolishness.

I surrendered the other wrist without a struggle. Looking down at my trapped hands, I saw the dab of blood on one of my fingers.

"Let's go," the first deputy said. He dropped my wallet in the side pocket of my jacket.

They herded me up the bank and into the back of their car. The driver of the fire truck leaned from his cab:

"Keep a close eye on him, fellows. He's a cool customer. He gave me a story about his car getting stolen, took me in completely."

"Not us," the first deputy said. "We're trained to spot these phonies, the way you're trained to put out fires. Don't let anybody else near the Jag. Leave a guard on it, eh? I'll send a man as soon as we can spare one."

"What did he do?"

"Knifed a man."

"Jesus, and I thought he was a citizen."

The first deputy climbed into the back seat beside me. "I got to warn you anything you say can be used against you. Why did you do it?"

"Do what?"

"Cut Peter Culligan."

"I didn't cut him."

"You got blood on your hand. Where did it come from?"

"Probably the Jaguar."

"Your car, you mean?"

"It isn't my car."

"The hell it isn't. I got a witness saw you drive away from the scene of the crime."

"I wasn't in it. The man who was in it just stole my car."

"Don't give me that. You can fool a fireman with it. I'm a cop."

"Was it woman trouble?" Barney said over his shoulder. "If it was a woman, we can understand it. Crime of passion, and all. Shucks," he added lightly, "it wouldn't even be second-degree, probably. You could be out in two-three years. Couldn't he, Conger?"

"Sure," Conger said. "You might as well tell us the truth now, get it over with."

I was getting bored with the game. "It wasn't a woman. It was seaweed. I'm a seaweed-fancier from way back. I like to sprinkle a little of it on my food."

"What's that got to do with Culligan?"

Barney said from the front seat: "He sounds to me like he's all hopped up."

Conger leaned across me. "Are you?"

"Am I what?"

"All hopped up?"

"Yeah. I chew seaweed, then I orbit. Take me to the nearest launching pad."

Conger looked at me pityingly. I was a hophead. The pity was gradually displaced by doubt. He had begun to grasp that he was being ragged. Very suddenly, his face turned dusky red under the tan. He balled his right fist on his knee. I could see the packed muscles tighten under the shoulder of his blouse. I pulled in my chin and got ready to roll with the punch. But he didn't hit me.

Under the circumstances, this made him a good cop. I almost began to like him, in spite of the handcuffs. I said:

"As I told you before, my name is Archer. I'm a licensed private detective, retired sergeant from the Long Beach P.D. The California Penal Code has a section on false arrest. Do you think you better take the jewelry off?"

Barney said from the front seat: "A poolroom lawyer, eh?"

Conger didn't say anything. He sat in pained silence for what seemed a long time. The effort of thought did unexpected things to his heavy face. It seemed to alarm him, like a loud noise in the night.

The car left the county road and climbed Sable's hill. A second sheriff's car stood in front of the glass house. Sable climbed out, followed by a heavy-set man in mufti.

Sable looked pale and shaken. "You took your time about getting here." Then he saw the handcuffs on my wrists. "For heaven's sake!"

The heavy-set man stepped past him, and yanked the car door open. "What's the trouble here?"

Conger's confusion deepened. "No trouble, Sheriff. We picked up a suspect, claims he's a private cop working for Mr. Sable."

The sheriff turned to Sable. "This your man?"

"Of course."

Conger was already removing the handcuffs, unobtrusively, as if perhaps I wouldn't notice they'd ever been on my wrists. The back of Barney's neck reddened. He didn't turn around, even when I stepped out of the car.

The Sheriff gave me his hand. He had a calm and weathered face in which quick bright eyes moved with restless energy. "I'm Trask. I won't apologize. We all make mistakes. Some of us more than others, eh, Conger?"

Conger didn't reply. I said: "Now that we've had our fun, maybe you'd like to get on the radio with the description of my car and the man that took it."

"What man are we talking about?" Trask said.

I told him, and added: "If you don't mind my saying so, Sheriff, it might be a good idea for you to check with the Highway Patrol yourself. Our friend took off in the direction of San Francisco, but he may have circled back."

"I'll put out the word."

Trask started toward his radio car. I held him for a minute: "One other thing. That Jaguar ought to be checked by an expert. It may be just another stolen car—"

"Yeah, let's hope it isn't."

6

THE dead man was lying where he had fallen, on a patch of blood-filmed grass, about ten feet from Sable's front door. The lower part of his white jacket was red-stained. His upturned face was gray and impervious-looking, like the stone faces on tombs.

A Sheriff's identification man was taking pictures of him with a tripod camera. He was a white-haired officer with a long inquisitive nose. I waited until he moved his camera to get another angle:

"Mind if I have a look at him?"

"Long as you don't touch him. I'll be through here in a minute."

When he had finished his work, I leaned over the body for a closer look. There was a single deep wound in the abdomen. The right hand had cuts across the palm and inside the curled fingers. The knife that had done the damage, a bloody five-inch switch-blade, lay on the grass in the angle between the torso and the outstretched right arm.

I took hold of the hand: it was still warm and limp: and turned it over. The skin on the tattooed knuckles was torn, probably by teeth.

"He put up quite a struggle," I said.

The identification officer hunkered down beside me. "Yeah. Be careful with those fingernails. There's some kind of debris under 'em, might be human skin. You notice the tattoo marks?"

"I'd have to be blind to miss them."

"I mean these." He took the hand away from me, and pointed out four dots arranged in a tiny rectangle between the first and second fingers. "Gang mark. He had it covered up later with a standard tattoo. A lot of old gang members do that. I see them on people we vag."

"What kind of gang?"

"I don't know. This is a Sac or Frisco gang. I'm no expert on the northern California insignia. I wonder if Lawyer Sable knew he had an old gang member working for him."

"We could ask him."

The front door was standing open. I walked in and found Sable in the front sitting-room. He raised a limp arm, and waved me into a chair:

"Sit down, Archer. I'm sorry about what happened. I can't imagine what they thought they were pulling."

"Eager-beavering. Forget it. We got off to a poor start, but the local boys seem to know what they're doing."

"I hope so," he said, not very hopefully.

"What do you know about your late houseman?"

"Not a great deal, I'm afraid. He only worked for me for a few months. I hired him originally to look after my yacht. He lived aboard the yacht until I sold it. Then he moved up here. He had no place to go, and he didn't ask for much. Peter wasn't very competent indoors, as you may have noticed. But it's hard for us to get help out in the country, and he was an obliging soul, so I let him stay on."

"What sort of a background did he have?"

"I gathered he was pretty much of a floater. He mentioned various jobs he'd held: marine cook, longshoreman, housepainter."

"How did you hire him? Through an employment agency?"

"No. I picked him up on the dock. I think he'd just come off a fishing-boat, a Monterey seiner. I was polishing brass, varnishing deck, and so on, and he offered to help me for a dollar an hour. He did a good day's work, so I took him on. He never failed to do a good day's work."

A cleft of pain, like a knife-cut, had appeared between Sable's eyebrows. I guessed that he had been fond of the dead man. I hesitated to ask my next question:

"Would you know if Culligan had a criminal record?"

The cleft in his brow deepened. "Good Lord, no. I trusted him with my boat and my house. What makes you ask such a question?"

"Two things mainly. He had a tattoo mark on his hand, four little black dots at the edge of the blue tattoo. Gangsters and drug addicts wear that kind of mark. Also, this has the look of a gang killing. The man who took my car is almost certainly the killer, and he has the earmarks of a pro."

Sable looked down at the polished terrazzo as if at any moment it might break up under his feet. "You think Peter Culligan was involved with criminals?"

"Involved is putting it mildly. He's dead."

"I realize that," he said rather shrilly.

"Did he seem nervous lately? Afraid of anything?"

"If he was, I never noticed. He didn't talk about himself."

"Did he have any visitors, before this last one?"

"Never. At least, not to my knowledge. He was a solitary person."

"Could he have been using your place and his job here as a sort of hide-out?"

"I don't know. It's hard to say."

An engine started up in front of the house. Sable rose and moved to the glass wall, parting the drapes. I looked out over his shoulder. A black panel truck rolled away from the house and started down the hill.

"Come to think of it," Sable said, "he certainly kept out of sight. He wouldn't chauffeur for me, said he'd had bad luck with cars. But he may have wanted to avoid going to town. He never went to town."

"He's on his way there now," I said. "How many people knew he was out here?"

"Just my wife and I. And you, of course. I can't think offhand of anyone else."

"Have you had visitors from out of town?"

"Not in the last few months. Alice has been having her ups and downs. It's one reason I took Peter on out here. We'd lost our house-keeper, and I didn't like to leave Alice by herself all day."

"How is Mrs. Sable now?"

"Not so good, I'm afraid."

"Did she see it happen?"

"I don't believe so. But she heard the sounds of the struggle, and saw the car drive away. That was when she phoned me. When I got here, she was sitting on the doorstep in a half daze. I don't know what it will do to her emotional state."

"Any chance of my talking to her?"

"Not now, please. I've already spoken to Dr. Howell, and he told me to give her sedation. The Sheriff has agreed not to question her for the present. There's a limit to what the human mind can endure."

Sable might have been talking about himself. His shoulders drooped as he turned from the window. In the harsh sunlight his face was a grainy white, and puffy like boiled rice. In murder cases, there are usually more victims than one.

Sable must have read the look on my face. "This is an unsettling thing to me, too. It can't conceivably relate to Alice and me. And yet it does, very deeply. Peter was a member of the household. I believe he was quite devoted to us, and he died in our front yard. That really brings it home."

"What?"

"*Timor mortis*," he said. "The fear of death."

"You say Culligan was a member of your household. I take it he slept in."

"Yes, of course."

"I'd like to have a look at his room."

He took me across the court and through a utility room to a back bedroom. The room was furnished with a single bed, a chest of drawers, a chair, and a reading-lamp.

"I'll just look in on Alice," Sable said, and left me.

I went through Peter Culligan's meager effects. The closet contained a pair of Levis, a couple of workshirts, boots, and a cheap blue suit which had been bought at a San Francisco department store. There was a Tanforan pari-mutuel stub in the outside breast pocket of the suit coat. A dirty comb and a safety razor lay on top of the chest of drawers. The drawers were practically empty: a couple of white shirts, a greasy blue tie, a T-shirt and a pair of floral shorts, socks and hand-kerchiefs, and a cardboard box containing a hundred shells for a .38-caliber automatic. Not quite a hundred: the box wasn't full. No gun.

Culligan's suitcase was under the bed. It was a limp old canvas affair, held together with straps, which looked as if it had been kicked around every bus station between Seattle and San Diego. I unstrapped it. The lock was broken, and it fell open. Its contents emitted a whiff of tobacco, sea water, sweat, and the subtler indescribable odor of masculine loneliness.

It contained a gray flannel shirt, a rough blue turtle-neck sweater, and other heavier work clothes. A broad-bladed fisherman's knife had fish scales still clinging like faded sequins to the cork handle. A crumpled greenish tuxedo jacket was preserved as a memento from some more sophisticated past.

A union card issued in San Francisco in 1941 indicated that Culligan had been a paid-up active member of the defunct Marine Cooks' Union. And there was a letter, addressed to Mr. Peter Culligan, General

Delivery, Reno, Nevada. Culligan hadn't been a loner all his life. The letter was written on pink notepaper in an unformed hand. It said:

Dear Pete,

Dear is not the word after all I suffered from you, which is all over now and I'm going to keep it that way. I hope you realize. Just so you do I'll spell it out, you never realized a fact in your life until you got hit over the head with it. So here goes, no I don't love you anymore. Looking back now I don't see how I ever did love you, I was "infatuated." When I think of all you made me suffer, the jobs you lost and the fights and the drinking and all. You certainly didn't love me, so don't try to "kid" me. No I'm not crying over "spilt milk." I had only myself to blame for staying with you. You gave me fair warning plenty of times. What kind of person you were. I must say you have your "guts" writing to me. I don't know how you got hold of my address. Probably from one of your crooked cop friends, but they don't scare me.

I am happily married to a wonderful man. He knows that I was married before. But he does not know about "us." If you have any decency, stay away from me and don't write any more letters. I'm warning you, don't make trouble for me. I could make trouble for you, double trouble. Remember L. Bay.

Wishing you all success in your new life (I hope youre making as much money as you claim),

Marian

Mrs. Ronald S. Matheson (and bear it in mind). Me come back to you? Don't ever give it another thought. Ronald is a very successful business exec! I wouldn't rub it in, only you really put me through the "wringer" and you know it. No hard feelings on my part, just leave me alone, please.

The letter had no return address, but it was postmarked San Mateo, Calif. The date was indecipherable.

I put everything back and closed the suitcase and kicked it under the bed.

I went out into the court. In a room on the other side of it, a woman or an animal was moaning. Sable must have been watching for me.

The sound became louder as he opened a sliding glass door, and was shut off as he closed it. He came toward me, his face tinged green by the reflected light from the foliage:

"Find anything significant?"

"He kept shells for an automatic in his drawer. I didn't come across the automatic."

"I didn't know Peter had a gun."

"Maybe he had, and sold it. Or it's possible the killer took it away from him."

"Anything else?"

"I have a tentative lead to his ex-wife, if you want me to explore his background."

"Why not leave it to the police? Trask is very competent, and an old friend of mind into the bargain. I wouldn't feel justified in taking you off the Galton case."

"The Galton case doesn't seem so very urgent."

"Possibly not. Still, I think you should stay with it for the present. Was Cassie Hildreth any help?"

"Some. I can't think of much more to be done around here. I was planning to drive to San Francisco."

"You can take a plane. I wrote you a check for two hundred dollars, and I'll give you a hundred in cash." He handed me the check and the money. "If you need any more, don't hesitate to call on me."

"I won't, but I'm afraid it's money down the drain."

Sable shrugged. He had worse problems. The moaning behind the glass door was louder, rising in peaks of sound which pierced my eardrums.

7
·

I HATE coincidences. Aboard the plane, I spent a fruitless hour trying to work out possible connections between Maria Galton's loss of her son and Peter Culligan's loss of life. I had a delayed gestalt after I'd given up on the subject.

I was flipping through the smudged pages of *Chisel*, the little magazine that Cassie Hildreth had given me. Somebody named Chad Bolling was listed on the masthead as editor and publisher. He also had a poem in the magazine, "Elegy on the Death of Bix Beiderbecke." It said that the inconsolable cornet would pipe Eurydice out of Boss Pluto's smoke-filled basement. I liked it better than the poem about Luna.

I reread Anthony Galton's poem, wondering if Luna was his wife. Then the gestalt clicked. There was a town named Luna Bay on the coast south of San Francisco. From where I sat, a few thousand feet above the Peninsula, I could practically spit on it. And Culligan's ex-wife had referred to an L. Bay" in her letter to him.

When the plane let down at International Airport, I headed for a telephone booth. The woman had signed herself Mrs. Ronald S. Matheson; the envelope had been postmarked in San Mateo.

I hardly expected a hit on such a random shot, after an indefinite lapse of time. But the name was in the directory: Ronald S. Matheson, 780 Sherwood Drive, Redwood City. I dialed the Emerson number.

I couldn't tell if it was a girl or a boy who answered. It was a child, pre-pubic: "Hello?"

"Is Mrs. Matheson there?"

"Just a minute, please. Mummy, you're wanted on the phone."

The child's voice trailed off, and a woman's took its place. It was cool and smooth and careful:

"Marian Matheson speaking. Who is calling, please?"

"My name is Archer. You've never heard of me."

"That's right, I haven't."

"Ever hear of a man named Culligan?"

There was a long pause. "Come again? I didn't catch the name."

"Culligan," I said. "Peter Culligan."

"What about him?"

"Did you ever know him?"

"Maybe I did, a long time ago. So what? Maybe I didn't."

"Let's not play games, Mrs. Matheson. I have some information, if you're interested."

"I'm not. Not if you're talking for Pete Culligan." Her voice had become harsher and deeper. "I don't care anything about him, as long as he leaves me alone. You can tell him that for me."

"I can't, though."

"Why not?"

"Because he's dead."

"Dead?" Her voice was a leaden echo.

"I'm investigating his murder." I'd just decided I was. "I'd like to talk to you about the circumstances."

"I don't see why. I had nothing to do with it. I didn't even know it happened."

"I'm aware of that. It's one reason I called."

"Who killed him?"

"I'll tell you when I see you."

"Who says you're seeing me?"

I waited.

"Where are you now?" she said.

"At the San Francisco Airport."

"I guess I can come there, if it has to be. I don't want you coming to the house. My husband—"

"I understand that. It's good of you to come at all. I'll be in the coffee shop."

"Are you in uniform?"

"Not at the moment." Or for the last ten years, but let her go on thinking I was law. "I'm wearing a gray suit. You won't miss me. I'll be sitting beside the windows close to the entrance."

"I'll be there in fifteen minutes. Did you say Archer?"

"Yes. Archer."

It took her twenty-five. I passed the time watching the big planes circling in, dragging their late-afternoon shadows along the runways.

A woman in a dark cloth coat came in, paused at the doorway, and looked around the huge room. Her eye lighted on me. She came toward my table, clutching her shiny leather purse as if it was a token of respectability. I got up to meet her:

"Mrs. Matheson?"

She nodded, and sat down hurriedly, as if she was afraid of being conspicuous. She was an ordinary-looking woman, decently dressed, who would never see forty again. There were flecks of gray in her carefully waved black hair, like little shards of iron.

She had once been handsome in a strong-boned way. Maybe she still was, under favorable lighting and circumstances. Her black eyes were her best feature, but they were hard with tension:

"I didn't want to come. But here I am."

"Will you have some coffee?"

"No, thanks. Let's have the bad news. I'll take it straight."

I gave it to her straight, leaving out nothing important. She began to twist the wedding ring on her finger, round and round.

"Poor guy," she said when I finished. "Why did they do it to him, do you know?"

"I was hoping you could help me answer that."

"You say you're not a policeman?"

"No. I'm a private investigator."

"I don't see why you come to me. We haven't been married for fifteen years. I haven't even seen him for ten. He wanted to come back to me, I guess he finally got tired of bucketing around. But I wasn't having any. I'm happily married to a good man—"

"When was the last time you heard from Culligan?"

"About a year ago. He wrote me a letter from Reno, claimed he'd struck it rich, that he could give me anything I wanted if I'd come back. Pete was always a dreamer. The first while after we were married, I used to believe in his dreams. But they all went blooey, one after another. I caught onto him so many years ago it isn't funny. I'm not laughing, notice."

"What kind of dreams did he dream?"

"Great big ones, the kind that never come off. Like he was going to open a chain of restaurants where food of all nations would be served. He'd hire the best chefs in the country, French, Chinese, Armenian, and so on. At which time he was a short-order cook on lower Market. Then there was the time he worked out a new system to beat the ponies. He took every cent we possessed to try it out. He even hocked my furniture. It took me all that winter to work it off." Her voice had the driving energy of old anger that had found an outlet. "That was Pete's idea of a honeymoon, me working and him playing the ponies."

"How did you get hooked up with him?"

"I was a dreamer, too, I guess you'd say. I thought I could straighten him out, make a man of him. That all he needed was the love of a good woman. I wasn't a good woman, and I don't pretend to be. But I was better than he was."

"Where did you meet?"

"In the San Francisco Hospital where I was working. I was a nurse's aide, and Pete was in the ward with a broken nose and a couple of broken ribs. He got beaten up in a gang fight."

"A gang fight?"

"That's all I know. Pete just said it was some rumble on the docks. I should have taken warning, but after he got out of the hospital I went on seeing him. He was young and good-looking, and like I said I thought he had the makings of a man. So I married him—the big mistake of my life, and I've made some doozies."

"How long ago was that?"

"Nineteen-thirty-six. That dates me, doesn't it? But I was only twenty-one at the time." She paused, and raised her eyes to my face. "I don't know why I'm telling you all this. I've never told a living soul in my life. Why don't you stop me?"

"I'm hoping you'll tell me something that will help. Did your husband go in for gambling?"

"Please don't call him that. I married Pete Culligan, but he was no husband to me." She lifted her head. "I have a real husband now. Incidentally, he'll be expecting me back to make his dinner." She leaned forward in her chair and started to get up.

"Can't you give me a few minutes more, Mrs. Matheson? I've told you all I know about Peter—"

She laughed shortly. "If I told you all *I* know, it would take all night. Okay, a few more minutes, if you promise me there won't be any publicity. My husband and me have a position to keep up. I'm a member of the PTA, the League of Women Voters."

"There won't be any publicity. Was he a gambler?"

"As much as he could afford to be. But he was always small-time."

"This money he said he made in Reno—did he tell you how he made it?"

"Not a word. But I don't think it was gambling. He was never that lucky."

"Do you still have his letter?"

"Certainly not. I burned it, the same day I got it."

"Why?"

"Because I didn't want it around the house. I felt like it was dirt tracked into the house."

"Was Culligan a crook, or a hustler?"

"Depends what you mean by that." Her eyes were wary.

"Did he break the law?"

"I guess everybody does from time to time."

"Was he ever arrested?"

"Yeah. Mostly for drunk and disorderly, nothing serious."

"Did he carry a gun?"

"Not when I was with him. I wouldn't let him."

"But the issue came up?"

"I didn't say that." She was becoming evasive. "I meant I wouldn't let him even if he wanted to."

"Did he own a gun?"

"I wouldn't know," she said.

I'd almost lost her. She wasn't talking frankly or willingly any more. So I threw her the question I didn't expect her to answer, hoping to gather something from her reaction to it:

"You mentioned an L. Bay in your letter to Culligan. What happened there?"

Her lips were pushed out stiff and pale, as if they were made of bone. The dark eyes seemed to shrink in her head:

"I don't know what makes you ask that." The tip of her tongue moved along her upper lip, and she tried again: "What was that about a bay in my letter? I don't remember any bay in my letter."

"I do, Mrs. Matheson." I quoted: " 'I could make trouble for you, double trouble. Remember L. Bay.' "

"If I said that, I don't know what I meant."

"There's a place called Luna Bay about twenty-five or thirty miles from here."

"Is there?" she said stupidly.

"You know it. What did Pete Culligan do there?"

"I don't remember. It must have been some dirty trick he played on me." She was a poor liar, as most honest people are. "Does it matter?"

"It seems to matter to you. Did you and Pete live in Luna Bay?"

"I guess you could call it living. I had a job there, doing practical nursing."

"When?"

"Way back when. I don't remember what year."

"Who were you working for?"

"Some people. I don't remember their name." She leaned toward me urgently, her eyes pointed like flints. "You have that letter with you?"

"I left it where I found it, in Culligan's suitcase in the house where he worked. Why?"

"I want it back. I wrote it, and it belongs to me."

"You may have to take that up with the police. It's probably in their hands by now."

"Will they be coming here?" She looked behind her, and all around the crowded restaurant, as if she expected to find a policeman bearing down on her.

"It depends on how soon they catch the killer. They may have him already, in which case they won't bother with secondary leads. Do you have any idea who it was, Mrs. Matheson?"

"How could I? I haven't seen Pete in ten years, I told you."

"What happened in Luna Bay?"

"Change the record, can't you? If anything happened, which I can't remember, it was strictly between me and Pete. Nothing to do with anybody else, understand?"

Her voice and looks were altering under pressure. She seemed to have broken through into a lower stratum of experience and a coarser personality. And she knew it. She pulled her purse toward her and held on to it with both hands. It was a good purse, beautifully cut from genuine lizard. In contrast with it, her hands were rough, their knuckles swollen and cracked by years of work.

She raised her eyes to mine. I caught the red reflection of fear in their centers. She was afraid of me, and she was afraid to leave me.

"Mrs. Matheson, Peter Culligan was murdered today—"

"You expect me to go into mourning?"

"I expect you to give me any information that might have a bearing on his death."

"I already did. You can leave me alone, understand? You're not getting me mixed up in no murder. Any murder."

"Did you ever hear of a man named Anthony Galton?"

"No."

"John Brown?"

"No."

I could see the bitter forces of her will gathering in her face. She exerted them, and got up, and walked away from me and her fear.

8

I WENT back to the telephone booths and looked up the name Chad Bolling in the Bay Area directories. I didn't expect to find it, after more than twenty years, but I was still running in luck. Bolling had a Telegraph Hill address. I immured myself in one of the booths and called him.

A woman's voice answered: "This is the Bolling residence."

"Is Mr. Bolling available?"

"Available for what?" she said abruptly.

"It has to do with magazine publication of a poem. The name is Archer," I added, trying to sound like a wealthy editor.

"I see." She softened her tone. "I don't know where Chad is at the moment. And I'm afraid he won't be home for dinner. I do know he'll be at The Listening Ear later this evening."

"The Listening Ear?"

"It's a new night club. Chad's giving a reading there tonight. If you're interested in poetry, you owe it to yourself to catch it."

"What time does he go on?"

"I think ten."

I rented a car and drove it up Bayshore to the city, where I parked it under Union Square. Above the lighted towers of the hotels, twilight had thickened into darkness. A damp chill had risen from the sea; I could feel it through my clothes. Even the colored lights around the square had a chilly look.

I bought a pint of whisky to ward off the chill and checked in at the Salisbury, a small side-street hotel where I usually stayed in San Francisco. The desk clerk was new to me. Desk clerks are always moving up or down. This one was old and on his way down; his sallow face drooped in the pull of gravity. He handed me my key reluctantly:

"No luggage, sir?"

I showed him my bottle in its paper bag. He didn't smile.

"My car was stolen."

"That's too bad." His eyes were sharp and incredulous behind fussy little pince-nez. "I'm afraid I'll have to ask you to pay in advance."

"All right." I gave him the five dollars and asked for a receipt.

The bellhop who took me up in the old open ironwork elevator had been taking me up in the same elevator for nearly twenty years. We shook hands. His was crumpled by arthritis.

"How are you, Coney?"

"Fine, Mr. Archer, fine. I'm taking a new pill, phenylbuta-something. It's doing wonders for me."

He stepped out and did a little soft-shoe step to prove it. He'd once been half of a brother act that played the Orpheum circuit. He danced me down the corridor to the door of my room.

"What brings you up to the City?" he said when we were inside. To San Franciscans, there's only one city.

"I flew up for a little entertainment."

"I thought Hollywood was the world's center of entertainment."

"I'm looking for something different," I said. "Have you heard of a new club called The Listening Ear?"

"Yeah, but you wouldn't like it." He shook his white head. "I hope you didn't come all the way up here for *that*."

"What's the matter with it?"

"It's a culture cave. One of these bistros where guys read poems to music. It ain't your speed at all."

"My taste is becoming more elevated."

His grin showed all his remaining teeth. "Don't kid an old man, eh?"

"Ever hear of Chad Bolling?"

"Sure. He promotes a lot of publicity for himself." Coney looked at me anxiously. "You really going in for the poetry kick, Mr. Archer? With music?"

"I have long yearned for the finer things."

Such as a good French dinner at a price I could pay. I took a taxi to the Ritz Poodle Dog, and had a good French dinner. When I finished eating, it was nearly ten o'clock.

The Listening Ear was full of dark blue light and pale blue music. A combo made up of piano, bass fiddle, trumpet, and drums was playing something advanced. I didn't have my slide rule with me, but the four musicians seemed to understand each other. From time to time they smiled and nodded like space jockeys passing in the night.

The man at the piano seemed to be the head technician. He smiled more distantly than the others, and when the melody had been done to death, he took the applause with more exquisite remoteness. Then he bent over his keyboard again like a mad scientist.

The tight-hipped waitress who brought my whisky-and-water was interchangeable with nightclub girls anywhere. Even her parts looked interchangeable. But the audience was different from other nightclub crowds. Most of them were young people with serious expressions on their faces. A high proportion of the girls had short straight hair through which they ran their fingers from time to time. Many of the boys had longer hair than the girls, but they didn't run their fingers through it so much. They stroked their beards instead.

Another tune failed to survive the operation, and then the lights went up. A frail-looking middle-aged man in a dark suit sidled through the blue curtains at the rear of the room. The pianist extended his hand and assisted him onto the bandstand. The audience applauded. The frail-looking man, by way of a bow, allowed his chin to subside on the big black bow tie which blossomed on his shirt front. The applause rose to a crescendo.

"I give you Mr. Chad Bolling," the pianist said. "Master of all the arts, singer of songs to be sung, painter of pictures, hepcat, man of letters. Mr. Chad Bolling."

The clapping went on for a while. The poet lifted his hand as if in benediction, and there was silence.

"Thank you, friends," he said. "With the support of my brilliant young friend Fingers Donahue, I wish to bring to you tonight, if my larynx will permit, my latest poem." His mouth twisted sideways as if in self-mockery. "It ain't chopped liver."

He paused. The instruments began to murmur behind him. Bolling took a roll of manuscript out of his inside breast pocket and unrolled it under the light.

" 'Death Is Tabu,' " he said, and begun to chant in a hoarse carrying voice that reminded me of a carnival spieler. He said that at the end of the night he sat in wino alley where the angels drink canned heat, and that he heard a beat. It seemed a girl came to the mouth of the alley and asked him what he was doing in death valley. " 'Death is the ultimate crutch,' she said," he said. She asked him to come home with her to bed.

He said that sex was the ultimate crutch, but he turned out to be wrong. It seemed he heard a gong. She fled like a ghost, and he was lost, at the end of the end of the night.

While the drummer and the bass fiddler made shock waves on the roof, Bolling raised his voice and began to belt it out. About how he followed her up and down and around and underground, up Russian Hill and Nob Hill and Telegraph Hill and across the Bay Bridge and back by way of the Oakland ferry. So he found the sphinx on Market Street cadging drinks and they got tight and danced on the golden asphalt of delight.

Eventually she fell upon her bed. "I'm star-transfixed," she said. He drank the canned hell of her lips, and it went on like that for quite a while, while the music tittered and moaned. She finally succeeded in convincing him that death was the ultimate crutch, whatever that meant. She knew, because it happened she was dead. "Good night, mister," she said, or he said she said. "Good night, sister," he said.

The audience waited to make sure that Bolling was finished, then burst into a surge of clapping, interspersed with *bravos* and *ole*'s. Bolling stood with pursed lips and absorbed it like a little boy sucking soda pop through a straw. While the lower part of his face seemed to be enjoying itself, his eyes were puzzled. His mouth stretched in a clownish grin:

"Thanks, cats. I'm glad you dig me. Now dig this."

He read a poem about the seven blind staggers of the soul, and one about the beardless wonders on the psycho wards who were going to be the *gurus* of the new truth. At this point I switched off my hearing aid, and waited for it to be over. It took a long time. After the reading there were books to be autographed, questions to be answered, drinks to be drunk.

It was nearly midnight when Bolling left a tableful of admirers and made for the door. I got up to follow him. A large girl with a very hungry face cut in in front of me. She attached herself to Bolling's arm and began to talk into his ear, bending over because she was taller than he was.

He shook his head. "Sorry, kiddie, I'm a married man. Also I'm old enough to be your father."

"What are years?" she said. "A woman's wisdom is ageless."

"Let's see you prove it, honey."

He shook her loose. Tragically clutching the front of her baggy black sweater, she said: "I'm not pretty, am I?"

"You're beautiful, honey. The Greek navy could use you for launching ships. Take it up with them, why don't you?"

He reached up and patted her on the head and went out. I caught up with him on the sidewalk as he was hailing a taxi.

"Mr. Bolling, do you have a minute?"

"It depends on what you want."

"I want to buy you a drink, ask you a few questions."

"I've had a drink. Several, in fact. It's late. I'm beat. Write me a letter, why don't you?"

"I can't write."

He brightened a little. "You mean to tell me you're not an unrecognized literary genius? I thought everybody was."

"I'm a detective. I'm looking for a man. You may have known him at one time."

His taxi had turned in the street and pulled into the curb. He signaled the driver to wait:

"What's his name?"

"John Brown."

"Oh sure, I knew him well at Harper's Ferry. I'm older than I look." His empty clowning continued automatically while he sized me up.

"In 1936 you printed a poem of his in a magazine called *Chisel.*"

"I'm sorry you brought that up. What a lousy name for a magazine. No wonder it folded."

"The name of the poem was 'Luna.'"

"I'm afraid I don't remember it. A lot of words have flowed under the bridge. I did know a John Brown back in the thirties. Whatever happened to John?"

"That's what I'm trying to find out."

"Okay, buy me a drink. But not at the Ear, eh? I get tired of the shaves and the shave-nots."

Bolling dismissed his taxi. We walked about sixty feet to the next bar. A pair of old girls on the two front stools flapped their eyelashes at us as we went in. There was nobody else in the place but a comatose bartender. He roused himself long enough to pour us a couple of drinks.

We sat down in one of the booths, and I showed Bolling my pictures of Tony Galton. "Do you recognize him?"

"I think so. We corresponded for a while, but I only met him once or twice. Twice. He called on us when we were living in Sausalito. And then one Sunday when I was driving down the coast by Luna Bay, I returned the visit."

"Were they living at Luna Bay?"

"A few miles this side of it, in an old place on the ocean. I had the very devil of a time finding it, in spite of the directions Brown had given me. I remember now, he asked me not to tell anyone else where he was living. I was the only one who knew. I don't know why he singled me out, except that he was keen to have me visit his home, and see his son. He may have had some sort of father feeling about me, though I wasn't much older than he was."

"He had a son?"

"Yes, they had a baby. He'd just been born, and he wasn't much bigger than my thumb. Little John was the apple of his father's eye. They were quite a touching little family."

Bolling's voice was gentle. Away from the crowd and the music he showed a different personality. Like other performers, he had a public face and a private one. Each of them was slightly phony, but the private face suited him better.

"You met the wife, did you?"

"Certainly. She was sitting on the front porch when I got there, nursing the baby. She had lovely white breasts, and she didn't in the least mind exposing them. It made quite a picture, there on the bluff above the sea. I tried to get a poem out of her, but it didn't come off. I never really got to know her."

"What sort of a girl was she?"

"Very attractive, I'd say, in the visual sense. She didn't have too much to say for herself. As a matter of fact, she massacred the English language. I suppose she had the fascination of ignorance for Brown. I've seen other young writers and artists fall for girls like that. I've been guilty of it myself, when I was in my pre-Freudian period." He added wryly: "That means before I got analyzed."

"Do you remember her name?"

"Mrs. Brown's name?" He shook his head. "Sorry. In the poem I botched I called her Stella Maris, star of the sea. But that doesn't help you, does it?"

"Can you tell me when you were there? It must have been toward the end of the year 1936."

"Yes. It was around Christmas, just before Christmas—I took along some bauble for the child. Young Brown was very pleased that I did."

Bolling pulled at his chin, lengthening his face. "It's queer I never heard from him after that."

"Did you ever try to get in touch with him?"

"No, I didn't. He may have felt I'd brushed him off. Perhaps I did, without intending to. The woods were full of young writers; it was hard to keep track of them all. I was doing valid work in those days, and a lot of them came to me. Frankly, I've hardly thought of Brown from that day to this. Is he still living on the coast?"

"I don't know. What was he doing in Luna Bay, did he tell you?"

"He was trying to write a novel. He didn't seem to have a job, and I can't imagine what they were living on. They couldn't have been completely destitute, either. They had a nurse to look after the mother and child."

"A nurse?"

"I suppose she was what you'd call a practical nurse. One of those young women who take charge," he added vaguely.

"Do you recall anything about her?"

"She had remarkable eyes, I remember. Sharp black eyes which kept watching me. I don't think she approved of the literary life."

"Did you talk to her at all?"

"I may have. I have a distinct impression of her, that she was the only sensible person in the house. Brown and his wife seemed to be living in Cloud-Cuckoo-Land."

"How do you mean?"

"They were out of touch with the ordinary run of life. I don't mean that as a criticism. I've been out of touch enough in my own life, God knows. I still am." He gave me his clown grin. "You can't make a Hamlet without breaking egos. But let's not talk about me."

"Getting back to the nurse, do you think you can remember her name?"

"I know perfectly well I can't."

"Would you recognize it if I said it?"

"That I doubt. But try me."

"Marian Culligan," I said. "C-u-l-l-i-g-a-n."

"It rings no bell with me. Sorry."

Bolling finished his drink and looked around the bar as if he expected something to happen. I guessed that most of the things that can happen to a man had already happened to him. He changed expressions like rubber masks, but between the masks I could see dismay in his face.

"We might as well have another drink," he said. "This one will be on me. I'm loaded. I just made a hundred smackers at the Ear." Even his commercialism sounded phony.

While I lit a fire under the bartender, Bolling studied the photographs I'd left on the table:

"That's John all right. A nice boy, and perhaps a talented one, but out of this world. All the way out of this world. Where did he get the money for horses and tennis?"

"From his family. They're heavily loaded."

"Good Lord, don't tell me he's the missing heir. Is that why you're making a search for him?"

"That's why."

"They waited long enough."

"You can say that again. Can you tell me how to get to the house the Browns were living in when you visited them?"

"I'm afraid not. I might be able to *show* you, though."

"When?"

"Tomorrow morning if you like."

"That's good of you."

"Not at all. I *liked* John Brown. Besides, I haven't been to Luna Bay for years. Eons. Maybe I'll rediscover my lost youth."

"Maybe." But I didn't think it likely.

Neither did he.

9
.

In the morning I picked up Bolling at his Telegraph Hill apartment. It was one of those sparkling days that make up for all the fog in San Francisco. An onshore wind had swept the air clear and tessellated the blue surface of the Bay. A white ship cutting a white furrow was headed out toward the Golden Gate. White gulls hung above her on the air.

Bolling looked at all this with a fishy eye. He was frowsy and gray and shivering with hangover. He crawled into the back seat and snored all the way to our destination. It was a dingy, formless town sprawling along the coast highway. Its low buildings were dwarfed by the hills rising behind it, the broad sea spreading out in front.

I stopped beside a filling-station where the inland road met Highway 1, and told Bolling to wake up.

"Wha' for?" he mumbled from the depths of sleep. "Wha' happen?"

"Nothing yet. Where do we go from here?"

He groaned and sat up and looked around. The glare from the ocean made his eyes water. He shaded them with his hand. "Where are we?"

"Luna Bay."

"It doesn't look the same," he complained. "I'm not sure whether I can find the place or not. Anyway, we turn north here. Just drive along slowly, and I'll try to spot the road."

Almost two miles north of Luna Bay, the highway cut inland across the base of a promontory. On the far side of the promontory, a new-looking asphalt road turned off toward the sea. A billboard stood at the intersection: "Marvista Manor. Three bedrooms and rumpus room. Tile bathrooms. Built-in kitchens. All utilities in. See our model home."

Bolling tapped my shoulder. "This is the place, I think."

I backed up and made a left turn. The road ran straight for several hundred yards up a gentle slope. We passed a rectangle of bare adobe as big as a football field, where earth-movers were working. A wooden sign at the roadside explained their activity: "Site of the Marvista Shopping Center."

From the crest of the slope we looked down over the roof-tops of a hundred or more houses. They stood along the hillside on raw earth terraces which were only just beginning to sprout grass. Driving along the winding street between them, I could see that most of the houses were occupied. There were curtains at the windows, children playing in the yards, clothes drying on the lines. The houses were painted different colors, which only seemed to emphasize their sameness.

The street unwound itself at the foot of the slope, paralleling the edge of the bluffs. I stopped the car and turned to look at Bolling.

"I'm sorry," he said. "It's changed so much, I can't be certain this is the place. There were some clapboard bungalows, five or six of them, scattered along the bluff. The Browns lived in one of them, if memory serves me."

We got out and walked toward the edge of the bluff. A couple of hundred feet below, the sea wrinkled like blue metal against its base, and burst in periodic white explosions. A mile to the south, under the shelter of the promontory, a cove of quiet water lay in a brown rind of beach.

Bolling pointed toward the cove. "This has to be the place. I remember Brown telling me that inlet was used as a harbor by rum-runners in the old Prohibition days. There used to be an old hotel on the bluff above it. You could see it from the Browns' front porch. Their bungalow must have stood quite near here."

"They probably tore it down when they put in the road. It wouldn't have done me much good to see it, anyway. I was hoping I'd run across a neighbor who remembered the Browns."

"I suppose you could canvass the tradesmen in Luna Bay."

"I could."

"Oh well, it's nice to get out in the country."

Bolling wandered off along the edge of the bluff. Suddenly he said: "Whee!" in a high voice like a gull's screak. He began to flap his arms.

I ran toward him. "What's the matter?"

"Whee!" he said again, and let out a childish laugh. "I was just imagining that I was a bird."

"How did you like it?"

"Very much." He flapped his arms some more. "I can fly! I breast the windy currents of the sky. I soar like Icarus toward the sun. The wax melts. I fall from a great height into the sea. Mother Thalassa."

"Mother who?"

"Thalassa, the sea, the Homeric sea. We could build another Athens. I used to think we could do it in San Francisco, build a new city of man on the great hills. A city measured with forgiveness. Oh, well."

His mood sank again. I pulled him away from the edge. He was so unpredictable I thought he might take a flying leap into space, and I was beginning to like him.

"Speaking of mothers," I said, "if John Brown's wife had just had a baby, she must have been going to a doctor. Did they happen to mention where the baby was born?"

"Yes. Right in their house. The nearest hospital is in Redwood City, and Brown didn't want to take his wife there. The chances are she had a local doctor."

"Let's hope he's still around."

I drove back through the housing-tract until I saw a young woman walking a pram. She shied like a filly when I pulled up beside her. In the daytime the tract was reserved for women and children; unknown men in cars were probably kidnappers. I got out and approached her, smiling as innocuously as I could.

"I'm looking for a doctor."

"Oh. Is somebody sick?"

"My friend's wife is going to have a baby. They're thinking of moving into Marvista Manor, and they thought they'd better check on the medical situation."

"Dr. Meyers is very good," she said. "I go to him myself."

"In Luna Bay?"

"That's right."

"How long has he practiced there?"

"I wouldn't know. We just moved out from Richmond month before last."

"How old is Dr. Meyers?"

"Thirty, thirty-five, I dunno."

"Too young," I said.

"If your friend will feel safer with an older man, I think there is one in town. I don't remember his name, though. Personally I like a young doctor, they know all the latest wonder drugs and all."

Wonder drugs. I thanked her, and drove back to Luna Bay in search of a drugstore. The proprietor gave me a rundown on the three local doctors. A Dr. George Dineen was the only one who had practiced there in the thirties. He was an elderly man on the verge of retirement. I'd probably find him in his office if he wasn't out on a call. It was only a couple of blocks from the drugstore.

I left Bolling drinking coffee at the fountain, and walked to the doctor's office. It occupied the front rooms of a rambling house with green shingle walls which stood on a dusty side street. A woman of about sixty answered the door. She had blue-white hair and a look on her face you don't see too often any more, the look of a woman who hasn't been disappointed:

"Yes, young man?"

"I'd like to see the doctor."

"His office hours are in the afternoon. They don't start till one-thirty."

"I don't want to see him as a patient."

"If you're a pharmaceutical salesman, you'd better wait till after lunch. Dr. Dineen doesn't like his mornings to be disturbed."

"I'm only in town for the morning. I'm investigating a disappearance. He may be able to help me to find a missing man."

She had a very responsive face, in spite of its slack lines of age. Her eyes imagined what it would be like to lose a loved one. "Well, that's different. Come in, Mr.—"

"Archer. I'm a private detective."

"My husband is in the garden. I'll bring him in."

She left me in the doctor's office. Several diplomas hung on the wall above the old oak desk. The earliest stated that Dr. Dineen had graduated from the University of Ohio Medical School in 1914. The room itself was like a preserve of prewar time. The cracked leather furniture had been molded by use into comfortable human shapes. A set of old chessmen laid out on a board stood like miniature armies stalled in the sunlight that fell slanting from the window.

The doctor came in and shook hands with me. He was a tall high-shouldered old man. His eyes were noncommittal under shaggy gray brows which hung like bird's-nests on the cliff of his face. He lowered himself into the chair behind his desk. His head was partly bald; a few strands of hair lay lankly across the top of his scalp.

"You mentioned a missing person to my wife. One of my patients, perhaps?"

"Perhaps. His name was John Brown. In 1936 he and his wife lived a few miles up the coast where the Marvista tract is now."

"I remember them very well," the doctor said. "Their son was in this office not so very long ago, sitting where you're sitting."

"Their son?"

"John, Junior. You may know him. He's looking for his father, too."

"No," I said, "I don't know him. But I'd certainly like to."

"I daresay that could be arranged." Dr. Dineen's deep voice rumbled to a stop. He looked at me intently, as if he was getting ready to make a diagnosis. "First, I'd want to know the reasons for your interest in the family."

"I was hired to make a search for the father, the senior John Brown."

"Has your search had any results?"

"Not until now. You say this boy who came to see you is looking for his father?"

"That is correct."

"What brought him to you?"

"He has the ordinary filial emotions. If his father is alive, he wants to be with him. If his father is dead, he wants to know."

"I mean what brought him here to your office specifically? Had you known him before?"

"I brought him into the world. In my profession, that constitutes the best possible introduction."

"Are you sure it's the same boy?"

"I have no reason to doubt it." The doctor looked at me with some distaste, as if I'd criticized some work he'd done with his hands. "Before we go any further, Mr. Archer, you can oblige me with a fuller response to my question. You haven't told me who hired you."

"Sorry, I can't do that. I've been asked to keep my client's identity confidential."

"No doubt you have. I've been keeping such matters confidential for the past forty years."

"And you won't talk unless I do, is that it?"

The doctor raised his hand and brushed the thought away from his face, like an annoying insect. "I suggested no bargain. I simply want to know who I'm dealing with. There may be grave matters involved."

"There are."

"I think you ought to elucidate that remark."

"I can't."

We faced each other in a stretching silence. His eyes were steady, and bright with the hostility of a proud old man. I was afraid of losing him entirely, just as the case seemed to be breaking open. While I didn't doubt his integrity, I had my own integrity to think of, too. I'd promised Gordon Sable and Mrs. Galton to name no names.

Dr. Dineen produced a pipe, and began to pack its charred bowl with tobacco from an oilskin pouch. "We seem to have reached a stalemate. Do you play chess, Mr. Archer?"

"Not as well as you do, probably. I've never studied the book."

"I would have thought you had." He finished packing his pipe, and lit it with a kitchen match. The blue smoke swirled in the hollow shafts of sunlight from the window. "We're wasting both our times. I suggest you make a move."

"I thought this was a stalemate."

"New game." A flicker of interest showed in his eyes for the first time. "Tell me about yourself. Why would a man of your sort spend his life doing the kind of work you do? Do you make much money?"

"Enough to live on. I don't do it for the money, though. I do it because I want to."

"Isn't it dirty work, Mr. Archer?"

"It depends on who's doing it, like doctoring or anything else. I try to keep it clean."

"Do you succeed?"

"Not entirely. I've made some bad mistakes about people. Some of them assume that a private detective is automatically crooked, and they act accordingly, as you're doing now."

The old man emitted a grunt which sounded like a seal's bark. "I can't act blindly in a matter of this importance."

"Neither can I. I don't know what makes it important to you—"

"I'll tell you," he said shortly. "Human lives are involved. A boy's love for his parents is involved. I try to handle these things with the care they deserve."

"I appreciate that. You seem to have a special interest in John Brown, Junior."

"I do have. The young fellow's had a rough time of it. I don't want him hurt unnecessarily."

"It's not my intention to hurt him. If the boy is actually John Brown's son, you'd be doing him a favor by leading me to him."

"You're going to have to prove that to me. I'll be frank to say I've had one or two experiences with private detectives in my time. One of them had to do with the blackmailing of a patient of mine—a young girl who had a child out of wedlock. I don't mean that reflects on you, but it makes a man leery."

"All right. I'll put my position hypothetically. Let's say I'd been hired to find the heir to several million dollars."

"I've heard that one before. You'll have to invent a better gambit than that."

"I didn't invent it. It happens to be the truth."

"Prove it."

"That will be easy to do when the time comes. Right now, I'd say the burden of proof is on this boy. Can he prove his identity?"

"The question never came up. As a matter of fact, the proof of his identity is on his face. I knew whose son he was as soon as he stepped in here. His resemblance to his father is striking."

"How long ago did he turn up?"

"About a month. I've seen him since."

"As a patient?"

"As a friend," Dineen said.

"Why did he come to you in the first place?"

"My name is on his birth certificate. Now hold your horses, young man. Give me a chance to think." The doctor smoked in silence for a while. "Do you seriously tell me that this boy is heir to a fortune?"

"He will be, if his father is dead. His grandmother is still living. She has the money."

"But you won't divulge her name?"

"Not without her permission. I suppose I could call her long distance. But I'd rather have a chance to talk to the boy first."

The doctor hesitated. He held his right hand poised in the air, then struck the desk-top with the flat of it. "I'll take a chance on you, though I may regret it later."

"You won't if I can help it. Where can I find him?"

"We'll come to that."

"What did he have to say about his origins?"

"It would be more appropriate if you got that from him. I'm willing to tell you what I know about his father and mother from my own direct observation. And this has more relevance than you may think." He paused. "What precisely did this anonymous client of yours hire you to do?"

"Find John Brown, Senior," I said.

"I take it that isn't his real name."

"That's right, it isn't."

"I'm not surprised," Dineen said. "At the time I knew him, I did some speculating about him. It occurred to me he might be a remittance man—one of those ne'er-do-wells whose families paid them to stay away from home. I remember when his wife was delivered, Brown paid me with a hundred-dollar-bill. It didn't seem to suit with their scale of living. And there were other things, his wife's jewels, for example—diamonds and rubies in ornate gold settings. One day she came in here like a walking jewelry store.

"I warned her not to wear them. They were living out in the country, near the old Inn, and it was fairly raw territory in those days. Also, people were poor. A lot of them used to pay me for my services in fish. I had so much fish during the Depression I've never eaten it since.

No matter. A public display of jewels was an incitement to robbery. I told the young lady so, and she left off wearing them, at least when I saw her."

"Did you see her often?"

"Four or five times, I'd say. Once or twice before the boy was born, and several times afterwards. She was a healthy enough wench, no complications. The main thing I did for her was to instruct her in the care of an infant. Nothing in her background had prepared her for motherhood."

"Did she talk about her background?"

"She didn't have to. It had left marks on her body, for one thing. She'd been beaten half to death with a belt buckle."

"Not by her husband?"

"Hardly. There had been other men in her life, as the phrase goes. I gathered that she'd been on her own from an early age. She was one of the wandering children of the thirties—quite a different sort from her husband."

"How old was she?"

"I think nineteen or twenty, perhaps older. She looked older. Her experiences hadn't hardened her, but as I said they left her unprepared for motherhood. Even after she was back on her feet, she needed a nurse to help her care for the child. Actually, she was a child herself in emotional development."

"Do you remember the nurse's name?"

"Let me see. I believe she was a Mrs. Kerrigan."

"Or Culligan?"

"Culligan, that was it. She was a good young woman, fairly well trained. I believe she took off at the same time the Brown family did."

"The Brown family took off?"

"They skipped, without a good-by or a thank-you to anybody. Or so it appeared at the time."

"When was this?"

"A very few weeks after the child was born. It was close to Christmas Day of 1936, I think a day or two after. I remember it so distinctly because I've gone into it since with the sheriff's men."

"Recently?"

"Within the last five months. To make a long story short, when they were clearing the land for the Marvista tract, a set of bones were unearthed. The local deputy asked me to look them over to see what

I could learn from them. I did so. They were human bones, which had probably belonged to a man of medium height, in his early twenties.

"It's not unlikely, in my opinion, that they are John Brown's bones. They were found buried under the house he lived in. The house was torn down to make way for the new road. Unfortunately, we had no means of making a positive identification. The skull was missing, which ruled out the possibility of dental evidence."

"It rules in the possibility of murder."

Dineen nodded gravely. "There's rather more than a possibility of murder. One of the cervical vertebrae had been cut through by a heavy instrument. I'd say John Brown, if that is who he is, was decapitated with an ax."

10
.

BEFORE I left Dr. Dineen, he gave me a note of introduction to the deputy in charge of the local sheriff's office, written on a prescription blank; and the address of the gas station where John Brown, Jr., worked. I walked back to the drugstore in a hurry. Bolling was still at the fountain, with a grilled cheese sandwich in his left hand and a pencil in his right. He was simultaneously munching the sandwich and scribbling in a notebook.

"Sorry to keep you waiting—"

"Excuse me, I'm writing a poem."

He went on scribbling. I ate an impatient sandwich while he finished, and dragged him out to the car:

"I want to show you somebody; I'll explain who he is later." I started the car and turned south on the highway. "What's your poem about?"

"The city of man. I'm making a break-through into the affirmative. It's going to be good—the first good poem I've written in years."

He went on telling me about it, in language which I didn't understand. I found the place I was looking for on the southern outskirts of the town. It was a small independent station with three pumps, one attendant. The attendant was a young man in white drill coveralls. He was busy gassing a pickup truck whose bed was piled with brown fishermen's nets. I pulled in behind it and watched him.

There was no doubt that he looked like Anthony Galton. He had the same light eyes set wide apart, the same straight nose and full mouth. Only his hair was different; it was dark and straight.

Bolling was leaning forward in the seat. "For Christ's sake! Is it Brown? It can't be Brown. He's almost as old as I am."

"He had a son, remember."

"Is this the son?"

"I think so. Do you remember the color of the baby's hair?"

"It was dark, what there was of it. Like his mother's."

Bolling started to get out of the car.

"Wait a minute," I said. "Don't tell him who you are."

"I want to ask him about his father."

"He doesn't know where his father is. Besides, there's a question of identity. I want to see what he says without any prompting."

Bolling gave me a frustrated look, but he stayed in the car. The driver of the pickup paid for his gas and rattled away. I pulled up even with the pumps, and got out for a better look at the boy.

He appeared to be about twenty-one or -two. He was very good-looking, as his putative father had been. His smile was engaging.

"What can I do for you, sir?"

"Fill her up. It'll only take a couple of gallons. I stopped because I want you to check the oil."

"I'll be glad to, sir."

He seemed like a willing boy. He filled the tank, and wiped the windshield spotless. But when he lifted the hood to check the oil, he couldn't find the dip-stick. I showed him where it was.

"Been working here long?"

He looked embarrassed. "Two weeks. I haven't caught on to all the new cars yet."

"Think nothing of it." I looked across the highway at the windswept shore where the long combers were crashing. "This is nice country. I wouldn't mind settling out here."

"Are you from San Francisco?"

"My friend is." I indicated Bolling, who was still in the car, sulking. "I came up from Santa Teresa last night."

He didn't react to the name.

"Who owns the beach property across the highway, do you know?"

"I'm sorry, I wouldn't know. My boss probably would, though."

"Where is he?"

"Mr. Turnell has gone to lunch. He should be back pretty soon, if you want to talk to him."

"How soon?"

He glanced at the cheap watch on his wrist. "Fifteen or twenty minutes. His lunch-hour is from eleven to twelve. It's twenty to twelve now."

"I might as well wait for him. I'm in no hurry."

Bolling was in visible pain by this time. He made a conspiratorial gesture, beckoning me to the car.

"Is it Brown's son?" he said in a stage whisper.

"Could be."

"Why don't you ask him?"

"I'm waiting for him to tell me. Take it easy, Mr. Bolling."

"May I talk to him?"

"I'd just as soon you didn't. This is a ticklish business."

"I don't see why it should be. Either he is or he isn't."

The boy came up behind me. "Is something the matter, sir? Anything more I can do?"

"Nothing on both counts. The service was fine."

"Thank you."

His teeth showed bright in his tanned face. His smile was strained, though. He seemed to sense the tension in me and Bolling. I said as genially as I knew how:

"Are you from these parts?"

"I could say I was, I guess. I was born a few miles from here."

"But you're not a local boy."

"That's true. How can you tell?"

"Accent. I'd say you were raised in the middle west."

"I was." He seemed pleased by my interest. "I just came out from Michigan this year."

"Have you had any higher education?"

"College, you mean? As a matter of fact I have. Why do you ask?"

"I was thinking you could do better for yourself than jockeying a gas pump."

"I hope to," he said, with a look of aspiration. "I regard this work as temporary."

"What kind of work would you like to do?"

He hesitated, flushing under his tan. "I'm interested in acting. I know that sounds ridiculous. Half the people who come to California probably want to be actors."

"Is that why you came to California?"

"It was one of the reasons."

"This is a way-stop to Hollywood for you, then?"

"I guess you could say that." His face was closing up. Too many questions were making him suspicious.

"Ever been to Hollywood?"

"No. I haven't."

"Had any acting experience?"

"I have as a student."

"Where?"

"At the University of Michigan."

I had what I wanted: a way to check his background, if he was telling the truth; if he was lying, a way to prove that he was lying. Universities kept full dossiers on their students.

"The reason I'm asking you all these questions," I said, "is this. I have an office on Sunset Boulevard in Hollywood. I'm interested in talent, and I was struck by your appearance."

He brightened up considerably. "Are you an agent?"

"No, but I know a lot of agents." I wanted to avoid the lie direct, on general principles, so I brought Bolling into the conversation: "My friend here is a well-known writer. Mr. Chad Bolling. You may have heard of him."

Bolling was confused. He was a sensitive man, and my underhanded approach to the boy troubled him. He leaned out of the car to shake hands:

"Pleased to meet you."

"I'm very glad to meet you, sir. My name is John Brown, by the way. Are you in the picture business?"

"No."

Bolling was tongue-tied by the things he wanted to say and wasn't supposed to. The boy looked from Bolling to me, wondering what he had done to spoil the occasion. Bolling took pity on him. With a defiant look at me, he said:

"Did you say your name was John Brown? I knew a John Brown once, in Luna Bay."

"That was my father's name. You must have known my father."

"I believe I did." Bolling climbed out of the car. "I met you when you were a very small baby."

I watched John Brown. He flushed up warmly. His gray eyes shone with pleasure, and then were moist with deeper feelings. I had to remind myself that he was a self-admitted actor.

He pumped Bolling's hand a second time. "Imagine your knowing my father! How long is it since you've seen him?"

"Twenty-two years—a long time."

"Then you don't know where he is now?"

"I'm afraid not, John. He dropped out of sight, you know, quite soon after you were born."

The boy's face stiffened. "And Mother?" His voice cracked on the word.

"Same story," I said. "Don't you remember either of your parents?"

He answered reluctantly: "I remember my mother. She left me in an orphanage in Ohio when I was four. She promised to come back for me, but she never did come back. I spent nearly twelve years in that institution, waiting for her to come back." His face was dark with emotion. "Then I realized she must be dead. I ran away."

"Where was it?" I said. "What town?"

"Crystal Springs, a little place near Cleveland."

"And you say you ran away from there?"

"Yes, when I was sixteen. I went to Ann Arbor, Michigan, to get an education. A man named Lindsay took me in. He didn't adopt me, but he let me use his name. I went to school under the name of John Lindsay."

"Why the name change?"

"I didn't want to use my own name. I had good reason."

"Are you sure it wasn't the other way around? Are you sure John Lindsay wasn't your real name, and you took the name of Brown later?"

"Why would I do that?"

"Somebody hired you, maybe."

He flushed up darkly. "Who are you?"

"A private detective."

"If you're a detective, what was all that bushwa about Hollywood and Sunset Boulevard?"

"I have my office on Sunset Boulevard."

"But what you said was deliberately misleading."

"Don't worry about me so much. I needed some information, and I got it."

"You could have asked me directly. I have nothing to hide."

"That remains to be seen."

Bolling stepped between us, sputtering at me in sudden anger: "Leave the boy alone now. He's obviously genuine. He even has his father's voice. Your implications are an insult."

I didn't argue with him. In fact, I was ready to believe he was right. The boy stepped back away from us as if we'd threatened his life. His eyes had turned the color of slate, and there were white rims on his nostrils:

"What is this, anyway?"

"Don't get excited," I said.

"I'm not excited." He was trembling all over. "You come here and ask me a bunch of questions and tell me you knew my father. Naturally I want to know what it means."

Bolling moved toward him and laid an impulsive hand on his arm. "It could mean a great deal to you, John. Your father belonged to a wealthy family."

The boy brushed him off. He was young for his age in some ways. "I don't care about that. I want to see my father."

"Why is it so important?" Bolling said.

"I never had a father." His working face was naked to the light. Tears ran down his cheeks. He shook them off angrily.

I bought him, and made a down payment: "I've asked enough questions for now, John. Have you talked to the local police, by the way?"

"Yes, I have. And I know what you're getting at. They have a box of bones at the sheriff's station. Some of them claim that they're my father's bones, but I don't believe it. Neither does Deputy Mungan."

"Do you want to come down there with me now?"

"I can't," he said. "I can't close up the station. Mr. Turnell expects me to stay on the job."

"What time do you get off?"

"About seven-thirty, week nights."

"Where can I get in touch with you tonight?"

"I live in a boardinghouse about a mile from here. Mrs. Gorgello's." He gave me the address.

"Aren't you going to tell him who his father was?" Bolling said.

"I will when it's been proved. Let's go, Bolling."

He climbed into the car reluctantly.

11
.

THE Sheriff's substation was a stucco shoebox of a building across the street from a sad-looking country hotel. Bolling said he would stay in the car, on the grounds that skeletons frightened him:

"It even horrifies me to think that I contain one. Unlike Webster in Mr. Eliot's poem, I like to remain oblivious to the skull beneath the skin."

I never knew whether Bolling was kidding me.

Deputy Mungan was a very large man, half a head taller than I was, with a face like unfinished sculpture. I gave him my name and occupation, and Dineen's note of introduction. When he'd read it, he reached across the counter that divided his little office, and broke all the bones in my hand:

"Any friend of Doc Dineen's is a friend of mine. Come on in around behind and tell me your business."

I went on in around behind and sat in the chair he placed for me at the end of his desk:

"It has to do with some bones that were found out in the Marvista tract. I understand you've made a tentative identification."

"I wouldn't go so far as to say that. Doc Dineen thinks it was a man he knew—fellow by the name of John Brown. It fits in with the location of the body, all right. But we haven't been able to nail it down. The trouble is, no such man was ever reported missing in these parts. We haven't been able to turn up any local antecedents. Naturally we're still working on it."

Mungan's broad face was serious. He talked like a trained cop, and his eyes were sharp as tacks. I said: "We may be able to help each other to clarify the issue."

"Any help you can give me will be welcome. This has been dragging on for five months now, more like six." He threw out a quick hooked question: "You represent his family, maybe?"

"I represent a family. They asked me not to use their name. And there's still a question whether they are the dead man's family. Was there any physical evidence found with the bones? A watch, or a ring? Shoes? Clothing?"

"Nothing. Not even a stitch of clothing."

"I suppose it could rot away completely in twenty-two years. What about buttons?"

"No buttons. Our theory is he was buried the way he came into the world."

"But without a head."

Mungan nodded gravely. "Doc Dineen filled you in, eh? I've been thinking about that head myself. A young fellow came in here a few weeks ago, claimed to be John Brown's son."

"Don't you think he is?"

"He acted like it. He got pretty upset when I showed him the bones. Unfortunately, he didn't know any more about his father than I do. Which is nil, absolutely nil. We know this John Brown lived out on the old Bluff Road for a couple of months in 1936, and that's the sumtotal of it. On top of that, the boy doesn't believe these are his father's bones. And he could just be right. I've been doing some thinking, as I said.

"This business about the head, now. We assumed when the body was first turned up, that he was killed by having his head cut off." Mungan made a snicking sound between tongue and palate, and sheared the air with the edge of his huge hand. "Maybe he was. Or maybe the head was chopped off after death, to remove identification. You know how much we depend on teeth and fillings. Back in the thirties, before we developed our modern lab techniques, teeth and fillings were the main thing we had to go on.

"If my hypothesis is right, the killer was a pro. And that fits in with certain other facts. In the twenties and thirties, the Bluff Road area was a stamping ground for hoods. It was until quite recently, as a matter of fact. In those days it was a real hotbed. A lot of the liquor that kept San Francisco going during Prohibition came in by sea and was funneled through Luna Bay. They brought in other things than liquor—drugs, for instance, and women from Mexico and Panama. You ever hear of the Red Horse Inn?"

"No."

"It stood on the coast about a mile south of where we found the skeleton. They tore it down a couple of years ago, after we put the stopper on it. That was a place with a history. It used to be a resort hotel for well-heeled people from the City and the Peninsula. The rum-runners took it over in the twenties. They converted it into a three-way operation: liquor warehouse in the basement, bars and gaming on the first floor, women upstairs. The reason I know so much about it, I had my first drink there back about 1930. And my first woman."

"You don't look that old."

"I was sixteen at the time. I think that's one of the reasons I went into law enforcement. I wanted to put bastards like Lempi out of circulation. Lempi was the boss hood who ran the place in the twenties. I knew him personally, but the law got to him before I grew up to his size. They got him for income tax in 1932, he died on the Rock a few years later. Some of his guns were sent up at the same time.

"I knew those boys, see, and this is the point I'm coming to. I knew what they were capable of doing. They killed for pay, and they killed because they enjoyed it. They bragged in public that nobody could touch them. It took a federal indictment to cool Lempi. Meantime a number of people lost their lives. Our Mr. Bones could be one of them."

"But you say Lempi and his boys were cleaned out in '32. Our man was killed in '36."

"We don't know that. We jumped to that conclusion on the basis of what Doc Dineen said, but we've got no concrete evidence to go on. The Doc himself admits that given the chemistry of that particular soil, he can't pinpoint time of burial closer than five years either way. Mr. Bones could have been knocked off as early as 1931. I say *could* have."

"Or as late as 1941?" I said.

"That's right. You see how little we have to go on."

"Do I get to take a look at what you have?"

"Why not?"

Mungan went into a back room and returned lugging a metal box about the size of a hope chest. He set it on top of his desk, unlocked it, lifted the lid. Its contents were jumbled like kindling. Only the vertebrae had been articulated with wire, and lay coiled on the heap like the skeleton of a snake. Mungan showed me where the neck bone had been severed by a cutting instrument.

The larger bones had been labeled: left femur, left fibula, and so on. Mungan picked out a heavy bone about a foot long; it was marked "right humerus."

"This is the bone of the upper arm," he said in a lecturer's tone. "Come along on over to the window here. I want to show you something."

He held the bone to the light. Close to one knobbed end, I made out a thin line filled and surrounded by deposits of calcium.

"A break?" I said.

"I hope in more senses than one. It's a mended fracture, the only unusual thing in the entire skeleton. Dineen says it was probably set by a trained hand, a doctor. If we could find the doctor that set it, it would answer some of our questions. So if you've got any ideas . . ." Mungan let his voice trail off, but his eyes stayed hard on my face.

"I'll do some telephoning."

"You can use my phone."

"A pay phone would suit me better."

"If you say so. There's one across the street, in the hotel."

I found the telephone booth at the rear of the dingy hotel lobby, and placed a call to Santa Teresa. Sable's secretary put him on the line.

"Archer speaking, the one-man dragnet," I said. "I'm in Luna Bay."

"You're where?"

"Luna Bay. It's a small town on the coast south of San Francisco. I have a couple of items for you: a dead man's bones, and a live boy. Let's start with the bones."

"Bones?"

"Bones. They were dug up by accident about six months ago, and they're in the sheriff's substation here. They're unidentified, but the chances are better than even that they belong to the man I'm looking for. The chances are also better than even that he was murdered twenty-two years ago."

The line was silent.

"Did you get that, Sable? He was probably murdered."

"I heard you. But you say the remains haven't been identified."

"That's where you can help me, if you will. You better write this down. There's a fracture in the right humerus, close to the elbow. It was evidently set by a doctor. I want you to check on whether Tony Galton ever had a broken right arm. If so, who was the doctor that looked after it? It may have been Howell, in which case there's no sweat. I'll call you back in fifteen minutes."

"Wait. You mentioned a boy. What's he got to do with all this?"

"That remains to be seen. He thinks he's the dead man's son."

"Tony's son?"

"Yes, but he isn't sure about it. He came here from Michigan in the hope of finding out who his father was."

"Do you think he's Tony's son?"

"I wouldn't bet my life savings on it. I wouldn't bet against it, either. He bears a strong resemblance to Tony. On the other hand, his story is weak."

"What story does he tell?"

"It's pretty long and complicated for the telephone. He was brought up in an orphanage, he says, went to college under an assumed name, came out here a month ago to find out who he really is. I don't say it couldn't have happened the way he says, but it needs to be proved out."

"What kind of a boy is he?"

"Intelligent, well spoken, fairly well mannered. If he's a con artist, he's smooth for his age."

"How old is he?"

"Twenty-two."

"You work very quickly," he said.

"I was lucky. What about your end? Has Trask got anything on my car?"

"Yes. It was found abandoned in San Luis Obispo."

"Wrecked?"

"Out of gas. It's in perfectly good shape, I saw it myself. Trask has it impounded in the county garage."

"What about the man who stole it?"

"Nothing definite. He probably took another car in San Luis. One disappeared late yesterday afternoon. Incidentally, Trask tells me that the Jaguar, the murder car, as he calls it, was another stolen car."

"Who was the owner?"

"I have no idea. The Sheriff is having the engine number traced."

I hung up, and spent the better part of fifteen minutes thinking about Marian Culligan Matheson and her respectable life in Redwood City which I was going to have to invade again. Then I called Sable back. The line was busy. I tried again in ten minutes, and got him.

"I've been talking to Dr. Howell," he said. "Tony broke his right arm when he was in prep school. Howell didn't set the break himself, but he knows the doctor who did. In any case, it was a fractured humerus."

"See if they can turn up the X-ray, will you? They don't usually keep X-ray pictures this long, but it's worth trying. It's the only means I can think of for making a positive identification."

"What about teeth?"

"Everything above the neck is missing."

It took Sable a moment to grasp this. Then he said: "Good Lord!" After another pause: "Perhaps I should drop everything and come up there. What do you think?"

"It might be a good idea. It would give you a chance to interview the boy."

"I believe I'll do that. Where is he now?"

"Working. He works at a gas station in town. How long will it take you to get here?"

"I'll be there between eight and nine."

"Meet me at the sheriff's substation at nine. In the meantime, is it all right if I take the local deputy into my confidence? He's a good man."

"I'd just as soon you didn't."

"You can't handle murder without publicity."

"I'm aware of that," Sable said acidly. "But then we don't know for certain that the victim was Tony, do we?"

Before I could give him any further argument, Sable hung up.

12
•
___

I PHONED the Santa Teresa courthouse. After some palaver, I got
Sheriff Trask himself on the other end of the line. He sounded harried:
"What is it?"

"Gordon Sable just told me you traced the murder car in the Culligan
case."

"A fat lot of good it did us. It was stolen in San Francisco night before last. The thief changed the license plates."

"Who owns it?"

"San Francisco man. I'm thinking of sending somebody up to talk
to him. Far as I can make out, he didn't report the theft."

"That doesn't sound so good. I'm near San Francisco now, in Luna
Bay. Do you want me to look him up?"

"I'd be obliged. I can't really spare anybody. His name is Roy Lemberg. He lives at a hotel called the Sussex Arms."

An hour later, I drove into the garage under Union Square. Bolling
said good-by to me at the entrance:

"Good luck with your case."

"Good luck with your poem. And thanks."

The Sussex Arms was another side-street hotel like the one I had
spent the night in. It was several blocks closer to Market Street, and
several degrees more dilapidated. The desk clerk had large sorrowful
eyes and a very flexible manner, as if he had been run through all the
wringers of circumstance.

He said Mr. Lemberg was probably at work.

"Where does he work?"

"He's supposed to be a car salesman."

"Supposed to be?"

"I don't think he's doing so good. He's just on commission with a
secondhand dealer. The reason I know, he tried to sell *me* a car." He
snickered, as if he possessed the secret of a more advanced type of
transportation.

"Has Lemberg lived here long?"

"A few weeks, more or less. This wouldn't happen to be a police matter?"

"I want to see him on personal business."

"Maybe Mrs. Lemberg is up in the room. She usually is."

"Try her, will you? My name is Archer. I'm interested in buying their car."

He went to the switchboard and relayed the message. "Mrs. Lemberg says come right on up. It's three-eleven. You can take the elevator."

The elevator jerked me up to the third floor. At the end of the dust-colored hallway, a blonde in a pink robe gleamed like a mirage. Closer up, her luster was dimmer. She had darkness at the roots of her hair, and a slightly desperate smile.

She waited until I was practically standing on her feet; then she yawned and stretched elastically. She had wine and sleep on her breath. But her figure was very good, lush-breasted and narrow-waisted. I wondered if it was for sale or simply on exhibition by the owner.

"Mrs. Lemberg?"

"Yeah. What's all this about the Jag? Somebody phones this morning and he tells them it was stole. And now you want to buy it."

"Was the car stolen?"

"That was just some of Roy's malarkey. He's full of it. You serious about buying?"

"Only if he has clear title," I said fussily.

My show of reluctance made her eager, as it was intended to. "Come in, we'll talk about it. The Jag is in his name, but I'm the one that makes the money decisions."

I followed her into the little room. At the chinks in the drawn blinds, daylight peered like a spy. She turned on a lamp and waved her hand vaguely toward a chair. A man's shirt hung on the back of it. A half-empty half-gallon jug of muscatel stood on the floor beside it.

"Siddown, excuse the mess. With all the outside work I do, I don't get time to houseclean."

"What do you do?"

"I model. Go ahead, siddown. That shirt is ready for the laundry, anyway."

I sat down against the shirt. She flung herself on the bed, her body falling automatically into a cheesecake pose:

"Were you thinking of paying cash?"

"If I buy."

"We sure could use a chunk of ready cash. What price did you have in mind? I'm warning you, I won't let it go too cheap. That's my chief recreation in life, driving out in the country. The trees and everything." Her own words seemed to bewilder her. "Not that he takes me out in it. I hardly ever see the car any more. That brother of his monopolizes it. Roy's so soft, he don't stick up for his rights the way he should. Like the other night."

"What happened the other night?"

"Just more of the same. Tommy comes up full of the usual. He's got another one of these big job opportunities that never pan out. All he needs is a car, see, and he'll be making a fortune in no time. So Roy lends him the car, just like that. Tommy could talk the fillings right out of his teeth."

"How long ago was this?"

"Night before last, I think. I lose count of the nights and days."

"I didn't know Roy had a brother," I prompted her.

"Yeah, he's got a brother." Her voice was flat. "Roy's all fixed up with a brother, till death doth us part. We'd still be in Nevada, living the life of O'Reilly, if it wasn't for that punk."

"How so?"

"I'm talking too much." But bad luck had dulled her brains, bad wine had loosened her tongue: "The Adult Authority said they'd give him a parole if he had somebody willing to be responsible. So back we move to California, to make a home for Tommy."

I thought: This is a home? She caught my look:

"We didn't always live here. We made a down payment on a real nice little place in Daly City. But Roy started drinking again, we couldn't hold onto it." She turned over onto her stomach, supporting her chin on her hand. Her china-blue eyes looked fractured in the light. "Not that I blame him," she added more softly. "That brother of his would drive a saint to drink. Roy never hurt nobody in his life. Except me, and you expect that from any man."

I was touched by her asphalt innocence. The long curve of her hip and thigh, the rich flesh of her bosom, were like the disguise of a frightened adolescent.

"What was Tommy in for?"

"He beat up a guy and took his wallet. The wallet had three bucks in it, and Tommy was in for six months."

"That works out to fifty cents a month. Tommy must be quite a mastermind."

"Yeah, to hear him tell it. It was supposed to be longer, but I guess he's good when he's in, with somebody watching him. It's just when he gets out." She cocked her head sideways, and her bright hair fell across her hand. "I don't know why I'm telling you all this. In my experience, the guys do most of the talking. I guess you have a talkable-attable face."

"You're welcome to the use of it."

"Sanctuary mucho. But you came here to buy a car. I was almost forgetting. I worry so much, I forget things." Her gaze slid down from my face to the muscatel jug. "I had a few drinkies, too, if the truth be knownst." She drew a lock of hair across her eyes and looked at me through it.

Her kittenish mood was depressing. I said: "When can I have a look at the Jaguar?"

"Any time, I guess. Maybe you better talk to Roy."

"Where can I find him?"

"Don't ask me. Tell you the truth, I don't even know if Tommy brought it back yet."

"Why did Roy say the car was stolen?"

"I dunno. I was half asleep when he left. I didn't ask him."

The thought of sleep made her yawn. She dropped her head and lay still. Traffic went by in the street like a hostile army. Then footsteps came down the corridor and paused outside the door. A man spoke softly through it:

"You busy, Fran?"

She raised herself on her arms like a fighter hearing a far-off count. "Is that you, hon?"

"Yeah. You busy?"

"Not so's you'd notice. Come ahead in."

He flung the door open, saw me, and hung back like an interloper. "Excuse me."

His dark eyes were quick and uncertain. He was still in his early thirties, but he had a look about him, intangible and definite as an odor. The look of a man who has lost his grip and is sliding. His suit was sharply pressed, but it hadn't been cleaned for too long. The very plumpness of his face gave it a lardlike inertness, as if it had stopped reacting to everything but crises.

His face interested me. Unless I was getting hipped on family re-
semblances, he was an older softer version of the boy who'd stolen my
car. This one's dark curls were thinner and limper. And the violence
of the younger man was petulance in him. He said to his wife:

"You told me you weren't busy."

"I'm not. I'm only resting." She rolled over and sat up. "This gentleman wants to buy the Jaguar."

"It's not for sale." Lemberg closed the door behind him. "Who told
you it was?"

"Grapevine."

"What else did you hear?"

He was quick on the uptake. I couldn't hope to con him for long,
so I struck at his vulnerable spot:

"Your brother's in trouble."

His gaze went to my shoulder, my hands, my mouth, and then my
eyes. I think in his extremity he would have liked to hit me. But I could
have broken him in half, and he must have known it. Still, anger or
frustration made him foolish:

"Did Schwartz send you to tell me this?"

"Who?"

"You needn't play dumb. Otto Schwartz." He gargled the words. "If
he sent you, you can take a message back for me. Tell him to take a
running jump in the Truckee River and do us all a favor."

I got up. Instinctively, one of Lemberg's arms rose to guard his
face. The gesture told a lot about him and his background.

"Your brother's in very bad trouble. So are you. He drove down south
to do a murder yesterday. You provided the car."

"I didn't know whah—" His jaw hung open, and then clicked shut.
"Who are you?"

"A friend of the family. Show me where Tommy is."

"But I don't know. He isn't in his room. He never came back."

The woman said: "Are you from the Adult Authority?"

"No."

"Who are you?" Lemberg repeated. "What do you want?"

"Your brother, Tommy."

"I don't know where Tommy is. I swear."

"What's Otto Schwartz got to do with you and Tommy?"

"I don't know."

"You brought up his name. Did Schwartz give Tommy a contract to murder Culligan?"

"Who?" the woman said. "Who did you say got murdered?"

"Peter Culligan. Know him?"

"No," Lemberg answered for her. "We don't know him."

I advanced on him: "You're lying, Lemberg. You better let down your back hair, tell me all about it. Tommy isn't the only one in trouble. You're accessory to any crime he did."

He backed away until the backs of his legs were touching the bed. He looked down at his wife as if she was his only source of comfort. She was looking at me:

"What did you say Tommy did?"

"He committed a murder."

"For gosh sake." She swung her legs down and stood up facing her husband. "And you lent him the car?"

"I had to. It was his car. It was only in my name."

"Because he was on parole?" I said.

He didn't answer me.

The woman took hold of his arm and shook it. "Tell the man where he is."

"I don't know where he is." Lemberg turned to me: "And that's the honest truth."

"What about Schwartz?"

"Tommy used to work for him, when we lived in Reno. They were always asking him to come back to work."

"Doing what?"

"Any dirty thing they could dream up."

"Including murder?"

"Tommy never did a murder."

"Before this one, you mean."

"I'll believe it when I hear it from him."

The woman groaned. "Don't be an idiot all your life. What did he ever do for you, Roy?"

"He's my brother."

"Do you expect to hear from him?" I said.

"I hope so."

"If you do, will you let me know?"

"Sure I will," he lied.

I went down in the elevator and laid a ten-dollar bill on the counter in front of the room clerk. He raised a languid eyebrow:

"What's this for? You want to check in?"

"Not today, thanks. It's your certificate of membership in the junior G-men society. Tomorrow you get your intermediate certificate."

"Another ten?"

"You catch on fast."

"What do I have to do for it?"

"Keep track of Lemberg's visitors, if he has any. And any telephone calls, especially long-distance calls."

"Can do." His hand moved quickly, flicking the bill out of sight. "What about *her* visitors?"

"Does she have many?"

"They come and go."

"She pay you to let them come and go?"

"That's between me and her. Are you a cop?"

"Not me," I said, as if his question was an insult. "Just keep the best track you can. If it works out, I may give you a bonus."

"If what works out?"

"Developments. Also I'll mention you in my memoirs."

"That will be just ducky."

"What's your name?"

"Jerry Farnsworth."

"Will you be on duty in the morning?"

"What time in the morning?"

"Any time."

"For a bonus I can be."

"An extra five," I said, and went outside.

There was a magazine shop on the opposite corner. I crossed to it, bought a *Saturday Review*, and punched a hole in the cover. For an hour or more, I watched the front of the Sussex Arms, trusting that Lemberg wouldn't penetrate my literate disguise.

But Lemberg didn't come out.

13
.

It was past five when I got to Redwood City. The commuting trains were running south every few minutes. The commuters in their uniforms, hat on head, briefcase in hand, newspaper under arm, marched wearily toward their waiting cars. The cop on traffic duty at the station corner told me how to get to Sherwood Drive.

It was in a junior-executive residential section, several cuts above the Marvista tract. The houses were set further apart, and differed from each other in architectural detail. Flowers bloomed competitively in the yards.

A bicycle lay on the grass in front of the Matheson house. A small boy answered my knock. He had black eyes like his mother's, and short brown hair which stuck up all over his head like visible excitement.

"I was doing pushups," he said, breathing hard. "You want my daddy? He ain't, I mean, he isn't home from the city yet."

"Is your mother home?"

"She went to the station to get him. They ought to be back in about eleven minutes. That's how old I am."

"Eleven minutes?"

"Eleven *years*. I had my birthday last week. You want to see me do some pushups?"

"All right."

"Come in, I'll show you."

I followed him into a living-room which was dominated by a large brick fireplace with a raised hearth. Everything in the room was so new and clean, the furniture so carefully placed around it, that it seemed forbidding. The boy flung himself down in the middle of the green broadloom carpet:

"Watch me."

He did a series of pushups, until his arms collapsed under him. He got up panting like a dog on a hot day:

"Now that I got the knack, I can do pushups all night if I want to."

"You wouldn't want to wear yourself out."

"Shucks, I'm strong. Mr. Steele says I'm very strong for my age, it's just my co-ordination. Here, feel my muscle."

He pulled up the sleeve of his jersey, flexed his biceps, and produced an egg-sized lump. I palpated this:

"It's hard."

"That's from doing pushups. You think I'm big for my age, or just average?"

"A pretty fair size, I'd say."

"As big as you when you were eleven?"

"Just about."

"How big are you now?"

"Six feet or so."

"How much do you weigh?"

"About one-ninety."

"Did you ever play football?"

"Some, in high school."

"Do you think, will I ever get to be a football player?" he said wistfully.

"I don't see why not."

"That's my ambition, to be a football player."

He darted out of the room and was back in no time with a football which he threw at me from the doorway.

"Y.A. Tittle," he said.

I caught the ball and said: "Hugh McElhenny."

This struck him as very funny. He laughed until he fell down. Being in position, he did a few pushups.

"Stop it. You're making me tired."

"I never get tired," he bragged exhaustedly. "When I get through doing pushups, I'm going to take a run around the block."

"Don't tell me. It wears me out."

A car turned into the driveway. The boy struggled to his feet:

"That's Mummy and Daddy now. I'll tell them you're here, Mr. Steele."

"My name is Archer. Who's Mr. Steele?"

"My coach in the Little League. I got you mixed up with him, I guess."

It didn't bother him, but it bothered me. It was a declaration of trust, and I didn't know what I was going to have to do to his mother.

She came in alone. Her face hardened and thinned when she saw me:

"What do you want? What are you doing with my son's football?"

"Holding it. He threw it to me. I'm holding it."

"We were making like Forty-niners," the boy said. But the laughter had gone out of him.

"Leave my son alone, you hear me?" She turned on the boy: "James, your father is in the garage. You can help him bring in the groceries. And take that football with you."

"Here." I tossed him the ball. He carried it out as if it was made of iron. The door closed behind him. "He's a likely boy."

"A lot you care, coming here to badger me. I talked to the police this morning. I don't have to talk to you."

"I think you want to, though."

"I can't. My husband—he doesn't know."

"What doesn't he know?"

"Please." She moved toward me rapidly, heavily, almost as though she was falling, and grasped my arm. "Ron will be coming in any minute. You won't force me to talk in front of him?"

"Send him away."

"How can I? He wants his dinner."

"You need something from the store."

"But we just came from the store."

"Think of something else."

Her eyes narrowed to two black glittering slits. "Damn you. You come in here disrupting my life. What did I do to bring this down on me?"

"That's the question that needs answering, Mrs. Matheson."

"Won't you go away and come back later?"

"I have other things to do later. Let's get this over with."

"I only wish I could."

The back door opened. She pulled away from me. Her face smoothed out and became inert, like the face of someone dying.

"Sit down," she said. "You might as well sit down."

I sat on the edge of an overstuffed chesterfield covered with hard shiny green brocade. Footsteps crossed the kitchen, and paper rustled. A man raised his voice:

"Marian, where are you?"

"I'm in here," she said tightly.

Her husband appeared in the doorway. Matheson was a thin small man in a gray suit who looked about five years younger than his wife. He stared at me through his glasses with the belligerence of his size. It was his wife he spoke to:

"I didn't know you had a visitor."

"Mr. Archer is Sally Archer's husband. You've heard me speak of Sally Archer, Ron." In spite of his uncomprehending look, she rushed on: "I promised to send her a cake for the church supper, and I forgot to bake it. What am I going to do?"

"You'll have to skip it."

"I can't. She's depending on me. Ron, would you go downtown and bring me a cake for Mr. Archer to take to Sally? Please?"

"Now?" he said with disgust.

"It's for tonight. Sally's waiting for it."

"Let her wait."

"But I can't. You wouldn't want it to get around that I didn't do my share."

He turned out his hands in resignation. "How big a cake does it have to be?"

"The two-dollar size will do. Chocolate. You know the bakery at the shopping center."

"But that's way over on the other side of town."

"It's got to be good, Ron. You don't want to shame me in front of my friends."

Some of her real feeling was caught in the words. His eyes jabbed at me and returned to her face, searching it:

"Listen, Marian, what's the trouble? Are you okay?"

"Certainly I'm okay." She produced a smile. "Now run along like a good boy and bring me that cake. You can take Jimmy with you, and I'll have supper ready when you get back."

Matheson went out, slamming the door behind him in protest. I heard his car engine start, and sat down again:

"You've got him well trained."

"Please leave my husband out of this. He doesn't deserve trouble."

"Does he know the police were here?"

"No, but the neighbors will tell him. And then I'll have to do some more lying. I hate this lying."

"Stop lying."

"And let him know I'm mixed up in a murder? That would be just great."

"Which murder are you talking about?"

She opened her mouth. Her hand flew up to cover it. She forced her hand down to her side and stood very still, like a sentinel guarding her hearth.

"Culligan's?" I said. "Or the murder of John Brown?"

The name struck her like a blow in the mouth. She was too shaken to speak for a minute. Then she gathered her forces and straightened up and said:

"I don't know any John Brown."

"You said you hated lying, but you're doing it. You worked for him in the winter of 1936, looking after his wife and baby."

She was silent. I brought out one of my pictures of Anthony Galton and thrust it up to her face:

"Don't you recognize him?"

She nodded resignedly. "I recognize him. It's Mr. Brown."

"And you worked for him, didn't you?"

"So what? Working for a person is no crime."

"Murder is the crime we're talking about. Who killed him, Marian? Was it Culligan?"

"Who says anybody killed him? He pulled up stakes and went away. The whole family did."

"Brown didn't go very far, just a foot or two underground. They dug him up last spring, all but his head. His head was missing. Who cut it off, Marian?"

The ugliness rose like smoke in the room, spreading to its far corners, fouling the light at the window. The ugliness entered the woman and stained her eyes. Her lips moved, trying to find the words that would exorcise it. I said:

"I'll make a bargain with you, and keep it if I can. I don't want to hurt your boy. I've got nothing against you or your husband. I suspect you're material witness to a murder. Maybe the law would call it accessory—"

"No." She shook her head jerkily. "I had nothing to do with it."

"Maybe not. I'm not interested in pinning anything on you. If you'll tell me the whole truth as you know it, I'll do my best to keep you out of it. But it has to be the whole truth, and I have to have it now. A lot depends on it."

"How could a lot depend, after all these years?"

"Why did Culligan die, after all these years? I think that the two deaths are connected. I also think that you can tell me how."

Her deeper, cruder personality rose to the surface. "What do you think I am, a crystal ball?"

"Stop fooling around," I said sharply. "We only have a few minutes. If you won't talk to me alone, you can talk in front of your husband."

"What if I refuse to talk at all?"

"You'll be having another visit from the cops. It'll start here and end up at the courthouse. And everybody west of the Rockies will have a chance to read all about it in the papers. Now talk."

"I need a minute to think."

"You've had it. Who murdered Brown?"

"I didn't know he was murdered, not for sure. Culligan wouldn't let me go back to the house after that night. He said the Browns moved on, bag and baggage. He even tried to give me money he said they left for me."

"Where did he get it?"

After a silence, she blurted: "He stole it from them."

"Did he murder Brown?"

"Not Culligan. He wouldn't have the nerve."

"Who did?"

"There was another man. It must have been him."

"What was his name?"

"I don't know."

"What did he look like?"

"I hardly remember. I only saw him the once, and it was at night."

Her story was turning vague, and it made me suspicious. "Are you sure the other man existed?"

"Of course he did."

"Prove it."

"He was a jailbird," she said. "He escaped from San Quentin. He used to belong to the same gang Culligan did."

"What gang is that?"

"I wouldn't know. It broke up long before I married Culligan. He never talked about his gang days. I wasn't interested."

"Let's get back to this man who broke out of 'Q.' He must have had a name. Culligan must have called him something."

"I don't remember what."

"Try harder."

She looked toward the window. Her face was drawn in the tarnished light.

"Shoulders. I think it was Shoulders."

"No last name?"

"Not that I remember. I don't think Culligan ever told me his last name."

"What did he look like?"

"He was a big man, dark-haired. I never really saw him, not in the light."

"What makes you think he murdered Brown?"

She answered in a low voice, to keep her house from hearing: "I heard them arguing that night, in the middle of the night. They were sitting out in my car arguing about money. The other man—Shoulders —said that he'd knock off Pete, too, if he didn't get his way. I heard him say it. The walls of the shack we lived in were paper thin. This Shoulders had a kind of shrill voice, and it cut through the walls like a knife. He wanted all the money for himself, and most of the jewels.

"Pete said it wasn't fair, that he was the finger man and should have an equal split. He needed money, too, and God knows that he did. He always needed money. He said that a couple of hot rubies were no good to him. That was how I guessed what happened. Little Mrs. Brown had these big red jewels, I always thought they were glass. But they were rubies."

"What happened to the rubies?"

"The other man took them, he must of. Culligan settled for part of the money, I guess. At least he was flush for a while."

"Did you ever ask him why?"

"No. I was afraid."

"Afraid of Culligan?"

"Not him so much." She tried to go on, but the words stuck in her throat. She plucked at the skin of her throat as if to dislodge them. "I was afraid of the truth, afraid he'd tell me. I didn't want to believe what happened, I guess. That argument I heard outside our house—I tried to pretend to myself it was all a dream. I was in love with Culligan in those days. I couldn't face my own part in it."

"You mean the fact that you didn't take your suspicions to the police?"

"That would have been bad enough, but I did worse. I was the one responsible for the whole thing. I've lived with it on my conscience for over twenty years. It was all my fault for not keeping my loud mouth shut." She gave me an up-from-under look, her eyes burning with pain: "Maybe I ought to be keeping it shut now."

"How were you responsible?"

She hung her head still lower. Her eyes sank out of sight under her black brows. "I told Culligan about the money," she said. "Mr. Brown kept it in a steel box in his room. I saw it when he paid me. There must have been thousands of dollars. And I had to go and mention it to my hus—to Culligan. I would have done better to go and cut my tongue out instead." She raised her head, slowly, as if she was balancing a weight. "So there you have it."

"Did Brown ever tell you where *he* got the money?"

"Not really. He made a joke about it—said he stole it. But he wasn't the type."

"What type was he?"

"Mr. Brown was a gentleman, at least he started out to be a gentleman. Until he married that wife of his. I don't know what he saw in her outside of a pretty face. She didn't know from nothing, if you ask me. But he knew plenty, he could talk your head off."

She gasped. The enormity of the image struck her. "God! They cut his head off?" She wasn't asking me. She was asking the dark memories flooding up from the basement of her life.

"Before death or after, we don't know which. You say you never went back to the house?"

"I never did. We went back to San Francisco."

"Do you know what happened to the rest of the family, the wife and son?"

She shook her head. "I tried not to think about them. What did happen to them?"

"I'm not sure, but I think they went east. The indications are they got away safe, at any rate."

"Thank God for that." She tried to smile, and failed. Her eyes were still intent on the guilty memory. She looked at the walls of her living-room as if they were transparent. "I guess you wonder what kind of a woman I am, that I could run out on a patient like that. Don't think it didn't bother me. I almost went out of my mind for a while that winter. I used to wake up in the middle of the night and listen to Culligan's breathing and wish it would stop. But I stuck to him for five more years after that. Then I divorced him."

"And now he's stopped breathing."

"What do you mean by that?"

"You could have hired a gun to knock him off. He was threatening to make trouble for you. You have a lot to lose." I didn't believe it, but I wanted to see what she would make of it.

Her two hands went to her breasts and grasped them cruelly. "Me? You think I'd do that?"

"To keep your husband and son, you would. Did you?"

"No. For God's sake, no."

"That's good."

"Why do you say that?" Her eyes were dull with the sickness of the past.

"Because I want you to keep what you have."

"Don't do me any favors."

"I'm going to, though. I'm going to keep you out of the Culligan case. As for the information you've given me, I'm going to use it for private reference only. It would be easier for me if I didn't—"

"So you want to be paid for your trouble, is that it?"

"Yes, but not in money. I want your confidence, and any other information you can give me."

"But there isn't any more. That's all there is."

"What happened to Shoulders?"

"I don't know. He must of got away. I never heard of him again."

"Culligan never mentioned him?"

"No. Honest."

"And you never brought the subject up?"

"No. I was too much of a coward."

A car entered the driveway. She started, and went to the window. The light outside was turning dusky gray. In the yard across the street, red roses burned like coals. She rubbed her eyes with her knuckles, as if she wanted to wipe out all her past experiences, live innocent in an innocent world.

The little boy burst through the door. Matheson came at his heels, balancing a cake box in his hands.

"Well, I got the darn thing." He thrust it into my hands. "That takes care of the church supper."

"Thanks."

"Don't mention it," he said brusquely, and turned to his wife: "Is supper ready? I'm starved."

She stood on the far side of the room, cut off from him by the ugliness. "I didn't make supper."

"You didn't make it? What is this? You said you'd have it ready when I got home."

Hidden forces dragged at her face, widening her mouth, drawing deep lines between her eyes. Suddenly her eyes were blind with tears. The tears ran in the furrows of her face. Sobbing, she sat on the edge of the hearth like an urchin on a curb.

"Marian? What's the matter? What's the trouble, kiddie?"

"I'm not a good wife to you."

Matheson went across the room to her. He sat on the hearth beside her and took her in his arms. She buried her face in his neck.

The boy started toward them, and then turned back to me. "Why is Mother crying?"

"People cry."

"I don't cry," he said.

14
.

I DROVE back across the ridge toward the last fading light in the sky. On the road that wound down to Luna Bay I passed an old man with a burlap bag on his back. He was one of the old-time hoboes who follow the sun like migratory birds. But the birds fly, and the men walk. The birds mate and nest; the old men have no nests. They pace out their lives along the roadsides.

I stopped and backed up and gave him the cake.

"Thank you very kindly." His mouth was a rent in shaggy fur. He put the cake in his bag. It was a cheap gift, so I gave him a dollar to go with it. "Do you want a ride into town?"

"No, thank you very kindly. I'd smell up your car."

He walked away from me with a long, slow, swinging purposeless stride, lost in a dream of timeless space. When I passed him, he didn't raise his bearded head. He was like a moving piece of countryside on the edge of my headlight beam.

I had fish and chips at a greasy spoon and went to the sheriff's sub-station. It was eight by the clock on the wall above Mungan's desk. He looked up from his paperwork:

"Where you been? The Brown kid's been looking for you."

"I want to see him. Do you know where he went?"

"Over to Doc Dineen's house. They're pretty good friends. He told me that the doc is teaching him how to play chess. That game was always a little over my head. Give me a hand of poker any time."

I went around the end of the counter and complied with his request, in a way:

"I've been doing some asking around. A couple of things came up that ought to interest you. You say you knew some of the hoods in these parts, back in the early thirties. Does the name Culligan mean anything to you?"

"Yeah. Happy Culligan, they called him. He was in the Red Horse mob."

"Who were his friends?"

"Let's see." Mungan stroked his massive chin. "There was Rossi, Shoulders Nelson, Lefty Dearborn—all of them Lempi's guns. Culligan was more the operator type, but he liked to hang around with the guns."

"What about Shoulders Nelson?"

"He was about the hardest limb in the bunch. Even his buddies were afraid of him." A trace of his boyhood admiration showed in Mungan's eyes. "I saw him beat Culligan to a pulp one night. They both wanted the same girl."

"What girl?"

"One of the girls upstairs at the Red Horse. I didn't know her name. Nelson shacked up with her for a while, I heard."

"What did Nelson look like?"

"He was a big man, almost as big as me. The women went for him, he must have been good-looking to them. I never thought so, though.

He was a mean-looking bastard, with a long sad face and mean eyes. Him and Rossi and Dearborn got sent up the same time as Lempi."

"To Alcatraz?"

"Lempi went there, when the Government took it over. But the others took the fall on a larceny charge. Highjacking. The three of them went to San Quentin."

"What happened to them after that?"

"I didn't keep any track of them. I wasn't in law enforcement at the time. Where is all this supposed to be leading?"

"Shoulders Nelson may be the killer you want," I said. "Would your Redwood City office have a dossier on him?"

"I doubt that. He hasn't been heard of around here in more than twenty-five years. It was a state case, anyway."

"Then Sacramento should have it. You could have Redwood City teletype them."

Mungan spread his hands on the desk-top and stood up, wagging his big head slowly from side to side. "If all you got is a hunch, you can't use official channels to test it out for you."

"I thought we were co-operating."

"I am. You're not. I've been doing the talking, you've been doing the listening. And this has been going on for quite some time."

"I told you Nelson's probably our killer. That's a fairly big mouthful."

"By itself, it doesn't do anything for me."

"It could if you let it. Try querying Sacramento."

"What's your source of information?"

"I can't tell you."

"Like that, eh?"

"I'm afraid so."

Mungan looked down at me in a disappointed way. Not surprised, just disappointed. We had had the beginning of a beautiful friendship, but I had proved unworthy.

"I hope you know what you're doing."

"I hope I do. You think about this Nelson angle. It's worth going into. You could earn yourself some very nice publicity."

"I don't give a damn about publicity."

"Good for you."

"And you can go to hell."

I didn't blame him for blowing off. It's tough to live with a case for half a year and then watch it elope with a casual pickup.

But I couldn't afford to leave him feeling sore. I didn't even want to. I went outside the counter and sat down on a wooden bench against the wall. Mungan resumed his place at his desk and avoided looking at me. I sat there like a penitent while the minute hand of the clock took little pouncing bites of eternity.

At eight-thirty-five Mungan got up and made an elaborate show of discovering me:

"You still here?"

"I'm waiting for a friend—a lawyer from down south. He said he'd be here by nine o'clock."

"What for? To help you to pick my brains?"

"I don't know why you're browned off, Mungan. This is a big case, bigger than you realize. It's going to take more than one of us to handle it."

"What makes it so big?"

"The people involved, the money, and the names. At this end we have the Red Horse gang, or what's left of it; at the other end, one of the richest and oldest families in California. It's their lawyer I'm expecting, a man named Sable."

"So what? I get down on my knees? I give everybody an even shake, treat 'em all alike."

"Mr. Sable may be able to identify those bones of yours."

Mungan couldn't repress his interest. "He the one you talked to on the phone?"

"He's the one."

"You're working on this case for him?"

"He hired me. And he may be bringing some medical data that will help us identify the remains."

Mungan went back to his paperwork. After a few minutes, he said casually:

"If you're working for a lawyer, it lets you off the hook. It gives you the same rights of privacy a lawyer has. You probably wouldn't know that, but I've made quite a study of the law."

"It's news to me," I lied.

He said magnanimously: "People in general, even law officers, they don't know all the fine points of the law."

His pride and his integrity were satisfied. He called the county courthouse and asked them to get a rundown on Nelson from Sacramento.

Gordon Sable walked in at five minutes to nine. He had on a brown topcoat and a brown Homburg, and a pair of yellow pigskin driving gloves. The lids of his gray eyes were slightly inflamed. His mouth was drawn down at the corners, and lines of weariness ran from them to the wings of his nose.

"You made a quick trip," I said.

"Too quick to suit me. I didn't get away until nearly three o'clock."

He looked around the small office as if he doubted that the trip had been worth making. Mungan rose expectantly.

"Mr. Sable, Deputy Mungan."

The two men shook hands, each of them appraising the other.

"Glad to meet you," Mungan said. "Mr. Archer tells me you've got some medical information about this—these remains we turned up last spring."

"That may be." Sable glanced sideways at me. "How much more detail did you go into?"

"Just that, and the fact that the family is important. We're not going to be able to keep them anonymous from here on in."

"I realize that," he snapped. "But let's get the identification established first, if we can. Before I left, I talked to the doctor who set the broken arm. He did have X-ray pictures taken, but unfortunately they don't survive. He has his written record, however, and he gave me the —ah—specifications of the fracture." Sable produced a folded piece of paper from an inner pocket. "It was a clean break in the right humerus, two inches above the joint. The boy sustained it falling off a horse."

Mungan said: "It figures."

Sable turned to him. "May we see the exhibit in question?"

Mungan went into the back room.

"Where's the boy?" Sable said in an undertone.

"At a friend's house, playing chess. I'll take you to him when we finish here."

"Tony was a chess-player. Do you really think he's Tony's son?"

"I don't know. I'm waiting to have my mind made up for me."

"By the evidence of the bones?"

"Partly. I've got hold of another piece of evidence that fits in. Brown has been identified from one of Tony Galton's pictures."

"You didn't tell me that before."

"I didn't know it before."

"Who's your witness?"

"A woman named Matheson in Redwood City. She's Culligan's ex-wife and Galton's ex-nurse. I've made a commitment to keep her name out of the police case."

"Is that wise?" Sable's voice was sharp and unpleasant.

"Wise or not, it's the way it is."

We were close to quarreling. Mungan came back into the room and cut it short. The bones rattled in his evidence box. He hoisted it onto the counter and raised the lid. Sable looked down at John Brown's leavings. His face was grave.

Mungan picked out the arm bone and laid it on the counter. He went to his desk and came back with a steel foot-rule. The break was exactly two inches from the end.

Sable was breathing quickly. He spoke in repressed excitement: "It looks very much as if we've found Tony Galton. Why is the skull missing? What was done to him?"

Mungan told him what he knew. On the way to the Dineen house I told Sable the rest of it.

"I have to congratulate you, Archer. You certainly get results."

"They fell into my lap. It's one of the things that made me suspicious. Too many coincidences came together—the Culligan murder, the Brown-Galton murder, the Brown-Galton boy turning up, if that's who he is. I can't help feeling that the whole business may have been planned to come out this way. There are mobsters involved, remember. Those boys look a long way ahead sometimes, and they're willing to wait for their payoff."

"Payoff?"

"The Galton money. I think the Culligan killing was a gang killing. I think it was no accident that Culligan came to work for you three months ago. Your house was a perfect hide-out for him, and a place where he could watch developments in the Galton family."

"For what possible purpose?"

"My thinking hasn't got that far," I said. "But I'm reasonably certain that Culligan didn't go there on his own."

"Who sent him?"

"That's the question." After a pause, I said: "How is Mrs. Sable, by the way?"

"Not good. I had to put her in a nursing home. I couldn't leave her by herself at home."

"I suppose it's the Culligan killing that got her down?"

"The doctors seem to think it's what triggered her breakdown. But she's had emotional trouble before."

"What sort of emotional trouble?"

"I'd just as soon not go into it," he said bleakly.

15

DR. DINEEN came to the door in an ancient smoking-jacket made of red velvet which reminded me of the plush in old railway coaches. His wrinkled face was set in a frown of concentration. He looked at me impatiently:

"What is it?"

"I think we've identified your skeleton."

"Really? How?"

"Through the mended break in the arm bone. Dr. Dineen, this is Mr. Sable. Mr. Sable's an attorney representing the dead man's family."

"Who were his family?"

Sable answered: "His true name was Anthony Galton. His mother is Mrs. Henry Galton of Santa Teresa."

"You don't say. I used to see her name on the society pages. She cut quite a swathe at one time."

"I suppose she did," Sable said. "She's an old woman now."

"We all grow older, don't we? But come in, gentlemen."

He stood back to let us enter. I turned to him in the hallway:

"Is John Brown with you?"

"He is, yes. I believe he was trying to locate you earlier in the evening. At the moment he's in my office studying the chessboard. Much good may it do him. I propose to beat him in six more moves."

"Can you give us a minute, Doctor, by ourselves?"

"If it's important, and I gather it is."

He steered us into a dining-room furnished in beautiful old mahogany. Light from a yellowing crystal chandelier fell on the dark wood and on the sterling tea set which stood in geometrical order on the tall buffet. The room recalled the feeling I'd had that morning, that the doctor's house was an enclave of the solid past.

He sat at the head of the table and placed us on either side of him. Sable leaned forward across the corner of the table. The events of the day and the one before it had honed his profile sharp:

"Will you give me your opinion of the young man's moral character?"

"I entertain him in my house. That ought to answer your question."

"You consider him a friend?"

"I do, yes. I don't make a practice of entertaining casual strangers. At my age you can't afford to waste your time on second-rate people."

"Does that imply that he's a first-rate person?"

"It would seem to." The doctor's smile was slow, and almost indistinguishable from his frown. "At least he has the makings. You don't ask much more from a boy of twenty-two."

"How long have you known him?"

"All his life, if you count our initial introduction. Mr. Archer may have told you that I brought him into the world."

"Are you certain this is the same boy that you brought into the world?"

"I have no reason to doubt it."

"Would you swear to it, Doctor?"

"If necessary."

"It may be necessary. The question of his identity is a highly important one. A very great deal of money is involved."

The old man smiled, or frowned. "Forgive me if I'm not overly impressed. Money is only money, after all. I don't believe John is particularly hungry for money. As a matter of fact, this development will be quite a blow to him. He came here in the hope of finding his father, alive."

"If he qualifies for a fortune," Sable said, "it ought to be some comfort to him. Were his parents legally married, do you know?"

"It happens that I can answer that question, in the affirmative. John has been making some inquiries. He discovered just last week that a John Brown and a Theodora Gavin were married in Benicia, by civil ceremony, in September 1936. That seems to make him legitimate, by a narrow margin."

Sable sat in silence for a minute. He looked at Dineen like a prosecutor trying to weigh the credibility of a witness.

"Well," the old man said. "Are you satisfied? I don't wish to appear inhospitable, but I'm an early riser, and it happens to be my bedtime."

"There are one or two other things, if you'll bear with me, Doctor. I'm wondering, for instance, just how you happen to be so close to the boy's affairs."

"I choose to be," Dineen said abruptly.

"Why?"

The doctor looked at Sable with faint dislike. "My motives are no concern of yours, Counselor. The young man knocked on my door a month ago, looking for some trace of his family. Naturally I did my best to help him. He has a moral right to the protection and support of his family."

"If he can prove that he's a member of it."

"There seems to be no question of that. I think you're being unnecessarily hard on him, and I see no reason why you should continue in that vein. Certainly there's no indication that he's an impostor. He has his birth certificate, which proves the facts of his birth. My name is on it as attending physician. It's why he came to me in the first place."

"Birth certificates are easy to get," I said. "You can write in, pay your money, and take your choice."

"I suppose you can, if you're a cheat and a scoundrel. I resent the implication that this boy is."

"Please don't." Sable moderated his tone. "As Mrs. Galton's attorney, it's my duty to be skeptical of these claims."

"John has been making no claims."

"Perhaps not yet. He will. And very important interests are involved, human as well as financial. Mrs. Galton is in uncertain health. I don't intend to present her with a situation that's likely to blow up in her face."

"I don't believe that's the case here. You asked me for my opinion, and now you have it. But no human situation is entirely predictable, is it?" The old man leaned forward to get up. His bald scalp gleamed like polished stone in the light from the chandelier. "You'll be wanting to talk to John, I suppose. I'll tell him you're here."

He left the room and came back with the boy. John was wearing flannel slacks and a gray sweater over an open-necked shirt. He looked like the recent college graduate that he was supposed to be, but he wasn't at ease in the situation. His eyes shifted from my face to Sable's. Dineen stood beside him in an almost protective posture.

"This is Mr. Sable," he said in a neutral tone. "Mr. Sable is an attorney from Santa Teresa, and he's very much interested in you."

Sable stepped forward and gave him a brisk handshake. "I'm glad to meet you."

"Glad to meet you." His gray eyes matched Sable's in watchfulness. "I understand you know who my father is."

"Was, John," I said. "We've identified those bones at the station, pretty definitely. They belonged to a man named Anthony Galton. The indications are that he was your father."

"But my father's name was John Brown."

"He used that name. It started out as a pen name, apparently." I looked at the lawyer beside me. "We can take it for granted, can't we, that Galton and Brown were the same man, and that he was murdered in 1936?"

"It appears so." Sable laid a restraining hand on my arm. "I wish you'd let me handle this. There are legal questions involved."

He turned to the boy, who looked as if he hadn't absorbed the fact of his father's death. The doctor laid an arm across his shoulders:

"I'm sorry about this, John. I know how much it means to you."

"It's funny, it doesn't seem to mean a thing. I never knew my father. It's simply words, about a stranger."

"I'd like to talk to you in private," Sable said. "Where can we do that?"

"In my room, I suppose. What are we going to talk about?"

"You."

He lived in a workingmen's boardinghouse on the other side of town. It was a ramshackle frame house standing among others which had known better days. The landlady intercepted us at the front door. She was a large-breasted Portuguese woman with rings in her ears and spice on her breath. Something in the boy's face made her say:

"Whatsamatter, Johnny? You in trouble?"

"Nothing like that, Mrs. Gorgello," he said with forced lightness. "These men are friends of mine. Is it all right if I take them up to my room?"

"It's your room, you pay rent. I cleaned it up today for you, real nice. Come right in, gentlemen," she said royally.

Not so royally, she jostled the boy as he passed her in the doorway. "Lift up the long face, Johnny. You look like judgment day."

His room was a small bare cubicle on the second floor at the rear. I guessed that it had been a servant's room in the days when the house was a private residence. Torn places and stains among the faded roses of the wallpaper hinted at a long history of decline.

The room was furnished with an iron cot covered by an army blanket, a stained pine chest of drawers topped by a clouded mirror, a teetery wardrobe, a kitchen chair standing beside a table. In spite of the books on the table, something about the room reminded me of the dead man Culligan. Perhaps it was the smell, compound of hidden dirt and damp and old grim masculine odors.

My mind skipped to Mrs. Galton's grandiose estate. It would be quite a leap from this place to that. I wondered if the boy was going to make it.

He was standing by the single window, looking at us with a sort of defiance. This was his room, his bearing seemed to say, and we could take it or leave it. He lifted the kitchen chair and turned it away from the table:

"Sit down if you like. One of you can sit on the bed."

"I'd just as soon stand, thanks," Sable said. "I had a long drive up here, and I'm going to have to drive back tonight."

The boy said stiffly: "I'm sorry to put you to all this trouble."

"Nonsense. This is my job, and there's nothing personal about it. Now I understand you have your birth certificate with you. May I have a look at it?"

"Certainly."

He pulled out the top drawer of the chest of drawers and produced a folded document. Sable put on horn-rimmed spectacles to read it. I read it over his shoulder. It stated that John Brown, Jr., had been born on Bluff Road in San Mateo County on December 2, 1936; father, John Brown; mother, Theodora Gavin Brown; attending physician, Dr. George T. Dineen.

Sable glanced up, snatching off his glasses like a politician:

"You realize this document means nothing in itself? Anyone can apply for a birth certificate, any birth certificate."

"This one happens to be mine, sir."

"I notice it was issued only last March. Where were you in March?"

"I was still in Ann Arbor. I lived there for over five years."

"Going to the University all that time?" I asked.

"Most of it. I attended high school for a year and a half, then I shifted over to the University. I graduated this spring." He paused, and caught with his teeth at his full lower lip. "I suppose you'll be checking all this, so I might as well explain that I didn't go to school under my own name."

"Why? Didn't you know your own name?"

"Of course I did. I always have. If you want me to go into the circumstances, I will."

"I think that's very much to be desiderated," Sable said.

The boy picked up one of the books from the table. Its title was *Dramas of Modernism*. He opened it to the flyleaf and showed us the name "John Lindsay" written in ink there.

"That was the name I used, John Lindsay. The Christian name was my own, of course. The surname belonged to Mr. Lindsay, the man who took me into his home."

"He lived in Ann Arbor?" Sable said.

"Yes, at 1028 Hill Street." The boy's tone was faintly sardonic. "I lived there with him for several years. His full name was Mr. Gabriel R. Lindsay. He was a teacher and counselor at the high school."

"Isn't it rather odd that you used his name?"

"I didn't think so, under the circumstances. The circumstances were odd—that's putting it mildly—and Mr. Lindsay was the one who took a real interest in my case."

"Your case?"

The boy smiled wryly. "I was a case, all right. I've come a long way in five years, thanks to Mr. Lindsay. I was a mess when I showed up at that high school—a mess in more ways than one. I'd been two days on the road, and I didn't have decent clothes, or anything. Naturally they wouldn't let me in. I didn't have a school record, and I wouldn't tell them my name."

"Why not?"

"I was mortally scared that they'd drag me back to Ohio and put me in training-school. They did that to some of the boys who ran away from the orphanage. Besides, the superintendent didn't like me."

"The superintendent of the orphanage?"

"Yes. His name was Mr. Merriweather."

"What was the name of the orphanage?"

"Crystal Springs. It's near Cleveland. They didn't call it an orphanage. They called it a Home. Which didn't make it any more homelike."

"You say your mother put you there?" I said.

"When I was four."

"Do you remember your mother?"

"Of course. I remember her face, especially. She was very pale and thin, with blue eyes. I think she must have been sick. She had a bad cough. Her voice was husky, very low and soft. I remember the last thing she ever said to me: 'Your daddy's name was John Brown, too, and you were born in California.' I didn't know what or where California was, but I held on to the word. You can see why I had to come here, finally." His voice seemed to have the resonance of his life behind it.

Sable was unimpressed by his emotion. "Where did she say that to you?"

"In the Superintendent's office, when she left me there. She promised to come back for me, but she never did. I don't know what happened to her."

"But you remember her words from the age of four?"

"I was bright for my age," he answered matter-of-factly. "I'm bright, and I'm not ashamed of it. It stood me in good stead when I was trying to get into the high school in Ann Arbor."

"Why did you pick Ann Arbor?"

"I heard it was a good place to get an education. The teachers in the Home were a couple of ignorant bullies. I wanted an education more than anything. Mr. Lindsay gave me an aptitude test, and he decided that I deserved an education, even if I didn't have any transcript. He put up quite a battle for me, getting me into the high school. And then he had to fight the welfare people. They wanted to put me in Juvenile, or find a foster-home for me. Mr. Lindsay convinced them that his home would do, even if he didn't have a wife. He was a widower."

"He sounds like a good man," I said.

"He was the best, and I ought to know. I lived with him for nearly four years. I looked after the furnace, mowed the lawn in the summer, worked around the house to pay for my board and room. But board and room was the least of what he gave me. I was a little bum when he took me in. He made a decent person out of me."

He paused, and his eyes looked past us, thousands of miles. Then they focused on me:

"I had no right today, to tell you that I never had a father. Gabe Lindsay was a father to me."

"I'd like to meet him," I said.

"So that you can check up on me?"

"Not necessarily. Don't take all this so hard, John. As Mr. Sable said, there's nothing personal about it. It's our business to get the facts."

"It's too late to get them from Mr. Lindsay. Mr. Lindsay died the winter before last. He was good to me right up to the end, and past it. He left me enough money to finish my studies."

"How much did he leave you?" Sable said.

"Two thousand dollars. I still have a little of it left."

"What did he die of?"

"Pneumonia. He died in the University Hospital in Ann Arbor. I was with him when he died. You can check that. Next question."

His irony was young and vulnerable. It failed to mask his feeling. I thought if his feeling was artificial, he didn't need the Galton money: he could make his fortune as an actor.

"What motivated you to come here to Luna Bay?" Sable said. "It couldn't have been pure coincidence."

"Who said it was?" Under the pressure of cross-questioning, the boy's poise was breaking down. "I had a right to come here. I was born here, wasn't I?"

"Were you?"

"You just saw my birth certificate."

"How did you get hold of it?"

"I wrote to Sacramento. Is there anything wrong with that? I gave them my birthdate, and they were able to tell me where I was born."

"Why the sudden interest in where you were born?"

"It wasn't a sudden interest. Ask any orphan how important it is to him. The only sudden part of it was my bright idea of writing to Sacramento. It hadn't occurred to me before."

"How did you know your birthdate?"

"My mother must have told the orphanage people. They always gave me a birthday present on December second." He grinned wryly. "Winter underwear."

Sable smiled, too, in spite of himself. He waved his hand in front of his face, as if to dissipate the tension in the room: "Are you satisfied, Archer?"

"I am for now. We've all had a long day. Why don't you lay over for the night?"

"I can't. I have an important probate coming up at ten tomorrow morning. Before that, I have to talk to the Judge in his chambers." He turned suddenly to the boy: "Do you drive a car?"

"I don't have one of my own, but I can drive."

"How would you like to drive me to Santa Teresa? Now."

"To stay?"

"If it works out. I think it will. Your grandmother will be eager to see you."

"But Mr. Turnell's counting on me at the station."

"He can get himself another boy," I said. "You better go, John. You're due for a big change, and this is the beginning of it."

"I'll give you ten minutes to pack," Sable said.

The boy seemed dazed for a minute. He looked around the walls of the mean little room as if he hated to leave it. Perhaps he was afraid to make the big leap.

"Come on," Sable said. "Snap into it."

John shook himself out of his apathy, and dragged an old leather suitcase from the wardrobe. We stood and watched him pack his meager belongings: a suit, a few shirts and socks, shaving gear, a dozen books, his precious birth certificate.

I wondered if we were doing him a favor. The Galton household had hot and cold running money piped in from an inexhaustible reservoir. But money was never free. Like any other commodity, it had to be paid for.

16
·

I SAT up late in my motel room, making notes on John Brown's story. It wasn't a likely story, on the face of it. His apparent sincerity made it plausible; that, and the fact that it could easily be checked. Some time in the course of the interview I'd made a moral bet with myself that John Brown was telling the truth. John Galton, that is.

In the morning I mailed my notes to my office in Hollywood. Then I paid a visit to the sheriff's substation. A young deputy with a crewcut was sitting at Mungan's desk.

"Yessir?"

"Is Deputy Mungan anywhere around?"

"Sorry, he's off duty. If you're Mr. Archer, he left a message for you."

He took a long envelope out of a drawer and handed it across the counter. It contained a hurried note written on yellow scratch-pad paper:

> R.C. phoned me some dope on Fred Nelson. Record goes back to S.F. docks in twenties. Assault with intent, nolle-prossed. Lempi gang enforcer 1928 on. Arrested suspicion murder 1930, habeas-corpused. Convicted grand theft 1932, sentenced "Q." Attempted escape 1933, extended sentence. Escaped December 1936, never apprehended.
>
> Mungan.

I walked across the street to the hotel and phoned Roy Lemberg's hotel, the Sussex Arms. The desk clerk answered:

"Sussex Arms. Mr. Farnsworth speaking."

"This is Archer. Is Lemberg there?"

"Who did you say it was?"

"Archer. I gave you ten dollars yesterday. Is Lemberg there?"

"Mr. and Mrs. Lemberg both checked out."

"When?"

"Yesterday aft, right after you left."

"Why didn't I see them go?"

"Maybe because they went out the back way. They didn't even leave a forwarding address. But Lemberg made a long-distance call before they took off. A call to Reno."

"Who did he call in Reno?"

"Car-dealer name of Generous Joe. Lemberg used to work for him, I think."

"And that's all there is?"

"That's all," Farnsworth said. "I hope it's what you want."

I drove across country to International Airport, turned in my rented car, and caught a plane to Reno. By noon I was parking another rented car in front of Generous Joe's lot.

A huge billboard depicted a smiling Santa Claus type scattering silver dollars. The lot had a kiosk on one corner, and a row of late-model cars fronting for half an acre of clunks. A big corrugated metal shed with a Cars Painted sign on the wall stood at the rear of the lot.

An eager young man with a rawhide tie cantered out of the kiosk almost before I'd brought my car to a halt. He patted and stroked the fender:

"Nice. Very nice. Beautiful condition, clean inside and out. Depending on your equity, you can trade up and still carry cash away."

"They'd put me in jail. I just rented this crate."

He gulped, performed a mental back somersault, and landed on his feet: "So why pay rent? On our terms, you can *own* a car for less money."

"You wouldn't be Generous Joe?"

"Mr. Culotti's in the back. You want to talk to him?"

I said I did. He waved me toward the shed, and yelled: "Hey, Mr. Culotti, customer!"

A gray-haired man came out, looking cheaply gala in an ice-cream suit. His face was swarthy and pitted like an Epstein bronze, and its two halves didn't quite match. When I got closer to him, I saw that one of his brown eyes was made of glass. He looked permanently startled.

"Mr. Culotti?"

"That's me." He smiled a money smile. "What can I do for you?" A trace of Mediterranean accent added feminine endings to some of his words.

"A man named Lemberg called you yesterday."

"That's right, he used to work for me, wanted his old job back. Nix." A gesture of his spread hand swept Lemberg into the dust-bin.

"Is he back in Reno? I'm trying to locate him."

Culotti picked at his nose and looked wise, in a startled way. He smiled expansively, and put a fatherly arm around my back. "Come in, we'll talk."

He propelled me toward the door. Hissing sounds came from the shed, and the sweet anesthetic odor of sprayed paint. Culotti opened the door and stepped back. A goggled man with a paint-gun turned from his work on a blue car.

I was trying to recognize him, when Culotti's shoulder caught me like a trunk-bumper in the small of the back. I staggered toward the goggled man. The paint-gun hissed in his hands.

A blue cloud stung my eyes. In the burning blue darkness, I recalled that the room clerk Farnsworth hadn't asked me for more money. Then I felt the sap's soft explosion against the back of my head. I glissaded down blue slopes of pain to a hole which opened for me.

Later there was talking.

"Better wash out his eyes," the first gravedigger said. "We don't want to blind him."

"Let him go blind," the second gravedigger said. "Teach him a lesson. I got a hook in the eye."

"Did it teach you a lesson, Blind-eye? Do what I tell you."

I heard Culotti breathe like a bull. He spat, but made no answer. My hands were tied behind me. My face was on cement. I tried to blink. My eyelids were stuck tight.

The fear of blindness is the worst fear there is. It crawled on my face and entered my mouth. I wanted to beg them to save my eyes. A persistent bright speck behind my eyes stared me down and shamed me into continued silence.

Liquid gurgled in a can.

"Not with gasoline, greaseball."

"Don't call me that."

"Why not? You're a blind-eye greaseball, hamburger that used to be a muscle." This voice was light and featureless, without feeling, almost without meaning. "You got any olive oil?"

"At home, plenty."

"Go and get it. I'll keep store."

My consciousness must have lapsed. Oil ran on my face like tears. I thought of a friend named Angelo who made his own oil from the olives he grew on his hillside in the Valley. The Maffia had killed his father.

A face came into blurred focus, Culotti's face, hanging slack-mouthed over me. I twisted from my side onto my back, and lashed at him with both feet. One heel caught him under the chin, and he went down. Something bounced and rolled on the floor. Then he stood one-eyed over me, bleeding at the mouth. He stamped my head back down into earthy darkness.

It was a bad afternoon. Quite suddenly it was a bad evening. Somebody had awakened me with his snoring. I listened to the snoring for a while. It stopped when I held my breath and started again when I let my breath out. For a long time I missed the significance of this.

There were too many other interesting things to do and think about.

The staring speck was back again in the center of my mind. It moved, and my hands moved with it. They felt my face. It bored me. Ruins always bored me.

I was lying in a room. The room had walls. There was a window in one of the walls. Snow-capped mountains rose against a yellow sky which darkened to green, then blue. Twilight hung like blue smoke in the room.

I sat up; springs creaked under me. A man I hadn't noticed moved away from the wall he'd been leaning on. I dropped my feet to the floor and turned to face him, slowly and carefully, so as not to lose my balance.

He was a thick young man with shiny black curls tumbling over his forehead. One of his arms was in a sling. The other arm had a gun at the end of it. His hot eyes and the cold eye of the gun triangulated my breastbone.

"Hello, Tommy," I tried to say. It came out: "Huddo, Tawy."

My mouth contained ropes of blood. I tried to spit them out. That started a chain-reaction which flung me back on the bed retching and cawing. Tommy Lemberg stood and watched me.

He said when I was still: "Mr. Schwartz is waiting to talk to you. You want to clean up a little?"

"Wheh do I do dat?" I said in my inimitable patois.

"There's a bathroom down the hall. Think you can walk?"

"I can walk."

But I had to lean on the wall to reach the bathroom. Tommy Lemberg stood and watched me wash my face and gargle. I tried to avoid looking into the mirror over the sink. I looked, though, finally, when I was drying my face. One of my front teeth was broken off short. My nose resembled a boiled potato.

All of this made me angry. I moved on Tommy. He stepped back into the doorway. I lost my footing and fell to my knees, took the barrel of his gun in the nape of my neck. Pain went through me so large and dull it scared me. I got up, supporting myself on the sink.

Tommy was grinning in an excited way. "Don't *do* things like that. I don't want to hurt you."

"Or Culligan, either, I bet." I was talking better now, but my eyes weren't focusing properly.

"Culligan? Who he? I never heard of any Culligan."

"And you've never been in Santa Teresa?"

"Where's that?"

He ushered me to the end of the corridor and down a flight of steps into a big dim room. In its picture windows, the mountains now stood black against the darkening sky. I recognized the mountains west of Reno. Tommy turned on lights which blotted them out. He moved around the room as if he was at home there.

I suppose it was the living-room of Otto Schwartz's house, but it was more like the lobby of a hotel or the recreation room of an institution. The furniture stood around in impersonal groupings, covered with plastic so that nothing could harm it. An antique bar and a wall of bottles took up one whole end. A jukebox, an electric player piano, a roulette layout, and several slot machines stood against the rear wall.

"You might as well sit down." Tommy waved his gun at a chair.

I sat down and closed my eyes, which still weren't focusing. Everything I looked at had a double outline. I was afraid of concussion. I was having a lot of fears.

Tommy turned on the player piano. It started to tinkle out a tune about a little Spanish town. Tommy did a few dance steps to it, facing me and holding the gun in his hand. He didn't seem to know what to do with himself.

I concentrated on wishing that he would put his gun away and give me some kind of chance at him. He never would, though. He loved holding the gun. He held it different ways, posturing in front of his reflection in the window. I began to draft a mental letter to my congressman advocating legislation prohibiting the manfacture of guns except for military purposes.

Mr. J. Edgar Hoover entered the room at this point. He must have been able to read minds, because he said that he approved of my plan and intended to present it to the President. I felt my forehead. It was hot and dry, like a heating-pad. Mr. Hoover faded away. The player piano went on hammering out the same tune: music to be delirious by.

The man who came in next radiated chill from green glacial eyes. He had a cruel nose and under it the kind of mouth that smiles by stretching horizontally. He must have been nearly sixty but he had a well-sustained tan and a lean quick body. He wore a light fedora and a top-coat.

So did the man who moved a step behind him and towered half a foot over him. This one had the flat impervious eyes, the battered face and pathological nervelessness of an old-fashioned western torpedo.

When his boss paused in front of me, he stood to one side in canine watchfulness. Tommy moved up beside him, like an apprentice.

"You're quite a mess." Schwartz's voice was chilly, too, and very soft, expecting to be listened to. "I'm Otto Schwartz, in case you don't know. I got no time to waste on two-bit private eyes. I got other things on my mind."

"What kind of things have you got on it? Murder?"

He tightened up. Instead of hitting me, he took off his hat and threw it to Tommy. His head was completely bald. He put his hands in his coat pockets and leaned back on his heels and looked down the curve of his nose at me:

"I was giving you the benefit, that you got in over your head without knowing. What's going to happen, you go on like this, talk about murder, crazy stuff like that?" He wagged his head solemnly from side to side. "Lake Tahoe is very deep. You could take a long dive, no Aqualung, concrete on the legs."

"You could sit in a hot seat, no cushion, electrodes on the bald head."

The big man took a step toward me, watching Schwartz with a doggy eye, and lunged around with his big shoulders. Schwartz surprised me by laughing, rather tinnily:

"You are a brave young man. I like you. I wish you no harm. What do you suggest? A little money, and that's that?"

"A little murder. Murder everybody. Then you can be the bigshot of the world."

"I am a bigshot, don't ever doubt it." His mouth pursed suddenly and curiously, like a wrinkled old wound: "I take insults from nobody! And nobody steals from me."

"Did Culligan steal from you? Is that why you ordered him killed?"

Schwartz looked down at me some more. His eyes had dark centers. I thought of the depths of Tahoe, and poor drowned Archer with concrete on his legs. I was in a susceptible mood, and fighting it. Tommy Lemberg spoke up:

"Can I say something, Mr. Schwartz? I didn't knock the guy off. The cops got it wrong. He must of fell down on the knife and stabbed himself."

"Yah! Moron!" Schwartz turned his contained fury on Tommy: "Go tell that to the cops. Just leave me out of it, please."

"They wouldn't believe me," he said in a misunderstood whine.

"They'd pin it on me, just because I tried to defend myself. I was the one got shot. He pulled a gun on me."

"Shut up! Shut up!" Schwartz spread one hand on top of his head and pulled at imaginary hair. "Why is there no intelligence left in the world? All morons!"

"The intelligent ones wouldn't touch your rackets with a ten-foot pole."

"I heard enough out of you."

He jerked his head at the big man, who started to take off his coat: "Want me to work him over, Mr. Schwartz?"

It was the light and meaningless voice that had argued with Culotti. It lifted me out of my chair. Because Schwartz was handy, I hit him in the stomach. He jackknifed, and went down gasping. It doesn't take much to make me happy, and that gave me a happy feeling which lasted through the first three or four minutes of the beating.

Then the big man's face began to appear in red snatches. When the light in the room failed entirely, the bright staring speck in my mind took over for a while. Schwartz's voice kept making tinny little jokes:

"Just promise to forget it, that will be that."

"All you gotta do, give me your word. I'm a man of my word, you're another."

"Back to L.A., that's all you gotta do. No questions asked, no harm done."

The bright speck stood like a nail in my brain. It wouldn't let me let go of the room. I cursed it, but it wouldn't go away. It wrote little luminous remarks on the red pounding darkness: This is it. You take a stand.

Then it was a light surging away from me like the light of a ship. I swam for it, but it rose away, hung in the dark heaven still as a star. I let go of the pounding room, and swung from it up and over the black mountains.

17

·

I CAME to early next morning in the accident ward of the Reno hospital. When I had learned to talk with a packed nose and a wired jaw, a couple of detectives asked me who took my wallet. I didn't bother disturbing their assumption that I was a mugging victim.

Anything I told them about Schwartz would be wasted words. Besides, I needed Schwartz. The thought of him got me through the first bad days, when I doubted from time to time that I would be very active in the future. Everything was still fuzzy at the edges. I got very tired of fuzzy nurses and earnest young fuzzy doctors asking me how my head felt.

By the fourth day, though, my vision was clear enough to read some of yesterday's newspapers which the voluntary aides brought around for the ward patients. There was hardware in the sky, and dissension on earth. A special dispatch in the back pages told how a real-life fairy-tale had reached its happy ending when the long-lost John Galton was restored to the bosom of his grandmother, the railroad and oil widow. In the accompanying photograph, John himself was wearing a new-looking sports jacket and a world-is-my-oyster grin.

This spurred me on. By the end of the first week, I was starting to get around. One morning after my Cream of Wheat I sneaked out to the nurses' station and put in a collect call to Santa Teresa. I had time to tell Gordon Sable where I was, before the head nurse caught me and marched me back to the ward.

Sable arrived while I was eating my Gerber's-baby-food dinner. He waved a checkbook. Before I knew it I was in a private room with a bottle of Old Forester which Sable had brought me. I sat up late with him, drinking highballs through a glass tube and talking through my remaining teeth like a gangster in very early sound.

"You're going to need a crown on that tooth," Sable said comfortingly. "Also, plastic surgery on the nose. Do you have any hospital insurance?"

"No."

"I'm afraid I can't commit Mrs. Galton." Then he took another look at me, and his manner softened: "Well, yes, I think I can. I think I can persuade her to underwrite the expense, even though you did exceed your instructions."

"That's mighty white of you and her." But the words didn't come out ironic. It had been a bad eight days. "Doesn't she give a good goddamn about who murdered her son? And what about Culligan?"

"The police are working on both cases, don't worry."

"They're the same case. The cops are sitting on their tails. Schwartz put the fix in."

Sable shook his head. "You're way off in left field, Lew."

"The hell I am. Tommy Lemberg's his boy. Have they arrested Tommy?"

"He dropped out of sight. Don't let it ride you. You're a willing man, but you can't take on responsibility for all the trouble in the world. Not in your present condition, anyway."

"I'll be on my feet in another week. Sooner." The whisky in the bottle was falling like a barometer. I was full of stormy optimism. "Give me another week after that and I'll break the case wide open for you."

"I hope so, Lew. But don't take too much on yourself. You've been hurt, and naturally your feelings are a bit exaggerated."

He was sitting directly under the light, but his face was getting fuzzy. I leaned out of bed and grabbed his shoulder. "Listen, Sable, I can't prove it, but I can feel it. That Galton boy is a phony, part of a big conspiracy, with the Organization behind it."

"I think you're wrong. I've spent hours on his story. It checks out. And Mrs. Galton is quite happy, for the first time in many years."

"I'm not."

He rose, and pushed me gently back against the pillows. I was still as weak as a cat. "You've talked enough for one night. Let it rest, and don't worry, eh? Mrs. Galton will take care of everything, and if she doesn't want to, I'll make her. You've earned her gratitude. We're all sorry this had to happen."

He shook my hand and started for the door.

"Flying back tonight?" I asked him.

"I have to. My wife's in bad shape. Take it easy, now, you'll hear from me. And I'll leave some money for you at the desk."

18

I SPRUNG myself out of the hospital three days later, and assembled myself aboard a plane for San Francisco. From International Airport I took a cab to the Sussex Arms Hotel.

The room clerk, Farnsworth, was sitting behind the counter at the rear of the dim little lobby, looking as if he hadn't moved in two weeks. He was reading a muscle magazine, and he didn't look up until I was close enough to see the yellows of his eyes. Even then he didn't recognize me right away: the bandages on my face made an effective mask.

"You wish a room, sir?"

"No. I came to see you."

"Me?" His eyebrows jumped, and then came down in a frown of concentration.

"I owe you something."

The color left his face. "No. No, you don't. That's all right."

"The other ten and the bonus. That makes fifteen I owe you. Excuse the delay. I got held up."

"That's too bad." He craned his neck around and looked behind him. There was nothing there but the switchboard, staring like a wall of empty eyes.

"Don't let it bother you, Farnsworth. It wasn't your fault. Was it?"

"No." He swallowed several times. "It wasn't my fault."

I stood and smiled at him with the visible parts of my face.

"What happened?" he said after a while.

"It's a long sad story. You wouldn't be interested."

I took the creaking new wallet out of my hip pocket and laid a five and a ten on the counter between us. He sat and looked at the money.

"Take it," I said.

He didn't move.

"Go ahead, don't be bashful. The money belongs to you."

"Well. Thanks."

Slowly and reluctantly, he reached out for the bills. I caught his wrist in my left hand, and held it. He jerked convulsively, reached under the counter and came up with a gun in his left hand:

"Turn me loose."

"Not a chance."

"I'll shoot!" But the gun was wavering.

I reached for his gun wrist, and twisted it until the gun dropped on the counter between us. It was a .32 revolver, a little nickel-plated suicide gun. I let go of Farnsworth and picked it up and pointed it at the knot of his tie. Without moving, he seemed to draw away from it. His eyes got closer together.

"Please. I couldn't help it."

"What couldn't you help?"

"I had orders to give you that contact in Reno."

"Who gave you the orders?"

"Roy Lemberg. It wasn't my fault."

"Lemberg doesn't give orders to anybody. He's the kind that takes them."

"Sure, he passed the word, that's what I meant."

"Who gave him the word?"

"Some gambler in Nevada, name of Schwartz." Farnsworth wet his mauve lips with his tongue. "Listen, you don't want to ruin me. I make a little book, lay off the heavy bets. If I don't do like the money boys say, I'm out of business. So have a heart, mister."

"If you level with me. Does Lemberg work for Schwartz?"

"His brother does. Not him."

"Where are the Lembergs now?"

"I wouldn't know about the brother. Roy took off like I said, him and his wife both. Put the gun down, mister. Jeeze. I got a nervous stomach."

"You'll have a perforated ulcer if you don't talk. Where did the Lembergs go?"

"Los Angeles, I think."

"Where in Los Angeles?"

"I dunno." He spread his hands. They had a tremor running through them, like dry twigs in a wind. "Honest."

"You know, Farnsworth," I said in my menacing new lockjaw voice, "I'll give you five seconds to tell me."

He looked around at the switchboard again, as if it was an instrument of execution, and swallowed audibly. "All right, I'll tell you.

Now will you put down the gun, mister?"

Before the rhythm of his fear ran down, I said: "Do you know a man named Peter Culligan?"

"Yeah. He roomed here for a while, over a year ago."

"What did he do for a living?"

"He was a horseplayer."

"That's a living?"

"I guess he hacked a little, too. Put the gun down, eh? I told you what you wanted to know."

"Where did Culligan go from here?"

"I heard he got a job in Reno."

"Working for Schwartz?"

"Could be. He told me once he used to be a stickman."

I dropped the gun in my jacket pocket.

"Hey," he said. "That's my gun. I bought it myself."

"You're better off without it."

Looking back from the door, I saw that Farnsworth was halfway between the counter and the switchboard. He stopped in mid-motion. I went back across the lobby:

"If it turns out you're lying, or if you tip off the Lembergs, I'll come back for you. Is that clear?"

A kind of moral wriggle moved up his body from his waist to his fish-belly face. "Yeah. Sure. Okay."

This time I didn't look back. I walked up to Union Square, where I made a reservation on an afternoon flight to L.A. Then I rented a car and drove down Bayshore past the airport.

The hangars of Moffett Field loomed up through the smog like gray leviathans. The Triton Motor Court stood in a wasteland of shacks on the edge of the flight pattern. Its buildings were a fading salmon pink. Its only visible attraction was the $3.00 Double sign. Jets snorted like flies in the sky.

I parked on the cinder driveway beside the chicken-coop office. The woman who ran it wore a string of fake pearls dirtied by her neck. She said that Mr. and Mrs. Lemberg weren't registered there.

"They may be going under their maiden name." I described them.

"Sounds like the girl in seven, maybe. She don't want to be disturbed, not in the daytime."

"She won't mind. I have no designs on her."

She bridled. "Who said you had? What kind of a place do you think this is, anyway?"

It was a tough question to answer. I said: "What name is she going under?"

"You from the cops? I don't want trouble with the cops."

"I was in an accident. She may be able to help me find the driver."

"That's different." The woman probably didn't believe me, but she chose to act as if she did. "They registered under the name Hamburg, Mr. and Mrs. Rex Hamburg."

"Is her husband with her?"

"Not for the last week. Maybe it's just as well," she added cryptically.

I knocked on the weathered door under the rusted iron seven. Footsteps dragged across the floor behind it. Fran Lemberg blinked in the light. Her eyes were puffed. The roots of her hair were darker. Her robe was taking on a grimy patina.

She stopped blinking when she recognized me.

"Go away."

"I'm coming in for a minute. You don't want trouble."

She looked past me, and I followed her look. The woman with the dirty pearls was watching us from the window of the office.

"All right, come in."

She let me come in past her, and slammed the door on daylight. The room smelled of wine and smoke, stale orange-peel and a woman's sleep, and a perfume I didn't recognize, Original Sin perhaps. When my eyes became night-adapted, I saw the confusion on the floor and the furniture: clothes and looped stockings and shoes and empty bottles, ashes and papers, the congealed remains of hamburgers and french fries.

She sat in a defensive posture on the edge of the unmade bed. I cleared a space for myself on the chair.

"What happened to you?" she said.

"I had a run-in with some of Tommy's playmates. Your husband set me up for the fall."

"Roy did?"

"Don't kid me, you were with him at the time. I thought he was a straight joe trying to help his brother, but he's just another errandboy for mobsters."

"No. He isn't."

"Is that what he told you?"

"I lived with him nearly ten years, I ought to know. He worked one time for a crooked car-dealer in Nevada. When Roy found out about the crookedness, he quit. That's the kind of guy he is."

"If you mean Generous Joe, that hardly qualifies Roy as a boy scout."

"I didn't say he was. He's just a guy trying to get through life."

"Some of us make it harder for the others."

"You can't blame Roy for trying to protect himself. He's wanted for accessory in a murder. But it isn't fair. You can't blame him for what Tommy did."

"You're a loyal wife," I said. "But where is it getting you?"

"Who says I want to get any place?"

"There are better places than this."

"You're telling me. I've lived in some of them."

"How long has Roy been gone?"

"Nearly two weeks, I guess. I don't keep track of the time. It goes faster that way."

"How old are you, Fran?"

"None of your business." After a pause she added: "A hundred and twenty-eight."

"Is Roy coming back?"

"He says he is. But he always sides with his brother when the chips are down." Emotion flooded up in her eyes, but drained away again. "I guess I can't blame him. This time the chips are really down."

"Tommy's staying in Nevada," I said, trying to find the wedge that would open her up.

"Tommy's in Nevada?"

"I saw him there. Schwartz is looking after him. And Roy, too, probably."

"I don't believe you. Roy said they were leaving the country."

"The state, maybe. Isn't that what he said, that they were leaving the state?"

"The country," she repeated stubbornly. "That's why they couldn't take me along."

"They were stringing you. They just don't want a woman in the way. So here you sit in a rundown crib on Bayshore. Hustling for hamburgers, while the boys are living high on the hog in Nevada."

"You're a liar!" she cried. "They're in Canada!"

"Don't let them kid you."

"Roy is going to send for me as soon as he can swing it."

"You've heard from him, then."

"Yeah, I've heard from him." Her loose mouth tightened, too late to hold back the words. "Okay, so you got it out of me. That's all you're going to get out of me." She folded her arms across her half-naked breasts, and looked at me grimly: "Why don't you beat it? You got nothing on me, you never will have."

"As soon as you show me Roy's letter."

"There was no letter. I got the message by word of mouth."

"Who brought it?"

"A guy."

"What guy?"

"Just a guy. Roy told him to look me up."

"He sent him from Nevada, probably."

"He did not. The guy drove a haulaway out from Detroit. He talked to Roy in Detroit."

"Is that where Roy and Tommy crossed the border?"

"I guess so."

"Where were they headed?"

"I don't know, and I wouldn't tell you if I did know."

I sat on the bed beside her. "Listen to me, Fran. You want your husband back, don't you?"

"Not in a convict suit, or on a slab."

"It doesn't have to be that way. Tommy's the one we're after. If Roy will turn him over to us, he'll be taking a long step out of trouble. Can you get that message to Roy from me?"

"Maybe if he phones me or something. All I can do is wait."

"You must have some idea where they went."

"Yeah, they said something about this town in Ontario near Windsor. Tommy was the one that knew about it."

"What's the name of the place?"

"They didn't say."

"Was Tommy ever in Canada before?"

"No, but Pete Culligan—"

She covered the lower part of her face with her hand and looked at me over it. Fear and distress hardened her eyes, but not for long. Her feelings were too diffuse to sustain themselves.

I said: "Tommy did know Culligan, then?"

She nodded.

"Did he have a personal reason for killing Culligan?"

"Not that I know of. Him and Pete were palsy-walsy."

"When did you see them together?"

"Last winter in Frisco. Tommy was gonna jump parole until Roy talked him out of it, and Pete told him about this place in Canada. It's sort of an irony of fate like, now Tommy's hiding out there for knocking Pete off."

"Did Tommy admit to you that he killed Culligan?"

"No, to hear him tell it he's innocent as an unborn babe. Roy even believes him."

"But you don't?"

"I swore off believing Tommy the day after I met him. But we won't go into that."

"Where is this hideout in Canada?"

"I don't know." Her voice was taking on an edge of hysteria. "Why don't you go away and leave me alone?"

"Will you contact me if you hear from them?"

"Maybe I will, maybe I won't."

"How are you fixed for money?"

"I'm loaded," she said. "What do you think? I park in this crib because I like the homey atmosphere."

I dropped a ten in her lap as I went out. Before my plane took off for Los Angeles, I had time to phone Sheriff Trask. I filled him in, with emphasis on Culligan's probable connection with Schwartz. In the rational light of day, I didn't want Schwartz all to myself.

19
•

IN THE morning, after a session with my dentist, I opened up my office on Sunset Boulevard. The mailbox was stuffed with envelopes, mostly bills and circulars. There were two envelopes mailed from Santa Teresa in the past few days.

The first one I opened contained a check for a thousand dollars and a short letter from Gordon Sable typed on the letterhead of his firm. Sad as was the fact of Anthony Galton's death, his client and he both felt that the over-all outcome was better than could have been hoped for. He hoped and trusted that I was back in harness, and none the worse for wear, and would I forward my medical bills as I received them.

The other letter was a carefully hand-written note from John Galton:

Dear Mr. Archer—

Just a brief note to thank you for your labours on my behalf. My father's death is a painful blow to all of us here. There is tragedy in the situation, which I have to learn to face up to. But there is also opportunity, for me. I hope to prove myself worthy of my patrimony.

Mr. Sable told me how you "fell among thieves." I hope that you are well again, and Grandmother joins me in this wish. For what it's worth, I did persuade Grandmother to send you an additional check in token of appreciation. She joins me in inviting you to visit us when you can make the trip up this way.

I myself would like very much to talk to you.

Respectfully yours,
John Galton.

It seemed to be pure gratitude undiluted by commercialism, until I reflected that he was taking credit for the check Sable had sent me. His letter stirred up the suspicions that had been latent in my mind since I'd talked to Sable in the hospital. Whatever John was, he was a bright boy and a fast worker. I wondered what he wanted from me.

After going through the rest of my mail, I called my answering-service. The girl at the switchboard expressed surprise that I was still in the land of the living, and told me that a Dr. Howell had been trying to reach me. I called the Santa Teresa number he'd left.

A girl's voice answered: "Dr. Howell's residence."

"This is Lew Archer. Miss Howell?" The temporary crown I'd just acquired that morning pushed out against my upper lip, and made me lisp.

"Yes, Mr. Archer."

"Your father has been trying to get in touch with me."

"Oh. He's just leaving for the hospital. I'll see if I can catch him."

After a pause, Howell's precise voice came over the line: "I'm glad to hear from you, Archer. You may recall that we met briefly at Mrs. Galton's house. I'd like to buy you a lunch."

"Lunch will be fine. What time and place do you have in mind?"

"The time is up to you—the sooner the better. The Santa Teresa Country Club would be the most convenient place for me."

"It's a long way for me to come for lunch."

"I had a little more than lunch in mind." He lowered his voice as though he suspected eavesdroppers. "I'd like to engage your services, if you're free."

"To do what?"

"I'd much prefer to discuss that in person. Would today be possible for you?"

"Yes. I'll be at the Country Club at one."

"You can't drive it in three hours, man."

"I'll take the noon plane."

"Oh, fine."

I heard the click as he hung up, and then a second click. Someone had been listening on an extension. I found out who it was when I got off the plane at Santa Teresa. A young girl with doe eyes and honey-colored hair was waiting for me at the barrier.

"Remember me? I'm Sheila Howell. I thought I'd pick you up."

"That was a nice thought."

"Not really. I have an ulterior motive."

She smiled charmingly. I followed her through the sunlit terminal to her car. It was a convertible with the top down.

Sheila turned to me as she slid behind the wheel: "I might as well be frank about it. I overheard what was said, and I wanted to talk to you about John before Dad does. Dad is a well-meaning person, but he's been a widower for ten years, and he has certain blind spots. He doesn't understand the modern world."

"But you do?"

She colored slightly, like a peach in the sun. "I understand it better than Dad does. I've studied social science at college, and people just don't go around any more telling other people who to be interested in. That sort of thing is as dead as the proverbial dodo. Deader." She nodded her small head, once, with emphasis.

"First-year social science?"

The color in her cheeks deepened. Her eyes were candid, the color

of the sky. "How did you know? Anyway, I'm a sophomore now." As
if this made all the difference between adolescence and maturity.

"I'm a mind reader. You're interested in John Galton."

Her pure gaze didn't waver. "I love John. I think he loves me."

"Is that what you wanted to say to me?"

"No." She was suddenly flustered. "I didn't mean to say it. But it's
true." Her eyes darkened. "The things that Dad believes aren't true,
though. He's just a typical patriarch type, full of prejudices against
the boy I happen to like. He believes the most awful things against
John, or pretends to."

"What things, Sheila?"

"I wouldn't even repeat them, so there. Anyway, you'll be hearing
them from him. I know what Dad wants you to do, you see. He let the
cat out of the bag last night."

"What does he want me to do?"

"Please," she said, "don't talk to me as if I were a child. I know that
tone so well, and I'm so tired of it. Dad uses it on me all the time. He
doesn't realize I'm practically grown up. I'm going to be nineteen on
my next birthday."

"Wow," I said softly.

"All right, go ahead and patronize me. Maybe I'm not mature. I'm
mature enough to know good people from bad people."

"We all make mistakes about people, no matter how ancient we are."

"But I couldn't be mistaken about John. He's the nicest boy I ever met
in my life."

I said: "I liked him, too."

"I'm so glad." Her hand touched my arm, like a bird alighting and
then taking off again: "John likes you, or I wouldn't be taking you
into our confidence."

"You wouldn't be planning on getting married?"

"Not just yet," she said, as if this was a very conservative approach.
"John has a lot of things he wants to do first, and of course I couldn't
go against Father's wishes."

"What things does John want to do?"

She answered vaguely: "He wants to make something of himself.
He's very ambitious. And of course the one big thing in his life is
finding out who killed his father. It's all he thinks about."

"Has he done anything about it?"

"Not yet, but I know he has plans. He doesn't tell me all he has on his mind. I probably wouldn't understand, anyway. He's much more intelligent than I am."

"I'm glad you realize that. It's a good thing to bear in mind."

"What do you mean?" she said in a small voice. But she knew what I meant: "It isn't true, what Father says, that John is an impostor. It can't be true!"

"What makes you so sure?"

"I know it here." Her hand touched her breast, ever so lightly. "He couldn't be lying to me. And Cassie says he's the image of his dad. So does Aunt Maria."

"Does John ever talk about his past to you?"

She regarded me with deepening distrust. "Now you sound just like Father again. You mustn't ask me questions about John. It wouldn't be fair to John."

"Give yourself some thought, too," I said. "I know it doesn't seem likely, but if he is an impostor, you could be letting yourself in for a lot of pain and trouble."

"I don't even care if he is!" she cried, and burst into tears.

A young man in airline coveralls came out of the terminal and glared at me. I was making a pretty girl cry, and there ought to be a law. I assumed a very legal expression. He went back inside again.

My plane took off with a roar. The roar diminished to a cicada humming in the northern sky. Sheila's tears passed like a summer shower. She started the engine and drove me into town, very efficiently, like a chauffeur who happened to be a deaf-mute.

John was a very fast worker.

20
.

BEFORE she deposited me in the main lounge of the clubhouse, Sheila apologized for her emotional outburst, as she called it, and said something inarticulate about not telling Daddy. I said that no apology was necessary, and that I wouldn't.

The windows of the lounge overlooked the golf course. The players were a shifting confetti of color on the greens and fairways. I watched them until Howell came in at five minutes after one.

He shook my hand vigorously. "Good to see you, Archer. I hope you don't mind eating right away. I have to meet a committee shortly after two."

He led me into a huge dining-room. Most of the tables were roped off and empty. We took one by a window which looked out across a walled swimming-pool enclosure where young people were romping and splashing. The waiter deferred to Howell as if he was a member of the stewardship committee.

Since I knew nothing about the man, I asked him the first question that occurred to me: "What kind of a committee are you meeting?"

"Aren't all committees alike? They spend hours making up their collective mind to do something which any one of their members could accomplish in half the time. I'm thinking of setting up a committee to work for the abolition of committees." His smile was a rapid flash. "As a matter of fact, it's a Heart Association committee. We're laying plans for a fund campaign, and I happen to be chairman. Will you have something to drink? I'm going to have a Gibson."

"That will do for me."

He ordered two Gibsons from the hovering waiter. "As a medical man, I feel it's my duty to perpetuate the little saving vices. It's probably safer to overdrink than it is to overeat. What will you have to eat?"

I consulted the menu.

"If you like sea food," he said executively, "the lobster Newberg is easy to chew. Gordon Sable told me about your little accident. How's the jaw?"

"Mending, thanks."

"What precisely was the trouble about, if you don't object to the question?"

"It's a long story, which boils down to something like this: Anthony Galton was killed for his money by a criminal named Nelson who had just escaped from prison. Your original guess was very close to the truth. But there's more to the case. I believe Tony Galton's murder and Pete Culligan's murder are related."

Howell leaned forward across the table, his short gray hair bristling. "How related?"

"That's the problem I was trying to solve when I got my jaw broken.

Let me ask you a question, Doctor. What's your impression of John Galton?"

"I was going to ask you the same question. Since you got to it first, I'll take first turn in answering. The boy *seems* open and aboveboard. He's certainly intelligent, and I suppose prepossessing if you like obvious charm. His grand—Mrs. Galton seems to be charmed with him."

"She doesn't question his identity?"

"Not in the slightest, she hasn't from the beginning. For Maria, the boy is practically the reincarnation of her son Tony. Her companion, Miss Hildreth, feels very much the same way. I have to admit myself that the resemblance is striking. But such things can be arranged, when a great deal of money is involved. I suppose there's no man alive who doesn't have a double somewhere in the world."

"You're suggesting that he was searched out and hired?"

"Hasn't the possibility occurred to you?"

"Yes, it has. I think it should be explored."

"I'm glad to hear you say that. I'll be frank with you. It occurred to me when the boy turned up here, that you might be a part of the conspiracy. But Gordon Sable vouches for you absolutely, and I've had other inquiries made." His gray eyes probed mine. "In addition to which, you have the marks of honesty on your face."

"It's the hard way to prove you're honest."

Howell smiled slightly, looking out over the pool. His daughter, Sheila, had appeared at the poolside in a bathing-suit. She was beautifully made, but the fact seemed to give her no pleasure. She sat by herself, with a pale closed look, undergoing the growing pains of womanhood. Howell's glance rested on her briefly, and a curious woodenness possessed his face.

The waiter brought our drinks, and we ordered lunch. When the waiter was out of hearing, Howell said:

"It's the boy's story that bothers me. I understand you were the first to hear it. What do you think about it?"

"Sable and I gave him quite a going-over. He took it well, and his story stood up. I made notes on it the same night. I've gone over the notes since I talked to you this morning, and couldn't find any self-contradictions."

"The story may have been carefully prepared. Remember that the stakes are very high. You may be interested to know that Maria is planning to change her will in his favor."

"Already?"

"Already. She may already have done. Gordon wouldn't agree to it, so she called in another attorney to draw up a will. Maria's half out of her mind—she's pent up her generous feelings for so long, that she's intoxicated with them."

"Is she incompetent?"

"By no means," he said hastily. "I don't mean to overstate the case. And I concede her perfect right to do what she wants to do with her own money. On the other hand, we can't let her be defrauded by a—confidence man."

"How much money is involved?"

He raised his eyes over my head as if he could see a mountain of gold in the distance. "I couldn't estimate. Something like the national debt of a medium-sized European country. I know Henry left her oil property that brings in a weekly income in the thousands. And she has hundreds of thousands in securities."

"Where does it all go if it doesn't go to the boy?"

Howell smiled mirthlessly. "I'm not supposed to know that. It happens that I do, but I'm certainly not supposed to tell."

"You've been frank with me," I said. "I'll be frank with you. I'm wondering if you have an interest in the estate."

He scratched at his jaw, violently, but gave no other sign of discomposure. "I have, yes, in several senses. Mrs. Galton named me executor in her original will. I assure you personal considerations are not influencing my judgment. I think I know my own motives well enough to say that."

It's a lucky man who does, I thought. I said: "Apart from the amount of money involved, what exactly is bothering you?"

"The young man's story. As he tells it, it doesn't really start till age sixteen. There's no way to go beyond that to his origins, whatever they may be. I tried, and came up against a stone wall."

"I'm afraid I don't follow you. The way John tells it, he was in an orphanage until he ran away at the age of sixteen. The Crystal Springs Home, in Ohio."

"I've been in touch with a man I know in Cleveland—chap I went to medical school with. The Crystal Springs Home burned to the ground three years ago."

"That doesn't make John a liar. He says he left there five and a half years ago."

"It doesn't make him a liar, no. But if he is, it leaves us with no way to prove that he is. The records of the Home were completely destroyed in the fire. The staff was scattered."

"The Superintendent should be traceable. What was his name—Merriweather?"

"Merriweather died in the fire of a heart attack. All of this suggests the possibility—I'd say probability—that John provided himself with a story *ex post facto*. Or was provided with one. He or his backers looked around for a foolproof background to equip him with—one that was uncheckable. Crystal Springs was it—a large institution which no longer existed, which had no surviving records. Who knows if John Brown ever spent a day there?"

"You've been doing a lot of thinking about this."

"I have, and I haven't told you all of it. There's the question of his speech, for instance. He represents himself as an American, born and raised in the United States."

"You're not suggesting he's a foreigner?"

"I am, though. National differences in speech have always interested me, and it happens I've spent some time in central Canada. Have you ever listened to a Canadian pronounce the word 'about'?"

"If I did, I never noticed. 'About'?"

"You say aba-oot, more or less. A Canadian pronounces the word more like 'aboat.' And that's the way John Brown pronounces it."

"Are you certain?"

"Of course I'm certain."

"About the theory, I mean?"

"It isn't a theory. It's a fact. I've taken it up with specialists in the subject."

"In the last two weeks?"

"In the last two days," he said. "I hadn't meant to bring this up, but my daughter, Sheila is—ah—interested in the boy. If he's a criminal, as I suspect—" Howell broke off, almost choking on the words.

Both our glances wandered to the poolside. Sheila was still alone, sitting on the edge and paddling her feet in the water. She turned to look toward the entrance twice while I watched her. Her neck and body were stiff with expectancy.

The waiter brought our food, and we ate in silence for a few minutes. Our end of the dining-room was slowly filling up with people in sports clothes. Slice and sand-trap seemed to be the passwords. Dr.

Howell glanced around independently from time to time, as if to let the golfers know that he resented their intrusion on his privacy.

"What do you intend to do, Doctor?"

"I propose to employ you myself. I understand that Gordon has terminated your services."

"So far as I know. Have you taken it up with him?"

"Naturally I have. He's just as keen as I am that there should be further investigation. Unfortunately Maria won't hear of it, and as her attorney he can't very well proceed on his own. I can."

"Have you discussed it with Mrs. Galton?"

"I've tried to." Howell grimaced. "She won't listen to a word against the blessed youth. It's frustrating, to say the least, but I can understand why she has to believe in him. The fact of her son Anthony's death came as a great shock to her. She had to hold on to something, and there was Anthony's putative son, ready and willing. Perhaps it was planned that way. At any rate, she's clinging to the boy as if her life depended on it."

"What will the consequences be if we prove he's crooked?"

"Naturally we'll put him in prison where he belongs."

"I mean the consequences to Mrs. Galton's health. You told me yourself that any great shock might kill her."

"That's true, I did."

"Aren't you concerned about that?"

His face slowly reddened, in blotches. "Of course I'm concerned. But there are ethical priorities in life. We can't sit still for a criminal conspiracy, merely because the victim has diseases. The longer we permit it to go on, the worse it will be in the long run for Maria."

"You're probably right. Anyway, her health is your responsibility. I'm willing to undertake the investigation. When do I begin?"

"Now."

"I'll probably have to go to Michigan, for a start. That will cost money."

"I understand that. How much?"

"Five hundred."

Howell didn't blink. He produced a checkbook and a fountain pen. While he was making out the check, he said:

"It might be a good idea if you talked to the boy first. That is, if you can do it without arousing suspicion."

"I think I can do that. I got an invitation from him this morning."

"An invitation?"

"A written invitation to visit the Galton house."

"He's making very free with Mrs. Galton's property. Do you happen to have the document with you?"

I handed him the letter. He studied it with growing signs of excitement. "I was right, by God!"

"What do you mean?"

"The dirty little hypocrite is a Canadian. Look here." He put the letter on the table between us, and speared at it with his forefinger. "He spells the word 'labor' l, a, b, o, u, r. It's the British spelling, still current in Canada. He isn't even American. He's an impostor."

"It's going to take more than this to prove it."

"I realize that. Get busy, man."

"If you don't mind, I'll finish my lunch first."

Howell didn't hear me. He was looking out of the window again, half out of his seat.

A dark-headed youth in a tan sport shirt was talking to Sheila Howell at the poolside. He turned his head slightly. I recognized John Galton. He patted the shoulder of her terrycloth robe familiarly. Sheila smiled up full into his face.

Howell's light chair fell over backwards. He was out of the room before I could stop him. From the front door of the clubhouse, I saw him striding across the lawn toward the entrance of the swimming-pool enclosure.

John and Sheila came out hand-in-hand. They were so intent on each other that they didn't see Howell until he was on top of them. He thrust himself between them, shaking the boy by the arm. His voice was an ugly tearing rent in the quietness:

"Get out of here, do you hear me? You're not a member of this club."

John pulled away and faced him, white and rigid. "Sheila invited me."

"I dis-invite you." The back of Howell's neck was carbuncle red.

Sheila touched his arm. "Please, Daddy, don't make a scene. There's nothing to be gained."

John was encouraged to say: "My grandmother won't like this, Doctor."

"She will when she knows the facts." But the threat had taken the wind out of Howell's sails. He wasn't as loud as he had been.

"Please," Sheila repeated. "John's done no harm to anyone."

"Don't you understand, Sheila, I'm trying to protect you?"

"From what?"

"From corruption."

"That's silly, Dad. To hear you talk, you'd think John was a criminal."

The boy's head tilted suddenly, as if the word had struck a nerve in his neck. "Don't argue with him, Sheila. I oughtn't to've come here."

He turned on his heel and walked head down toward the parking-lot. Sheila went in the other direction. Molded in terrycloth, her body had a massiveness and mystery that hadn't struck me before. Her father stood and watched her until she entered the enclosure. She seemed to be moving heavily and fatally out of his control.

I went back to the dining-room and let Howell find me there. He came in pale and slack-faced, as if he'd had a serious loss of blood. His daughter was in the pool now, swimming its length back and forth with slow and powerful strokes. Her feet churned a steady white wake behind her.

She was still swimming when we left. Howell drove me to the court-house. He scowled up at the barred windows of the county jail:

"Put him behind bars, that's all I ask."

21

·

SHERIFF TRASK was in his office. Its walls were hung with testi-monials from civic organizations and service clubs; recruiting certifi-cates from Army, Navy, and Air Force; and a number of pictures of the Sheriff himself taken with the Governor and other notables. Trask's actual face was less genial than the face in the photographs.

"Trouble?" I said.

"Sit down. You're the trouble. You stir up a storm, and then you drop out of the picture. The trouble with you private investigators is ir-responsibility."

"That's a rough word, Sheriff." I fingered the broken bones in my face, thoughtfully and tenderly.

"Yeah, I know you got yourself hurt, and I'm sorry. But what can I do about it? Otto Schwartz is outside my jurisdiction."

"Murder raps cross state lines, or haven't you heard."

"Yeah, and I also heard at the same time that you can't extradite without a case. Without some kind of evidence, I can't even get to Schwartz to question him. And you want to know why I have no evidence?"

"Let me guess. Me again."

"It isn't funny, Archer. I was depending on you for some discretion. Why did you have to go and spill your guts to Roy Lemberg? Scare my witnesses clear out of the damn country?"

"I got overeager, and made a mistake. I wasn't the only one."

"What is that supposed to mean?"

"You told me Lemberg's car had been stolen."

"That's what switched license plates usually mean." Trask sat and thought about this for a minute, pushing out his lower lip. "Okay. We made mistakes. I made a medium-sized dilly and you made a peacheroo. So you took a beating for it. We won't sit around and cry. Where do we go from here?"

"It's your case, Sheriff. I'm just your patient helper."

He leaned toward me, heavy-shouldered and earnest. "You really mean to help? Or have you got an angle?"

"I mean to help, that's my angle."

"We'll see. Are you still working for Sable—for Mrs. Galton, that is?"

"Not at the moment."

"Who's bankrolling you. Dr. Howell?"

"News travels fast."

"Heck, I knew it before you did. Howell came around asking me to check your record with L.A. You seem to have some good friends down south. If you ever conned any old ladies, you never got caught."

"Young ones are more my meat."

Trask brushed aside the badinage with an impatient gesture. "I assume you're being hired to go into the boy's background. Howell wanted me to. Naturally I told him I couldn't move without some indication that law's been broken. You got any such indication?"

"Not yet."

"Neither have I. I talked to the boy, and he's as smooth as silk. He doesn't even make any definite claims. He merely says that people tell him he's his father's son, so it's probably so."

"Do you think he's been coached, Sheriff?"

"I don't know. He may be quarterbacking his own plays. When he came in to see me, it had nothing to do on the face of it with establishing his identity. He wanted information about his father's murder, if this John Brown was his father."

"Hasn't that been proved?"

"As close as it ever will be. There's still room for doubt, in my opinion. But what I started to say, he came in here to tell *me* what to do. He wanted more action on that old killing. I told him it was up to the San Mateo people, so what did he do? He made a trip up there to build a fire under the San Mateo sheriff."

"It's barely possible he's serious."

"Either that, or he's a psychologist. That kind of behavior doesn't go with consciousness of guilt."

"The Syndicate hires good lawyers."

Trask pondered this, his eyes withdrawing under the ledges of his brows. "You think it's a Syndicate job, eh? A big conspiracy?"

"With a big payoff, in the millions. Howell tells me Mrs. Galton's rewriting her will, leaving everything to the boy. I think her house should be watched."

"You honestly believe they'd try to knock her off?"

"They kill people for peanuts. What wouldn't they do to get hold of the Galton property?"

"Don't let your imagination run away. It won't happen, not in Santa Teresa County."

"It started to happen two weeks ago, when Culligan got it. That has all the marks of a gang killing, and in your territory."

"Don't rub it in. That case isn't finished yet."

"It's the same case," I said. "The Brown killing and the Culligan killing and the Galton impersonation, if it is one, all hang together."

"That's easy to say. How do we prove it?"

"Through the boy. I'm taking off for Michigan tonight. Howell thinks his accent originated in central Canada. That ties in with the Lembergs. Apparently they crossed the border into Canada from Detroit, and were headed for an address Culligan gave them. If you could trace Culligan that far back—"

"We're working on it." Trask smiled, rather forbiddingly. "Your Reno lead was a good one, Archer. I talked long distance last night to a friend in Reno, captain of detectives. He called me back just before lunch. Culligan was working for Schwartz about a year ago."

"Doing what?"

"Steerer for his casino. Another interesting thing: Culligan was arrested in Detroit five-six years ago. The FBI has a rap sheet on him."

"What was this particular rap?"

"An old larceny charge. It seems he left the country to evade it, got nabbed as soon as he showed his face on American soil, spent the next couple of years in Southern Michigan pen."

"What was the date of his arrest in Detroit?"

"I don't remember exactly. It was about five-and-a-half years ago. I could look it up, if it matters."

"It matters."

"What's on your mind?"

"John Galton turned up in Ann Arbor five-and-a-half years ago. Ann Arbor is practically a suburb of Detroit. I'm asking myself if he crossed the Canadian border with Culligan."

Trask whistled softly, and flicked on the switch of his squawk-box: "Conger, bring me the Culligan records. Yeah, I'm in my office."

I remembered Conger's hard brown face. He didn't remember me at first, then did a double take:

"Long time no see."

I quipped lamely: "How's the handcuff business?"

"Clicking."

Trask rustled the papers Conger had brought, and frowned impatiently. When he looked up his eyes were crackling bright:

"A little over five-and-a-half years. Culligan got picked up in Detroit January 7. Does that fit with your date?"

"I haven't pinned it down yet, but I will."

I rose to go. Trask's parting handshake was warm. "If you run into anything, call me collect, anytime day or night. And keep the hard nose out of the chopper."

"That's my aspiration."

"By the way, your car's in the county garage. I can release it to you if you want."

"Save it for me. And take care of the old lady, eh?"

The Sheriff was giving Conger orders to that effect before I reached the door.

22

I CASHED Howell's check at his bank just before it closed for business at three. The teller directed me to a travel agency where I made a plane reservation from Los Angeles to Detroit. The connecting plane didn't leave Santa Teresa for nearly three hours.

I walked the few blocks to Sable's office. The private elevator let me out into the oak-paneled anteroom.

Mrs. Haines looked up from her work, and raised her hand to smooth her dyed red hair. She said in maternal dismay:

"Why, Mr. Archer, you were *badly* injured. Mr. Sable *told* me you'd been hurt, but I had no idea—"

"Stop it. You're making me feel sorry for myself."

"What's the matter with feeling sorry for yourself? I do it all the time. It bucks me up no end."

"You're a woman."

She dipped her bright head as if I'd paid her a compliment. "What's the difference?"

"You don't want me to spell it out."

She tittered, not unpleasantly, and tried to blush, but her experienced face resisted the attempt. "Some other time, perhaps. What can I do for you now?"

"Is Mr. Sable in?"

"I'm sorry, he isn't back from lunch."

"It's three-thirty."

"I know. I don't expect he'll be in again today. He'll be sorry he missed you. The poor man's schedule has been all broken up, ever since that trouble at his house."

"The murder, you mean?"

"That, and other things. His wife isn't well."

"So I understand. Gordon told me she had a breakdown."

"Oh, did he tell you that? He doesn't do much talking about it to anyone. He's awfully sensitive on the subject." She made a confidential gesture, raising her red-tipped hand vertically beside her mouth. "Just between you and me, this isn't the first time he's had trouble with her."

"When was the other time?"

"Times, in the plural. She came here one night in March when we were doing income tax, and accused me of trying to steal her husband. I could have told her a thing or two, but of course I couldn't say a word in front of Mr. Sable. I tell you, he's a living saint, what he's taken from that woman, and he goes right on looking after her."

"What did she do to him?"

Color dabbed her cheekbones. She was slightly drunk with malice. "Plenty. Last summer she took off and went rampaging around the country spending his good money like water. Spending it on other men, too, can you imagine? He finally tracked her down in Reno, where she was *living* with another man."

"Reno?"

"Reno," she repeated flatly. "She probably intended to divorce him or something, but she gave up on the idea. She'd have been doing him a favor, if you ask me. But the poor man talked her into coming back with him. He seems to be infatuated with her." Her voice was disconsolate. After a moment's thought, she said: "I oughtn't to be telling you all this. Ought I?"

"I knew she had a history of trouble. Gordon told me himself that he had to put her in a nursing home."

"That's right, he's probably there with her now. He generally goes over to eat lunch with her, and most of the time he stays the rest of the day. Wasted devotion, I call it. If you ask me, that's one marriage doomed to failure. I did a horoscope on it, and you never saw such antagonism in the stars."

Not only in the stars.

"Where is the nursing home she's in, Mrs. Haines?"

"It's Dr. Trenchard's, on Light Street. But I wouldn't go there, if that's what you're thinking of. Mr. Sable doesn't like to be disturbed when he's visiting Mrs. Sable."

"I'll take my chances. And I won't mention that I've been here. Okay?"

"I guess so," she said dubiously. "It's over on the west side, 235 Light Street."

I took a cab across town. The driver looked me over curiously as I got out. Perhaps he was trying to figure out if I was patient or just a visitor.

"You want me to wait?"

"I think so. If I don't come out, you know what that will mean."

I left him having a delayed reaction. The "home" was a long stucco building set far back from the street on its own acre. Nothing indicated its specialness, except for the high wire fence which surrounded the patio at the side.

A man and a woman were sitting in a blue canvas swing behind the fence. Their backs were to me, but I recognized Sable's white head. The woman's blond head rested on his shoulder.

I resisted the impulse to call out to them. I climbed the long veranda, which was out of sight of the patio, and pressed the bellpush beside the front door. The door was unlocked and opened by a nurse in white, without a cap. She was unexpectedly young and pretty.

"Yes, sir?"

"I'd like to speak to Mr. Sable."

"And who shall I say is calling?"

"Lew Archer."

She left me in a living-room or lounge whose furniture was covered with bright chintz. Two old ladies in shawls were watching a baseball game on televison. A young man with a beard squatted on his heels in a corner, watching the opposite corner of the ceiling. His lips were moving.

One of the half-curtained windows looked out across the sun-filled patio. I saw the young nurse cross to the blue swing, and Sable's face come up as if from sleep. He disengaged himself from his wife. Her body relaxed into an awkward position. Blue-shadowed by the canvas shade of the swing, her face had the open-eyed blankness of a doll's.

Sable dragged his shadow across the imitation flagstone. He looked small, oddly diminished, under the sky's blue height. The impression persisted when he entered the lounge. Age had fallen on him. He needed a haircut, and his tie was pulled to one side. The look he gave me was red-eyed; his voice was cranky.

"What brings you here, anyway?"

"I wanted to see you. I don't have much time in town."

"Well. You see me." He lifted his arms from his sides, and dropped them.

The old ladies, who had greeted him with smiles and nods, reacted like frightened children to his bitterness. One of them hitched her shawl high around her neck and slunk out of the room. The other stretched her hand out toward Sable as if she wanted to comfort him. She remained frozen in that position while she went on watching the ball game. The bearded man watched the corner of the ceiling.

"How is Mrs. Sable?"

"Not well." He frowned, and drew me out into the corridor. "As a matter of fact, she's threatened with melancholia. Dr. Trenchard tells me she's had a similar illness before—before I married her. The shock she suffered two weeks ago stirred up the old trouble. Good Lord, was that only two weeks ago?"

I risked asking: "What sort of background does she have?"

"Alice was a model in Chicago, and she's been married before. She lost a child, and her first husband treated her badly. I've tried to make it up to her. With damn poor success."

His voice sank toward despair.

"I take it she's having therapy."

"Of course. Dr. Trenchard is one of the best psychiatrists on the coast. If she gets any worse, he's going to try shock treatment." He leaned on the wall, looking down at nothing in particular. His red eyes seemed to be burning.

"You should go home and get some sleep."

"I haven't been sleeping much lately. It's easy to say, sleep. But you can't will yourself to sleep. Besides, Alice needs me with her. She's much calmer when I'm around." He shook himself, and straightened. "But you didn't come here to discuss my woes with me."

"That's true, I didn't. I came to thank you for the check, and to ask you a couple of questions."

"You earned the money. I'll answer the questions if I can."

"Dr. Howell has hired me to investigate John Galton's background. Since you brought me into the case, I'd like to have your go-ahead."

"Of course. You have it, as far as I'm concerned. I can't speak for Mrs. Galton."

"I understand that. Howell tells me she's sold on the boy. Howell himself is convinced that he's a phoney."

"We've discussed it. There seems to be some sort of romance between John and Howell's daughter."

"Does Howell have any other special motive?"

"For doing what?"

"Investigating John, trying to prevent Mrs. Galton from changing her will."

Sable looked at me with some of his old sharpness. "That's a good question. Under the present will, Howell stands to benefit in several ways. He himself is executor, and due to inherit a substantial sum, I really mustn't say how much. His daughter, Sheila, is in for another substantial sum, very substantial. And after various other bequests have been met, the bulk of the estate goes to various charities, one of which is the Heart Association. Henry Galton died of cardiovascular trouble. Howell is an officer of the Heart Association. All of which makes him a highly interested party."

"And highly interesting. Has the will been changed yet?"

"I can't say. I told Mrs. Galton I couldn't conscientiously draw up a new will for her, under the circumstances. She said she'd get someone else. Whether she has or not, I can't say."

"Then you're not sold on the boy, either."

"I was. I no longer know what to think. Frankly, I haven't been giving the matter much thought." He moved impatiently, and made a misstep to one side, his shoulder thudding against the wall. "If you don't mind, I think I'll get back to my wife."

The young nurse let me out.

I looked back through the wire fence. Mrs. Sable remained in the same position on the swing. Her husband joined her in the blue shadow. He raised her inert head and insinuated his shoulder behind it. They sat like a very old couple waiting for the afternoon shadows to lengthen and merge into night.

23
·

THE cab-driver stopped at the curb opposite the gates of the Galton estate. He hung one arm over the back of the seat and gave me a quizzical look:

"No offense, Mister, but you want the front entrance or the service entrance?"

"The front entrance."

"Okay. I just didn't want to make a mistake."

He let me off under the porte-cochere. I paid him, and told him not to wait. The Negro maid let me into the reception hall, and left me to cool my heels among the ancestors.

I moved over to one of the tall, narrow windows. It looked out across the front lawn, where the late afternoon sunlight lay serenely. I got some sense of the guarded peace that walled estates like this had once provided. In the modern world the walls were more like prison walls, or the wire fence around a nursing-home garden. When it came right down to it, I preferred the service entrance. The people in the kitchen usually had more fun.

Quick footsteps descended the stairs, and Cassie Hildreth came into the room. She had on a skirt and a sweater which emphasized her figure. She looked more feminine in other, subtler, ways. Something had happened to change her style.

She gave me her hand. "It's good to see you, Mr. Archer. Sit down. Mrs. Galton will be down in a minute."

"Under her own power?"

"Yes, isn't it remarkable? She's becoming much more active than she was. John takes her out for a drive nearly every day."

"That's nice of him."

"He actually seems to enjoy it. They hit it off from the start."

"He's the one I really came to see. Is he around?"

"I haven't seen him since lunch. Probably he's out in his car somewhere."

"His car?"

"Aunt Maria bought him a cute little Thunderbird. John's crazy about it. He's like a child with a new toy. He told me he's never had a car of his own before."

"I guess he has a lot of things he never had before."

"Yes. I'm so happy for him."

"You're a generous woman."

"Not really. I've a lot to be thankful for. Now that John's come home, I wouldn't trade my life for any other. It may sound like a strange thing to say, but life is suddenly just as it was in the old days—before the war, before Tony died. Everything seems to have fallen into harmony."

She sounded as if she had transferred her lifelong crush from Tony to John Galton. A dream possessed her face. I wanted to warn her not to bank too heavily on it. Everything could fall into chaos again.

Mrs. Galton was fussing on the stairs. Cassie went to the door to meet her. The old lady had on a black tailored suit with something white at her throat. Her hair was marcelled in hard gray corrugations which resembled galvanized iron. She extended her bony hand:

"I'm most pleased to see you. I've been wanting to express my personal appreciation to you. You've made my house a happier one."

"Your check was a very nice expression," I said.

"The laborer is worthy of his hire." Perhaps she sensed that that wasn't the most tactful way to put it, because she added: "Won't you stay for tea? My grandson will want to see you. I expect him back for tea. He should be here now."

The querulous note was still in her voice. I wondered how much of her happiness was real, how much sheer will to believe that something good could happen to a poor old rich lady. She lowered herself into a chair, exaggerating the difficulty of her movements. Cassie began to look anxious.

"I think he's at the country club, Aunt Maria."

"With Sheila?"

"I think so," Cassie said.

"Is he still seeing a lot of her?"

"Just about every day."

"We'll have to put a stop to that. He's much too young to think of taking an interest in any one girl. Sheila is a dear sweet child, of course, but we can't have her monopolizing John. I have other plans for him."

"What plans," I said, "if you don't mind my asking?"

"I'm thinking of sending John to Europe in the fall. He needs broadening, and he's very much interested in the modern drama. If the interest persists, and deepens, I'll build him a repertory theater here in Santa Teresa. John has great talent, you know. The Galton distinction comes out in a different form in each generation."

As if to demonstrate this proposition, a red Thunderbird convertible careened up the long driveway. A door slammed. John came in. His face was flushed and sullen. He stood inside the doorway and pushed his fists deep in his jacket pockets, his head thrust forward in a peering attitude.

"Well!" he said. "Here we all are. The three fates, Clotho, Lachesis, and Mr. Archer."

"That isn't funny, John," Cassie said in a voice of warning.

"I think it's funny. Very, very funny."

He came toward us, weaving slightly, exaggerating the movements of his shoulders. I went to meet him:

"Hello, John."

"Get away from me. I know why you're here."

"Tell me."

"I'll tell you all right."

He threw a wild fist in my direction, staggering off balance. I moved in close, turned him with his back to me, took hold of his jacket collar with both hands and pulled it halfway down his arms. He sputtered words at me which smelled like the exhalations from a still. But I could feel the lethal force vibrating through him.

"Straighten up and quiet down," I said.

"I'll knock your block off."

"First you'll have to load yourself up with something solider than whisky."

Mrs. Galton breathed at my shoulder. "Has he been drinking?"

John answered her himself, in a kind of small-boy defiance: "Yes I have been drinking. And I've been thinking. Thinking and drinking. I say it's a lousy setup."

"What?" she said. "What's happened?"

"A lot of things have happened. Tell this man to turn me loose."

"Let him go," Mrs. Galton said commandingly.

"Do you think he's ready?"

"Damn you, let me go."

He made a violent lunge, and tore loose from the arms of his jacket. He whirled and faced me with his fists up:

"Come on and fight. I'm not afraid of you."

"This is hardly the time and place."

I tossed his jacket to him. He caught and held it, looking down at it stupidly. Cassie stepped between us. She took the jacket and helped him on with it. He submitted almost meekly to her hands.

"You need some black coffee, John. Let me get you some black coffee."

"I don't want coffee, I'm not drunk."

"But you've been drinking." Mrs. Galton's voice rose almost an octave and stayed there on a querulous monotone: "Your *father* started drinking young, you mustn't let it happen all over again. Please, you must promise me."

The old lady hung on John's arm, making anxious noises, while Cassie tried to soothe her. John's head swung around, his eyes on me: "Get that man out of here! He's spying for Dr. Howell."

Mrs. Galton turned on me, the bony structure of her face pushing out through the seamed flesh:

"I trust my grandson is mistaken about you. I know Dr. Howell is incapable of committing disloyal acts behind my back."

"Don't be too sure of that," John said. "He doesn't want me seeing Sheila. There's nothing he wouldn't do to break it up."

"I'm asking you, Mr. Archer. Did Dr. Howell hire you?"

"I'll have to ask you to take it up with Howell."

"It is true, then?"

"I can't answer that, Mrs. Galton."

"In that case please leave my house. You entered it under false pretenses. If you trespass again, I'll have you prosecuted. I've a good mind to go to the authorities as it is."

"No, don't do that," John said. "We can handle it, Grandma."

He seemed to be sobering rapidly. Cassie chimed in:

"You mustn't get so excited about nothing. You know what Dr. Howell—"

"Don't mention his name in my presence. To be betrayed by an old and trusted friend—well, that's what it is to have money. They think they have a right to it simply because it's there. I see now what August Howell has been up to, insinuating himself and his chit of a daughter into my life. Well, he's not getting a cent of my money. I've seen to that."

"Please calm down, Aunt Maria."

Cassie tried to lead her back to her chair. Mrs. Galton wouldn't budge. She called hoarsely in my direction:

"You can go and tell August Howell he's overreached himself. He won't get a cent of my money, not a cent. It's going to my own kith and kin. And tell him to keep that daughter of his from flinging herself at my grandson. I have other plans for him."

The breath rustled and moaned in her head. She closed her eyes; her face was like a death mask. She tottered and almost fell. John held her around the shoulders.

"Get out," he said to me. "My grandmother is a sick woman. Can't you see what you're doing to her?"

"Somebody's doing it to her."

"Are you going to get out, or do I call the police?"

"You'd better go," Cassie said. "Mrs. Galton has a heart condition."

Mrs. Galton's hand went to her heart automatically. Her head fell loosely onto John's shoulder. He stroked her gray hair. It was a very touching scene.

I wondered as I went out how many more scenes like that the old lady's heart would stand. The question kept me awake on the night plane to Chicago.

24
·

I PUT in two days of legwork in Ann Arbor, where I represented myself as a personnel investigator for a firm with overseas contracts. John's account of his high school and college life checked out in detail. I established one interesting additional detail: He had enrolled in the high school under the name of John Lindsay five-and-a-half years before, on January 9. Peter Culligan had been arrested in Detroit, forty miles away, on January 7 of the same year. Apparently it had taken the boy just two days to find a new protector in Gabriel Lindsay.

I talked to friends of Lindsay's, mostly high-school teachers. They remembered John as a likely boy, though he had been, as one of them said: "A tough little egg to start with." They understood that Lindsay had taken him off the streets.

Gabriel Lindsay had gone in for helping young people in trouble. He was an older man who had lost a son in the war, and his wife soon after the war. He died himself in the University Hospital in February of the previous year, of pneumonia.

His doctor remembered John's constant attendance at his bedside. The copy of his will on file in the Washtenaw County courthouse left two thousand dollars to "my quasi-foster-son, known as John Lindsay, for the furtherance of his education." There were no other specific bequests in Lindsay's will; which probably meant it was all the money he had.

John had graduated from the University in June, as a Speech major, with honors. His counselor in the Dean's office said that he had been a student without any overt problems; not exactly popular perhaps: he seemed to have no close friends. On the other hand, he had been active in campus theatrical productions, and moderately successful as an actor in his senior year.

His address at the time of his graduation had been a rooming-house on Catherine Street, over behind the Graduate School. The landlady's name was Mrs. Haskell. Maybe she could help me.

Mrs. Haskell lived on the first floor of an old three-story gingerbread mansion. I guessed from the bundles of mail on the table inside the door that the rest of her house was given over to roomers. She led me along the polished parquetry hallway into a half-blinded parlor. It was a cool oasis in the heat of the Michigan July.

Somewhere over our heads, a typewriter pecked at the silence. The echo of a southern drawl twanged like a mandolin in Mrs. Haskell's voice:

"Do sit down and tell me how John is. And how is he doing in his position?" Mrs. Haskell clasped her hands enthusiastically on her flowered print bosom. The curled bangs on her forehead shook like silent bells.

"He hasn't started with us yet, Mrs. Haskell. The purpose of my investigation is to clear him for a confidential assignment."

"Does that mean the other thing has fallen through?"

"What other thing is that?"

"The acting thing. You may not know it, but John Lindsay's a very fine actor. One of the most talented boys I've ever had in my house. I never missed an appearance of his at the Lydia Mendelssohn. In *Hobson's Choice* last winter, he was rich."

"I bet he was. And you say he had acting offers?"

"I don't know about offers in the plural, but he had one very good one. Some big producer wanted to give him a personal contract and train him professionally. The last I heard, John had accepted it. But I guess he changed his mind, if he's going with your firm. Security."

"It's interesting about his acting," I said. "We like our employees to be well-rounded people. Do you remember the producer's name?"

"I'm afraid I never knew it."

"Where did he come from?"

"I don't know. John was very secretive about his private affairs. He didn't even leave a forwarding address when he left in June. All I really know about this is what Miss Reichler told me after he left."

"Miss Reichler?"

"His friend. I don't mean she was his girlfriend exactly. Maybe she thought so, but he didn't. I warned him not to get mixed up with a rich young lady like her, riding around in her Cadillacs and her convertibles. My boys come and go, but I try to keep them from overstepping themselves. Miss Reichler is several years older than John." Her lips moved over his name with a kind of maternal greed. The mandolin twang was becoming more pronounced.

"He sounds like the kind of young man we need. Socially mobile, attractive to the ladies."

"Oh, he was always that. I don't mean he's girl-crazy. He paid the girls no mind, unless they forced themselves on his attention. Ada Reichler practically beat a path to his door. She used to drive up in her Cadillac every second or third day. Her father's a big man in Detroit. Auto parts."

"Good," I said. "A high-level business connection."

Mrs. Haskell sniffed. "Don't count too much on that one. Miss Reichler was sore as a boil when John left without even saying good-by. She was really let down. I tried to explain to her that a young man just starting out in the world couldn't carry any excess baggage. Then she got mad at me, for some god-forsaken reason. She slam-banged into her car and ground those old Cadillac gears to a pulp."

"How long did they know each other?"

"As long as he was with me, at least a year. I guess she had her nice qualities, or he wouldn't have stuck with her so long. She's pretty enough, if you like that slinky type."

"Do you have her address? I'd like to talk to her."

"She might tell you a lot of lies. You know: 'Hell hath no fury like a woman scorned.'"

"I can discount anything like that."

"See that you do. John's a fine young man, and your people will be lucky if he decides to go with them. Her father's name is Ben, I think, Ben Reichler. They live over in the section by the river."

I drove on winding roads through a semi-wooded area. Eventually I found the Reichlers' mailbox. Their driveway ran between rows of maples to a low brick house with a sweeping roof. It looked small from a distance, and massive when I got up close to it. I began to understand how John could have made the leap from Mrs. Gorgello's boardinghouse to the Galton house. He'd been training for it.

A man in overalls with a spraygun in his hands climbed up the granite steps of a sunken garden.

"The folks aren't home," he said. "They're never home in July."

"Where can I find them?"

"If it's business, Mr. Reichler's in his office in the Reichler Building three-four days a week."

"Miss Ada Reichler's the one I want."

"Far as I know, she's in Kingsville with her mother. Kingsville, Canada. They have a place up there. You a friend of Miss Ada's?"

"Friend of a friend," I said.

It was early evening when I drove into Kingsville. The heat hadn't let up, and my shirt was sticking to my back. The lake lay below the town like a blue haze in which white sails hung upright by their tips.

The Reichlers' summer place was on the lakeshore. Green terraces descended from the house to a private dock and boathouse. The house itself was a big old lodge whose brown shingled sides were shaggy with ivy. The Reichlers weren't camping out, though. The maid who answered the door wore a fresh starched uniform, complete with cap. She told me that Mrs. Reichler was resting and Miss Ada was out in one of the boats. She was expected back at any time, if I cared to wait.

I waited on the dock, which was plastered with No Trespassing signs. A faint breeze had begun to stir, and the sailboats were leaning shoreward. Mild little land-locked waves lapped at the pilings. A motorboat went by like a bird shaking out wings of white water. Its wash rocked the dock. The boat turned and came in, slowing down. A girl with dark hair and dark glasses was at the wheel. She pointed a finger at her brown chest, and cocked her head questioningly.

"You want me?"

I nodded, and she brought the boat in. I caught the line she threw and helped her onto the dock. Her body was lean and supple in black

Capris and a halter. Her face, when she took off her glasses, was lean and intense.

"Who are you?"

I had already decided to discard my role. "My name is Archer. I'm a private detective from California."

"You came all this way to see me?"

"Yes."

"Why on earth?"

"Because you knew John Lindsay."

Her face opened up, ready for anything, wonderful or otherwise. "John sent you here?"

"Not exactly."

"Is he in some kind of trouble?"

I didn't answer her. She jerked at my arm like a child wanting attention.

"Tell me, is John in trouble? Don't be afraid, I can take it."

"I don't know whether he is or not, Miss Reichler. What makes you jump to the conclusion that he is?"

"Nothing, I don't mean that." Her speech was staccato. "You said that you're a detective. Doesn't that indicate trouble?"

"Say he is in trouble. What then?"

"I'd want to help him, naturally. Why are we talking in riddles?"

I liked her rapid, definite personality, and guessed that honesty went along with it:

"I don't like riddles any more than you do. I'll make a bargain with you, Miss Reichler. I'll tell you my end of the story if you'll tell me yours."

"What is this, true confession hour?"

"I'm serious, and I'm willing to do my talking first. If you're interested in John's situation—"

"Situation is a nice neutral word."

"That's why I used it. Is it a bargain?"

"All right." She gave me her hand on it, as a man would have. "I warn you in advance, though, I won't tell you anything against him. I don't *know* anything against him, except that he treated me—well, I was asking for it." She lifted her high thin shoulders, shrugging off the past. "We can talk in the garden, if you like."

We climbed the terraces to a walled garden in the shadow of the house. It was crowded with the colors and odors of flowers. She placed me in a canvas chair facing hers. I told her where John was and what he was doing.

Her eyes were soft and black, lit tremulously from within. Their expression followed all the movements of my story. She said when I'd finished:

"It sounds like one of Grimm's fairy tales. The goatherd turns out to be the prince in disguise. Or like Œdipus. John had an Œdipus theory of his own, that Œdipus killed his father because he banished him from the kingdom. I thought it was very clever." Her voice was brittle. She was marking time.

"John's a clever boy," I said. "And you're a clever girl, and you knew him well. Do you believe he's who he claims to be?"

"Do you?" When I failed to answer, she said: "So he has a girl in California, already." Her hands lay open on her slender thighs. She hugged them between her thighs.

"The girl's father hired me. He thinks John is a fraud."

"And you do, too?"

"I don't like to think it, but I'm afraid I do. There are some indications that his whole story was invented to fit the occasion."

"To inherit money?"

"That's the general idea. I've been talking to his landlady in Ann Arbor, Mrs. Haskell."

"I know her," the girl said shortly.

"Do you know anything about this offer John had from a producer?"

"Yes, he mentioned it to me. It was one of these personal contracts that movie producers give to promising young actors. This man saw him in *Hobson's Choice*."

"When?"

"Last February."

"Did you meet the man?"

"I never did. John said he flew back to the coast. He didn't want to discuss it after that."

"Did he mention any names before he dried up?"

"Not that I recall. Do you think John was lying about him, that it wasn't an acting job he was offered?"

"That could be. Or it could be John was sucked in. The conspirators made their approach as movie producers or agents, and later told him what was required of him."

"Why would John fall in with their plans? He's not a criminal."

"The Galton estate is worth millions. He stands to inherit all of it, any day. Even a small percentage of it would make him a rich man."

"But he never cared about money, at least not the kind you inherit. He could have married me: Barkis was willing. My father's money was one of the reasons he didn't. At least that's what he said. The real reason, I guess, was that he didn't love me. Does he love her?"

"My client's daughter? I couldn't say for sure. Maybe he doesn't love anybody."

"You're very honest, Mr. Archer. I gave you an opening, but you didn't try to use her on me as a wedge. You could have said that he was crazy about her, thus fanning the fires of jealousy." She winced at her own self-mockery.

"I try to be honest with honest people."

She gave me a flashing look. "That's intended to put me on the spot."

"Yes."

She turned her head and looked out over the lake as if she could see all the way to California. The last sails were converging toward shore, away from the darkness falling like soot along the horizon. As light drained from the sky, it seemed to gather more intensely on the water.

"What will they do to him if they find out he's an impostor?"

"Put him in jail."

"For how long?"

"It's hard to say. It'll be easier on him if we get it over with soon. He hasn't made any big claims yet, or taken any big money."

"You really mean, really and truly, that I'd be doing him a favor by puncturing his story?"

"That's my honest opinion. If it's all a pack of lies, we'll find out sooner or later. The sooner the better."

She hesitated. Her profile was stark. One cord in her neck stood out under the skin. "You say that he claims that he was brought up in an orphanage in Ohio."

"Crystal Springs, Ohio. Did he ever mention the place to you?"

She shook her head in a quick short arc. I said:

"There are some indications that he was raised here in Canada."

"What indications?"

"Speech. Spelling."

She rose suddenly, walked to the end of the garden, stooped to pick a snapdragon, threw it away with a spurning gesture. She came back toward me and stood with her face half-averted. She said in a rough dry voice:

"Just don't tell him I was the one that told you. I couldn't bear to have him hate me, even if I never see him again. The poor damn silly fool was born and raised right here in Ontario. His real name is Theodore Fredericks, and his mother runs a boardinghouse in Pitt, not more than sixty miles from here."

I stood up, forcing her to look at me. "How do you know, Miss Reichler?"

"I talked to Mrs. Fredericks. It wasn't a very fortunate meeting. It didn't do anything for either of us. I should never have gone there."

"Did he take you to meet his mother?"

"Hardly. I went to see her myself a couple of weeks ago, after John left Ann Arbor. When I didn't hear from him I got it into my head that perhaps he'd gone home to Pitt."

"How did you learn about his home in Pitt? Did he tell you?"

"Yes, but I don't believe he intended to. It happened on the spur of the moment, when he was spending a week-end here with us. It was the only time he ever came to visit us here in Kingsville, and it was a bad time for me—the worst. I hate to think of it."

"Why?"

"If you have to know, he turned me down. We went for a drive on Sunday morning. I did the driving, of course. He'd never touch the wheel of my car. That's the way he was with me, so proud, and I had no pride at all with him. I got carried away by the flowers and the bees, or something, and I asked him to marry me. He gave me a flat refusal.

"He must have seen how hurt I was, because he asked me to drive him to Pitt. We weren't too far from there, and he wanted to show me something. When we got there he made me drive down a street that runs along by the river on the edge of the Negro section. It was a dreadful neighborhood, filthy children of all colors playing in the mud, and slatternly women screaming at them. We stopped across from an old red brick house where some men in their undershirts were sitting on the front steps passing around a wine jug.

"John asked me to take a good look, because he said he belonged there. He said he'd grown up in that neighborhood, in that red house. A woman came out on the porch to call the men in for dinner. She had a voice like a kazoo, and she was a hideous fat pig of a woman. John said that she was his mother.

"I didn't believe him. I thought he was hoaxing me, putting me to some kind of silly test. It was a test, in a way, but not in the way I imagined. He wanted to be *known*, I think. He wanted me to accept him as he actually was. But by the time I understood that, it was too late. He'd gone into one of his deep freezes." She touched her mournful mouth with the tips of her long fingers.

"When did this happen?"

"Last spring. It must have been early in March, there was still some snow on the ground."

"Did you see John after that?"

"A few times, but it wasn't any good. I think he regretted telling me about himself. In fact I know he did. That Sunday in Pitt was the end of any real communication between us. There were so many things we couldn't talk about, finally we couldn't talk at all. The last time I saw him was humiliating, for him, and for me, too. He asked me not to mention what he'd said about his origins, if anyone ever brought it up."

"Who did he expect to bring it up? The police?"

"The immigration authorities. Apparently there was something irregular about his entry into the United States. That fitted in with what his mother told me afterwards. He'd run away with one of her boarders when he was sixteen, and apparently crossed over into the States."

"Did she give you the boarder's name?"

"No. I'm surprised Mrs. Fredericks told me as much as she did. You know how the lower classes are, suspicious. But I gave her a little money, and that loosened her up." Her tone was contemptuous, and she must have overheard herself: "I know, I'm just what John said I was, a dollar snob. Well, I had my comeuppance. There I was prowling around the Pitt slums on a hot summer day like a lady dog in season. And I might as well have stayed at home. His mother hadn't laid eyes on him for over five years, and she never expected to see him again, she said. I realized that I'd lost him, for good."

"He was easy to lose," I said, "and no great loss."

She looked at me like an enemy. "You don't know him. John's a fine person at heart, fine and deep. I was the one who failed in our relationship. If I'd been able to understand him that Sunday, say the right thing and hold him, he mightn't have gone into this fraudulent life. I'm the one who wasn't good for anything."

She screwed up her face like a monkey and tugged at her hair, making herself look ugly.

"I'm just a hag."

"Be quiet."

She looked at me incredulously, one hand flat against her temple. "Who do you think you're talking to?"

"Ada Reichler. You're worth five of him."

"I'm not. I'm no good. I betrayed him. Nobody could love me. *Nobody* could."

"I told you to be quiet." I'd never been angrier in my life.

"Don't you dare speak to me like that. Don't you dare!"

Her eyes were as bright and heavy as mercury. She ran blind to the end of the garden, knelt at the edge of the grass, and buried her face in flowers.

Her back was long and beautiful. I waited until she was still, and lifted her to her feet. She turned toward me.

The last light faded from the flowers and from the lake. Night came on warm and moist. The grass was wet.

25

·

THE town of Pitt was dark except for occasional street lights and the fainter lights that fell from the heavily starred sky. Driving along the street Ada Reichler had named, I could see the moving river down between the houses. When I got out of the car, I could smell the river. A chanting chorus of frogs made the summer night pulsate at its edges.

On the second floor of the old red house, a bleary light outlined a window. The boards of the veranda groaned under my weight. I knocked on the alligatored door. A card offering "Rooms for Rent" was stuck inside the window beside the door.

A light went on over my head. Moths swirled up around it like unseasonable snow. An old man peered out, cocking his narrow gray head at me out of a permanent stoop.

"Something you want?" His voice was a husky whisper.

"I'd like to speak to Mrs. Fredericks, the landlady."

"I'm Mr. Fredericks. If it's a room you want, I can rent you a room just as good as she can."

"Do you rent by the night?"

"Sure, I got a nice front room you can have. It'll cost you—let's see." He stroked the bristles along the edge of his jaw, making a rasping noise. His dull eyes looked me over with stupid cunning. "Two dollars?"

"I'd like to see the room first."

"If you say so. Try not to make too much noise, eh? The old woman —Mrs. Fredericks is in bed."

He must have been just about to go himself. His shirt was open so that I could have counted his ribs, and his broad striped suspenders were hanging down. I followed him up the stairs. He moved with elaborate secrecy, and turned at the top to set a hushing finger to his lips. The light from the hall below cast his hunched condor shadow on the wall.

A woman's voice rose from the back of the house: "What are you creeping around for?"

"Didn't want to disturb the boarders," he said in his carrying whisper.

"The boarders aren't in yet, and you know it. Is somebody with you?"

"Nope. Just me and my shadow."

He smiled a yellow-toothed smile at me, as if he expected me to share the joke.

"Come to bed then," she called.

"In a minute."

He tiptoed to the front of the hallway, beckoned me through an open door, and closed the door quietly behind me. For a moment we were alone in the dark, like conspirators. I could hear his emotional breathing.

Then he reached up to pull on a light. It swung on its cord, throwing lariats of shadow up to the high ceiling, and shifting gleam and gloom on the room's contents. These included a bureau, a washstand with pitcher and bowl, and a bed which had taken the impress of many bodies. The furnishings reminded me of the room John Brown had had in Luna Bay.

John Brown? John Nobody.

I looked at the old man's face. It was hard to imagine what quirk of his genes had produced the boy. If Fredericks had ever possessed good looks, time had washed them out. His face was patchily furred leather, stretched on gaunt bones, held in place by black nailhead eyes.

"The room all right?" he said uneasily.

I glanced at the flowered paper on the walls. Faded morning-glories climbed brown lattices to the watermarked ceiling. I didn't think I could sleep in a room with morning-glories crawling up the walls all night.

"If it's bugs you're worried about," he said, "we had the place fumigated last spring."

"Oh. Good."

"I'll let in some fresh air." He opened the window and sidled back to me. "Pay me cash in advance, and I can let you have it for a dollar and a half."

I had no intention of staying the night, but I decided to let him have the money. I took out my wallet and gave him two ones. His hand trembled as he took them:

"I got no change."

"Keep it. Mr. Fredericks, you have a son."

He gave me a long slow cautious look. "What if I have?"

"A boy named Theodore."

"He's no boy. He'll be grown up now."

"How long is it since you've seen him?"

"I dunno. Four-five years, maybe longer. He ran away when he was sixteen. It's a tough thing to have to say about your own boy, but it was good riddance of bad rubbish."

"Why do you say that?"

"Because it's the truth. You acquainted with Theo?"

"Slightly."

"Is he in trouble again? Is that why you're here?"

Before I could answer, the door of the room flew open. A short stout woman in a flannelette nightgown brushed past me and advanced on Fredericks: "What you think you're doing, renting a room behind my back?"

"I didn't."

But the money was still in his hand. He tried to crumple it in his fist and hide it. She grabbed for it:

"Give me my money."

He hugged his valuable fist against his washboard chest. "It's just as much my money as it is yours."

"Aw no it isn't. I work myself to the bone keeping our heads above water. And what do you do? Drink it up as fast as I can make it."

"I ain't had a drink for a week."

"You're a liar." She stamped her bare foot. Her body shook under the nightgown, and her gray braids swung like cables down her back. "You were drinking wine last night with the boys in the downstairs bedroom."

"That was free," he said virtuously. "And you got no call to talk to me like this in front of a stranger."

She turned to me for the first time. "Excuse us, mister. It's no fault of yours, but he can't handle money." She added unnecessarily: "He drinks."

While her eyes were off him, Fredericks made for the door. She intercepted him. He struggled feebly in her embrace. Her upper arms were as thick as hams. She pried open his bony fist and pushed the crumpled bills down between her breasts. He watched the money go as though it represented his hope of heaven:

"Just give me fifty cents. Fifty cents won't break you."

"Not one red cent," she said. "If you think I'm going to help you get the d.t.'s again, you got another think coming."

"All I want is one drink."

"Sure, and then another and another. Until you feel the rats crawling up under your clothes, and I got to nurse you out of it again."

"There's all different kinds of rats. A woman that won't give her lawful husband four bits to settle his stomach is the worst kind of rat there is."

"Take that back."

She moved on him, arms akimbo. He backed into the hallway:

"All right, I take it back. But I'll get a drink, don't worry. I got good friends in this town, they know my worth."

"Sure they do. They feed you stinking rotgut across the river, and then they come to me asking for money. Don't you set foot outside this house tonight."

"You're not going to order me around, treat me like a has-been. It ain't my fault I can't work, with a hole in my belly. It ain't my fault I can't sleep without a drink to ease the pain."

"Scat," she said. "Go to bed, old man."

He shambled away, trailing his slack suspenders. The fat woman turned to me.

"I apologize for my husband. He's never been the same since his accident."

"What happened to him?"

"He got hurt bad." Her answer seemed deliberately vague. Under folds of fat, her face showed traces of her son's stubborn intelligence. She changed the subject: "I notice you paid with American money. You from the States?"

"I just drove over from Detroit."

"You live in Detroit? I never been over there, but I hear it's an interesting place."

"It probably is. I was just passing through on my way from California."

"What brings you all the way from California?"

"A man named Peter Culligan was murdered there several weeks ago. Culligan was stabbed to death."

"Stabbed to death?"

I nodded. Her head moved slightly in unison with mine. Without shifting her eyes from my face, she moved around me and sat on the edge of the bed.

"You know him, don't you, Mrs. Fredericks?"

"He boarded with me for a while, years ago. He had this very room."

"What was he doing in Canada?"

"Don't ask me. I don't ask my boarders where their money comes from. Mostly he sat in this room and studied his racing sheets." She looked up shrewdly from under frowning brows. "Would you be a policeman?"

"I'm working with the police. Are you sure you don't know why Culligan came here?"

"I guess it was just a place like any other. He was a loner and a drifter—I get quite a few of them. He probably covered a lot of territory in his time." She looked up at the shadows on the ceiling. The light was still now, and the shadows were concentric, spreading out like ripples on a pool. "Listen, mister, who stabbed him?"

"A young hoodlum."

"My boy? Was it my boy that done it? Is that why you come to me?"

"I think your son is involved."

"I knew it." Her cheeks shuddered. "He took a knife to his father before he was out of high school. He would of killed him, too. Now he really is a murderer." She pressed her clenched hands deep into her bosom; it swelled around her fists like rising dough. "I didn't have enough trouble in my life. I had to give birth to a murderer."

"I don't know about that, Mrs. Fredericks. He committed fraud. I doubt that he committed murder." Even as I said it, I was wondering if he had been within striking distance of Culligan, and if he had an alibi for that day. "Do you have a picture of your son?"

"I have when he was in high school. He ran away before he graduated."

"May I have a look at the picture, Mrs. Fredericks? It's barely possible we're talking about two different people."

But any hope of this died a quick death. The boy in the snapshot she brought was the same one, six years younger. He stood on a riverbank, his back to the water, smiling with conscious charm into the camera.

I gave the picture back to Mrs. Fredericks. She held it up to the light and studied it as if she could re-create the past from its single image.

"Theo was a good-looking boy," she said wistfully. "He was doing so good in school and all, until he started getting those ideas of his."

"What kind of ideas did he have?"

"Crazy ideas, like he was the son of an English lord, and the gypsies stole him away when he was a baby. When he was just a little tyke, he used to call himself Percival Fitzroy, like in a book. That was always his way—he thought he was too good for his own people. I worried about where all that daydreaming was going to land him."

"He's still dreaming," I said. "Right now he's representing himself as the grandson of a wealthy woman in Southern California. Do you know anything about that?"

"I never hear from him. How would I know about it?"

"Apparently Culligan put him up to it. I understand he ran away from here with Culligan."

"Yeah. The dirty scamp talked him into it, turned him against his own father."

"And you say he knifed his father?"

"That very same day." Her eyes widened and glazed. "He stabbed him with a butcher knife, gave him an awful wound. Fredericks was on his back for weeks. He's never got back on his feet entirely. Neither have I, to think my own boy would do a thing like that."

"What was the trouble about, Mrs. Fredericks?"

"Wildness and willfulness," she said. "He wanted to leave home and make his own way in the world. That Culligan encouraged him. He

pretended to have Theo's welfare at heart and I know what you're thinking, that Theo did right to run away from home with his old man a
bum and the kind of boarders I get. But the proof of the pudding is in
the eating. Look at how Theo turned out."

"I have been, Mrs. Fredericks."

"I knew he was headed for a bad end," she said. "He didn't show
natural feelings. He never wrote home once since he left. Where has
he been all these years?"

"Going to college."

"To college? He went to college?"

"Your son's an ambitious boy."

"Oh, he always had an ambition, if that's what you want to call it.
Is that what he learned in college, how to cheat people?"

"He learned that someplace else."

Perhaps in this room, I thought, where Culligan spun his fantasies
and laid a long-shot bet on an accidental resemblance to a dead man.
The room had Culligan's taint on it.

The woman stirred uncomfortably, as if I'd made a subtle accusation:

"I don't claim we were good parents to him. He wanted more than
we could give him. He always had a dream of himself, like."

Her face moved sluggishly, trying to find the shape of truth and feeling. She leaned back on her arms and let her gaze rest on the swollen
slopes of her body, great sagging breasts, distended belly from which a
son had struggled headfirst into the light. Over her bowed head, insects
swung in eccentric orbits around the hanging bulb, tempting hot death.

She managed to find some hope in the situation: "At least he didn't
murder anybody, eh?"

"No."

"Who was it that knifed Culligan? You said it was a young hoodlum."

"His name is Tommy Lemberg. Tommy and his brother Roy are supposed to be hiding out in Ontario—"

"Hamburg, did you say?"

"They may be using that name. Do you know Roy and Tommy?"

"I hope to tell you. They been renting the downstairs room for the
last two weeks. They told me their name was Hamburg. How was I to
know they were hiding out?"

26

I WAITED for the Lembergs on the dark porch. They came home after midnight, walking a bit unsteadily down the street. My parked car attracted their attention, and they crossed the street to look it over. I went down the front steps and across the street after them.

They turned, so close together that they resembled a single amorphous body with two white startled faces. Tommy started toward me, a wide lopsided shape. His arm was still in a white sling under his jacket.

Roy lifted his head with a kind of hopeless alertness. "Come back here, kid."

"The hell. It's old man trouble himself." He walked up to me busily, and spat in the dust at my feet.

"Take it easy, Tommy." Roy came up behind him. "Talk to him."

"Sure I'll talk to him." He said to me: "Didn't you get enough from Mr. Schwartz? You came all this way looking for more?"

Without giving the matter any advance thought, I set myself on my heels and hit him with all my force on the point of the jaw. He went down and stayed. His brother knelt beside him, making small shocked noises which resolved themselves into words:

"You had no right to hit him. He wanted to talk to you."

"I heard him."

"He's been drinking, and he was scared. He was just putting on a big bluff."

"Put away the violin. It doesn't go with a knifing rap."

"Tommy never knifed anybody."

"That's right, he was framed. Culligan framed him by falling down and stabbing himself. Tommy was just an innocent bystander."

"I don't claim he was innocent. Schwartz sent him there to throw his weight around. But nobody figured he was going to run into Culligan, let alone Culligan with a knife and a gun. He got shot taking the gun away from Culligan. Then he knocked Culligan out, and that's the whole thing as far as Tommy's concerned."

"At which point the Apaches came out of the hills."

"I thought maybe you'd be interested in the truth," Roy said in a shaking voice. "But your thinking is the same as all the others. Once a fellow takes a fall, he's got no human rights."

"Sure, I'm unfair to organized crime."

The wisecrack sounded faintly tinny, even to me. Roy made a disgusted sound in his throat. Tommy groaned as if in response. His eyes were still turned up, veined white between half-closed lids. Roy inserted one arm under his brother's head and lifted it.

Peering down at the dim face, unconscious and innocent-looking, I had a pang of doubt. I knew my bitterness wasn't all for Tommy Lemberg. When I hit him I was lashing out at the other boy, too, reacting to a world of treacherous little hustlers that wouldn't let a man believe in it.

I scraped together a nickel's worth of something, faith or gullibility, and invested it:

"Lemberg, do you believe this yarn your brother told you?"

"Yes."

"Are you willing to put it to the test?"

"I don't understand you." But his white face slanted up fearfully. "If you're talking about him going back to California, no. They'd put him in the gas chamber."

"Not if his story is true. He could do a lot to back it up by coming back with me voluntarily."

"He can't. He's been in jail. He has a record."

"That record of his means a lot to you, doesn't it? More than it does to other people, maybe."

"I don't dig you."

"Why don't you dissolve the brother act? Commit yourself where there's some future. Your wife could do with a piece of you. She's in a bad way, Lemberg."

He didn't answer me. He held his brother's head possessively against his shoulder. In the light of the stars they seemed like twins, mirror images of each other. Roy looked at Tommy in a puzzled way, as if he couldn't tell which was the real man and which was the reflection. Or which was the possessor and which was the possessed.

Footfalls thudded in the dust behind me. It was Mrs. Fredericks, wearing a bathrobe and carrying a pan of water.

"Here," was all she said.

She handed me the pan and went back into the house. She wanted no part of the trouble in the street. Her house was well supplied with trouble.

I sprinkled some water on Tommy's face. He snorted and sat up blinking. "Who hit me?" Then he saw me, and remembered: "You sucker-punched me. You sucker-punched a cripple."

He tried to get up. Roy held him down with both hands on his shoulders:

"You had it coming, you know that. I've been talking to Mr. Archer. He'll listen to what you have to say."

"I'm willing to listen to the truth," I said. "Anything else is a waste of time."

With his brother's help, Tommy got onto his feet. "Go ahead," Roy prompted him. "Tell him. And no more kid stuff."

"The whole truth, remember," I said, "including the Schwartz angle."

"Yeah. Yeah." Tommy was still dazed. "Schwartz was the one hired me in the first place. He sent one of his boys to look me up, promised me a hundred bucks to put a little fear into this certain party."

"A little death, you mean?"

He shook his head violently. "Nothing like that, just a little working over."

"What did Schwartz have against Culligan?"

"Culligan wasn't the one. He wasn't supposed to be there, see. He got in the picture by mistake."

"I told you that," Roy said.

"Be quiet. Let Tommy do the talking."

"Yeah, sure," Tommy said. "It was this beast that I was supposed to put on a little show for. I wasn't supposed to hurt her, nothing like that, just put the fear of God in her so she'd cough up what she owed Schwartz. It was like a collection agency, y'unnerstan'? Legit."

"What was her name?"

"Alice Sable. They sent me because I knew what she looked like. Last summer in Reno she used to run around with Pete Culligan. But he wasn't supposed to be there at her house, for God sake. The way they told it to me, she was alone by herself out there all day. When Culligan came marching out, armed up to the teeth, you could of knocked me over with a 'dozer.

"I moved in on him, very fast, very fast reflexes I got, talking all the time. Got hold of the gun but it went off, the slug plowed up my arm, same time he dropped the gun. I picked it up. By that time he had his knife out. What could I do? He was going to gut me. I slammed him on the noggin with the gun and chilled him. Then I beat it."

"Did you see Alice Sable?"

"Yeah, she came surging out and yelled at me. I was starting the Jag, and I couldn't hear what she said over the engine. I didn't stop or turn around. Hell, I didn't want to rough up no beast, anyway."

"Did you pick up Culligan's knife before you left, and cut him with it?"

"No sir. What would I do that for? Man, I was hurt. I wanted out."

"What was Culligan doing when you left?"

"Laying there." He glanced at his brother. "Lying there."

"Who coached you to say that?"

"Nobody did."

"That's true," Roy said. "It's just the way he told it to me. You've got to believe him."

"I'm not the important one. The man he has to convince is Sheriff Trask of Santa Teresa County. And planes are taking off for there all the time."

"Aw, no." Tommy's gaze swiveled frantically from me to Roy. "They'll throw the book at me if I go back."

"Sooner or later you have to go back. You can come along peaceably now, or you can force extradition proceedings and make the trip in handcuffs and leg-chains. Which way do you want it, hard or easy?"

For once in his young life, Tommy Lemberg did something the easy way.

27

I PHONED Sheriff Trask long distance. He agreed to wire me transportation authorization for the Lemberg brothers. I picked it up at Willow Run, and the three of us got aboard an early plane. Trask had an official car waiting to meet the connecting plane when it landed in Santa Teresa.

Before noon we were in the interrogation room in the Santa Teresa courthouse. Roy and Tommy made statements, which were recorded by a court reporter on steno and tape-machine. Tommy seemed to be awed by the big room with its barred windows, the Sheriff's quiet power, the weight of the law which both man and building represented. There were no discrepancies in the part of his statement I heard.

Trask motioned me out before Tommy was finished. I followed him down the corridor to his office. He took off his coat and opened the neck of his shirt. Blotches of sweat spread from his armpits. He filled a paper cup with water from a cooler, drained the cup, and crushed it in his fist.

"If we buy this," he said at last, "it puts us back at the beginning. You buy it, don't you, Archer?"

"I've taken an option on it. Naturally I think it should be investigated. But that can wait. Have you questioned Theo Fredericks about the Culligan killing?"

"No."

"Is Fredericks doing any talking at all?"

"Not to me he isn't."

"But you picked him up last night?"

Trask's face had a raw red look. I thought at first that he was on the verge of a heart attack. Then I realized that he was painfully embarrassed. He turned his back on me, walked over to the wall, and stood looking at a photograph of himself shaking hands with the Governor.

"Somebody tipped him off," he said. "He flew the coop five minutes before I got there." He turned to face me: "The worst part of it is, he took Sheila Howell with him."

"By force?"

"You kidding? She was probably the one who tipped him off. I made the mistake of phoning Dr. Howell before I moved on the little rat. In any case, she went along with him willingly—walked out of her father's house and drove away with him in the middle of the night. Howell's been on my back ever since."

"Howell's very fond of his daughter."

"Yeah, I know how he feels, I have a daughter of my own. I was afraid for a while that he was going to take off after her with a shotgun, and I mean literally. Howell's a trap-shooter, one of the best in the county. But I got him calmed down. He's in the communications room, waiting to hear some word of them."

"They're traveling by car?"

"The one Mrs. Galton bought for him."

"A red Thunderbird should be easy to spot."

"You'd think so. But they've been gone over eight hours without a trace. They may be in Mexico by now. Or they may be cuddled up in an L.A. motel under one of his aliases." Trask scowled at the image. "Why do so many nice young girls go for the dangerous ones?"

The question didn't expect an answer, and that was just as well. I hadn't any.

Trask sat down heavily behind his desk. "Just how dangerous is he? When we talked on the telephone last night, you mentioned a knifing he did before he left Canada."

"He stabbed his father. Apparently he meant to kill him. The old man is no saint, either. In fact, the Fredericks' boardinghouse is a regular thieves' kitchen. Peter Culligan was staying there at the time of the knifing. The boy ran away with him."

Trask took up a pencil and broke it in half, abstractedly, dropping the pieces on his blotter. "How do we know the Fredericks boy didn't murder Culligan? He had a motive: Culligan was in a position to call his bluff and tell the world who he really was. And M.O. figures, with his knifing record."

"We've been thinking the same thing, Sheriff. There's even a strong likelihood that Culligan was his partner in the conspiracy. That would give him a powerful motive to silence Culligan. We've been assuming that Fredericks was in Luna Bay that day. But has his alibi ever been checked?"

"There's no time like the present."

Trask picked up his phone and asked the switchboard to put through a call to the San Mateo County sheriff's office in Redwood City.

"I can think of one other possibility," I said. "Alice Sable was involved with Culligan last year in Reno, and maybe since. Remember how she reacted to his death. We put it down to nervous shock, but it could have been something worse."

"You're not suggesting that she killed him?"

"As a hypothesis."

Trask shook his head impatiently. "Even putting it hypothetically, it's pretty hard to swallow about a lady like her."

"What kind of a lady is she? Do you know her?"

"I've met her, that's about all. But hell, Gordon Sable's one of the top lawyers in the city."

The politician latent in every elected official was rising to the surface and blurring Trask's hard, clear attitudes. I said:

"That doesn't put his wife above suspicion. Have you questioned her?"

"No." Trask became explanatory, as though he felt that he had missed a move: "I haven't been able to get to her. Sable was opposed, and the head-shrinkers backed him up. They say she shouldn't be questioned on painful subjects. She's been borderline psychotic since the killing, and any more pressure might push her over the edge."

"Howell's her personal doctor, isn't he?"

"He is. As a matter of fact, I tried to get to her through Howell. He was dead set against it, and as long as it looked like an open-and-shut case, I didn't press the point."

"Howell should be ready to change his mind. Did you say he's somewhere around the courthouse?"

"Yeah, he's down in Communications. But wait a minute, Archer." Trask rose and came around the desk. "This is a touchy business, and you don't want to hang too much weight on the Lemberg brothers' story. They're not disinterested witnesses."

"They don't know enough to invent the story, either."

"Schwartz and his lawyers do."

"Are we back on the Schwartz kick again?"

"You were the one that got me on it in the first place. You were convinced that the Culligan killing was a gang killing."

"I was wrong."

"Maybe. We'll let the facts decide when they all come out. But if you were wrong, you could be wrong again." Trask punched me in the stomach in a friendly way. "How about that, Archer?"

His telephone chirped, and he lifted the receiver. I couldn't make out the words that came scratchily over the wire, but I saw their effect on Trask. His body stiffened, and his face seemed to grow larger.

"I'll use my Aero Squadron," he said finally, "and I ought to be there in two hours. But don't sit around waiting for me." He slammed down the receiver and reached for the coat draped over the back of his chair.

"They made the red Thunderbird," he said. "Fredericks abandoned it in San Mateo. They were just going to put the word on the teletype when they got my call."

"Where in San Mateo?"

"Parking-lot of the S.P. station. Fredericks and the girl probably took a train into San Francisco."

"Are you flying up?"

"Yeah, I've had a volunteer pilot standing by all morning. Ride along with us if you want. He has a four-passenger Beechcraft."

"Thanks, I've had enough flying to last me for a while. You didn't ask them to check Fredericks's alibi."

"I forgot," Trask said lightly. "I'll take it up with Fredericks personally."

He seemed glad to be leaving Alice Sable in my lap.

28
.

THE communications center of the courthouse was a windowless room on the basement level, full of the chatter and whine of short-wave radio signals. Dr. Howell was sitting with his head down in front of a quiet teletype machine. He raised his head abruptly when I spoke to him. His face was gray in the white overhead light:

"So here you are. While you've been junketing around the country at my expense, she's gone away with him. Do you understand what that means?"

His voice rose out of control. The two deputies monitoring the radios looked at him and then at each other. One of them said: "If you two gentlemen want to talk in private, this is no place to do it."

"Come outside," I said to Howell: "You're not accomplishing anything here. They'll be picked up soon, don't worry."

He sat in inert silence. I wanted to get him away from the teletype machine before the message from San Mateo hit it. It would send him off to the Bay area, and I had a use for him here:

"Doctor, is Alice Sable still under your care?"

He looked up questioningly. "Yes."

"Is she still in the nursing home?"

"Yes. I should try to get out there today." He brushed his forehead with his fingertips. "I've been neglecting my patients, I'm afraid."

"Come out there with me now."

"What on earth for?"

"Mrs. Sable may be able to help us terminate this case, and help us reach your daughter."

He rose, but stood irresolute beside the teletype machine. Sheila's defection had robbed him of his force. I took hold of his elbow and steered him out into the basement corridor. Once moving, he went ahead of me up the iron stairs into the hot white noon.

His Chevrolet was in the county parking-lot. He turned to me as he started the engine:

"How can Mrs. Sable help us to find Sheila?"

"I'm not certain she can. But she was involved with Culligan, the Fredericks boy's probable partner in the conspiracy. She may know more about Theo Fredericks than anyone else does."

"She never said a word about him to me."

"Has she been talking to you about the case?"

He said after some hesitation: "Not being a practicing psychiatrist, I haven't encouraged that line of discussion with her. The matter has come up, however. Unavoidably so, since it's part and parcel of her mental condition."

"Can you be more specific?"

"I prefer not to. You know the ethics of my profession. The doctor-patient relationship is sacrosanct."

"So is human life. Don't forget a man was murdered. We have evidence that Mrs. Sable knew Culligan before he came to Santa Teresa. She was also a witness to his death. Anything she has to say about it may be very significant."

"Not if her memory of the event is delusional."

"Does she have delusions on the subject?"

"She has indeed. Her account doesn't agree with the actual event as we know it. I've gone into this with Trask, and there's no doubt whatever that a thug named Lemberg stabbed the man."

"There's a good deal of doubt," I said. "The Sheriff just took a statement from Lemberg. A Reno gambler sent Lemberg to collect money from Alice Sable, and maybe rough her up a bit. Culligan got in the way. Lemberg knocked him out, was shot in the process, left him unconscious on the ground. He claims that somebody else did the knifing after he left."

Howell's face underwent a curious change. His eyes became harder and brighter. He wasn't looking at me, or at anything external. The lines around his eyes and at the corners of his mouth curved and deepened, as if he was being forced to look against his will at something horrible.

"But Trask said Lemberg was undeniably guilty."

"Trask was wrong. We all were."

"Do you honestly mean to say that Alice Sable has been speaking the truth all along?"

"I don't know what she's been saying, Doctor. You do."

"But Trenchard and the other psychiatrists were convinced that her self-accusations were fantasies. They had me convinced."

"What does she accuse herself of? Does she blame herself for Culligan's death?"

Howell sat over the wheel in silence. He had been shaken, and wide open, for a few minutes. Now his personality closed up again:

"You have no right to cross-examine me about the intimate affairs of one of my patients."

"I'm afraid I have to, Doctor. If Alice Sable murdered Culligan, there's no way you can cover up for her. I'm surprised you want to. You're not only breaking the law, you're violating the ethics you set such store by."

"I'll be the judge of my own ethics," he said in a strained voice.

He sat and wrestled with his unstated problem. His gaze was inward and glaring. Sweat-drops studded his forehead. I got some sense of the empathy he felt for his patient. Even his daughter was forgotten.

"She has confessed the murder to you, Doctor?"

Slowly his eyes remembered me again. "What did you say?"

"Has Mrs. Sable confessed Culligan's murder?"

"I'm going to ask you not to question me further."

Abruptly, he released the emergency brake. I kept quiet all the way to the nursing home, hoping my patience might earn me an interview with Alice Sable herself.

A gray-haired nurse unlocked the front door, and smiled with special intensity at Howell. "Good morning, Doctor. We're a little late this morning."

"I'm having to skip my regular calls today. I do want to see Mrs. Sable."

"I'm sorry, Doctor, she's already gone."

"Gone where, for heaven's sake?"

"Mr. Sable took her home this morning, didn't you know? He said it was all right with you."

"It certainly is not. You don't release disturbed patients without specific orders from a doctor. Haven't you learned that yet, nurse?"

Before she could answer, Howell turned on his heel and started back to his car. I had to run to catch him.

"The man's a fool!" he cried above the roar of the engine. "He can't be permitted to take a chance like this with his wife's safety. She's dangerous to herself and other people."

I said when we were underway: "Was she dangerous to Culligan, Doctor?"

His answer was a sigh which seemed to rise from the center of his body. The outskirts of Santa Teresa gave place to open country. The hills of Arroyo Park rose ahead of us. With his eyes on the green hills, Howell said:

"The poor wretch of a woman told me that she killed him. And I didn't have sense enough to believe her. Somehow her story didn't ring true to me. I was convinced that it was fantasy masking the actual event."

"Is that why you wouldn't let Trask talk to her?"

"Yes. The present state of the law being what it is, a doctor has a duty to protect his patients, especially the semi-psychotic ones. We can't run off to the police with every sick delusion they come up with. But in this case," he added reluctantly, "it seems I was mistaken."

"You're not sure."

"I'm no longer sure about anything."

"Exactly what did she say to you?"

"She heard the sounds of a struggle, two men fighting and calling each other names. A gun went off. She was terrified, of course, but she forced herself to go to the front door. Culligan was lying on the lawn. The other man was just driving away in the Jaguar. When he was out of sight, she went out to Culligan. Her intention was to help him, she said, but she saw his knife in the grass. She picked it up and—used it."

We had reached the foot of Sable's hill. Howell wrestled his car up the climbing curves. The tires shuddered and screeched like lost souls under punishment.

29

SABLE must have heard the car, and been waiting behind the door for Howell's knock. He opened the door at once. His bloodshot eyes began to water in the strong sunlight, and he sneezed.

"Where is your wife?" Howell said.

"In her own room, where she belongs. There was so much noise and confusion in the nursing home—"

"I want to see her."

"I don't think so, Doctor. I understand you've been grilling her about the unfortunate crime that occurred on our premises. It's been most disturbing to Alice. You told me yourself that she shouldn't be forced to talk about it."

"She brought up the subject of her own accord. I demand to be allowed to see her."

"Demand, Doctor? How can you do that? I should make it clear, I suppose, that I'm terminating your services as of now. I intend to hire a new crew of doctors, and find a place where Alice can rest in peace."

The phrase set up whispering echoes which Howell's voice cut through:

"You don't hire doctors, Sable, and you don't fire them."

"Your law is rusty. Perhaps you should hire a lawyer. You're certainly going to need one if you try to force your way into my house." Sable's voice was controlled, but queerly atonal.

"I have a duty to my patient. You had no right to remove her from nursing care."

"From your third-degree methods, you mean? Let me remind you, if you need reminding, that anything Alice has said to you is privileged.

I employed you and the others in my capacity as her lawyer in order to have your assistance in determining certain facts. Is that clear? If you communicate these facts or alleged facts to anyone, official or unofficial, I'll sue you for criminal libel."

"You're talking doubletalk," I said. "You won't be suing anybody."

"Won't I, though? You're in roughly the same position as Dr. Howell. I employed you to make a certain investigation, and ordered you to communicate the results orally to me. Any further communication is a breach of contract. Try it out, and by God I'll have your license."

I didn't know if he was legally right. I didn't care. When he started to swing the door shut, I set my foot against it:

"We're coming in, Sable."

"I think not," his queer new voice said.

He reached behind the door and stepped back with a gun in his hands. It was a long, heavy gun, a deer rifle with a telescopic sight. He raised it deliberately. I looked directly into the muzzle, at the clean, glinting spiral of the rifling.

Sable curled his finger on the trigger, and cuddled the polished stock against his cheek. His face had a fine glaze on it, like porcelain. I realized that he was ready to kill me.

"Put it down," Howell said.

He moved ahead of me into the doorway, taking my place in the line of fire:

"Put it down, Gordon. You're not yourself, you're feeling upset, you're terribly worried about Alice. But we're your friends, we're Alice's friends, too. We want to help you both."

"I have no friends," Sable said. "I know why you're here, why you want to talk to Alice. And I'm not going to let you."

"Don't be silly, Gordon. You can't look after a sick woman by yourself. I know you don't care about your personal safety, but you have to consider Alice's safety. She needs looking after, Gordon. So put it down now, let me in to see her."

"Get back. I'll shoot."

Sable's voice was a high sharp yell. His wife must have heard it. From deep inside the house, she cried out in answer:

"No!"

Sable blinked against the light. He looked like a sleepwalker waking up on the verge of a precipice. Behind him his wife's crying went on, punctuated by resounding blows and then a crash of glass.

Caught between impossible pressures, Sable half-turned toward the noise. The rifle swung sideways with his movement. I went in past Howell and got one hand on the gun-barrel and the other on the knot of Sable's tie. I heaved. Man and rifle came apart.

Sable thudded against the wall and almost fell. He was breathing hard. His hair was in his eyes. He bore a strange resemblance to an old woman peering out through the fringes of a matted white wig.

I opened the breech of the rifle. While I was unloading it, running feet slapped the pavement of the inner court. Alice Sable appeared at the end of the hallway. Her light hair was ruffled, and her nightgown was twisted around her slender body. Blood ran down over her naked foot from a cut in her leg.

"I hurt myself on the window," she said in a small voice. "I cut myself on the glass."

"Did you have to break it?" Sable made an abrupt, threatening movement toward her. Then he remembered us, and sweetened his tone: "Go back to your room, dear. You don't want to run around half-dressed in front of visitors."

"Dr. Howell isn't a visitor. You came to fix it where I hurt myself, didn't you?"

She moved uncertainly toward the doctor. He went to meet her with his hands out. "Of course I did. Come back to your room with me and we'll fix it now."

"But I don't want to go back in there. I hate it in there, it depresses me. Peter used to visit me in there."

"Be quiet!" Sable said.

She moved behind the doctor, making her body small as if to claim a child's irresponsibility. From the protection of Howell's shoulder, she peered sadly at her husband:

"Be quiet is all you say to me. Be quiet, hush it up. But what's the use, Gordon? Everybody knows about me and Peter. Dr. Howell knows. I made a clean breast of it to him." Her hand went to her breast, and fingered the rosebuds embroidered on her nightgown. Her heavy gaze swung to me. "This man knows about me, too, I can see it in his face."

"Did you kill him, Mrs. Sable?"

"Don't answer," Sable said.

"But I want to confess. I'll feel better then, won't I?" Her smile was bright and agonized. It faded, leaving its lines in her face and her teeth bare: "I did kill him. The fellow in the black car knocked him out, and I went out and stabbed him."

Her hand jerked downward from her breast, clenched on an imaginary knife. Her husband watched her like a poker-player.

"Why did you do it?" I said.

"I don't know. I guess I just got sick of him. Now it's time for me to take my punishment. I killed, and I deserve to die."

The tragic words had an unreal quality. She spoke them like a life-size puppet activated by strings and used by a voice that didn't belong to her. Only her eyes were her own, and they contained a persistent stunned innocence.

"I deserve to die," she repeated. "Don't I, Gordon?"

He flushed up darkly. "Leave me out of this."

"But you said—"

"I said nothing of the sort."

"You're lying, Gordon," she chided him. Perhaps there was an undertone of malice in her voice. "You told me after all my crimes that I deserved to die. And you were right. I lost your good money gambling and went with another man and now on top of it all I'm a murderer."

Sable appealed to Howell: "Can't we put an end to this? My wife is ill and hurt. It's inconceivable that you should let her be questioned. This man isn't even a policeman—"

"I'll take the responsibility for what I do," I said. "Mrs. Sable, do you remember stabbing Peter Culligan?"

She raised one hand to her forehead, pushing back her hair as if it got in the way of her thoughts. "I don't remember exactly, but I must have."

"Why do you say you must have, if you don't remember?"

"Gordon saw me."

I looked at Sable. He wouldn't look at me. He stood against the wall, trying to merge with the wall.

"Gordon wasn't here," I said. "He was at Mrs. Galton's house when you telephoned."

"But he came. He came right over. Peter was lying there on the grass for a long time. He was making a funny noise, it sounded like snoring. I unbuttoned the top of his shirt to help him breathe."

"You remember all this, but you don't remember stabbing him?"

"I must have blanked out on that part. I'm always blanking out on things, ask Gordon."

"I'm asking you, Mrs. Sable."

"Let me think. I remember, I slid my hand down under his shirt, to see if his heart was beating properly. I could feel it there thumping and jumping. You'd think it was a little animal trying to get out. The hair on his chest was scratchy, like wire."

Sable made a noise in his throat.

"What did you do then?" I said.

"I—nothing. I just sat for a while and looked at him and his poor old beatup face. I put my arms around him and tried to coax him awake. But he went on snoring at me. He was still snoring when Gordon got there. Gordon was angry, catching me with him like that. I ran into the house. But I watched from the window."

Suddenly her face was incandescent. "I didn't kill him. It wasn't me out there. It was Gordon, and I watched him from the window. He picked up Peter's knife and pushed it into his stomach." Her clenched hand repeated its downward gesture, striking her own soft abdomen. "The blood spurted out and ran red on the grass. It was all red and green."

Sable thrust his head forward. The rest of his body, even his arms and hands, remained stuck to the wall:

"You can't believe her. She's hallucinating again."

His wife seemed not to hear him. Perhaps she was tuned to a higher frequency, singing like salvation in her head. Tears streamed from her eyes:

"I didn't kill him."

"Hush now." Howell quieted her face against his shoulder.

"This is the truth, isn't it?" I said.

"It must be. I'm certain of it. Those self-accusations of hers were fantasy after all. This account is much more circumstantial. I'd say she's taken a long step toward reality."

"She's crazier than she ever was," Sable said. "If you think you can use this against me, you're crazier than she is. Don't forget I'm a lawyer—"

"Is that what you are—a lawyer?" Howell turned his back on Sable and spoke to his wife: "Come on, Alice, we'll put a bandage on that cut and you can get some clothes on. Then we'll take a little ride, back to the nice place with the other ladies."

"It isn't a nice place," she said.

Howell smiled down at her. "That's the spirit. Keep saying what you really think and know, and we'll get you out of there to stay. But not for a while yet, eh?"

"Not for a while yet."

Holding her with one arm, Howell stretched out his other hand to Sable. "The key to your wife's room. You won't be needing it."

Sable produced a flat brass key which Howell accepted from him without a word. The doctor walked Alice Sable down the hallway toward the court.

30

.

GORDON SABLE watched them go with something approaching relief. The bright expectancy had left his eyes. He had had it.

"I wouldn't have done it," he said, "if I'd known what I know now. There are factors you don't foresee—the factor of human change, for example. You think you can handle anything, that you can go on forever. But your strength wears away under pressure. A few days, or a few weeks, and everything looks different. Nothing seems worth struggling for. It all goes blah." He made a loose bumbling sound with his lips: "All gone to bloody blah. So here we are."

"Why did you kill him?"

"You heard her. When I got back here she was crying and moaning over him, trying to wake him up with kisses. It made me sick to death."

"Don't tell me it was a sudden crime of passion. You must have known about them long before."

"I don't deny that." Sable shifted his stance, as if to prepare himself for a shift in his story. "Culligan picked her up in Reno last summer. She went there to divorce me, but she ended up on a gambling spree with Culligan egging her on. No doubt he collected commissions on the money she lost. She lost a great deal, all the ready money I could raise. When it was gone, and her credit was exhausted, he let her share his apartment for a while. I had to go there and beg her to come home with me. She didn't want to come. I had to pay him to send her away."

I didn't doubt the truth of what he was saying. No man would invent such a story against himself. It was Sable who didn't seem to believe his own words. They fell weightlessly from his mouth, like a memorized report of an accident he didn't understand, which had happened to people in a foreign country:

"I never felt quite the same about myself after that. Neither of us did. We lived in this house I'd built for her as if there were always a glass partition between us. We could see each other, but we couldn't really speak. We had to act out our feelings like clowns, or apes in separate cages. Alice's gestures became queerer, and no doubt mine did, too. The things we acted out got uglier. She would throw herself on the floor and strike herself with her fist until her face was bruised and swollen. And I would laugh at her and call her names.

"We did such things to each other," he said. "I think we were both glad, in a strange way, when Culligan turned up here in the course of the winter. Anthony Galton's bones had been unearthed, and Culligan had read about it in the papers. He knew who they belonged to, and came to me with the information."

"How did he happen to pick you?"

"It's a good question. I've often asked myself that good question. Alice had told him that I was Mrs. Galton's lawyer, of course. It may have been the source of his interest in her. He knew that her gambling losses had put me in financial straits. He needed expert help with the plan he had; he wasn't clever enough to execute it alone. He was just clever enough to realize that I was infinitely cleverer."

And he knew other things about you, I thought. You were a loveless man who could be bent and finally twisted.

"How did Schwartz get in on the deal?"

"Otto Schwartz? He wasn't in on it." Sable seemed offended by the notion. "His only connection with it was the fact that Alice owed him sixty thousand dollars. Schwartz had been pressing for payment, and it finally reached the point where he was threatening both of us with a beating. I had to raise money somehow. I was desperate. I didn't know which way to turn."

"Leave out the drama, Sable. You didn't go into this conspiracy on the spur of the moment. You've been working on it for months."

"I'm not denying that. There was a lot of work to be done. Culligan's idea didn't look too promising at first. He'd been carrying it around ever since he ran into the Fredericks boy in Canada five or six years ago. He'd known Anthony Galton in Luna Bay, and was struck by the boy's resemblance to him. He even brought Fredericks into the States in the hope of cashing in on the resemblance in some way. But he ran into trouble with the law, and lost track of the boy. He believed that if I'd stake him, he could find him again.

"Culligan did find him, as you know, going to school in Ann Arbor. I went east myself in February, and saw him in one of the student plays. He was a fairly good actor, with a nice air of sincerity about him. I decided when I talked to him that he could carry the thing off if anyone could. I introduced myself as a Hollywood producer interested in his talent. Once he was hooked on that, and had taken money from me, he wasn't too hard to talk around to the other.

"I prepared his story for him, of course. It required considerable thought. The most difficult problem was how to lead investigation of his actual Canadian background into a blind alley. The Crystal Springs orphanage was my inspiration. But I realized that the success of the imposture depended primarily on him. If he did succeed in bringing it off, he would be entitled to the lion's share. I was modest in my own demands. He simply gave me an option to buy, at a nominal price, a certain amount of producing oil property."

I watched him, trying to understand how a man with so much foresight could have ended where Sable was. Something had cut off the use of his mind from constructive purposes. Perhaps it was the shallow pride which he seemed to take in his schemes, even at this late date.

"They talk about the crime of the century," he said. "This would have been the greatest of all—a multi-million-dollar enterprise with no actual harm done to anyone. The boy was simply to let himself be discovered, and let the facts speak for themselves."

"The facts?" I said sharply.

"The apparent facts, if you like. I'm not a philosopher. We lawyers don't deal in ultimate realities. Who knows what they are? We deal in appearances. There was very little manipulation of the facts in this case, no actual falsification of documents. True, the boy had to tell one or two little lies about his childhood and his parents. What did a few little lies matter? They made Mrs. Galton just as happy as if he was her real grandson. And if she chose to leave him her money, that was her affair."

"Has she made a new will?"

"I believe so. I had no part in it. I advised her to get another lawyer."

"Wasn't that taking a chance?"

"Not if you know Maria Galton as I know her. Her reactions are so consistently contrary that you can depend on them. I got her to make a new will by urging her not to. I got her interested in looking for Tony by telling her it was hopeless. I persuaded her to hire you by opposing the whole idea of a detective."

"Why me?"

"Schwartz was prodding me, and I had to get the ball rolling. I couldn't take the chance of finding the boy for myself. I had to have someone to do it for me, someone I could trust. I thought, too, if we could get past you, we could get past anyone. And if we failed to get past you, I thought you'd be—more flexible, shall we say?"

"Crooked, shall we say?"

Sable winced at the word. Words meant more to him than the facts they stood for.

A door opened at the end of the corridor, and Alice Sable and Dr. Howell came toward us. She hung on the doctor's arm, dressed and freshly groomed and empty-faced under her makeup. He was carrying a white leather suitcase in his free hand.

"Sable has made a full confession," I said to Howell. "Phone the Sheriff's office, will you?"

"I already have. They ought to be here shortly. I'm taking Mrs. Sable back where she'll be properly attended to." He added in an undertone: "I hope this will be a turning-point for her."

"I hope so, too," Sable said. "Honestly I do."

Howell made no response. Sable tried again:

"Good-by, Alice. I really do wish you well, you know."

Her neck stiffened, but she didn't look at him. She went out leaning on Howell. Her brushed hair shone like gold in the sunlight. Fool's gold. I felt a twinge of sympathy for Sable. He hadn't been able to carry her weight. In the stretching gap between his weakness and her need, Culligan had driven a wedge, and the whole structure had fallen.

Sable was a subtle man, and he must have noticed some change in my expression:

"You surprise me, Lew. I didn't expect you to bear down so hard. You have a reputation for tempering the wind to the shorn lamb."

"Stabbing Culligan to death wasn't exactly a lamblike gesture."

"I had to kill him. You don't seem to understand."

"On account of your wife?"

"My wife was only the beginning. He kept moving in on me. He wasn't content to share my wife and my house. He was very hungry, always wanting more. I finally saw that he wanted it all to himself. Everything." His voice trembled with indignation. "After all my contributions, all my risks, he was planning to shut me out."

"How could he?"

"Through the boy. He had something on Theo Fredericks. I never learned what it was, I couldn't get it out of either of them. But Culligan said that it was enough to ruin my whole plan. It was his plan, too, of course, but he was irresponsible enough to wreck it unless he got his way."

"So you killed him."

"The chance offered itself, and I took it. It wasn't premeditated."

"No jury will believe that, after what you did to your wife. It looks as premeditated as hell. You waited for your chance to knock off a defenseless man, and then tried to push the guilt onto a sick woman."

"She asked for it," he said coldly. "She wanted to believe that she killed him. She was half-convinced before I talked to her, she felt so guilty about her affair with him. I only did what any man would do under the circumstances. She'd seen me stab him. I had to do something to purge her mind of the memory."

"Is that what you've been doing on your long visits, pounding guilt into her mind?"

He struck the wall with the flat of his hand. "She was the cause of the trouble. She brought him into our life. She deserved to suffer for it. Why should I do all the suffering?"

"You don't have to. Spread it around a little. Tell me how to get to the Fredericks boy."

He glanced at me from the corners of his eyes. "I'd want a quid pro quo." The legal phrase seemed to encourage him. He went on in quickening tempo until he was almost chattering: "As a matter of fact, he should take the blame for most of this frightful mess. If it will help to clear up the matter, I'm willing to turn state's evidence. Alice can't be made to testify against me. You don't even know that what she said was true. How do you know her story is true? I may be simply covering up for her." His voice was rising like a manic hope.

"How do you know you're alive, Sable? I want your partner. He was in San Mateo this morning. Where is he headed for?"

"I haven't the faintest idea."

"When did you see him last?"

"I don't know why I should co-operate with you if you won't co-operate with me."

I still had his empty rifle in my hands. I reversed it and raised it like a club. I was angry enough to use it if I had to.

"This is why."

He pulled his head back so sharply it rapped the wall. "You can't use third-degree methods on me. It isn't legal."

"Stop blowing bubbles, Sable. Was Fredericks here last night?"

"Yes. He wanted me to cash a check for him. I gave him all the cash I had in the house. It amounted to over two hundred dollars."

"What did he want it for?"

"He didn't tell me. Actually, he wasn't making too much sense. He talked as if the strain had been too much for him."

"What did he say?"

"I can't reproduce it verbatim. I was upset myself. He asked me a lot of questions, which I wasn't able to answer, about Anthony Galton and what happened to him. The imposture must have gone to his head; he seemed to have himself convinced that he actually was Galton's son."

"Was Sheila Howell with him?"

"Yes, she was present, and I see what you mean. He may have been talking for her benefit. If it was an act, she was certainly taken in by it. But as I said, he seemed to be taken in by it himself. He became very excited, and threatened me with force unless I told him who murdered Galton. I didn't know what to tell him. I finally thought of the name of that woman in Redwood City—the Galtons' former nurse."

"Mrs. Matheson?"

"Yes. I had to tell him something, get rid of him somehow."

A patrol car whined up the hill and stopped in front of the house. Conger and another deputy climbed out. Sable was going to have a hard time getting rid of them.

31
·

THEY dropped me at the airport, and I got aboard a plane. It was the same two-engine bucket, on the same flight, that had taken me north three weeks ago. Even the stewardess was the same. Somehow she looked younger and more innocent. Time had stood still for her while it had been rushing me along into premature middle age.

She comforted me with Chiclets and coffee in paper cups. And there was the blessed Bay again, and the salt flats.

The Matheson house was closed up tight, with the drapes pulled over the windows, as if there was sickness inside. I asked my cab-driver to wait and knocked on the front door. Marian Matheson answered it herself.

She had been living on my time-schedule, and growing old rapidly. There was more gray in her hair, more bone in her face. But the process of change had softened her. Even her voice was gentler:

"I've been sort of expecting you. I had another visitor this morning."

"John Galton?"

"Yes. John Galton—the little boy I looked after in Luna Bay. It was quite an experience meeting him after all these years. And his girl, too. He brought his girl along." She hesitated, then opened the door wider. "Come in if you want."

She took me into the darkened living-room and placed me in a chair.

"What did they come to you for, Mrs. Matheson?"

"The same thing you did. Information."

"What about?"

"That night. I thought he had a right to know the truth, so I told him all I told you, about Culligan and Shoulders." Her answer was vague; perhaps she was trying to keep the memory vague in her mind.

"What was his reaction?"

"He was very interested. Naturally. He really pricked up his ears when I told him about the rubies."

"Did he explain his interest in the rubies?"

"He didn't explain anything. He got up and left in a hurry, and they rocketed off in that little red car of his. They didn't even wait to drink the coffee I was brewing."

"Were they friendly?"

"To me, you mean? Very friendly. The girl was lovely to me. She confided they were going to get married as soon as her young man worked his way out of the darkness."

"What did she mean by the darkness?"

"I don't know, that was just the phrase she used." But she squinted at the sunlight filtering through the drapes, like someone who understood what darkness meant. "He seemed to be very concerned about his father's death."

"Did he say what he was going to do next, or where he was going?"

"No. He did ask me how to get to the airport—if there were buses running. It seemed kind of funny, him asking about buses when he had a brand-new sports car standing out front."

"He's evading arrest, Mrs. Matheson. He knew his car would be spotted right away if he parked it at the airport."

"Who wants to arrest him?"

"I do, for one. He isn't Galton's son, or Brown's son. He's an impostor."

"How can that be? Why, he's the spitting image of his father."

"Appearances can be deceiving, and you're not the first one to be taken in by his appearance. His real name is Theo Fredericks. He's a small-time crook from Canada with a record of violence."

Her hand went to her mouth. "From Canada, did you say?"

"Yes. His parents run a boardinghouse in Pitt, Ontario."

"But that's where they're going, Ontario. I heard him say to her, when I was out in the kitchen, that there were no direct flights to Ontario. That was just before they took off from here."

"What time were they here?"

"It was early in the morning, just past eight. They were waiting out front when I got back from driving Ron to the station."

I looked at my watch. It was nearly five. They had had almost nine hours. With the right connections, they could be in Canada by now.

And with the right connections, I could be there in another eight or nine hours.

Mrs. Matheson followed me to the door. "Is this trouble going to go on forever?"

"We're coming to the end of it," I said. "I'm sorry I couldn't keep you out of it after all."

"It's all right. I've talked it out with Ron. Whatever comes up—if I have to testify in court or anything—we can handle it together. My husband is a very good man."

"He has a good wife."

"No." She shook the compliment off her fingers. "But I love him and the boy, and that's something. I'm glad it all came out between me and Ron. It's been a big load off my heart." She smiled gravely. "I hope it works out some way for that young girl. It's hard to believe that her boy is a criminal. But I know how these things can be in life."

She looked up at the sun.

On the way to International Airport my taxi passed the Redwood City courthouse. I thought of stopping and getting in touch with Trask. Then I decided not to. It was my case, and I wanted to end it.

Perhaps I had a glimmering of the truth.

32

I DROVE my rented car into Pitt at three o'clock, the darkest hour of the night. But there were lights in the red house on the riverbank. Mrs. Fredericks came to the door fully dressed in rusty black. Her heavy face set stubbornly when she saw me.

"You got no call coming here again. What do you think you're after? I didn't know those Hamburg fellows were wanted by the police."

"They're not the only ones. Has your son been here?"

"Theo?" Her eyes and mouth sought obtusely for an answer. "He hasn't come near me for years."

A husky whisper rose from the shadows behind her. "Don't believe her, mister." Her husband came forward, supporting himself with one hand against the wall. He looked and sounded very drunk: "She'd lie her false heart out for him."

"Hold your tongue, old man."

Dark anger filled her eyes like a seepage of ink: I'd seen the same thing happen to her son. She turned on Fredericks, and he backed away. His face looked porous and moist like a deliquescent substance. His clothes were covered with dust.

"Have you seen him, Mr. Fredericks?"

"No. Lucky for him I was out, or I'd of shown him what's what." His hatchet profile chopped the air. "She saw him, though."

"Where is he, Mrs. Fredericks?"

Her husband answered for her: "She told me they went to check in at the hotel, him and the girl both."

Some obscure feeling, guilt or resentment, made the woman say: "They didn't have to go to the hotel. I offered them the use of my house. I guess it isn't good enough for mucky-mucks like her."

"Is the girl all right?"

"I guess so. Theo's the one that's got me worried. What did he want to come here for, after all these years? I can't figure him out."

"He always did have crazy ideas," Fredericks said. "But he's crazy like a fox, see. Watch him close when you go to nab him. He talks smooth, but he's a real snake-in-the-grass."

"Where is this hotel?"

"Downtown. The Pitt Hotel—you can't miss it. Just keep us out of it, eh? He'll try to drag us into his trouble, but I'm a respectable man—"

His wife cried: "Shut up, you. I want to see him again if you don't."

I left them locked in the combat which seemed the normal condition of their nights.

The hotel was a three-story red brick building with one lighted window on the second floor corner. One other light was burning in the lobby. I punched the hand-bell on the desk. A middle-aged little man in a green eyeshade came yawning out of a dark room behind it.

"You're up early," he said.

"I'm up late. Can you rent me a room?"

"Sure can. I got more vacancies than you can shake a stick at. With or without bath?"

"With."

"That will be three dollars." He opened the heavy leather-cornered register, and pushed it across the desk. "Sign on the line."

I signed. The registration above my signature was: Mr. and Mrs. John Galton, Detroit, Michigan.

"I see you have some other Americans staying here."

"Yeah. Nice young couple, checked in late last night. I believe they're honeymooners, probably on their way to Niagara Falls. Anyway, I put them in the bridal chamber."

"Corner room on the second floor?"

He gave me a sharp dry look. "You wouldn't want to disturb them, mister."

"No, I thought I'd say hello to them in the morning."

"Better make it late in the morning." He took a key from a hook and dropped it on the desk. "I'm putting you in two-ten, at the other end. I'll show you up if you want."

"Thanks, I can find it by myself."

I climbed the stairs that rose from the rear of the lobby. My legs were heavy. In the room, I took my .32 automatic out of my overnight bag and inserted one of the clips I had brought for it. The carpet in the dim corridor was threadbare, but it was thick enough to silence my footsteps.

There was still light in the corner room, spilling over through the open transom. A sleeper's heavy breathing came over, too, a long sighing choked off and then repeated. I tried the door. It was locked.

Sheila Howell spoke clearly from the darkness: "Who is that?"

I waited. She spoke again:

"John. Wake up."

"What is it?" His voice sounded nearer than hers.

"Somebody's trying to get in."

I heard the creak of bed springs, the pad of his feet. The brass doorknob rotated.

He jerked the door open, stepped out with his right fist cocked, saw me and started to swing, saw the gun and froze. He was naked to the waist. His muscles stood out under his pale skin.

"Easy, boy. Raise your hands."

"This nonsense isn't necessary. Put the gun down."

"I'm giving the orders. Clasp your hands and turn around, walk slowly into the room."

He moved reluctantly, like stone forced into motion. When he turned, I saw the white scars down his back, hundreds of them, like fading cuneiform cuts.

Sheila was standing beside the rumpled bed. She had on a man's shirt which was too big for her. The shirt and the lipstick smudged on her mouth gave her a dissolute air.

"When did you two have time to get married?"

"We didn't. Not yet." A blush mounted like fire from her neck to her cheekbones. "This isn't what you think. John shared my room because I asked him to. I was frightened. And he slept across the foot of the bed, so there."

He made a quelling gesture with his raised hands. "Don't tell him anything. He's on your father's side. Anything we say he'll twist against us."

"I'm not the twister, Theo."

He turned on me, so suddenly I almost shot him. "Don't call me by that name."

"It belongs to you, doesn't it?"

"My name is John Galton."

"Come off it. Your partner, Sable, made a full confession to me yesterday afternoon."

"Sable is not my partner. He never was."

"Sable tells a different story, and he tells it very well. Don't get the idea that he's covering up for you. He'll be turning state's witness on the conspiracy charge to help him with the murder charge."

"Are you trying to tell me that Sable murdered Culligan?"

"It's hardly news to you, is it? You sat on the information while we were wasting weeks on a bum lead."

The girl stepped between us. "Please. You don't understand the situation. John had his suspicions of Mr. Sable, it's true, but he wasn't in any position to go to the police with them. He was under suspicion himself. Won't you put that awful gun away, Mr. Archer? Give John a chance to explain?"

Her blind faith in him made me angry. "His name isn't John. He's Theo Fredericks, a local boy who left Pitt some years ago after knifing his father."

"The Fredericks person is not his father."

"I have his mother's word for it."

"She's lying," the boy said.

"Everybody's lying but you, eh? Sable says you're a phony, and he ought to know."

"I let him think it. The fact is, when Sable first approached me I didn't know who I was. I went into the deal he offered me partly in the hope of finding out."

"Money had nothing to do with it?"

"There's more than money to a man's inheritance. Above everything else, I wanted to be sure of my identity."

"And now you are?"

"Now I am. I'm Anthony Galton's son."

"When did this fortunate revelation strike you?"

"You don't want a serious answer, but I'll give you one anyway. It grew on me gradually. I think it began when Gabe Lindsay saw something in me I didn't know was there. And then Dr. Dineen recognized me as my father's son. When my grandmother accepted me, too, I thought it must be true. I didn't know it was true until these last few days."

"What happened in the last few days?"

"Sheila believed me. I told her everything, my whole life, and she believed me."

He glanced at her, almost shyly. She reached for his hand. I began to feel like an intruder in their room. Perhaps he sensed this shift in the moral balance, because he began to talk about himself in a deeper, quieter tone:

"Actually, it goes back much further. I suspected the truth about myself, or part of it, when I was a little kid. Nelson Fredericks never treated me as if I belonged to him. He used to beat me with a belt-buckle. He never gave me a kind word. I knew he couldn't possibly be my father."

"A lot of boys feel like that about their real fathers."

Sheila moved closer to him, in a tender protective movement, pressing his hand unconsciously to her breast. "Please let him tell his story. I know it sounds wild, but it's only as wild as life. John's telling you the honest truth, so far as he knows it."

"Assuming that he is, how far does he know it? Some very earnest people have fantastic ideas about who they are and what they've got coming to them."

I expected him to flare up again. He surprised me by saying: "I know, it's what I was scared of, that I was hipped on the subject. I really used to be hipped when I was a boy. I imagined I was the prince in the poorhouse, and so on. My mother encouraged me. She used to dress me up in velvet suits and tell me I was different from the other kids.

"Even before that, though, long before, she had a story that she used to tell me. She was a young woman then. I remember her face was thin, and her hair hadn't turned gray. I was only a toddler, and I used to think it was a fairytale. I realize now it was a story about myself. She wanted me to know about myself, but she was afraid to come right out with it.

"She said that I was a king's son, and we used to live in a palace in the sun. But the young king died and the bogeyman stole us away to the caves of ice where nothing was nice. She made a sort of rhyme of it. And she showed me a gold ring with a little red stone set in it that the king had left her for a remembrance."

He gave me a curious questioning look. Our eyes met solidly for the first time. I think the reality formed between us then.

"A ruby?" I said.

"It must have been. I talked to a woman named Matheson yesterday in Redwood City. You know her, don't you, and you've heard her story? It made sense of some of the things that had puzzled me, and it confirmed what Culligan told me long before. He said that my stepfather was an ex-convict whose real name was Fred Nelson. He had taken my mother out of a place called the Red Horse Inn and made her his— lover. She married my father after Nelson was sent to prison. But he escaped, and found them, and murdered my father." His voice had sunk almost out of hearing.

"When did Culligan tell you this?"

"The day I ran away with him. He'd just had a fight with Fredericks about his board bill. I listened to it from the cellar stairs. They were always fighting. Fredericks was older than Culligan, but he gave him an awful lacing, worse than usual, and left him unconscious on the kitchen floor. I poured water on Culligan's face and brought him to. It was then he told me that Fredericks killed my father. I got a butcher knife out of the drawer, and hid it upstairs in my room. When Fredericks tried to lock me in, I stabbed him in the guts.

"I thought I'd killed him. By the time I saw a newspaper and found out that I hadn't, I was across the border. I rode through the Detroit tunnel under the burlaps in an empty truck-trailer. The border police didn't find me, but they caught Culligan. I didn't see him again until last winter. Then he claimed that he'd been lying to me. He said that

Fredericks had nothing to do with my father's death, that he'd simply blamed Fredericks to get back at him, through me.

"You can see why I decided to play along with Culligan and his scheme. I didn't know which of his stories was true, or if the truth was something else again. I even suspected that Culligan had killed my father himself. How else would he know about the murder?"

"He was involved in it," I said. "It's why he changed his story when he wanted to use you again. It's also the reason he couldn't admit to other people, even Sable, that he knew who you were."

"How was he involved?"

How wasn't he? I thought. His life ran through the case like a dirty piece of cord. He had marked Anthony Galton for the ax and Anthony Galton's murderer for the knife. He had helped a half-sane woman to lose her money, then sold her husband a half-sane dream of wealth. Which brought him to the ironic day when his half-realities came together in a final reality, and Gordon Sable killed him to preserve a lie.

"I don't understand," John said. "What did Culligan have to do with my father's death?"

"Apparently he was the finger man. Have you talked to your mother about the circumstances of the killing? She was probably a witness."

"She was more than that." The words almost strangled him.

Sheila turned to him anxiously. "John?" she said. "Johnny?"

He made no response to her. His gaze was dark and inward:

"Even last night she was lying to me, trying to pretend that I was Fredericks's son, that I never had another father. She's stolen half my life away already. Isn't she satisfied?"

"You haven't seen Fredericks?"

"Fredericks has gone away, she wouldn't tell me where. But I'll find him."

"He can't be far. He was at home an hour ago."

"Damn you! Why didn't you say so?"

"I just did. I'm wondering now if I made a mistake."

John got the message. He didn't speak again until we were a few blocks from his mother's house. Then he turned in the seat and said across Sheila:

"Don't worry about me. There's been enough death and violence. I don't want any more of it."

Along the riverside street the rooftops thrust their dark angles up against a whitening sky. I watched the boy as he got out of the car. His face was pinched and pale as a revenant's. Sheila held his arm, slowing his abrupt movements.

I knocked on the front door. After a long minute, the door was unlocked from the inside. Mrs. Fredericks peered out at us.

"Yes? What now?"

John brushed past me, and faced her on the threshold:

"Where is he?"

"He went away."

"You're a liar. You've lied to me all your life." His voice broke, and then resumed on a different, higher note. "You knew he killed my father, you probably helped him. I know you helped him to hush it up. You left the country with him, changed your name when he did."

"I'm not denying that much," she said levelly.

His whole body heaved as if in nausea. He called her an ugly name. In spite of his promise to me, he was on the thin edge of violence. I laid one hand on his shoulder, heavily:

"Don't be too hard on your mother. Even the law admits mitigation, when a woman is dominated or threatened by a man."

"But that isn't the case. She's still trying to protect him."

"Am I?" the woman said. "Protect him from what?"

"From punishment for murder."

She shook her head solemnly. "It's too late for that, son. Fredericks has took his punishment. He said he would rather have digger get him than go back behind walls. Fredericks hung himself, and I didn't try to argue him out of doing it."

We found him in a back room on the second floor. He was on an old brass bed, in a half-sitting position. A piece of heavy electrical cord was tied to the head of the bed and wrapped several times around his neck. The free end of the cord was clenched in his right hand. There was no doubt that he had been his own executioner.

"Get Sheila out of here," I said to John.

She stood close to him. "I'm all right. I'm not afraid."

Mrs. Fredericks came into the doorway, heavy and panting. She looked at her son with her head up:

"This is the end of it. I told him it was him or you, and which it was going to be. I couldn't go on lying for him, and let you get arrested instead of him."

He faced her, still the accuser. "Why did you lie for so long? You stayed with him after he killed my father."

"You got no call to judge me for doing that. It was to save your life that I married him. I saw him cut off your daddy's head with an ax, fill it with stones, and chunk it in the sea. He said that if I ever told a living soul, that he would kill you, too. You were just a tiny baby, but that wouldn't of stopped him. He held up the bloody ax over your crib and made me swear to marry him and keep my lips shut forever. Which I have done until now."

"Did you have to spend the rest of your life with him?"

"That was my choice," she said. "For sixteen years I stood between you and him. Then you ran away and left me alone with him. I had nobody else left in my life excepting him. Do you understand what it's like to have nobody at all, son?"

He tried to speak, to rise to the word, but the gorgon past held him frozen.

"All I ever wanted in my life," she said, "was a husband and a family and a place I could call my own."

Sheila made an impulsive movement toward her. "You have us."

"Aw, no. You don't want me in your life. We might as well be honest about it. The less you see of me, the better you'll like it. Too much water flowed under the bridge. I don't blame my son for hating me."

"I don't hate you," John said. "I'm sorry for you, Mother. And I'm sorry for what I said."

"You and who else is sorry?" she said roughly. "You and who else?"

He put his arm around her, awkwardly, trying to comfort her. But she was past comforting, perhaps beyond sorrow, too. Whatever she felt was masked by unfeeling layers of flesh. The stiff black silk she was wearing curved over her breast like armor.

"Don't bother about me. Just take good care of your girl."

Somewhere outside, a single bird raised its voice for a few notes, then fell into abashed silence. I went to the window. The river was white. The trees and buildings on its banks were resuming their colors and shapes. A light went on in one of the other houses. As if at this human signal, the bird raised its voice again.

Sheila said: "Listen."

John turned his head to listen. Even the dead man seemed to be listening.

THE
CHILL

␣␣␣␣␣

1
..

THE heavy red-figured drapes over the courtroom windows were incompletely closed against the sun. Yellow daylight leaked in and dimmed the electric bulbs in the high ceiling. It picked out random details in the room: the glass water cooler standing against the panel wall opposite the jury box, the court reporter's carmine-tipped fingers playing over her stenotype machine, Mrs. Perrine's experienced eyes watching me across the defense table.

It was nearly noon on the second and last day of her trial. I was the final witness for the defense. Her attorney had finished questioning me. The deputy D.A. waived cross-examination, and several of the jurors looked at him with puzzled frowns. The judge said I could go.

From my place on the witness stand I'd noticed the young man sitting in the front row of spectators. He wasn't one of the regular trial-watchers, housewives and pensioners filling an empty morning with other people's troubles. This one had troubles of his own. His brooding blue gaze stayed on my face, and I had the uncomfortable feeling that he might be willing to share his troubles with me.

He rose from his seat as I stepped down and intercepted me at the door. "Mr. Archer, may I talk to you?"

"All right."

The bailiff opened the door and gestured urgently. "Outside, gentlemen. Court is still in session."

We moved out into the corridor. The young man scowled at the automatically closing door. "I don't like being pushed around."

"I'd hardly describe that as being pushed around. What's eating you, friend?"

I shouldn't have asked him. I should have walked briskly out to my car and driven back to Los Angeles. But he had that clean, crewcut All-American look, and that blur of pain in his eyes.

"I just got thrown out of the Sheriff's office. It came on top of a couple of other brushoffs from the local authorities, and I'm not used to that kind of treatment."

"They don't mean it personally."

"You've had a lot of detective experience, haven't you? I gathered that from what you said on the witness stand. Incidentally, you did a wonderful job for Mrs. Perrine. I'm sure the jury will acquit her."

"We'll see. Never bet on a jury." I distrusted his compliment, which probably meant he wanted something more substantial from me. The trial in which I had just testified marked the end of a long uninteresting case, and I was planning a fishing trip to La Paz. "Is that all you wanted to say to me?"

"I have a lot to say, if you'll only listen. I mean, I've got this problem about my wife. She left me."

"I don't ordinarily do divorce work, if that's what you have in mind."

"Divorce?" Without making a sound, he went through the motions of laughing hollowly, once. "I was only married one day—less than one day. Everybody including my father keeps telling me I should get an annulment. But I don't want an annulment or a divorce. I want her back."

"Where is your wife now?"

"I don't know." He lit a cigarette with unsteady hands. "Dolly left in the middle of our honeymoon weekend, the day after we were married. She may have met with foul play."

"Or she may have decided she didn't want to be married, or not to you. It happens all the time."

"That's what the police keep saying: it happens all the time. As if that's any comfort! Anyway, I know that wasn't the case. Dolly loved me, and I loved—I love her."

He said this very intensely, with the entire force of his nature behind the words. I didn't know his nature but there was sensitivity and feeling there, more feeling than he could handle easily.

"You haven't told me your name."

"I'm sorry. My name is Kincaid. Alex Kincaid."

"What do you do for a living?"

"I haven't been doing much lately, since Dolly—since this thing happened. Theoretically I work for the Channel Oil Corporation. My father is in charge of their Long Beach office. You may have heard of him. Frederick Kincaid?"

I hadn't. The bailiff opened the door of the courtroom, and held it open. Court had adjourned for lunch, and the jurors filed out past him. Their movements were solemn, part of the ritual of the trial. Alex Kincaid watched them as if they were going out to sit in judgment on him.

"We can't talk here," he said. "Let me buy you lunch."

"I'll have lunch with you. Dutch." I didn't want to owe him anything, at least till I'd heard his story.

There was a restaurant across the street. Its main room was filled with smoke and the roar of conversation. The red-checkered tables were all occupied, mainly with courthouse people, lawyers and sheriff's men and probation officers. Though Pacific Point was fifty miles south of my normal beat, I recognized ten or a dozen of them.

Alex and I went into the bar and found a couple of stools in a dim corner. He ordered a double scotch on the rocks. I went along with it. He drank his down like medicine and tried to order a second round immediately.

"You set quite a pace. Slow down."

"Are you telling me what to do?" he said distinctly and unpleasantly.

"I'm willing to listen to your story. I want you to be able to tell it."

"You think I'm an alcoholic or something?"

"I think you're a bundle of nerves. Pour alcohol on a bundle of nerves and it generally turns into a can of worms. While I'm making suggestions you might as well get rid of those chips you're wearing on both shoulders. Somebody's liable to knock them off and take a piece of you with them."

He sat for a while with his head down. His face had an almost fluorescent pallor, and a faint humming tremor went through him.

"I'm not my usual self, I admit that. I didn't know things like this could happen to people."

"It's about time you told me what did happen. Why not start at the beginning?"

"You mean when she left the hotel?"

"All right. Start with the hotel."

"We were staying at the Surf House," he said, "right here in Pacific Point. I couldn't really afford it but Dolly wanted the experience of staying there—she never had. I figured a three-day weekend wouldn't break me. It was the Labor Day weekend. I'd already used my vacation time, and we got married that Saturday so that we could have at least a three-day honeymoon."

"Where were you married?"

"In Long Beach, by a judge."

"It sounds like one of these spur-of-the-moment weddings."

"I suppose it was, in a way. We hadn't known each other too long. Dolly was the one, really, who wanted to get married right now. Don't think I wasn't eager. I was. But my parents thought we should wait a bit, until we could find a house and have it furnished and so on. They would have liked a church wedding. But Dolly wanted to be married by a judge."

"What about her parents?"

"They're dead. She has no living relatives." He turned his head slowly and met my eyes. "Or so she claims."

"You seem to have your doubts about it."

"Not really. It's just that she got so upset when I asked her about her parents. I naturally wanted to meet them, but she treated my request as though I was prying. Finally she told me her entire family was dead, wiped out in an auto accident."

"Where?"

"I don't know where. When it comes right down to it, I don't know too much about my wife. Except that she's a wonderful girl," he added in a rush of loyal feeling slightly flavored with whisky. "She's beautiful and intelligent and good and I know she loves me." He was almost chanting, as though by wishful thinking or sheer incantation he could bend reality back into shape around him.

"What was her maiden name?"

"Dolly McGee. Her name is really Dorothy. She was working in the university library and I was taking a summer course in Business Ad—"

"Just this summer?"

"That's correct." He swallowed, and his adam's apple throbbed like a grief in his throat. "We only knew each other for six weeks—six-and-a-half weeks—before we were married. But we saw each other every day of those six-and-a-half weeks."

"What did you do together?"

"I don't see that it matters."

"It could. I'm trying to get a line on her personal habits."

"She had no *bad* habits, if that's what you're looking for. She never let me drink when we were out together. She wasn't very keen on the coffee houses, either, or the movies. She was—she's a very serious girl. Most of our time we talked—we talked and walked. We must have covered most of West Los Angeles."

"What did you talk about?"

"The meaning of life," he said, as if this went without saying. "We were trying to work out a plan to live by, a set of rules for our marriage and our children. The main thing for Dolly was the children. She wanted to bring them up to be real people. She thought it was more important to be an honest individual than to have security and worldly possessions and so on. I don't want to bore you with all this."

"You're not. I take it she was completely sincere?"

"Nobody was ever more sincere. I mean it. She actually wanted me to give up my job and go back and finish my M.A. She didn't think I should take money from my family. She was willing to go on working to help me through. But we decided against that plan, when we made up our minds to get married."

"It wasn't a forced marriage?"

He looked at me stonily. "There was nothing like that between us. As a matter of fact we didn't even—I mean, I didn't touch her on our wedding night. The Surf House and Pacific Point seemed to get on her nerves, even though she was the one who wanted to come here. So we decided to postpone the physical bit. A lot of couples do that nowadays."

"How does Dolly feel about sex?"

"Fine. We talked about it very frankly. If you think she left me because she's afraid of it, you're way off the beam. She's a warm person."

"Why did she leave you, Alex?"

His eyes clouded with pain, which had scarcely left them. "I haven't been able to figure it out. It wasn't anything between me and Dolly, I'm sure of that. The man with the beard must have had something to do with it."

"How does he get into the picture?"

"He came to the hotel that afternoon—the day she left. I was down on the beach having a swim, and afterward I went to sleep in the sun. I must have been away from the room for a couple of hours. She was gone, bag and baggage, when I got back. The desk clerk told me she had this visitor before she left, a man with a short gray beard who stayed in the room about an hour."

"No name?"

"He didn't mention his name."

"Did he and your wife leave together?"

"The desk clerk said they didn't. The man left first. Then Dolly took a taxi to the bus station, but so far as I could find out she didn't buy a ticket. She didn't buy a railroad ticket or an airline ticket, either. She had no car. So I've been going on the assumption that she's still here in Pacific Point. She couldn't walk down the freeway."

"She could hitchhike."

"Not Dolly."

"Where did she live before you were married?"

"In Westwood, in a furnished apartment. She gave it up and we moved her typewriter and things into my apartment on Saturday morning just before the ceremony. All the stuff is still there, and it's one of the things that worry me. I've been over it with a fine-toothed comb for clues, but she didn't leave any behind—nothing really personal at all."

"Do you think she planned to marry you and leave you?"

"No, I don't. What would be the point?"

"I can think of several possibilities. Do you carry much insurance, for example?"

"A fair amount. Dad insured me when I was born. But he's still the beneficiary."

"Does your family have money?"

"Not that much. Dad makes a good living, but he works for it. Anyway, what you're hinting at is out of the question. Dolly's completely honest, and she doesn't even care about money."

"What does she care about?"

"I thought she cared about me," he said with his head down. "I still believe she does. Something must have happened to her. She may have gone out of her mind."

"Is she mentally unstable?"

He considered the question, and his answer to it. "I don't think so. She had her black spells. I guess most people do. I was talking loosely."

"Keep on talking loosely. You can't tell what may be important. You've been making a search for her, of course?"

"As much of a search as I could. But I can't do it all by myself, without any cooperation from the police. They write down what I say on little pieces of paper and put them away in a drawer and give me pitying looks. They seem to think Dolly found out something shameful about me on our wedding night."

"Could there be any truth in that?"

"No! We're crazy about each other. I tried to tell that to the Sheriff this morning. He gave me one of those knowing leers and said he couldn't act unless there was some indication of a breach of the peace. I asked him if a missing woman wasn't some indication, and he said no.

She was free and twenty-one and she left under her own power and I had no legal right to force her to come back. He advised me to get an annulment. I told him what he could do with his advice, and he ordered two of his men to throw me out of his office. I found out where the deputy D.A. was, in court, and I was waiting to put in a complaint when I saw you on the stand."

"Nobody sent you to me, then?"

"No, but I can give you references. My father—"

"You told me about your father. He thinks you should get an annulment, too."

Alex nodded dolefully. "Dad thinks I'm wasting my time, on a girl who isn't worth it."

"He could be right."

"He couldn't be more wrong. Dolly is the only one I've ever loved and the only one I ever will love. If you won't help me, I'll find somebody who will!"

I liked his insistence. "My rates are high. A hundred a day and expenses."

"I've got enough to pay you for at least a week." He reached for his billfold and slammed it down on the bar, so hard that the bartender looked at him suspiciously. "Do you want a cash advance?"

"There's no hurry," I said. "Do you have a picture of Dolly?"

He removed a folded piece of newspaper from the billfold and handed it to me with a certain reluctance, as if it was more valuable than money. It was a reproduction of a photograph which had been unfolded and refolded many times.

"Among happy honeymooners at the Surf House," the caption said, "are Mr. and Mrs. Alex Kincaid of Long Beach." Alex and his bride smiled up at me through the murky light. Her face was oval and lovely in a way of its own, with a kind of hooded intelligence in the eyes and humor like a bittersweet taste on the mouth.

"When was this taken?"

"Three weeks ago Saturday, when we arrived at the Surf House. They do it for everybody. They printed it in the Sunday morning paper, and I clipped it. I'm glad I did. It's the only picture I have of her."

"You could get copies."

"Where?"

"From whoever took it."

"I never thought of that. I'll see the photographer at the hotel about it. How many copies do you think I should ask him for?"

"Two or three dozen, anyway. It's better to have too many than too few."

"That will run into money."

"I know, and so will I."

"Are you trying to talk yourself out of a job?"

"I don't need the work, and I could use a rest."

"To hell with you then."

He snatched at the flimsy picture between my fingers. It tore across the middle. We faced each other like enemies, each of us holding a piece of the happy honeymooners.

Alex burst into tears.

2

I AGREED over lunch to help him find his wife. That and the chicken pot pie calmed him down. He couldn't remember when he had eaten last, and he ate ravenously.

We drove out to the Surf House in separate cars. It was on the sea at the good end of town: a pueblo hotel whose Spanish gardens were dotted with hundred-dollar-a-day cottages. The terraces in front of the main building descended in wide green steps to its own marina. Yachts and launches were bobbing at the slips. Further out on the water, beyond the curving promontory that gave Pacific Point its name, white sails leaned against a low gray wall of fog.

The desk clerk in the Ivy League suit was very polite, but he wasn't the one who had been on duty on the Sunday I was interested in. That one had been a summer replacement, a college boy who had gone back to school in the East. He himself, he regretted to say, knew nothing about Mrs. Kincaid's bearded visitor or her departure.

"I'd like to talk to the hotel photographer. Is he around today?"

"Yes, sir. I believe he's out by the swimming pool."

We found him, a thin spry man wearing a heavy camera like an albatros around his neck. Among the colored beach clothes and bathing costumes, his dark business suit made him look like an undertaker. He was taking some very candid pictures of a middle-aged woman in a Bikini who didn't belong in one. Her umbilicus glared at the camera like an eyeless socket.

When he had done his dreadful work, the photographer turned to Alex with a smile. "Hi. How's the wife?"

"I haven't seen her recently," Alex said glumly.

"Weren't you on your honeymoon a couple of weeks ago? Didn't I take your picture?"

Alex didn't answer him. He was peering around at the poolside loungers like a ghost trying to remember how it felt to be human. I said:

"We'd like to get some copies made of that picture you took. Mrs. Kincaid is on the missing list, and I'm a private detective. My name is Archer."

"Fargo. Simmy Fargo." He gave me a quick handshake, and the kind of glance a camera gives you when it records you for posterity. "In what sense on the missing list?"

"We don't know. She left here in a taxi on the afternoon of September the second. Kincaid has been looking for her ever since."

"That's tough," Fargo said. "I suppose you want the prints for circularization. How many do you think you'll be needing?"

"Three dozen?"

He whistled, and slapped himself on his narrow wrinkled forehead. "I've got a busy weekend coming up, and it's already started. This is Friday. I could let you have them by Monday. But I suppose you want them yesterday?"

"Today will do."

"Sorry." He shrugged loosely, making his camera bob against his chest.

"It could be important, Fargo. What do you say we settle for a dozen, in two hours?"

"I'd like to help you. But I've got a job." Slowly, almost against his will, he turned and looked at Alex. "Tell you what I'll do. I'll call the wife in, and you can have your pictures. Only don't stand me up, the way the other one did."

"What other one?" I said.

"Big guy with a beard. He ordered a print of the same picture and never came back for it. I can let you have that print now if you like."

Alex came out of his dark trance. He took hold of Fargo's arm with both hands and shook it. "You saw him then. Who is he?"

"I thought maybe you knew him." Fargo disengaged himself and stepped back. "As a matter of fact, I thought I knew him, too. I could have sworn I took his picture once. But I couldn't quite place the face. I see too many faces."

"Did he give you his name?"

"He must have. I don't take orders without a name. I'll see if I can find it for you, eh?"

We followed him into the hotel and through a maze of corridors to his small cluttered windowless office. He phoned his wife, then burrowed into the pile of papers on his desk and came up with a photographer's envelope. Inside, between two sheets of corrugated paper, was a glossy print of the newlyweds. On the front of the envelope Fargo had written in pencil: "Chuck Begley, Wine Cellar."

"I remember now," he said. "He told me he was working at the Wine Cellar. That's a liquor store not too far from here. When Begley didn't claim his picture I called them. They said Begley wasn't working for them any more." Fargo looked from me to Alex. "Does the name Begley mean anything to you?"

We both said that it didn't. "Can you describe him, Mr. Fargo?"

"I can describe the part of him that wasn't covered with seaweed, I mean the beard. His hair is gray, like the beard, and very thick and wavy. Gray eyebrows and gray eyes, an ordinary kind of straight nose, I noticed it was peeling from the sun. He's not bad-looking for an older man, apart from his teeth, which aren't good. And he looks as though he's taken a beating or two in his time. Personally I wouldn't want to go up against him. He's a big man, and he looks pretty rough."

"How big?"

"Three or four inches taller than I am. That would make him six feet one or two. He was wearing a short-sleeved sport shirt, and I noticed the muscles in his arms."

"How did he talk?"

"Nothing special. He didn't have a Harvard accent, and he didn't say ain't."

"Did he give you any reason for wanting the picture?"

"He said he had a sentimental interest. He saw it in the paper, and it reminded him of somebody. I remember thinking he must have dashed right over. The paper with the picture in it came out Sunday morning, and he came in around Sunday noon."

"He must have gone to see your wife immediately afterward," I said to Alex. And to Fargo: "How did this particular picture happen to be used by the newspaper?"

"They picked it out of a batch I sent over. The *Press* often uses my pictures, as a matter of fact I used to work for them. Why they used this one instead of some of the others I couldn't say." He held up the print in the fluorescent light, then handed it to me. "It did turn out well, and Mr. Kincaid and his wife make an attractive couple."

"Thanks very much," Alex said sardonically.

"I was paying you a compliment, fellow."

"Sure you were."

I took the print from Fargo and shunted Alex out of the place before it got too small for him. Black grief kept flooding up in him, changing to anger when it reached the air. It wasn't just grief for a one-day wife, it was also grief for himself. He didn't seem to know if he was a man or not.

I couldn't blame him for his feelings, but they made him no asset to the kind of work I was trying to do. When I found the Wine Cellar, on a motel strip a few blocks inland, I left him outside in his little red sports car.

The interior of the liquor store was pleasantly cool. I was the only potential customer, and the man behind the counter came out from behind it to greet me.

"What can I do for you, sir?"

He wore a plaid waistcoat, and he had the slightly muzzy voice and liquid eyes and dense complexion of a man who drank all day and into the night.

"I'd like to see Chuck Begley."

He looked vaguely pained, and his voice took on a note of mild complaint. "I had to fire Chuck. I'd send him out with a delivery, and sometimes it'd arrive when it was supposed to, and sometimes it wouldn't."

"How long ago did you fire him?"

"Couple of weeks. He only worked for me a couple of weeks. He isn't cut out for that kind of work. I told him more than once it was beneath his capacity. Chuck Begley is a fairly bright man if he'd straighten up, you know."

"I don't know."

"I thought perhaps you were an acquaintance of his."

I showed him my photostat.

He blew the smell of peppermint in my face. "Is Begley on the run?"

"He may be. Why?"

"I wondered when he first came in why a man like him would take a part-time delivery job. What's he wanted for?"

"I wouldn't know. Can you give me his home address?"

"I think I can at that." He stroked his veined nose, watching me over his fingers. "Don't tell Begley I gave you the word. I don't want him bouncing back on me."

"I won't."

"He spends a lot of time in the home of one of my customers. You might say he's a non-paying guest of hers. I certainly wouldn't want to make trouble for her. But then," he reasoned, "if Begley's on the run I'm doing her a favor in seeing that he's picked up. Isn't that right?"

"I'd say so. Where does she live?"

"On Shearwater Beach, cottage number seventeen. Her name's Madge Gerhardi. Take the freeway south and you'll see the Shearwater turnoff about two miles down the line. Only just don't tell either of them that it was me sent you. Okay?"

"Okay." I left him with his bottles.

3
..

WE PARKED our cars at the top of the access lane, and I persuaded Alex to stay in his, out of sight. Shearwater Beach turned out to be a kind of expensive slum where several dozen cottages stood in a row. The changing blue reflection of the sea glared through the narrow gaps between them. Beyond their peaked rooftops, out over the water, a tern circled on flashing wings, looking for fish.

Number seventeen needed paint, and leaned on its pilings like a man on crutches. I knocked on the scabbed gray door. Slowly, like bodies being dragged, footsteps approached the other side. The bearded man opened it.

He was a man of fifty or so wearing an open-necked black shirt from which his head jutted like weathered stone. The sunlight struck mica glints from his eyes. The fingers with which he was holding the edge of the door were bitten down to the quick. He saw me looking at them and curled them into a fist.

"I'm searching for a missing girl, Mr. Begley." I had decided on the direct approach. "She may have met with foul play and if she did, you may have been one of the last people who saw her alive."

He rubbed the side of his face with his clenched knuckles. His face bore marks of old trouble, some of them done by hand: faintly quilted patches around the eyes, a thin scar on his temple divided like a miniature ruler by stitch-marks. Old trouble and the promise of further trouble.

"You must be crazy. I don't even know any girls."

"You know *me*," a woman said behind him.

She appeared at his shoulder and leaned on him, waiting for somebody to second the self-administered flattery. She was about Begley's age, and may have been older. Her body was very assertive in shorts and a halter. Frizzled by repeated dyeings and bleachings, her hair stuck up on her head like a yellow fright wig. Between their deep blue artificial shadows, her eyes were the color of gin.

"I'm very much afraid that you must be mistaken," she said to me with a cultivated Eastern-seaboard accent which lapsed immediately. "I swear by all that's holy that Chuck had nothing to do with any girl. He's been too busy looking after little old me." She draped a plump white arm across the back of his neck. "Haven't you, darling?"

Begley was immobilized between the woman and me. I showed him Fargo's glossy print of the honeymooners.

"You know this girl, don't you? Her name, her married name, is Dolly Kincaid."

"I never heard of her in my life."

"Witnesses tell me different. They say you went to see her at the Surf House three weeks ago this coming Sunday. You saw this picture of her in the paper and ordered a copy of it from the photographer at the Surf House."

The woman tightened her arm around his neck, more like a wrestling partner than a lover. "Who is she, Chuck?"

"I have no idea." But he muttered to himself: "So it's started all over again."

"What has started all over again?"

She was stealing my lines. "Could I please talk to Mr. Begley alone?"

"He has no secrets from me." She looked up at him proudly, with a wilted edge of anxiety on her pride. "Have you, darling? We're going to be married, aren't we, darling?"

"Could you stop calling me darling? Just for five minutes? Please?"

She backed away from him, ready to cry, her downturned red mouth making a lugubrious clown face.

"Please go inside," he said. "Let me talk to the man."

"This is my place. I have a right to know what goes on in my own place."

"Sure you do, Madge. But I have squatter's privileges, at least. Go in and drink some coffee."

"Are you in trouble?"

"No. Of course I'm not." But there was resignation in his voice. "Beat it, eh, like a good girl?"

His last word seemed to mollify her. Dawdling and turning, she disappeared down the hallway. Begley closed the door and leaned on it.

"Now you can tell me the truth," I said.

"All right, so I went to see her at the hotel. It was a stupid impulse. It doesn't make me a murderer."

"Nobody suggested that, except you."

"I thought I'd save you the trouble." He spread out his arms as if for instant crucifixion. "You're the local law, I gather."

"I'm working with them," I said hopefully. "My name is Archer. You haven't explained why you went to see Mrs. Kincaid. How well did you know her?"

"I didn't know her at all." He dropped his outspread arms in emphasis. The sensitive areas around his mouth were hidden by his beard, and I couldn't tell what he was doing with them. His gray eyes were unrevealing. "I thought I knew her, but I didn't."

"What do you mean?"

"I thought she might be my daughter. There was quite a resemblance to her in the newspaper picture, but not so much in the flesh. The mistake on my part was natural. I haven't seen my daughter for so long."

"What's your daughter's name?"

He hesitated. "Mary. Mary Begley. We haven't been in touch for over ten years. I've been out of the country, on the other side of the world." He made it sound as remote as the far side of the moon.

"Your daughter must have been quite young when you left."

"Yeah. Ten or eleven."

"And you must have been quite fond of her," I said, "to order a picture just because it reminded you of her."

"I was fond of her."

"Why didn't you go back for the picture then?"

He went into a long silence. I became aware of something impressive in the man, the untouchable still quality of an aging animal.

"I was afraid that Madge would be jealous," he said. "I happen to be living on Madge."

I suspected he was using the bald statement to tell a lie. But it may have come from a deeper source. Some men spend their lives looking for ways to punish themselves for having been born, and Begley had some of the stigmata of the trouble-prone. He said:

"What do you think happened to Mrs. Kincaid?" His question was cold and formal, disclaiming all interest in the answer to it.

"I was hoping you'd have some ideas on the subject. She's been missing for nearly three weeks. I don't like it. It's true that girls are always disappearing, but not on their honeymoons—not when they love their husbands."

"She loves hers, does she?"

"He thinks so. How was she feeling when you saw her? Was she depressed?"

"I wouldn't say that. She was surprised to see me."

"Because she hadn't seen you for so long?"

He sneered at me hairily. "Don't bother trying to trap me. I told you she wasn't my daughter. She didn't know me from Adam."

"What did you find to talk about with her?"

"We didn't talk." He paused. "Maybe I asked her a few questions."

"Such as?"

"Who her father was. Who her mother was. Where she came from. She said she came from Los Angeles. Her maiden name was Dolly something—I forget the name. Her parents were both dead. That's about all."

"It took you quite a while to get that much out of her."

"I was only there five or ten minutes, maybe fifteen."

"The desk clerk said an hour."

"He made a mistake."

"Or maybe you did, Mr. Begley. Time passes very rapidly sometimes."

He clutched at this dubious excuse. "Maybe I did stay longer than I realized. I remember now, she wanted me to stay and meet her husband." His eyes held steady, but they had taken on a faint lying sheen. "He didn't come and didn't come, so I left."

"Did you suggest seeing her again?"

"No. She wasn't that interested in my story."

"You told her your story?"

"I told her about my daughter, naturally, just like I told you."

"I don't understand it. You say you were out of the country for ten years. Where?"

"In New Caledonia, mostly. I worked for a chrome mine there. They shut it down last spring and shipped us home."

"And now you're looking for your daughter?"

"I'd certainly like to put my hands on her."

"So she can be a bridesmaid at your wedding?" I wanted to see how sharp a needle he would take.

He took this one without a word.

"What happened to your wife?"

"She died." His eyes were no longer steady. "Look, do we have to go into all this? It's bad enough losing your loved ones without having it raked up and pushed in your face." I couldn't tell if his self-pity was false: self-pity always is to some extent.

"It's too bad you lost your family," I said. "But what did you expect when you left the country for ten years?"

"It wasn't my choice. How would you like to get shanghaied and not be able to get back?"

"Is that your story? It isn't a likely one."

"My story is wilder than that, but we won't go into it. You wouldn't believe me, anyway. Nobody else has."

"You could always try me."

"It would take all day. You've got better things to do than talk to me."

"Name one."

"You said there's a young lady missing. Go and find her."

"I was hoping you could help me. I still am hoping, Mr. Begley."

He looked down at his feet. He was wearing huaraches. "I've told you all I know about her. I should never have gone to that hotel in the first place. Okay, so I made a mistake. You can't hang a man for a little mistake in judgment."

"You've mentioned murder once, and hanging once. I wonder why."

"It was just a manner of speaking." But the confidence was seeping out of him through the holes my needle had made. He said with a rising inflection: "You think I murdered her?"

"No. I do think this. Something happened between you, or something was said, that might explain why she left so suddenly. Give it some thought, will you?"

Slowly, perhaps involuntarily, he raised his head and looked up at the sun. Under his tilted beard his neck was pale and scrawny. It gave the impression that he was wearing the kind of mask Greek actors wore, covering him completely from my eyes.

"No. Nothing was said like that."

"Was there any trouble between you?"

"No."

"Why did she let you come to her room?"

"I guess she was interested in my story. I talked to her on the house phone, said she resembled my daughter. It was just a foolish impulse. I knew as soon as I saw her that she wasn't."

"Did you make arrangements to see her again?"

"No. I'd certainly like to."

"Did you wait outside the hotel for her, or agree to meet her at the bus station?"

"I did not. What are you trying to nail me for? What do you want?"

"Just the truth. I'm not satisfied I've been getting it from you."

He said in a sudden spurt of fury: "You've got as much as—" He began to regret the outburst before it was over, and swallowed the rest of the words.

But he turned his back on me and went inside, slamming the door. I waited for a little while, and gave up on him. I walked back along the sandy access lane to our cars.

The blonde woman, Madge Gerhardi, was sitting beside Alex in his red Porsche. He looked up with shining eyes.

"Mrs. Gerhardi has seen her. She's seen Dolly."

"With Begley?"

"No, not with him." She opened the door and squeezed out of the little car. "It was at that garage that specializes in fixing foreign cars. I drive an MG myself, and I had it in for a lube job. The girl was there with an old woman. They went away together in an old brown Rolls. The girl was doing the driving."

"Are you certain of the identification?" I showed her the picture again.

She nodded over it emphatically. "I'm certain, unless she has a twin. I noticed her because she was so stunning."

"Do you know who the old woman was?"

"No, but the man at the garage ought to be able to tell you." She gave us directions, and started to edge away. "I better get back to the house. I snuck out along the beach, and Chuck will be wondering where I am."

4
..

A MECHANIC lying face up on a creeper rolled out from under the raised front end of a Jaguar sedan. I saw when he stood up that he was a plump Mediterranean type with "Mario" embroidered on his coverall. He nodded enthusiastically when I asked him about the old Rolls and the old lady.

"That's Mrs. Bradshaw. I been looking after her Rolls for the last twelve years, ever since she bought it. It's running as good now as the day she bought it." He looked at his greasy hands with some satisfaction, like a surgeon recalling a series of difficult but successful operations. "Some of the girls she gets to drive her don't know how to treat a good car."

"Do you know the girl who's driving her at present?"

"I don't know her name. Mrs. Bradshaw has quite a turnover with her drivers. She gets them from the college mostly. Her son is Dean at the college, and he won't let the old lady do her own driving. She's crippled with rheumatics, and I think she was in a smashup at one time."

I cut in on Mario's complicated explanations and showed him the print. "This girl?"

"Yeah. She was here with Mrs. Bradshaw the other day. She's a new one. Like I said, Mrs. Bradshaw has quite a turnover. She likes to have her own way, and these college girls don't take orders too well. Personally I always hit it off with Mrs. Bradshaw—"

"Where does she live?"

Alex sounded anxious, and Mario was slightly infected by his anxiety. "What is it you want with her?"

"She's not the one I'm interested in. The girl is my wife."

"You and her are on the outs?"

"I don't know. I have to talk to her."

Mario looked up at the high corrugated-iron roof of the garage. "My wife divorced me a couple years ago. I been putting on weight ever since. A man don't have the same motivation."

"Where does Mrs. Bradshaw live?" I said.

"Foothill Drive, not too far from here. Take the first cross street to the right, it runs into it. You can look up the house number in the phone book, on the desk there. It's in her son's name, Roy Bradshaw."

I thanked him. He lay down on the creeper and slid back under the Jaguar. The directory was under the telephone on top of the battered desk which stood in a corner. I found the listing: "Roy Bradshaw, 311 Foothill Drive."

"We could phone from here," Alex said.

"It's always better in person."

In spite of the housing tracts and the smokeless industries proliferating around it, Pacific Point had kept its identity. Foothill Drive was lined with trees, and had a dusty changeless quality. Settled old families still lived here behind mortised walls that had resisted earthquakes, or hedges that had outlived generations of gardeners.

The towering cypress hedge of 311 masked the house completely from the road. I turned in through the open iron gates with Alex following me. We passed a small white gatehouse with a green door and green shutters, rounded a bend in the driveway, and came in sight of the white Colonial house.

A woman with a wide straw hat tied under her chin was kneeling shoulder deep among the flowers in front of it. She had a pair of clippers in her gloved hands. They snicked in the silence when our engines died.

She rose cumbrously to her feet and came toward us, tucking wisps of gray hair under her hat. She was just an old lady in dirty tennis shoes but her body, indeterminate in a loose blue smock, carried itself with heavy authority, as if it recalled that it had once been powerful or handsome. The architecture of her face had collapsed under the weight of flesh and years. Still her black eyes were alert, like unexpected animal or bird life in the ruins of a building.

"Mrs. Bradshaw?" Alex said eagerly.

"I am Mrs. Bradshaw. What do you gentlemen want? I'm very busy, as you can see." She flourished the clippers. "I never trust anyone else to clip my roses. And still they die, poor things." Regret rustled in her voice.

"They look very beautiful to me," I said in an encouraging way. "Mr. Kincaid and I hate to bother you. But he seems to have misplaced his wife, and we have reason to think she's working for you."

"For me? I employ no one but my Spanish couple. My son," she added with a trace of pride, "keeps me to a strict budget."

"Don't you have a girl driving for you?"

She smiled. "I completely forgot about her. She's just on a part-time basis. What's her name? Molly? Dolly? I never can remember the girls' names."

"Dolly," I said, and showed her the print. "Is this Dolly?"

She removed one gardening glove to take the picture. Her hand was gnarled by arthritis.

"I do believe it is. But she said nothing to me about being married. I'd never have hired her if I'd known, it makes for too much involvement. I like to take my little drives on schedule."

Alex interrupted her rather garrulous chatter. "Where is she now?"

"I couldn't say. She's done her day's stint for me. She may have walked over to the college, or she may be in the gatehouse. I let my girls use the gatehouse. Sometimes they abuse the privilege, but so far this one hasn't." She gave Alex a sharp black glance. "I hope she won't begin to, now that you've turned up."

"I don't expect she'll be going on—"

I cut him short. "Go and see if she's in the gatehouse." I turned back to Mrs. Bradshaw: "How long has she been with you?"

"About two weeks. The semester started two weeks ago."

"Is she attending the college?"

"Yes. I get all my girls from there, except when I have to have a regular attendant, as I did when my son was abroad last summer. I hope I don't lose Dolly. She's brighter than most of them. But if she goes I sup-

pose there are always others. You'll realize, when you've lived as long
as I have, that the young ones leave the old ones . . ."

She turned to her roses, glowing red and yellow in the sunlight. She
seemed to be looking for some way to finish the thought. None occurred
to her. I said:

"What name is she using? What surname?"

"I'm afraid I don't remember. I call them by their first names. My son
could tell you."

"Is he here?"

"Roy is at the college. He happens to be the Dean there."

"Is it far from here?"

"You can see it from where you stand."

Her arthritic hand curled on my elbow and turned me gently.
Through a gap in the trees I could make out the metal cupola of a small
observatory. The old lady spoke close to my ear, in a gossipy way:

"What happened between your young friend and his wife?"

"They came here on their honeymoon and she walked out on him.
He's trying to find out why."

"What a strange thing to do," she said. "I'd never have acted like that
on my honeymoon, I had too much respect for my husband. But girls
are different nowadays, aren't they? Loyalty and respect mean nothing
to them. Are you married, young man?"

"I have been."

"I see. Are you the boy's father?"

"No. My name is Archer. I'm a private detective."

"Really? What do you make of all this?" She gestured vaguely with
her clippers toward the gatehouse.

"Nothing so far. She may have left him on account of a girlish whim.
Or she may have had deep dark reasons. All I can do is ask her. By the
way, Mrs. Bradshaw, have you ever heard her mention a man named
Begley?"

"Begley?"

"He's a big man with a short gray beard. He visited her at the Surf
House the day she left her husband. There's some possibility that he's
her father."

She wet her seamed lips with the purple tip of her tongue. "She didn't
mention him to me. I don't encourage the girls to unburden themselves
to me. Perhaps I should."

"What kind of a mood has Dolly been in lately?"

"It's hard to say. She's always the same. Quiet. She thinks her own thoughts."

Alex appeared, walking rapidly around the bend in the driveway. His face was bright.

"It's her definitely. I found her things in the closet."

"You weren't authorized to go in there," Mrs. Bradshaw said.

"It's her house, isn't it?"

"It happens to be mine."

"But she has the use of it, hasn't she?"

"She does. You don't."

A quarrel with Dolly's employer was the last thing Alex needed. I stepped between them, turned him around, and walked him away from trouble for the second time.

"Get lost," I said when he was in his car. "You're in my way."

"But I have to see her."

"You'll see her. Go and check in at the Mariner's Rest Motel for both of us. It's on the strip between here and the Surf House—"

"I know where it is. But what about Dolly?"

"I'm going over to the college to talk to her. I'll bring her back with me, if she's willing."

"Why can't I go along to the college?" he said like a spoiled child.

"Because I don't want you to. Dolly has a separate life of her own. You may not like it, but you have no right to jump in and wreck it for her. I'll see you at the motel."

He drove away rapidly and angrily, spinning the wheels of his car. Mrs. Bradshaw was back among her roses. I asked her very politely for permission to examine Dolly's things. She said that would have to be up to Dolly.

5

··

THE CAMPUS was an oasis of vivid green under the brown September foothills. Most of the buildings were new and very modern, ornamented with pierced concrete screens and semi-tropical plantings. A barefoot boy sitting under a roadside palm took time out from his Salinger to show me where the Administration Building was.

I parked in the lot behind it, among a scattering of transportation clunks with faculty stickers. A new black Thunderbird stood out among them. It was late Friday afternoon by now, and the long collegiate weekend was setting in. The glass information booth opposite the entrance of the building was empty. The corridors were practically deserted.

I found the Dean's office without much trouble. The paneled anteroom was furnished with convertible Danish pieces, and with a blonde secretary who sat at a typewriter guarding the closed inner door. She had a pale thin face, strained blue eyes that had worked too long under fluorescent light, and a suspicious voice:

"Can I help you, sir?"

"I'd like to see the Dean."

"Dean Bradshaw is very busy, I'm afraid. Perhaps I can assist you?"

"Perhaps. I'm trying to get in touch with one of your girl students. Her name is Dolly McGee, or Dolly Kincaid."

"Which?" she said with a little gasp of irritation.

"Her maiden name is McGee, her married name is Kincaid. I don't know which she's using."

"Are you a parent?" she said delicately.

"No. I'm not her father. But I have good reason for wanting to see her."

She looked at me as if I was a self-confessed kingpin in the white slave traffic. "We have a policy of not giving out information about students, except to parents."

"What about husbands?"

"You're her husband?"

"I represent her husband. I think you'd better let me talk to the Dean about her."

"I can't do that," she said in a final tone. "Dean Bradshaw is in conference with the department heads. About what do you wish to see Miss McGee?"

"It's a private matter."

"I see."

We had reached an impasse. I said in the hope of making her smile: "We have a policy of not giving out information."

She looked insulted, and went back to her typewriter. I stood and waited. Voices rose and fell behind the door of the inner office. "Budget" was the word I caught most frequently. After a while the secretary said:

"I suppose you could try Dean Sutherland, if she's in. Dean Sutherland is Dean of Women. Her office is just across the hall."

Its door was standing open. The woman in it was the well-scrubbed ageless type who looks old in her twenties and young in her forties. She wore her brown hair rolled in a bun at the back of her neck. Her only concession to glamour was a thin pink line of lipstick accenting her straight mouth.

She was a good-looking woman in spite of this. Her face was finely chiseled. The front of her blouse curved out over her desk like a spinnaker going downwind.

"Come in," she said with a severity that I was getting used to. "What are you waiting for?"

Her fine eyes had me hypnotized. Looking into them was like looking into the beautiful core of an iceberg, all green ice and cold blazing light.

"Sit down," she said. "What is your problem?"

I told her who I was and why I was there.

"But we have no Dolly McGee or Dolly Kincaid on campus."

"She must be using a third name, then. I know she's a student here. She has a job driving for Dean Bradshaw's mother." I showed her my photograph.

"But this is Dorothy Smith. Why would she register with us under a false name?"

"That's what her husband would like to know."

"Is this her husband in the picture with her?"

"Yes."

"He appears to be a nice enough boy."

"Apparently she didn't think so."

"I wonder why." Her eyes were looking past me, and I felt cheated. "As a matter of fact, I don't see how she *could* register under a false name, unless she came to us with forged credentials." She rose abruptly. "Excuse me for a minute, Mr. Archer."

She went into the next room, where filing cabinets stood like up-ended metal coffins, and came back with a folder which she opened on her desk. There wasn't much in it.

"I see," she said more or less to herself. "She's been admitted provisionally. There's a note here to the effect that her transcript is on the way."

"How long is provisional admission good for?"

"Until the end of September." She consulted her desk calendar. "That gives her nine days to come up with a transcript. But she'll have to come up with an explanation rather sooner. We don't look with favor on this sort of deception. And I had the impression that she was a straightforward girl." Her mouth turned down at the corners.

"You know her personally, Dean Sutherland?"

"I make a point of contacting all the new girls. I went out of my way to be useful to Miss or Mrs. Smith-Kincaid. In fact I helped to get her a part-time job in the library."

"And the job with old Mrs. Bradshaw?"

She nodded. "She heard that there was an opening there, and I recommended her." She looked at her watch. "She may be over there now."

"She isn't. I just came from Mrs. Bradshaw's. Your Dean lives pretty high on the hog, by the way. I thought academic salaries were too low."

"They are. Dean Bradshaw comes from a wealthy old family. What was his mother's reaction to this?" She made an impatient gesture which somehow included me.

"She seemed to take it in stride. She's a smart old woman."

"I'm glad you found her so," she said, as if she had had other kinds of experience with Mrs. Bradshaw. "Well, I suppose I'd better see if Mrs. Smith-Kincaid is in the library."

"I could go over there and ask."

"I think not. I had better talk to her first, and try to find out what's going on in her little head."

"I didn't want to make trouble for her."

"Of course not, and you didn't. The trouble is and was there. You merely uncovered it. I'm grateful to you for that."

"Could your gratitude," I said carefully, "possibly take the form of letting me talk to her first?"

"I'm afraid not."

"I've had a lot of experience getting the facts out of people."

It was the wrong thing to say. Her mouth turned down at the corners again. Her bosom changed from a promise to a threat.

"I've had experience, too, a good many years of it, and I am a trained counselor. If you'll be good enough to wait outside, I'm going to try and phone her at the library." She flung a last shaft as I went out: "And please don't try to intercept her on the way here."

"I wouldn't dream of it, Miss Sutherland."

"Dean Sutherland, if you please."

I went and read the bulletin board beside the information booth. The jolly promises of student activities, dances and get-togethers and poetry clubs and breakfasts where French was spoken, only saddened me. It was partly because my own attempt at college hadn't worked out, partly because I'd just put the kibosh on Dolly's.

A girl wearing horn-rimmed glasses, and a big young fellow in a varsity sweater drifted in from outside and leaned against the wall. She was explaining something to him, something about Achilles and the tortoise. Achilles was chasing the tortoise, it seemed, but according to Zeno he would never catch it. The space between them was divisible into an infinite number of parts; therefore it would take Achilles an infinite period of time to traverse it. By that time the tortoise would be somewhere else.

The young man nodded. "I see that."

"But it isn't so," the girl cried. "The infinite divisibility of space is merely theoretical. It doesn't affect actual *movement* across space."

"I don't get it, Heidi."

"Of course you do. Imagine yourself on the football field. You're on the twenty-yard line and there's a tortoise crawling away from you toward the thirty-yard line."

I stopped listening. Dolly was coming up the outside steps toward the glass door, a dark-haired girl in a plaid skirt and a cardigan. She leaned on the door for a moment before she pushed it open. She seemed to have gone to pieces to some extent since Fargo had taken her picture. Her skin was sallow, her hair not recently brushed. Her dark uncertain glance slid over me without appearing to take me in.

She stopped short before she reached Dean Sutherland's office. Turning in a sudden movement, she started for the front door. She stopped again, between me and the two philosophers, and stood considering. I was struck by her faintly sullen beauty, her eyes dark and blind with thought. She turned around once more and trudged back along the hallway to meet her fate.

The office door closed behind her. I strolled past it after a while and heard the murmur of female voices inside, but nothing intelligible. From Dean Bradshaw's office across the hall the heads of departments emerged in a body. In spite of their glasses and their foreheads and their scholars' stoops, they looked a little like schoolboys let out for recess.

A woman with a short razorblade haircut came into the building and drew all their eyes. Her ash-blonde hair shone against the deep tan of her face. She attached herself to a man standing by himself in the doorway of the Dean's office.

He seemed less interested in her than she was in him. His good looks were rather gentle and melancholy, the kind that excite maternal passions in women. Though his brown wavy hair was graying at the temples, he looked rather like a college boy who twenty years after graduation glanced up from his books and found himself middle-aged.

Dean Sutherland opened the door of her office and made a sign to him. "Can you spare me a minute, Dr. Bradshaw? Something serious has come up." She was pale and grim, like a reluctant executioner.

He excused himself. The two Deans shut themselves up with Dolly. The woman with the short and shining haircut frowned at the closed door. Then she gave me an appraising glance, as if she was looking for a substitute for Bradshaw. She had a promising mouth and good legs and a restless predatory air. Her clothes had style.

"Looking for someone?" she said.

"Just waiting."

"For Lefty or for Godot? It makes a difference."

"For Lefty Godot. The pitcher."

"The pitcher in the rye?"

"He prefers bourbon."

"So do I," she said. "You sound like an anti-intellectual to me, Mr.—"

"Archer. Didn't I pass the test?"

"It depends on who does the grading."

"I've been thinking maybe I ought to go back to school. You make it seem attractive, and besides I feel so out of things when my intellectual friends are talking about Jack Kerouac and Eugene Burdick and other great writers, and I can't read. Seriously, if I were thinking of going back to college, would you recommend this place?"

She gave me another of her appraising looks. "Not for you, Mr. Archer. I think you'd feel more at home in some larger urban university, like Berkeley or Chicago. I went to Chicago myself. This college presents quite a contrast."

"In what way?"

"Innumerable ways. The quotient of sophistication here is very low, for one thing. This used to be a denominational college, and the moral atmosphere is still in Victorian stays." As if to demonstrate that she was not, she shifted her pelvis. "They tell me when Dylan Thomas visited here—but perhaps we'd better not go into that. *De mortuis nil nisi bonum.*"

"Do you teach Latin?"

"No, I have small Latin and less Greek. I try to teach modern languages. My name is Helen Haggerty, by the way. As I was saying, I wouldn't really recommend Pacific Point to you. The standards are improving every year, but there's still a great deal of dead wood around. You can see some of it from here."

She cast a sardonic glance toward the entrance, where five or six of her fellow professors were conducting a post-mortem of their conference with the Dean.

"That was Dean Bradshaw you were talking to, wasn't it?"

"Yes. Is he the one you want to see?"

"Among others."

"Don't be put off by his rather forbidding exterior. He's a fine scholar —the only Harvard doctor on the faculty—and he can advise you better than I ever could. But tell me honestly, are you really serious about going back to college? Aren't you kidding me a little?"

"Maybe a little."

"You could kid me more effectively over a drink. And I could use a drink, preferably bourbon."

"It's a handsome offer." And a sudden one, I thought. "Give me a rain check, will you? Right now I have to wait for Lefty Godot."

She looked more disappointed than she had any right to be. We parted on fairly good, mutually suspicious terms.

The fatal door I was watching opened at last. Dolly backed out thanking the two Deans effusively, and practically curtsying. But I saw when she turned around and headed for the entrance that her face was white and set.

I went after her, feeling a little foolish. The situation reminded me of a girl I used to follow home from Junior High. I never did work up enough nerve to ask her for the privilege of carrying her books. But I began to identify Dolly with that unattainable girl whose name I couldn't even remember now.

She hurried along the mall that bisected the campus, and started up the steps of the library building. I caught up with her.

"Mrs. Kincaid?"

She stopped as though I had shot her. I took her arm instinctively. She flung away my hand, and opened her mouth as if to call out for help. No sound came out. The other students around us, passing on the wide mall or chatting on the steps, paid no attention to her silent scream.

"I'd like very much to talk to you, Mrs. Kincaid."

She pushed her hair back, so forcefully that one of her eyes slanted up and gave her a Eurasian look. "Who are you?"

"A friend of your husband's. You've given Alex a bad three weeks."

"I suppose I have," she said, as if she had only just thought of it.

"You must have had a bad three weeks yourself, if you're fond of him at all. Are you?"

"Am I what?" She seemed to be slightly dazed.

"Fond of Alex."

"I don't know. I haven't had time to think about it. I don't wish to discuss it, with you or anyone. Are you really a friend of Alex's?"

"I think I can claim to be. He doesn't understand what you're doing to him. He's a pretty sad young man."

"No doubt he caught it from me. Spreading ruin is my specialty."

"It doesn't have to be. Why don't you call it off, whatever you're doing, and give it another try with Alex? He's waiting for you here in town right now."

"He can wait till doomsday, I'm not going back to him."

Her young voice was surprisingly firm, almost harsh. There was something about her eyes I didn't like. They were wide and dry and fixed, eyes which had forgotten how to cry.

"Did Alex hurt you in some way?"

"He wouldn't hurt a fly. You know that, if you're really a friend of his. He's a nice harmless boy, and *I* don't want to hurt *him*." She added with conscious drama: "Tell him to congratulate himself on his narrow escape."

"Is that the only message you have for your husband?"

"He isn't my husband, not really. Tell him to get an annulment. Tell him I'm not ready to settle down. Tell him I've decided to finish my education."

She made it sound like a solitary trip to the moon, one-way.

I went back to the Administration Building. The imitation flagstone pavement of the mall was flat and smooth, but I had the feeling that I was walking knee-deep in gopher holes. Dean Sutherland's door was closed and, when I knocked, her "Come in" was delayed and rather muffled.

Dean Bradshaw was still with her, looking more than ever like a college student on whom light frost had fallen during the night.

She was flushed, and her eyes were bright emerald green. "This is Mr. Archer, Brad, the detective I told you about."

He gave my hand a fiercely competitive grip. "It's a pleasure to meet you, sir. Actually," he said with an attempt at a smile, "it's rather a mixed pleasure under the circumstances. I very much regret the necessity of your coming here to our campus."

"The kind of work I do has to be done," I said a little defensively. "Mrs. Kincaid ran out on her husband, and some explanation is due him. Did she give any to you?"

Dean Sutherland put on her grim face. "She's not returning to him. She found out something on their wedding night so dreadful—"

Bradshaw raised his hand. "Wait a minute, Laura. The facts she divulged to you are in the nature of professional confidences. We certainly don't want this chap running back to her husband with them. The poor girl is frightened enough as it is."

"Frightened of her husband? I find that hard to believe," I said.

"She didn't pour out her heart to you," Laura Sutherland cried warmly. "Why do you suppose the poor child used a fake name? She was mortally afraid that he would track her down."

"You're being melodramatic, you know." Bradshaw's tone was indulgent. "The boy can't be as bad as all that."

"You didn't hear her, Brad. She told me things, as woman to woman, that I haven't even told you, and I don't intend to."

I said: "Perhaps she was lying."

"She most assuredly was not! I know the truth when I hear it. And my advice to you is to go back to that husband of hers, wherever he is, and tell him that you haven't been able to find her. She'll be safer and happier if you do."

"She seems to be safe enough. She certainly isn't happy. I talked to her outside for a minute."

Bradshaw tilted his head in my direction. "What did she say?"

"Nothing sensational. She made no accusations against Kincaid. In fact she blamed herself for the breakup. She says she wants to go on with her education."

"Good."

"Are you going to let her stay here?"

Bradshaw nodded. "We've decided to overlook her little deception. We believe in giving young people a certain amount of leeway, so long as it doesn't impinge on the rights of others. She can stay, at least for the present, and continue to use her pseudonym if she likes." He added with dry academic humor: " 'A rose by any other name,' you know."

"She's going to have her transcripts sent to us right away," Dean Sutherland said. "Apparently she's had two years of junior college and a semester at the university."

"What's she planning to study here?"

"Dolly is majoring in psychology. According to Professor Haggerty, she has a flair for it."

"How would Professor Haggerty know that?"

"She's Dolly's academic counselor. Apparently Dolly is deeply interested in criminal and abnormal psychology."

For some reason I thought of Chuck Begley's bearded head, with eyes opaque as a statue's. "When you were talking with Dolly, did she say anything about a man named Begley?"

"Begley?" They looked at each other and then at me. "Who," she asked, "is Begley?"

"It's possible he's her father. At any rate he had something to do with her leaving her husband. Incidentally I wouldn't put too much stock in her husband's Asiatic perversions or whatever it was she accused him of. He's a clean boy, and he respects her."

"You're entitled to your opinion," Laura Sutherland said, as though I wasn't. "But please don't act on it precipitately. Dolly is a sensitive young woman, and something has happened to shake her very deeply. You'll be doing them both a service by keeping them apart."

"I agree," Bradshaw said solemnly.

"The trouble is, I'm being paid to bring them together. But I'll think about it, and talk it over with Alex."

6
..

In the parking lot behind the building Professor Helen Haggerty was sitting at the wheel of the new black Thunderbird convertible. She had put the top down and parked it beside my car, as if for contrast. The late afternoon sunlight slanting across the foothills glinted on her hair and eyes and teeth.

"Hello again."

"Hello again," I said. "Are you waiting for me?"

"Only if you're left-handed."

"I'm ambidextrous."

"You would be. You threw me a bit of a curve just now."

"I did?"

"I know who you are." She patted a folded newspaper on the leather seat beside her. The visible headline said: "Mrs. Perrine Acquitted." Helen Haggerty said: "I think it's very exciting. The paper credits you with getting her off. But it's not quite clear how you did it."

"I simply told the truth, and evidently the jury believed me. At the time the alleged larceny was committed here in Pacific Point, I had Mrs. Perrine under close surveillance in Oakland."

"What for? Another larceny?"

"It wouldn't be fair to say."

She made a mock-sorrowful mouth, which fitted the lines of her face too well. "All the interesting facts are confidential. But I happened to be checked out for security. In fact my father is a policeman. So get in and tell me all about Mrs. Perrine."

"I can't do that."

"Or I have a better idea," she said with her bright unnatural smile. "Why don't you come over to my house for a drink?"

"I'm sorry, I have work to do."

"Detective work?"

"Call it that."

"Come *on*." With a subtle movement, her body joined in the invitation. "All work and no play makes Jack a dull boy. You don't want to be a dull boy and make me feel rejected. Besides, we have things to talk about."

"The Perrine case is over. Nothing could interest me less."

"It was the Dorothy Smith case I had in mind. Isn't that why you're on campus?"

"Who told you that?"

"The grapevine. Colleges have the most marvelously efficient grapevines, second only to penitentiaries."

"Are you familiar with penitentiaries?"

"Not intimately. But I wasn't lying when I told you my father was a policeman." A gray pinched expression touched her face. She covered it over with another smile. "We do have things in common. Why don't you come along?"

"All right. I'll follow you. It will save you driving me back."

"Wonderful."

She drove as rapidly as she operated, with a jerky nervousness and a total disregard for the rules of the road. Fortunately the campus was almost empty of cars and people. Diminished by the foothills and by their own long shadows, the buildings resembled a movie lot which had shut down for the night.

She lived back of Foothill Drive in a hillside house made out of aluminum and glass and black enameled steel. The nearest rooftop floated among the scrub oaks a quarter of a mile down the slope. You could stand in the living room by the central fireplace and see the blue mountains rising up on one side, the gray ocean falling away on the other. The offshore fog was pushing in to the land.

"Do you like my little eyrie?"

"Very much."

"It isn't really mine, alas. I'm only renting at present, though I have hopes. Sit down. What will you drink? I'm going to have a tonic."

"That will do nicely."

The polished tile floor was almost bare of furniture. I strolled around the large room, pausing by one of the glass walls to look out. A wild pigeon lay on the patio with its iridescent neck broken. Its faint spread-eagled image outlined in dust showed where it had flown against the glass.

I sat on a rope chair which probably belonged on the patio. Helen

Haggerty brought our drinks and disposed herself on a canvas chaise, where the sunlight would catch her hair again, and shine on her polished brown legs.

"I'm really just camping for now," she said. "I haven't sent for my furniture, because I don't know if I want it around me any more. I may just leave it in storage and start all over, and to hell with the history. Do you think that's a good idea, Curveball Lefty Lew?"

"Call me anything, I don't mind. I'd have to know the history."

"Ha. You never will." She looked at me sternly for a minute, and sipped her drink. "You might as well call me Helen."

"All right, Helen."

"You make it sound so formal. I'm not a formal person, and neither are you. Why should we be formal with each other?"

"You live in a glass house, for one thing," I said smiling. "I take it you haven't been in it long."

"A month. Less than a month. It seems longer. You're the first really interesting man I've met since I arrived here."

I dodged the compliment. "Where did you live before?"

"Here and there. There and here. We academic people are such nomads. It doesn't suit me. I'd like to settle down permanently. I'm getting old."

"It doesn't show."

"You're being gallant. Old for a woman, I mean. Men never grow old."

Now that she had me where she apparently wanted me, she wasn't crowding so hard, but she was working. I wished that she would stop, because I liked her. I downed my drink. She brought me a second tonic with all the speed and efficiency of a cocktail waitress. I couldn't get rid of the dismal feeling that each of us was there to use the other.

With the second tonic she let me look down her dress. She was smooth and brown as far as I could see. She arranged herself on the chaise with one hip up, so that I could admire the curve. The sun, in its final yellow flareup before setting, took possession of the room.

"Shall I pull the drapes?" she said.

"Don't bother for me. It'll be down soon. You were going to tell me about Dolly Kincaid alias Dorothy Smith."

"Was I?"

"You brought the subject of her up. I understand you're her academic counselor."

"And that's why you're interested in me, *n'est-ce pas?*" Her tone was mocking.

"I was interested in you before I knew of your connection with Dolly."

"Really?"

"Really. Here I am to prove it."

"Here you are because I lured you with the magic words Dorothy Smith. What's she doing on this campus anyway?" She sounded almost jealous of the girl.

"I was sort of hoping you knew the answer to that."

"Don't you?"

"Dolly gives conflicting stories, probably derived from romantic fiction—"

"I don't think so," she said. "She's a romantic all right—one of these romantic idealists who are always a jump or two behind her unconscious mind. I ought to know, I used to be one myself. But I also think she has some real trouble—appalling trouble."

"What was her story to you?"

"It was no story. It was the lousy truth. We'll come to it later on, if you're a good boy." She stirred like an odalisque in the dying light, and recrossed her polished legs. "How brave are you, Mr. Lew?"

"Men don't talk about how brave they are."

"You're full of copybook maxims," she said with some malice. "I want a serious answer."

"You could always try me."

"I may at that. I have a use—I mean, I need a man."

"Is that a proposal, or a business proposition, or are you thinking about some third party?"

"You're the man I have in mind. What would you say if I told you that I'm likely to be killed this weekend?"

"I'd advise you to go away for the weekend."

She leaned sideways toward me. Her breast hardly sagged. "Will you take me?"

"I have a prior commitment."

"If you mean little Mr. Alex Kincaid, I can pay you better than he can. Not to mention fringe benefits," she added irrepressibly.

"That college grapevine is working overtime. Or is Dolly the source of your information?"

"She's one of them. I could tell you things about that girl that would curl your hair."

"Go ahead. I've always wanted curly hair."

"Why should I? You don't offer a *quid pro quo*. You don't even take me seriously. I'm not used to being turned down flat, by the way."

"It's nothing personal. I'm just the phlegmatic type. Anyway, you don't need me. There are roads going in three directions—Mexico, the desert, or Los Angeles—and you have a nice fast car."

"I'm too nervous to drive any distance."

"Scared?"

She nodded.

"You put up a good front."

"A good front is all I have."

Her face looked closed and dark, perhaps because the sunlight had faded from the room. Only her hair seemed to hold the light. Beyond the slopes of her body I could see the mountains darkening down.

"Who wants to kill you, Helen?"

"I don't know exactly. But I've been threatened."

"How?"

"Over the telephone. I didn't recognize the voice. I couldn't tell if it was a man or a woman, or something in between." She shuddered.

"Why would anybody threaten you?"

"I don't know," she said without meeting my eyes.

"Teachers do get threatened from time to time. It usually isn't too serious. Have you had a run-in with any local crackpots?"

"I don't even know any local people. Except the ones at the college, of course."

"You may have a psychoneurotic in one of your classes."

She shook her head. "It's nothing like that. This is serious."

"How do you know?"

"I have my ways of knowing."

"Is it anything to do with Dolly Kincaid?"

"Perhaps. I can't say for sure. The situation is so complicated."

"Tell me about the complicated situation."

"It goes a long way back," she said, "all the way back to Bridgeton."

"Bridgeton?"

"The city where I was born and raised. The city where everything happened. I ran away, but you can't run away from the landscape of your dreams. My nightmares are still set in the streets of Bridgeton.

That voice on the telephone threatening to kill me was Bridgeton catching up with me. It was the voice of Bridgeton talking out of the past."

She was unconscious of herself, caught in a waking nightmare, but her description of it sounded false. I still didn't know whether to take her seriously.

"Are you sure you're not talking nonsense out of the present?"

"I'm not making this up," she said. "Bridgeton will be the death of me. Actually I've always known it would."

"Towns don't kill people."

"You don't know the proud city of my birth. It has quite a record along those lines."

"Where is it?"

"In Illinois, south of Chicago."

"You say that everything happened there. What do you mean?"

"Everything important—it was all over before I knew it had started. But I don't want to go into the subject."

"I can't very well help you unless you do."

"I don't believe you have any intention of helping me. You're simply trying to pump me for information."

It was true. I didn't care for her as she wished to be cared for by someone. I didn't entirely trust her. Her handsome body seemed to contain two alternating persons, one sensitive and candid, one hard and evasive.

She rose and went to the glass wall that faced the mountains. They had turned lavender and plum, with dark nocturnal blue in their clefts and groins. The entire evening, mountains and sky and city, was inundated with blue.

"*Die blaue Stunde,*" she said more or less to herself. "I used to love this hour. Now it gives me the mortal shivers."

I got up and stood behind her. "You're deliberately working on your own emotions."

"You know so much about me."

"I know you're an intelligent woman. Act like one. If the place is getting you down leave it, or stay here and take precautions. Ask for police protection."

"You're very free with brilliant suggestions not involving you. I asked for protection yesterday after I got the threatening telephone call. The Sheriff sent a man out. He said such calls were common, and usually involved teenagers."

"Could it have been a teenager?"

"I didn't think so. But the deputy said they sometimes disguise their voices. He told me not to worry."

"So don't worry."

"I can't help it. I'm afraid, Lew. Stay with me?"

She turned and leaned on my chest, moving her body tentatively against me. The only real feeling I had for her was pity. She was trying to use me, and using herself in order to use me.

"I have to run along," I said. "I told you at the start I have a prior commitment. But I'll check back on you."

"Thanks so much!"

She pulled away from me, so violently that she thudded like a bird against the glass wall.

7
..

I DROVE downhill through deepening twilight toward the Mariner's Rest Motel, telling myself in various tones of voice that I had done the right thing. The trouble was, in the scene I had just walked out of, there was no right thing to do—only sins of commission or omission.

A keyboy wearing a gold-braided yachting cap who looked as though he had never set foot on a dock told me that Alex Kincaid had registered and gone out again. I went to the Surf House for dinner. The spotlit front of the big hotel reminded me of Fargo and all the useless pictures I had ordered from him.

He was in the dark room adjoining his little office. When he came out he was wearing rectangular dark glasses against the light. I couldn't see his eyes, but his mouth was hostile. He picked up a bulky manila envelope from the desk and thrust it at me.

"I thought you were in a hurry for these prints."

"I was. Things came up. We found her."

"So now you don't want 'em? My wife worked in this sweatbox half the afternoon to get 'em ready."

"I'll take them. Kincaid will have a use for them if I don't. How much?"

"Twenty-five dollars including tax. It's actually $24.96."

I gave him two tens and a five, and his mouth went through three stages of softening. "Are they getting back together?"

"I don't know yet."

"Where did you find her?"

"Attending the local college. She has a job driving for an old lady named Bradshaw."

"The one with the Rolls?"

"Yes. You know her?"

"I wouldn't say that. She and her son generally eat Sunday buffet lunch in the dining room. She's quite a character. I took a candid picture of them once, on the chance they'd order some copies, and she threatened to smash my camera with her cane. I felt like telling the old biddy her face was enough to smash it."

"But you didn't?"

"I can't afford such luxuries." He spread out his chemical-stained hands. "She's a local institution, and she could get me fired."

"I understand she's loaded."

"Not only that. Her son is a big wheel in educational circles. He seems like a nice enough joe, in spite of the Harvard lah-de-dah. As a matter of fact he calmed her down when she wanted to smash my Leica. But it's hard to figure a guy like that, a good-looking guy in his forties, still tied to his old lady's apron-strings."

"It happens in the best of families."

"Yeah, especially in the best. I see a lot of these sad cookies waiting around for the money, and by the time they inherit it's too late. At least Bradshaw had the guts to go out and make a career for himself." Fargo looked at his watch. "Speaking of careers, I've already put in a twelve-hour day and I've got about two hours of developing to do. See you."

I started toward the hotel coffee shop. Fargo came running after me along the corridor. The rectangular dark glasses lent his face a robot-like calm which went oddly with the movements of his legs and arms.

"I almost forgot to ask you. You get a line on this Begley?"

"I talked to him for quite a while. He didn't give too much. He's living with a woman on Shearwater Beach."

"Who's the lucky woman?" Fargo said.

"Madge Gerhardi is her name. Do you know her?"

"No, but I think I know who he is. If I could take another look at
him—"

"Come over there now."

"I can't. I'll tell you who I *think* he is under all that seaweed, if you
promise not to quote me. There's such a thing as accidental resemblance, and a libel suit is the last thing I need."

"I promise not to quote you."

"See that you don't." He took a deep breath like a skin diver getting
ready to go for the bottom. "I think he's a fellow named Thomas Mc-
Gee who murdered his wife in Indian Springs about ten years ago. I
took a picture of McGee when I was a cub reporter on the paper, but
they never used the picture. They never play up those Valley cases."

"You're sure he murdered his wife?"

"Yeah, it was an open-and-shut case. I don't have time to go into details, in fact they're getting pretty hazy at this late date. But most of
the people around the courthouse thought he should have been given
first degree. Gil Stevens convinced the jury to go for second degree,
which explains how he's out so quick."

Remembering Begley's story about his ten years on the other side of
the world, the other side of the moon, I thought that ten years wasn't
so very quick.

The fog was dense along Shearwater Beach. It must have been high
tide: I could hear the surf roaring up under the cottages and sucking
at their pilings. The smell of iodine hung in the chilly air.

Madge Gerhardi answered the door and looked at me rather vaguely.
The paint on her eyelids couldn't hide the fact that they were swollen.

"You're the detective, aren't you?"

"Yes. May I come in?"

"Come in if you want. It won't do any good. He's gone."

I'd already guessed it from her orphaned air. I followed her along
a musty hallway into the main room, which was high and raftered.
Spiders had been busy in the angles of the rafters, which were webbed
and blurred as if fog had seeped in at the corners. The rattan furniture
was coming apart at the joints. The glasses and empty bottles and half-
empty bottles standing around on the tables and the floor suggested that
a party had been going on for some days and might erupt again if I
wasn't careful.

The woman kicked over an empty bottle on the way to the settee, where she flung herself down.

"It's your fault he's gone," she complained. "He started to pack right after you were here this afternoon."

I sat on a rattan chair facing her. "Did Begley say where he was going?"

"Not to me he didn't. He did say I wasn't to expect him back, that it was all off. Why did you have to scare him, anyway? Chuck never did anybody any harm."

"He scares very easily."

"Chuck is sensitive. He's had a great deal of trouble. Many's the time he told me that all he wanted was a quiet nook where he could write about his experiences. He's writing an autobiographical novel about his experiences."

"His experiences in New Caledonia?"

She said with surprising candor: "I don't think Chuck ever set foot in New Caledonia. He got that business about the chrome mine out of an old *National Geographic* magazine. I don't believe he ever left this country."

"Where has he been?"

"In the pen," she said. "You know that, or you wouldn't be after him. I think it's a dirty crying shame, when a man has paid his debt to society and proved that he can rehabilitate himself—"

It was Begley she was quoting, Begley's anger she was expressing, but she couldn't sustain the anger or remember the end of the quotation. She looked around the wreckage of the room in dim alarm, as if she had begun to suspect that his rehabilitation was not complete.

"Did he tell you what he was in for, Mrs. Gerhardi?"

"Not in so many words. He read me a piece from his book the other night. This character in the book was in the pen and he was thinking about the past and how they framed him for a murder he didn't commit. I asked him if the characters stood for him. He wouldn't say. He went into one of his deep dark silences."

She went into one of her own. I could feel the floor trembling under my feet. The sea was surging among the pilings like the blithe mindless forces of dissolution. The woman said:

"Was Chuck in the pen for murder?"

"I was told tonight that he murdered his wife ten years ago. I haven't confirmed it. Can you?"

She shook her head. Her face had lengthened as if by its own weight, like unbaked dough. "It must be a mistake."

"I hope so. I was also told that his real name is Thomas McGee. Did he ever use that name?"

"No."

"It does tie in with another fact," I said, thinking aloud. "The girl he went to visit at the Surf House had the same name before she was married. He said the girl resembled his daughter. I think she is his daughter. Did he ever talk about her?"

"Never."

"Or bring her here?"

"No. If she's his daughter, he wouldn't bring her here." She reached for the empty bottle she had kicked over, set it on its base, and slumped back onto the settee, as if morally exhausted by the effort.

"How long did Begley, or McGee, live here with you?"

"A couple of weeks is all. We were going to be married. It's lonely living here without a man."

"I can imagine."

She drew a little life from the sympathy in my voice: "They just don't stay with me. I try to make things nice for them, but they don't stay. I should have stuck with my first husband." Her eyes were far away and long ago. "He treated me like a queen but I was young and foolish. I didn't know any better than to leave him."

We listened to the water under the house.

"Do you think Chuck went away with this girl you call his daughter?"

"I doubt it," I said. "How did he leave here, Mrs. Gerhardi? By car?"

"He wouldn't let me drive him. He said he was going up to the corner and catch the L.A. bus. It stops at the corner if you signal it. He walked up the road with his suitcase and out of sight." She sounded both regretful and relieved.

"About what time?"

"Around three o'clock."

"Did he have any money?"

"He must have had some for the bus fare. He couldn't have had much. I've been giving him a little money, but he would only take what he needed from me, and then it always had to be a loan. Which he said he would pay back when he got his book of experiences on the market. But I don't care if he never pays me back. He was nice to have around."

"Really?"

"Really he was. Chuck is a smart man. I don't care what he's done in the course of his life. A man can change for the better. He never gave me a bad time once." She made a further breakthrough into candor: "I was the one who gave him the bad times. I have a drinking problem. He only drank with me to be sociable. He didn't want me to drink alone." She blinked her gin-colored eyes. "Would you like a drink?"

"No thanks. I have to be on my way." I got up and stood over her. "You're sure he didn't tell you where he was going?"

"Los Angeles is all I know. He promised I'd hear from him but I don't expect it. It's over."

"If he should write or phone will you let me know?"

She nodded. I gave her my card, and told her where I was staying. When I went out, the fog had moved inland as far as the highway.

8

I STOPPED at the motel again on my way to the Bradshaw house. The keyboy told me that Alex was still out. I wasn't surprised when I found his red Porsche parked under the Bradshaws' hedge beside the road.

The moon was rising behind the trees. I let my thoughts rise with it, imagining that Alex had got together with his bride and they were snug in the gatehouse, talking out their troubles. The sound of the girl's crying wiped out the hopeful image. Her voice was loud and terrible, almost inhuman. Its compulsive rhythms rose and fell like the ululations of a hurt cat.

The door of the gatehouse was slightly ajar. Light spilled around its edges, as if extruded by the pressure of the noise inside. I pushed it open.

"Get out of here," Alex said.

They were on a studio bed in the tiny sitting room. He had his arms around her, but the scene was not domestic. She seemed to be fighting him, trying to struggle out of his embrace. It was more like a scene in a closed ward where psychiatric nurses will hold their violent patients, sometimes for hours on end, rather than strap them in canvas jackets.

Her blouse was torn, so that one of her breasts was almost naked. She twisted her unkempt head around and let me see her face. It was gray and stunned, and it hardly changed expression when she screamed at me:

"Get out!"

"I think I better stick around," I said to both of them.

I closed the door and crossed the room. The rhythm of her crying was running down. It wasn't really crying. Her eyes were dry and fixed in her gray flesh. She hid them against her husband's body.

His face was shining white.

"What happened, Alex?"

"I don't really know. I was waiting for her when she got home a few minutes ago. I couldn't get much sense out of her. She's awfully upset about something."

"She's in shock," I said, thinking that he was close to it himself. "Was she in an accident?"

"Something like that."

His voice trailed off in a mumble. His look was inward, as if he was groping for the strength to handle this new problem.

"Is she hurt, Alex?"

"I don't think so. She came running down the road, and then she tried to run away again. She put up quite a battle when I tried to stop her."

As if to demonstrate her prowess as a battler, she freed her hands and beat at his chest. There was blood on her hands. It left red dabs on his shirt-front.

"Let me go," she pleaded. "I want to die. I deserve to."

"She's bleeding, Alex."

He shook his head. "It's somebody else's blood. A friend of hers was killed."

"And it's all my fault," she said in a flat voice.

He caught her wrists and held her. I could see manhood biting into his face. "Be quiet, Dolly. You're talking nonsense."

"Am I? She's lying in her blood, and I'm the one who put her there."

"Who is she talking about?" I said to Alex.

"Somebody called Helen. I've never heard of her."

I had.

The girl began to talk in her wispy monotone, so rapidly and imprecisely that I could hardly follow. She was a devil and so was her father before her and so was Helen's father and they had the bond of murder between them which made them blood sisters and she had betrayed her blood sister and done her in.

"What did you do to Helen?"

"I should have kept away from her. They die when I go near them."

"That's crazy talk," Alex said softly. "You never hurt anybody."

"What do you know about me?"

"All I need to. I'm in love with you."

"Don't say that. It only makes me want to kill myself." Sitting upright in the circle of his arms, she looked at her bloody hands and cried some more of her terrible dry tears. "I'm a criminal."

Alex looked up at me, his eyes blue-black. "Can you make any sense of it?"

"Not much."

"You can't really think she killed this Helen person?" We were talking past Dolly as if she was deaf or out of her head, and she accepted this status.

"We don't even know that anybody's been killed," I said. "Your wife is loaded with some kind of guilt, but it may belong to somebody else. I found out a little tonight about her background, or I think I did." I sat on the shabby brown studio bed beside them and said to Dolly: "What's your father's name?"

She didn't seem to hear me.

"Thomas McGee?"

She nodded abruptly, as if she'd been struck from behind. "He's a lying monster. He made me into a monster."

"How did he do that?"

The question triggered another nonstop sentence. "He shot her," she said with her chin on her shoulder, "and left her lying in her blood but I told Aunt Alice and the policemen and the court took care of him but now he's done it again."

"To Helen?"

"Yes, and I'm responsible. I caused it to happen."

She seemed to take a weird pleasure in acknowledging her guilt. Her gray and jaded looks, her tearless crying, her breathless run-on talking and her silences, were signs of an explosive emotional crisis. Under the raw melodrama of her self-accusations, I had the sense of something valuable and fragile in danger of being permanently broken.

"We'd better not try to question her any more," I said. "I doubt right now she can tell the difference between true and false."

"Can't I?" she said malignly. "Everything I remember is true and I can remember everything from year one, the quarrels and the beatings, and then he finally shot her in her blood—"

I cut in: "Shut up, Dolly, or change the record. You need a doctor. Do you have one in town here?"

"No. I don't need a doctor. Call the police. I want to make a confession."

She was playing a game with us and her own mind, I thought, performing dangerous stunts on the cliff edge of reality, daring the long cloudy fall.

"You want to confess that you're a monster," I said.

It didn't work. She answered matter-of-factly: "I am a monster."

The worst of it was, it was happening physically before my eyes. The chaotic pressures in her were changing the shape of her mouth and jaw. She peered at me dully through a fringe of hair. I'd hardly have recognized her as the girl I talked to on the library steps that day.

I turned to Alex. "Do you know any doctors in town?"

He shook his head. His short hair stood up straight as if live electricity was running through him from his contact with his wife. He never let go of her.

"I could call Dad in Long Beach."

"That might be a good idea, later."

"Couldn't we take her to the hospital?"

"Not without a private doctor to protect her."

"Protect her from what?"

"The police, or the psycho ward. I don't want her answering any official questions until I have a chance to check on Helen."

The girl whimpered. "I don't want to go to the psycho ward. I had a doctor in town here a long time ago." She was sane enough to be frightened, and frightened enough to cooperate.

"What's his name?"

"Dr. Godwin. Dr. James Godwin. He's a psychiatrist. I used to come in and see him when I was a little girl."

"Do you have a phone in the gatehouse?"

"Mrs. Bradshaw lets me use her phone."

I left them and walked up the driveway to the main house. I could smell fog even at this level now. It was rolling down from the mountains, flooding out the moon, as well as rising from the sea.

The big white house was quiet, but there was light behind some of the windows. I pressed the bell push. Chimes tinkled faintly behind the heavy door. It was opened by a large dark woman in a cotton print dress. She was crudely handsome, in spite of the pitted acne scars on her cheekbones. Before I could say anything she volunteered that Dr. Bradshaw was out and Mrs. Bradshaw was on her way to bed.

"I just want to use the phone. I'm a friend of the young lady in the gatehouse."

She looked me over doubtfully. I wondered if Dolly's contagion had given me a wild irrational look.

"It's important," I said. "She needs a doctor."

"Is she sick?"

"Quite sick."

"You shouldn't ought to leave her alone."

"She isn't alone. Her husband's with her."

"But she is not married."

"We won't argue about it. Are you going to let me call a doctor?"

She stepped back reluctantly and ushered me past the foot of a curved staircase into a book-lined study where a lamp burned like a night light on the desk. She indicated the telephone beside it, and took up a watchful position by the door.

"Could I have a little privacy, please? You can search me on the way out."

She sniffed, and withdrew out of sight. I thought of calling Helen's house, but she wasn't in the telephone directory. Dr. James Godwin fortunately was. I dialed his number. The voice that eventually answered was so quiet and neutral that I couldn't tell if it was male or female.

"May I speak to Dr. Godwin?"

"This is Dr. Godwin." He sounded weary of his identity.

"My name is Lew Archer. I've just been talking to a girl who says she used to be your patient. Her maiden name was Dolly or Dorothy McGee. She's not in a good way."

"Dolly? I haven't seen her for ten or eleven years. What's troubling her?"

"You're the doctor, and I think you'd better see her. She's hysterical, to put it mildly, talking incoherently about murder."

He groaned. With my other ear I could hear Mrs. Bradshaw call hoarsely down the stairs:

"What's going on down there, Maria?"

"The girl Dolly is sick, he says."

"Who says?"

"I dunno. Some man."

"Why didn't you tell me she was sick?"

"I just did."

Dr. Godwin was talking in a small dead voice that sounded like the whispering ghost of the past: "I'm not surprised this material should come up. There was a violent death in her family when she was a child, and she was violently exposed to it. She was in the immediate pre-pubic period, and already in a vulnerable state."

I tried to cut through the medical jargon: "Her father killed her mother, is that right?"

"Yes." The word was like a sigh. "The poor child found the body. Then they made her testify in court. We permit such barbarous things—" He broke off, and said in a sharply different tone: "Where are you calling from?"

"Roy Bradshaw's house. Dolly is in the gatehouse with her husband. It's on Foothill Drive—"

"I know where it is. In fact I just got in from attending a dinner with Dean Bradshaw. I have another call to make, and then I'll be right with you."

I hung up and sat quite still for a moment in Bradshaw's leather-cushioned swivel chair. The walls of books around me, dense with the past, formed a kind of insulation against the present world and its disasters. I hated to get up.

Mrs. Bradshaw was waiting in the hallway. Maria had disappeared. The old woman was breathing audibly, as if the excitement was a strain on her heart. She clutched the front of her pink wool bathrobe against her loosely heaving bosom.

"What's the trouble with the girl?"

"She's emotionally upset."

"Did she have a fight with her husband? He's a hothead, I could hardly blame her."

"The trouble goes a little deeper than that. I just called Dr. Godwin the psychiatrist. She's been his patient before."

"You mean to tell me the girl is—?" She tapped her veined temple with a swollen knuckle.

A car had stopped in the driveway, and I didn't have to answer her question. Roy Bradshaw came in the front door. The fog had curled his hair tight, and his thin face was open. It closed up when he saw us standing together at the foot of the stairs.

"You're late," Mrs. Bradshaw said in an accusing tone. "You go out wining and dining and leave me here to cope all by myself. Where were you, anyway?"

"The Alumni banquet. You can't have forgotten that. You know how those banquets drag on, and I'm afraid I made my own contribution to the general boredom." He hesitated, becoming aware of something in the scene more serious than an old woman's possessiveness. "What's up, Mother?"

"This man tells me the little girl in the gatehouse has gone out of her mind. Why did you have to send me a girl like that, a psychiatric patient?"

"I didn't send her."

"Who did?"

I tried to break in on their foolishness, but neither of them heard me. They were intent on their game of emotional ping-pong, which had probably been going on since Roy Bradshaw was a boy.

"It was either Laura Sutherland or Helen Haggerty," he was saying. "Professor Haggerty is her counselor, and it was probably she."

"Whichever one it was, I want you to instruct her to be more careful next time. If you don't care about my personal safety—"

"I *do* care about your safety. I care very much about your safety." His voice was strained thin between anger and submissiveness. "I had no idea there was anything the matter with the girl."

"There probably wasn't," I said. "She's had a shock. I just called a doctor for her. Dr. Godwin."

Bradshaw turned slowly in my direction. His face was strangely soft and empty, like a sleeping boy's.

"I know Dr. Godwin," he said. "What kind of a shock did she sustain?"

"It isn't clear. I'd like to talk to you in private."

Mrs. Bradshaw announced in a trembling voice: "This is my house, young man."

She was telling me, but she was also reminding Bradshaw, flicking the economic whip at him. He felt its sting:

"I live here, too. I have my duties to you, and I try to perform them satisfactorily. I also have my duties to the students."

"You and your precious students." Her bright black eyes were scornful. "Very well. You can have your privacy. I'll go outside."

She actually started for the front door, drawing her bathrobe around her lumpy body as if she was being cast out into a blizzard. Bradshaw went after her. There were pullings and haulings and cajolings and a final goodnight embrace, from which I averted my eyes, before she climbed heavily up the stairs, with his assistance.

"You mustn't judge Mother too harshly," he said when he came down. "She's getting old, and it makes it hard for her to adjust to crises. She's really a generous-hearted soul, as I have good reason to know."

I didn't argue with him. He knew her better than I did.

"Well, Mr. Archer, shall we go into my study?"

"We can save time if we talk on the road."

"On the road?"

"I want you to take me to Helen Haggerty's place if you know where it is. I'm not sure I can find it in the dark."

"Why on earth? Surely you're not taking Mother seriously? She was simply talking to hear herself talk."

"I know. But Dolly's been doing some talking, too. She says that Helen Haggerty is dead. She has blood on her hands, by way of supporting evidence. I think we'd better go up there and see where the blood came from."

He gulped. "Yes. Of course. It isn't far from here. In fact it's only a few minutes by the bridle path. But at night we'll probably get there faster in my car."

We went out to his car. I asked him to stop at the gatehouse, and glanced in. Dolly was lying on the studio bed with her face turned to the wall. Alex had covered her with a blanket. He was standing by the bed with his hands loose.

"Dr. Godwin is on his way," I said in a low voice. "Keep him here till I get back, will you?"

He nodded, but he hardly appeared to see me. His look was still inward, peering into depths he hadn't begun to imagine until tonight.

9

BRADSHAW'S compact car was equipped with seat-belts, and he made me fasten mine before we set out. Between his house and Helen's I told him as much as I thought he needed to know about Dolly's outpourings. His response was sympathetic. At my suggestion, he left his car by the mailbox at the foot of Helen's lane. When we got out I could hear a foghorn moaning from the low sea.

Another car, a dark convertible whose shape I could barely make out through the thickening air, was parked without lights down the road. I ought to have shaken it down. But I was pressed by my own private guilt, and eager to see if Helen was alive.

Her house was a faint blur of light high among the trees. We started up the hairpinning gravel driveway. An owl flew low over our heads, silent as a traveling piece of fog. It lit somewhere in the gray darkness, called to its mate, and was answered. The two invisible birds seemed to be mocking us with their sad distant foghorn voices.

I heard a repeated crunching up ahead. It resolved itself into footsteps approaching in the gravel. I touched Bradshaw's sleeve, and we stood still. A man loomed up above us. He had on a topcoat and a snap-brim hat. I couldn't quite see his face."

"Hello."

He didn't answer me. He must have been young and bold. He ran straight at us, shouldering me, spinning Bradshaw into the bushes. I tried to hold him but his downhill momentum carried him away.

I chased his running footfalls down to the road, and got there in time to see him climbing into the convertible. Its engine roared and its parking lights came on as I ran toward it. Before it leaped away, I caught a glimpse of a Nevada license and the first four figures of the license number. I went back to Bradshaw's car and wrote them down in my notebook: FT37.

I climbed up the driveway a second time. Bradshaw had reached the house. He was sitting on the doorstep with a sick look on his face. Light poured over him from the open door and cast his bowed shadow brokenly on the flagstones.

"She *is* dead, Mr. Archer."

I looked in. Helen was lying on her side behind the door. Blood had run from a round bullet hole in her forehead and formed a pool on the tiles. It was coagulating at the edges, like frost on a dark puddle. I touched her sad face. She was already turning cold. It was nine-seventeen by my watch.

Between the door and the pool of blood I found a faint brown hand-print still sticky to the touch. It was about the size of Dolly's hand. She could have fallen accidentally, but the thought twisted through my head that she was doing her best to be tried for murder. Which didn't necessarily mean that she was innocent.

Bradshaw leaned like a convalescent in the doorway. "Poor Helen. This is a heinous thing. Do you suppose the fellow who attacked us—?"

"I'd say she's been dead for at least two hours. Of course he may have come back to wipe out his traces or retrieve his gun. He acted guilty."

"He certainly did."

"Did Helen Haggerty ever mention Nevada?"

He looked surprised. "I don't believe so. Why?"

"The car our friend drove away in had a Nevada license."

"I see. Well, I suppose we must call the police."

"They'll resent it if we don't."

"Will you? I'm afraid I'm feeling rather shaken."

"It's better if you do, Bradshaw. She worked for the college, and you can keep the scandal to a minimum."

"Scandal? I hadn't even thought of that."

He forced himself to walk past her to the telephone on the far side of the room. I went through the other rooms quickly. One bedroom was completely bare except for a kitchen chair and a plain table which she had been using as a working desk. A sheaf of test papers conjugating French irregular verbs lay on top of the table. Piles of books, French and German dictionaries and grammars and collections of poetry and prose, stood around it. I opened one at the flyleaf. It was rubber-stamped in purple ink: Professor Helen Haggerty, Maple Park College, Maple Park, Illinois.

The other bedroom was furnished in rather fussy elegance with new French Provincial pieces, lambswool rugs on the polished tile floor, soft heavy handwoven drapes at the enormous window. The wardrobe contained a row of dresses and skirts with Magnin and Bullocks labels, and under them a row of new shoes to match. The chest of drawers was stuffed with sweaters and more intimate garments, but nothing really intimate. No letters, no snapshots.

The bathroom had wall-to-wall carpeting and a triangular sunken tub. The medicine chest was well supplied with beauty cream and cosmetics and sleeping pills. The latter had been prescribed by a Dr. Otto Schrenk and dispensed by Thompson's Drug Store in Bridgeton, Illinois, on June 17 of this year.

I turned out the bathroom wastebasket on the carpet. Under crumpled wads of used tissue I found a letter in an airmail envelope postmarked in Bridgeton, Illinois, a week ago and addressed to Mrs. Helen Haggerty. The single sheet inside was signed simply "Mother," and gave no return address.

Dear Helen

It was thoughtful of you to send me a card from sunny Cal my favorite state of the union even though it is years since I was out there. Your father keeps promising to make the trip with me on his vacation but something always comes up to put it off. Anyway his blood pressure is some better and that is a blessing. I'm glad you're well. I wish you would reconsider about the divorce but I suppose that's all over and done with. It's a pity you and Bert couldn't stay together. He is a good man in his way. But I suppose distant pastures look greenest.

Your father is still furious of course. He won't let me mention your name. He hasn't really forgiven you for when you left home in the first place, or forgiven himself either I guess, it takes two to make a quarrel. Still you are his daughter and you shouldn't have talked to him the way you did. I don't mean to recriminate. I keep hoping for a reconcilement between you two before he dies. He is not getting any younger, you know, and I'm not either, Helen. You're a smart girl with a good education and if you wanted to you could write him a letter that would make him feel different about "things." You are his only daughter after all and you've never taken it back that he was a crooked stormtrooper. That is a hard word for a policeman to swallow from anybody and it still rankles him after more than twenty years. Please write.

I put the letter back in the wastebasket with the other discarded paper. Then I washed my hands and returned to the main room. Bradshaw was sitting in the rope chair, stiffly formal even when alone. I wondered if this was his first experience of death. It wasn't mine by a long shot, but this death had hit me especially hard. I could have prevented it.

The fog outside was getting denser. It moved against the glass wall of the house, and gave me the queer sensation that the world had dropped away, and Bradshaw and I were floating together in space, unlikely *gemini* encapsulated with the dead woman.

"What did you tell the police?"

"I talked to the Sheriff personally. He'll be here shortly. I gave him only the necessary minimum. I didn't know whether or not to say anything about Mrs. Kincaid."

"We have to explain our discovery of the body. But you don't have to repeat anything she said. It's purely hearsay so far as you're concerned."

"Do you seriously regard her as a suspect in this?"

"I have no opinion yet. We'll see what Dr. Godwin has to say about her mental condition. I hope Godwin is good at his job."

"He's the best we have in town. I saw him tonight, oddly enough. He sat at the speaker's table with me at the Alumni dinner, until he was called away."

"He mentioned seeing you at dinner."

"Yes. Jim Godwin and I are old friends." He seemed to lean on the thought.

I looked around for something to sit on, but there was only Helen's canvas chaise. I squatted on my heels. One of the things in the house that puzzled me was the combination of lavish spending and bare poverty, as if two different women had taken turns furnishing it. A princess and a pauper.

I pointed this out to Bradshaw, and he nodded: "It struck me when I was here the other evening. She seems to have spent her money on inessentials."

"Where did the money come from?"

"She gave me to understand she had a private income. Heaven knows she didn't dress as she did on an assistant professor's salary."

"Did you know Professor Haggerty well?"

"Hardly. I did escort her to one or two college functions, as well as the opening concert of the fall season. We discovered a common passion for Hindemith." He made a steeple of his fingers. "She's a—she was a very presentable woman. But I wasn't close to her, in any sense. She didn't encourage intimacy."

I raised my eyebrows. Bradshaw colored slightly.

"I don't mean sexual intimacy, for heaven's sake. She wasn't my type at all. I mean that she didn't talk about herself to any extent."

"Where did she come from?"

"Some small college in the Middle West, Maple Park I believe. She'd already left there and come out here when we appointed her. It was an emergency appointment, necessitated by Dr. Farrand's coronary. Fortunately Helen was available. I don't know what our Department of Modern Languages will do now, with the semester already under way."

He sounded faintly resentful of the dead woman's absenteeism. While it was natural enough for him to be thinking of the college and its problems, I didn't like it. I said with deliberate intent to jolt him:

"You and the college are probably going to have worse problems than finding a teacher to take her place."

"What do you mean?"

"She wasn't an ordinary female professor. I spent some time with her this afternoon. She told me among other things that her life had been threatened."

"How dreadful," he said, as though the threat of murder were somehow worse than the fact. "Who on earth—?"

"She had no idea, and neither have I. I thought perhaps you might. Did she have enemies on the campus?"

"I certainly can't think of any. You understand, I didn't know Helen at all well."

"I got to know her pretty well, in a hurry. I gathered she'd had her share of experience, not all of it picked up in graduate seminars and faculty teas. Did you go into her background before you hired her?"

"Not too thoroughly. It was an emergency appointment, as I said, and in any case it wasn't my responsibility. The head of her department, Dr. Geisman, was favorably impressed by her credentials and made the appointment."

Bradshaw seemed to be delicately letting himself off the hook. I wrote down Geisman's name in my notebook.

"Her background ought to be gone into," I said. "It seems she was married, and recently divorced. I also want to find out more about her relations with Dolly. Apparently they were close."

"You're not suggesting a Lesbian attachment? We have had—" He decided not to finish the sentence.

"I'm not suggesting anything. I'm looking for information. How did Professor Haggerty happen to become Dolly's counselor?"

"In the normal way, I suppose."

"What is the normal way of acquiring a counselor?"

"It varies. Mrs. Kincaid was an upperclassman, and we usually permit upperclassmen to choose their own counselors, so long as the counselor in question has an opening in his or her schedule."

"Then Dolly probably chose Professor Haggerty, and initiated the friendship herself?"

"She had every chance to. Of course it may have been pure accident."

As if we had each received a signal on a common wavelength, we turned and looked at Helen Haggerty's body. It seemed small and lonely at the far end of the room. Our joint flight with it through cloudy space had been going on for a long time. I looked at my watch. It was only nine-thirty-one, fourteen minutes since our arrival. Time seemed to have slowed down, dividing itself into innumerable fractions, like Zeno's space or marijuana hours.

With a visible effort, Bradshaw detached his gaze from the body. His moment of communion with it had cost him the last of his boyish look. He leaned toward me with deep lines of puzzlement radiating from his eyes and mouth:

"I don't understand what Mrs. Kincaid said to you. Do you mean to say she actually confessed this—this murder?"

"A cop or a prosecutor might say so. Fortunately none was present. I've heard a lot of confessions, good ones and phony ones. Hers was a phony one, in my opinion."

"What about the blood?"

"She may have slipped and fallen in it."

"Then you don't think we should mention any of it to the Sheriff?"

"If you don't mind stretching a point."

His face showed that he minded, but after some hesitation he said: "We'll keep it to ourselves, at least for the present. After all she was a student of ours, however briefly."

Bradshaw didn't notice his use of the past tense, but I did, and it depressed me. I think we were both relieved by the sound of the Sheriff's car coming up the hill. It was accompanied by a mobile laboratory. Within a few minutes a fingerprint man and a deputy coroner and a photographer had taken over the room and changed its character. It became impersonal and drab like any room anywhere in which murder had been committed. In a curious way the men in uniform seemed to be doing the murder a second and final time, annulling Helen's rather garish aura, converting her into laboratory meat and courtroom exhibits. My raw nerves jumped when the bulbs flashed in her corner.

Sheriff Herman Crane was a thick-shouldered man in a tan gabardine suit. His only suggestion of uniform was a slightly broad-brimmed hat with a woven leather band. His voice had an administrative ring, and his manner had the heavy ease of a politician, poised between bullying and flattery. He treated Bradshaw with noisy deference, as if Bradshaw was a sensitive plant of undetermined value but some importance.

Me he treated the way cops always treated me, with occupational suspicion. They suspected me of the misdemeanor of doing my own thinking. I did succeed in getting Sheriff Crane to dispatch a patrol car in pursuit of the convertible with the Nevada license. He complained that his department was seriously understaffed, and he didn't think road blocks were indicated at this stage of the game. At this stage of the game I made up my mind not to cooperate fully with him.

The Sheriff and I sat in the chaise and the rope chair respectively and had a talk while a deputy who knew speedwriting took notes. I told him that Dolly Kincaid, the wife of a client of mine, had discovered the body of her college counselor Professor Haggerty and reported the discovery to me. She had been badly shocked, and was under a doctor's care.

Before the Sheriff could press me for further details, I gave him a *verbatim* account, or as close to *verbatim* as I could make it, of my conversation with Helen about the death threat. I mentioned that she had reported it to his office, and he seemed to take this as a criticism:

"We're understaffed, like I said. I can't keep experienced men. Los Angeles lures 'em away with salaries we can't pay and pie in the sky." I was from Los Angeles, as he knew, and the implication was that I was obscurely to blame. "If I put a man on guard duty in every house that got a crank telephone call, I wouldn't have anybody left to run the department."

"I understand that."

"I'm glad you do. Something I don't understand—how did this conversation you had with the decedent happen to take place?"

"Professor Haggerty approached me and asked me to come up here with her."

"What time was this?"

"I didn't check the time. It was shortly before sundown. I was here for about an hour."

"What did she have in mind?"

"She wanted me to stay with her, for protection. I'm sorry I didn't." Simply having the chance to say this made me feel better.

"You mean she wanted to hire you, as a bodyguard?"

"That was the idea." There was no use going into the complex interchange that had taken place between Helen and me, and failed.

"How did she know you were in the bodyguard business?"

"I'm not, exactly. She knew I was an investigator because she saw my name in the paper."

"Sure enough," he said. "You testified in the Perrine case this morning. Maybe I ought to congratulate you because Perrine got off."

"Don't bother."

"No, I don't think I will. The Perrine broad was guilty as hell and you know it and I know it."

"The jury didn't think so," I said mildly.

"Juries can be fooled and witnesses can be bought. Suddenly you're very active in our local crime circles, Mr. Archer." The words had the weight of an implied threat. He flung out a heavy careless hand toward the body. "This woman, this Professor Haggerty here, you're sure she wasn't a friend of yours?"

"We became friends to a certain extent."

"In an hour?"

"It can happen in an hour. Anyway, we had a previous conversation at the college today."

"What about before today? Did you have other previous conversations?"

"No. I met her today for the first time."

Bradshaw, who had been hanging around us in various anxious attitudes, spoke up: "I can vouch for the truth of that, Sheriff, if it will save you any time."

Sheriff Crane thanked him and turned back to me: "So it was a purely business proposition between her and you?"

"It would have been if I had been interested." I wasn't telling the precise truth, but there was no way to tell it to Crane without sounding foolish.

"You weren't interested. Why not?"

"I had other business."

"What other business?"

"Mrs. Kincaid had left her husband. He employed me to locate her."

"I heard something about that this morning. Did you find out why she left him?"

"No. My job was to locate her. I did."

"Where?"

I glanced up at Bradshaw. He gave me a reluctant nod. I said: "She's a student at the college."

"And now you say she's under a doctor's care? What doctor?"

"Dr. Godwin."

"The psychiatrist, eh?" The Sheriff uncrossed his heavy legs and leaned toward me confidentially. "What does she need a psychiatrist for? Is she out of her head?"

"She was hysterical. It seemed like a good idea to call one."

"Where is she now?"

I looked at Bradshaw again. He said: "At my house. My mother employed her as a driver."

The Sheriff got up with a rowing motion of his arms. "Let's get over there and talk to her."

"I'm afraid that won't be possible," Bradshaw said.

"Who says so?"

"I do, and I'm sure the doctor would concur."

"Naturally Godwin says what his patients pay him to say. I've had trouble with him before."

"I know that." Bradshaw had turned pale, but his voice was under rigid control. "You're not a professional man, Sheriff, and I rather doubt that you understand Dr. Godwin's code of ethics."

Crane reddened under the insult. He couldn't think of anything to say. Bradshaw went on:

"I very seriously doubt that Mrs. Kincaid can or should be questioned at the present time. What's the point of it? If she had anything to hide, she wouldn't have rushed to the nearest detective with her dreadful news. I'm sure we don't want to subject the girl to cruel and unusual punishment, simply for doing her duty as a citizen."

"What do you mean, cruel and unusual punishment? I'm not planning to third-degree her."

"I hope and trust you're not planning to go near the child tonight. That would be cruel and unusual punishment in my opinion, Sheriff, and I believe I speak for informed opinion in this county."

Crane opened his mouth to expostulate, perhaps realized the hopelessness of trying to outtalk Bradshaw, and shut it again. Bradshaw and I walked out unaccompanied. I said when we were out of hearing of the house:

"That was quite a job you did of facing down the Sheriff."

"I've always disliked that blustering bag of wind. Fortunately he's vulnerable. His majority slipped badly in the last election. A great many people in this county, including Dr. Godwin and myself, would like to see more enlightened and efficient law enforcement. And we may get it yet."

Nothing had changed visibly in the gatehouse. Dolly was still lying on the studio bed with her face turned to the wall. Bradshaw and I hesitated at the door. Walking with his head down, Alex crossed the room to speak to us.

"Dr. Godwin went up to the house to make a phone call. He thinks she ought to be in a nursing home, temporarily."

Dolly spoke in a monotone: "I know what you're saying. You might as well say it out loud. You want to put me away."

"Hush, darling." It was a brave word.

The girl relapsed into silence. She hadn't moved at all. Alex drew us outside, keeping the door open so that he could watch her. He said in a low voice:

"Dr. Godwin doesn't want to run the risk of suicide."

"It's that bad, eh?" I said.

"I don't think so. Neither does Dr. Godwin, really. He says it's simply a matter of taking reasonable security precautions. I told him I could sit up with her, but he doesn't think I should try to do it myself."

"You shouldn't," Bradshaw said. "You'll need to have something left for tomorrow."

"Yeah. Tomorrow." Alex kicked at the rusty boot-scraper attached to the side of the doorstep. "I better call Dad. Tomorrow's a Saturday, he ought to be able to come."

Footsteps approached from the direction of the main house. A big man in an alligator coat emerged from the fog, his bald head gleaming in the light from the doorway. He greeted Bradshaw warmly:

"Hello, Roy. I enjoyed your speech, what I heard of it. You'll elevate us yet into the Athens of the West. Unfortunately a patient dragged me out in the middle of it. She wanted to know if it was safe for her to see a Tennessee Williams movie all by herself. She really wanted me to go along with her and protect her from bad thoughts." He turned to me. "Mr. Archer? I'm Dr. Godwin."

We shook hands. He gave me a look of lingering intensity, as if he was going to paint my portrait from memory. Godwin had a heavy, powerful face, with eyes that changed from bright to dark like lamps being turned down. He had authority, which he was being careful not to use.

"I'm glad you called me. Miss McGee—Mrs. Kincaid needed something to calm her down." He glanced in through the doorway. "I hope she's feeling better now."

"She's much quieter," Alex said. "Don't you think it will be all right for her to stay here with me?"

Godwin made a commiserating face. His mouth was very flexible, like an actor's. "It wouldn't be wise, Mr. Kincaid. I've made arrangements for a bed in a nursing home I use. We don't want to take any chances with her life."

"But why should she try to kill herself?"

"She has a lot on her mind, poor girl. I always pay attention to suicide threats, or even the slightest hint of them."

"Have you found out just what she does have on her mind?" Bradshaw said.

"She didn't want to talk much. She's very tired. It can wait till morning."

"I hope so," Bradshaw said. "The Sheriff wants to question her about the shooting. I did my best to hold him off."

Godwin's mobile face became grave. "There actually has been a murder then? Another murder?"

"One of our new professors, Helen Haggerty, was shot in her home tonight. Mrs. Kincaid apparently stumbled on the body."

"She's had dreadful luck." Godwin looked up at the low sky. "I sometimes feel as though the gods have turned their backs on certain people."

I asked him to explain what he meant. He shook his head: "I'm much too tired to tell you the bloody saga of the McGees. A lot of it has faded out of my memory, mercifully. Why don't you ask the courthouse people for the details?"

"That wouldn't be a good idea, under the circumstances."

"It wouldn't, would it? You can see how tired I am. By the time I get my patient safely disposed of for the night I'll have just enough energy left to make it home and to bed."

"We still need to talk, doctor."

"What about?"

I didn't like to say it in front of Alex but I said it, watching him: "The possibility that she committed this second murder, or let's say the possibility that she'll be accused of it. She seems to want to be."

Alex rose to her defense: "She was out of her head, temporarily, and you can't use what she said—"

Godwin laid a hand on his shoulder. "Take it easy, Mr. Kincaid. We can't settle anything now. What we all need is a night's sleep—especially your wife. I want you to come along with me to the nursing home in case I need help with her on the way. You," he said to me, "can follow along in your car and bring him back. You'll want to know where the nursing home is, anyway, because I'll meet you there tomorrow morning at eight, after I've had an opportunity to talk to Mrs. Kincaid. Got that?"

"Tomorrow morning at eight."

He turned to Bradshaw. "Roy, if I were you I'd go and see how Mrs. Bradshaw is feeling. I gave her a sedative, but she's alarmed. She thinks, or pretends to think, that she's surrounded by maniacal assassins. You can talk her out of it better than I could."

Godwin seemed to be a wise and careful man. At any rate, his authority imposed itself. All three of us did as he said.

So did Dolly. Propped between him and Alex, she came out to his car. She didn't struggle or make a sound, but she walked as though she was on her way to the execution chamber.

10

An hour later I was sitting on one of the twin beds in my motel room. There was nothing more I could do right now, except possibly stir up trouble if I went for information to the local authorities. But my mind kept projecting on the plaster wall rapid movies of actions I could be performing. Run down Begley-McGee. Capture the man from Nevada.

I shut off the violent images with an effort of will and forced myself to think about Zeno, who said that Achilles could never traverse the space between him and the tortoise. It was a soothing thought, if you were a tortoise, or maybe even if you were Achilles.

I had a pint of whisky in my bag. I was getting it out of its sock when I thought of Arnie Walters, a Reno colleague of mine who had split more than one pint with me. I put in a long-distance call to his office, which happened to be the front room of his house. Arnie was at home.

"Walters Detective Agency," he said in a reluctant midnight voice.

"This is Lew Archer."

"Oh. Good. I didn't really want to go to bed. I was only modeling my pajamas."

"Irony isn't your forte, so drop it. All I'm asking for is a small service which I will repay in kind at the earliest opportunity. Are you recording?"

I heard the click of the machine, and told it and Arnie about Helen's death. "A couple of hours after the shooting, the man I'm interested in came out of the murder house and drove away in a black or dark blue convertible, I think a late-model Ford, with a Nevada license. I think I got the first four figures—"

"You think?"

"It's foggy here, and it was dark. First four figures are probably FT37. The subject is young and athletic, height about five-eleven, wearing a dark topcoat and dark snap-brim fedora. I couldn't make out his face."

"Have you seen your oculist lately?"

"You can do better than that, Arnie. Try."

"I hear senior citizens can get free glaucoma tests nowadays."

Arnie was older than I was, but he didn't like to have this pointed out. "What's bugging you? Trouble with the wife?"

"No trouble," he said cheerfully. "She's waiting for me in bed."

"Give Phyllis my love."

"I'll give her my own. In case I come up with anything, which seems unlikely in view of the fragmentary information, where do I contact you?"

"I'm staying at the Mariner's Rest Motel in Pacific Point. But you better call my answering service in Hollywood."

He said he would. As I hung up, I heard a gentle tapping on my door. It turned out to be Alex. He had pulled on his trousers over his pajamas.

"I heard you talking in here."

"I was on the phone."

"I didn't mean to interrupt."

"I'm through phoning. Come in and have a drink."

He entered the room cautiously, as if it might be booby-trapped. In the last few hours his movements had become very tentative. His bare feet made no sound on the carpet.

The bathroom cupboard contained two glasses wrapped in wax paper. I unwrapped and filled them. We sat on the twin beds, drinking to nothing in particular. We faced each other like mirror images separated by an invisible wall of glass.

I was conscious of the differences between us, particularly of Alex's youth and lack of experience. He was at the age when everything hurts.

"I was thinking of calling Dad," he said. "Now I don't know whether I should or not."

There was another silence.

"He won't say 'I told you so,' in so many words. But that will be the general idea. Fools rush in where angels fear to tread and all that jazz."

"I think it makes just as much sense if you reverse it. Angels rush in where fools are afraid to tread. Not that I know any angels."

He got the message. "You don't think I'm a fool?"

"You've handled yourself very well."

"Thank you," he said formally. "Even if it isn't actually true."

"It is, though. It must have taken some doing."

Whisky and the beginnings of human warmth had dissolved the glass wall between us. "The worst of it," he said, "was when I put her in the nursing home just now. I felt as if I was—you know, consigning her to oblivion. The place is like something out of Dante, with people crying and groaning. Dolly's a sensitive girl. I don't see how she'll be able to take it."

"She can take it better than some other things, such as wandering around loose in her condition."

"You think she's insane, don't you?"

"What I think doesn't matter. We'll get an expert opinion tomorrow. There's no doubt she's temporarily off base. I've seen people further off, and I've seen them come back."

"You think she'll be all right then?"

He'd grabbed at what I said like a flying trapeze and swung up into hopefulness. Which I didn't think ought to be encouraged:

"I'm more concerned about the legal situation than the psychiatric one."

"You can't really believe she killed this friend of hers—Helen? I know she said so, but it isn't possible. You see, I know Dolly. She isn't aggressive at all. She's one of the really pro-life people. She doesn't even like to kill a spider."

"It is possible, Alex, and that was all I said. I wanted Godwin to be aware of the possibility from the start. He's in a position to do a lot for your wife."

Alex said, "My wife," with a kind of wonder.

"She is your wife, legally. But nobody would consider that you owe her much. You have an out, if you want to use it."

The whisky slopped in his glass. I think he barely restrained himself from throwing it in my face.

"I'm not going to ditch her," he said. "If you think I ought to, you can go to hell."

I hadn't liked him thoroughly until now. "Somebody had to mention the fact that you have an out. A lot of people would take it."

"I'm not a lot of people."

"So I gather."

"Dad would probably call me a fool, but I don't care if she's guilty of murder. I'm staying."

"It's going to cost money."

"You want more money, is that it?"

"I can wait. So can Godwin. I was thinking about the future. Also there's the strong possibility that you'll need a lawyer tomorrow."

"What for?" He was a good boy, but a little slow on the uptake.

"Judging by tonight, your main problem is going to be to prevent Dolly from talking herself into deep trouble. That means keeping her out of the hands of the authorities, in a place where she can be properly looked after. A good lawyer can be a help in that. Lawyers generally don't wait for their money in criminal cases."

"Do you really think she's in such danger—such legal jeopardy? Or are you just trying to put the iron in my soul?"

"I talked to the local sheriff tonight, and I didn't like the gleam in his eye when we got on the subject of Dolly. Sheriff Crane isn't stupid. He knew that I was holding back on him. He's going to bear down on her when he catches on to the family connection."

"The family connection?"

"The fact that her father murdered her mother." It was cruel to hit him with it again, on top of everything else. Still it was better for him to hear it from me than from the dreary voice that talks from under the twisted pillow at three o'clock in the morning. "Apparently he was tried and convicted in the local courts. Sheriff Crane probably gathered the evidence for the prosecution."

"It's almost as though history is repeating itself." There was something approaching awe in Alex's voice. "Did I hear you say that this Chuck Begley character, the man with the beard, is actually her father?"

"He seems to be."

"He was the one who started the whole thing off," he said, as much to himself as to me. "It was after he visited her that Sunday that she walked out on me. What do you think happened between them, to make her do that?"

"I don't know, Alex. Maybe he bawled her out for testifying against him. In any case he brought back the past. She couldn't handle the old mess and her new marriage together, so she left you."

"I still don't get it," he said. "How could Dolly have a father like that?"

"I'm not a geneticist. But I do know most non-professional killers aren't criminal types. I intend to find out more about Begley-McGee and his murder. I suppose it's no use asking if Dolly ever talked about it to you?"

"She never said a word about either of her parents, except that they were dead. Now I can understand why. I don't blame her for lying—" He cut the sentence short, and amended it: "I mean, for not telling me certain things."

"She made up for it tonight."

"Yeah. It's been quite a night." He nodded several times, as though he was still absorbing its repercussions. "Tell me the honest truth, Mr. Archer. Do you believe the things she said about being responsible for this woman's death? And her mother?"

"I can't even remember half of them."

"That's not an answer."

"Maybe we'll get some better answers tomorrow. It's a complex world. The human mind is the most complex thing in it."

"You don't give me much comfort."

"It's not my job to."

Making a bitter face over this and the last of his whisky, he rose slowly. "Well, you need your sleep, and I have a phone call to make. Thanks for the drink." He turned with his hand on the doorknob. "And thanks for the conversation."

"Any time. Are you going to call your father?"

"No. I've decided not to."

I felt vaguely gratified. I was old enough to be his father, with no son of my own, and that may have had something to do with my feeling.

"Who are you going to call, or is that a private matter?"

"Dolly asked me to try and get in touch with her Aunt Alice. I guess I've been putting it off. I don't know what to say to her aunt. I didn't even know she had an Aunt Alice until tonight."

"I remember she mentioned her. When did Dolly ask you to make the call?"

"In the nursing home, the last thing. She wants her aunt to come and see her. I didn't know if that was a good idea or not."

"It would depend on the aunt. Does she live here in town?"

"She lives in the Valley, in Indian Springs. Dolly said she's in the county directory. Miss Alice Jenks."

"Let's try her."

I found her name and number in the phone book, placed the toll call, and handed the receiver to Alex. He sat on the bed, looking at the instrument as if he had never seen one before.

"What am I going to say to her?"

"You'll know what to say. I want to talk to her when you're finished."

A voice rasped from the receiver: "Yes? Who is this?"

"I'm Alex Kincaid. Is that Miss Jenks? . . . We don't know each other, Miss Jenks, but I married your niece a few weeks ago . . . Your niece, Dolly McGee. We were married a few weeks ago, and she's come down with a rather serious illness . . . No, it's more emotional. She's emotionally disturbed, and she wants to see you. She's in the Whitmore Nursing Home here in Pacific Point. Dr. Godwin is looking after her."

He paused again. There was sweat on his forehead. The voice at the other end went on for some time.

"She says she can't come tomorrow," he said to me; and into the receiver: "Perhaps Sunday would be possible? . . . Yes, fine. You can contact me at the Mariner's Rest Motel, or . . . Alex Kincaid. I'll look forward to meeting you."

"Let me talk to her," I said.

"Just a minute, Miss Jenks. The gentleman here with me, Mr. Archer, has something to say to you." He handed over the receiver.

"Hello, Miss Jenks."

"Hello, Mr. Archer. And who are you, may I ask, at one o'clock in the morning?" It wasn't a light question. The woman sounded anxious and irritated, but she had both feelings under reasonable control.

"I'm a private detective. I'm sorry to disrupt your sleep with this, but there's more to the situation than simple emotional illness. A woman has been murdered here."

She gasped, but made no other comment.

"Your niece is a material witness to the murder. She may be more deeply involved than that, and in any case she's going to need support. So far as I know you're her only relative, apart from her father—"

"You can leave him out. He doesn't count. He never has, except in a negative way." Her voice was flat and harsh. "Who was killed?"

"A friend and counselor of your niece's, Professor Helen Haggerty."

"I never heard of the woman," she said with combined impatience and relief.

"You'll be hearing a great deal about her, if you're at all interested in your niece. Are you close to her?"

"I was, before she grew away from me. I brought her up after her mother's death." Her voice became flat again: "Does Tom McGee have anything to do with this new killing?"

"He may have. He's in town here, or he was."

"I knew it!" she cried in bleak triumph. "They had no business letting him out. They should have put him in the gas chamber for what he did to my little sister."

She was choked with sudden emotion. I waited for her to go on. When she didn't, I said:

"I'm anxious to go into the details of that case with you, but I don't think we should do it over the phone. It really would be helpful if you could come here tomorrow."

"I simply can't. There's no use badgering me. I have a terribly important meeting tomorrow afternoon. Several state officials will be here from Sacramento, and it will probably go on into the evening."

"What about the morning?"

"I have to prepare for them in the morning. We're shifting over to a new state-county welfare program." Latent hysteria buzzed in her voice, the hysteria of a middle-aged spinster who has to make a change. "If I walked out on this project, I could lose my position."

"We don't want that to happen, Miss Jenks. How far is it from there to Pacific Point?"

"Seventy miles, but I tell you I can't make it."

"I can. Will you give me an hour in the morning, say around eleven?"

She hesitated. "Yes, if it's important. I'll get up an hour earlier and do my paperwork. I'll be at home at eleven. You have my address? It's just off the main street of Indian Springs."

I thanked her and got rid of Alex and went to bed, setting my mental alarm for six-thirty.

11

ALEX was still sleeping when I was ready to leave in the morning. I let him sleep, partly for selfish reasons, and partly because sleep was kinder to him than waking was likely to be.

The fog was thick outside. Its watery mass overlay Pacific Point and transformed it into a kind of suburb of the sea. I drove out of the motel enclosure into a gray world without perspective, came abruptly to an access ramp, descended onto the freeway where headlights swam in pairs like deep-sea fish, and arrived at a truck stop on the east side without any real sense that I had driven across the city.

I'd been having a little too much talk with people whose business was talking. It was good to sit at the counter of a working-class restaurant where men spoke when they wanted something, or simply to kid the waitress. I kidded her a little myself. Her name was Stella, and she was so efficient that she threatened to take the place of automation. She said with a flashing smile that this was her aim in life.

My destination was near the highway, on a heavily used thoroughfare lined mainly with new apartment buildings. Their faddish pastel colors and scant transplanted palms seemed dingy and desolate in the fog.

The nursing home was a beige stucco one-storied building taking up most of a narrow deep lot. I rang the bell at eight o'clock precisely. Dr. Godwin must have been waiting behind the door. He unlocked it and let me in himself.

"You're a punctual man, Mr. Archer."

His changeable eyes had taken the stony color of the morning. I noticed when he turned to shut the door behind us that his shoulders were permanently stooped. He was wearing a fresh white smock.

"Sit down, won't you? This is as good a place to talk as any."

We were in a small reception room or lounge. I sat in one of several worn armchairs aimed at a silent television set in one corner. Through the inner door I could hear the rattle of dishes and the bright voices of nurses beginning the day.

"Is this your place, doctor?"

"I have an interest in it. Most of the patients here are mine. I've just been giving some shock treatments." He smoothed the front of his smock. "I'd feel less like a witch-doctor if I knew why electric shocks make depressed people feel better. So much of our science, or art, is still in the empirical stage. But the people do get better," he said with a sudden grin, too sudden to touch his watching, waiting eyes.

"Is Dolly?"

"Yes, I think she's somewhat better. We don't have overnight cures, of course. I want to keep an eye on her for at least a week. Here."

"Is she fit to be questioned?"

"I don't want you to question her, or anyone else remotely con- nected with the—the world of crime and punishment." As if to remove the curse from his refusal, he flung himself loosely into the armchair beside me, asked me for a cigarette and let me light it.

"Why not?"

"I do not love the law in its current primitive state, where sick people are trapped into betraying themselves in their sickness and then treated by the courts as if they were well. I've been fighting the situa- tion for a long time." He rested his ponderous bald head on the back of the chair, and blew smoke toward the ceiling.

"What you say suggests that Dolly is in danger from the law."

"I was making a general statement."

"Which applied specifically to Dolly. We don't have to play games, doctor. We're both on the same side. I don't assume the girl is guilty of anything. I do think she has information which may help me to clear up a murder."

"But what if she's guilty?" he said, watching for my reaction.

"Then I'd want to cooperate with you in getting charges reduced, finding mitigating circumstances, making a case for merciful treatment by the court. Remember I'm working for her husband. Is she guilty?"

"I don't know."

"You have talked to her this morning?"

"She did most of the talking. I don't ask many questions. I wait and I listen. In the end you learn more that way." He gave me a meaningful look, as if I should start applying this principle.

I waited and listened. Nothing happened. A plump woman with

long black hair straggling down the back of her cotton robe appeared in the inside doorway. She stretched out her arms to the doctor.

He lifted his hand like a weary king. "Good morning, Nell."

She gave him a bright agonized smile and softly withdrew, like a woman walking backward in her sleep. Her outstretched arms were the last I saw of her.

"It would be helpful if you told me what Dolly had to say this morning."

"And possibly dangerous." Godwin crushed out his cigarette in a blue ceramic ashtray which looked homemade. "There is after all a difference between you and me. What a patient says to me is a professional confidence. You have no professional standing. If you refused to repeat information in court you could be jailed for contempt. I could, under the law, but I'm not likely to be."

"I've sweated out contempt before. And the police won't get anything out of me that I don't choose to tell them. That's a guarantee."

"Very well." Godwin nodded his head once, decisively. "I'm concerned about Dolly and I'll try to tell you why without any professional jargon. You may be able to put together the objective jigsaw puzzle while I'm reconstructing the subjective one."

"You said no professional jargon, doctor."

"Sorry. First there's her history. Her mother Constance McGee brought her to me at the instigation of her sister Alice, a woman I know slightly, when Dolly was ten years old. She wasn't a happy child. In fact she was in some danger of becoming really withdrawn, for good reason. There's always good reason. Her father McGee was an irresponsible and violent man who couldn't handle the duties of fatherhood. He blew hot and cold on the child, spoiled her and punished her, constantly fought with his wife and eventually left her, or was left, it hardly matters. I would have preferred to treat him instead of Dolly, since he was the main source of the trouble in the family. But he was unreachable."

"Did you ever see him?"

"He wouldn't even come in for an interview," Godwin said with regret. "If I could have reached him, I might have been able to prevent a murder. Perhaps not. From what I've been told he was a severely maladjusted man who needed help but never got it. You can understand my bitterness about the gap between psychiatry and the law. People like McGee are allowed to run around loose, without preventive action of any kind, until they commit a crime. Then of course they're hauled into court and sent away for ten or twenty years. But not to a hospital. To a prison."

"McGee's out now. He's been in town here. Did you know that?"

"Dolly told me this morning. It's one of the many severe pressures on her. You can understand how a sensitive child brought up in an atmosphere of violence and instability would be plagued by anxiety and guilt. The worst guilt often arises when a child is forced, by sheer instinctive self-preservation, to turn against her parents. A clinical psychologist I work with helped Dolly to express her feelings in clay and doll-play and so on. There wasn't too much I could do for her myself, since children don't have the mental equipment to be analyzed. But I did try to assume the role of the calm and patient father, provide some of the stability that was missing in her young life. And she was doing pretty well, until the disaster occurred."

"You mean the murder?"

He swung his head in sorrow. "McGee worked himself into a self-pitying rage one night, came to the aunt's house in Indian Springs where they were staying, and shot Constance through the head. Dolly was alone in the house with her mother. She heard the shot and saw McGee taking off. Then she discovered the body."

His head went on swinging slowly like a heavy silent bell. I said:

"What was her reaction at the time?"

"I don't know. One of the peculiar difficulties of my work is that I often have to perform a public function with private means. I can't go out and lasso patients. Dolly never came back to me. She no longer had her mother to bring her in from the Valley, and Miss Jenks, her aunt, is a busy woman."

"But didn't you say that Alice Jenks suggested treatment for Dolly in the first place?"

"She did. She also paid for it. Perhaps with all the trouble in the family she felt she couldn't afford it any longer. At any rate, I didn't see Dolly again until last night, with one exception. I went to court the day she testified against McGee. As a matter of fact I bearded the judge in his chambers and told him that it shouldn't be allowed. But she was a key witness, and they had her aunt's permission, and they put her through her sad little paces. She acted like a pale little automaton lost in a world of hostile adults."

His large body trembled with feeling. His hands burrowed under his smock, searching for a cigarette. I gave him one and lit it, and lit one for myself.

"What did she say in court?"

"It was very short and simple. I suspect that she was thoroughly rehearsed. She heard the shot and looked out her bedroom window and saw her father running away with the gun in his hand. One other question had to do with whether McGee had threatened Constance with bodily harm. He had. That was all."

"You're sure?"

"Yes. This isn't my unaided recollection, as they say. I took written notes at the time, and I scanned them this morning."

"Why?"

"They're part of her history, evidently a crucial part." He blew out smoke and looked at me through it, long and cautiously.

I said: "Does she tell a different story now?"

His face was working with complex passions. He was a man of feeling, and Dolly was his office daughter lost for many years.

"She tells an absurd story," he burst out. "I not only can't believe it, I can't believe that she believes it. She isn't that sick."

He paused, drawing deep on his cigarette, trying to get himself under full control. I waited and listened. This time he did go on:

"She claims now that she didn't see McGee that night, and that in fact he had nothing to do with the murder. She says she lied on the witness stand because the various adults wanted her to."

"Why would she say that now?"

"I don't pretend to understand her. After an interval of ten years we've naturally lost what rapport we had. And of course she hasn't forgiven me for what she considers my betrayal—my failure to look after her in the disaster. But what could I do? I couldn't go to Indian Springs and kidnap her out of her aunt's house."

"You care about your patients, doctor."

"Yes. I care. It keeps me tired." He stubbed his cigarette in the ceramic ashtray. "Nell made this ashtray, by the way. It's rather good for a first attempt."

I murmured something in agreement. Above the subsiding clamor of dishes, a wild old complaining voice rose in the depths of the building.

"That story of hers," I said, "may not be so very absurd. It fits in with the fact that McGee visited her on the second day of her honeymoon and hit her so hard with something that it knocked her right off the tracks."

"You're acute, Mr. Archer. That's precisely what happened. He treated her to a long tirade on the subject of his innocence. You mustn't forget that she loved her father, however ambivalently. He was able to convince her that her memory was at fault, that he was innocent and she was guilty. Childhood memories are powerfully influenced by emotion."

"That she was guilty of perjury, you mean?"

"Murder." He leaned toward me. "She told me this morning she killed her mother herself."

"With a gun?"

"With her tongue. That's the absurd part. She claims she killed her mother and her friend Helen, and sent her father to prison into the bargain, all with her poisonous tongue."

"Does she explain what she means by that?"

"She hasn't yet. It's an expression of guilt which may be only superficially connected with these murders."

"You mean she's using the murders to unload guilt which she feels about something else?"

"More or less. It's a common enough mechanism. I know for a fact that she didn't kill her mother, or lie about her father, essentially. I'm certain McGee was guilty."

"Courts can make mistakes, even in a capital case."

He said with a kind of muted arrogance: "I know more about that case than ever came out in court."

"From Dolly?"

"From various sources."

"I'd be obliged if you'd let me in on it."

His eyes veiled themselves. "I can't do that. I have to respect the confidences of my patients. But you can take my word for it that McGee killed his wife."

"Then what's Dolly feeling so guilty about?"

"I'm sure that will come out, in time. It probably has to do with her resentment against her parents. It's natural she'd want to punish them for the ugly failure of their marriage. She may well have fantasied her mother's death, her father's imprisonment, before those things emerged into reality. When the poor child's vengeful dreams came true, how else could she feel but guilty? McGee's tirade the other weekend stirred up the old feelings, and then this dreadful accident last night—" He ran out of words and spread his hands, palms upward and fingers curling, on his heavy thighs.

"The Haggerty shooting was no accident, doctor. The gun is missing, for one thing."

"I realize that. I was referring to Dolly's discovery of the body, which was certainly accidental."

"I wonder. She blames herself for that killing, too. I don't see how you can explain that in terms of childhood resentments."

"I wasn't attempting to." There was irritation in his voice. It made him pull a little professional rank on me: "Nor is there any need for you to understand the psychic situation. You stick to the objective facts, and I'll handle the subjective." He softened this with a bit of philosophy: "Objective and subjective, the outer world and the inner, do correspond of course. But sometimes you have to follow the parallel lines almost to infinity before they touch."

"Let's stick to the objective facts then. Dolly said she killed Helen Haggerty with her poisonous tongue. Is that all she said on the subject?"

"There was more, a good deal more, of a rather confused nature. Dolly seems to feel that her friendship with Miss Haggerty was somehow responsible for the latter's death."

"The two women were friends?"

"I'd say so, yes, though there was twenty years' difference in their ages. Dolly confided in her, poured out everything, and Miss Haggerty reciprocated. Apparently she'd had severe emotional problems involving her own father, and she couldn't resist the parallel with Dolly. They both let down their back hair. It wasn't a healthy situation," he said dryly.

"Does she have anything to say about Helen's father?"

"Dolly seems to think he was a crooked policeman involved in a murder, but that may be sheer fantasy—a kind of secondary image of her own father."

"It isn't. Helen's father is a policeman, and Helen at least regarded him as a crook."

"How in the world would you know that?"

"I read a letter from her mother on the subject. I'd like to have a chance to talk to her parents."

"Why don't you?"

"They live in Bridgeton, Illinois."

It was a long jump, but not so long as the jump my mind made into blank possibility. I had handled cases which opened up gradually like fissures in the firm ground of the present, cleaving far down through the strata of the past. Perhaps Helen's murder was connected with an obscure murder in Illinois more than twenty years ago, before Dolly was born. It was a wishful thought, and I didn't mention it to Dr. Godwin.

"I'm sorry I can't be more help to you," he was saying. "I have to go now, I'm already overdue for my hospital rounds."

The sound of a motor detached itself from the traffic in the street, and slowed down. A car door was opened and closed. Men's footsteps came up the walk. Moving quickly for a big man, Godwin opened the door before they rang.

I couldn't see who his visitors were, but they were unwelcome ones. Godwin went rigid with hostility.

"Good morning, Sheriff," he said.

Crane responded folksily: "It's a hell of a morning and you know it. September's supposed to be our best month, but the bloody fog's so thick the airport's socked in."

"You didn't come here to discuss the weather."

"That's right, I didn't. I heard you got a fugitive from justice holed up here."

"Where did you hear that?"

"I have my sources."

"You'd better fire them, Sheriff. They're giving you misleading information."

"Somebody is, doctor. Are you denying that Mrs. Dolly Kincaid née McGee is in this building?"

Godwin hesitated. His heavy jaw got heavier. "She is."

"You said a minute ago she wasn't. What are you trying to pull, doc?"

"What are *you* trying to pull? Mrs. Kincaid is not a fugitive. She's here because she's ill."

"I wonder what made her ill. Can't she stand the sight of blood?"

Godwin's lips curled outward. He looked ready to spit in the other man's face. I couldn't see the Sheriff from where I sat, and I made no attempt to. I thought it was best for me to stay out of sight.

"It isn't just the weather that makes it a lousy day, doc. We had a lousy murder in town last night. I guess you know that, too. Probably Mrs. Kincaid told you all about it."

"Are you accusing her?" Godwin said.

"I wouldn't say that. Not yet, anyway."

"Then beat it."

"You can't talk like that to me."

Godwin held himself motionless but his breath shook him as though he had a racing engine inside of him. "You accused me in the presence of witnesses of harboring a fugitive from justice. I could sue you for slander and by God I will if you don't stop harassing me and my patients."

"I didn't mean it that way." Crane's voice was much less confident. "Anyway, I got a right to question a witness."

"At some later time perhaps you have. At the present time Mrs. Kincaid is under heavy sedation. I can't permit her to be questioned for at least a week."

"A week?"

"It may be longer. I strongly advise you not to press the point. I'm prepared to go before a judge and certify that police questioning at the present time would endanger her health and perhaps her life."

"I don't believe it."

"I don't care what you believe."

Godwin slammed the door and leaned on it, breathing like a runner. A couple of white-uniformed nurses who had been peeking through the inner door tried to look as if they had business there. He waved them away.

I said with unfeigned admiration: "You really went to bat for her."

"They did enough damage to her when she was a child. They're not going to compound it if I can help it."

"How did they know she was here?"

"I have no idea. I can usually trust the staff to keep their mouths shut." He gave me a probing look. "Did you tell anyone?"

"Nobody connected with the law. Alex did mention to Alice Jenks that Dolly was here."

"Perhaps he shouldn't have. Miss Jenks has worked for the county a long time, and Crane and she are old acquaintances."

"She wouldn't tattle on her own niece, would she?"

"I don't know what she'd do." Godwin tore off his smock and threw it at the chair where I had been sitting. "Well, shall I let you out?"

He shook his keys like a jailer.

12

ABOUT HALFWAY up the pass road I came out into sunlight. The fog below was like a sea of white water surging into the inlets of the mountains. From the summit of the pass, where I paused for a moment, further mountains were visible on the inland horizon.

The wide valley between was full of light. Cattle grazed among the live oaks on the hillsides. A covey of quail marched across the road in front of my car like small plumed tipsy soldiers. I could smell new-mown hay, and had the feeling that I had dropped down into a pastoral scene where nothing much had changed in a hundred years.

The town of Indian Springs didn't entirely dispel the feeling, though it had its service stations and its drive-ins offering hamburgers and tacos. It had a bit of old-time Western atmosphere, and more than a bit of the old-time sun-baked poverty of the West. Prematurely aging women watched over their brown children in the dooryards of crumbling adobes. Most of the loiterers in the main street had Indian faces under their broad-brimmed hats. Banners advertising Old Rodeo Days hung limply over their heads.

Alice Jenks lived in one of the best houses on what appeared to be the best street. It was a two-storied white frame house, with deep porches upstairs and down, standing far back from the street behind a smooth green lawn. I stepped onto the grass and leaned on a pepper tree, fanning myself with my hat. I was five minutes early.

A rather imposing woman in a blue dress came out on the veranda. She looked me over as if I might possibly be a burglar cleverly creeping up on her house at eleven o'clock in the morning. She came down the steps and along the walk toward me. The sun flashed on her glasses and lent her searchlight eyes.

Close up, she wasn't so alarming. The brown eyes behind the glasses were strained and anxious. Her hair was streaked with gray. Her mouth was unexpectedly generous and even soft, but it was tweezered like a live thing between the harsh lines that thrust down from the base of her nose. The stiff blue dress that curved like armor plate over her monolithic bosom was old-fashioned in cut, and gave her a dowdy look. The valley sun had parched and roughened her skin.

"Are you Mr. Archer?"

"Yes. How are you, Miss Jenks?"

"I'll survive." Her handshake was like a man's. "Come up on the porch, we can talk there."

Her movements, like her speech, were so abrupt that they suggested the jitters. The jitters under firm, perhaps lifelong, control. She motioned me into a canvas glider and sat on a reed chair facing me, her back to the street. Three Mexican boys on one battered bicycle rode by precariously like high-wire artists.

"I don't know just what you want from me, Mr. Archer. My niece appears to be in very serious trouble. I talked to a friend in the courthouse this morning—"

"The Sheriff?"

"Yes. He seems to think that Dolly is hiding from him."

"Did you tell Sheriff Crane where she was?"

"Yes. Shouldn't I have?"

"He trotted right over to the nursing home to question her. Dr. Godwin wouldn't let him."

"Dr. Godwin is a great one for taking matters into his own hands. I don't believe myself that people in trouble should be coddled and swaddled in cotton wool, and what I believe for the rest of the world holds true for my own family. We've always been a law-abiding family, and if Dolly is holding something back, she ought to come out with it. I say let the truth be told, and the chips fall where they may."

It was quite a speech. She seemed to be renewing her old disagreement with Godwin about Dolly's testimony at the trial.

"Those chips can fall pretty hard, sometimes, when they fall on people you love."

She watched me, her sensitive mouth held tight, as if I had accused her of a weakness. "People I love?"

I had only an hour, and no sure intuition of how to reach her. "I'm assuming you love Dolly."

"I haven't seen her lately—she seems to have turned against me—but I'll always be fond of her. That doesn't mean"—and the deep lines reasserted themselves at the corners of her mouth—"that I'll condone any wrongdoing on her part. I have a public position—"

"Just what is your position?"

"I'm senior county welfare worker for this area," she announced. Then she looked anxiously behind her at the empty street, as if a posse might be on its way to relieve her of her post.

"Welfare begins at home."

"Are you instructing me in the conduct of my private life?" She didn't wait for an answer. "Let me tell you, you don't have to. Who do you think took the child in when my sister's marriage broke up? I did, of course. I gave them both a home, and after my sister was killed I brought my niece up as if she was my own daughter. I gave her the best of food and clothes, the best of education. When she wanted her own independence, I gave her that, too. I gave her the money to go and study in Los Angeles. What more could I do for her?"

"You can give her the benefit of the doubt right now. I don't know what the Sheriff said to you, but I'm pretty sure he was talking through his little pointed hat."

Her face hardened. "Sheriff Crane does not make mistakes."

I had the sense of doubleness again, of talking on two levels. On the surface we were talking about Dolly's connection with the Haggerty killing but underneath this, though McGee had not been mentioned, we were arguing the question of McGee's guilt.

"All policemen make mistakes," I said. "All human beings make mistakes. It's even possible that you and Sheriff Crane and the judge and the twelve jurors and everybody else were mistaken about Thomas McGee, and convicted an innocent man."

She laughed in my face, not riotously. "That's ridiculous, you didn't know Tom McGee. He was capable of anything. Ask anybody in this town. He used to get drunk and come home and beat her. More than once I had to stand him off with a gun, with the child holding onto my legs. More than once, after Constance left him, he came to this house and battered on the door and said he would drag her out of here by the hair. But I wouldn't let him." She shook her head vehemently, and a strand of iron-gray hair fell like twisted wire across her cheek.

"What did he want from her?"

"He wanted domination. He wanted her under his thumb. But he had no right to her. We Jenks are the oldest family in town. The McGees across the river are the scum of the earth, most of them are on welfare to this day. He was one of the worst of them but my sister couldn't see it when he came courting her in his white sailor suit. He married her against Father's bitter objections. He gave her a dozen years of hell on earth and then he finally killed her. Don't tell me he was innocent. You don't know him."

A scrub jay in the pepper tree heard her harsh obsessive voice and raised his own voice in counter-complaint. I said under his noise:

"Why did he kill your sister?"

"Out of sheer diabolical devilment. What he couldn't have he chose to destroy. It was as simple as that. It wasn't true that there was another man. She was faithful to him to the day she died. Even though they were living in separate houses, my sister kept herself pure."

"Who said there was another man?"

She looked at me. The hot blood left her face. She seemed to lose the confidence that her righteous anger had given her.

"There were rumors," she said weakly. "Foul, dirty rumors. There always are when there's bad blood between a husband and wife. Tom McGee may have started them himself. I know his lawyer kept hammering away at the idea of another man. It was all I could do to sit there and listen to him, trying to destroy my sister's reputation after that murdering client of his had already destroyed her life. But Judge Gahagan made it clear in his instructions to the jury that it was just a story he invented, with no basis in fact."

"Who was McGee's lawyer?"

"An old fox named Gil Stevens. People don't go to him unless they're guilty, and he takes everything they have to get them off."

"But he didn't get McGee off."

"He practically did. Ten years is a small price to pay for first-degree murder. It should have been first-degree. He should have been executed."

The woman was implacable. With a firm hand she pressed her stray lock of hair back into place. Her graying head was marcelled in neat little waves, all alike, like the sea in old steel engravings. Such implacability as hers, I thought, could rise from either one of two sources: righteous certainty, or a guilty dubious fear that she was wrong. I hesitated to tell her what Dolly had said, that she had lied her father into prison. But I intended to tell her before I left.

"I'm interested in the details of the murder. Would it be too painful for you to go into them?"

"I can stand a lot of pain. What do you want to know?"

"Just how it happened."

"I wasn't here myself. I was at a meeting of the Native Daughters. I was president of the local group that year." The memory of this helped to restore her composure.

"Still I'm sure you know as much about it as anyone."

"No doubt I do. Except Tom McGee," she reminded me.

"And Dolly."

"Yes, and Dolly. The child was here in the house with Constance. They'd been living with me for some months. It was past nine o'clock, and she'd already gone to bed. Constance was downstairs sewing. My sister was a fine seamstress, and she made most of the child's clothes. She was making a dress for her that night. It got all spotted with blood. They made it an exhibit at the trial."

Miss Jenks couldn't seem to forget the trial. Her eyes went vague, as if she could see it like a ritual continually being repeated in the courtroom of her mind.

"What were the circumstances of the shooting?"

"It was simple enough. He came to the front door. He talked her into opening it."

"It's strange that he could do that, after her bad experiences with him."

She brushed my objection aside with a flat movement of her hand. "He could talk a bird out of a tree when he wanted to. At any rate, they had an argument. I suppose he wanted her to come back with him, as usual, and she refused. Dolly heard their voices raised in anger."

"Where was she?"

"Upstairs in the front bedroom, which she shared with her mother." Miss Jenks pointed upward at the boarded ceiling of the veranda. "The argument woke the child up, and then she heard the shot. She went to the window and saw him run out to the street with the smoking gun in his hand. She came downstairs and found her mother in her blood."

"Was she still alive?"

"She was dead. She died instantaneously, shot through the heart."

"With what kind of a gun?"

"A medium-caliber hand-gun, the Sheriff thought. It was never found. McGee probably threw it in the sea. He was in Pacific Point when they arrested him next day."

"On Dolly's word?"

"She was the only witness, poor child."

We seemed to have an unspoken agreement that Dolly existed only in the past. Perhaps because we were both avoiding the problem of Dolly's present situation, some of the tension between us had evaporated. I took advantage of this to ask Miss Jenks if I could look over the house.

"I don't see what for."

"You've given me a very clear account of the murder. I want to try and relate it to the physical layout."

She said doubtfully: "I don't have much more time, and frankly I don't know how much more of this I can stand. My sister was very dear to me."

"I know."

"What are you trying to prove?"

"Nothing. I just want to understand what happened. It's my job."

A job and its imperatives meant something to her. She got up, opened the front door, and pointed out the place just inside it where her sister's body had lain. There was of course no trace of the ten-year-old crime on the braided rag rug in the hall. No trace of it anywhere, except for the blind red smear it had left in Dolly's mind, and possibly in her aunt's.

I was struck by the fact that Dolly's mother and her friend Helen had both been shot at the front door of their homes by the same caliber gun, possibly held by the same person. I didn't mention this to Miss Jenks. It would only bring on another outburst against her brother-in-law McGee.

"Would you like a cup of tea?" she said unexpectedly.

"No thanks."

"Or coffee? I use instant. It won't take long."

"All right. You're very kind."

She left me in the living room. It was divided by sliding doors from the dining room, and furnished with stiff old dark pieces reminiscent of a nineteenth-century parlor. There were mottoes on the walls instead of pictures, and one of them brought back with a rush and a pang my grandmother's house in Martinez. It said: "He is the Silent Listener at Every Conversation." My grandmother had hand-embroidered the same motto and hung it in her bedroom. She always whispered.

An upright grand piano with a closed keyboard stood in one corner of the room. I tried to open it, but it was locked. A photograph of two women and a child stood in the place of honor on the piano top. One of the women was Miss Jenks, younger but just as stout and overbearing. The other woman was still younger and much prettier. She held herself with the naïve sophistication of a small-town belle. The child between them, with one hand in each of theirs, was Dolly aged about ten.

Miss Jenks had come through the sliding doors with a coffee tray. "That's the three of us." As if two women and a little girl made a complete family. "And that's my sister's piano. She played beautifully. I never could master the instrument myself."

She wiped her glasses. I didn't know whether they were clouded by emotion or by the steam from the coffee. Over it she related some of Constance's girlhood triumphs. She had won a prize for piano, another for voice. She did extremely well in high school, especially in French, and she was all set to go to college, as Alice had gone before her, when that smooth-talking devil of a Tom McGee—

I left most of my coffee and went out into the hallway. It smelled of the mold that invades old houses. I caught a glimpse of myself in the clouded mirror beside the deer-horn hatrack. I looked like a ghost from the present haunting a bloody moment in the past. Even the woman behind me had an insubstantial quality, as if her large body was a husk or shell from which the essential being had departed. I found myself associating the smell of mold with her.

A rubber-treaded staircase rose at the rear of the hall. I was moving toward it as I said:

"Do you mind if I look at the room Dolly occupied?"

She allowed my momentum to carry her along and up the stairs. "It's my room now."

"I won't disturb anything."

The blinds were drawn, and she turned on the overhead light for me. It had a pink shade which suffused the room with pinkness. The floor was thickly carpeted with a soft loose pink material. A pink decorator spread covered the queen-sized bed. The elaborate three-mirrored dressing-table was trimmed with pink silk flounces, and so was the upholstered chair in front of it.

A quilted pink long chair stood by the window with an open magazine across its foot. Miss Jenks picked up the magazine and rolled it in her hands so that its cover wasn't visible. But I knew a *True Romance* when I saw one.

I crossed the room, sinking to the ankles in the deep pink pile of her fantasy, and raised the blind over the front window. I could see the wide flat second-story porch, and through its railings the pepper tree, and my car in the street. The three Mexican boys came by on their bicycle, one on the handlebars, one on the seat, one on the carrier, trailed by a red mongrel which had joined the act.

"They have no right to be riding like that," Miss Jenks said at my shoulder. "I have a good mind to report them to the deputy. And that dog shouldn't be running around loose."

"He's doing no harm."

"Maybe not, but we had a case of hydrophobia two years ago."

"I'm more interested in ten years ago. How tall was your niece at that time?"

"She was a good big girl for her age. About four feet and a half. Why?"

I adjusted my height by getting down on my knees. From this position I could see the lacy branches of the pepper tree, and through them most of my car, but nothing nearer. A man leaving the house would scarcely be visible until he passed the pepper tree, at least forty feet away. A gun in his hand could not be seen until he reached the street. It was a hasty and haphazard experiment, but its result underlined the question in my mind.

I got up off my knees. "Was it dark that night?"

She knew which night I meant. "Yes. It was dark."

"I don't see any street lights."

"No. We have none. This is a poor town, Mr. Archer."

"Was there a moon?"

"No. I don't believe so. But my niece has excellent eyesight. She can spot the markings on a bird—"

"At night?"

"There's always some light. Anyway, she'd know her own father." Miss Jenks corrected herself: "She *knew* her own father."

"Did she tell you this?"

"Yes. I was the first one she told."

"Did you question her about it in any detail?"

"I didn't, no. She was quite broken up, naturally. I didn't want to subject her to the strain."

"But you didn't mind subjecting her to the strain of testifying to these things in court."

"It was necessary, necessary to the prosecution's case. And it did her no harm."

"Dr. Godwin thinks it did her a lot of harm, that the strain she went through then is partly responsible for her breakdown."

"Dr. Godwin has his ideas and I have mine. If you want my opinion, he's a dangerous man, a troublemaker. He has no respect for authority, and I have no respect for a man like that."

"You used to respect him. You sent your niece to him for treatment."

"I know more about him now than I did then."

"Do you mind telling me why she needed treatment?"

"No. I don't mind." She was still trying to preserve a friendly surface, though we were both conscious of the disagreement simmering under it. "Dolly wasn't doing well in school. She wasn't happy or popular. Which was natural enough with her parents—I mean, her father, making a shambles of their home together.

"This isn't the backwoods," she said as if she suspected maybe it was, "and I thought the least I could do was see that she got a little help. Even the people on welfare get family counseling when they need it. So I persuaded my sister to take her into Pacific Point to see Dr. Godwin. He was the best we had at that time. Constance drove her in every Saturday morning for about a year. The child showed considerable improvement, I'll say that much for Godwin. So did Constance. She seemed brighter and happier and surer of herself."

"Was she getting treatment, too?"

"I guess she had a little, and of course it did her good to get into town every Saturday. She wanted to move into town but there was no money for it. She left McGee and moved in with me instead. That took some of the strain off her. He couldn't stand to see that. He couldn't stand to see her getting her dignity back. He killed her like a dog in the manger."

After ten years her mind was still buzzing like a fly around the bloody moment.

"Why didn't you continue Dolly's therapy? She probably needed it more than ever afterward."

"It wasn't possible. I work Saturday mornings. I have to get my paperwork done some time." She fell silent, confused and tongue-tied as honest people can be by their own deviousness.

"Also you had a disagreement with Godwin about your niece's testimony at the trial."

"I'm not ashamed of it, no matter what *he* says. It did her no harm to speak out about her father. It probably did her good. She had to get it out of her system somehow."

"It isn't out of her system, though. She's still hung up on it." Just as you are, Miss Jenks. "But now she's changed her story."

"Changed her story?"

"She says now that she didn't see her father the night of the murder. She denies that he had anything to do with it."

"Who told you that?"

"Godwin. He'd just been talking to her. She told him she lied in court to please the adults." I was tempted to say more, but remembered in time that it would almost certainly be relayed to her friend the Sheriff.

She was looking at me as if I had questioned a basic faith of her life. "He's twisting what she said, I'm sure. He's using her to prove that he was right when he was wrong."

"I doubt that, Miss Jenks. Godwin doesn't believe her new story himself."

"You see! She's either crazy or she's lying! Don't forget she's got McGee blood in her!" She was appalled by her own outburst. She turned her eyes away, glancing around the pink room as though it might somehow vouch for the girlish innocence of her intentions. "I didn't really mean that," she said. "I love my niece. It's just—it's harder than I thought to rake over the past like this."

"I'm sorry, and I'm sure you love your niece. Feeling about her the way you do, and did, you couldn't have fed her a false story to tell in court."

"Who says I did?"

"No one. I'm saying you couldn't have. You're not the sort of woman who could bring herself to corrupt the mind of a twelve-year-old child."

"No," she said. "I had nothing to do with Dolly's accusation against her father. She came to me with it, the night it happened, within half-an-hour of the *time* it happened. I never questioned it for a minute. It had all the accents of truth."

But she had not. I didn't think she was lying, exactly. More likely she was suppressing something. She spoke carefully and in a low voice, so that the motto in the living room wouldn't hear her. She still wasn't meeting my eyes. A slow dull flush rose from her heavy neck to her face. I said:

"I doubt that it was physically possible for her to identify anyone, even her own father, at this distance on a dark night—let alone pick out a smoking gun in his hand."

"But the police accepted it. Sheriff Crane and the D.A. both believed her."

"Policemen and prosecutors are usually glad to accept the facts, or the pseudo-facts, that fit their case."

"But Tom McGee was guilty. He was guilty."

"He may have been."

"Then why are you trying to convince me that he wasn't?" The flush of shame in her face was going through the usual conversion into a flush of anger. "I won't listen."

"You might as well listen. What can you lose? I'm trying to open up that old case because it's connected, through Dolly, with the Haggerty case."

"Do you believe she killed Miss Haggerty?" she said.

"No. Do you?"

"Sheriff Crane seems to regard her as the main suspect."

"Did he say so to you, Miss Jenks?"

"He as much as said so. He was feeling me out on what my reaction would be if he took her in for questioning."

"And what was your reaction?"

"I hardly know, I was so upset. I haven't seen Dolly for some time. She went and married behind my back. She was always a good girl, but she may have changed."

I had the feeling that Miss Jenks was talking out of her deepest sense of herself: She had always been a good girl, but she might have changed.

"Why don't you call Crane up and tell him to lay off? Your niece needs delicate handling."

"You don't believe she's guilty of this murder?"

"I said I didn't. Tell him to lay off or he'll lose the next election."

"I couldn't do that. He's my senior in county work." But she was thinking about it. She shook the thought off. "Speaking of which, I've given you all the time I possibly can. It must be past twelve."

I was ready to leave. It had been a long hour. She followed me downstairs and out onto the veranda. I had the impression as we said goodbye that she wanted to say something more. Her face was expectant. But nothing came.

13

THE FOG had thinned out a little along the coastline, but you still couldn't see the sun, only a sourceless white glare that hurt the eyes. The keyboy at the Mariner's Rest told me that Alex had driven away with an older man in a new Chrysler. His own red sports car was still in the parking enclosure, and he hadn't checked out.

I bought a sandwich at a drive-in down the street and ate it in my room. Then I made a couple of frustrating phone calls. The switchboard operator at the courthouse said there wasn't a chance of getting hold of a trial transcript this afternoon: everything was locked up tight for the weekend. I called the office of Gil Stevens, the lawyer who had unsuccessfully defended Tom McGee. His answering service said he was in Balboa. No, I couldn't reach him there. Mr. Stevens was racing his yacht today and tomorrow.

I decided to drop in on Jerry Marks, the young lawyer who had acted as Mrs. Perrine's defense counsel. His office was in a new shopping center not too far from the motel strip. Jerry was unmarried and ambitious, and he might be in it, even on a Saturday afternoon.

The front door was open and I walked into the waiting room, which was furnished with maple and chintz. The secretary's cubicle behind the glass half-wall on the left was deserted for the weekend, but Jerry Marks was in the inner office.

"How are you, Jerry?"

"I'm all right."

He looked at me guardedly over the book he was reading, an enormous tome entitled *Rules of Evidence*. He wasn't very experienced in criminal practice, but he was competent and honest. His homely Middle-European face was warmed and lit by intelligent brown eyes.

"How's Mrs. Perrine?" I said.

"I haven't seen her since she was released, and I don't expect to. I seldom see much of my ex-clients. I smell of the courtroom to them."

"I have the same experience. Are you free?"

"Yeah, and I'm going to stay that way. I promised myself a clear week-end of study, murder or no murder."

"You know about the Haggerty murder then."

"Naturally, it's all over town."

"What have you heard?"

"Really not very much. Somebody at the courthouse told my secretary that this lady professor was shot by a girl student at the college. I forget her name."

"Dolly Kincaid. Her husband is my client. She's in a nursing home, under a doctor's care."

"Psycho?"

"It depends on your definition of psycho. It's a complex situation, Jerry. I doubt that she's legally insane under the McNaghten rule. On the other hand I very much doubt that she did the shooting at all."

"You're trying to get me interested in the case," he said suspiciously.

"I'm not trying to do anything to you. Actually I came to you for in-formation. What's your opinion of Gil Stevens?"

"He's the local old master. Get him."

"He's out of town. Seriously, is he a good lawyer?"

"Stevens is the most successful criminal lawyer in the county. He has to be good. He knows law, and he knows juries. He does pull some old-fashioned courtroom shenanigans that I wouldn't use myself. He's quite an actor, heavy with the emotion. It works, though. I can't remember when he's lost an important case."

"I can. About ten years ago he defended a man named Tom McGee who was convicted of shooting his wife."

"That was before my time."

"Dolly Kincaid is McGee's daughter. Also, she was the key witness for the prosecution at her father's trial."

Jerry whistled. "I see what you mean by complex." After a pause, he said: "Who's her doctor?"

"Godwin."

He pushed out his heavy lips. "I'd go easy with him."

"What do you mean?"

"I'm sure he's a good psychiatrist, but maybe not so much in the forensic department. He's a very bright man and he doesn't hide his light under a bushel, in fact he sometimes acts like a mastermind. Which puts people's backs up, especially if their name is Gahagan and they're sitting on the Superior Court bench. So I'd use him sparingly."

"I can't control the use that's made of him."

"No, but you can warn her attorney—"

"It would be a lot simpler if you were her attorney. I haven't had a chance to talk to her husband today, but I think he'll go along with my recommendation. His family isn't poverty-stricken, by the way."

"It wasn't the money I was thinking about," Jerry said coldly. "I promised myself that I'd spend this weekend with my books."

"Helen Haggerty should have picked another weekend to get herself shot."

It came out harsher than I intended. My own failure to do anything for Helen was eating me.

Jerry regarded me quizzically. "This case is a personal matter with you?"

"It seems to be."

"Okay, okay," he said. "What do you want me to do?"

"Just hold yourself in readiness for the present."

"I'll be here all afternoon. After that my answering service will be able to contact me."

I thanked him and went back to the motel. Alex's room next to mine was still empty. I checked with my own answering service in Hollywood. Arnie Walters had left his number for me and I called Reno.

Arnie was out of the office, but his wife and partner Phyllis took the call. Her exuberant femininity bounced along the wires:

"I never *see* you, Lew. All I hear is your voice on the telephone. For all I know you don't exist any more, but simply made some tapes a number of years ago and somebody plays them to me from time to time."

"How do you explain the fact that I'm responsive? Like now."

"Electronics. I explain everything I don't understand electronically. It saves me no end of trouble. But when am I going to *see* you?"

"This weekend, if Arnie's tabbed the driver of the convertible."

"He hasn't quite done that, but he does have a line on the owner. She's a Mrs. Sally Burke and she lives right here in Reno. She claims her car was stolen a couple of days ago. But Arnie doesn't believe her."

"Why not?"

"He's very intuitive. Also she didn't report the alleged theft. Also she has boy friends of various types. Arnie's out doing legwork on them now."

"Good."

"I gather this is important," Phyllis said.

"It's a double murder case, maybe a triple. My client's a young girl with emotional problems. She's probably going to be arrested today or tomorrow, for something she almost certainly didn't do."

"You sound very intense."

"This case has gotten under my skin. Also I don't know where I'm at."

"I never heard you admit that before, Lew. Anyway, I was thinking before you called, maybe I could strike up an acquaintance with Mrs. Sally Burke. Does that sound like a good idea to you?"

"An excellent idea." Phyllis was an ex-Pinkerton operative who looked like an ex-chorus girl. "Remember Mrs. Burke and her playmates may be highly dangerous. They may have killed a woman last night."

"Not this woman. I've got too much to live for." She meant Arnie.

We exchanged some further pleasantries in the course of which I heard people coming into Alex's room next door. After I said goodbye to Phyllis I stood by the wall and listened. Alex's voice and the voice of another man were raised in argument, and I didn't need a contact mike to tell what the argument was about. The other man wanted Alex to clear out of this unfortunate mess and come home.

I knocked on his door.

"Let me handle them," the other man said, as if he was expecting the police.

He stepped outside, a man of about my age, good-looking in a grayish way, with a thin face, narrow light eyes, a pugnacious chin. The mark of organization was on him, like an invisible harness worn under his conservative gray suit.

There was some kind of desperation in him, too. He didn't even ask who I was before he said: "I'm Frederick Kincaid and you have no right to chivvy my son around. He has nothing to do with that girl and her crimes. She married him under false pretenses. The marriage didn't last twenty-four hours. My son is a respectable boy—"

Alex stepped out and pulled at the older man's arm. His face was miserable with embarrassment. "You'd better come inside, Dad. This is Mr. Archer."

"Archer, eh? I understand you've involved my son in this thing—"

"On the contrary, he hired me."

"I'm firing you." His voice sounded as if it had often performed this function.

"We'll talk it over," I said.

The three of us jostled each other in the doorway. Kincaid senior didn't want me to come in. It was very close to turning into a brawl. Each of us was ready to hit at least one of the others.

I bulled my way into the room and sat down in a chair with my back to the wall. "What's happened, Alex?"

"Dad heard about me on the radio. He phoned the Sheriff and found out where I was. The Sheriff called us over there just now. They found the murder gun."

"Where?"

Alex was slow in answering, as though the words in his mouth would make the whole thing realer when he let them out. His father answered for him:

"Where she hid it, under the mattress of the bed in that little hut she's been living in—"

"It isn't a hut," Alex said. "It's a gatehouse."

"Don't contradict me, Alex."

"Did you see the gun?" I said.

"We did. The Sheriff wanted Alex to identify it, which naturally he couldn't do. He didn't even know she had a gun."

"What kind of a gun is it?"

"It's a Smith and Wesson revolver, .38 caliber, with walnut grips. Old, but in pretty fair condition. She probably bought it at a pawn shop."

"Is this the police theory?"

"The Sheriff mentioned the possibility."

"How does he know it's hers?"

"They found it under her mattress, didn't they?" Kincaid talked like a prosecutor making a case, using it to bring his son into line. "Who else could have hidden it there?"

"Practically anybody else. The gatehouse was standing open last night, wasn't it, Alex?"

"It was when I got there."

"Let me do the talking," his father said. "I've had more experience in these matters."

"It hasn't done you a hell of a lot of good. Your son is a witness, and I'm trying to get at the facts."

He stood over me with his hands on his hips, vibrating. "My son has nothing whatever to do with this case."

"Don't kid yourself. He's married to the girl."

"The marriage is meaningless—a boyish impulse that didn't last one full day. I'm having it annulled. It wasn't even consummated, he tells me."

"You can't annul it."

"Don't tell me what I can do."

"I think I will, though. All you can do is annul yourself and your son. There's more to a marriage than sexual consummation or legal technicalities. The marriage is real because it's real for Alex."

"He wants out of it now."

"I don't believe you."

"It's true, isn't it, Alex, you want to come home with me and Mother? She's terribly worried about you. Her heart is kicking up again." Kincaid was throwing everything but the kitchen sink.

Alex looked from him to me. "I don't know. I just want to do what's right."

Kincaid started to say something, probably having to do with the kitchen sink, but I talked over him:

"Then answer another question or two, Alex. Was Dolly carrying a gun when she came running back to the gatehouse last night?"

"I didn't see one."

Kincaid said: "She probably had it concealed under her clothes."

"Shut up, Kincaid," I said calmly from my sitting position. "I don't object to the fact that you're a bloodless bastard. You obviously can't help it. I do object to your trying to make Alex into one. Leave him a choice, at least."

Kincaid sputtered a couple of times, and walked away from me. Alex said without looking at either of us: "Don't talk to my father that way, Mr. Archer."

"All right. She was wearing a cardigan and a blouse and skirt. Anything else?"

"No."

"Carrying a bag?"

"I don't think so."

"Think."

"She wasn't."

"Then she couldn't have been carrying a concealed .38 revolver. You didn't see her hide it under the mattress?"

"No."

"And were you with her all the time, between the time she got back and the time she left for the nursing home?"

"Yes. I was with her all the time."

"Then it's pretty clear it isn't Dolly's gun, or at least it wasn't Dolly who hid it under the mattress. Do you have any idea who it could have been?"

"No."

"You said it was the murder gun. How did they establish that? They haven't had time for ballistics tests."

Kincaid spoke up from the far corner where he had been sulking: "It's the right caliber to fit the wound, and one shell had been fired, recently. It stands to reason it's the gun she used."

"Do you believe that, Alex?"

"I don't know."

"Have they questioned her?"

"They intend to. The Sheriff said something about waiting until they nailed it down with ballistic evidence, Monday."

That gave me a little time, if I could believe Alex. The pressures of the night and morning, on top of the uncertainties of the last three weeks, had left him punchy. He looked almost out on his feet.

"I think we all should wait," I said, "before we make up our minds about your wife. Even if she's guilty, which I very strongly doubt, you owe her all the help and support you can give her."

"He owes her nothing," Kincaid said. "Not a thing. She married him fraudulently. She lied to him again and again."

I kept my voice and temper down, for contrast. "She still needs medical care, and she needs a lawyer. I have a good local lawyer waiting to step in, but I can't retain him myself."

"You're taking quite a lot into your hands, aren't you?"

"Somebody has to assume responsibility. There's a lot of it floating around loose at the moment. You can't avoid it by crawling into a hole and pulling the hole in after you. The girl's in trouble, and whether you like it or not she's a member of your family."

Alex appeared to be listening. I didn't know if he was hearing me. His father shook his narrow gray head:

"She's no member of my family, and I'll tell you one thing for certain. She's not going to drag my son down into the underworld. And neither are you." He turned to Alex. "How much have you already paid this man?"

"A couple of hundred."

Kincaid said to me: "You've been amply paid, exorbitantly paid. You heard me fire you. This is a private room and if you persist in intruding I'll call the management. If they can't handle you I'll call the police."

Alex looked at me and lifted his hands, not very far, in a helpless movement. His father put an arm around his shoulders:

"I'm only doing what's best for you, son. You don't belong with these people. We'll go home and cheer up Mother. After all you don't want to drive her into her grave."

It came out smooth and pat, and it was the clincher. Alex didn't look at me again. I went back to my own room and phoned Jerry Marks and told him I had lost a client and so had he. Jerry seemed disappointed.

14
..

ALEX and his father vacated their room and drove away. I didn't go out to see them off but I could hear the sound of their engines, quickly muffled by the fog. I sat and let my stomach unknot, telling myself I should have handled them better. Kincaid was a frightened man who valued his status the way some previous generations valued their souls.

I drove up Foothill to the Bradshaw house. The Dean was probably another breakable reed, but he had money, and he had shown some sympathy for Dolly, over and above his official interest in the case. I had no desire to continue it on my own. I needed a principal, preferably one who swung some weight locally. Alice Jenks met this requirement, more or less, but I didn't want her for a client.

A deputy was standing guard at the gatehouse. He wouldn't let me in to look around but he didn't object to my going up to the main house. The Spanish woman Maria answered the door.

"Is Dr. Bradshaw home?"

"No sir."

"Where can I find him?"

She shrugged. "I dunno. I think Mrs. Bradshaw said he's gone for the weekend."

"That's queer. I'd like to talk to Mrs. Bradshaw."

"I'll see if she's busy."

I stepped inside uninvited and sat on a gilt chair in the entrance hall while Maria went upstairs. She came down and told me that Mrs. Bradshaw would be with me shortly.

It was at least half-an-hour before she came limping down. She had primped her gray head and rouged her cheeks and put on a dress with lace at her slack throat held in place by a diamond brooch. I wondered, as she made me the dubious gift of her hand, if all this had been done for my benefit.

The old lady seemed glad to see me. "How are you, Mr.—it's Mr. Archer, isn't it? I've been so hoping somebody would call. This fog makes one feel so isolated, and with my driver gone—" She seemed to hear the note of complaint rising in her voice, and cut it off. "How is the girl?" she said briskly.

"She's being taken care of. Dr. Godwin thinks she's better than she was last night."

"Good. You'll be glad to know," she said with a bright ironic stare, "that I'm somewhat better myself than I was last night. My son informed me this morning that I staged one of my exhibitions, as he calls them. Frankly, I was upset. Nights aren't my best season."

"It was a rough night for everybody."

"And I'm a selfish old woman. Isn't that what you're thinking?"

"People don't seem to change much as they get older."

"That has all the earmarks of an insult." But she was smiling, almost flirtatiously. "You imply that I've always been this way."

"You'd know better than I would."

She laughed outright. It wasn't a joyous sound, but there was humor in it. "You're a bold young man, and a bright one. I like bright young men. Come into the study and I'll see that you get a drink."

"Thank you, but I can't stay—"

"Then I'll sit here." She lowered herself carefully onto the gilt chair. "My moral qualities may not have altered for the worse. My physical capabilities certainly have. This fog is very bad for my arthritis." She added, with a gingerly shake of her head: "But I mustn't complain. I promised my son, in penance for last night, that I would go through an entire day without uttering a word of complaint."

"How are you doing?"

"Not so well," she said with her wry and wrinkled smile. "It's like solitaire, you always cheat a little. Or don't you?"

"I don't play the game."

"You're not missing a great deal, but it helps to pass the days for me. Well, I won't keep you if you have business."

"I have business with Dr. Bradshaw. Do you know where I can contact him?"

"Roy flew to Reno this morning."

"Reno?"

"Not to gamble, I assure you. He hasn't an iota of gambling instinct. In fact I sometimes think he's excessively cautious. Roy is a bit of a mother's boy, wouldn't you say?" She looked up at me with complex irony, unembarrassed by his condition or her complicity in it.

"I'm a little surprised that he'd go away in the middle of this murder case."

"So was I, but there was no stopping him. He isn't exactly running away from it. They're holding a conference of small-college deans at the University of Nevada. It's been planned for months, and Roy is slated as one of the principal speakers. He felt it was his duty to be there. But I could see very well that he was eager to go. He loves the public eye, you know—he's always been a bit of an actor—but he isn't so terribly fond of the responsibilities that go with it."

I was amused and intrigued and a little appalled by her realism. She seemed to be enjoying it herself. Conversation was better than solitaire.

Mrs. Bradshaw rose creakingly and leaned on my arm. "You might as well come into the study. It's drafty here. I've taken a fancy to you, young man."

I didn't know if this was a blessing or a curse. She grinned up into my face as if she could read my doubts there. "Don't worry, I won't eat you." She placed the emphasis on the final word, as though she had already eaten her son for breakfast.

We went into the study together and sat in facing highbacked leather chairs. She rang for Maria and ordered me a highball. Then she leaned back and scanned the bookshelves. The phalanxes of books seemed to remind her of Bradshaw's importance.

"Don't misunderstand me. I love my son profoundly and I'm proud of him. I'm proud of his good looks and I'm proud of his brains. He graduated *summa cum laude* from Harvard and went on to take a most distinguished doctorate. One of these days he's going to be the president of a major university or a great foundation."

"Is he ambitious, or are you?"

"I used to be, for him. As Roy became more ambitious, I became less so. There are better things in life than climbing an endless ladder. I haven't entirely given up hope that he'll marry." She cocked a bright old eye at me. "He *likes* women, you know."

"I'm sure he does."

"In fact I was beginning to persuade myself that he was interested in Miss Haggerty. I've never known him to pay so much attention to any other woman." She dropped the statement so that it became a question.

"He mentioned to me that he took her out several times. But he also said that they were never close in any way. His reaction to her death confirmed that."

"What was his reaction to her death?"

I'd done a lot of pumping in my time, and I knew when it was being done to me. "I mean his general reaction. He wouldn't have flown to Reno this morning, deans' conference or no deans' conference, if he had been really fond of Helen Haggerty. He'd be here in Pacific Point trying to find out who did her in."

"You seem quite let down about it."

"I was looking for his help. He seemed genuinely concerned about Dolly Kincaid."

"He is. We both are. In fact Roy asked me at breakfast to do what I could for the girl. But what can I do?" She displayed her crumpled hands, making a show of her helplessness.

Maria came in with my clinking highball, handed it to me unceremoniously, and asked her employer if there was anything else. There wasn't. I sipped my drink, wondering if Mrs. Bradshaw was a client I could possibly handle, if she became my client. She had the money, all right. The diamonds winking at her throat would have bought my services for several years.

"You can hire me," I said.

"Hire you?"

"If you really want to do something for Dolly, and not just sit there paying lip-service to the idea. Do you think we could get along?"

"I was getting along with men when you were in the cradle, Mr. Archer. Are you implying I can't get along with people?"

"I seem to be the one who can't. Alex Kincaid just fired me, with a strong assist from his father. They want no part of Dolly and her problems, now that the chips are down."

Her black eyes flashed. "I saw through that boy immediately. He's a mollycoddle."

"I don't have the resources to go on by myself. It isn't good practice, anyway. I need somebody to back me, preferably somebody with local standing and—I'll be frank—a substantial bank balance."

"How much would it cost me?"

"It depends on how long the case goes on and how many ramifications develop. I get a hundred a day and expenses. Also I have a team of detectives in Reno working on a lead that may be a hot one."

"A lead in Reno?"

"It originated here, last night."

I told her about the man in the convertible which belonged to Mrs. Sally Burke, a woman with many boy friends. She leaned forward in her chair in mounting interest:

"Why aren't the police working on that lead?"

"They may be. If they are, I don't know about it. They seem to have settled for the idea that Dolly's guilty and everything else is irrelevant. It's simpler that way."

"You don't accept that idea?"

"No."

"In spite of the gun they found in her bed?"

"You know about that, then."

"Sheriff Crane showed it to me this morning. He wanted to know if I recognized it. Of course I didn't. I abhor the very sight of guns myself. I've never permitted Roy to own a gun."

"And you have no idea who owned that one?"

"No, but the Sheriff appeared to take it for granted that it was Dolly's, and that it tied her to the murder."

"We have no reason to think it was hers. If it was, the last place she'd put it would be under her own mattress. Her husband denies she did, and he was with her continuously once she got back to the gatehouse. There's the further point that there's no definite proof it's the murder weapon."

"Really?"

"Really. It will take ballistics tests, and they're not scheduled until Monday. If my luck holds, I think I can throw more light on the situation by then."

"Do you have a definite theory of your own, Mr. Archer?"

"I have an idea that the ramifications of this thing go far back beyond Dolly. It wasn't Dolly who threatened Miss Haggerty's life. She would have recognized her voice, they were close friends. I think Dolly walked up to her house simply to ask her advice about whether to go back to her husband. She stumbled over the body and panicked. She's still in panic."

"Why?"

"I'm not prepared to explain it. I want to go into her background further. I also want to go into Miss Haggerty's background."

"That might be interesting," she said, as if she was considering attending a double-feature movie. "How much is all this going to cost me?"

"I'll keep it as low as I can. But it could mount up in the thousands, two or three or even four."

"That's rather an expensive penance."

"Penance?"

"For all my selfishness, past and present and future. I'll think about it, Mr. Archer."

"How long do you need to think about it?"

"Call me tonight. Roy will be telephoning me around dinnertime— he telephones me every night when he's away—and I couldn't possibly give you an answer before I discuss it with him. We live on a tighter budget than you might think," she said earnestly, fingering the diamonds at her throat.

15
##

I DROVE up under the dripping trees to Helen Haggerty's place. Two deputies messing around outside the front door wouldn't let me in or answer any questions. It was turning out to be a bad day.

I drifted over to the campus and into the Administration Building. I had some idea of talking to Laura Sutherland, the Dean of Women, but her office was locked. All the offices were locked. The building was deserted except for a white-headed man in blue jeans who was sweeping the corridor with a long-handled push-broom. He looked like Father Time, and I had a nightmare moment of thinking that he was sweeping Helen's last vestiges away.

In a kind of defensive reflex I got out my notebook and looked up the name of the chairman of the modern languages department. Dr. Geisman. The old man with the push-broom knew where his office was:

"It's in the new Humanity Building, down the line." He pointed. "But he won't be there on a Saturday afternoon."

The old man was mistaken. I found Geisman in the department office on the first floor of the Humanities Building, sitting with a telephone receiver in one hand and a pencil in the other. I had seen him coming out of Bradshaw's conference the day before, a heavy middle-aged man with thick spectacles imperfectly masking anxious little eyes.

"One moment," he said to me; and into the telephone: "I'm sorry you can't help us, Mrs. Bass. I realize you have your family responsibilities and of course the remuneration is not great for a special lecturer."

He sounded foreign, though he had no accent. His voice was denatured, as if English was just another language he had learned.

"I am Dr. Geisman," he said as he hung up and stroked out a name on the list in front of him. "Are you Dr. de Falla?"

"No. My name is Archer."

"What are your qualifications? Do you have an advanced degree?"

"In the university of hard knocks."

He didn't respond to my smile. "A member of our faculty is defunct, as you must know, and I've had to give up my Saturday to an attempt to find a replacement for her. If you expect me to take your application seriously—"

"I'm not applying for anything, doctor, except possibly a little information. I'm a private detective investigating Professor Haggerty's death, and I'm interested in how she happened to land here."

"I have no time to go into all that again. There are classes which must be met on Monday. If this Dr. de Falla doesn't arrive, or proves impossible, I don't know what to do." He peered at his wristwatch. "I'm due at the Los Angeles airport at six-thirty."

"You can spare five minutes, anybody can."

"Very well. Five minutes." He tapped the crystal of his watch. "You wish to know how Miss Haggerty came here? I can't say, except that she appeared in my office one day and asked for a position. She had heard about Professor Farrand's heart attack. This is our second emergency in a month."

"Who told her about the heart attack?"

"I don't know. Perhaps Dean Sutherland. She gave Dean Sutherland as a local reference. But it was common knowledge, it was in the paper."

"Was she living here before she applied for a job with you?"

"I believe so. Yes, she was. She told me she already had a house. She liked the place, and wished to remain. She was very eager for the post. Frankly, I had some doubts about her. She had a master's degree from Chicago but she wasn't fully qualified. The school where she had been teaching, Maple Park, is not credentialed on our level. But Dean Sutherland told me she needed the position and I let her have it, unfortunately."

"I understood she had a private income."

He pursed his lips and shook his head. "Ladies with a private income don't take on four sections of French and German, plus counseling duties, at a salary of less than five thousand dollars. Perhaps she meant her alimony. She told me she was having difficulty collecting her alimony." His spectacles glinted as he looked up. "You knew that she had been recently divorced?"

"I heard that. Do you know where her ex-husband is?"

"No. I had very few words with her at any time. Do you suspect him?"

"I have no reason to. But when a woman is killed you normally look for a man who had a motive to kill her. The local police have other ideas."

"You don't agree with them?"

"I'm keeping my mind open, doctor."

"I see. They tell me one of our students is under suspicion."

"So I hear. Do you know the girl?"

"No. She was registered for none of our departmental courses, fortunately."

"Why 'fortunately'?"

"She is psychoneurotic, they tell me." His myopic eyes looked as vulnerable as open oysters under the thick lenses of his glasses. "If the administration employed proper screening procedures we would not have students of that sort on the campus, endangering our lives. But we are very backward here in some respects." He tapped the crystal of his watch again. "You've had your five minutes."

"One more question, doctor. Have you been in touch with Helen Haggerty's family?"

"Yes, I phoned her mother early this morning. Dean Bradshaw asked me to perform that duty, though properly I should think it was his duty. The mother, Mrs. Hoffman, is flying out here and I have to meet her at the Los Angeles airport."

"At six-thirty?"

He nodded dismally. "There seems to be no one else available. Both of our deans are out of town—"

"Dean Sutherland, too?"

"Dean Sutherland, too. They've gone off and left the whole business on my shoulders." His glasses blurred with self-pity, and he took them off to wipe them. "It's foggy, and I can't see to drive properly. My eyesight is so poor that without my glasses I can't tell the difference between you and the Good Lord himself."

"There isn't much difference."

He put on his glasses, saw that this was a joke, and emitted a short barking laugh.

"What plane is Mrs. Hoffman coming in on, doctor?"

"United, from Chicago. I promised to meet her at the United baggage counter."

"Let me."

"Are you serious?"

"It will give me a chance to talk to her. Where do you want me to bring her?"

"I reserved her a room at the Pacific Hotel. I could meet you there, at eight, say."

"Fine."

He got up and came around the desk and shook my hand vigorously. As I was leaving the building, a small, old man in a black hat and a greenish black cloak came sidling out of the fog. He had a dyed-looking black mustache, hectic black eyes, a wine flush on his hollow cheeks.

"Dr. de Falla?"

He nodded. I held the door for him. He swept off his hat and bowed.

"Merci beaucoup."

His rubber-soled shoes made no more sound than a spider. I had another one of my little nightmare moments. This one was Doctor Death.

16
..

IT WAS a slow drive up the coast but the fog lifted before I reached the airport, leaving a thickish twilight in the air. I parked my car at the United building. It was exactly six-twenty-five, according to the ticket the girl in the parking lot handed me. I crossed the road to the bright enormous building and found the baggage carrousel, besieged by travelers.

A woman who looked like a dried-up older Helen was standing on the edge of the crowd beside her suitcase. She had on a black dress under a black coat with a ratty fur collar, black hat, and black gloves.

Only her garish red hair was out of keeping with the occasion. Her eyes were swollen, and she seemed dazed, as if a part of her mind was still back in Illinois.

"Mrs. Hoffman?"

"Yes. I'm Mrs. Earl Hoffman."

"My name is Archer. Your daughter's department head, Dr. Geisman, asked me to pick you up."

"That was nice of him," she said with a poor vague smile. "And nice of you."

I picked up her suitcase, which was small and light. "Would you like something to eat, or drink? There's a pretty good restaurant here."

"Oh no thanks. I had dinner on the plane. Swiss steak. It was a very interesting flight. I never flew in a jet before. But I wasn't the least bit frightened."

She didn't know what she was. She stared around at the bright lights and the people. The muscles of her face were tensing up as if she might be getting ready to cry some more. I got hold of her thin upper arm and hustled her out of there and across the road to my car. We circled the parking lot and got onto the freeway.

"They didn't have this when I was here before. I'm glad you decided to meet me. I'd get lost," she said in a lost voice.

"How long is it since you were here before?"

"Nearly twenty years. It was when Hoffman was in the Navy, he was a warrant officer in the Shore Patrol. They assigned him to San Diego and Helen had already run—left home, and I thought I might as well get the benefit of the travel. We lived in San Diego for over a year, and it was very nice." I could hear her breathing as if she was struggling up to the rim of the present. She said carefully: "Pacific Point is quite near San Diego, isn't it?"

"About fifty miles."

"Is that right?" After another pause, she said: "Are you with the college?"

"I happen to be a detective."

"Isn't that interesting? My husband is a detective. He's been on the Bridgeton force for thirty-four years. He's due to retire next year. We've talked about retiring in California but this will probably turn him against it. He pretends not to care, but he cares. I think he cares just as much as I do." Her voice floated along above the highway noises like a disembodied spirit talking to itself.

"It's too bad he couldn't fly out with you today."

"He could have, if he'd wanted to. He could have taken time off. I think he was afraid he couldn't face it. And he has his blood pressure to consider." She hesitated again. "Are you investigating my daughter's murder?"

"Yes."

"Dr. Geisman said on the phone that you have a suspect, a young girl. What would make a student shoot one of her teachers? I never heard of such a thing."

"I don't think she did, Mrs. Hoffman."

"But Dr. Geisman said it was practically open and shut." The sorrow in her voice had changed into a kind of vengeful justice.

"That may be." I had no desire to argue with a potentially valuable witness. "I'm investigating other angles, and you may be able to help me."

"How is that?"

"Your daughter's life was threatened. She talked to me about it before she was shot. Somebody called her on the telephone. It was a voice she didn't recognize, but she said a strange thing about it. She said it sounded like the voice of Bridgeton."

"Bridgeton? That's where we live."

"I know that, Mrs. Hoffman. Helen said it was Bridgeton catching up with her. Do you have any idea what she meant?"

"She always hated Bridgeton. From the time that she was in high school she blamed it for everything that went wrong with her life. She couldn't wait to get out of Bridgeton."

"I understand she ran away from home."

"I wouldn't put it that way," although she almost had. "She only dropped out of sight for the one summer, and she was working all the time. She had a job with a newspaper in Chicago. Then she started in at the University, and she let me know where she was. It was just her father—" She cut this sentence off short. "I used to help her out of my housekeeping money until we went into the Navy."

"What was the trouble between her and her father?"

"It had to do with his professional work. At least that was what the final big battle was about."

"When Helen called him a crooked stormtrooper?"

She turned in the seat to look at me. "Helen told you that, eh? Are you—were you her boy friend or something like that?"

"We were friends." I found that I could say it with some conviction. We had spent a single angry hour together but her death had turned a light on it which hurt my eyes.

She leaned closer to study my face. "What else did she tell you?"

"There was murder involved in her quarrel with her father."

"That's a lie. I don't mean Helen was lying, but she was mistaken. The Deloney shooting was an accident pure and simple. If Helen thought she knew more about it than her father, she was dead wrong."

"Dead" and "wrong" were heavy words to lay on the dead. Her black-gloved hand flew up to her mouth. She rode for a while in hunched and fearful silence, a thin dry cricket of a woman who had lost her chirp.

"Tell me about the Deloney shooting, Mrs. Hoffman."

"I don't see the point of doing that. I never talk about my husband's cases. He doesn't like me to."

"But he isn't here."

"In a way he is. We've been together so long. Anyway it's all past history."

"History is always connected with the present. That case may have something to do with Helen's death."

"How could that be? It was twenty years ago, longer than that, and it didn't amount to anything at the time. The only reason it made an impression on Helen was that it happened in our apartment building. Mr. Deloney was cleaning a gun, and it went off and shot him, and that was the whole story."

"Are you sure?"

"Hoffman said so, and Hoffman doesn't lie." It sounded like an incantation which she had used before.

"What made Helen think he was lying?"

"Imagination pure and simple. She said she talked to a witness who saw somebody shoot Mr. Deloney, but I say she dreamed it. No witness ever turned up, and Hoffman said there couldn't have been a witness. Mr. Deloney was alone in the apartment when it happened. He tried to clean a loaded gun and shot himself in the face. Helen must have dreamed the other. She had a bit of a crush on Mr. Deloney. He was a good-looking man, and you know how young girls are."

"How old was she?"

"Nineteen. That was the summer she left home."

It was full dark now. Away off to the right the lights of Long Beach, where I had spent my own uneasy youth, were reflected like a dying red fire from the overcast.

"Who was Mr. Deloney?"

"Luke Deloney," she said. "He was a very successful contractor in Bridgeton and throughout the state. He owned our apartment building and other buildings in town. Mrs. Deloney still owns them. They're worth a lot more than they were then, and even then he was close to a millionaire."

"Deloney has a surviving widow?"

"Yes, but don't go jumping to conclusions. She was miles away, in their main house, when it happened. Sure there was a lot of talk in town, but she was as innocent as a newborn babe. She came from a very good family. She was one of the famous Osborne sisters in Bridgeton."

"What were they famous for?"

"Their father was the U. S. Senator. I remember when I was in grade school, back before the World War One, they used to ride to hounds in red coats. But they were always very democratic."

"Good for them." I brought her back to the Deloney case. "You say Deloney was shot in the building where you had your own apartment?"

"Yes. We were in an apartment on the ground floor. We got it dirt cheap because we used to collect the rent for Mr. Deloney. He kept the roof apartment for himself. He used it for a kind of private office, and a place to throw parties for visiting firemen and so on. A lot of big men from the state house were friends of his. We used to see them coming and going," she said in a privileged way.

"And he shot himself in this penthouse apartment?"

"The gun shot him," she corrected me. "It was an accident."

"What sort of a man was Deloney?"

"He was a self-made man, I guess you'd say. He came from the same section of town Hoffman and I did, which is how we got the job collecting rent for him, and that *helped*, in the depression. The depression didn't faze Luke Deloney. He borrowed the money to start his own contracting business and came up fast on his own initiative, and married Senator Osborne's oldest daughter. There's no telling where he might have got to. He was only a young man of forty when he died."

"Helen was interested in him, you say?"

"Not seriously, I don't mean that. I doubt if they ever said two words to each other. But you know how young girls are, dreaming about older men. He was the most successful man around, and Helen was always very ambitious. It's funny, she blamed her father for being a failure, which he isn't. But when she finally got around to marrying she had to pick Bert Haggerty, and he's a failure if there ever was one."

She was talking much more freely, but her loquacity tended to fly off in all directions. It was natural enough. Her daughter's murder had dropped a depth charge into her life.

"Assume there is a connection," I said, "between Helen's death and the Deloney shooting—do you have any notion what it could be?"

"No, she must have been imagining things. She was always a great one for that."

"But she said she knew a witness who saw Deloney shot by someone else?"

"She was talking foolishness."

"Why?"

"You mean why would she say such things to her father? To get under his skin. There was always bad blood between them, from the time that Hoffman first raised his hand to her. Once they got arguing, there wasn't anything she wouldn't say."

"Did she name the witness?"

"How could she? There was no such person. Her father challenged her to mention a name. She admitted that she couldn't, that she was just talking."

"She admitted it?"

"She had to. Hoffman made her. But she never took back the hard words she spoke to him."

"Is it possible that Helen herself was the witness?"

"That's crazy and you know it. How could she be a witness to something that never happened?" But there was a shrill edge on her certitude.

"Deloney's dead, remember. So is she. It tends to confirm the things she told her friends before she died."

"About Bridgeton, you mean?"

"Yes."

She lapsed into silence again. Below the harbor cities we entered the fog zone. I was afraid of running into a pileup and I slowed down. Mrs. Hoffman kept looking back as if she could feel Bridgeton catching up.

"I hope Hoffman isn't drinking," she said after a while. "It isn't good for his blood pressure. I'll blame myself if anything happens to him."

"One of you had to come out here."

"I suppose so. Anyway Bert is with him and whatever else he may be Bert is no drunk."

"Helen's ex-husband is staying with her father?"

"Yes. He came over from Maple Park this morning and drove me to the airport. Bert's a good boy. I shouldn't call him a boy, he's a grown man in his forties, but he always seems younger than he is."

"Does he teach at Maple Park?"

"That's right, only he hasn't got his degree. He's been working on it for years. He teaches journalism and English, and he helps put out the school paper. He used to be a newspaperman, that was how Helen met him."

"When she was nineteen?"

"You have a good memory. You and Hoffman would get along. Hoffman's middle name is memory. There was a time before we got our wartime expansion when he knew every building in Bridgeton. Every factory, every warehouse, every residence. Pick any house on any street and he could tell you who built it and who owned it. He could tell you who lived there and who used to live there and how many children they had and how much income and anything else you wanted to know about them. I'm not exaggerating, ask any of his fellow officers. They used to predict great things for him, but he never made it higher than Lieutenant."

I wondered why the great things hadn't materialized. She gave me a kind of answer, which I suspected was more of a legend than a fact:

"Helen got her memory from him. They were more alike than either of them admitted. And they were crazy about each other, under all the trouble there was between them. It broke his heart when Helen left home and never wrote. He never asked about her, either, but he did a lot of brooding. He was never the same man again."

"Did she marry Bert Haggerty right away?"

"No, she kept him dangling for five or six years. He was away in the army part of that time. Bert did well in the war—a lot of men did well in the war that never did so well before or since—and he was full of confidence for a while. He was going to write a book, start his own newspaper, take her to Europe on their honeymoon. They did get to Europe, on the G. I. Bill—I gave them part of the money to make the trip—but that was all that ever came of his plans. He never could settle down to any one thing, and when he finally did it was too late. Last spring they came to the parting of the ways. I didn't like it, but

I can hardly blame her. She always did better than he did, from the time that they were married. And one thing I'll say for Helen, she always had class."

"I agree."

"But maybe she should have stuck with Bert. Who knows? Maybe this wouldn't have happened. I sometimes think that any man is better than no man at all."

Later, as we were entering Pacific Point, she said: "Why couldn't Helen marry an upstanding husband? It's funny. She had brains and looks *and* class, but she never could attract an upstanding man."

I could feel her eyes on my profile, trying to chart the lost continent of her daughter's life.

17
..

THE PACIFIC HOTEL stood on a corner just above the economic equator that divided the main street into a prosperous section and a not so prosperous one. The lobby was almost empty on this Saturday night. Four old men were playing bridge in the light of a standing lamp. The only other human being in sight was Dr. Geisman, if he qualified.

He got up out of a shabby green plastic armchair and shook hands formally with Mrs. Hoffman.

"I see that you've arrived safely. How are you?"

"I'm all right, thanks."

"Your daughter's unexpected demise came as quite a blow to us."

"To me, too."

"In fact I've been endeavoring all day to find a replacement for her. I still haven't succeeded. This is the worst possible time of year to try to recruit teaching personnel."

"That's too bad."

I left them trying to breathe life into their stillborn conversation and went into the bar for a drink. A single customer sat trading sorrows with the fat lugubrious bartender. Her hair was dyed black, with a greenish sheen on it like certain ducks.

I recognized the woman—I could have spotted Mrs. Perrine at a thousand yards—and I started to back out of the room. She turned and saw me.

"Fancy meeting you here." She made a large gesture which almost upset the empty glass in front of her, and said to the bartender: "This is my friend Mr. Archer. Pour my friend a drink."

"What'll you have?"

"Bourbon. I'm paying. What is the lady drinking?"

"Planter's punch," she said, "and thanks for the 'lady.' Thanks for everything in fact. I'm celebrating, been celebrating all day."

I wished she hadn't been. The granite front she had kept up at her trial had eroded, and the inner ruin of her life showed through. While I didn't know all of Mrs. Perrine's secrets, I knew the record she had left on the police blotters of twenty cities. She had been innocent of this one particular crime, but she was a hustler who had worked the coasts from Acapulco to Seattle and from Montreal to Key West.

The bartender limped away to make our drinks. I sat on the stool beside her. "You should pick another town to celebrate in."

"I know. This town is a graveyard. I felt like the last living inhabitant, until you sashayed in."

"That isn't what I mean, Mrs. Perrine."

"Hell, call me Bridget, you're my pal, you've earned the right."

"Okay, Bridget. The police didn't like your acquittal, you couldn't expect them to. They'll pick you up for any little thing."

"I haven't stepped out of line. I have my own money."

"I'm thinking about what you might do if you go on celebrating. You can't afford to jaywalk in this town."

She considered this problem, and her twisting face mimicked the efforts of her mind. "You may be right at that. I been thinking of going to Vegas in the morning. I have a friend in Vegas."

The bartender brought our drinks. Mrs. Perrine sipped at hers, making a sour face, as if she'd suddenly lost her taste for it. Her gaze strayed to the mirror behind the bar.

"My gosh," she said, "is that me? I look like the wrath of God."

"Take a bath and get some sleep."

"It isn't so easy to sleep. I get lonely at night." She ogled me, more or less automatically.

She wasn't my baby. I finished my drink and put two dollar bills on the bar.

"Good night, Bridget. Take it easy. I have to make a phone call."

"Sure you do. See you at the Epworth League."

The bartender limped toward her as I walked out. Mrs. Hoffman and Dr. Geisman were no longer in the lobby. I found the telephone booths in a cul-de-sac behind the main desk and called the Bradshaw house.

Before the phone had rung more than once, the old lady's voice came quavering over the line. "Roy? Is that you, Roy?"

"This is Archer."

"I was so hoping it would be Roy. He always telephones by this time. You don't suppose something has happened to him?"

"No. I don't."

"Have you seen the paper?"

"No."

"There's an item to the effect that Laura Sutherland went to the Reno conference with him. Roy didn't tell me that. Do you suppose he's interested in Laura?"

"I wouldn't know."

"She's a lovely young woman, don't you think?"

I wondered if she'd had some wine at dinner that made her silly. "I have no opinion on the subject, Mrs. Bradshaw. I called to see if you're willing to follow through on our conversation this afternoon."

"I'm afraid I couldn't possibly, not without Roy's consent. He handles the money in the family, you know. Now I'm going to ask you to cut this short, Mr. Archer. I'm expecting to hear from Roy at any moment."

She hung up on me. I seemed to be losing my touch with little old ladies. I went into the washroom and looked at my face in the mirror above the row of basins. Someone had written in pencil on the wall: Support Mental Health or I'll kill you.

A small brown newsboy came into the washroom and caught me grinning at my reflection. I pretended to be examining my teeth. He looked about ten years old, and conducted himself like a miniature adult.

"Read all about the murder," he suggested.

I bought a local paper from him. The lead story was headlined:

"PPC Teacher Shot," with the subhead: "Mystery Student to be Questioned." In effect, it tried and convicted Dolly. She had "registered fraudulently, using an alias." Her friendship with Helen was described as "a strange relationship." The S and W thirty-eight found in her bed was "the murder weapon." She had "a dark secret in her past"— the McGee killing—and was "avoiding questioning by the police."

No other possible suspect was mentioned. The man from Reno didn't appear in the story.

In lieu of doing something constructive I tore the paper to pieces and dropped the pieces in the trash basket. Then I went back to the telephone booths. Dr. Godwin's answering service wanted to know if it was an emergency.

"Yes. It has to do with a patient of Dr. Godwin's."

"Are you the patient, sir?"

"Yes," I lied, wondering if this meant I needed help.

The switchboard girl said in a gentler voice: "The last time the doctor called in he was at home."

She recited his number but I didn't use it. I wanted to talk to Godwin face to face. I got his address out of the directory and drove across town to his house.

It was one of a number of large houses set on the edge of a mesa which normally overlooked the harbor and the city. Tonight it was islanded by the fog.

Behind the Arizona fieldstone front of the house a tenor and a soprano were singing a heartbreaking duet from *La Bohème*.

The door was answered by a handsome woman wearing a red silk brocade coat and the semi-professional smile that doctors' wives acquire. She seemed to recognize my name.

"I'm sorry, Mr. Archer. My husband was here until just a few minutes ago. We were actually listening to music for a change. Then a young man called—the husband of one of his patients—and he agreed to meet him at the nursing home."

"It wasn't Alex Kincaid who called?"

"I believe it was. Mr. Archer?" She stepped outside, a brilliant and very feminine figure in her red coat. "My husband has spoken of you. I understand you're working on this criminal case he's involved with."

"Yes."

Her hand touched my arm. "I'm worried about him. He's taking this thing so seriously. He seems to think that he let the girl down

when she was his patient before, and that it makes him responsible
for everything that's happened." Her fine long eyes looked up at me,
asking for reassurance.

"He isn't," I said.

"Will you tell him so? He won't listen to me. There are very few
people he will listen to. But he seems to have some respect for you,
Mr. Archer."

"It's mutual. I doubt that he'd want my opinion on the subject of
his responsibility, though. He's a very powerful and temperamental
man, easy to cross."

"You're telling me," she said. "I suppose I had no right to ask you
to speak to him. But the way he pours his life away into those patients
of his—" Her hand moved from her breast in an outward gesture.

"He seems to thrive on it."

"I don't." She made a wry face. "Physician's wife, heal thyself, eh?"

"You're thriving by all appearances," I said. "That's a nice coat, by
the way."

"Thank you. Jim bought it for me in Paris last summer."

I left her smiling less professionally, and went to the nursing home.
Alex's red Porsche was standing at the curb in front of the big plain
stucco building. I felt my heartbeat pounding in my ears. Something
good could still happen.

A Spanish American nurse's aide in a blue and white uniform unlocked the door and let me into the front room to wait for Dr. Godwin.
Nell and several other bathrobed patients were watching a television
drama about a pair of lawyers, father and son. They paid no attention
to me. I was only a real-life detective, unemployed at the moment. But
not, I hoped, for long.

I sat in an empty chair to one side. The drama was well directed
and well played but I couldn't keep my mind on it. I began to watch
the four people who were watching it. Nell the somnambulist, her
black hair hanging like tangled sorrows down her back, held cupped
in her hands the blue ceramic ashtray she had made. A young man
with an untrimmed beard and rebellious eyes looked like a conscien-
tious objector to everything. A thin-haired man, who was trembling
with excitement, went on trembling right through the commercial. An
old woman had a translucent face through which her life burned like
a guttering candle. Step back a little and you could almost imagine

that they were three generations of one family, grandmother, parents, and son, at home on a Saturday night.

Dr. Godwin appeared in the inner doorway and crooked his finger at me. I followed him down the hallway through a thickening hospital odor, into a small cramped office. He switched on a lamp over the desk and sat behind it. I took the only other chair.

"Is Alex Kincaid with his wife?"

"Yes. He called me at home and seemed very eager to see her, though he hasn't been around all day. He also wanted to talk to me."

"Did he say anything about running out on her?"

"No."

"I hope he's changed his mind." I told Godwin about my meeting with Kincaid senior, and Alex's departure with his father.

"You can't entirely blame him for falling by the wayside momentarily. He's young, and under great strain." Godwin's changeable eyes lit up. "The important thing, for him as well as Dolly, is that he decided to come back."

"How is she?"

"Calmer, I think. She didn't want to talk tonight, at least not to me."

"Will you let me have a try at her?"

"No."

"I almost regret bringing you into this case, doctor."

"I've been told that before, and less politely," he said with a stubborn smile. "But once I'm in I'm in, and I'll continue to do as I think best."

"I'm sure you will. Did you see the evening paper?"

"I saw it."

"Does Dolly know what's going on outside? About the gun, for instance?"

"No."

"Don't you think she should be told?"

He spread out his hands on the scarred desk-top. "I'm trying to simplify her problems, not add to them. She had so many pressures on her last night, from both the past and the present, that she was on the verge of a psychotic breakthrough. We don't want that to happen."

"Will you be able to protect her from police questioning?"

"Not indefinitely. The best possible protection would be a solution to this case absolving her."

"I'm working on it. I talked to her Aunt Alice this morning, and looked over the scene of the McGee killing. I became pretty well convinced that even if McGee did kill his wife, which I doubt, Dolly couldn't have identified him as he left the house. In other words her testimony at his trial was cooked."

"Alice Jenks convinced you of this?"

"The physical layout did. Miss Jenks did her best to convince me of the opposite, that McGee was guilty. I wouldn't be surprised if she was the main motive power behind the case against him."

"He *was* guilty."

"So you've said. I wish you'd go into your reasons for believing that."

"I'm afraid I can't. It has to do with the confidences of a patient."

"Constance McGee?"

"Mrs. McGee wasn't formally a patient. But you can't treat a child without treating the parents."

"And she confided in you?"

"Naturally, to some extent. For the most part we talked about her family problems." Godwin was feeling his way carefully. His face was bland. Under the lamp his bald head gleamed like a metal dome in moonlight.

"Her sister Alice made an interesting slip. She said there was no other man in Constance's life. I didn't ask her. Alice volunteered the information."

"Interesting."

"I thought so. Was Constance in love with another man at the time she was shot?"

Godwin nodded almost imperceptibly.

"Who was he?"

"I have no intention of telling you. He's suffered enough." A shadow of the suffering passed across his own face. "I've told you this much because I want you to understand that McGee had a motive, and was certainly guilty."

"I think he was framed, just as Dolly is being framed."

"We agree on the latter point. Why can't we settle for that?"

"Because there have been three killings, and they're connected. They're connected subjectively, as you would say, in Dolly's mind. I believe they're objectively connected, too. They may all have been done by the same person."

Godwin didn't ask me who. It was just as well. I was talking over my head, and I had no suspect.

"What third killing are you referring to?"

"The death of Luke Deloney, a man I never heard of until tonight.
I met Helen Haggerty's mother at the L.A. airport and had a talk with
her on the way down here. According to her, Deloney shot himself
by accident while cleaning a gun. But Helen claimed he was murdered
and said she knew a witness. The witness may have been herself. At
any rate she quarreled with her father on the issue—he seems to have
been the detective in charge of the case—and ran away from home.
All this was over twenty years ago."

"You seriously think it's connected with the present case?"

"Helen thought so. Her death makes her an authority on the
subject."

"What do you propose to do about it?"

"I'd like to fly to Illinois tonight and talk to Helen's father. But I
can't afford to do it on my own hook."

"You could phone him."

"I could. My sense of the situation is that it would do more harm
than good. He may be a tough nut to crack."

Godwin said after a minute's thought: "I might consider backing
you."

"You're a generous man."

"A curious one," he said. "Remember I've been living with this case
for over ten years. I'd give a good deal to see it ended."

"Let me talk to Alex first, and ask him how he feels about laying
out more money."

Godwin inclined his head and remained bowing as he stood up. He
wasn't bowing to me. It was more of a general and habitual bow, as if
he could feel the weight of the stars and was asking their permission to
take part of the weight on human shoulders.

"I'll get him out of there. He's stayed long enough."

Godwin disappeared down the hallway. A few minutes later Alex
came back alone. He walked like a man in a tunnel underground, but
his face was more serene than I'd ever seen it.

He paused in the doorway. "Dr. Godwin said you were here."

"I'm surprised to see you."

Hurt and embarrassment flickered across the upper part of his face.
He brushed at it impatiently with his fingers. Then he stepped into the
office, shutting the door behind him and leaning on it.

"I made a fool of myself today. I tried to chicken out."

"It takes guts to admit it."

"Don't gloss it over," he said sharply. "I was really lousy. It's funny, when Dad gets upset it has a peculiar effect on me. It's like sympathetic vibrations: he goes to pieces, I go to pieces. Not that I'm blaming *him.*"

"I'm blaming him."

"Please don't. You have no right to." His eyebrows knitted. "The company's talking about bringing in computers to handle most of the work in the office. Dad's afraid he can't adjust, and I guess it makes him afraid of things in general."

"You've been doing some thinking."

"I had to. You started me off with what you said about annulling myself. I felt that way when I went home with Dad—as though I wasn't a man any more." He pushed himself clear of the door and balanced himself on his feet, his arms swinging slightly at his sides. "It's really amazing, you know? You really can make a decision inside yourself. You can decide to be one thing or the other."

The only trouble was that you had to make the decision every hour on the hour. But he would have to find that out for himself.

"How is your wife?" I said.

"She actually seemed glad to see me. Have you talked to her?"

"Dr. Godwin wouldn't let me."

"He wouldn't let me, either, till I promised not to ask her any questions. I didn't, but the subject of the revolver came up. She'd heard two of the aides talking about some newspaper story—"

"It's in the local paper. What did she have to say about the gun?"

"It isn't hers. Somebody must have hidden it under her mattress. She asked me to describe it, and she said it sounded like her Aunt Alice's revolver. Her aunt used to keep it on her bedside table at night. Dolly was sort of fascinated by it when she was a little girl." He breathed deeply. "Apparently she saw her aunt threaten her father with it. I didn't want her to go into all that stuff but I couldn't prevent her. She calmed down again after a while."

"At least she's stopped blaming herself for Helen Haggerty's death."

"She hasn't, though. She still says it was her fault. Everything's her fault."

"In what way?"

"She didn't go into it. I didn't want her to."

"You mean Dr. Godwin didn't want you to."

"That's right. He's calling the shots. I guess he knows more about her than I ever will."

"I take it you're going on with your marriage?" I said.

"We have to. I realized that today. People can't walk out on each other when they're in this kind of trouble. I think maybe Dolly realizes it, too. She didn't turn her back on me or anything."

"What else did you talk about?"

"Nothing important. The other patients, mostly. There's one old lady with a broken hip who doesn't want to stay in bed. Dolly's been sort of looking after her." It seemed important to him. "She can't be so very sick herself." It was an implied question.

"You'll have to take that up with the doctor."

"He isn't saying much. He wants to give her some psychological tests tomorrow. I told him to go ahead."

"Do I have your go-ahead, too?"

"Naturally. I was hoping you'd take that for granted. I want you to do everything you can to settle this thing. I'll give you a written contract—"

"That won't be necessary. But it's going to cost you money."

"How much money?"

"A couple of thousand, maybe a good deal more."

I told him about the Reno end of the case, which Arnie and Phyllis Walters were handling, and about the Bridgeton situation which I wanted to explore. I also advised him to talk to Jerry Marks first thing in the morning.

"Will Mr. Marks be available on a Sunday?"

"Yes. I've already set him up for you. Of course you're going to have to give him a retainer."

"I have some savings bonds," he said thoughtfully, "and I can borrow on my insurance policy. Meantime I can sell the car. It's paid for, and I've been offered two five for it. I was getting pretty tired of sports car rallies and all that jazz. It's kid stuff."

18

THE front doorbell rang. Someone trotted past the office door to answer it. It was getting late for visitors, and I went out and followed the aide along the hallway. The four patients were still watching the television screen as if it was a window on the outside world.

Whoever had rung the bell was knocking now, rather violently.

"Just a minute," the aide said through the door. She got her key into the lock and opened it partly. "Who is it? Who do you want to see?"

It was Alice Jenks. She tried to push her way in, but the aide had her white shoe against the door.

"I wish to see my niece, Dolly McGee."

"We have no such patient."

"She calls herself Dolly Kincaid now."

"I can't let you in to see anyone without doctor's permission."

"Is Godwin here?"

"I think so."

"Get him," Miss Jenks said peremptorily.

The girl's Latin temper flared. "I don't take orders from you," she said in a hissing whisper. "And keep your voice down. We have people trying to rest."

"Get Dr. Godwin."

"Don't worry, I intend to. But you'll have to wait outside."

"It will be a pleasure."

I stepped between them before the nurse closed the door and said to Miss Jenks: "May I speak to you for a minute?"

She peered at me through fogged glasses. "So you're here, too."

"I'm here, too."

I stepped out under the outside light and heard the door shut behind me. The air was chilly after the hot-house atmosphere of the nursing home. Miss Jenks had on a thick fur-collared coat which made her figure massive in the gloom. Droplets of water glistened in the fur, and in her graying hair.

"What do you want with Dolly?"

"It's none of your business. She's my flesh and blood, not yours."

"Dolly has a husband. I represent him."

"You can go and represent him in some other constituency. I'm not interested in you *or* her husband."

"But suddenly you're interested in Dolly. Does it have anything to do with the story in the paper?"

"Maybe it has and maybe it hasn't." In her language, that meant yes. She added defensively: "I've been interested in Dolly since she was born. I know better than a lot of strangers what's good for her."

"Dr. Godwin isn't a stranger."

"No. I wish he was."

"I hope you're not thinking of taking her out of here."

"Maybe I am and maybe I'm not." She dug some Kleenex out of her purse and used it to clean her glasses. I could see a newspaper folded small in the purse.

"Miss Jenks, did you read the description of the revolver that was found in Dolly's bed?"

She replaced her glasses quickly, as though to cover the startled look in her eyes. "Naturally I read it."

"Did it ring any bell with you?"

"Yes. It sounded like the revolver I used to have, so I came into town to the courthouse to have a look at it. It looks like mine all right."

"You admit that?"

"Why shouldn't I? I haven't seen it for over ten years."

"Can you prove it?"

"Of course I can prove it. It was stolen from my house before Constance was shot. Sheriff Crane theorized at the time that it might have been the gun McGee used on her. He still thinks so. McGee could easily have taken it. He knew where it was, in my bedroom."

"You didn't tell me all this this morning."

"I didn't think of it. It was only theory, anyway. You were interested in facts."

"I'm interested in both, Miss Jenks. What's the police theory now? That McGee killed Miss Haggerty and tried to frame his daughter?"

"I wouldn't put it past him. A man who would do what he did to his wife—" Her voice sank out of hearing in her throat.

"And they want to use his daughter to nail McGee again?"

She didn't answer me. Lights went on inside, and there were sounds of movement culminating in Godwin's opening the door. He shook his keys at us, grinning fiercely.

"Come inside, Miss Jenks."

She stamped up the concrete steps. Godwin had cleared the front room of everyone but Alex, who was sitting on a chair against the wall. I stood unobtrusively in the corner beside the silent television set.

She faced him, almost as tall in heels as he was, almost as wide in her coat, almost as stubborn in her pride. "I don't approve of what you're doing, Dr. Godwin."

"What am I doing?" He sat on the arm of a chair and crossed his legs.

"You know what I'm referring to. My niece. Keeping her cooped up here in defiance of the constituted authorities."

"There's no defiance involved. I try to do my duty, the Sheriff tries to do his. Sometimes we come into conflict. It doesn't necessarily mean that Sheriff Crane is right and I'm wrong."

"It does to me."

"I'm not surprised. We've disagreed before, on a similar issue. You and your friend the Sheriff had your way on that occasion, unfortunately for your niece."

"It did her no harm to testify. Truth is truth."

"And trauma is trauma. It did her incalculable harm, which she's still suffering under."

"I'd like to see that for myself."

"So you can make a full report to the Sheriff?"

"Good citizens cooperate with the law," she said sententiously. "But I'm not here on the Sheriff's behalf. I came here to help my niece."

"How do you propose to help her?"

"I'm going to take her home with me."

Godwin stood up shaking his head.

"You can't stop me. I've been her guardian since her mother died. The law will back me up."

"I think not," Godwin said coldly. "Dolly's of age, and she's here of her own free will."

"I'd like to ask her that question for myself."

"You're not going to ask her any questions."

The woman took a step toward him and thrust her head forward on her neck. "You think you're a little tin god, don't you, masterminding my family's affairs? I say you've got no right to keep her here under duress, making us all look bad. I've got a position to keep up in this county. I spent the day with some very high-level people from Sacramento."

"I'm afraid I don't follow your logic. But keep your voice down, please." Godwin himself was using the slow weary monotone that I had first heard on the telephone twenty-four hours before. "And let me assure you again, your niece is here of her own free will."

"That's right." Alex came forward into the verbal line of fire. "I don't believe we've met. I'm Alex Kincaid, Dolly's husband."

She disregarded his hand.

"I think it's important for her to stay here," he said. "I have confidence in the doctor, and so has my wife."

"I'm sorry for you then. He had me bamboozled, too, until I found out what went on in his office."

Alex looked inquiringly at Godwin. The doctor turned his hands out as if he was feeling for rain. He said to Miss Jenks:

"You graduated in sociology, I believe."

"What if I did?"

"From a woman of your training and background, I'd expect a more professional attitude toward the practice of psychiatry."

"I'm not talking about the practice of psychiatry. I'm talking about the practice of other things."

"What other things?"

"I wouldn't soil my tongue with them. But please don't think I didn't know my sister and what went on in her life. I've been remembering things—the way she used to primp and preen Saturday mornings before she came in to town. And then she wanted to move here, to be closer."

"Closer to me?"

"So she told me."

Godwin's face was white, as if all its color had been drawn into the darkness of his eyes. "You're a silly woman, Miss Jenks, and I've had enough of you. I'll ask you to leave now."

"I'm staying here till I see my niece. I want to know what you're practicing on her."

"It would do her no good. In your present mood you'd do no good to anyone." He moved around her to the door and held it open. "Good night."

She didn't move or look at him. She stood with her head down, a little dazed by the anger that had gone through her like a storm.

"Do you wish to be forcibly removed?"

"Try it. You'll end up in court."

But a kind of shame had begun to invade her face. Her mouth was twitching like a small injured thing. It had said more than she intended.

When I took her by the arm and said, "Come on, Miss Jenks," she let me lead her to the door. Godwin closed it on her.

"I have no patience with fools," he said.

"Have a little patience with me, though, will you, doctor?"

"I'll give it a try, Archer." He took a deep breath and let it out as a sigh. "You want to know if there's any truth in her innuendo."

"You make it easy for me."

"Why not? I love the truth. My entire life is a search for it."

"Okay, was Constance McGee in love with you?"

"I suppose she was, in a way. Women patients traditionally fall in love with their doctors, particularly in my field. It didn't persist in her case."

"This may strike you as a foolish question, but did you love her?"

"I'll give you a foolish answer, Mr. Archer. Of course I loved her. I loved her the way a doctor loves his patients, if he's any good. It's a love that's more maternal than erotic." He spread his large hands on his chest, and spoke from there: "I wanted to serve her. I didn't succeed too well."

I was silenced.

"And now, gentlemen, if you'll excuse me, I have hospital rounds in the morning." He swung his keys.

Alex said to me in the street: "Do you believe him?"

"Unless or until I have proof that he's lying. He's not telling all he knows but people seldom do, let alone doctors. I'd take his word ahead of Alice Jenks's."

He started to climb into his car, then turned back toward me, gesturing in the direction of the nursing home. Its plain rectangular façade loomed in the fog like a blockhouse, the visible part of an underground fortress.

"You think she's safe there, Mr. Archer?"

"Safer than she'd be on the streets, or in jail, or in a psycho ward with a police psychiatrist quizzing her."

"Or at her aunt's?"

"Or at her aunt's. Miss Jenks is one of these righteous women who doesn't let her left lobe know what her right lobe is doing. She's quite a tiger."

His eyes were still on the front of the nursing home.

Deep inside the building, the wild old voice I had heard that morning rose again. It faded like the cry of a seabird flying away, intermitted by wind.

"I wish I could stay with Dolly, and protect her," Alex said.

He was a good boy.

I broached the subject of money. He gave me most of the money in his wallet. I used it to buy an airline ticket to Chicago and return, and caught a late flight from International Airport.

19
..

I LEFT the toll road, which bypassed Bridgeton, and drove my rented car through the blocks of housing tracts on the outskirts of the city. I could see the clump of sawed-off skyscrapers in the business district ahead, and off to the left, across the whole south side, the factories. It was Sunday morning, and only one of their stacks was pouring smoke into the deep blue sky.

I stopped for gas at a service station and looked up Earl Hoffman's address in the telephone directory. When I asked the attendant how to get to Cherry Street, where Hoffman lived, he pointed in the general direction of the factories.

It was a middle-class street of substantial two-story houses which had been touched but not destroyed by the blight that creeps outward from the centers of cities. Hoffman's house was of grimy white brick like the others, but the front porch had been painted within living memory. An old Chevrolet coupé stood at the curb in front of it.

The doorbell didn't work. I knocked on the screen door. An old young man with more nose than chin opened the inner door and looked at me through the screen in a sad way.

"Mr. Haggerty?"

"Yes."

I told him my name and trade and where I was from. "I was with your wife—your ex-wife—shortly before she was killed."

"It's a dreadful thing."

He stood absently in the doorway, forgetting to ask me in. He had a frowzy sleepless look as if he'd been up most of the night. Though there was no gray on his head, white hairs glistened in his day-old beard. His small eyes had the kind of incandescence that goes with conscious suffering.

"May I come in, Mr. Haggerty?"

"I don't know if it's such a good idea. Earl's pretty broken up."

"I thought he and his daughter had been on the outs for a long time."

"They were. It only makes it harder for him, I think. When you're angry with someone you love, you always expect at the back of your mind there'll be a reconciliation some day. But now there will never be anything."

He was speaking for his father-in-law but also for himself. His empty hands moved aimlessly at his sides. The fingers of his right hand were stained dark yellow by nicotine.

"I'm sorry," I said, "that Mr. Hoffman isn't feeling well. I'm afraid I'll have to talk to him anyway. I didn't come from California for the ride."

"No. Obviously not. What is it you have to discuss with him?"

"His daughter's murder. He may be able to help me understand it."

"I thought it was already solved."

"It isn't."

"Has the girl student been cleared?"

"She's in process of being cleared," I said with deliberate vagueness. "You and I can go into all that later. Right now I'm very eager to talk to Hoffman."

"If you insist. I only hope you can get some sense out of him."

I saw what he meant when he took me through the house to "Earl's den," as Haggerty called it. It was furnished with a closed roll-top desk, an armchair, a studio couch. Through a haze compounded of whisky fumes and smoke I could see a big old man sprawled in orange pajamas on the couch, his head propped up by bolsters. A strong reading light shone on his stunned face. His eyes seemed out of focus, but he was holding a magazine with an orange cover that almost matched his pajamas. The wall above him was decorated with rifles and shotguns and hand guns.

"When I recall the loss of all my perished years," he said huskily.

Old cops didn't talk like that, and Earl Hoffman looked like no exception to the rule. His body was massive, and could have belonged to a professional football player or a wrestler gone to pot. His nose had once been broken. He had a clipped gray head and a mouth like bent iron.

"That's beautiful poetry, Bert," the iron mouth said.

"I suppose it is."

"Who's your friend, Bert?"

"Mr. Archer, from California."

"California, eh? That's where my poor little Helen got knocked off."

He sobbed, or hiccuped, once. Then he swung himself onto the edge of the couch, letting his bare feet fall heavily to the floor.

"Do you know—did you know my little daughter Helen?"

"I knew her."

"Isn't that remarkable." He rose swaying and clasped my hands in both of his, using me to support him. "Helen was a remarkable girl. I've just been reading over one of her poems. Wrote it when she was just a teen-age girl at City College. Here, I'll show you."

He made a fairly elaborate search for the orange-covered magazine, which was lying in plain sight on the floor where he had dropped it. The name of it was the *Bridgeton Blazer*, and it looked like a school production.

Haggerty picked it up and handed it to him: "Please don't bother with it, Earl. Helen didn't write it anyway."

"Didn't write it? 'Course she wrote it. It's got her initials on it." Hoffman flipped through the pages. "See?"

"But she was only translating from Verlaine."

"Never heard of him." Hoffman turned to me, thrusting the magazine into my hands. "Here, read this. See what a remarkable gift poor little Helen had."

I read:

> When the violins
> Of the autumn winds
> Begin to sigh
> My heart is torn
> With their forlorn
> Monotony.
>
> And when the hour
> Sounds from the tower
> I weep tears
> For I recall
> The loss of all
> My perished years.
>
> And then I go
> With the winds that blow
> And carry me
> There and here
> Like a withered and sere
> Leaf from a tree.—H.H.

Hoffman looked at me with one of his unfocused eyes. "Isn't that beautiful poetry, Mr. Arthur?"

"Beautiful."

"I only wisht I understood it. Do you understand it?"

"I think so."

"Then keep it. Keep it in memory of poor little Helen."

"I couldn't do that."

"Sure you can. Keep it." He snatched it out of my hands, rolled it up, and thrust it into my jacket pocket, breathing whisky in my face.

"Keep it," Haggerty whispered at my shoulder. "You don't want to cross him."

"You heard him. You don't want to cross me."

Hoffman grinned loosely at me. He clenched his left fist, examined it for defects, then used it to strike himself on the chest. He walked on spraddled legs to the roll-top desk and opened it. There were bottles and a single smeared tumbler inside. He half-filled the tumbler from a fifth of bourbon and drank most of it down. His son-in-law said something under his breath, but made no move to stop him.

The heavy jolt squeezed sweat out on Hoffman's face. It seemed to sober him a little. His eyes focused on me.

"Have a drink?"

"All right. I'll take water and ice in mine, please." I didn't normally drink in the morning but this was an abnormal occasion.

"Get some ice and a glass, Bert. Mr. Arthur wants a drink. If you're too mucky-muck to drink with me, Mr. Arthur isn't."

"The name is Archer."

"Get *two* glasses," he said with his foolish grin. "Mr. Archer wants a drink, too. Sit down," he said to me. "Take the load off your feet. Tell me about poor little Helen."

We sat on the couch. I filled him in quickly on the circumstances of the murder, including the threat that preceded it, and Helen's feeling that Bridgeton was catching up with her.

"What did she mean by that?" The lines of the grin were still in his face like clown marks but the grin had become a rictus.

"I've come a long way to see if you can help me answer that question."

"Me? Why come to me? I never knew what went on in her mind, she never *let* me know. She was too bright for me." His mood swayed into heavy drunken self-pity. "I sweated and slaved to buy her an education like I never had, but she wouldn't give her poor old father the time of day."

"I understand you had a bad quarrel and she left home."

"She told you, eh?"

I nodded. I had decided to keep Mrs. Hoffman out of it. He was the kind of man who wouldn't want his wife ahead of him in anything.

"She tell you the names she called me, crook and Nazi, when all I was doing was my bounden duty? You're a cop, you know how a man feels when your own family undermines you." He peered at me sideways. "You are a cop, aren't you?"

"I have been."

"What do you do for a living now?"

"Private investigation."

"Who for?"

"A man named Kincaid, nobody you know. I knew your daughter

slightly, and I have a personal interest in finding out who killed her. I think the answer may be here in Bridgeton."

"I don't see how. She never set foot in this town for twenty years, until last spring. She only came home then to tell her mother she was getting a divorce. From *him*." He gestured toward the back of the house, where I could hear ice being chipped.

"Did she do any talking to you?"

"I only saw her the once. She said hello-how-are-you and that was about it. She told her mother that she'd had it with Bert and her mother couldn't talk her out of it. Bert even followed her out to Reno to try and convince her to come back, but it was no go. He isn't enough of a man to hold a woman."

Hoffman finished his drink and set his tumbler down on the floor. He remained slumped forward for about a minute, and I was afraid he was going to get sick or pass out on me. But he came back up to a sitting position and muttered something about wanting to help me.

"Fine. Who was Luke Deloney?"

"Friend of mine. Big man in town back before the war. She told you about him, too, eh?"

"You could tell me more, Lieutenant. I hear you have a memory like an elephant."

"Did Helen say that?"

"Yes." The lie didn't cost me anything, not even a pang of conscience.

"At least she had some respect for her old man, eh?"

"A good deal."

He breathed with enormous relief. It would pass, as everything passes when a man is drinking seriously to kill awareness. But for the moment he was feeling good. He believed his daughter had conceded a point in their bitter life-long struggle.

"Luke was born in nineteen-oh-three on Spring Street," he said with great care, "in the twenty-one-hundred block, way out on the south side—two blocks over from where I lived when I was a kid. I knew him in grade school. He was the kind of a kid who saved up his paper-route money to buy a Valentine for everybody in his class. He actually did that. The principal used to take him around to the various rooms to show off his mental arithmetic. He did have a good head on his shoulders, I'll give him that. He skipped two grades. He was a comer.

"Old man Deloney was a cement finisher, and cement started to come in strong for construction after the World War. Luke bought himself a mixer with money he'd saved and went into business for himself. He did real well in the twenties. At his peak he had over five hundred men working for him all over the state. Even the depression didn't cramp his style. He was a wheeler and a dealer as well as a builder. The only things going up in those days were public works, so he went out in a big way for the federal and state contracts. He married Senator Osborne's daughter, and that didn't do him any harm, either."

"I hear Mrs. Deloney's still alive."

"Sure she is. She lives in the house the Senator built in nineteen-oh-one on Glenview Avenue on the north side. Number one-oh-three, I think." He was straining to live up to his encyclopedic reputation.

I made a mental note of the address. Preceded by clinking, Bert Haggerty came into the room with ice and water and glasses on a tin tray. I cleared a space on the desk and he set the tray down. It had originally belonged to the Bridgeton Inn.

"You took long enough," Hoffman said offhandedly.

Haggerty stiffened. His eyes seemed to regroup themselves more closely at the sides of his nose.

"Don't talk to me like that, Earl. I'm not a servant."

"If you don't like it you know what you can do."

"I realize you're tight, but there's a limit—"

"Who's tight? I'm not tight."

"You've been drinking for twenty-four hours."

"So what? A man has a right to drown his sorrows. But my brain is as clear as a bell. Ask Mr. Arthur here. Mr. Archer."

Haggerty laughed, mirthlessly, falsetto. It was a very queer sound, and I tried to cover it over with a broad flourish:

"The Lieutenant's been filling me in on some ancient history. He has a memory like an elephant."

But Hoffman wasn't feeling good any more. He rose cumbrously and advanced on Haggerty and me. One of his eyes looked at each of us. I felt like a man in a cage with a sick bear and his keeper.

"What's funny, Bert? You think my sorrow is funny, is that it? She wouldn't be dead if you were man enough to keep her at home. Why didn't you bring her home from Reno with you?"

"You can't blame me for everything," Haggerty said a little wildly. "I got along with her better than you did. If she hadn't had a father-fixation—"

"Don't give me that, you lousy intellectual. Ineffectual. Ineffectual intellectual. You're not the only one that can use four-bit words. And stop calling me Earl. We're not related. We never would have been if I had any say in the matter. We're not even related and you come into my house spying on my personal habits. What are you, an old woman?"

Haggerty was speechless. He looked at me helplessly.

"I'll break your neck," his father-in-law said.

I stepped between them. "Let's have no violence, Lieutenant. It wouldn't look good on the blotter."

"The little pipsqueak accused me. He said I'm drunk. You tell him he's mistaken. Make him apologize."

I turned to Haggerty, closing one eye. "Lieutenant Hoffman is sober, Bert. He can carry his liquor. Now you better get out of here before something happens."

He was glad to. I followed him out into the hall.

"This is the third or fourth time," he said in a low voice. "I didn't mean to set him off again."

"Let him cool for a bit. I'll sit with him. I'd like to talk to you afterward."

"I'll wait outside in my car."

I went back into the bear cage. Hoffman was sitting on the edge of the couch with his head supported by his hands.

"Everything's gone to hell in a hand-car," he said. "That pussy willow of a Bert Haggerty gets under my skin. I dunno what he thinks he's sucking around for." His mood changed. "You haven't deserted me, anyway. Go ahead, make yourself a drink."

I manufactured a light highball and brought it back to the couch. I didn't offer Hoffman any. In wine was truth, perhaps, but in whisky, the way Hoffman sluiced it down, was an army of imaginary rats climbing your legs.

"You were telling me about Luke Deloney and how he grew."

He squinted at me. "I don't know why you're so interested in Deloney. He's been dead for twenty-two years. Twenty-two years and three months. He shot himself, but I guess you know that, eh?" A hard intelligence glinted momentarily in his eyes and drew them into focus on my face.

I spoke to the hard intelligence: "Was there anything between Helen and Deloney?"

"No, she wasn't interested in *him*. She had a crush on the elevator boy. George. I ought to know, she made me get him the job. I was sort

330 · *Archer* AT LARGE

of managing the Deloney Apartments at the time. Luke Deloney and me, we were like that."

He tried to cross his second finger over his forefinger. It kept slipping. He finally completed the maneuver with the help of his other hand. His fingers were thick and mottled like uncooked breakfast sausages.

"Luke Deloney was a bit of a womanizer," he said indulgently, "but he didn't mess around with the daughters of his friends. He never cared for the young stuff, anyway. His wife must of been ten years older than he was. Anyway, he wouldn't touch my daughter. He knew I'd kill him."

"Did you?"

"That's a lousy question, mister. If I didn't happen to like you I'd knock your block off."

"No offense."

"I had nothing against Luke Deloney. He treated me fair and square. Anyway, I told you he shot himself."

"Suicide?"

"Naw. Why would he commit suicide? He had everything, money and women and a hunting lodge in Wisconsin. He took me up there personally more than once. The shooting was an accident. That's the way it went into the books and that's the way it stays."

"How did it happen, Lieutenant?"

"He was cleaning his .32 automatic. He had a permit to tote it on his person—I helped him get it myself—because he used to carry large sums of money. He took the clip out all right but he must of forgot the shell that was in the chamber. It went off and shot him in the face."

"Where?"

"Through the right eye."

"I mean where did the accident occur?"

"In one of the bedrooms in his apartment. He kept the roof apartment in the Deloney building for his private use. More than once I drank with him up there. Prewar Green River, boy." He slapped my knee, and noticed the full glass in my hand. "Drink up your drink."

I knocked back about half of it. It wasn't prewar Green River. "Was Deloney drinking at the time of the shooting?"

"Yeah, I think so. He knew guns. He wouldn't of made that mistake if he was sober."

"Was anybody with him in the apartment?"

"No."

"Can you be sure?"

"I can be sure. I was in charge of the investigation."

"Did anybody share the apartment with him?"

"Not on a permanent basis, you might say. Luke Deloney had various women on the string. I checked them out, but none of them was within a mile of the place at the time it happened."

"What kind of women?"

"All the way from floozies to one respectable married woman here in town. Their names didn't go into the record then and they're not going to now."

There was a growl in his voice. I didn't pursue the subject. Not that I was afraid of Hoffman exactly. I had at least fifteen years on him, and a low alcohol content. But if he went for me I might have to hurt him badly.

"What about Mrs. Deloney?" I said.

"What about her?"

"Where was she when all this was going on?"

"At home, out on Glenview. They were sort of separated. She didn't believe in divorce."

"People who don't believe in divorce sometimes believe in murder."

Hoffman moved his shoulders belligerently. "You trying to say that I hushed up a murder?"

"I'm not accusing you of anything, Lieutenant."

"You better not. I'm a cop, remember, first last and always." He raised his fist and rotated it before his eyes like a hypnotic device. "I been a good cop all my life. In my prime I was the best damn cop this burg ever saw. I'll have a drink on that." He picked up his tumbler. "Join me?"

I said I would. We were moving obscurely on a collision course. Alcohol might soften the collision, or sink him. I finished my drink and handed him my glass. He filled it to the brim with neat whisky. Then he filled his own. He sat down and stared into the brown liquid as if it was a well where his life had drowned.

"Bottoms up," he said.

"Take it easy, Lieutenant. You don't want to kill yourself." It occurred to me as I said it that maybe he did.

"What are you, another pussy willow? Bottoms up."

He drained his glass and shuddered. I held mine in my hand. After a while he noticed this.

"You didn't drink your drink. What you trying to do, pull a fast one on me? Insult my hosh—my hoshpit—?" His lips were too numb to frame the word.

"No insult intended. I didn't come here for a drinking party, Lieutenant. I'm seriously interested in who killed your daughter. Assuming Deloney was murdered—"

"He wasn't."

"Assuming he was, the same person may have killed Helen. In view of everything I've heard, from her and other people, I think it's likely. Don't you?"

I was trying to get his mind under my control: the sloppy drunken sentimental part, and the drunken violent part, and the hard intelligent part hidden at the core.

"Deloney was an accident," he said clearly and stubbornly.

"Helen didn't think so. She claimed it was murder, and that she knew a witness to the murder."

"She was lying, trying to make me look bad. All she ever wanted to do was make her old man look bad."

His voice had risen. We sat and listened to its echoes. He dropped his empty glass, which bounced on the rug, and clenched the fist which seemed to be his main instrument of expression. I got ready to block it, but he didn't throw it at me.

Heavily and repeatedly, he struck himself in the face, on the eyes and cheeks, on the mouth, under the jaw. The blows left dull red welts in his clay-colored flesh. His lower lip split.

Hoffman said through the blood: "I clobbered my poor little daughter. I chased her out of the house. She never came back."

Large tears the color of pure distilled alcohol or grief rolled from his puffing eyes and down his damaged face. He fell sideways on the couch. He wasn't dead. His heart was beating strongly. I straightened him out—his legs were as heavy as sandbags—and put a bolster under his head. With blind eyes staring straight up into the light, he began to snore.

I closed the roll-top desk. The key was in it, and I turned it on the liquor and switched off the light and took the key outside with me.

20

BERT HAGGERTY was sitting in the Chevrolet coupé, wearing a stalled expression. I got in beside him and handed him the key.

"What's this?"

"The key to the liquor. You better keep it. Hoffman's had as much as he can take."

"Did he throw you out?"

"No. He passed out, while hitting himself in the face. Hard."

Haggerty thrust his long sensitive nose toward me. "Why would Earl do a thing like that?"

"He seemed to be punishing himself for hitting his daughter a long time ago."

"Helen told me about that. Earl treated her brutally before she left home. It's one thing I can't forgive him for."

"He can't forgive himself. Did Helen tell you what they quarreled about?"

"Vaguely. It was something to do with a murder here in Bridgeton. Helen believed, or pretended to believe, that her father deliberately let the murderer go free."

"Why do you say she pretended to believe it?"

"My dear dead wife," he said, wincing at the phrase, "had quite a flair for the dramatic, especially in her younger days."

"Did you know her before she left Bridgeton?"

"For a few months. I met her in Chicago at a party in Hyde Park. After she left home I helped her to get a job as a cub reporter. I was working for the City News Bureau then. But as I was saying, Helen always had this dramatic flair and when nothing happened in her life for it to feed on she'd *make* something happen or pretend that it had happened. Her favorite character was Mata Hari," he said with a chuckle that was half a sob.

"So you think she invented this murder?"

"I suppose I thought so at the time, because I certainly didn't take it seriously. I have no opinion now. Does it matter?"

"It could matter very much. Did Helen ever talk to you about Luke Deloney?"

"Who?"

"Luke Deloney, the man who was killed. He owned the apartment building they lived in, and occupied the penthouse himself."

Haggerty lit a cigarette before he answered. His first few words came out as visible puffs of smoke: "I don't recall the name. If she talked about him, it couldn't have made much of an impression on me."

"Her mother seems to think Helen had a crush on Deloney."

"Mrs. Hoffman's a pretty good woman, and I love her like a mother, but she gets some wild ideas."

"How do you know that this one is so wild? Was Helen in love with *you* then?"

He took a deep drag on his cigarette, like an unweaned child sucking on a dry bottle. It burned down to his yellow fingers. He tossed it into the street with a sudden angry gesture.

"She never was in love with me. I was useful to her, for a while. Later, in some sense, I was the last chance. The faithful follower. The last chance for gas before the desert."

"The desert?"

"The desert of love. The desert of *un*love. But I don't think I'll go into the long and dreary chronicle of my marriage. It wasn't a lucky one, for either of us. I loved her, as far as I'm able to love, but she didn't love me. Proust says it's always that way. I'm teaching Proust to my sophomore class this fall, if I can summon up the *élan* to go on teaching."

"Who did Helen love?"

"It depends on which year you're talking about. Which month of which year." He didn't move, but he was hurting himself, hitting himself in the face with bitter words.

"Right at the beginning, before she left Bridgeton."

"I don't know if you'd call it love, but she was deeply involved with a fellow-student at the City College. It was a Platonic affair, the kind bright young people have, or used to have. It consisted largely of reading aloud to each other from their own works and others'. According to Helen, she never went to bed with him. I'm pretty sure she was a virgin when I met her."

"What was his name?"

"I'm afraid I don't remember. It's a clear case of Freudian repression."

"Can you describe him?"

"I never met him. He's a purely legendary figure in my life. But obviously he isn't the elusive murderer you're searching for. Helen would have been happy to see *him* go free." He had withdrawn from the pain of memory and was using an almost flippant tone, as if he was talking about people in a play, or watching ceiling movies at the dentist's. "Speaking of murder, as we seem to be doing, you were going to tell me about my ex-wife's death. She's completely ex now, isn't she, exed out?"

I cut in on his sad nonsense and gave him the story in some detail, including the man from Reno who ran away in the fog, and my attempts to get him identified. "Earl tells me you went to Reno last summer to see your wife. Did you run into any of her acquaintances there?"

"Did I not. Helen played a trick on me involving a couple of them. Her purpose was to stall off any chance for an intimate talk with me. Anyway, the one evening we spent together she insisted on making it a foursome with this woman named Sally something and her alleged brother."

"Sally Burke?"

"I believe that *was* her name. The hell of it was, Helen arranged it so that I was the Burke woman's escort. She wasn't a bad-looking woman, but we had nothing in common, and in any case it was Helen I wanted to talk to. But she spent the entire evening dancing with the brother. I'm always suspicious of men who dance too well."

"Tell me more about this brother. He may be our man."

"Well, he struck me as a rather sleazy customer. That may be projected envy. He was younger than I am, and healthier, and better looking. Also, Helen seemed to be fascinated by his line of chatter, which I thought was pointless—all about cars and horses and gambling odds. How a highly educated woman like Helen could be interested in such a man—" He tired of the sentence, and dropped it.

"Were they lovers?"

"How would I know? She wasn't confiding in me."

"But you know your own wife, surely."

He lit another cigarette and smoked half of it. "I'd say they weren't lovers. They were simply playmates. Of course she was using him to hit at me."

"For what?"

"For being her husband. For having been her husband. Helen and I parted on bad terms. I tried to put the marriage together again in Reno, but she wasn't even remotely interested."

"What broke up your marriage?"

"It had a major fracture in it from the beginning." He looked past me at the house where Earl Hoffman was lying senseless under the past. "And it got worse. It was both our faults. I couldn't stop nagging her and she couldn't stop—doing what she was doing."

I waited and listened. The church-bells were ringing, in different parts of the city.

"She was a tramp," Haggerty said. "A campus tramp. I started her on it when she was a nineteen-year-old babe in the woods in Hyde Park. Then she went on without me. Toward the end she was even taking money."

"Who from?"

"Men with money, naturally. My wife was a corrupt woman, Mr. Archer. I played a part in making her what she was, so I have no right to judge her." His eyes were brilliant with the pain that came and went like truth in him.

I felt sorry for the man. It didn't prevent me from saying: "Where were you Friday night?"

"At home in Maple Park in our—in my apartment, grading themes."

"Can you prove it?"

"I have the marked papers to prove it. They were turned in to me Friday, and I marked them Friday night. I hope you're not imagining I did something fantastic like flying to California and back?"

"When a woman is murdered, you ask her estranged husband where he was at the time. It's the corollary of *cherchez la femme.*"

"Well, you have my answer. Check it out if you like. But you'll save yourself time and trouble simply by believing me. I've been completely frank with you—inordinately frank."

"I appreciate that."

"But then you turn around and accuse me—"

"A question isn't an accusation, Mr. Haggerty."

"It carried that implication," he said in an aggrieved and slightly nagging tone. "I thought the man in Reno was your suspect."

"He's one of them."

"And I'm another?"

"Let's drop it, shall we?"

"You brought it up."

"Now I'm dropping it. Getting back to the man in Reno, can you remember his name?"

"I was introduced to him, of course, but I don't recall his surname. The women called him Jud. I'm not sure whether it was a given name or a nickname."

"Why did you refer to him as Mrs. Burke's alleged brother?"

"They didn't strike me as brother and sister. They acted toward each other more like—oh—intimate friends who were simply going along with Helen's gag. I intercepted a couple of knowing glances, for example."

"Will you describe the man in detail for me?"

"I'll try. My visual memory isn't too good. I'm strictly the verbal type."

But under repeated questions, he built up an image of the man: age about thirty-two or -three, height just under six feet, weight about 175; muscular and active, good-looking in an undistinguished way; thinning black hair, brown eyes, no scars. He had worn a light gray silk or imitation silk suit and pointed low black shoes in the Italian style. Haggerty had gathered that the man Jud worked in some undetermined capacity for one of the gambling clubs in the Reno-Tahoe area.

It was time I went to Reno. I looked at my watch: nearly eleven: and remembered that I would gain time on the flight west. I could still have a talk with Luke Deloney's widow, if she was available, and get to Reno at a reasonable hour.

I went into the house with Haggerty, called O'Hare Airport, and made a reservation on a late afternoon flight. Then I called Mrs. Deloney. She was at home, and would see me.

Bert Haggerty offered to drive me out to her house. I told him he'd better stay with his father-in-law. Hoffman's snores were sounding through the house like muffled lamentations, but he could wake up at any time and go on the rampage.

21
..

GLENVIEW AVENUE wound through the north side of the north side, in a region of estates so large that it almost qualified as country. Trees lined the road and sometimes met above it. The light that filtered through their turning leaves onto the great lawns was the color of sublimated money.

I turned in between the brick gate-posts of 103 and shortly came in sight of an imposing old red brick mansion. The driveway led to a brick-columned *porte-cochère* on the right. I was hardly out of my car when a Negro maid in uniform opened the door.

"Mr. Archer?"

"Yes."

"Mrs. Deloney is expecting you, in the downstairs sitting-room."

She was sitting by a window looking out on a countryside where red sumac blazed among less brilliant colors. Her hair was white, and bobbed short. Her blue silk suit looked like Lily Daché. Her face was a mass of wrinkles but its fine bones remained in all their delicacy. She was handsome in the way an antique object can be handsome without regard to the condition of the materials. Her mind must have been very deep in the past, because she didn't notice us until the maid spoke.

"Mr. Archer is here, Mrs. Deloney."

She rose with the ease of a younger woman, putting down a book she was holding. She gave me her hand and a long look. Her eyes were the same color as her blue silk suit, unfaded and intelligent.

"So you've come all the way from California to see me. You must be disappointed."

"On the contrary."

"You don't need to flatter me. When I was twenty I looked like everybody else. Now I'm past seventy, I look like myself. It's a liberating fact. But do sit down. This chair is the most comfortable. My father Senator Osborne preferred it to any other."

She indicated a red leather armchair polished and dark with use. The chair she sat in opposite me was a ladderbacked rocker with worn cushions attached to it. The rest of the furnishings in the room were equally old and unpretentious, and I wondered if she used it as a place to keep the past.

"You've had a journey," she reminded herself. "Can I give you something to eat or drink?"

"No thanks."

She dismissed the maid. "I'm afraid you're going to be doubly disappointed. I can add very little to the official account of my husband's suicide. Luke and I hadn't been in close touch for some time before it occurred."

"You already have added something," I said. "According to the official account it was an accident."

"So it was. I'd almost forgotten. It was thought best to omit the fact of suicide from the public reports."

"Who thought it best?"

"I did, among others. Given my late husband's position in the state, his suicide was bound to have business and political repercussions. Not to mention the personal ugliness."

"Some people might think it was uglier to alter the facts of a man's death."

"Some people might think it," she said with a *grande dame* expression. "Not many of them would say it in my presence. In any case the fact was not altered, only the report of it. I've had to live with the fact of my husband's suicide."

"Are you perfectly certain that it is a fact?"

"Perfectly."

"I've just been talking to the man who handled the case, Lieutenant Hoffman. He says your husband shot himself by accident while he was cleaning an automatic pistol."

"That was the story we agreed upon. Lieutenant Hoffman naturally sticks to it. I see no point in your trying to change it at this late date."

"Unless Mr. Deloney was murdered. Then there would be some point."

"No doubt, but he was *not* murdered." Her eyes came up to mine, and they hadn't changed, except that they may have become a little harder.

"I've heard rumors that he was, as far away as California."

"Who's been spreading such nonsense?"

"Lieutenant Hoffman's daughter Helen. She claimed she knew a witness to the killing. The witness may have been herself."

The insecurity that had touched her face changed into cold anger. "She has no right to tell such lies. I'll have her stopped!"

"She's been stopped," I said. "Somebody stopped her Friday night, with a gun. Which is why I'm here."

"I see. Where in California was she killed?"

"Pacific Point. It's on the coast south of Los Angeles."

Her eyes flinched, ever so slightly. "I'm afraid I never heard of it. I'm naturally sorry that the girl is dead, though I never knew her. But I can assure you that her death had nothing to do with Luke. You're barking up the wrong tree, Mr. Archer."

"I wonder."

"There's no need to. My husband wrote me a note before he shot himself which made the whole thing very clear. Detective Hoffman brought it to me himself. No one knew it existed except him and his superiors. I hadn't intended to tell you."

"Why?"

"Because it was ugly. In effect he blamed me and my family for what he intended to do. He was in financial hot water, he'd been gambling in stocks and other things, his business was overextended. We refused to help him, for reasons both personal and practical. His suicide was an attempt to strike back at us. It succeeded, even though we altered the facts, as you put it." She touched her flat chest. "I was hurt, as I was meant to be."

"Was Senator Osborne alive at the time?"

"I'm afraid you don't know your history," she chided me. "My father died on December 14, 1936, three-and-a-half years before my husband killed himself. At least my father was spared that humiliation."

"You referred to family."

"I meant my sister Tish and my late Uncle Scott, the guardian of our trust. He and I were responsible for refusing further assistance to Luke. The decision was essentially mine. Our marriage had ended."

"Why?"

"The usual reason, I believe. I don't care to discuss it." She rose and went to the window and stood there straight as a soldier looking out. "A number of things ended for me in 1940. My marriage, and then my husband's life, and then my sister's. Tish died in the summer of that same year, and I cried for her all that fall. And now it's fall again," she said with a sigh. "We used to ride together in the fall. I taught her to ride when she was five years old and I was ten. That was before the turn of the century."

Her mind was wandering off into remoter and less painful times. I said:

"Forgive me for laboring the point, Mrs. Deloney, but I have to ask you if that suicide note still exists."

She turned, trying to smooth the marks of grief from her face. They persisted. "Of course not. I burned it. You can take my word as to its contents."

"It isn't your word that concerns me so much. Are you absolutely certain your husband wrote it?"

"Yes. I couldn't be mistaken about his handwriting."

"A clever forgery can fool almost anybody."

"That's absurd. You're talking the language of melodrama."

"We live it every day, Mrs. Deloney."

"But who would forge a suicide note?"

"It's been done, by other murderers."

She flung back her white head and looked at me down her delicate curved nose. She resembled a bird, even in the sound of her voice:

"My husband was not murdered."

"It seems to me you're resting a great deal of weight on a single handwritten note which might have been forged."

"It was not forged. I know that by internal evidence. It referred to matters that only Luke and I were privy to."

"Such as?"

"I have no intention of telling you, or anyone. Besides, Luke had been talking for months about killing himself, especially when he was in his cups."

"You said you hadn't been close to him for months."

"No, but I got reports, from mutual friends."

"Was Hoffman one of them?"

"Hardly. I didn't consider him a friend."

"Yet he hushed up your husband's suicide for you. Your husband's alleged suicide."

"He was ordered to. He had no choice."

"Who gave the order?"

"Presumably the Commissioner of Police. He *was* a friend of mine, and a friend of Luke's."

"And that made it all right for him to order the falsification of records?"

"It's done every day," she said, "in every city in the land. Spare me your moralizing, Mr. Archer. Commissioner Robertson is long since dead. The case itself is a dead issue."

"Maybe it is to you. It's very much on Hoffman's mind. His daughter's murder revived it."

"I'm sorry for both of them. But I can't very well alter the past to accommodate some theory you may have. What are you trying to prove, Mr. Archer?"

"Nothing specific. I'm trying to find out what the dead woman meant when she said that Bridgeton had caught up with her."

"No doubt she meant something quite private and personal. Women usually do. But as I said, I never knew Helen Hoffman."

"Was she involved with your husband?"

"No. She was not. And please don't ask me how I can be sure. We've scratched enough at Luke's grave, don't you think? There's nothing hidden there but a poor suicide. I helped to put him there, in a way."

"By cutting off his funds?"

"Precisely. You didn't think I was confessing to shooting him?"

"No," I said. "Would you like to?"

Her face crinkled up in a rather savage smile. "Very well. I shot him. What do you propose to do about it?"

"Nothing. I don't believe you."

"Why would I say it if it wasn't true?" She was playing the kind of fantastic girlish game old women sometimes revert to.

"Maybe you wanted to shoot your husband. I have no doubt you did want to. But if you actually had, you wouldn't be talking about it."

"Why not? There's nothing you could possibly do. I have too many good friends in this city, official and otherwise. Who incidentally would be greatly disturbed if you persisted in stirring up that old mess."

"Am I to take that as a threat?"

"No, Mr. Archer," she said with her tight smile, "I have nothing against you except that you're a zealot in your trade, or do you call it a profession? Does it really matter so much how people died? They're dead, as we all shall be, sooner or later. Some of us sooner. And I feel I've given you enough of my remaining time on earth."

She rang for the maid.

22

I STILL HAD TIME for another try at Earl Hoffman. I drove back toward his house, through downtown streets depopulated by the Sabbath. The questions Mrs. Deloney had raised, or failed to answer, stuck in my mind like fishhooks which trailed their broken lines into the past.

I was almost certain Deloney hadn't killed himself, by accident or intent. I was almost certain somebody else had, and that Mrs. Deloney knew it. As for the suicide note, it could have been forged, it could have been invented, it could have been misread or misremembered. Hoffman would probably know which.

As I turned into Cherry Street, I saw a man in the next block walking away from me. He had on a blue suit and he moved with the heavy forcefulness of an old cop, except that every now and then he staggered and caught himself. I saw when I got closer that it was Hoffman. The orange cuffs of his pajama legs hung below his blue trousers.

I let him stay ahead of me, through slums that became more blighted as we went south. We entered a Negro district. The adult men and women on the sidewalk gave Hoffman a wide berth. He was walking trouble.

He wasn't walking too well. He stumbled and fell on his hands and knees by a gap-toothed picket fence. Some children came out from behind the fence and followed him, prancing and hooting, until he turned on them with upraised arms. He turned again and went on.

We left the Negro district and came to a district of very old three-storied frame houses converted into rooming houses and business buildings. A few newer apartment buildings stood among them, and Hoffman's destination was one of these.

It was a six-story concrete structure with a slightly rundown aspect: cracked and yellowing blinds in the rows of windows, brown watermarks below them. Hoffman went in the front entrance. I could see the inscription in the concrete arch above it: Deloney Apartments, 1928. I parked my car and followed Hoffman into the building.

He had evidently taken the elevator up. The tarnished brass arrow above the elevator door slowly turned clockwise to seven and stuck there. I gave up pushing the button after a while—Hoffman had probably left the door ajar—and found the fire stairs. I was breathing hard by the time I reached the metal door that let out onto the roof.

I opened the door a crack. Except for some pigeons coo-hooing on a neighboring rooftop, everything outside seemed very quiet. A few potted shrubs and a green plexiglass windscreen jutting out at right angles from the wall of the penthouse had converted a corner of the roof into a terrace.

A man and a woman were sunning themselves there. She was lying face down on an air mattress with the brassière of her Bikini unfastened. She was blonde and nicely made. He sat in a deck chair, with a half-empty cola bottle on the table beside him. He was broad and dark, with coarse black hair matting his chest and shoulders. He wore a diamond ring on the little finger of his left hand, and had a faint Greek accent.

"So you think the restaurant business is low class? When you say that you're biting the hand that feeds you. The restaurant business put mink on your back."

"I didn't say it. What I said, the insurance business is a nice clean business for a man."

"And restaurants are dirty? Not my restaurants. I even got violet rays in the toilets—"

"Don't talk filthy," she said.

"Toilet is not a filthy word."

"It is in my family."

"I'm sick of hearing about your family. I'm sick of hearing about your good-for-nothing brother Theo."

"Good-for-nothing?" She sat up, exposing a pearly flash of breast before she fastened its moorings. "Theo made the Million Dollar Magic Circle last year."

"Who bought the policy that put him over the top? I did. Who set him up in the insurance agency in the first place? I did."

"Mr. God." Her face was a beautiful blank mask. It didn't change when she said: "Who's that moving around in the house? I sent Rosie home after breakfast."

"She came back maybe."

"It doesn't sound like Rosie. It sounds like a man."

"Could be Theo coming to sell me this year's Magic Circle policy."

"That isn't funny."

"I think it's very funny."

He laughed to prove it. He stopped laughing when Earl Hoffman came out from behind the plexiglass windscreen. Every mark on his face was distinct in the sunlight. His orange pajamas were down over his shoes.

The dark man got out of his deck chair and pushed air toward Hoffman with his hands. "Beat it. This is a private roof."

"I can't do that," Hoffman said reasonably. "We got a report of a dead body. Where is it?"

"Down in the basement. You'll find it there." The man winked at the woman.

"The basement? They said the penthouse." Hoffman's damaged mouth opened and shut mechanically, like a dummy's, as if the past was ventriloquizing through him. "You moved it, eh? It's against the law to move it."

"*You* move yourself out of here." The man turned to the woman, who had covered herself with a yellow terrycloth robe: "Go in and phone the you-know-who."

"I am the you-know-who," Hoffman said. "And the woman stays. I have some questions to ask her. What's your name?"

"None of your business," she said.

"Everything's my business." Hoffman flung one arm out and almost lost his balance. "I'm detective inves'gating murder."

"Let's see your badge, detective."

The man held out his hand, but he didn't move toward Hoffman. Neither of them had moved. The woman was on her knees, with her beautiful scared face slanting up at Hoffman.

He fumbled in his clothes, produced a fifty-cent piece, looked at it in a frustrated way, and flung it spinning over the parapet. Faintly, I heard it ring on the pavement six stories down.

"Must of left it home," he said mildly.

The woman gathered herself together and made a dash for the penthouse. Moving clumsily and swiftly, Hoffman caught her around the waist. She didn't struggle, but stood stiff and white-faced in the circle of his arm.

"Not so fast now, baby. Got some questions to ask you. You the broad that's been sleeping with Deloney?"

She said to the man: "Are you going to let him talk to me this way? Tell him to take his hands off me."

"Take your hands off my wife," the man said without force.

"Then tell her to sit down and cooperate."

"Sit down and cooperate," the man said.

"Are you crazy? He smells like a still. He's crazy drunk."

"I know that."

"Then *do* something."

"I am doing something. You got to humor them."

Hoffman smiled at him like a public servant who was used to weathering unjust criticism. His hurt mouth and mind made the smile grotesque. The woman tried to pull away from him. He only held her closer, his belly nudging her flank.

"You look a little bit like my dau'er Helen. You know my dau'er Helen?"

The woman shook her head frantically. Her hair fluffed out.

"She says there was a witness to the killing. Were you there when it happened, baby?"

"I don't even know what you're talking about."

"Sure you do. Luke Deloney. Somebody drilled him in the eye and tried to make it look like suicide."

"I remember Deloney," the man said. "I waited on him in my father's hamburg joint once or twice. He died before the war."

"Before the war?"

"That's what I said. Where you been the last twenty years, detective?"

Hoffman didn't know. He looked around at the rooftops of his city as if it was a strange place. The woman cried out:

"Let me go, fatso."

He seemed to hear her from a long way off. "You speak with some respect to your old man."

"If you were my old man I'd kill myself."

"Don't give me no more of your lip. I've had as much of your lip as I'm going to take. You hear me?"

"Yes I hear you. You're a crazy old man and take your filthy paws off me."

Her hooked fingers raked at his face, leaving three bright parallel tracks. He slapped her. She sat down on the gravel roof. The man picked up the half-empty cola bottle. Its brown contents gushed down his arm as he raised it, advancing on Hoffman.

Hoffman reached under the back of his coat and took a revolver out of his belt. He fired it over the man's head. The pigeons flew up from the neighboring rooftop, whirling in great spirals. The man dropped the bottle and stood still with his hands raised. The woman, who had been whimpering, fell silent.

Hoffman glared at the glaring sky. The pigeons diminished into it. He looked at the revolver in his hand. With my eyes focused on the same object, I stepped out into the sunlight.

"You need any help with these witnesses, Earl?"

"Naw, I can handle 'em. Everythin's under control." He squinted at me. "What was the name again? Arthur?"

"Archer." I walked toward him, pushing my squat shadow ahead of me across the uneven surface of the gravel. "You'll get some nice publicity out of this, Earl. Solving the Deloney killing singlehanded."

"Yeah. Sure." His eyes were deeply puzzled. He knew I was talking nonsense, as he knew he had been acting nonsense out, but he couldn't admit it, even to himself. "They hid the body in the basement."

"That means we'll probably have to dig."

"Is everybody crazy?" the man said between his upraised arms.

"Keep quiet, you," I said. "You better call for reinforcements, Earl. I'll hold the gun on these characters."

He hesitated for a stretching moment. Then he handed me the revolver and went into the penthouse, bumping the doorframe heavily with his shoulder.

"Who are you?" the man said.

"I'm his keeper. Relax."

"Did he escape from the insane asylum?"

"Not yet."

The man's eyes were like raisins thumbed deep into dough. He helped his wife to her feet, awkwardly brushing off the seat of her robe. Suddenly she was crying in his arms and he was patting her back with his diamonded hand and saying something emotional in Greek.

Through the open door I could hear Hoffman talking on the phone: "Six men with shovels an' a drill for concrete. Her body's under the basement floor. Want 'em here in ten minutes or somebody gets reamed!"

The receiver crashed down, but he went on talking. His voice rose and fell like a wind, taking up scattered fragments of the past and blowing them together in a whirl. "He never touched her. Wouldn't do that to the daughter of a friend. She was a good girl, too, a clean little daddy's girl. 'Member when she was a little baby, I used to give her her

bath. She was soft as a rabbit. I held her in my arms, she called me da."
His voice broke. "What happened?"

He was silent. Then he screamed. I heard him fall to the floor with a
thud that shook the penthouse. I went inside. He was sitting with his
back against the kitchen stove, trying to remove his trousers. He waved
me back.

"Keep away from me. There's spiders on me."

"I don't see any spiders."

"They're under my clothes. Black widows. The killer's trying to
poison me with spiders."

"Who is the killer, Earl?"

His face worked. "Never found out who put the chill on Deloney.
Word came down from the top, close off the case. What can a man—?"
Another scream issued from his throat. "My God, there's hundreds of
'em crawling on me."

He tore at his clothes. They were in blue and orange rags when the
police arrived, and his old wrestler's body was naked and writhing on
the linoleum.

The two patrolmen knew Earl Hoffman. I didn't even have to explain.

23
..

THE RED SUN sank abruptly when the plane came down into the
shadow of the mountains. I had wired my ETA to the Walters agency,
and Phyllis was waiting for me at the airport.

She took my hand and offered me her cheek. She had a peaches-
and-cream complexion, a little the worse for sun, and opaque smiling
eyes the color of Indian enamel.

"You look tired, Lew. But you do exist."

"Don't tell me. It makes me feel tireder. You look wonderful."

"It gets more difficult as I get older. But then some other things get
easier." She didn't say what things. We walked toward her car in the

sudden evening. "What were you doing in Illinois, anyway? I thought you were working on a case in Pacific Point."

"It's in both places. I found an old prewar murder in Illinois which seems to be closely tied in with the current ones. Don't ask me how. It would take all night to explain, and we have more important things to do."

"You do, anyway. You have a dinner date at eight-thirty with Mrs. Sally Burke. You're an old friend of mine from Los Angeles, business unspecified. You take it from there."

"How did you fix it?"

"It wasn't hard. Sally dotes on free dinners and unattached men. She wants to get married again."

"But how did you get to know her?"

"I sort of happened into her at the bar where she hangs out and we got drunk together last night. One of us got drunk, anyway. She did some talking about her brother Judson, who may be the man you want."

"He is. Where does he live?"

"Somewhere on the South Shore. It's a hard place to find people, as you know. Arnie's out there looking for him now."

"Lead me to the sister."

"You sound like a lamb asking to be led to the slaughter. Actually she's a pretty nice gal," she said with female solidarity. "Not bright, but she has her heart in the right place. She's very fond of her brother."

"So was Lucrezia Borgia."

Phyllis slammed the car door. We drove toward Reno, a city where nothing good had ever happened to me, but I kept hoping.

Mrs. Sally Burke lived close in on Riley Street, in the upper flat of an old two-story house. Phyllis dropped me off in front of it at eight-twenty-nine, having extracted my promise to come back and spend the night with Arnie and her. Mrs. Burke was waiting in full panoply on the upper landing: tight black sheath with foxes, pearls and earrings, four-inch heels. Her hair was mingled brown and blonde, as if to express the complexity of her personality. Her brown eyes appraised me, as I came up to her level, the way an antebellum plantation owner might look over an able-bodied slave on the auction block.

She smelled nice, anyway, and she had a pleasant friendly anxious smile. We exchanged greetings and names. I was to call her Sally right away.

"I'm afraid I can't ask you in, the place is a mess. I never seem to get anything done on Sunday. You know the old song, 'Gloomy Sunday'? That is, since my divorce. Phyllis says you're divorced."

"Phyllis is right."

"It's different for a man," she said with some faint resentment. "But I can see you could use a woman to look after you."

She was one of the fastest and least efficient workers I'd ever met. My heart went down toward my boots. She was looking at my boots, and at the clothes I had slept in on the plane. On the other hand I was able-bodied. I had climbed the stairs unaided.

"Where shall we eat?" she said. "The Riverside is nice."

It was nice and expensive. After a couple of drinks I ceased to care about spending Alex's money. I began to be fascinated, in a way, by Sally Burke's conversation. Her ex-husband, if I could believe her, was a combination of Dracula, Hitler, and Uriah Heep. He made at least twenty-five thousand a year as a salesman in the Northwest, but more than once she had to attach his salary to collect her measly six hundred a month alimony. She was having a rough time making ends meet, especially now that her little brother had lost his job at the club.

I ordered her another drink and indicated mild sympathy.

"Jud's a good boy," she said, as if somebody had just denied it. "He played football at Washington State and led the team in rushing. A lot of people in Spokane thought he would have made All-American if he'd played for a better-known school. But he never got due recognition, he never has. He lost his coaching job out of sheer politics pure and simple. The charges they made were a lot of poppycock, he told me so himself."

"What charges?"

"Nothing. They were a lot of poppycock, I mean it." She finished her fourth martini and regarded me with simple cunning over the empty glass. "I don't believe you told me what kind of business that you're in. Lew?"

"I don't believe I did. I run a small agency in Hollywood."

"Isn't that interesting? Jud has always been interested in acting. He hasn't done any, actually, but he's said to be a very handsome boy. Jud was down in Hollywood last week."

"Looking for an acting job?"

"Anything," she said. "He's a willing worker, but the trouble is he isn't trained for anything, I mean after he lost his teaching credentials, and then the dance studio folded. Do you think you could get him something to do in Hollywood?"

"I'd certainly like to talk to him," I said truthfully.

She was tipsy and hopeful, and she wasn't surprised by my interest in her brother.

"*That* can be arranged," she said. "As a matter of fact he's at my apartment right now. I could call him and tell him to come over here."

"Let's have dinner first."

"*I* don't mind paying for Jud's dinner." She realized she had made a tactical error, and quickly back-tracked: "But I guess three's company, eh? I mean two."

She talked so much about her brother at dinner that it was almost like having him there. She recited his old football statistics. She told me, with a kind of vicarious enthusiasm, all about his prowess with the ladies. She explained about the brilliant ideas Jud was always hatching. The one I liked best was a plan for a condensed version of the Bible, with all the offensive passages removed, for family reading.

Sally couldn't drink. She was coming apart by the time we finished eating. She wanted to pick up her brother and go and hell around in the clubs, but my heart wasn't in it. I took her home. In the cab she went to sleep on my shoulder. This I didn't mind.

I woke her up on Riley Street and got her into the house and up the stairs. She seemed very large and loosely put together, and the foxes kept slipping. I felt as if I'd been nursing drunks all weekend.

A man in shirtsleeves and form-fitting trousers opened the door of her flat. With Sally leaning on me, I got a quick impression of him: a man of half-qualities who lived in a half-world: he was half-handsome, half-lost, half-spoiled, half-smart, half-dangerous. His pointed Italian shoes were scuffed at the toes.

"Need any help?" he said to me.

"Don't be ridic," Sally said. "I'm in perfect control. Mr. Archer, meet brother Jud, Judson Foley."

"Hello," he said. "You shouldn't have let her drink. She's got a weak head for liquor. Here, I'll take her."

With weary skill he looped her arm over his shoulders, clasped her around the waist, walked her through the front room into a lighted bedroom, laid her out on the Hollywood bed, and turned off the light.

He seemed unpleasantly surprised to find me still in the front room. "Good night, Mr. Archer, or whatever your name is. We're closing up for the night now."

"You're not very hospitable."

"No. My sister is the hospitable one." He cast a sour glance around the little room, at overflowing ashtrays, clouded glasses, scattered newspapers. "I never saw you before, I'll never see you again. Why should I be hospitable?"

"You're sure you never saw me before? Think hard."

His brown eyes studied my face, and then my body. He scratched nervously at the front of his thinning hair. He shook his head.

"If I ever saw you before I must have been drunk at the time. Did Sally bring you here when I was drunk?"

"No. Were you drinking last Friday night?"

"Let's see, what night was that? I think I was out of town. Yeah. I didn't get back here until Saturday morning." He was trying to sound casual and look unconcerned. "It must have been two other guys."

"I don't think so, Jud. I ran into you, or you ran into me, about nine last Friday night in Pacific Point."

Panic brightened his face like a flash of lightning. "Who are you?"

"I chased you down Helen Haggerty's driveway, remember? You were too fast for me. It took me two days to catch up."

He was breathing as if he'd just finished the run. "Are you from the police?"

"I'm a private detective."

He sat down in a Danish chair, gripping the fragile arms so hard I thought they might break. He snickered. It was very close to a sob.

"This is Bradshaw's idea, isn't it?"

I didn't answer him. I cleared a chair and sat in it.

"Bradshaw said he was satisfied with my story. Now he sends you up against me." His eyes narrowed. "I suppose you were pumping my sister about me."

"She doesn't need much priming."

Twisting in the chair, he threw a wicked look in the direction of her bedroom. "I wish she'd keep her mouth shut about my business."

"Don't blame her for what you did yourself."

"But the hell of it is I didn't *do* anything. I *told* Bradshaw that, and he believed me, at least he said he did."

"Are you talking about Roy Bradshaw?"

"Who else? He recognized me the other night, or thought he did. I didn't know who it was I bumped in the dark. I just wanted out of there."

"Why?"

He lifted his heavy shoulders and sat with them lifted, head down between them. "I didn't want trouble with the law."

"What were you doing at Helen's?"

"She *asked* me to come. Hell, I went there as a good Samaritan. She called me at the motel in Santa Monica and practically begged me to come and spend the night. It wasn't my beautiful blue eyes. She was frightened, she wanted company."

"What time did she call you?"

"Around seven or seven-thirty. I was just coming in from getting something to eat." He dropped his shoulders. "Listen, you know all this, you got it from Bradshaw, didn't you? What are you trying to do, trap me into a mistake?"

"It's an idea. What sort of a mistake did you have in mind?"

He shook his head, and went on shaking it as he spoke. "I didn't have anything particular in mind. I mean, I can't afford to make any mistakes."

"You already made the big one, when you ran."

"I know. I panicked." He shook his head some more. "There she was with a bullet hole in her skull and there I was a natural setup for a patsy. I heard you fellows coming, and I panicked. You've got to believe me."

They always said that. "Why do I have to believe you?"

"Because I'm telling the truth. I'm innocent as a little child."

"That's pretty innocent."

"I didn't mean in general, I meant in this particular situation. I went a long way out of my way to give Helen a helping hand. It doesn't make sense I'd go there to knock her off. I *liked* the girl. She and I had a lot in common."

I didn't know if this was a compliment to either of them. Bert Haggerty had described his ex-wife as corrupt. The man in front of me was a dubious character. Behind the mask of his good looks he seemed dilapidated, as if he'd painfully bumped down several steps in the social scale. In spite of this, I half-believed his story. I would never more than half-believe anything he said.

"What did you and Helen have in common?"

He gave me a quick sharp up-from-under look. This wasn't the usual line of questioning. He thought about his answer. "Sports. Dancing. Fun and games. We had some real fun times, I mean it. I almost died when I found her the other night."

"How did you happen to meet her?"

"You *know* all this," he said impatiently. "You're working for Bradshaw, aren't you?"

354 · *Archer* AT LARGE

"Put it this way: Bradshaw and I are on the same side." I wanted to know why Roy Bradshaw loomed so large in Foley's mind, but other questions had priority. "Now why don't you humor me and tell me how you knew Helen?"

"It's simple enough." He jabbed his thumb downward like a decadent emperor decreeing death. "She rented the downstairs apartment when she was putting in her six weeks this summer. She and my sister hit it off, and eventually I got into the act. The three of us used to go places together."

"In Sally's car?"

"I had my own car then—sixty-two Galaxie five hundred," he said earnestly. "This was back in August before I lost my job and couldn't keep up with the payments."

"How did you happen to lose your job?"

"That wouldn't interest you. It had nothing to do with Helen Haggerty, nothing whatever."

His overinsistence on the point made me suspicious. "What were you working at?"

"I said you wouldn't be interested."

"I can easily find out where you were working. You might as well tell me."

He said with his eyes down: "I was in the cashier's cage at the Solitaire in Stateline. I guess I made one mistake too many." He looked at his strong square fumbling hands.

"So you were looking for work in Los Angeles?"

"Correcto." He seemed relieved to get away from the subject of his job and why he lost it. "I didn't make a connection, but I've got to get out of this place."

"Why?"

He scratched his hair. "I can't go on living on my sister. It *cuts* me, being on the ding. I'm going down to L.A. again and have another look around."

"Let's get back to the first time. You say Helen called you at your motel Friday night. How did she know you were there?"

"I already called her earlier in the week."

"What for?"

"The usual. I mean, I thought we could get together, have some fun." He kept talking about having fun but he looked as if he hadn't had any for years. "Helen already had a date that night, Wednesday night. As a matter of fact she had a date with Bradshaw. They were going to some concert. She said she'd call me back another time. Which she did, Friday night."

"What did she say on the telephone?"

"That somebody threatened to kill her, and she was scared. I never heard her talk like that before. She said that she had nobody to turn to but me. And I got there too late." There seemed to be grief in him, but even this was ambiguous, as if he felt defrauded by Helen's death.

"Were Helen and Bradshaw close?"

He answered cautiously: "I wouldn't say that. I guess they lucked into each other last summer the same way Helen and I did. Anyway, he was busy Friday night. He had to give a speech at some big dinner. At least that's what he told me this morning."

"He wasn't lying. Did Bradshaw and Helen meet here in Reno?"

"Where else?"

"I thought Bradshaw spent the summer in Europe."

"You thought wrong. He was here all through August, anyway."

"What was he doing here?"

"He told me once he was doing some kind of research at the University of Nevada. He didn't say what kind. I hardly knew him, actually. I ran into him a couple of times with Helen, and that was it. I didn't see him again until today."

"And you say he recognized you Friday night and came here to question you?"

"That's the truth. He came here this morning, gave me quite a grilling. *He* believed I didn't do that murder. I don't see why you can't believe me."

"I'll want to talk to Bradshaw before I make up my mind. Where is he now, do you know?"

"He said he was staying at the Lakeview Inn, on the North Shore. I don't know if he's still there or not."

I stood up and opened the door. "I think I'll go and see."

I suggested to Jud that he stay where he was, because a second runout would make him look very bad. He nodded. He was still nodding when a counter-impulse took hold of him and he rushed me. His heavy shoulder caught me under the ribs and slammed me back against the doorframe wheezing for air.

He threw a punch at my face. I shifted my head. His fist crunched into the plaster wall. He yipped with pain. He hit me low in the belly with his other hand. I slid down the doorframe. He kneed me, a glancing blow on the side of the jaw.

This impelled me to get up. He rushed me again, head down. I stepped to one side and chopped the back of his neck as he went by. He staggered rapidly through the door and across the landing, and plunged down. At the foot of the stairs he lay still.

But he was conscious when the police arrived. I rode along to the station to make sure they nailed him down. We hadn't been there five minutes when Arnie came in. He had an understanding with the officers. They booked Foley for assault and related charges, and promised to hold him.

24

Arnie drove me out to the Lakeview Inn, a rambling California Gothic pile which must have dated from the early years of the century. Generations of summer visitors had marched through the lobby and trampled out any old-world charm it might once have had. It seemed an unlikely place for Roy Bradshaw to be staying.

But Bradshaw was there, the elderly night clerk said. He took a railroad watch out of his vest pocket and consulted it. "It's getting pretty late, though. They may be asleep."

"They?"

"Him and his wife. I can go up and call him, if you want me to. We never did put telephones in the rooms."

"I'll go up. I'm a friend of Dr. Bradshaw's."

"I didn't know he was a doctor."

"A doctor of philosophy," I said. "What's his room number?"

"Thirty-one, on the top floor." The old man seemed relieved at not having to make the climb.

I left Arnie with him and went up to the third floor. Light shone through the transom of 31, and I could hear the indistinct murmur of voices. I knocked. There was a silence, followed by the noise of slippered feet.

Roy Bradshaw spoke through the door. "Who is it?"

"Archer."

He hesitated. A sleeper in the room across the hall, perhaps disturbed by our voices, began to snore. Bradshaw said:

"What are you doing here?"

"I have to see you."

"Can't it wait till morning?" His voice was impatient, and he had temporarily mislaid his Harvard accent.

"No. It can't. I need your advice on what to do about Judson Foley."

"Very well. I'll get dressed."

I waited in the narrow ill-lit hallway. It had the faintly acrid smell which old buildings seem to absorb from the people who pass through them night by night, the smell of transient life. The snoring man was uttering terrible moans between his snores. A woman told him to turn over, and he subsided.

I could hear a quick interchange of voices in Bradshaw's room. The woman's voice seemed to want something, which Bradshaw's voice denied. I thought I recognized the woman's voice, but I couldn't be sure.

I was sure when Bradshaw finally opened the door. He tried to slip out without letting me see in, but I caught a glimpse of Laura Sutherland. She was sitting upright on the edge of the unmade bed in a severely cut Paisley robe. Her hair was down around her shoulders, and she was rosy and beautiful.

Bradshaw jerked the door shut. "So now you know."

He had pulled on slacks and a black turtleneck sweater which made him look more undergraduate than ever. In spite of the tension in him, he seemed quite happy.

"I don't know what I know," I said.

"This is not an illicit liaison, believe me. Laura and I were married some time ago. We're keeping our marriage secret, for the present. I'm going to ask you to go along with that."

I didn't say whether I would or not. "Why all the secrecy?"

"We have our reasons. For one thing, under the college regulations, Laura would have to give up her post. She intends to, of course, but not immediately. And then there's Mother. I don't know how I'm going to break it to her."

"You could just tell her. She'll survive."

"It's easy enough to say. It isn't possible."

The thing that made it impossible, I thought, was Mother's money.

Having money and looking forward to inheriting more were difficult habits for a man to break in early middle age. But I felt a sneaking admiration for Bradshaw. He had more life in him than I'd suspected.

We went downstairs and through the lobby, where Arnie was playing gin rummy with the night clerk. The bar was a gloomy cavern with antlers on the walls instead of stalactites and customers instead of stalagmites. One of the customers, a local man wearing a cap and windbreaker and carrying a load, wanted to buy Bradshaw and me a drink. The bartender told him it was time to go home. Surprisingly, he went, and most of the others drifted out after him.

We sat at the bar. Bradshaw ordered a double bourbon and insisted on one for me, though I didn't need it. There was some aggression in his insistence. He hadn't forgiven me for stumbling on his secret, or for dragging him away from his wife's bed.

"Well," he said, "what about Judson Foley?"

"He tells me you recognized him Friday night."

"I had an intuition that it was he." Bradshaw had recovered his accent, and was using it as a kind of vocal mask.

"Why didn't you say so? You could have saved a lot of legwork and expense."

He looked at me solemnly over his drink. "I had to be certain and I was very far from being that. I couldn't accuse a man, and set the police on his trail, unless I were certain."

"So you came here to make certain?"

"It happened to work out that way. There are times in a man's life when everything seems to fall together into place, have you noticed?" A momentary flash of glee broke through his earnestness. "Laura and I had been planning to steal a weekend here for some time, and the conference gave us the opportunity. Foley was a side issue, but of course a very important one. I looked him up this morning and questioned him thoroughly. He seems completely innocent to me."

"Innocent of what?"

"Of Helen's murder. Foley went to her house to give her what protection he could, but she was already beyond protection when he got there. He lost his nerve and ran."

"What was he afraid of?"

"A false accusation, what he calls a frameup. He's had some trouble with the law in the past. It had to do with shaving points, as they call it, in football games."

"How do you know?"

"He told me. I have," he said with a chuckle of vanity, "a certain capacity to inspire confidence in these—ah—disaffiliates. The man was utterly forthright with me, and in my considered opinion he had nothing to do with Helen's murder."

"You're probably right. I'd still like to find out more about him."

"I know very little about him. He was a friend of Helen's. I saw him once or twice in her company."

"In Reno."

"Yes. I spent a part of the summer in Nevada. It's another fact about myself that I'm not publicizing." He added rather vaguely: "A man has a right to some private life, surely."

"You mean you were here with Laura?"

He dropped his eyes. "She was with me a part of the time. We hadn't quite made up our minds to get married. It was quite a decision. It meant the end of her career and the end of my—life with Mother," he concluded lamely.

"I can understand your reason for keeping it quiet. Still I wish you'd told me that you met Foley and Helen last month in Reno."

"I should have. I apologize. One acquires the habit of secrecy." He added in a different, passionate voice: "I'm deeply in love with Laura. I'm jealous of anything that threatens to disturb our idyl." His words were formal and old-fashioned, but the feeling behind them seemed real.

"What was the relationship between Foley and Helen?"

"They were friends, nothing more, I'd say. Frankly I was a little surprised at her choice of companion. But he was younger than she, and I suppose that was the attraction. Presentable escorts are at a premium in Reno, you know. I had quite a time myself fending off the onslaughts of various predatory females."

"Does that include Helen?"

"I suppose it does." Through the gloom I thought I could discern a faint blush on his cheek. "Of course she didn't know about my—my *thing* with Laura. I've kept it a secret from everyone."

"Is that why you don't want Foley taken back for questioning?"

"I didn't say that."

"I'm asking you."

"I suppose that's partly it." There was a long silence. "But if you think it's necessary, I won't argue. Laura and I have nothing really to hide."

The bartender said: "Drink up, gentlemen. It's closing time."

We drank up. In the lobby Bradshaw gave me a quick nervous handshake, muttering something about getting back to his wife. He went up the stairs two at a time, on his toes.

I waited for Arnie to finish his game of gin. One of the things that made him a first-rate detective was his ability to merge with almost any group, nest into almost any situation, and start a conversation rolling. He and the night man shook hands when we left the hotel.

"The woman your friend registered with," he said in the car, "is a good-looking brownette type, well stacked, who talks like a book."

"She's his wife."

"You didn't tell me Bradshaw was married," he said rather irritably.

"I just found out. The marriage is *sub rosa*. The poor beggar has a dominating mother in the background. In the foreground. The old lady has money, and I think he's afraid of being disinherited."

"He better come clean with her, and take his chances."

"That's what I told him."

Arnie put the car in gear and as we drove west and south along the lakeshore, recounted a long story about a client he had handled for Pinkerton in San Francisco before the war. She was a well-heeled widow of sixty or so who lived in Hillsborough with her son, a man in his thirties. The son was always home by midnight, but seldom before, and the mother wanted to know what he was doing with his evenings. It turned out he had been married for five years to an ex-waitress whom he maintained, with their three small children, in a row house in South San Francisco.

Arnie seemed to think that this was the end of the story.

"What happened to the people?" I asked him.

"The old lady fell in love with her grandchildren and put up with the daughter-in-law for their sake. They all lived happily ever after, on her money."

"Too bad Bradshaw hasn't been married long enough to have any children."

We drove in silence for a while. The road left the shore and tunneled among trees which enclosed it like sweet green coagulated night. I kept thinking about Bradshaw and his unsuspected masculinity.

"I'd like you to do some checking on Bradshaw, Arnie."

"Has this marriage business escalated him into a suspect?"

"Not in my book. Not yet, anyway. But he did suppress the fact that he met Helen Haggerty in Reno last summer. I want to know exactly what he was doing here in the month of August. He told Judson Foley he was doing research at the University of Nevada, but that doesn't seem likely."

"Why not?"

"He's got a doctorate from Harvard, and he'd normally do his research there or at Berkeley or Stanford. I want you to do some checking on Foley, too. Find out if you can why Foley was fired by the Solitaire Club."

"That shouldn't be too hard. Their top security man is an old friend of mine." He looked at his watch in the light from the dash. "We could go by there now but he probably won't be on duty this late on a Sunday night."

"Tomorrow will do."

Phyllis was waiting for us with food and drink. We sat up in her kitchen foolishly late, getting mildly drunk on beer and shared memories and exhaustion. Eventually the conversation came full circle, back to Helen Haggerty and her death. At three o'clock in the morning I was reading aloud her translated poem in the *Bridgeton Blazer* about the violins of the autumn winds.

"It's terribly sad," Phyllis said. "She must have been a remarkable young girl, even if it is only a translation."

"That was her father's word for her. Remarkable. He's remarkable, too, in his own way."

I tried to tell them about the tough old drunken heartbroken cop who had sired Helen. Suddenly it was half-past three and Phyllis was asleep with her head resting like a tousled dahlia among the bottles on the kitchen table. Arnie began gathering up the bottles, carefully, so as not to wake her unnecessarily soon.

Alone in their guest room I had one of those intuitions that come sometimes when you're very tired and emotionally stirred up. I became convinced that Hoffman had given me the *Blazer* for a reason. There was something in it he wanted me to see.

I sat in my underwear on the edge of the open fresh-smelling bed and read the little magazine until my eyes crossed. I learned a good deal about student activities at Bridgeton City College twenty-two years ago, but nothing of any apparent consequence to my case.

I found another poem I liked, though. It was signed with the initials G.R.B., and it went:

> If light were dark
> And dark were light,
> Moon a black hole
> In the blaze of night,
>
> A raven's wing
> As bright as tin,
> Then you, my love,
> Would be darker than sin.

I read it aloud at breakfast. Phyllis said she envied the woman it had been written to. Arnie complained that his scrambled eggs weren't moist. He was older than Phyllis, and it made him touchy.

We decided after breakfast to leave Judson Foley sitting for the present. If Dolly Kincaid were arrested and arraigned, Foley would make a fairly good surprise witness for the defense. Arnie drove me to the airport, where I caught a Pacific flight to Los Angeles.

I picked up an L.A. paper at International Airport, and found a brief account of the Haggerty killing in the Southland News on an inside page. It informed me that the wife-slayer Thomas McGee, released from San Quentin earlier in the year, was being sought for questioning. Dolly Kincaid wasn't mentioned.

25

AROUND NOON I walked into Jerry Marks's store-front office. His secretary told me that Monday was the day for the weekly criminal docket and Jerry had spent the morning in court. He was probably having lunch somewhere near the courthouse. Yes, Mr. Kincaid had got in touch with Mr. Marks on Sunday, and retained him.

I found them together in the restaurant where Alex and I had lunched the day it began. Alex made room for me on his side of the booth, facing the front. Business was roaring, and there was a short lineup inside the front door.

"I'm glad the two of you got together," I said.

Alex produced one of his rare smiles. "So am I. Mr. Marks has been wonderful."

Jerry flapped his hand in a depreciating way. "Actually I haven't been able to do anything yet. I had another case to dispose of this morning. I did make an attempt to pick Gil Stevens's brains, but he told me I'd better go to the transcript of the trial, which I plan to do this afternoon. Mrs. Kincaid," he said, with a sidelong glance at Alex, "was just as uncommunicative as Stevens."

"You've talked to Dolly then?"

He lowered his voice. "I tried, yesterday. We've got to know where we stand before the police get to her."

"Is that going to happen?"

Jerry glanced around him at the courthouse crowd, and lowered his voice still further. "According to the grapevine, they were planning to make their move today, when they completed their ballistics tests. But something's holding them up. The Sheriff and the experts he brought in are still down in the shooting gallery under the courthouse."

"The bullet may be fragmented. It often is in head wounds. Or they may have shifted their main attention to another suspect. I see in the paper they've put out an APB for Thomas McGee."

"Yes, it was done yesterday. He's probably over the Mexican border by now."

"Do you consider him a major suspect, Jerry?"

"I'll want to read that transcript before I form an opinion. Do you?"

It was a hard question. I was spared having to answer it by a diversion. Two elderly ladies, one in serviceable black and one in fashionable green, looked in through the glass front door. They saw the waiting queue and turned away. The one in black was Mrs. Hoffman, Helen's mother. The other was Luke Deloney's widow.

I excused myself and went out after them. They had crossed the street in the middle of the block and were headed downtown, moving through light and shadow under the giant yuccas that hedged the courthouse grounds. Though they seemed to keep up an incessant conversation, they walked together like strangers, out of step and out of sympathy. Mrs. Deloney was much the older, but she had a horsewoman's stride. Mrs. Hoffman stubbed along on tired feet.

I stayed on the other side of the street and followed them at a distance. My heart was thudding. Mrs. Deloney's arrival in California confirmed my belief that her husband's murder and Helen's were connected, and that she knew it.

They walked two blocks to the main street and went into the first restaurant they came to, a tourist trap with empty tables visible through its plate glass windows. There was an open-fronted cigar store diagonally across the street. I looked over its display of paperbacks, bought a pack of cigarettes, and smoked three or four which I lit at the old-fashioned gas flame, and eventually bought a book about ancient Greek philosophy. It had a chapter on Zeno which I read standing. The old ladies were a long time over lunch.

"Archer will never catch the old ladies," I said.

The man behind the counter cupped his ear. "What was that?"

"I was thinking aloud."

"It's a free country. I like to talk to myself when I'm off work. In the store here it wouldn't be appropriate." He smiled over the word, and his gold teeth flashed like jewelry.

The old ladies came out of the restaurant and separated. Mrs. Hoffman limped south, toward her hotel. Mrs. Deloney strode in the opposite direction, moving rapidly now that she was unencumbered by her companion. From the distance you could have taken her for a young woman who had unaccountably bleached her hair white.

She turned off the main street in the direction of the courthouse, and halfway down the block disappeared into a modern concrete and glass building. "Law Offices of Stevens and Ogilvy," said the brass sign beside the entrance. I walked on to the next corner, sat on a bench at a bus stop, and read in my new book about Heraclitus. All things flow like a river, he said; nothing abides. Parmenides, on the other hand, believed that nothing ever changed, it only seemed to. Both views appealed to me.

A cab pulled up in front of the Stevens and Ogilvy office. Mrs. Deloney came out, and the cab took her away. I made a note of its license number before I went into the building.

It was a large office, and a working one. Typewriters were clacking in a row of cubicles behind the waiting room. A very junior attorney in a flannel suit was telling the middle-aged woman at the front desk how he wanted a brief set up on her typewriter.

He went away. Her steel-gray glance met mine, and we happened to smile at each other. She said:

"I was typing briefs when he was just a gleam in his daddy's eye. Can I help you?"

"I'm very eager to see Mr. Gil Stevens. My name is Archer."

She looked in her appointment book, and then at her watch. "Mr. Stevens is due for lunch in ten minutes. He won't be coming back to the office today. I'm sorry."

"It has to do with a murder case."

"I see. I may be able to slip you in for five minutes if that will do any good."

"It might."

She talked to Stevens on the phone and waved me past the cubicles to an office at the end of the hall. It was large and sumptuous. Stevens sat on leather behind mahogany, flanked by a glass-faced cabinet of yachting trophies. He was lion-faced, with a big soft masterful mouth, a high brow overhung by broken wings of yellowish white hair, pale blue eyes that had seen everything at least once and were watching the second time around. He wore tweeds and a florid bow tie.

"Close the door behind you, Mr. Archer, and sit down."

I parked myself on a leather settee and started to tell him what I was doing there. His heavy voice interrupted me:

"I have only a very few minutes. I know who you are, sir, and I believe I know what you have in mind. You want to discuss the McGee case with me."

I threw him a curve: "And the Deloney case."

His eyebrows went up, forcing the flesh above them into multiple corrugations. Sometimes you have to give away information on the chance of gaining other information. I told him what had happened to Luke Deloney.

He leaned forward in his chair. "You say this is connected in some way with the Haggerty murder?"

"It has to be. Helen Haggerty lived in Deloney's apartment building. She said she knew a witness to Deloney's murder."

"Strange she didn't mention it." He wasn't talking to me. He was talking to himself about Mrs. Deloney. Then he remembered that I was there. "Why do you come to me with this?"

"I thought you'd be interested, since Mrs. Deloney is your client."

"Is she?"

"I assumed she was."

"You're welcome to your assumptions. I suppose you followed her here."

"I happened to see her come in. But I've wanted to get in touch with you for a couple of days."

"Why?"

"You defended Tom McGee. His wife's death was the second in a series of three related murders which started with Deloney and ended with Helen Haggerty. Now they're trying to pin the Haggerty death on McGee or his daughter, or both of them. I believe McGee is innocent, and has been all along."

"Twelve of his peers thought otherwise."

"Why did they, Mr. Stevens?"

"I get no pleasure from discussing past mistakes."

"This could be very relevant to the present. McGee's daughter admits she lied on the witness stand. She says she lied her father into prison."

"Does she now? The admission comes a little belatedly. I should have borne down on her in cross, but McGee didn't want me to. I made the mistake of respecting his wishes."

"What was the motive behind them?"

"Who can say? Paternal love, perhaps, or his feeling that the child had been made to suffer enough. Ten years in prison is a big price to pay for such delicacies of feeling."

"You're convinced that McGee was innocent?"

"Oh, yes. The daughter's admission that she was lying removes any possible doubt." Stevens took a blotched green cigar out of a glass tube, clipped it and lit it. "I take it that is highly confidential advice."

"On the contrary, I'd like to see it publicized. It might help to bring McGee in. He's on the run, as you probably know."

Stevens neither affirmed nor denied this. He sat like a mountain behind a blue haze of smoke.

"I'd like to ask him some questions," I said.

"What about?"

"The other man, for one thing—the man Constance McGee was in love with. I understand he played some part in your case."

"He was my hypothetical alternative." Stevens's face crumpled in a rueful smile. "But the judge wouldn't let him in, except in my summing-up, unless I put McGee on the stand. Which didn't seem advisable. That other man was a two-edged weapon. He was a motive for McGee, as well as an alternative suspect. I made the mistake of going for an outright acquittal."

"I don't quite follow."

"It doesn't matter. It's only history." He waved his hand, and the smoke shifted around him like strata of time in an old man's memory.

"Who was the other man?"

"Come now, Mr. Archer, you can't expect to walk in off the street and pump me dry. I've been practicing law for forty years."

"Why did you take McGee's case?"

"Tom used to do some work on my boats. I rather liked him."

"Aren't you interested in clearing him?"

"Not at the expense of another innocent man."

"You know who the other man is?"

"I know who he is, if Tom can be believed." While he still sat solidly in his chair, he was withdrawing from me like a magician through dissolving mirrors. "I don't divulge the secrets that come to me. I bury 'em, sir. That's why they come to me."

"It would be a hell of a thing if they put Tom back in San Quentin for the rest of his life, or gassed him."

"It certainly would. But I suspect you're trying to enlist me in your cause, rather than Tom's."

"We could certainly use you."

"Who are 'we'?"

"McGee's daughter Dolly and her husband Alex Kincaid, Jerry Marks and me."

"And what *is* your cause?"

"The solution of those three murders."

"You make it sound very simple and neat," he said. "Life never is. Life always has loose ends, and it's sometimes best to let them ravel out."

"Is that what Mrs. Deloney wants?"

"I wasn't speaking on behalf of Mrs. Deloney. I don't expect to." He worked a speck of tobacco onto the tip of his tongue, and spat it out.

"Did she come to you for information about the McGee case?"

"No comment."

"That probably means yes. It's a further indication that the McGee case and the Deloney killing are connected."

"We won't discuss it," he said shortly. "As for your suggestion that I join forces with you, Jerry Marks had the same idea this morning. As I told him, I'll think about it. In the meantime I want you and Jerry to think about something. Tom McGee and his daughter may be on opposite sides of this issue. They certainly were ten years ago."

"She was a child then, manipulated by adults."

"I know that." He rose, bulking huge in his light tweed suit. "It's

368 · *Archer* AT LARGE

been interesting talking to you but I'm overdue for a luncheon meeting." He moved past me to the door, gesturing with his cigar. "Come along."

26
..

I WALKED down the main street to the Pacific Hotel and asked for Mrs. Hoffman. She had just checked out, leaving no forwarding address. The bellhop who handled her bag said she had ridden away in a taxi with another old lady wearing a green coat. I gave him five dollars and my motel address, and told him it would be worth another five to find out where they'd gone.

It was past two o'clock, and my instinct told me this was the crucial day. I felt cut off from what was happening in the private offices of the courthouse, in the shooting gallery and laboratory where the ballistics tests were being conducted, behind the locked door of the nursing home. Time was slipping away, flowing past me like Heraclitus' river, while I was checking up on the vagaries of old ladies.

I went back to the telephone booths behind the hotel lobby and called Godwin's office. The doctor was with a patient, and wouldn't be available until ten minutes to three. I tried Jerry Marks. His secretary told me he was still out.

I made a collect call to the Walters agency in Reno. Arnie answered the phone:

"Nice timing, Lew. I just got the word on your boy."

"Which one? Bradshaw or Foley?"

"Both of them in a way. You wanted to know why Foley lost his job at the Solitaire Club. The answer is he used his position in the cashier's cage to find out how much Bradshaw was worth."

"How did he do that?"

"You know how the clubs check up on their customers when they open an account. They put in a query to the customer's bank, get an approximate figure on his bank balance, and set a limit to his credit accordingly. 'Low three' means a three-figure bank balance on the low side, and maybe a limit of a couple of hundred. A 'high four' might be seven or eight thousand, and a 'low five' maybe twenty or thirty thousand. Which incidentally is Bradshaw's bracket."

"Is he a gambler?"

"He isn't. That's the point. He never opened an account at the Solitaire, or anywhere else that I know of, but Foley put in a query on him anyway. The club caught it, did a double check on Foley, and got him out of there fast."

"It smells like possible blackmail, Arnie."

"More than possible," he said. "Foley admits to a bit of a record in that line."

"What else does he admit?"

"Nothing else yet. He claims he got the information for a friend."

"Helen Haggerty?"

"Foley isn't saying. He's holding back in the hope of making a deal."

"Go ahead and deal with him. He got hurt worse than I did. I'm willing to drop charges."

"It may not be necessary, Lew."

"Deal with him. Assuming blackmail, which I do, the question is what makes Bradshaw blackmailable."

"Could be his divorce," Arnie said smoothly. "You were interested in what Bradshaw was doing in Reno between the middle of July and the end of August. The answer is on the court record. He was establishing residence for a divorce from a woman named Letitia O. Macready."

"Letitia who?"

"Macready." He spelled it out. "I haven't been able to get any further information on the woman. According to the lawyer who handled the divorce, Bradshaw didn't know where she lived. Her last known address was in Boston. The official notice of the proceedings came back from there with a 'Gone—No Order' stamp."

"Is Bradshaw still at Tahoe?"

"He and his new wife checked out this morning. They were on their way back to Pacific Point. That makes him your baby."

"Baby isn't quite the word for Bradshaw. I wonder if his mother knows about the first marriage."

"You could always ask her."

I decided to try and talk to Bradshaw first. I got my car out of the courthouse lot and drove out to the college. The students on the mall and in the corridors, particularly the girls, wore subdued expressions.

The threat of death and judgment had invaded the campus. I felt a little like its representative.

The blonde secretary in the Dean's outer office looked tense, as if only her will was holding her, and the whole institution, together.

"Dean Bradshaw isn't in."

"Not back from the weekend yet?"

"Of course he's back." She added in a defensive tone: "Dean Bradshaw was here this morning for over an hour."

"Where is he now?"

"I don't know. I guess he went home."

"You sound kind of worried about him."

She answered me with a machine-gun burst from her typewriter. I retreated, across the hall to Laura Sutherland's office. Her secretary told me she hadn't come in today. She'd phoned in the middle of the morning that she was afraid she was coming down with something. I hoped it wasn't something serious, like death and judgment.

I drove back to Foothill and along it to the Bradshaw house. Wind rustled in the trees. The fog had been completely dissipated, and the afternoon sky was a brilliant aching blue. The mountains rising into it were distinct in every scarred and wrinkled detail.

I was more aware than usual of these things, but I felt cut off from them. I must have had some empathy for Roy Bradshaw and his new wife and was afraid of being hurt in my empathy. I drove past his gate without seeing it and had to turn in the next driveway and come back to the Bradshaw house. I was somewhat relieved to be told by the Spanish woman, Maria, that Bradshaw wasn't there and hadn't been all day.

Mrs. Bradshaw called from the stairs in a cracked penetrating voice: "Is that you, Mr. Archer? I want to talk to you."

She came down the steps in a quilted dressing robe and cloth slippers. The weekend had aged her. She looked very old and haggard.

"My son hasn't been home for three days," she complained, "and he hasn't telephoned once. What do you suppose has happened to him?"

"I'd like to discuss that question with you, in private."

Maria, who had been listening with her entire body, went off in a hip-swinging dudgeon. Mrs. Bradshaw took me to a room I hadn't been in before, a small sitting room opening on a patio at the side of the house. Its furnishings were informal and old-fashioned, and they reminded me slightly of the room where I had interviewed Mrs. Deloney.

This room was dominated by an oil painting over the fireplace. It was a full-length portrait, almost life-size, of a handsome gentleman wearing sweeping white mustaches and a cutaway. His black eyes followed me across the room to the armchair which Mrs. Bradshaw indicated. She sat in an upholstered platform rocker with her slippered feet on a small petit point hassock.

"I've been a selfish old woman," she said unexpectedly. "I've been thinking it over, and I've decided to pay your expenses after all. I don't like what they're doing to that girl."

"You probably know more about it than I do."

"Probably. I have some good friends in this city." She didn't elaborate.

"I appreciate the offer," I said, "but my expenses are being taken care of. Dolly's husband came back."

"Really? I'm so glad." She tried to warm herself at the thought, and failed. "I'm deeply concerned about Roy."

"So am I, Mrs. Bradshaw." I decided to tell her what I knew, or part of it. She was bound to find out soon about his marriage, his marriages. "You don't have to worry about his physical safety. I saw him last night in Reno, and he was in good shape. He checked in at the college today."

"His secretary lied to me then. I don't know what they're trying to do to me out there, or what my son is up to. What was he really doing in Reno?"

"Attending a conference, as he said. He also went there to look into a suspect in Helen Haggerty's murder."

"He must have been very fond of her, after all, to go to such lengths."

"He was involved with Miss Haggerty. I don't think the involvement was romantic."

"What was it then?"

"Financial. I think he was paying her money, and incidentally he got her a job at the college, through Laura Sutherland. To put it bluntly, the Haggerty woman was blackmailing your son. She may have called it something different herself. But she used a crooked friend in Reno to check on his bank balance before she ever came here. This was the same man Roy went to Reno to talk to."

Mrs. Bradshaw didn't throw a fit, as I was afraid she might. She said in a grave tone: "Are these facts, Mr. Archer, or are you exercising your imagination?"

"I wish I were. I'm not."

"But how could Roy be blackmailed? He's led a blameless life, a dedicated life. I'm his mother. I ought to know."

"That may be. But the standard varies for different people. A rising college administrator has to be lily-white. An unfortunate marriage, for instance, would queer his chances for that university presidency you were telling me about."

"An unfortunate marriage? But Roy has never been married."

"I'm afraid he has," I said. "Does the name Letitia Macready mean anything to you?"

"It does not."

She was lying. The name drew a net of lines across her face, reduced her eyes to bright black points and her mouth to a purse with a drawstring. She knew the name and hated it, I thought; perhaps she was even afraid of Letitia Macready.

"The name ought to mean something to you, Mrs. Bradshaw. The Macready woman was your daughter-in-law."

"You must be insane. My son has never married."

She spoke with such force and assurance that I had a moment of doubt. It wasn't likely that Arnie had made a mistake—he seldom did—but it was possible that there were two Roy Bradshaws. No, Arnie had talked to Bradshaw's lawyer in Reno, and must have made a positive identification.

"You have to get married," I said, "before you can get a divorce. Roy got a Reno divorce a few weeks ago. He was in Nevada establishing residence for it from the middle of July till the end of August."

"Now I know you're insane. He was in Europe all that time, and I can prove it." She got up, on creaking reluctant limbs, and went to the eighteenth-century secretary against one wall. She came back toward me with a sheaf of letters and postcards in her shaking hands. "He sent me these. You can see for yourself that he was in Europe."

I looked over the postcards. There were about fifteen of them, arranged in order: the Tower of London (postmarked London, July 18), the Bodleian Library (Oxford, July 21), York Cathedral (York, July 25), Edinburgh Castle (Edinburgh, July 29), The Giant's Causeway (Londonderry, August 3), The Abbey Theatre (Dublin, August 6), Land's End (St. Ives, August 8), The Arc de Triomphe (Paris, August 12), and so on through Switzerland and Italy and Germany. I read the card from Munich (a view of the English Gardens, postmarked August 25):

Dear Moms:

Yesterday I visited Hitler's eyrie at Berchtesgaden—a beautiful setting made grim by its associations—and today, by way of contrast, I took a bus to Oberammergau, where the Passion Play is performed. I was struck by the almost Biblical simplicity of the villagers. This whole Bavarian countryside is studded with the most stunning little churches. How I wish you could enjoy them with me! I'm sorry to hear that your summer companion is presenting certain prickly aspects. Well, the summer will soon be over and I for one will be happy to turn my back on the splendors of Europe and come home. All my love.

Roy

I turned to Mrs. Bradshaw. "Is this your son's handwriting?"

"Yes. It's unmistakable. I know he wrote those cards, and these letters, too."

She brandished several letters under my nose. I looked at the postmarks: London, July 19; Dublin, August 7; Geneva, August 15; Rome, August 20; Berlin, August 27; Amsterdam, August 30. I started to read the last one ("Dear Moms: Just a hasty note, which may arrive after I do, to tell you how I loved your letter about the blackbirds . . .") but Mrs. Bradshaw snatched it out of my hand.

"Please don't *read* the letters. My son and I are very close, and he wouldn't like me to show our correspondence to a stranger." She gathered all the letters and cards and locked them up in the secretary. "I believe I've proved my point, that Roy couldn't have been in Nevada when you say he was."

For all her assurance, her voice was questioning. I said:

"Did you write letters to him while he was away?"

"I did. That is to say, I dictated them to Miss What's-her-name, except for once or twice when my arthritis allowed me to write. I had a nurse-companion during the summer. Miss Wadley, her name was. She was one of these completely self-centered young women—"

I cut in: "Did you write a letter about the blackbirds?"

"Yes. We had an invasion of them last month. It was more of a fanciful little tale than a letter, having to do with blackbirds baked in a pie."

"Where did you send the blackbird letter?"

"Where? I think to Rome, to American Express in Rome. Roy gave me an itinerary before he left here."

"He was supposed to be in Rome on August 20. The blackbird letter was answered from Amsterdam on August 30."

"You have an impressive memory, Mr. Archer, but I fail to see what you're getting at."

"Just this. There was a lapse of at least ten days between the receiving and the answering of that letter—time enough for an accomplice to pick it up in Rome, airmail it to Roy in Reno, get his airmail reply in Amsterdam, and remail it to you here."

"I don't believe it." But she half-believed it. "Why would he go to such lengths to deceive his mother?"

"Because he was ashamed of what he was actually doing—divorcing the Macready woman in Reno—and he didn't want you, or anyone else, to know about it. Has he been to Europe before?"

"Of course. I took him there soon after the war, when he was in graduate school at Harvard."

"And did you visit many of these same places?"

"Yes. We did. Not Germany, but most of the others."

"Then it wouldn't have been hard for him to fake the letters. As for the postcards, his accomplice must have bought them in Europe and mailed them to him."

"I dislike your use of the word 'accomplice' in connection with my son. There is, after all, nothing criminal about this—this deception. It's a purely personal matter."

"I hope so, Mrs. Bradshaw."

She must have known what I meant. Her face went through the motions of swallowing pain. She turned her back on me and went to the window. Several white-eyed blackbirds were walking around on the tiles of the patio. I don't suppose she saw them. One of her hands combed roughly at her hair, over and over, until it stuck up like molting thistles. When she turned around at last, her eyes were half-closed, and her face seemed tormented by the light.

"I'm going to ask you to keep all this in confidence, Mr. Archer."

Roy Bradshaw had used very similar language last night, about his marriage to Laura.

"I can try," I said.

"Please do. It would be tragic if Roy's career were to be ruined by a youthful indiscretion. That's all it was, you know—a youthful indiscretion. It would never have happened if his father had lived to give him a father's guidance." She gestured toward the portrait over the fireplace.

"By 'it' you mean the Macready woman?"

"Yes."

"You know her then?"

"I know her."

As if the admission had exhausted her, she collapsed in the platform rocker, leaning her head on the high cushioned back. Her loose throat seemed very vulnerable.

"Miss Macready came to see me once," she said. "It was before we left Boston, during the war. She wanted money."

"Blackmail money?"

"That's what it amounted to. She asked me to finance a Nevada divorce for her. She'd picked Roy up on Scollay Square and tricked the boy into marrying her. She was in a position to wreck his future. I gave her two thousand dollars. Apparently she spent it on herself and never bothered getting a divorce." She sighed. "Poor Roy."

"Did he know that you knew about her?"

"I never told him. I thought I had ended the threat by paying her money. I wanted it over with and forgotten, with no recriminations between my son and me. But apparently she's been haunting him all these years."

"Haunting him in the flesh?"

"Who knows? I thought I understood my son, and all the details of his life. It turns out that I don't."

"What sort of a woman is she?"

"I saw her only once, when she came to my house in Belmont. I formed a most unfavorable impression. She claimed to be an actress, unemployed, but she dressed and talked like a member of an older profession than that." Her voice rasped with irony. "I suppose I have to admit that the redheaded hussy was handsome, in a crude way. But she was utterly unsuitable for Roy, and of course she knew it. He was an innocent lad, hardly out of his teens. She was obviously an experienced woman."

"How old was she?"

"Much older than Roy, thirty at least."

"So she'd be pushing fifty now."

"At least," she said.

"Have you ever seen her in California?"

She shook her head so hard that her face went loose and wobbly.

"Has Roy?"

"He's never mentioned her to me. We've lived together on the assumption that the Macready woman never existed. And I beg you not to tell him what I've told you. It would destroy all confidence between us."

"There may be more important considerations, Mrs. Bradshaw."

"What could be more important?"

"His neck."

She sat with her thick ankles crossed, more stunned than impassive. Her broad sexless body made her resemble a dilapidated Buddha. She said in a hushed voice:

"Surely you can't suspect my son of murder?"

I said something vague and soothing. The eyes of the man in the portrait followed me out. I was glad the father wasn't alive, in view of what I might have to do to Roy.

27
..

I HADN'T eaten since breakfast, and on my way into town I stopped at a drive-in. While I was waiting for my sandwich, I made another call to Arnie Walters from an outside booth.

Arnie had made his deal with Judson Foley. It was Helen Haggerty who had wanted the word on Bradshaw's financial status. Foley couldn't or wouldn't swear that she had blackmail in mind. But shortly after he sold her the information she came into sudden wealth, by Foley's standards.

"How much did she pay Foley?"

"Fifty dollars, he says. Now he feels cheated."

"He always will," I said. "Did she tell Foley what she had on Bradshaw?"

"No. She was very careful not to, apparently. But there's a piece of negative evidence: She didn't mention to Foley that Bradshaw had been married, or was getting a divorce. Which probably means that that information was worth money to her."

"It probably does."

"One other fact came out, Lew. The Haggerty woman knew Bradshaw long before they met in Reno."

"Where and how?"

"Foley says he doesn't know, and I believe him. I offered to pay him for any information that checked out. It broke his heart when he couldn't do business with me."

I found Jerry Marks in the law library on the second floor of the courthouse. Several bound volumes of typescript were piled on the table in front of him. There was dust on his hands, and a smudge on the side of his nose.

"Have you turned up anything, Jerry?"

"I've come to one conclusion. The case against McGee was weak. It consisted of two things, mainly: prior abuse of his wife, and the little girl's testimony, which some judges would have thrown out of court. I've been concentrating on her testimony, because I'm going to have a chance to question her under pentothal."

"When?"

"Tonight at eight, at the nursing home. Dr. Godwin isn't free till then."

"I want to be there."

"That suits me, if Godwin can be persuaded. It was all I could do to get myself invited, and I'm her lawyer."

"I think Godwin is sitting on something. There's a job that needs doing between now and eight. It's properly my job but this is your town and you can do it faster. Find out if Roy Bradshaw's alibi for Helen Haggerty's murder is waterproof and dustproof and antimagnetic."

Jerry sat up straight and used his forefinger to smudge his nose some more. "How should I go about it?"

"Bradshaw addressed an alumni banquet Friday evening. I want to know if he could have slipped out during one of the other speeches, or left in time to kill her. You have a right to any facts the sheriff's men and the pathologist can provide about time of death."

"I'll do my best," he said, pushing his chair back.

"One other thing, Jerry. Is there any word on the ballistics tests?"

"The rumor says they're still going on. The rumor doesn't say why. Do you suppose they're trying to fake something?"

"No, I don't. Ballistics experts don't go in for fakery."

I left him gathering up his transcripts and walked downtown to the Pacific Hotel. My bellhop had contacted Mrs. Deloney's cab-driver, and told me in return for a second five that the two elderly ladies had checked in at the Surf House. I bought a drip-dry shirt and some underwear and socks and went back to my motel to shower and change. I needed that before I tackled Mrs. Deloney again.

Someone was knocking as I stepped out of the shower, tapping ever so gently as if the door was fragile.

"Who's there?"

"Madge Gerhardi. Let me in."

"As soon as I'm dressed."

It took a little time. I had to pick the pins out of my new shirt, and my hands were jerking.

"*Please* let me in," the woman said at the door. "I don't want to be seen."

I pulled on my trousers and went to the door in my bare feet. She pressed in past me as if there was a storm at her back. Her garish blonde hair was windblown. She took hold of my hands with both of her clammy ones.

"The police are watching my house. I don't know if they followed me here or not. I came along the beach."

"Sit down," I said, and placed a chair for her. "I'm sure the police aren't after you. They're looking for your friend Begley-McGee."

"Don't call him that. It sounds as though you're making fun of him." It was an avowal of love.

"What do you want me to call him?"

"I still call him Chuck. A man has a right to change his name, after what they did to him, and what they're doing. Anyway, he's a writer, and writers use pen names."

"Okay, I'll call him Chuck. But you didn't come here to argue about a name."

She fingered her mouth, pushing her full lower lip from side to side. She wasn't wearing lipstick or any other makeup. Without it she looked younger and more innocent.

"Have you heard from Chuck?" I said.

She nodded almost imperceptibly, as if too great a movement would endanger him.

"Where is he, Madge?"

"In a safe place. I'm not to tell you where unless you promise not to tell the police."

"I promise."

Her pale eyes brightened. "He wants to talk to you."

"Did he say what about?"

"I didn't talk to him personally. A friend of his down at the harbor telephoned the message."

"I take it he's somewhere around the harbor then."

She gave me another of her barely visible nods.

"You've told me this much," I said. "You might as well tell me the rest. I'd give a lot for an interview with Chuck."

"And you won't lead the police to him?"

"Not if I can help it. Where is he, Madge?"

She screwed up her face and made the plunge: "He's on Mr. Stevens's yacht, the *Revenant*."

"How did he get aboard her?"

"I'm not sure. He knew that Mr. Stevens was racing her at Balboa over the weekend. I think he went there and surrendered to Mr. Stevens."

I left Madge in my room. She didn't want to go out again by herself, or ride along with me. I took the waterfront boulevard to the harbor. While a few tugboats and tuna-fishers used its outer reaches, most of the boats moored at the slips or anchored within the long arm of the jetty were the private yachts and cruisers of weekend sailors.

On a Monday, not many of them were at sea, but I noticed a few white sails on the horizon. They were headed shoreward, like homing dreams.

A man in the harbormaster's glass-enclosed lookout pointed out Stevens's yacht to me. Though she rode at the far end of the outer slip, she was easy to spot because of her towering mast. I walked out along the floating dock to her.

Revenant was long and sleek, with a low streamlined cabin and a racing cockpit. Her varnish was smooth and clear, her brass was bright. She rocked ever so slightly on the enclosed water, like an animal trembling to run.

I stepped aboard and knocked on the hatch. No answer, but it opened when I pushed. I climbed down the short ladder and made my way past some short-wave radio equipment, and a tiny galley smelling of burned coffee, into the sleeping quarters. An oval of sunlight from one of the ports, moving reciprocally with the motion of the yacht, fluttered against the bulkhead like a bright and living soul. I said to it: "McGee?"

Something stirred in an upper bunk. A face appeared at eye level. It was a suitable face for the crew of a boat named *Revenant*. McGee had shaved off his beard, and the lower part of his face had a beard-

shaped pallor. He looked older and thinner and much less sure of himself.

"Did you come here by yourself?" he whispered.

"Naturally I did."

"That means you don't think I'm guilty, either." He was reduced to
such small momentary hopefulness.

"Who else doesn't think you're guilty?"

"Mr. Stevens."

"Was this his idea?" I said, with a gesture that included McGee and
myself.

"He didn't say I *shouldn't* talk to you."

"Okay, McGee, what's on your mind?"

He lay still watching me. His mouth was twitching, and his eyes held
a kind of beseeching brightness. "I don't know where to start. I've been
living in my thoughts for ten years—so long it hardly seems real. I know
what happened to me but I don't know why. Ten years in the pen,
with no chance of parole because I wouldn't admit that I was guilty.
How could I? I was bum-rapped. And now they're getting ready to do
it again."

He gripped the polished mahogany edge of the bunk. "I can't go back
to 'Q', brother. I did ten years and it was *hard* time. There's no time as
hard as the time you do for somebody else's mistake. God, but the days
crawled. There weren't enough jobs to go round and half the time I
had nothing to do but sit and think.

"I'll kill myself," he said, "before I let them send me back again."

He meant it, and I meant what I said in reply: "It won't happen,
McGee. That's a promise."

"I only wish I could believe you. You get out of the habit of believing
people. They don't believe you, you don't believe them."

"Who killed your wife?"

"I don't know."

"Who do you think killed her?"

"I'm not saying."

"You've gone to a lot of trouble, and taken quite a risk, to get me out
here and tell me you're not saying. Let's go back to where it started,
McGee. Why did your wife leave you?"

"I left her. We had been separated for months when she was killed.
I wasn't even in Indian Springs that night, I was here in the Point."

"Why did you leave her?"

"Because she asked me to. We weren't getting along. We never did get along after I came back from the service. Constance and the kid spent the war years living with her sister, and she couldn't adjust to me after that. I admit I was a wild man for a while then. But her sister Alice promoted the trouble between us."

"Why?"

"She thought the marriage was a mistake. I guess she wanted Constance all to herself. I just got in the way."

"Did anybody else get in the way?"

"Not if Alice could help it."

I phrased my question more explicitly: "Was there another man in Constance's life?"

"Yeah. There was." He seemed ashamed, as if the infidelity had been his. "I've given it a lot of thought over the years, and I don't see much point in opening it up now. The guy had nothing to do with her death, I'm sure of that. He was crazy about her. He wouldn't hurt her."

"How do you know?"

"I talked to him about her, not long before she was killed. The kid told me what was going on between him and her."

"You mean your daughter Dolly?"

"That's right. Constance used to meet the guy every Saturday, when she brought Dolly in to see the doctor. On one of my visiting days with the kid—the last one we ever had together, in fact—she told me about those meetings. She was only eleven or twelve and she didn't grasp the full significance, but she knew something fishy was going on.

"Every Saturday afternoon Constance and the guy used to park her in a double-feature movie and go off by themselves someplace, probably some motel. Constance asked the kid to cover for her, and she did. The guy even gave her money to tell Alice that Constance went to those movies with her. I thought that was a lousy trick." McGee tried to warm over his old anger but he had suffered too much, and thought too much, to be able to. His face hung like a cold moon over the edge of the bunk.

"We might as well use his name," I said. "Was it Godwin?"

"Hell no. It was Roy Bradshaw. He used to be a professor at the college." He added with a kind of mournful pride: "Now he's the Dean out there."

He wouldn't be for long, I thought; his sky was black with chickens coming home to roost.

"Bradshaw was one of Dr. Godwin's patients," McGee was saying.

"That's where he and Connie met, in Godwin's waiting room. I think the doctor kind of encouraged the thing between them."

"What makes you think that?"

"Bradshaw told me himself the doctor said it was good for them, for their emotional health. It's a funny thing, I went to Bradshaw's house to get him to lay off Connie, even if I had to beat him up. But by the time he was finished talking he had me half-convinced that he and Connie were right, and I was wrong. I still don't know who was right and who was wrong. I know I never gave her any real happiness, after the first year. Maybe Bradshaw did."

"Is that why you didn't inject him into your trial?"

"That was one reason. Anyway, what was the use of fouling it up? It would only make me look worse." He paused. A deeper tone rose from a deeper level of his nature: "Besides, I loved her. I loved Connie. It was the one way I had to prove I loved her."

"Did you know that Bradshaw was married to another woman?"

"When?"

"For the last twenty years. He divorced her a few weeks ago."

McGee looked shocked. He'd been living on illusions for a long time, and I was threatening his sustenance. He pulled himself back into the bunk, almost out of sight.

"Her name was Letitia Macready—Letitia Macready Bradshaw. Have you ever heard of her?"

"No. How could he be married? He was living at home with his mother."

"There are all kinds of marriages," I said. "He may not have seen his wife in years, and then again he may have. He may have had her living here in town, unknown to his mother or any of his friends. I suspect that was the case, judging from the lengths he went to to cover up his divorce."

McGee said in a confused and shaken voice: "I don't see what it has to do with me."

"It may have a very great deal. If the Macready woman was in town ten years ago, she had a motive for killing your wife—a motive as strong as your own."

He didn't want to think about the woman. He was too used to thinking about himself. "I *had* no motive. I wouldn't hurt a hair of her head."

"You did, though, once or twice."

He was silent. All I could see of him was his wavy gray hair, like a dusty wig, and his large dishonest eyes trying to be honest:

"I hit her a couple of times, I admit it. I suffered the tortures of the damned afterward. You've got to understand, I used to get mean when I got plastered. That's why Connie sent me away, I don't blame her. I don't blame her for anything. I blame myself." He drew in a long breath and let it out slowly.

I offered him a cigarette, which he refused. I lit one for myself. The bright trembling patch of sunlight was climbing the bulkhead. It would soon be evening.

"So Bradshaw had a wife," McGee said. He had had time to absorb the information. "And he told me he intended to marry Connie."

"Maybe he did intend to. It would strengthen the woman's motive."

"You honestly think she did it?"

"She's a prime suspect. Bradshaw is another. He must have been a suspect to your daughter, too. She enrolled in his college and took a job in his household to check on him. Was that your idea, McGee?"

He shook his head.

"I don't understand her part in all this. She hasn't been much help in explaining it, either."

"I know," he said. "Dolly's done a lot of lying, starting away back when. But when a little kid lies you don't put the same construction on it as you would an adult."

"You're a forgiving man."

"Oh no I'm not. I went to her with anger in my heart that Sunday I saw her picture in the paper, with her husband. What right did she have to a happy marriage after what she did to me? That's what was on my mind."

"Did you tell her what was on your mind?"

"Yessir, I did. But my anger didn't last. She reminded me so of her mother in appearance. It was like going back twenty years to happier times, when we were first married. We had a real good year when I was in the Navy and Connie was pregnant, with her."

His mind kept veering away from his current troubles. I could hardly blame him, but I urged him back to them:

"You gave your daughter a hard time the other Sunday, didn't you?"

"I did at first. I admit that. I asked her why she lied about me in court. That was a legitimate question, wasn't it?"

"I should say so. What was her reaction?"

"She went into hysterics and said she wasn't lying, that she saw me with the gun and everything and heard me arguing with her mother.

Which was false, and I told her so. I wasn't even in Indian Springs that night. That stopped her cold."

"Then what?"

"I asked her why she lied about me." He licked his lips and said in a hushed voice: "I asked her if she shot her mother herself, maybe by accident, the way Alice kept that revolver lying around loose. It was a terrible question, but it had to come out. It'd been on my mind for a long time."

"As long ago as your trial?"

"Yeah. Before that."

"And that's why you wouldn't let Stevens cross-examine her?"

"Yeah. I should have let him go ahead. I ended up cross-questioning her myself ten years later."

"What was the result?"

"More hysterics. She was laughing and crying at the same time. I never felt so sorry for anybody. She was as white as a sheet and the tears popped out of her eyes and ran down her face. Her tears looked so *pure.*"

"What did she say?"

"She said she didn't do it, naturally."

"Could she have? Did she know how to handle a gun?"

"A little. I gave her a little training, and so did Alice. It doesn't take much gun-handling to pull a trigger, especially by accident."

"You still think it could have happened that way?"

"I don't know. It's mainly what I wanted to talk to you about."

These words seemed to release him from an obscure bondage. He climbed down out of the upper bunk and stood facing me in the narrow aisle. He had on a seaman's black turtleneck, levis, and rubber-soled deck shoes.

"You're in a position to go and talk to her," he said. "I'm not. Mr. Stevens won't. But you can go and ask her what really happened."

"She may not know."

"I realize that. She got pretty mixed up the other Sunday. God knows I wasn't trying to mix her up. I only asked her some questions. But she didn't seem to know the difference between what happened and what she said in court."

"That story she told in court—did she definitely admit she made it up?"

"She made it up with a lot of help from Alice. I can imagine how it went. 'This is the way it happened, isn't it?' Alice would say. 'You saw

your old man with the gun, didn't you?' And after a while the kid had
her story laid out for her."

"Would Alice deliberately try to frame you?"

"She wouldn't put it that way to herself. She'd know for a fact I was
guilty. All she was doing was making sure I got punished for my crime.
She probably fed the kid her lines without knowing she was faking
evidence. My dear sister-in-law was always out to get me, anyway."

"Was she out to get Connie, too?"

"Connie? She doted on Connie. Alice was more like her mother than
her sister. There was fourteen-fifteen years' difference in their ages."

"You said she wanted Connie to herself. Her feelings for Connie
could have changed if she found out about Bradshaw."

"Not *that* much. Anyway, who would tell her?"

"Your daughter might have. If she told you, she'd tell Alice."

McGee shook his head. "You're really reaching."

"I have to. This is a deep case, and I can't see the bottom of it yet.
Did Alice ever live in Boston, do you know?"

"I think she always lived here. She's a Native Daughter. I'm a native
son, but nobody ever gave me a medal for it."

"Even Native Daughters have been known to go to Boston. Did
Alice ever go on the stage, or marry a man named Macready, or dye her
hair red?"

"None of those things sound like Alice."

I thought of her pink fantastic bedroom, and wondered.

"They sound more," McGee was saying, and then he stopped. He
was silent for a watching moment. "I'll take that cigarette you offered
me."

I gave him a cigarette and lighted it. "What were you going to say?"

"Nothing. I must have been thinking aloud."

"Who were you thinking about?"

"Nobody you know. Forget it, eh?"

"Come on, McGee. You're supposed to be leveling with me."

"I still have a right to my private thoughts. It kept me alive in
prison."

"You're out of prison now. Don't you want to stay out?"

"Not if somebody else has to go in."

"Sucker," I said. "Who are you covering for now?"

"Nobody."

"Madge Gerhardi?"

"You must be off your rocker."

I couldn't get anything more out of him. The long slow weight of prison forces men into unusual shapes. McGee had become a sort of twisted saint.

28
..
———————

HE WAS about to be given another turn of the screw. When I climbed out into the cockpit I saw three men approaching along the floating dock. Their bodies, their hatted heads, were dark as iron against the exploding sunset.

One of them showed me a deputy's badge and a gun, which he held on me while the others went below. I heard McGee cry out once. He scrambled up through the hatch with blue handcuffs on his wrists and a blue gun at his back. The single look he gave me was full of fear and loathing.

They didn't handcuff me, but they made me ride to the courthouse with McGee in the screened rear compartment of the Sheriff's car. I tried to talk to him. He wouldn't speak to me or look in my direction. He believed I had turned him in, and perhaps I had without intending to.

I sat under guard outside the interrogation room while they questioned him in tones that rose and fell and growled and palavered and yelled and threatened and promised and refused and wheedled. Sheriff Crane arrived, looking tired but important. He stood over me smiling, with his belly thrust out.

"Your friend's in real trouble now."

"He's been in real trouble for the last ten years. You ought to know, you helped to cook it for him."

The veins in his cheeks lit up like intricate little networks of infra-red tubing. He leaned toward me spewing martini-scented words:

"I could put you in jail for loose talk like that. You know where your friend is going? He's going all the way to the green room this time."

"He wouldn't be the first innocent man who was gassed."

"Innocent? McGee's a mass murderer, and we've got the evidence to prove it. It took my experts all day to nail it down: The bullet in the Haggerty corpse came from the same gun as the bullet we found in McGee's wife—the same gun he stole from Alice Jenks in Indian Springs."

I'd succeeded in provoking the Sheriff into an indiscretion. I tried for another. "You have no proof he stole it. You have no proof he fired it either time. Where's he been keeping the gun for the last ten years?"

"He cached it someplace, maybe on Stevens's boat. Or maybe an accomplice kept it for him."

"Then he hid it in his daughter's bed to frame her?"

"That's the kind of man he is."

"Nuts!"

"Don't talk to me like that!" He menaced me with the cannon ball of his belly.

"Don't talk like that to the Sheriff," the guard said.

"I don't know of any law against the use of the word 'nuts.' And incidentally I wasn't violating anything in the California Code when I went out to the yacht to talk to McGee. I'm cooperating with a local attorney in this investigation and I have a right to get my information where I can and keep it confidential."

"How did you know he was there?"

"I got a tip."

"From Stevens?"

"Not from Stevens. You and I could trade information, Sheriff. How did *you* know he was there?"

"I don't make deals with suspects."

"What do you suspect me of? Illegal use of the word 'nuts'?"

"It isn't so funny. You were taken with McGee. I have a right to hold you."

"I have a right to call an attorney. Try kicking my rights around and see where it gets you. I have friends in Sacramento."

They didn't include the Attorney General or anybody close to him, but I liked the sound of the phrase. Sheriff Crane did not. He was half a politician, and like most of his kind he was an insecure man. He said after a moment's thought:

"You can make your call."

The Sheriff went into the interrogation room—I caught a glimpse of McGee hunched gray-faced under a light—and added his voice to the difficult harmony there. My guard took me into a small adjoining room and left me by myself with a telephone. I used it to call Jerry Marks.

He was about to leave for his appointment with Dr. Godwin and Dolly, but he said he'd come right over to the courthouse and bring Gil Stevens with him if Stevens was available.

They arrived together in less than fifteen minutes. Stevens shot me a glance from under the broken white wings of his hair. It was a covert and complex glance which seemed to mean that for the record we were strangers. I suspected the old lawyer had advised McGee to talk to me, and probably set up the interview. I was in a position to use McGee's facts in ways that he couldn't.

With soft threats of *habeas corpus* proceedings, Jerry Marks sprung me out. Stevens remained behind with the Sheriff and a Deputy D.A. It was going to take longer to spring his client.

A moon like a fallen fruit reversing gravity was hoisting itself above the rooftops. It was huge and slightly squashed.

"Pretty," Jerry said in the parking lot.

"It looks like a rotten orange to me."

"Ugliness is in the eye of the beholder. I learned that at my mother's knee and other low joints, as a well-known statesman said." Jerry always felt good when he tried something he learned in law school, and it worked. He walked to his car swiftly, on the balls of his feet, and made the engine roar. "We're late for our appointment with Godwin."

"Did you have time to check on Bradshaw's alibi?"

"I did. It seems to be impregnable." He gave me the details as we drove across town. "Judging by temperature loss, rate of blood coagulation, and so on, the Deputy Coroner places the time of Miss Haggerty's death as no later than eight-thirty. From about seven until about nine-thirty Dean Bradshaw was sitting, or standing up talking, in front of over a hundred witnesses. I talked to three of them, three alumni picked more or less at random, and they all agreed he didn't leave the speaker's table during that period. Which lets him out."

"Apparently it does."

"You sound disappointed, Lew."

"I'm partly that, and partly relieved. I rather like Bradshaw. But I was pretty certain he was our man."

In the remaining minutes before we reached the nursing home, I told him briefly what I'd learned from McGee, and from the Sheriff. Jerry whistled, but made no other comment.

Dr. Godwin opened the door for us. He wore a clean white smock and an aggrieved expression.

"You're late, Mr. Marks. I was just about ready to call the whole thing off."

"We had a little emergency. Thomas McGee was arrested about seven o'clock tonight. Mr. Archer happened to be with him, and he was arrested, also."

Godwin turned to me. "*You* were with McGee?"

"He sent for me, and he talked. I'm looking forward to comparing his story with his daughter's."

"I'm afraid you aren't—ah—co-opted to this session," Godwin said with some embarrassment. "As I pointed out to you before, you don't have professional immunity."

"I do if I'm acting on Mr. Marks's instructions. Which I am."

"Mr. Archer is correct, on both counts," Jerry said.

Godwin let us in reluctantly. We were outsiders, interlopers in his shadowy kingdom. I had lost some of my confidence in his benevolent despotism, but I kept it to myself for the present.

He took us to the examination room where Dolly was waiting. She was sitting on the end of a padded table, wearing a sleeveless white hospital gown. Alex stood in front of her, holding both her hands. His eyes stayed on her face, hungry and worshipping, as if she was the priestess or the goddess of a strange one-member cult.

Her hair was shining and smooth. Her face was composed. Only her eyes had a sullen restlessness and inwardness. They moved across me and failed to give any sign of recognition.

Godwin touched her shoulder. "Are you ready, Dolly?"

"I suppose I am."

She lay back on the padded table. Alex held on to one of her hands.

"You can stay if you like, Mr. Kincaid. It might be easier if you didn't."

"Not for me," the girl said. "I feel safer when he's with me. I want Alex to know all about—everything."

"Yes. I want to stay."

Godwin filled a hypodermic needle, inserted it in her arm, and taped it to the white skin. He told her to count backward from one hundred. At ninety-six the tension left her body and an inner light left her face. It flowed back in a diffused form when the doctor spoke to her:

"Do you hear me, Dolly?"

"I hear you," she murmured.

"Speak louder. I can't hear you."

"I hear you," she repeated. Her voice was faintly slurred.

"Who am I?"

"Dr. Godwin."

"Do you remember when you were a little girl you used to come and visit me in my office?"

"I remember."

"Who used to bring you to see me?"

"Mommy did. She used to bring me in in Aunt Alice's car."

"Where were you living then?"

"In Indian Springs, in Aunt Alice's house."

"And Mommy was living there, too?"

"Mommy was living there, too. She lived there, too."

She was flushed, and talking like a drunken child. The doctor turned to Jerry Marks with a handing-over gesture. Jerry's dark eyes were mournful.

"Do you remember a certain night," he said, "when your Mommy was killed?"

"I remember. Who are you?"

"I'm Jerry Marks, your lawyer. It's all right to talk to me."

"It's all right," Alex said.

The girl looked up at Jerry sleepily. "What do you want me to tell you?"

"Just the truth. It doesn't matter what I want, or anybody else. Just tell me what you remember."

"I'll try."

"Did you hear the gun go off?"

"I heard it." She screwed up her face as if she was hearing it now. "I am—it frightened me."

"Did you see anyone?"

"I didn't go downstairs right away. I was scared."

"Did you see anyone out the window?"

"No. I heard a car drive away. Before that I heard her running."

"You heard *who* running?" Jerry said.

"I thought it was Aunt Alice at first, when she was talking to Mommy at the door. But it couldn't have been Aunt Alice. She wouldn't shoot Mommy. Besides, her gun was missing."

"How do you know?"

"She said I took it from her room. She spanked me with a hairbrush for stealing it."

"When did she spank you?"

"Sunday night, when she came home from church. Mommy said she had no right to spank me. Aunt Alice asked Mommy if *she* took the gun."

"Did she?"

"She didn't say—not while I was there. They sent me to bed."

"*Did* you take the gun?"

"No. I never touched it. I was afraid of it."

"Why?"

"I was afraid of Aunt Alice."

She was rosy and sweating. She tried to struggle up onto her elbows. The doctor eased her back into her supine position, and made an adjustment to the needle. The girl relaxed again, and Jerry said:

"Was it Aunt Alice talking to your Mommy at the door?"

"I thought it was at first. It sounded like her. She had a big scary voice. But it couldn't have been Aunt Alice."

"Why couldn't it?"

"It just couldn't."

She turned her head in a listening attitude. A lock of hair fell over her half-closed eyes. Alex pushed it back with a gentle hand. She said:

"The lady at the door said it had to be true, about Mommy and Mr. Bradshaw. She said she got it from Daddy's own lips, and Daddy got it from me. And then she shot my Mommy and ran away."

There was silence in the room, except for the girl's heavy breathing. A tear as slow as honey was exuded from the corner of one eye. It fell down her temple. Alex wiped the blue-veined hollow with his handkerchief. Jerry leaned across her from the other side of the table:

"Why did you say your Daddy shot your Mommy?"

"Aunt Alice wanted me to. She didn't say so, but I could tell. And I was afraid she'd think that I did it. She spanked me for taking the gun, and I *didn't* take it. I said it was Daddy. She made me say it over and over and over."

There were more tears than one now. Tears for the child she had been, frightened and lying, and tears for the woman she was painfully becoming. Alex wiped her eyes. He looked close to tears himself.

"Why," I said, "did you try to tell us that you killed your mother?"

"Who are you?"

"I'm Alex's friend Lew Archer."

"That's right," Alex said.

She lifted her head and let it fall back. "I forget what you asked me."

"Why did you say you killed your mother?"

"Because it was all my fault. I told my Daddy about her and Mr. Bradshaw, and that's what started everything."

"How do you know?"

"The lady at the door said so. She came to shoot Mommy because of what Daddy told her."

"Do you know who she was?"

"No."

"Was it your Aunt Alice?"

"No."

"Was it anyone you knew?"

"No."

"Did your mother know her?"

"I don't know. Maybe she did."

"Did she talk as if she knew her?"

"She called her by name."

"What name?"

"Tish. She called her Tish. I could tell Mommy didn't like her, though. She was afraid of her, too."

"Why haven't you ever told anyone this before?"

"Because it was all my fault."

"It wasn't," Alex said. "You were only a child. You weren't responsible for what the adults did."

Godwin shushed him with his finger to his lips. Dolly rolled her head from side to side:

"It was all my fault."

"This has gone on long enough," Godwin whispered to Jerry. "She's made some gains. I want to have a chance to consolidate them."

"But we haven't even got to the Haggerty case."

"Make it short then." Godwin said to the girl: "Dolly, are you willing to talk about last Friday night?"

"Not about finding her." She screwed up her face until her eyes were hidden.

"You needn't go into the details of finding the body," Jerry said. "But what were you doing there?"

"I wanted to talk to Helen. I often walked up the hill to talk to her. We were friends."

"How did that happen to be?"

"I ingratiated myself with Helen," she said with queer blank candor. "I thought at first she might be the lady—the woman who shot my mother. The rumor was going around the campus that she was close to Dean Bradshaw."

"And you were on the campus to find that woman?"

"Yes. But it wasn't Helen. I found out she was new in town, and she told me herself there was nothing between her and Bradshaw. I had no right to drag her into this."

"How did you drag her in?"

"I told her everything, about my mother and Bradshaw and the murder and the woman at the door. Helen was killed because she knew too much."

"That may be," I said, "but she didn't learn it from you."

"She did! I told her everything."

Godwin pulled at my sleeve. "Don't argue with her. She's coming out of it fast, but her mind is still operating below the conscious level."

"Did Helen ask you questions?" I said to the girl.

"Yes. She asked me questions."

"Then you didn't force the information on her."

"No. She wanted to know."

"What did she want to know?"

"All about Dean Bradshaw and my mother."

"Did she say why?"

"She wanted to help me in my crusade. I went on a sort of crusade after I talked to Daddy in the hotel. A children's crusade." Her giggle turned into a sob before it left her throat. "The only thing it accomplished was the death of my good friend Helen. And when I found her body—"

Her eyes opened wide. Then her mouth opened wide. Her body went rigid, as if it was imitating the rigor of the dead. She stayed like that for fifteen or twenty seconds.

"It was like finding Mommy again," she said in a small voice, and came fully awake. "Is it all right?"

"It's all right," Alex said.

He helped her up to a sitting position. She leaned on him, her hair mantling his shoulder. A few minutes later, still leaning on him, she walked across the hallway to her room. They walked like husband and wife.

Godwin closed the door of the examination room. "I hope you gentlemen got what you wanted," he said with some distaste.

"She talked very freely," Jerry said. The experience had left him drained.

"It was no accident. I've been preparing her for the last three days. Pentothal, as I've told you before, is no guarantee of truth. If a patient is determined to lie, the drug can't stop him."

"Are you implying she wasn't telling the truth?"

"No. I believe she was, so far as she knows the truth. My problem now is to enlarge her awareness and make it fully conscious. If you gentlemen will excuse me?"

"Wait a minute," I said. "You can spare me a minute, doctor. I've spent three days and a lot of Kincaid's money developing facts that you already had in your possession."

"Have you indeed?" he said coldly.

"I have indeed. You could have saved me a good deal of work by filling me in on Bradshaw's affair with Constance McGee."

"I'm afraid I don't exist for the purpose of saving detectives work. There's a question of ethics involved here which you probably wouldn't understand. Mr. Marks probably would."

"I don't understand the issue," Jerry said, but he edged between us as if he expected trouble. He touched my shoulder. "Let's get out of here, Lew, and let the doctor get about his business. He's cooperated beautifully and you know it."

"Who with? Bradshaw?"

Godwin's face turned pale. "My first duty is to my patients."

"Even when they murder people?"

"Even then. But I know Roy Bradshaw intimately and I can assure you he's incapable of killing anyone. Certainly he didn't kill Constance McGee. He was passionately in love with her."

"Passion can cut two ways."

"He didn't kill her."

"A couple of days ago you were telling me McGee did. You can be mistaken, doctor."

"I know that, but not about Roy Bradshaw. The man has lived a tragic life."

"Tell me about it."

"He'll have to tell you himself. I'm not a junior G-man, Mr. Archer. I'm a doctor."

"What about the woman he recently divorced, Tish or Letitia? Do you know her?"

He looked at me without speaking. There was sad knowledge in his eyes. "You'll have to ask Roy about her," he said finally.

29

On his way to the courthouse to question McGee, Jerry dropped me at the harbor, where my car had been left sitting. The moon was higher now, and had regained its proper shape and color. Its light converted the yachts in the slips into a ghostly fleet of Flying Dutchmen.

I went back to my motel to talk to Madge Gerhardi. She had evaporated, along with the rest of the whisky in my pint bottle. I sat on the edge of the bed and tried her number and got no answer.

I called the Bradshaw house. Old Mrs. Bradshaw seemed to have taken up a permanent position beside the telephone. She picked up the receiver on the first ring and quavered into it:

"Who is that, please?"

"It's only Archer. Roy hasn't come home, has he?"

"No, and I'm worried about him, deeply worried. I haven't seen him or heard from him since early Saturday morning. I've been calling his friends—"

"I wouldn't do that, Mrs. Bradshaw."

"I have to do something."

"There are times when it's better to do nothing. Keep still and wait."

"I can't. You're telling me there's something terribly wrong, aren't you?"

"I think you know it."

"Does it have to do with that dreadful woman—that Macready woman?"

"Yes. We have to find out where she is. I'm pretty sure your son could tell me, but he's made himself unavailable. Are you sure you haven't seen the woman since Boston?"

"I'm quite certain. I saw her only once, when she came to me for money."

"Can you describe her for me?"

"I thought I had."

"In more detail, please. It's very important."

She paused to think. I could hear her breathing over the line, a faint rhythmic huskiness. "Well, she was quite a large woman, taller than I, red-haired. She wore her hair bobbed. She had quite a good figure, rather lush, and quite good features, too—a kind of brassy good looks. And she had green eyes, murky green eyes which I didn't like at all. She wore very heavy makeup, more appropriate for the stage than the street, and she was hideously overdressed."

"What was she wearing?"

"It hardly seems relevant, after twenty years. But she had on a leopardskin—an imitation leopardskin coat, as I recall, and under it something striped. Sheer hose, with runs in them. Ridiculously high heels. A good deal of costume jewelry."

"How did she talk?"

"Like a woman of the streets. A greedy, pushing, lustful woman." The moral indignation in her voice hardly surprised me. She had almost lost Roy to the woman, and might yet.

"Would you know her if you saw her again, in different clothes, with her hair perhaps a different color?"

"I think so, if I had a chance to study her."

"You'll have that chance when we find her."

I was thinking that the color of a woman's eyes was harder to change than her hair. The only green-eyed woman connected with the case was Laura Sutherland. She had a conspicuously good figure and good features, but nothing else that seemed to jibe with the description of the Macready woman. Still, she might have changed. I'd seen other women change unrecognizably in half the time.

"You know Laura Sutherland, Mrs. Bradshaw?"

"I know her slightly."

"Does she resemble the Macready woman?"

"Why do you ask that?" she said on a rising note. "Do you suspect Laura?"

"I wouldn't go that far. But you haven't answered my question."

"She couldn't possibly be the same woman. She's a wholly different type."

"What about her basic physical characteristics?"

"I suppose there is some resemblance," she said dubiously. "Roy has always been attracted to women who are obviously mammals."

And obviously mother figures, I thought. "I have to ask you one other question, a more personal question."

"Yes?" She seemed to be bracing herself for a blow.

"I suppose you're aware that Roy was Dr. Godwin's patient."

"Dr. Godwin's patient? I don't believe it. He wouldn't go behind my back." For all her half-cynical insight into his nature, she seemed to know very little about him.

"Dr. Godwin says he did, apparently for some years."

"There must be a mistake. Roy has nothing the matter with his mind." There was a vibrating silence. "Has he?"

"I was going to ask you, but I'm sorry I brought it up. Take it easy, Mrs. Bradshaw."

"How can I, with my boy in jeopardy?"

She wanted to hold me on the line, siphoning comfort into her frightened old ears, but I said good night and hung up. One suspect had been eliminated: Madge Gerhardi: the description didn't fit her and never could have. Laura was still in the running.

It wouldn't make sense, of course, for Bradshaw to divorce her and remarry her immediately. But I had only Bradshaw's word for his recent marriage to Laura. I was gradually realizing that his word stretched like an elastic band, and was as easily broken. I looked up Laura's address—she lived in College Heights—and was copying it into my notebook when the phone rang.

It was Jerry Marks. McGee denied having told the woman Tish or anyone else about the affair between Bradshaw and his wife. The only one he had discussed the subject with was Bradshaw.

"Bradshaw may have told the woman himself," I said. "Or possibly the woman overheard McGee."

"Possibly, but hardly likely. McGee says his conversation with Bradshaw took place in Bradshaw's house."

"He could have had the woman there while his mother was away."

"You think she lives around here?"

"Somewhere in Southern California, anyway. I believe Bradshaw's been leading a split-level life with her, and that she's responsible for both the McGee and the Haggerty killings. I just got an improved description of her from Bradshaw's mother. Better pass it along to the police. Do you have something to write on?"

"Yes. I'm sitting at the Sheriff's desk."

I recited Letitia Macready's description, but I didn't say anything about Laura Sutherland. I wanted to talk to her myself.

College Heights was a detached suburb on the far side of the campus from the city. It was a hodgepodge of tract houses and fraternity houses, duplexes and apartment buildings, interspersed with vacant lots

sprouting for-sale signs. A boy with a guitar in one of the lighted fraternity houses was singing that this land belongs to you and me.

Laura lived in one of the better apartments, a garden apartment
built around an open court with a swimming pool. A shirt-sleeved man
slapping mosquitoes in a deck chair by the pool pointed out her door to
me and mentioned with some complacency that he owned the place.

"Is anybody with her?"

"I don't think so. She did have a visitor, but he went home."

"Who was he?"

The man peered up at my face. "That's her private business, mister."

"I expect it was Dean Bradshaw, from the college."

"If you know, why ask?"

I walked to the back of the court and knocked on her door. She
opened it on a chain. Her face had lost a good deal of its rosy beauty.
She had on a dark suit, as if she was in mourning.

"What do you want? It's late."

"Too late for us to have a talk, Mrs. Bradshaw?"

"I'm not Mrs. Bradshaw," she said without much conviction. "I'm not
married."

"Roy said you were last night. Which one of you is lying?"

"Please, my landlord's out there." She unchained the door and stepped
back out of the widening light. "Come inside if you must."

She closed the door and chained it behind me. I was looking at her
instead of the room, but I had the impression of a tastefully decorated
place where shaded lights gleamed peacefully on wooden and ceramic
surfaces. I was searching her face for traces of a past wholly different
from her present. There were no visible traces, no cruel lines or
pouches of dissipation. But she hadn't much peace in her. She was
watching me as though I was a burglar.

"What are you afraid of?"

"I'm not afraid," she said in a frightened voice. She tried to control
it with her hand at her throat. "I resent your barging into my home
and making personal remarks."

"You invited me in, more or less."

"Only because you were talking indiscreetly."

"I called you by your married name. What's your objection to it?"

"I *have* no objection," she said with a wan smile. "I'm very proud of
it. But my husband and I are keeping it a secret."

"A secret from Letitia Macready?"

She showed no particular reaction to the name. I'd already given up

on the idea that it could be hers. No matter how well preserved her
body or her skin might be, she was clearly too young. When Bradshaw
married Letitia, Laura couldn't have been more than a girl in her teens.

"Letitia who?" she said.

"Letitia Macready. She's also known as Tish."

"I have no idea who you're talking about."

"I'll tell you if you really want to know. May I sit down?"

"Please do," she said without much warmth. I was the messenger
who brought bad tidings, the kind they used to kill in the old days.

I sat on a soft leather hassock with my back against the wall. She
remained standing.

"You're in love with Roy Bradshaw, aren't you?"

"I wouldn't have married him if I weren't."

"Just when did you marry him?"

"Two weeks ago last Saturday, September the tenth." A little color
returned to her cheeks with the memory of the day. "He'd just got back
from his European tour. We decided to go to Reno on the spur of the
moment."

"Had you spent some time with him there earlier in the summer?"

She frowned in a puzzled way, and shook her head.

"Whose idea was it to go to Reno?"

"Roy's of course, but I was willing. I've been willing for some time,"
she added in a spurt of candor.

"What held up the marriage?"

"It wasn't held *up*, exactly. We postponed it, for various reasons. Mrs.
Bradshaw is a very possessive mother, and Roy has nothing of his own
except his salary. It may sound mercenary—" She paused in some embarrassment, and tried to think of a better way to phrase it.

"How old is his mother?"

"Somewhere in her sixties. Why?"

"She's a vigorous woman, in spite of her infirmities. She may be
around for a long time yet."

Her eyes flashed with some of their fine old iceberg fire. "We're not
waiting for her to die, if that's what you think. We're simply waiting
for the psychological moment. Roy hopes to persuade her to take a more
reasonable view of—of me. In the meantime—" She broke off, and
looked at me distrustfully. "But none of this is any concern of yours.
You promised to tell me about the Macready person, whoever she is.
Tish Macready? The name sounds fictitious."

"I assure you the woman isn't. Your husband divorced her in Reno shortly before he married you."

She moved to a chair and sat down very suddenly, as if her legs had lost their strength. "I don't believe it. Roy has never been married before."

"He has, though. Even his mother admitted it, after a struggle. It was an unfortunate marriage, contracted when he was a student at Harvard. But he waited until this summer to end it. He spent part of July and all of August establishing residence in Nevada."

"Now I know you're mistaken. Roy was in Europe all that time."

"I suppose you have letters and postcards to prove it?"

"Yes, I do," she said with a relieved smile.

She went into another room and came back with a handful of mail tied with a red ribbon. I riffled through the postcards and put them in chronological order: Tower of London (postmarked London, July 18), Bodleian Library (Oxford, July 21), and so on down to the view of the English Gardens (Munich, August 25). Bradshaw had written on the back of this last card:

Dear Laura:

Yesterday I visited Hitler's eyrie at Berchtesgaden—a beautiful setting made grim by it associations—and today, by way of contrast, I took a bus to Oberammergau, where the Passion Play is performed. I was struck by the almost Biblical simplicity of the villagers. This whole Bavarian countryside is studded with the most stunning little churches. How I wish you could enjoy them with me! I'm sorry to hear that your summer has turned out to be a lonely one. Well, the summer will soon be over and I for one will be happy to turn my back on the splendors of Europe and come home. All my love.

Roy

I sat and reread the incredible message. It was almost word by word the same as the one Mrs. Bradshaw had shown me. I tried to put myself in Bradshaw's place, to understand his motive. But I couldn't imagine what helpless division in a man's nature, what weary self-mockery or self-use, would make him send identical lying postcards to his mother and his fiancée.

"What's the matter?" Laura said.

"Merely everything."

I gave her back her documents. She handled them lovingly. "Don't try to tell me Roy didn't write these. They're in his writing and his style."

"He wrote them in Reno," I said, "and shipped them for remailing to a friend or accomplice who was traveling in Europe."

"Do you *know* this?"

"I'm afraid I do. Can you think of any friend of his who might have helped him?"

She bit her lower lip. "Dr. Godwin spent the late summer traveling in Europe. He and Roy are very close. In fact Roy was his patient for a long time."

"What was Godwin treating him for?"

"We haven't discussed it, really, but I expect it had something to do with his excessive—his excessive dependence on his mother." A slow angry flush mounted from her neck to her cheekbones. She turned away from the subject. "But why would two grown men collaborate in such a silly letter-writing game?"

"It isn't clear. Your husband's professional ambitions probably enter into it. He obviously didn't want anyone to know about his previous, bad marriage, or his divorce, and he went to great lengths to keep everything quiet. He got off a similar set of European postcards and letters to his mother. He may have sent a third set to Letitia."

"Who *is* she? *Where* is she?"

"I think she's here in town, or was as recently as last Friday night. She's very likely been here for the last ten years. I'm surprised your husband never gave it away, even to someone as close as you."

She was still standing over me, and I looked up into her face. Her eyes were heavy. She shook her head.

"Or maybe it isn't so surprising. He's very good at deceiving people, living on several levels, maybe deceiving himself to a certain extent. Mother's boys get that way sometimes. They need their little escape hatches from the hothouse."

Her bosom rose. "He isn't a mother's boy. He may have had a problem when he was younger, but now he's a virile man, and I *know* he loves me. There must be a reason for all this." She looked down at the cards and letters in her hand.

"I'm sure there is. I suspect the reason has to do with our two murders. Tish Macready is the leading suspect for both of them."

"*Two* murders?"

"Actually there have been three, spaced over a period of twenty-two years: Helen Haggerty on Friday night, Constance McGee ten years ago, Luke Deloney in Illinois before the war."

"Deloney?"

"Luke Deloney. You wouldn't know about him, but I think Tish Macready does."

"Is he connected with the Mrs. Deloney at the Surf House?"

"She's his widow. You know her?"

"Not personally. But Roy was talking to her on the telephone shortly before he left here."

"What did he say?"

"Simply that he was coming over to see her. I asked him who she was, but he was in too great a hurry to explain."

I got up. "If you'll excuse me, I'll see if I can catch him at the hotel. I've been trying to catch him all day."

"He was here, with me." She smiled slightly, involuntarily, but her eyes were confused. "Please don't tell him I told you. Don't tell him I told you anything."

"I'll try, but it may come out."

I moved to the door and tried to open it. The chain delayed my exit.

"Wait," she said behind me. "I've remembered something—something he wrote in a book of poems he lent me."

"What did he write?"

"Her name."

She started into the other room. Her hip bumped the doorframe, and Bradshaw's cards and letters fell from her hands. She didn't pause to pick them up.

She returned with an open book and thrust it at me a little blindly. It was a well-worn copy of Yeats's *Collected Poems*, open to the poem "Among School Children." The first four lines of the fourth stanza were underlined in pencil, and Bradshaw had written in the margin beside them the single word, "Tish."

I read the four lines to myself:

> Her present image floats into the mind—
> Did Quattrocento finger fashion it
> Hollow of cheek as though it drank the wind
> And took a mess of shadows for its meat?

I wasn't certain what they meant, and said so.

Laura answered bitterly: "It means that Roy still loves her. Yeats was writing about Maud Gonne—the woman he loved all his life. Roy may even have lent me the Yeats to let me know about Tish. He's very subtle."

"He probably wrote her name there long ago, and forgot about it. If he still loved her, he wouldn't have divorced her and married you. I have to warn you, though, that your marriage may not be legal."

"Not legal?" She was a conventional woman, and the possibility jarred her. "But we were married in Reno by a judge."

"His divorce from Tish," I said, "is probably voidable. I gather she wasn't properly informed of Bradshaw's action. Which means that under California law he's still married to her if she wants it that way."

Shaking her head, she took the book of poems from my hands and tossed it with some violence into a chair. A piece of paper fluttered from between the leaves. I picked it up from the floor.

It was another poem, in Bradshaw's handwriting:

To Laura

If light were dark
And dark were light,
Moon a black hole
In the blaze of night,

A raven's wing
As bright as tin,
Then you, my love,
Would be darker than sin.

At breakfast I had read the same poem aloud to Arnie and Phyllis. It had been printed twenty-odd years ago in the Bridgeton *Blazer*, over the initials G.R.B. I had a gestalt, and Bridgeton and Pacific Point came together in a roaring traffic of time. G.R.B. George Roy Bradshaw.

"When did he write this poem to you, Laura?"

"Last spring, when he lent me the Yeats."

I left her reading it over to herself, trying to recapture the spring.

30
..

PASSING THROUGH the lobby of the Surf House, I noticed Helen's mother sitting by herself in a far corner. She was deep in thought and she didn't look up until I spoke:

"You're sitting up late, Mrs. Hoffman."

"I don't have much choice," she said resentfully. "I'm supposed to be sharing a cottage with Mrs. Deloney, and it was entirely her idea. But she put me out so she can entertain her friend in private."

"You mean Roy Bradshaw?"

"That's what he calls himself now. I knew George Bradshaw when he was glad to be given a good hot meal, and I served him more than one in my own kitchen."

I pulled up a chair beside hers. "All this adds up to an interesting coincidence."

"I think it does, too. But I'm not supposed to talk about it."

"Who says so?"

"Mrs. Deloney."

"Does she tell you what to do?"

"No, but it was nice of her to take me out of that crummy room in the Pacific Hotel and—" She paused, considering.

"And stash you in the lobby here?"

"It's only temporary."

"So is life. Are you and your husband going to take orders from people like the Deloneys until the day you die? You get nothing out of it, you know, except the privilege of being pushed around."

"Nobody pushes Earl around," she said defensively. "You leave Earl out of this."

"Have you heard from him?"

"I haven't, and I'm worried about Earl. I tried to phone home two nights in a row, and nobody answered. I'm afraid he's drinking."

"He's in the hospital," I said.

"Is he sick?"

"He made himself sick with too much whisky."

"How do you know that?"

"I helped to get him to the hospital. I was in Bridgeton yesterday morning. Your husband talked to me, quite freely toward the end. He admitted Luke Deloney had been murdered but he had orders from the top to let it go as an accident."

Her eyes darted around the lobby, shyly and shamefully. There was no one in sight but the night clerk and a couple who didn't look married renting a room from him. But Mrs. Hoffman was as nervous as a cricket on a crowded floor.

"You might as well tell me what you know," I said. "Let me buy you a cup of coffee."

"I'd be up all night."

"A cup of cocoa then."

"Cocoa sounds good."

We went into the coffee shop. Several orchestra members in mauve jackets were drinking coffee at the counter and complaining in the language of their tribe about the pay. I sat in a booth facing Mrs. Hoffman and the plate glass door, so that I could see Bradshaw if he came out through the lobby.

"How did you come to know Bradshaw, Mrs. Hoffman?"

"Helen brought him home from City College. I think she was stuck on him for a while, but I could see that he wasn't stuck on her. They were more friends. They had interests in common."

"Like poetry?"

"Like poetry and play-acting. Helen said he was very talented for a boy his age, but he was having a hard time staying in college. We wangled him a part-time job running the elevator in the apartments. All it paid was five a week, but he was glad to have it. He was as thin as a rake and as poor as Job's turkey when we knew him. He claimed he came from a wealthy family in Boston, that he ran away from his freshman year at Harvard to be on his own. I never really believed him at the time—I thought he was maybe ashamed of his folks and putting on the dog—but I guess it was true after all. They tell me his mother is loaded." She gave me a questioning look.

"Yes. I know her."

"Why would a young fellow run away from all that money? I spent most of my own life trying to get a little to stick to my fingers."

"Money usually has strings attached to it."

I didn't go into a fuller explanation. The waitress brought Mrs.

Hoffman's cocoa and my coffee. I said when she had retreated behind the counter:

"Have you ever known a woman named Macready? Letitia O. Macready?"

Mrs. Hoffman's hand fumbled with her cup and spilled some brown liquid in the saucer. I was fleetingly conscious that her hair was dyed an unlikely shade of red and that she might once have been a handsome woman with a good figure and a gaudy taste in clothes. But she couldn't be Tish Macready. She'd been married to Earl Hoffman for over forty years.

She put a folded paper napkin under her cup to absorb the spillage. "I knew her to say hello to."

"In Bridgeton?"

"I'm not supposed to talk about Letitia. Mrs. Deloney—"

"Your daughter's in a refrigerated drawer and all you give me is Mrs. Deloney."

She bowed her head over the shiny formica table. "I'm afraid of her," she said, "of what she can do to Earl."

"Be afraid of what she's already done to him. She and her political pals made him seal up the Deloney case, and it's been festering inside of him ever since."

"I know. It's the first time Earl ever laid down on the job deliberately."

"You admit that?"

"I guess I have to. Earl never said it out in so many words, but I knew, and Helen knew. It's why she left us."

And why, perhaps, in the long run Helen couldn't stay honest.

"Earl had a great respect for Luke Deloney," the woman was saying, "even if Luke did have his human failings. He was the one who made good for all of us in a manner of speaking. His death hit Earl real hard, and he started drinking right after, seriously I mean. I'm worried about Earl." She reached across the table and touched the back of my hand with her dry fingertips. "Do you think he'll be all right?"

"Not if he keeps on drinking. He ought to survive this bout. I'm sure he's being well taken care of. But Helen isn't."

"Helen? What can anybody do for Helen?"

"You can do something for her by telling the truth. Her death deserves an explanation at least."

"But I don't know who killed her. If I did I'd shout it from the housetops. I thought the police were after that man McGee who killed his wife."

"McGee has been cleared. Tish Macready killed his wife, and probably your daughter as well."

She shook her head solemnly. "You're mistaken, mister. What you say isn't possible. Tish Macready—Tish Osborne that was—she died long ago before either of those tragedies happened. I admit there were rumors about her at the time of Luke Deloney's death, but then she had her own tragedy, poor thing."

"You said 'Tish Osborne that was.'"

"That's right. She was one of Senator Osborne's girls—Mrs. Deloney's sister. I told you about them the other night when we were driving down here from the airport, how they used to ride to hounds." She smiled faintly, nostalgically, as if she had caught a flash of red coats from her childhood.

"What were the rumors about her, Mrs. Hoffman?"

"That she was carrying on with Luke Deloney before his death. Some people said she shot him herself, but I never believed that."

"Was she having an affair with Luke Deloney?"

"She used to spend some time in his apartment, that was no secret. She was kind of his unofficial hostess when Luke and Mrs. Deloney were separated. I didn't think too much about it. She was already divorced from Val Macready. And she was Luke's sister-in-law after all, I guess she had a right to be in his penthouse."

"Did she have red hair?"

"More auburn, I'd say. She had beautiful auburn hair." Mrs. Hoffman absently stroked her own dyed curls. "Tish Osborne had a lot of life in her. I was sorry to hear when she died."

"What happened to her?"

"I don't know exactly. She died in Europe when the Nazis ran over France. Mrs. Deloney still hasn't got over it. She was talking about her sister's death today."

Something that felt like a spider with wet feet climbed up the back of my neck into the short hairs and made them bristle. The ghost of Tish or a woman (or a man?) using her name had come to the door of the house in Indian Springs ten years ago, more than ten years after the Germans overran France.

"Are you certain she's dead, Mrs. Hoffman?"

She nodded. "There was quite a writeup in the papers, even the Chicago papers. Tish Osborne was the belle of Bridgeton in her time. I can remember back in the early twenties her parties were famous.

The man she married, Val Macready, had meat-packing money on his mother's side."

"Is he still alive?"

"The last I heard of him, he married an Englishwoman during the war and was living in England. He wasn't a Bridgeton boy and I never really knew him. I just read the society pages, and the obituaries."

She sipped her cocoa. Her look, her self-enclosed posture, seemed to be telling me that she had survived. Her daughter Helen had been brighter, Tish Osborne had been wealthier, but she was the one who had survived. She would survive Earl, too, and probably make a shrine of the study where he kept his liquor in the roll-top desk.

Well, I had caught one of the old ladies. The other one would be tougher.

"Why did Mrs. Deloney fly out here?"

"I guess it was just a rich woman's whim. She said she wanted to help me out in my time of trouble."

"Were you ever close to her?"

"I hardly knew her. Earl knows her better."

"Was Helen close to her?"

"No. If they ever met each other, it's news to me."

"Mrs. Deloney came a long way to help out a comparative stranger. Has she given you any particular help, apart from changing hotels?"

"She bought me lunch and dinner. I didn't want her to pay, but she insisted."

"What were you to do in return for the free room and board?"

"Nothing."

"Didn't she ask you not to talk about her sister Tish?"

"That's true, she did. I wasn't to say anything about her carrying on with Luke Deloney, or the rumors that went around about his death. She's very sensitive about her sister's reputation."

"Abnormally sensitive, if Tish has really been dead for over twenty years. Who weren't you supposed to mention these things to?"

"Anybody, especially you."

She drowned her nervous little giggle in the remains of her cocoa.

31

I WENT OUT into the grounds of the hotel. The high moon floated steadily in the sky and in the ornamental pools of the Spanish garden. There was yellower light behind the shutters of Mrs. Deloney's cottage, and the sound of voices too low to be eavesdropped on.

I knocked on the door.

"What is it?" she said.

"Service." Detective service.

"I didn't order anything."

But she opened the door. I slipped in past her and stood against the wall. Bradshaw was sitting on an English sofa beside the fireplace in the opposite wall. A low fire burned in the grate, and gleamed on the brass fittings.

"Hello," he said.

"Hello, George."

He jumped visibly.

Mrs. Deloney said: "Get out of here." She seemed to have perfectly round blue eyes in a perfectly square white face, all bone and will. "I'll call the house detective."

"Go ahead, if you want to spread the dirt around."

She shut the door.

"We might as well tell him," Bradshaw said. "We have to tell someone."

The negative jerk of her head was so violent it threw her off balance. She took a couple of backward steps and regrouped her forces, looking from me to Bradshaw as if we were both her enemies.

"I absolutely forbid it," she said to him. "Nothing is to be said."

"It's going to come out anyway. It will be better if we bring it out ourselves."

"It is *not* going to come out. Why should it?"

"Partly," I said, "because you made the mistake of coming here. This isn't your town, Mrs. Deloney. You can't put a lid on events the way you could in Bridgeton."

She turned her straight back on me. "Pay no attention to him, George."

"My name is Roy."

"Roy," she corrected herself. "This man tried to bluff me yesterday in Bridgeton, but he doesn't know a thing. All we have to do is remain quiet."

"What will that get us?"

"Peace."

"I've had my fill of that sort of peace," he said. "I've been living close up to it all these years. You've been out of contact. You have no conception of what I've been through." He rested his head on the back of the sofa and lifted his eyes to the ceiling.

"You'll go through worse," she said roughly, "if you let down your back hair now."

"At least it will be different."

"You're a spineless fool. But I'm not going to let you ruin what remains of my life. If you do, you'll get no financial help from me."

"Even that I can do without."

But he was being careful to say nothing I wanted to know. He'd been wearing a mask so long that it stuck to his face and controlled his speech and perhaps his habits of thought. Even the old woman with her back turned was playing to me as if I was an audience.

"This argument is academic, in more than one sense," I said. "The body isn't buried any longer. I know your sister Letitia shot your husband, Mrs. Deloney. I know she later married Bradshaw in Boston. I have his mother's word for it—"

"His mother?"

Bradshaw sat up straight. "I do have a mother after all." He added in his earnest cultivated voice, with his eyes intent on the woman's: "I'm still living with her, and she has to be considered in this matter, too."

"You lead a very complicated life," she said.

"I have a very complicated nature."

"Very well, young Mr. Complexity, the ball is yours. Carry it." She went to a love-seat in a neutral corner of the room and sat down there.

"I thought the ball was mine," I said, "but you're welcome to it, Bradshaw. You can start where everything started, with the Deloney killing. You were Helen's witness, weren't you?"

He nodded once. "I shouldn't have gone to Helen with that heavy knowledge. But I was deeply upset and she was the only friend I had in the world."

"Except Letitia."

"Yes. Except Letitia."

"What was your part in the murder?"

"I was simply there. And it wasn't a murder, properly speaking. Deloney was killed in self-defense, virtually by accident."

"This is where I came in."

"It's true. He caught us in bed together in his penthouse."

"Did you and Letitia make a habit of going to bed together?"

"It was the first time. I'd written a poem about her, which the college magazine printed, and I showed it to her in the elevator. I'd been watching her, admiring her, all through the spring. She was much older than I was, but she was fascinating. She was the first woman I ever had." He spoke of her with a kind of awe still.

"What happened in the penthouse bedroom, Bradshaw?"

"He caught us, as I said. He got a gun out of the chest of drawers and hit me with the butt of it. Tish tried to stop him. He beat her face in with the gun. She got her hands on it somehow, and it went off and killed him."

He touched the lid of his right eye, and nodded toward the old woman. She was watching us from the corner, from the distance of her years.

"Mrs. Deloney hushed the matter up, or had it hushed up. You can hardly blame her, under the circumstances. Or blame us. We went to Boston, where Tish spent months in and out of the hospital having her face rebuilt. Then we were married. I was in love with her, in spite of the discrepancy in our ages. I suppose my feeling for my own mother prepared me to love Tish."

His hooded intelligence flared up in his eyes so bright it was half-insane. His mouth was wry.

"We went to Europe on our honeymoon. My mother put French detectives on our trail. I had to leave Tish in Paris and come home to make my peace with Mother and start my sophomore year at Harvard. The war broke out in Europe that same month. I never saw Tish again. She fell sick and died before I knew it."

"I don't believe you. There wasn't time for all that."

"It happened very rapidly, as tragedy does."

"Not yours, it's been dragging on for twenty-two years."

"No," Mrs. Deloney said. "He's telling the truth, and I can prove it to you."

She went into another room of the cottage and came back with a heavily creased document which she handed me. It was an *acte de décès* issued in Bordeaux and dated July 16, 1940. It stated in French that Letitia Osborne Macready, aged 45, had died of pneumonia.

I gave it back to Mrs. Deloney. "You carry this with you wherever you go?"

"I happened to bring it with me."

"Why?"

She couldn't think of an answer.

"I'll tell you why. Because your sister is very much alive and you're afraid she'll be punished for her crimes."

"My sister committed no crime. The death of my husband was either justifiable homicide or accident. The police commissioner realized that or he'd never have quashed the case."

"That may be. But Constance McGee and Helen Haggerty weren't shot by accident."

"My sister died long before either of those women."

"Your own actions deny it, and they mean more than this phony death certificate. For instance, you visited Gil Stevens today and tried to pump him about the McGee case."

"He broke my confidence, did he?"

"There was nothing there to be broken. You're not Stevens's client. He's still representing McGee."

"He didn't tell me."

"Why should he? This isn't your town."

She turned in confusion to Bradshaw. He shook his head. I crossed the room and stood over him:

"If Tish is safely buried in France, why did you go to such elaborate trouble to divorce her?"

"So you know about the divorce. You're quite a digger for facts, aren't you, quite a Digger Indian? I begin to wonder if there's anything you don't know about my private life."

He sat there, looking up at me brightly and warily. I was a little carried away by the collapse of his defenses, and I said:

"Your private life, or your private lives, are something for the book. Have you been keeping up two establishments, dividing your time between your mother and your wife?"

"I suppose it's obvious that I have," he said tonelessly.

"Does Tish live here in town?"

"She lived in the Los Angeles area. I have no intention of telling you where, and I can assure you you'll never find the place. There'd be no point in it, anyway, since she's no longer there."

"Where and how did she die this time?"

"She isn't dead. That French death certificate is a fake, as you guessed. But she is beyond your reach. I put her on a plane to Rio de Janeiro on Saturday, and she'll be there by now."

Mrs. Deloney said: "You didn't tell me that!"

"I hadn't intended to tell anyone. However, I have to make Mr. Archer see that there's no point in pressing this thing any further. My wife—my ex-wife—is an old woman, and a sick one, and she's beyond extradition. I've arranged for her to have medical care, psychiatric care, in a South American city which I won't name."

"You're admitting that she killed Helen Haggerty?"

"Yes. She confessed to me when I went to see her in Los Angeles early Saturday morning. She shot Helen and hid the gun in my gatehouse. I contacted Foley in Reno primarily to find out if he had witnessed anything. I didn't want him blackmailing me—"

"I thought he already was."

"Helen was," he said. "She learned about my pending divorce in Reno, and she jumped to a number of conclusions, including the fact that Tish was still alive. I gave her a good deal of money, and got her a job here, in order to protect Tish."

"And yourself."

"And myself. I do have a reputation to protect, though I've done nothing illegal."

"No. You're very good at arranging for other people to do your dirty work. You brought Helen here as a kind of decoy, didn't you?"

"I'm afraid I don't understand you." But he shifted uneasily.

"You took Helen out a few times and passed the word that she was your intended. She wasn't, of course. You were already married to Laura and you hated Helen, with good reason."

"That's not true. We were on quite a friendly basis, in spite of her demands. She was a very old friend, after all, and I couldn't help sympathizing with her feeling that she deserved something from the world."

"I know what she got—a bullet in the head. The same thing Constance McGee got. The same thing Laura would have got if you hadn't set Helen up as a substitute victim for Tish."

"I'm afraid you're getting much too complicated."

"For a complicated nature like yours?"

He looked around the room as if he felt imprisoned in it, or in the maze of his own nature. "You'll never prove any complicity on my part in Helen's death. It came as a fearful shock to me. Letitia's confession was another shock."

"Why? You must have known she killed Constance McGee."

"I didn't know it till Saturday. I admit I had my suspicions. Tish was always savagely jealous. I've lived with the dreadful possibility for ten years, hoping and praying that my suspicions were unfounded—"

"Why didn't you ask her?"

"I suppose I couldn't face it. Things were already so difficult between us. It would have meant admitting my love for Connie." He heard his own words, and sat quiet for a moment, his eyes downcast, as if he was peering down into a chasm in himself. "I really did love her, you know. Her death almost finished me."

"But you survived to love again."

"Men do," he said. "I'm not the sort of man who can live without love. I loved even Tish as long and as well as I could. But she got *old*, and sick."

Mrs. Deloney made a spitting sound. He said to her:

"I wanted a wife, one who could give me children."

"God help any children of yours, you'd probably abandon them. You broke all your promises to my sister."

"Everyone breaks promises. I didn't intend to fall in love with Connie. It simply happened. I met her in a doctor's waiting room quite by accident. But I didn't turn my back on your sister. I never have. I've done more for her than she ever did for me."

She sneered at him with the arrogance of a second-generation aristocrat. "My sister lifted you out of the gutter. What were you—an elevator boy?"

"I was a college student, and an elevator boy by my own choice."

"Very likely."

He leaned toward her, fixing her with his bright eyes. "I had family resources to draw on if I had wished."

"Ah yes, your precious mother."

"Be careful what you say about my mother."

There was an edge on his words, the quality of a cold threat, and it silenced her. This was one of several moments when I sensed that the two of them were playing a game as complex as chess, a game of

power on a hidden board. I should have tried to force it into the open.
But I was clearing up my case, and as long as Bradshaw was willing
to talk I didn't care about apparent side-issues.

"I don't understand the business of the gun," I said. "The police
have established that Connie McGee and Helen were shot with the
same gun—a revolver that belonged originally to Connie's sister Alice.
How did Tish get hold of it?"

"I don't really know."

"You must have some idea. Did Alice Jenks give it to her?"

"She very well may have."

"That's nonsense, Bradshaw, and you know it. The revolver was
stolen from Alice's house. Who stole it?"

He made a steeple of his fingers and admired its symmetry. "I'm
willing to tell you if Mrs. Deloney will leave the room."

"Why should I?" she said from her corner. "Anything my sister could
endure to live through I can endure to hear."

"I'm not trying to spare your sensibilities," Bradshaw said. "I'm trying to spare myself."

She hesitated. It became a test of wills. Bradshaw got up and opened
the inner door. Through it I could see across a hall into a bedroom
furnished in dull luxury. The bedside table held an ivory telephone
and a leather-framed photograph of a white-mustached gentleman who
looked vaguely familiar.

Mrs. Deloney marched into the bedroom like a recalcitrant soldier
under orders. Bradshaw closed the door sharply behind her.

"I'm beginning to hate old women," he said.

"You were going to tell me about the gun."

"I was, wasn't I?" He returned to the sofa. "It's not a pretty story.
None of it is. I'm telling you the whole thing in the hope that you'll
be completely satisfied."

"And not bring in the authorities?"

"Don't you see there's nothing to be gained by bringing them in?
The sole effect would be to turn the town on its ear, wreck the standing of the college which I've worked so hard to build up, and ruin
more than one life."

"Especially yours and Laura's?"

"Especially mine and Laura's. She's waited for me, God knows. And
even I deserve something more than I've had. I've lived my entire adult
life with the consequences of a neurotic involvement that I got into
when I was just a boy."

"Is that what Godwin was treating you for?"

"I needed *some* support. Tish hasn't been easy to deal with. She drove me half out of my mind sometimes with her animal violence and her demands. But now it's over." His eyes changed the statement into a question and a plea.

"I can't make any promises," I said. "Let's have the entire story, then we'll think about the next step. How did Tish get hold of Alice's revolver?"

"Connie took it from her sister's room and gave it to me. We had some wild idea of using it to cut the Gordian knot."

"Do you mean kill Tish with it?"

"It was sheer fantasy," he said, *"folie à deux.* Connie and I would never have carried it out, desperate as we were. You'll never know the agony I went through dividing myself between two wives, two lovers—one old and rapacious, the other young and passionate. Jim Godwin warned me that I was in danger of spiritual death."

"For which murder is known to be a sure cure."

"I'd never have done it. I couldn't. Actually Jim made me see that. I'm not a violent man."

But there was violence in him now, pressing against the conventional fears that corseted his nature and held him still, almost formal, under my eyes. I sensed his murderous hatred for me. I was forcing all his secrets into the open, as I thought.

"What happened to the gun Connie stole for you?"

"I put it away in what I thought was a safe place, but Tish must have found it."

"In your house?"

"In my mother's house. I sometimes took her there when Mother was away."

"Was she there the day McGee called on you?"

"Yes." He met my eyes. "I'm amazed that you should know about that day. You're very thorough. It was the day when everything came to a head. Tish must have found the gun in the lockbox in my study where I'd hidden it. Before that she must have heard McGee complaining to me about my interest in his wife. She took the gun and turned it against Constance. I suppose there was a certain poetic justice in that."

Bradshaw might have been talking about an event in someone else's past, the death of a character in history or fiction. He no longer cared for the meaning of his own life. Perhaps that was what Godwin meant by spiritual death.

"Do you still maintain you didn't know Tish killed her until she confessed it last Saturday?"

"I suppose I didn't let myself realize. So far as I knew the gun had simply disappeared. McGee might very well have taken it from my study when he was in the house. The official case against him seemed very strong."

"It was put together with old pieces of string, and you know it. McGee and his daughter are my main concern. I won't be satisfied until they're completely cleared."

"But surely that can be accomplished without dragging Letitia back from Brazil."

"I have only your word that she's in Brazil," I said. "Even Mrs. Deloney was surprised to hear it."

"Good heavens, don't you believe me? I've literally exposed my entrails to you."

"You wouldn't do that unless you had a reason. I think you're a liar, Bradshaw, one of those virtuosos who use real facts and feelings to make their stories plausible. But there's a basic implausibility in this one. If Tish was safe in Brazil, it's the last thing you'd ever tell me. I think she's hiding out here in California."

"You're quite mistaken."

His eyes came up to mine, candid and earnest as only an actor's can be. A telephone chirring behind the bedroom door interrupted our staring contest. Bradshaw moved toward the sound. I was on my feet and I moved more rapidly, shouldering him against the doorframe, picking up the bedside phone before it rang a third time.

"Hello."

"Is that you, darling?" It was Laura's voice. "Roy, I'm frightened. She *knows* about us. She called here just a minute ago and said she was coming over."

"Keep the door locked and chained. And you better call the police."

"That isn't Roy. Is it?"

Roy was behind me. I turned in time to see the flash of brass as the poker in his fist came down on my head.

32
··
───────

Mrs. Deloney was slapping my face with a wet towel. I told her
to quit it. The first thing I saw when I got up was the leather-framed
photograph beside her telephone. It seemed to my blurred vision to be
a photograph of the handsome old black-eyed gentleman whose portrait hung over the fireplace in Mrs. Bradshaw's sitting room.

"What are you doing with a picture of Bradshaw's father?"

"It happens to be my own father, Senator Osborne."

I said: "So Mrs. Bradshaw's a virtuoso, too."

Mrs. Deloney looked at me as if my brains had been addled by the
poker. But the blow had been a glancing one, and I couldn't have
been out for more than a few seconds. Bradshaw was leaving the hotel
parking lot when I got there.

His light car turned uphill away from the ocean. I followed him
to Foothill Drive and caught him long before he reached his house.
He made it easy for me by braking suddenly. His car slewed sideways
and came to a shuddering halt broadside across the road.

It wasn't me he was trying to stop. Another car was coming downhill toward us. I could see its headlights approaching under the trees
like large calm insane eyes, and Bradshaw silhouetted in their beam.
He seemed to be fumbling with his seat-belt. I recognized Mrs. Bradshaw's Rolls in the moment before, with screeching brakes, it crashed
into the smaller car.

I pulled off the road, set out a red blinker, and ran uphill toward
the point of impact. My footsteps were loud in the silence after the
crash. The crumpled nose of the Rolls was nuzzled deep in the caved-in
side of Bradshaw's car. He lolled in the driver's seat. Blood ran down
his face from his forehead and nose and the corners of his mouth.

I went in through the undamaged door and got his seat-belt un-
buckled. He toppled limply into my arms. I laid him down in the road.
The jagged lines of blood across his face resembled cracks in a mask
through which live tissue showed. But he was dead. He lay pulseless
and breathless under the iron shadows of the tree branches.

Old Mrs. Bradshaw had climbed down out of her high protected seat. She seemed unhurt. I remember thinking at the moment that she was an elemental power which nothing could ever kill.

"It's Roy, isn't it? Is he all right?"

"In a sense he is. He wanted out. He's out."

"What do you mean?"

"I'm afraid you've killed him, too."

"But I didn't mean to hurt him. I wouldn't hurt my own son, the child of my womb."

Her voice cracked with maternal grief. I think she half-believed she was his mother, she had lived the rôle so long. Reality had grown dim as the moonlit countryside around her.

She flung herself on the dead man, holding him close, as if her old body could somehow warm him back to life and rekindle his love for her. She wheedled and cooed in his ear, calling him a naughty malingering boy for trying to scare her.

She shook him. "Wake up! It's Moms."

As she had told me, night wasn't her best season. But she had a doubleness in her matching Roy's, and there was an element of playacting in her frenzy.

"Leave him alone," I said. "And let's drop the mother bit. The situation is ugly enough without that."

She turned in queer slow furtiveness and looked up at me. "The mother bit?"

"Roy Bradshaw wasn't your son. The two of you put on a pretty good act—Godwin would probably say it fitted both your neurotic needs—but it's over."

She got up in a surge of anger which brought her close to me. I could smell her lavender, and feel her force.

"I *am* his mother. I have his birth certificate to prove it."

"I bet you do. Your sister showed me a death certificate which proves that you died in France in 1940. With your kind of money you can document anything. But you can't change the facts by changing them on paper. Roy married you in Boston after you killed Deloney. Eventually he fell in love with Constance McGee. You killed her. Roy lived with you for another ten years, if you can call it living, terrified that you'd kill again if he ever dared to love anyone again. But finally he dared, with Laura Sutherland. He managed to convince you that it was Helen Haggerty he was interested in. So you went up the bridle path on Friday night and shot her. Those are all facts you can't change."

Silence set in between us, thin and bleak like a quality of the moonlight. The woman said:

"I was only protecting my rights. Roy owed me faithfulness at least. I gave him money and background, I sent him to Harvard, I made all his dreams come true."

We both looked down at the dreamless man lying in the road.

"Are you ready to come downtown with me and make a formal statement about how you protected your rights over the years? Poor Tom McGee is back in jail, still sweating out your rap."

She pulled herself erect. "I won't permit you to use such language to me. I'm not a criminal."

"You were on your way to Laura Sutherland's, weren't you? What were you planning to do to her, old woman?"

She covered the lower part of her face with her hand. I thought she was ill, or overcome with shame. But she said:

"You mustn't call me that. I'm not old. Don't look at my face, look into my eyes. You can see how young I am."

It was true in a way. I couldn't see her eyes clearly, but I knew they were bright and black and vital. She was still greedy for life, like the imaginary Letitia, the weird projection of herself in imitation leopard-skin she had used to hide behind.

She shifted her hand to her heavy chin and said: "I'll give you money."

"Roy took your money. Look what happened to him."

She turned abruptly and started for her car. I guessed what was in her mind: another death, another shadow to feed on: and got to the open door of the Rolls before her. Her black leather bag was on the floor where it had fallen in the collision. Inside the bag I found the new revolver which she had intended to use on Roy's new wife.

"Give me that."

She spoke with the authority of a Senator's daughter and the more terrible authority of a woman who had killed two other women and two men.

"No more guns for you," I said.

No more anything, Letitia.

BLACK
MONEY

1
•••

I'D BEEN HEARING about the Tennis Club for years, but I'd never been inside of it. Its courts and bungalows, its swimming pool and cabanas and pavilions, were disposed around a cove of the Pacific a few miles south of the Los Angeles County border. Just parking my Ford in the asphalt lot beside the tennis courts made me feel like less of a dropout from the affluent society.

The carefully groomed woman at the front desk of the main building told me that Peter Jamieson was probably in the snack bar. I walked around the end of the fifty-meter pool, which was enclosed on three sides by cabanas. On the fourth side the sea gleamed through a ten-foot wire fence like a blue fish alive in a net. A few dry bathers were lying around as if the yellow eye of the sun had hypnotized them.

When I saw my prospective client, in the sunny courtyard outside the snack bar, I recognized him instinctively. He looked like money about three generations removed from its source. Though he couldn't have been out of his early twenties, his face was puffy and apologetic, the face of a middle-aged boy. Under his carefully tailored Ivy League suit he wore a layer of fat like easily penetrable armor. He had the kind of soft brown eyes which are very often short-sighted.

When I approached his table he got up quickly, almost knocking over his double malted. "You must be Mr. Archer."

I acknowledged that I was.

"I'm glad to see you." He let me feel his large amorphous hand. "Let me get you something. The Monday hot lunch is New England boiled dinner."

"Thanks, I had lunch before I left Los Angeles. A cup of coffee, maybe."

He went and got it for me. In the creeping fig that covered one wall of the court, a pair of house finches were discussing family matters. The male, which had a splash of red on its front, took off on an errand. My eye followed him across the framed blue sky, then out of the frame.

"It's a beautiful day," I said to Peter Jamieson. "Also this coffee is good."

"Yes, they make good coffee." He sipped dolefully at his malted, then said abruptly: "Can you get her back for me?"

"I can't make your girl come back if she doesn't want to. I told you that on the phone."

"I know. I put it wrong. Even assuming she doesn't come back to me, we can still save her from ruining her life." He rested his arms on the table and leaned towards me, trying to imbue me with crusading fervor. "We can't let her marry this man. And I'm not talking out of jealousy. Even if I can't have her, I want to protect her."

"From the other man."

"I'm serious, Mr. Archer. This man is apparently wanted by the police. He claims to be a Frenchman, a French aristocrat no less, but nobody really knows who he is or where he comes from. He may not even be Caucasian."

"Where did you get that idea?"

"He's so dark. And Ginny is so fair. It nauseates me to see her with him."

"But it doesn't nauseate her."

"No. Of course she doesn't know what I know about him. He's a wanted man, probably some kind of a criminal."

"How did you find that out?"

"From a detective. He caught me—I mean, I was watching the house last night, waiting to see if Ginny came home with him."

"Do you make a practice of watching Martel's house?"

"Just this last weekend. I didn't know if they were coming back from the weekend."

"She went away for the weekend with him?"

He nodded dismally. "Before she left she gave me back my engagement ring. She said she had no further use for it. Or me."

He fumbled in his watch pocket and produced the ring, as if it was evidence. In a way it was. The diamonds that encrusted the platinum band must have been worth several thousand dollars. Its return meant that Ginny was serious about Martel.

"What did the man say?"

Peter didn't seem to hear me. He was absorbed in the ring. He turned it slowly so that the diamonds caught and refracted the light from the sky. He winced, as if their cold fire had burned his fingers.

"What did the detective say about Martel?"

"He didn't actually say anything outright. He asked me what I was doing there sitting in my car, and I told him I was waiting for Martel. He wanted to know where Martel came from, how long he'd been in Montevista, where he got his money—"

"Martel has money?"

"He seems to have. He certainly flings it around. But as I told the man, I don't know where it came from or where he came from. Then he tried to ask me some questions about Ginny—he must have seen her with Martel. I refused to discuss her, and he let me go."

"Was he a local detective?"

"I don't know. He showed me some kind of a badge, but I couldn't see it in the dark. He got in the car beside me all of a sudden and started talking. He was a very fast talker."

"Describe him. Young or old?"

"In between, around thirty-five or so. He had on some kind of a tweed jacket, and a light gray hat pulled down over his eyes. He was about my size, I think—I'm five-foot-ten—but not so heavy. I really can't describe his face, but I didn't like the sound of him. I thought at first he was some kind of crook trying to hold me up."

"Did he have a gun?"

"If he had, I didn't see it. When he finished asking me questions, he told me to be on my way. That was when I decided to buy a detective of my own."

There was a touch of arrogance in the phrase, reminding me that he was in the habit of buying things and people. But the boy was a little different from some other rich people I'd known. He heard himself, and apologized:

"I'm sorry. I didn't mean that the way it sounded."

"It's all right, as long as you realize that all you can do is rent me. What kind of a girl is Ginny?"

The question silenced him for a minute. The ring was still on the table, and his brown eyes focused on it until they crossed. I could hear the clatter of pans and conversation from the snack bar, interspersed with the sweeter notes of the finches.

"She's a beautiful girl," he said with a dreamy cross-eyed expression, "and really quite innocent. Undeveloped for her age, in spite of her brains. She can't possibly realize what she's getting into. I tried to show her the pitfalls, marrying a man with no real information about his background. But she wouldn't listen. She said she intended to marry him no matter what I said."

"Did she say why?"

"He reminds her of her father, that was one thing."

"Is Martel an older man?"

"I don't know how old he is. He must be thirty at least, maybe older than that."

"Is money one of the attractions?"

"It can't be. She could have married me, in fact we were due to be married next month. And I'm not poor." He added, with the caution of old money: "We're not the Rockefellers, but we're not poor."

"Good. I charge a hundred dollars a day and expenses."

"Isn't that quite a lot?"

"I don't think so. Actually it's just enough to get by on. I don't work all the time, and I have to maintain an office."

"I see."

"I'll take three hundred dollars advance from you." I knew from experience that very rich people were the hardest to collect from after the event.

He shied at the amount, but he didn't object. "I'll write you a check," he said, reaching into his inside breast pocket.

"First, tell me just what you expect in return for your money."

"I want you to find out who Martel is and where he came from and where his money came from. And why he came here to Montevista in the first place. Once I know something about him, I'm sure I can make Ginny see reason."

"And marry you?"

"And *not* marry him. That's all I hope to accomplish. I don't suppose she'll ever marry me."

But he carefully put the engagement ring away in the watch pocket of his trousers. Then he wrote me a check for three hundred dollars drawn on the Pacific Point National Bank.

I got out my little black book. "What's Ginny's full name?"

"Virginia Fablon. She lives with her mother, Marietta. Mrs. Roy Fablon. Their house is next door to ours on Laurel Drive." He gave me both addresses.

"Would Mrs. Fablon be willing to talk to me?"

"I don't know why not. She's Ginny's mother, she's interested in her welfare."

"How does Mrs. Fablon feel about Martel?"

"I haven't discussed him with her. I think she's taken in, like every-one else."

"What about Ginny's father?"

"He isn't around any more."

"What does that mean, Peter?"

The question bothered him. He fidgeted and said without meeting my eyes: "Mr. Fablon died."

"Recently?"

"Six or seven years ago. Ginny still hasn't got over it. She was crazy about her father."

"You knew her then?"

"All my life. I've been in love with her since I was eleven."

"How long is that?"

"Thirteen years. I realize it's an unlucky number," he added, as if he was collecting signs of bad luck.

"How old is Ginny?"

"Twenty-four. We're the same age. But she looks younger and I look older."

I asked him some questions about the other man. Francis Martel had driven his own black Bentley into Montevista about two months ago, on a rainy day in March, and moved into the Bagshaw house, which he leased furnished from General Bagshaw's widow. Old Mrs. Bag-shaw had apparently got him into the Tennis Club. Martel seldom appeared there and when he did appear he hid himself in his second-floor cabana. The hell of it was that Ginny had taken to hiding there with him, too.

"She even dropped out of school," Peter said, "so she could be with him all the time."

"What school was she going to?"

"Montevista State. She was majoring in French. Virginia's always been crazy about French language and literature. But she dropped it, just like that." He tried to snap his fingers: they made a sad squeaking sound.

"Maybe she wanted more of the real thing."

"You mean because he claims to be a Frenchman?"

"How do you know he isn't?"

"I know a phony when I see one," Peter said.

"But Ginny doesn't?"

"He has her hypnotized. It isn't a normal healthy relationship. It's all mixed up with her father and the fact that he was part French. She flung herself into this whole French business the same year that he died, and now it's coming to a head."

"I don't quite follow."

"I know, I don't express myself too well. But I'm worried sick about her. I've been eating so much I've given up weighing myself. I must weigh over two hundred." He palpated his stomach, cautiously.

"Roadwork would help."

He looked at me in a puzzled way. "I beg your pardon?"

"Get out on the beach and run."

"I couldn't, I'm much too depressed." He sucked up the last of his malted, making a noise like a death-rattle. "You'll get to work on this right away, won't you, Mr. Archer?"

2
...

MONTEVISTA IS a residential community adjacent to and symbiotic with the harbor city of Pacific Point. It has only one small shopping center, which calls itself the Village Square. Among its mock-rustic shops the Montevistans play at being simple villagers the way the courtiers of Versailles pretended to be peasants.

I cashed Peter's check at the Village branch of the Pacific Point National Bank. The transaction had to be okayed by the manager, a sharp-eyed young man in a conservative gray suit whose name was McMinn. He volunteered that he knew the Jamieson family very well; in fact the older Peter Jamieson was on the bank's board of directors.

McMinn seemed to take a dim but lofty pleasure in mentioning this, as if money conferred spiritual grace, which could be shared by talking about people who had it. I enhanced his pleasure by asking him how to get to the Bagshaw house.

"It's away back in the foothills. You'll need a map." He rummaged in the bottom drawer of his desk and produced a map, on which he made some markings. "I suppose you know that General Bagshaw is dead."

"I'm sorry to hear it."

"We were devastated here at the bank. He always did his local banking with us. Mrs. Bagshaw still does, of course. If it's Mrs. Bagshaw you want to see, she's moved into one of the cottages at the Tennis Club. The house is leased to a fellow by the name of Martel."

"You know him?"

"I've seen him. He does his banking at our main office downtown."

McMinn gave me a quick suspicious look. "Are you acquainted with Mr. Martel?"

"Not yet."

I drove back into the foothills. The slopes were still green from the rains. The white and purple flowers on the brush gave out a smell like the slow breath of sunlight.

When I stopped my car at the Bagshaw mailbox, I could see the ocean below, hung on the horizon like unevenly blued washing. I had climbed only a few hundred feet but I could feel the change in temperature, as if I had risen much nearer to the noon sun.

The house sat alone in its own canyon head, several hundred feet above the road. It looked almost as tiny as a birdhouse. A blacktop driveway hairpinned up to it from where I was parked.

A convertible with a snarl in the gearbox was toiling up behind me from the direction of town. It passed me, an old black Caddie, gray with dust, and stopped in front of my car.

The driver got out and came toward me. He was a middle-sized man wearing a hound's-tooth jacket and a good-looking pearl gray fedora, which he wore at a cocky slant. He moved with a kind of quick embarrassed belligerence. I had no doubt that he was Peter's "detective," but he didn't look like a detective to me. An air of desperate failure hung about him like a personal odor.

I got out my black book and made a note of the Cadillac's license number. It had California plates.

"What are you writing?"

"A poem."

He reached though the open window for my notebook. "Let's see it," he said in a loud unimpressive voice. His eyes were anxious.

"I never show work in progress."

I closed the book and put it back in my inside breast pocket. Then I started to turn up the window on his arm. He yanked his arm away and pressed his face against the glass, blurring it momentarily with his breath.

"I want to see what you wrote about me." He took a miniature camera out of his pocket and rapped on the window with it, foolishly and frantically. "What did you write about me?"

It was the kind of situation I liked to avoid, or terminate quickly. As the century wore on—I could feel it wearing on—angry pointless encounters like this one tended more and more to erupt in violence. I got out on the right-hand side and walked around the front of the car toward him.

As long as I was in my car, he had been yelling at a machine, a Cadillac yelling at a Ford. Now we were both men, and he was shorter and narrower than I was. He stopped yelling. His whole personality changed. He wiped his mouth with the back of his hand, as if to disclaim the evil spirit that had invaded him and made him yell at me. Self-doubt pulled at his face like a surgically hidden scar.

"I didn't do anything out of line, did I? You got no call to write down my license number."

"That remains to be seen," I said in a semi-official tone. "What are you doing here?"

"Sightseeing. I'm a tourist." His pale eyes glanced around at the sparsely inhabited hills as if he had never been out in the country before. "This is a public road, isn't it?"

"We've had a report of a man who was representing himself as a law officer last night."

His glance lighted briefly on my face, then jumped away. "It couldn't be me. I never been here before in my life."

"Let's see your driver's license."

"Listen," he said, "we can get together on this. I don't have much with me but I got other resources." He drew a lonely ten from a worn calfskin billfold and tucked it in the breast pocket of my jacket. "Here. Buy something for the kids. And call me Harry."

He smiled with conscious charm. But the charm he was conscious of, if it had ever existed, had dried up and blown away. His front teeth glared at me like a pair of chisels. I removed the ten from my pocket, tore it in half, and gave him back the pieces.

His face fell apart. "That's a ten-dollar bill. You must be a kook to tear up money like that."

"You can put it together with Scotch tape. Now let me see your license before you commit another felony."

"Felony?" He said it the way a sick man pronounces the name of his disease.

"Bribery and impersonating an officer are felonies, Harry."

He looked around at the daylight as if it had betrayed him, again. A little pale moon hung in a corner of the sky, faint as a thumbprint on a windowpane.

A fiercer light flashed down the canyon above us and almost dazzled me. It seemed to come from the head of a man who was standing with a girl on the terrace of the Bagshaw house. For a second I had the impression that he had great round eyes and that they had emitted the flashing light. Then I realized he was watching us through binoculars.

The man and the girl with him were as small as figures on a wedding cake. Their height and distance from me gave me a queer feeling, as if they were somehow unattainable, out of reach, out of time.

Harry Felony scrambled into his car and tried to start the engine. It turned over slowly like a dead man turning over in his grave. I had time to open the far door and get in on the gnawed leather seat.

"Where are we going, Harry?"

"Nowhere." He turned off the ignition and dropped his hands. "Why don't you leave me alone?"

"Because you stopped a young man on this road last night and said you were a detective and asked him a lot of questions."

He was silent while his malleable face went through new adjustments. "I am a detective, in a way."

"Where's your badge?"

He reached into his pocket for something, probably a dime-store badge, then changed his mind. "I don't have one," he admitted. "I'm just a kind of amateur dick, you might say, looking into something for a friend. She"—he swallowed the pronoun—"they didn't say anything about this kind of trouble."

"Maybe we can make a deal after all. Let me see your driver's license."

He got out his worn billfold and handed me a photostat.

HARRY HENDRICKS
10750 Vanowen, Apt. 12
Canoga Park, Calif

SEX M   COLOR HAIR brn   COLOR EYES blu   HEIGHT 5'9"   WEIGHT
165   MARRIED no   DATE OF BIRTH Apr 12 1928   AGE 38

From the lower left-hand corner a photograph of Harry grinned at me. I took down the address and the number of the license in my notebook.

"What do you want all that stuff for?" he said in a worried voice.

"So I can keep track of you. What do you do for a living, Harry?"

"Sell cars."

"I don't believe you."

"*Used* cars, on commission," he said bitterly. "I used to be an insurance adjuster but the little fellows can't compete with the big boys anymore. I've done a lot of things in my time. Name it and I done it."

"Ever do time?"

He gave me a hurt look. "Of course not. You said something about a deal."

"I like to know who I'm dealing with."

"Hell, you can trust me. I've got connections."

"In the used car business?"

"You'd be surprised," he said.

"And what do your connections want you to do to Martel?"

"Nothing *to* him. I'm just supposed to case the joint and find out who he is if I can."

"Who is he?"

Harry spread his hands on top of the steering wheel. "I only been in town less than twenty-four hours, and the local yokels don't know a thing about him." He peered at me sideways. "If you're a cop like you say—"

"I didn't say. I'm a private detective. This area is strictly patrolled." The two facts were true, but unrelated.

Harry related them. "Then you should be able to get the information. There's money in it, we could split it two ways."

"How much?"

"A hundred I could promise you."

"I'll see what I can find out. Where are you staying in town?"

"The Breakwater Hotel. That's on the waterfront."

"And who is the woman who put you up to this?"

"Nobody said anything about a woman."

"You said 'she.'"

"I must have been thinking of my wife. She's got nothing to do with this."

"I can't believe that. Your driver's license says you aren't married."

"I am married, though." The point seemed important to him, as if I'd denied him membership in the human race. "That's a mistake on the license. I forgot I was married that day, I mean—"

His explanation was interrupted by the smooth mutter of a car coming down the winding driveway above us. It was Martel's black Bentley. The man behind the wheel wore rectangular dark glasses which covered the upper part of his face like a mask.

The girl beside him had on dark glasses, too. They almost made her look like any Hollywood blonde.

Harry got out his miniature camera, which was hardly bigger than a cigarette lighter. He ran across the road and planted himself in the entrance to the driveway, holding the camera concealed in his right hand.

The driver of the Bentley got out facing him. He was compact and muscular, dressed in English-looking sports clothes, tweeds and brogues, which didn't go with his own swarthy sleekness. He said in a controlled, faintly accented voice: "Can I help you in any way?"

"Yeah. Watch the birdie." Harry raised the camera and took his picture. "Thanks, Mr. Martel."

"You are not welcome." Martel's fleshy mouth became ugly. "Give me that camera please."

"Nuts. It's worth a hundred and fifty bucks."

"It's worth two hundred to me," Martel said, "with the film in it. I have a passion for privacy, you see." He pronounced the word 'passion' with a long nasal 'o,' like a Frenchman. But he was dark for a Frenchman.

I looked at the blonde girl in the car. Though I couldn't see her eyes, she seemed to be looking back across the road at me. The lower part of her face was immobile, as if she was afraid to react to the situation. It had the dead beauty of marble.

Harry was calculating in his head, almost audibly. "You can have it for three hundred."

"*Trés bien*, three hundred. That should include a—what is the word? —receipt, with your signature and address."

"Uh—uh." I had a quick impression of Harry's whole life: he didn't know how to stop when he was winning.

The girl leaned out of the open door of the Bentley. "Don't let him hold you up, Francis."

"I have no intention of that."

Martel moved suddenly on Harry and plucked the camera out of his hand. He stepped back, dropped it on the asphalt, and ground it under his heel.

Harry was appalled. "You can't do that!"

"But I have. It's a *fait accompli.*"

"I want my money."

"No money. *Pas d'argent. Rien du tout.*"

Martel got into the black car and slammed the door. Harry followed him yelling:

"You can't do that to me! That camera doesn't belong to me! You've got to pay for it."

"Pay him, Francis," the girl said.

"No. He had his chance." Martel made another sudden movement. His fist appeared at the window, with the small round eye of a gun peering over his index finger. "Listen to me my friend. I do not like to be bothered by *canaille.* If you come this way again or trespass on my privacy in any way, I will kill you." He clicked his tongue.

Harry backed away from him. He backed to the edge of the driveway, lost his footing, and almost fell. Unimpeded by false shame, he came up like a sprinter and ran for the Cadillac. He got in wheezing and sweating.

"He almost shot me. You're a witness to that."

"You're lucky he didn't."

"Arrest him. Go ahead. He can't get away with that. He's nothing but a cheap crook. That French act he puts on is as queer as a three-dollar bill."

"Can you prove it?"

"Not right now. But I'm gonna get that dago. He can't get away with smashing my camera. It's a valuable camera, and it wasn't mine, either." His voice was aggrieved: the world had let him down for the thousandth time. "You wouldn't just sit there if you were a security cop like you say."

The Bentley rolled out of the driveway into the road. One wheel passed over the broken camera and flattened it. Martel drove away sedately toward town.

"I've got to think of something," Harry said more or less to himself.

He took off his hat as if it limited the sweep and scope of his mind, and held it on his knees like a begging bowl. The printing on the silk lining said that it came from The Haberdashery in Las Vegas. The gold printing on the leather sweatband said L. Spillman. Harry stole his hat, I thought. Or else he was carrying a false driver's license.

He turned to me as if he had heard my unspoken accusation. With carefully rationed hostility, he said: "You don't have to feel you have to stick around. You've been no help."

I said I would see him later at the hotel. The prospect didn't seem to excite him much.

3
...

LAUREL DRIVE ran deep between hedges like an English lane. An immense green barricade of pittosporum hid Mrs. Fablon's garden from the road. On the far side of the garden a woman who at a distance looked like Ginny's sister was sitting with a man at an umbrella table, eating lunch.

The man had a long jaw which hardened when I appeared in the driveway. He stood up wiping his mouth with a napkin. He was tall and erect, and his face was handsome in a bony pugnacious way.

"I'll be shoving off," I heard him say under his breath.

"Don't hurry away. I'm not expecting anyone."

"Neither was I," he said shortly.

He flung his napkin down on top of his half-eaten salmon mayonnaise. Without speaking again, or looking at me, he walked to a Mercedes parked under an oak, got in, and drove out the other side of the semi-circular driveway. He acted like a man who was anxious for an excuse to get away.

Mrs. Fablon stayed at the table, looking quite composed. "Who on earth are you?"

"My name is Archer. I'm a private detective."

"Does Dr. Sylvester know you?"

"If he does, I don't know him. Why?"

"He rushed off in such a hurry when he saw you."

"I'm sorry about that."

"You needn't be. The luncheon was no great success. Don't tell me Audrey Sylvester is having him followed."

"Possibly. Not by me. Should she have?"

"Certainly not to my doorstep. George Sylvester has been my family doctor for ten years, and the relationship between us is about as highly seasoned as a tongue-depressor." She smiled at her own elaborate wit. "Do you follow people, Mr. Archer?"

I looked at her eyes to see if she was kidding. If she was, they didn't show it. They were pale blue, with a kind of pastel imperviousness. I was interested in her eyes, because I hadn't seen her daughter's.

They were innocent eyes, not youthful but innocent, as if they perceived only pre-selected facts. Such eyes went with the carefully dyed blonde hair whipped like cream on her pretty skull, with the impossibly good figure under her too-youthful dress, and with the guileless way she let me look at her. But under her serenity she was tense.

"I must be wanted for something," she said with a half-smile. "Am I wanted for something?"

I didn't reply. I was trying to think of a tactful way to broach the subject of Ginny and Martel.

"I keep asking you questions," she said, "and you don't say anything. Is that the way detectives operate?"

"I have my own ways of working."

"Mysterious ways your wonders to perform? I was beginning to suspect as much. Now tell me what wonders you're bent on performing."

"It has to do with your daughter Ginny."

"I see." But her eyes didn't change. "Sit down if you like." She indicated the metal chair across from her. "Is Virginia in some kind of trouble? She never has been."

"That's the question I'm trying to answer."

"Who put you up to it?" she said rather sharply. "It wasn't George Sylvester?"

"What makes you think it was?"

"The way he ran off just now." She was watching me carefully. "But it wasn't George, was it? He's quite infatuated with Virginia—all the men are—but he wouldn't expose himself—" She paused.

"Expose himself?"

She frowned with her meager out-of-place eyebrows. "You're drawing me out and making me say things I don't want to." She caught her breath. "I know, it must have been Peter. Was it?"

"I can't go into that."

"If it was Peter, he's even more helpless than I supposed. It was Peter, wasn't it? He's been threatening to hire detectives for some time. Peter is mad with jealousy, but I had no idea he'd go this far."

"This isn't very far. He asked me to look into the background of the man she's planning to marry. I suppose you know Francis Martel."

"I've met him, naturally. He's a fascinating person."

"No doubt. But something happened in the last hour which makes it seem worthwhile to investigate him. I saw it happen, in the road below his house. A man tried to take a picture of him. Martel scared him off with a gun. He threatened to kill him."

She nodded calmly. "I don't blame him at all."

"Does he make a habit of threatening to murder people?"

"It wouldn't be murder, it would be self-protection." She sounded as if she was quoting somebody else. "There are reasons for what you saw, I'm sure. He doesn't want his identity to be known."

"Do you know who he is?"

"I'm pledged to secrecy." She touched her red lips with a finger tipped with the same red.

"Who is he," I said, "the lost Dauphin of France?"

Without trying, I had succeeded in startling her. She stared at me with her mouth open. Then she remembered that it looked better closed, and closed it.

"I can't tell you who he is," she said after a while. "There could be very serious international repercussions if Francis were discovered here." Once again she seemed to be reciting. "I'm sure you mean well in what you're doing—I'm not so sure about Peter—but I'm going to ask you to cease and desist, Mr. Archer."

She wasn't kidding me now. Her voice was grave.

"Are you trying to tell me Martel is a political figure?"

"He was. He will be again, when the conditions are ripe. Right now he's an exile from his native country," she said dramatically.

"France?"

"He's a Frenchman, yes, he makes no secret of that."

"But his name isn't Francis Martel?"

"He has a right to use it, but it isn't his actual name."

"What is his name?"

"I don't know. But it's one of the great names of France."

"Do you have evidence to support all this?"

"Evidence?" she smiled at me as if she had superior knowledge piped in directly from the infinite. "You don't ask your friends for evidence."

"I do."

"Then you probably don't have many friends. I can see you have a suspicious nature. You and Peter Jamieson make a good pair."

"Have you known him long?"

I meant Martel, but she misunderstood my question, I think deliberately. "Peter has been underfoot in our house for twenty years." She gestured toward the rambling one-story house behind her. "I swear I've been wiping his nose for at least that long. When Peter's mother died, I sort of took him over for a while. He was just a little boy. But little boys grow up, and when he did he fell in love with Ginny, which he had no right to do. She doesn't care for Peter in that way, doesn't and didn't. He simply wore down her resistance because there was nobody else."

She sounded fond of Peter in spite of herself. I said so.

"Of course, you get fond of anyone if you see him every day for twenty years. Also I detest him, especially at the moment. My daughter has a brilliant chance. She's a beautiful girl"—she lifted her chin as if Ginny's beauty belonged to both of them, like a family heirloom—"and she deserves her chance. I don't want Peter, or you, fouling it up."

"I don't intend to foul anything up."

She sighed. "Can't I persuade you simply to drop it?"

"Not without some further checking."

"Will you promise me one thing then? Will you try to handle yourself without spoiling matters for Ginny? The thing she has with Francis Martel is very bright and shining, and very new. Don't tarnish it."

"I won't if it's real."

"It's real, believe me. Francis Martel worships the ground she walks on. And Virginia's quite mad about him."

I thought I could hear a self-fulfilling wish in what she said, and I threw her a curve:

"Is that why she went away for the weekend with him?"

Her blue eyes, impervious till now, winced away from mine. "You have no right to ask such questions. You're not a gentleman, are you?"

"But Martel is?"

"I've had about enough of you and your innuendos, Mr. Archer."
She stood up. It was a dismissal.

4
...

I WENT next door to the Jamieson house. It was a great Spanish
mansion, grimy white, which had the barren atmosphere of an
institution.

The woman who answered the door, after repeated ringing, wore
a striped gray dress which might have been a uniform but wasn't quite.
She was handsome and dark, with the slightly imperious look of the
only woman in a big house.

"You didn't have to keep ringing. I heard you the first time."

"Why didn't you answer the first time?"

"I've got better things to do than to answer the door," she said tartly.
"I was putting a goose in the oven." She looked down at her greasy
hands, and wiped them on her apron. "What did you want?"

"I'd like to see Peter Jamieson."

"Junior or senior?"

"Junior."

"He's probably still down at the Tennis Club. I'll ask his father."

"Maybe I could talk to Mr. Jamieson. My name is Archer."

"Maybe. I'll see."

I waited in the dim hallway on a high-backed Spanish chair which
Torquemada had made with his own hands. The housekeeper returned
eventually, and said with some surprise that Mr. Jamieson would see
me. She led me past closed oak doors to an oak-paneled library whose
deeply embrasured windows looked out on the mountains.

A man was sunk in an armchair by the windows, reading a book.
His hair was gray, and his face was very nearly the same colorless color.
When he took off his reading glasses and peered up at me, I could see
that his look was faint and faraway.

Half of a highball stood on a low table beside him, and close at hand on a larger table were a bottle of bourbon and a pitcher of water. I caught the housekeeper glaring at the highball and the bottle as if they represented everything she hated. She had violent black eyes, and she looked like a good hater.

"Mr. Archer," she said.

"Thank you, Vera. Hello, Mr. Archer. Sit down, here." He waved his hand at an armchair facing his. His hand was almost transparent against the light. "Would you like a drink before Vera goes?"

"Not so early in the day, thanks."

"I don't often drink so early myself." I noticed that the book in his hands was upside down. He hadn't wanted to be found just drinking. He closed the book and laid it on the table. "*The Book of the Dead*," he said. "Egyptian stuff. You may go, Vera. I'm perfectly competent to entertain Mr. Archer myself."

"Yessir," she said in a dubious voice, and went out closing the door sharply.

"Vera is a powerful woman," Jamieson said. "She's the bane of my existence, but also the blessing. I don't know how this household would function without her. She's been like a mother to my poor boy. My wife has been dead for many years, you know." The flesh around his eyes seemed to crumple, as if the blow of her death was about to fall again. He took a long sip of his highball to ward it off. "Sure you won't have a drink?"

"Not while I'm working."

"I understand you're working for my son. He asked my advice about hiring you. I told him to go ahead."

"I'm glad you know about it. I won't have to beat around the bush. Do you think Francis Martel is an impostor?"

"We all are, to some extent, wouldn't you say? Take me, for instance. I'm a solitary drinker, as you can see. The more I drink, the more sorely I am tempted to conceal it. The only way I can preserve any integrity at all is by drinking openly, and facing the music with Peter and of course with Vera."

"You got that off your chest," I said smiling, "but it doesn't tell me much about Martel."

"I don't know. Anything I've learned about people I've had to learn by examining myself. It's a slow painful process," he said with an inward look. "If Martel is an impostor, he's taking some big chances."

"Have you met him?"

"No. But sequestered as my life is, I do get bulletins from the world of men. Martel has aroused a good deal of local interest."

"What's the consensus?"

"There are two camps. There always are. That's the worst thing about democracy: there have to be two opinions about every issue." He talked like a man who needed a listener. "Those who know Martel and like him, mainly the women, accept him at his face value as a distinguished young Frenchman of independent means. Others think he's more or less a fraud."

"A con man?"

He raised his transparent hand. "Hardly that. There's not much question that he's a cultivated European."

"And no question that he has independent means?"

"I'm afraid not. I happen to know that his initial deposit at the local bank was in six figures."

"I understand you're on the board of the bank."

"So you've investigated *me*," he said with some resentment. "You do me too much honor."

"I got it accidentally from Mr. McMinn, when I cashed a check. Can you find out where Martel's money came from?"

"I suppose I can try."

"It could be borrowed money," I said. "I've known con men who used borrowed money, sometimes borrowed from gangsters, to get local status quickly."

"For what possible purpose?"

"I know of one who bought a municipal bus system on terms, cannibalized it, then moved out and left it bankrupt. In the last few years they've even been buying banks."

"Martel hasn't been buying anything that I know of."

"Except Virginia Fablon."

Jamieson wrinkled his forehead. He picked up his highball, saw that it was nearly gone, and got up to make himself another. He was tall, but thin and frail. He moved like an old man, but I suspected he wasn't much older than I was—fifty at most.

When he'd made his fresh drink and comforted himself with part of it and resettled himself in his leather armchair, I said:

"Does Ginny have money?"

"Hardly enough to interest a confidence man. She isn't a girl who needs money to interest any kind of a man—in fact she's probably turned down more advances than most young women dream of. Frankly, I was surprised when she accepted Peter, and not so very surprised when she broke the engagement. I tried to tell him that last night. It was safe enough when they were high school kids. But a beautiful young wife can be a curse to an ordinary man, especially if he loses her." The flesh around his eyes was crumpling again. "It's dangerous to get what you want, you know. It sets you up for tragedy. But my poor son can't see that. Young people can't learn from the misfortunes of their elders."

He was becoming faintly garrulous. Looking past him at the mountains, I had a feeling of unreality, as if the sunlit world had moved back out of reach.

"We were talking about the Fablons and their money."

Jamieson visibly pulled himself together. "Yes, of course. They can't have a great deal. The Fablons did have money at one time, but Roy gambled a lot of it away. The rumor was that that was one reason he committed suicide. Fortunately Marietta has her own small private income. They have enough to live comfortably, but as I said, certainly not enough to tempt a fortune-hunter. Let alone a fortune-hunter with a hundred thousand dollars in cash of his own."

"Is a hundred grand in the bank all that Martel would need to get into the club?"

"The Tennis Club? Certainly not. You have to be sponsored by at least one member and passed on by the membership committee."

"Who sponsored him?"

"Mrs. Bagshaw, I believe. It's a common enough practice, when members lease their houses in town here. It's nothing against the tenant."

"And nothing in his favor. Do you accept the idea that Martel is some kind of political refugee?"

"He may very well be. Frankly, I didn't discourage Peter from hiring you because I'd like to satisfy my curiosity. And I'd also like him to get this business of Ginny out of his system. It's hurting him more than you perhaps realize. I'm his father, and I can see it. I may not be much of a father to him, but I do know my son. And I know Ginny, too."

"You don't want Ginny as a daughter-in-law?"

"On the contrary. She'd brighten any house, even this one. But I'm very much afraid she doesn't love my poor son. I'm afraid she agreed to marry him because she felt sorry for him."

"Mrs. Fablon said very much the same thing."

"So you've talked to Marietta?"

"A little."

"She's a much more serious woman than she pretends. So is Ginny. Ginny has always been a very serious young woman, even when she was a child. She used to sit in my study here whole weekends at a time, reading the books."

"*The Book of the Dead?*"

"I wouldn't be at all surprised."

"You mentioned that her father committed suicide."

"Yes." Jamieson stirred uneasily, and reached for his highball, as if the little death it provided was homeopathic medicine against the big one waiting. "The decimation among my friends these last ten years has been horrendous. Not to mention my enemies."

"Which was Roy Fablon, friend or enemy?"

"Roy was a friend, a very good friend at one time. Of course I disapproved of what he did to his wife and daughter. Ginny was only sixteen or seventeen at the time, and it hit her hard."

"What did he do?"

"Walked into the ocean with his clothes on one night. They found his body about ten days later. The sharks had been at it, and he was scarcely identifiable." He passed his hand over his gray face, and took a long drink.

"Did you see the body?"

"Yes. They made me look at it. It was a very humiliating experience."

"Humiliating?"

"It's dreadful to realize how mortal we are, and what time and tide will do to us. I can remember Roy Fablon when he was one of the best-looking men at Princeton, and one of the finest athletes."

"You knew him at Princeton?"

"Very well. He was my roommate. I was really the one who brought him out here to Montevista."

I rose to leave, but he held me at the door. "There's something I should ask you, Mr. Archer. How well do you know Montevista? I don't mean topographically. Socially."

"Not well. It's rich for my blood."

"There's something I should tell you, then, as an old Montevista hand. Almost anything can happen here. Almost everything has. It's partly the champagne climate and partly, to be frank, the presence of inordinate amounts of money. Montevista's been an international watering resort for nearly a century. Deposed maharajahs rub shoulders with Nobel prize-winners and Chicago meat packers' daughters marry the sons of South American billionaires.

"In this context, Martel isn't so extraordinary. In fact when you compare him with some of our Montevista denizens, he's quite routine. You really should bear that in mind."

"I'll try to."

I thanked him and left.

5
...

THE HEAT of the day was waning with the sun. Approaching the Tennis Club, I could feel a cool wind from the ocean on my face. The flag on top of the main building was whipping.

The woman at the front desk informed me that Peter was probably in the showers. She'd seen him come up from the beach a few minutes ago. I could go in and wait for him by the pool.

The lifeguard's blue canvas chair was unoccupied, and I sat in it. The afternoon wind had driven away most of the sun-bathers. On the far side of the pool, in a sheltered corner behind a plate-glass screen, four white-haired ladies were playing cards with the grim concentration of bridge players. The three fates plus one, I thought, wishing there was someone I could say it to.

A large boy in trunks who didn't look like a possible audience came out of the dressing rooms. He disposed his statuesque limbs on the tile deck near me. His smooth simple face was complicated by a certain wildness of the eye. His blond head had not been able to resist the bleach bottle. I noticed that his hair was wet and striated as if he had just been combing it.

"Is Peter Jamieson inside?"

"Yeah. He's getting dressed. You got my chair, but that's all right. I can sit here." He patted the tiles beside him. "You a guest of his?"

"I'm just meeting him here."

"He was running on the beach. I told him he better take it easy. You got to work up to it."

"But you have to start somewhere."

"I guess so. I don't run much, myself. It wears down the muscles." With quiet pride, he glanced down at his bronze pectorals. "I like to look like a typical California lifeguard."

"You do."

"Thank you," he said. "I put a lot of time and work into it. Like surfing. I took this job here on account of the surfing opportunities. I go to college, too," he added.

"What college?"

"Montevista State College. The one here."

"Who runs the French department?"

"I wouldn't know. I'm studying business ad and real estate. Very interesting." He reminded me of the dumb blondes who had cluttered up the California landscape when I was his age. Now a lot of them were boys. "You planning to study French, mister?"

"I just want to get the answers to a few questions."

"Maybe Mr. Martel could help you. He's a Frenchman."

"Is he here?"

"Yeah. I just been talking to him—he talks English, too, just like you and I."

He pointed toward the second-floor cabana nearest the sea. Through its open front I could see a man moving in the shadow of the awning. He was carrying a multicolored armful.

"He's moving his things out," the lifeguard said. "I offered to help him but he didn't want me messing with his personal stuff."

"Is he leaving?"

"He's giving up the cabana, anyway. The beauty of it is, he said I could have the furniture he bought for it. It's outdoor furniture but it's practically brand new and it must of cost him a fortune. It'll look swell in my apartment. All I have is a sleeping bag right now. All my money goes to keep up the cars."

"Cars?"

"I have a wagon for surfing," he said. "And me and my buddy have a sports car for out-of-town trips. You can save a lot of time with a sports car."

The boy was driving me crazy. The trouble was that there were thousands of him, neo-primitives who didn't seem to belong in the modern world. But it came to me with a jolt that maybe they were better adapted to it than I was. They could live like happy savages on the beach while computers and computer-jockeys did most of the work and made all the decisions.

"Why is Mr. Martel moving out of the cabana? It looks like a good one."

"The best. You can see down the coast as far as the surfing reef." He flung out his muscled arm. "Mr. Martel used to sit there and watch us surfing. He told me once he did some surfing himself in his younger days."

"Did he say where?"

"On that same reef, I think."

"Has he been here before?"

"I wouldn't know about that. Not in my time, anyway."

"And you don't know why he's leaving the cabana?"

"He didn't like it here. He was always complaining about something, like the water in the pool being fresh—he thought it should be salt. And he didn't get along with some of the members." The boy fell silent. His mind rubbed two facts together and struck a brief spark. "Listen, don't tell Peter Jamieson that Mr. Martel is giving me his furniture. He wouldn't like it."

"Why not?"

"He's one of the ones that didn't get along with Mr. Martel. A couple of times they almost had a fight."

"Over Ginny Fablon?"

"I guess you know all about it, eh?"

"No, I don't."

"I better not tell you, anyway. Peter Jamieson will find out and I get called on the rug for talking about the members."

He was embarrassed by all the talking he had already done. One of the bridge players rescued him from my questions. She called across the pool:

"Stan, will you bring us four coffees? Black?"

He rose and trudged away.

I put on sunglasses and in their sudden twilight climbed the wooden stairs to the second-floor deck and walked along it to the end. A rattan table in the middle of Martel's cabana was piled with things: bathing suits and robes and beach outfits for both men and women, flippers and masks, bottles of bourbon and brandy, a small electric heater, a bamboo cane. Martel came out of one of the two inner dressing rooms carrying a miniature television set which he put on the table.

"Moving out?"

He looked up sharply. Now I was wearing sunglasses and he wasn't. His eyes were very dark and bright, focusing the dark-bright intensity of his face. He had a long nose, slightly curved, which appeared both self-assertive and inquisitive. He didn't appear to recognize me.

"What if I am?" he said in a guarded tone.

"I thought I might take it over."

"That won't be possible. I have it leased for the season."

"But you're not going to use it."

"I haven't made up my mind yet."

He was talking to himself more than to me. His dark gaze had moved past me down the coast. I turned and followed it. A blue wave crumbled white on the reef. Further out a dozen boys knelt on their boards like worshippers.

"Ever do any surfing?"

"No."

"Skin diving? I notice you have some equipment there."

"Yes, I've done some skin diving."

I was listening carefully to him. He still had an accent but it was much less pronounced than in the argument with Harry Hendricks, and he wasn't using any French words. Of course he was less excited now.

"Ever try skin diving in the Mediterranean? They say skin diving originated in the Mediterranean."

"It did and I have," he said. "I happen to be a native of France."

"What part?"

"Paris."

"That's interesting. I was in Paris during the war."

"A great many Americans were," he answered dryly. "Now if you will excuse me I have to dispose of these things."

"Can I help?"

"No. Thank you. Good day."

He bowed curtly. I wandered away along the deck, trying to analyze my impression of him. His tar-black hair and smooth solid face and the unblunted sharpness of his eyes placed his age at not more than thirty. He had the controlled force and reticence of an older man. I didn't know what to make of him.

I found my way into the labyrinth of the downstairs dressing rooms. School was out by now and a gang of small boys were snapping towels at each other's legs and emitting shouts of menace and horrible laughter. I told them to shut up. They waited until I was out of sight, and laughed more horribly than they had before.

Peter was tying his tie in front of a steam-fogged mirror. He caught a glimpse of me in it and turned with a smile, the first I'd seen on his face. He was shiny and red.

"I didn't know you were here. I was running on the beach."

"Good," I said. "I've just been talking to Martel. He's moving the stuff out of his cabana. He may be planning to skip."

"With Ginny?"

"I didn't think I'd better ask him that. Under ordinary circumstances I wouldn't have approached him at all. It's not a good way to operate. But we may be running short of time."

I'd wiped out Peter's smile and started him biting his mouth. "I was hoping you could do something to stop him."

"I haven't quit. The trouble is I don't know what questions to ask. I've never been to France, and I don't remember much of my high school French."

"Neither do I. I took a freshman course from Professor Tappinger, but he flunked me."

"Was this at the local college?"

"Yes." He felt called upon to explain that he had been supposed to go to Princeton, and failed to make the grade. "But I did graduate from Montevista State last year."

"And Ginny was supposed to graduate this year?"

"Yes. She took a couple of years out. She was a receptionist at Dr. Sylvester's clinic, but she got sick of that and went back to school last year."

"Was your man Tappinger one of her professors?"

"He taught most of her French courses."

"Is Tappinger good at his subject?"

"Ginny thought so, and she was one of his best students."

"Then he should be willing to help us out."

I told Peter to make an appointment with the professor, for this afternoon if possible, and said I would meet him in the parking lot. I didn't want Martel to see us leaving together.

6
· · ·

"Mr. Jamieson just left," the woman at the front desk said. "I don't know how you missed him."

She had a gently modulated voice, and she sounded really concerned. I took a closer look at her. She was a subdued young woman dressed in a brown tweed suit. Her dark hair framed an oval, piquant face. She was too heavily made up, but that was occupational.

"I talked to Mr. Jamieson inside, but don't mention it to anyone."

"Why should I mention it to anyone?" she said.

"Somebody might ask you."

"I never discuss the goings and comings of the members and their guests. Besides, I don't remember your name."

"Archer. Lew Archer."

"I'm Ella Strome." The nameplate on the desk in front of her said: Mrs. Strome, Club Secretary. She saw me looking at it and added in a neutral tone: "I'm not married at present."

"Neither am I. What time do you get off for dinner?"

"Tonight I don't. We're having a dinner-dance. But thank you."

"Don't mention it."

In the parking lot by the tennis courts, Peter was waiting for me in his Corvette. The place was surrounded by massed green clouds of eucalyptus trees, and their faintly medicinal scent flavored the air. Only one of the half-dozen courts was in use: a pro in a "Tennis Club" sweatshirt was showing a very small girl how to serve, while her mother watched from the sidelines.

"Professor Tappinger isn't in his office and he isn't at home," Peter said. "His wife said he should be on his way home."

"I can use a little more time here. I understand Mrs. Bagshaw lives at the club."

"She's in one of the cottages." He gestured toward the trees at the back of the lot.

"Have you asked her any questions about Martel?"

"No."

"But you know Mrs. Bagshaw?"

"Not that well. I know everyone in Montevista," he added without enthusiasm. "And they know me, I guess."

I went through the eucalyptus grove and through a gate in a picket fence which enclosed an expanse of lawn next to the pool enclosure. A dozen or so gray-painted brick cottages were dispersed around the lawn, shielded from their neighbors by patio walls and flowering shrubs. A small Mexican in a khaki coverall was manipulating a hose among the shrubbery.

"*Buenos días.*"

"It is a fine day," he said with a white flash of teeth, and turned the stream from his hose toward the sky, like a fountain. "You looking for somebody?"

"Mrs. Bagshaw."

"That's her cottage there." Its roof was half-hidden by a purple avalanche of bougainvillea. "She just came back a couple of minutes ago."

Mrs. Bagshaw turned out to be one of the poolside bridge players, the one who had ordered the coffee. She was an alert-looking seventy or so.

"Didn't I see you talking to Stanley just now?" she asked me at the door.

"I was, yes."

"And then to Mr. Martel?"

"Yes."

"And now you come to me. It's an interesting progression." She shook her white curls. "I don't know whether to be flattered or discomfited."

"Don't be either, Mrs. Bagshaw. My name is Archer, and I'm a detective, as you may have guessed."

She let me into a sitting room which contained too much furniture. The Oriental rug on the floor was so good I hated to step on it. She noticed my noticing it.

"It doesn't go with this place at all. But I couldn't bear to leave it behind." Without changing her tone, she said: "Sit down. I suppose you're engaged in the current village sport of prying into Francis Martel's affairs."

"It's my profession, not my sport."

"Who brought you here?" she said brusquely.

"A local family."

"Marietta Fablon?"

"She's interested in the outcome of my researches, yes."

"Researches is a glossy word for what you do, Mr. Archer. You're driving Mr. Martel out of town. Is that your purpose?"

"No."

"I wonder about that. He's leaving, you know. He told me so not fifteen minutes ago."

"Is Ginny Fablon going with him?"

She lowered her eyes to her lap. "Miss Fablon was not discussed. She is in any case a young woman of twenty-four—at her age I had been married for five years—and she's perfectly capable of looking after herself and making her own choices." Her voice, which had faltered for a moment, regained its strength. "More capable than most young women, in my opinion."

"So you think she's going with him."

"I don't know. But this is a free country, I believe."

"It is for people who know what and who they're dealing with. You can't make valid choices without facts."

She shook her curls. Her face remained unshaken, like cement. "I don't wish to be lectured at. I brought Francis Martel into Montevista—ah—circles, and I feel perfectly sanguine about doing so. I like him. It's true I can't provide you with a copy of his genealogical tree. But I'm sure it's a good one. He's one of the most distinguished young Frenchmen of my acquaintance."

"He is a Frenchman, then?"

"Is there any doubt of that?"

"There's always doubt, until the facts are established."

"And you are the great arbiter of the facts, are you?"

"In my own investigations I naturally tend to be."

It was a fairly sharp interchange, and it made her angry. She resolved her anger by laughing out loud at me. "You talk up, don't you?"

"I might as well. I'm not getting anywhere anyway."

"That's because there's nowhere to get. Merely because Mr. Martel doesn't look like other people, they assume there's some dark secret in his past. The trouble with my neighbors is a simple one. They haven't enough to do, and they live like the Scilly islanders by taking in each other's dirty linen. If there isn't enough dirty linen to go around, they manufacture it."

She must be uncertain, I thought, or she wouldn't be talking so much and so well. Martel was in some degree her responsibility. She said into the silence between us:

"Have you found out anything against him?"

"Not really. Not yet."

"You imply that you expect to."

"I don't know. How did you become acquainted with him, through a real-estate broker?"

"Oh no, we have friends in common."

"Here in Montevista?"

"In Washington," she said, "more precisely, in Georgetown. General Bagshaw and I once lived in Georgetown."

"And you met Martel there?"

"I didn't say that. He knew some old neighbors of ours—" She hesitated, looking at me doubtfully. "I don't believe I ought to give you their name."

"It would help if you did."

"No. They're very fine and gentle people, and I don't want them bothered with this sort of thing."

"Martel used them as a reference. They might not approve of that. They may not even know him."

"I'm sure they do."

"Did they give him a letter of introduction?"

"No."

"Then all you have is his word?"

"It seems—it seemed to be enough. He talked very freely and fully about them." But the doubt with which she regarded me was spreading and deepening, undercutting her confidence in her own judgment. "Do you seriously believe he's some sort of an impostor?"

"My mind is open on the subject. I'm trying to open yours."

"And pry a name out of me," she said rather grimly.

"I don't need the name if you'll help."

"How can I help?"

"Call your Georgetown friends and ask them what they know about Martel."

She lifted her head. "I may do that."

"Please do. They're the only real lead I have."

"I will. Tonight."

"May I check with you later then?"

"I suppose you may."

"I'm sorry if I've upset you."

"You haven't. It's the moral question, really. Did I do right or wrong? Of course if we stopped to consider the possible consequences of everything we do, we'd end up doing nothing."

"How soon is he leaving?"

"Immediately, I think. Today or tomorrow."

"Did he say why?"

"No. He's very reticent. But I know why. Everyone's suspicious of him. He's made no friends here."

"Except Ginny."

"He didn't mention her."

"Or say where he was going?"

"No."

7
...

PETER MET me at the gate in the picket fence. Professor Tappinger was home now, and would see us.

He lived in the adjoining harbor city, in a rather rundown tract whose one obvious advantage was a view of the ocean. The sun, heavy and red, was almost down on the horizon now. Its image floated like spilled fire on the water.

The Tappinger house was a green stucco cottage which except for its color duplicated every third house in the block. The cement walk which led up to the front door was an obstacle course of roller skates, a bicycle, a tricycle. A girl of six or seven answered the door. She had a dutch bob and enormous watching eyes.

"Daddy says that you can join him in the study."

She led us through the trampled-looking living room into the kitchen. A woman was bowed over the sink in a passive-aggressive attitude, peeling potatoes. A boy of about three was butting her in the legs and chortling. She paid no attention to him and very little to us. She was a good-looking woman, no more than thirty, with a youthful ponytail, and blue eyes which passed over me coolly.

"He's in the study," she said, and gestured with one elbow toward a door.

It let us into a converted garage lined with bookshelves. A fluorescent fixture hung on a chain over a work table cluttered with open books and papers. The professor was seated there with his back to us. He didn't turn around when Peter spoke to him. The implication seemed to be that we were interrupting important brainwork.

"Professor Tappinger?" Peter said again.

"I hear you." His voice was impatient. "Excuse me for another minute, please. I'm trying to finish a sentence."

He scratched at his head with the blunt end of his pen, and jotted something down. His coppery brown hair had a frost of gray at the edges. I saw when he eventually got up that he was a short man, and at least ten years older than his handsome wife. He had probably been handsome, too, with his sensitive mouth and clean features. But he looked as if he had had a recent illness, and the eyes behind his reading glasses were haunted by the memory of it. His handshake was cold.

"How are you, Mr. Archer? How are you, Peter? Forgive me for keeping you waiting. I snatch these precious moments of concentration from the Bergsonian flux. With a twelve-hour teaching load and all the preparation it entails, it isn't easy to get anything written. I envy Flaubert the luxury he had of spending whole days in search of the right word, *le mot juste*—"

Tappinger seemed to have the professional habit of nonstop talking. I interrupted him: "What are you working on?"

"A book, if I can ever get the time to do it. My subject is the French influence on modern American literature—at the moment I'm studying the vexed question of Stephen Crane. But that wouldn't interest you. Peter tells me you're a detective."

"Yes. I'm trying to get some information about a man named Francis Martel. Have you run into him?"

"I doubt it, but his name is certainly interesting. It's one of the ancient names of France."

"Martel is supposed to be a Frenchman. His story is that he's a political refugee."

"How old is he?"

"About thirty." I described him: "He's a man of medium height, trim and fast on his feet. Black hair, black eyes, dark complexion. He has a French accent which varies from strong to weak."

"And you think he's putting it on?"

"I don't know. If he's a phony, he's fooled quite a few people. I'm trying to find out who and what he really is."

"Reality is an illusive thing," Tappinger said sententiously. "What do you want me to do—listen to his French and pronounce on its authenticity?"

He was only half-serious, but I answered him seriously: "That might be a good idea, if we could work it out. But Martel is on the point of leaving town. I thought if you could provide me with a few questions that only an educated Frenchman could answer—"

"You wish me to prepare a test, is that it?"

"With the answers."

"I suppose I can do that. When do you need it? Tomorrow?"

"Right now."

"That's simply impossible."

"But he may be leaving any minute."

"I can't help that!" Tappinger's voice had risen womanishly. "I have forty papers to read tonight—those bureaucrats at the college don't even provide me with a student reader. I have no time for my own children—"

I said: "Okay, we'll skip it. It wasn't a very good idea in the first place."

"But we have to do something," Peter said. "I'll be glad to pay you for your time, professor."

"I don't want your money. All I want is the free use of my own days." Tappinger was practically wailing.

His wife opened the kitchen door and looked out. Her face was set in a look of concern which somehow gave the impression that it had been blunted by use.

"What's the trouble, Daddy?"

"Nothing, and don't call me Daddy. I'm not that much older than you are."

She lifted and dropped one shoulder in a gesture of physical contempt, and looked at me. "Is something the matter out here?"

"We seem to be getting on your husband's nerves. This wasn't a good time to come."

Tappinger said to his wife in a quieter tone: "It's nothing that need concern you, Bess. I'm supposed to prepare some questions to test a certain man's knowledge of French."

"Is that all?"

"That's all."

She closed the kitchen door. Tappinger turned to us: "Forgive the elevation of the voice. I've got a headache." He pressed his hand to his pale rounded forehead. "I suppose I can do this work for you now —I've expended twice the energy just talking about it—but I don't understand the hurry."

Peter said: "Martel is taking Ginny with him. We have to stop him."

"Ginny?" Tappinger looked puzzled.

"I thought you told him about her," I said to Peter.

"I tried to, on the phone, but he wouldn't listen." He turned back to Tappinger. "You remember Virginia Fablon, professor."

"Naturally I do. Is she involved in this?"

"Very much so. She says she intends to marry Martel."

"And you're in love with her yourself, is that it?"

Peter blushed. "Yes, but I'm not doing this merely for selfish reasons. Ginny doesn't realize the mess she's getting into."

"Have you talked to her about it?"

"I've tried to. But she's infatuated with Martel. He was the reason she dropped out of school last month."

"Really? I thought she was ill. That was the word that went around the college."

"There's nothing the matter with her," Peter said. "Except him."

"What's her opinion of his Frenchness?"

"She's completely taken in," Peter said.

"Then he probably is French. Miss Fablon has a fair grasp of the language."

"He could be both a Frenchman and a phony," I said. "We're really trying to find out if he's the cultivated aristocrat he pretends to be."

For the first time Tappinger really looked interested. "That should be possible. Let me try." He sat down at his cluttered table and picked up his pen. "Just give me ten minutes, gentlemen."

We retreated to the living room. Mrs. Tappinger followed us from the kitchen, trailed by the three-year-old.

"Is Daddy all right?" she asked me in a little-girl voice so thin and sweet it sounded like self-parody.

"I think so."

"He hasn't been well, ever since last year. They turned him down for his full professorship. It was a terrible disappointment to him. He tends to take it out on—well, anybody available. Especially me." She made her shoulder gesture. This time her contempt seemed to be for herself.

"Please," Peter said in embarrassment. "Professor Tappinger has already apologized."

"That's good. He usually doesn't. Especially when his own family is involved."

She meant herself. In fact it was herself she wanted to talk about, and it was me she wanted to talk about herself to. Her body leaning in the doorway, the blue side glances of her eyes, the drooping movements of her mouth more than the words it uttered, said that she was a sleeping beauty imprisoned in a tract house with a temperamental professor who had failed to be promoted.

The three-year-old butted at her, pressing her cotton dress tight between her round thighs.

"You're a pretty girl," I said, with Peter standing there as a chaperone.

"I used to be prettier—twelve years ago when I married him." She gestured with her hip. Then she picked up the child and carried him into the kitchen like a penitential burden.

A married woman with young children wasn't exactly my dish, but she interested me. I looked around her living room. It was shabby, with a worn rug and beat-up maple furniture. The walls were virtually papered with Post-Impressionist reproductions, visions of an ideally brilliant world.

The sunset at the window competed in brilliance with the Van Goghs and the Gauguins. The sun burned like a fire ship on the water, sinking slowly till only a red smoke was left trailing up the sky. A fishing boat was headed into the harbor, black and small against the enormous west. Above its glittering wake a few gulls whirled like sparks which had gone out.

"I'm worried about Ginny," Peter said at my shoulder.

I was worried, too, though I didn't say so. The sudden moment when Martel pulled a gun on Harry Hendricks, which hadn't seemed quite real at the time, was real in my memory now. Beside it the idea of testing Martel in French seemed faintly preposterous.

A redheaded boy about eleven came in the front door. He tramped importantly into the kitchen and announced to his mother that he was going next door to watch some television.

"No you're not." Her sharp maternal tone was quite different from the one she had used on her husband and me. "You're staying right here. It's nearly dinnertime."

"I'm starved," Peter said to me.

The boy asked his mother why they didn't have a television set.

"Two reasons. We've been into them before. One, your father doesn't approve of television. Two, we can't afford it."

"You're always buying books and records," the boy said. "Television is better than books and records."

"Is it?"

"Much better. When I have my own house I'm going to have color television in every room. And you can come and watch it," he concluded grandly.

"Maybe I will at that."

The door to the garage study opened, ending the interchange. Professor Tappinger came into the living room waving a sheet of paper in each hand.

"The questions and the answers," he said. "I've devised five questions which a well-educated Frenchman should be able to answer. I don't think anyone else could, except possibly a graduate student of French. The answers are simple enough so that you can check them without having to know too much French."

"That's good. Let's hear them, Professor."

He read aloud from his sheets: "One. Who wrote the original *Les Liaisons dangereuses* and who made the modernized film version? Choderlos de Laclos wrote the original, and Roger Vadim made the movie.

"Two. Complete the phrase: '*Hypocrite lecteur . . .*' Answer: *Hypocrite lecteur, mon semblable, mon frère*—from the opening poem of Baudelaire's *Fleurs du mal*.

"Three. Name a great French painter who believed Dreyfus was guilty. Answer: Degas.

"Four. What gland did Descartes designate as the residence of the human soul? Answer: the pineal gland.

"Five. Who was mainly responsible for getting Jean Genet released from prison? Answer: Jean-Paul Sartre. Is this the sort of thing you had in mind?"

"Yes, but the emphasis seems to be a little one-sided. Shouldn't there be something about politics or history?"

"I disagree. If this man is an impostor passing himself off as a political refugee, the first thing he'd bone up on would be history and politics. My questions are subtler, and they cover a range that it would take years to bone up on." His eye brightened. "I wish I could put them to him myself."

"I wish you could, too. But it might be dangerous."

"Really?"

"Martel pulled a gun on another man today. I think you'd better let me go up against him."

"And me," Peter said. "I insist on going along."

Tappinger followed us out to our cars, as if to make up for his earlier impatience. I thought of offering him money for his work, five or ten dollars, but decided not to risk it. It might only remind him that he needed money and make him angry again.

8

I FOLLOWED Peter's Corvette inland into the foothills. Their masses had been half-absorbed by the blue darkness of the mountains. A few lights, bright as evening stars, were scattered up their slopes. One of them shone from Martel's house.

Peter stopped just short of the mailbox. The name stenciled on it stood out black in his headlights: Major General Hiram Bagshaw, U.S.A. (ret.). He cut the lights and started to get out.

The quiet of the evening shivered like a crystal. A high thin quavering cry came down from the direction of the house. It might have been a peacock, or a girl screaming.

Peter ran toward me. "It's Ginny! Did you hear her?"

"I heard something."

I tried to persuade him to wait in his car. But he insisted on riding up to the house with me.

It was a massive stone-and-glass building set on a pad which had been excavated above the floor of the canyon. A floodlight above the door illuminated the flagstone courtyard where the Bentley was parked. The door itself was standing open.

Peter started in. I held him back. "Take it easy. You'll get yourself shot."

"She's my girl," he said, in the teeth of all the evidence so far.

The girl appeared in the doorway. She had on a gray suit, the kind women use for traveling. Her movements seemed shaky and her eyes a little dull, as if she had already traveled too far and too fast.

Perhaps it was the brilliant light shining down on her face, but its skin appeared grayish and grainy. She had the sort of beauty—shape of head, slant of cheekbone and chin, curve of mouth—that made these other things irrelevant.

She held herself on the concrete stoop with a kind of forlorn elegance. Peter went to her and tried to put his arm around her. She disengaged herself.

"I told you not to come here."

"That was you screaming, wasn't it? Did he hurt you?"

"Don't be silly. I saw a rat." She turned her lusterless eyes on me. "Who are you?"

"My name is Archer. Is Mr. Martel home?"

"Not to you, I'm afraid."

"Tell him I'm here, anyway. All I want is a chance to talk to him."

She said to Peter: "Please go. Take your friend with you. You have no right to interfere with us." She managed to produce a little spurt of anger: "Go away now or I'll never speak to you again."

His large face contorted itself in the light, as if it could transform its homeliness by sheer expression. "I wouldn't care, Ginny, as long as you were safe."

"I'm perfectly safe with my husband," she said, and waited demurely for his surprise.

"You married him?"

"We were married on Saturday and I've never been happier in my life," she said without any visible sign of happiness.

"You can get it annulled."

"You don't seem to understand, I love my husband." Her voice was soft but there was a sting in the words which made him wince. "Francis is everything I've ever dreamed of in a man. You can't change that, and please stop trying."

"Thank you, *ma chérie*."

It was Martel, with his accent full on. No doubt he had been listening for an entrance cue. He appeared in the hallway behind Ginny and took hold of her upper arm. His hand against her light gray sleeve looked almost as dark as a mourning band.

Peter began to bite his mouth. I moved closer to him. Whether he was a French aristocrat or a cheap crook or a muddy mixture of the two, Ginny's husband would be a dangerous man to hit.

"Congratulations on your marriage," I said without much irony.

He bowed, touching his chest. "*Merci beaucoup*."

"Where were you married?"

"In the chambers of a judge, by the judge himself. That makes it legal, I believe."

"I meant what place."

"The place doesn't matter. Life has its private occasions, you know, and I confess to a passion for privacy. Which my dear wife shares." He smiled down into her face. His smile had changed when he looked up at me. It was wide and mocking. "Didn't we meet at the swimming pool today?"

"We did."

"This man was here before," Ginny said, "when the fellow tried to take your picture. I saw him in the fellow's car."

Martel stepped around his wife and came toward me. I wondered if his little gun was going to come into play. I also wondered what dark liquid had left a partial heelprint on the concrete stoop. More of it glistened on the heel of Martel's right shoe.

"Just who are you, *m'sieu*? And what gives you the right to ask questions?"

I told him my name. "I'm a detective, and I'm hired to ask them."

"Hired by this one here?" He gave Peter a black look of contempt.

"That's right," Peter said. "And we're going to keep after you until we know what you want."

"But I have what I want." He turned to Ginny with his arm stretched out. It was just a little like a scene from opera, more light than grand. Next minute the merry villagers would troop in for the nuptial dance.

I said to fend them off: "One question that interests me at the moment—is that blood on your heel?"

He looked down at his feet, then quickly back to me. "I expect it is blood."

Ginny's curled fingers had gone to her mouth, both hands, as if another peacock cry was surging up in her throat. Martel said quietly and smoothly:

"My wife was alarmed by a rat, as she told you." He had been listening. "I killed it."

"With your heel?"

"Yes." He stamped on the asphalt. "I am a fencer, very fast on my feet."

"I bet you are. May I see the corpse?"

"It would be hard to find, perhaps impossible. I threw it into the undergrowth for the bobcats. We have wild animals up here in the hills, don't we, *ma chérie?*"

Ginny dropped her hands and said yes. She was looking at Martel with a combination of respect and fear. Perhaps it was a form of love, I thought, but not one of the usual forms. His voice filled the vacuum again:

"My wife and I are very fond of the wild animals."

"But not the rats."

"No. Not the rats." He offered me his wide cold grin. Above it his eyes and forceful nose seemed to be probing at me. "Can I persuade you to leave now, Mr. Archer? I've been quite patient with you and your questions. And please take this one with you." He jerked his head toward Peter as if the fat young man didn't quite belong to the human race.

Peter said: "Ask him the five questions, why don't you?"

Martel raised his eyebrows. "Five questions? About myself?"

"Not directly." Now that the time had come to ask the questions, they seemed childish, even ludicrous. The light-operatic note on which the scene had balanced was giving way to *opéra bouffe*. The courtyard under the light, surrounded by the amphitheater of the canyon, was like a stage where nothing real could happen.

I said reluctantly: "The questions are about French culture. I've been told that an educated Frenchman ought to be able to answer them."

"And you doubt that I am an educated Frenchman?"

"You have a chance to prove it once and for all. Will you take a stab at the questions?"

He shrugged. *"Pourquoi pas? Why not?"*

I got out two sheets of paper. "One. Who wrote the original *Les Liaisons dangereuses* and who made the modernized film version?"

"Les Liaisons dangereuses," he said slowly, correcting my pronunciation. "Choderlos de Laclos wrote the novel. Roger Vadim made the cinema version. I believe that Vadim collaborated with Roger Vailland on the screen play. Is that enough, or do you want me to outline the plot for you? It's quite complex, having to do with a diabolical sexual intrigue and the corruption of innocence." His voice was sardonic.

"We won't bother with that just now. Question two. Complete the phrase: *'Hypocrite lecteur—'* "

" 'Hypocrite lecteur, mon semblable, mon frère.' Hypocritical reader, my brother, my—*comment-à-dire?*—duplicate?" He appealed to Ginny.

"Mirror image," she said with a small half-smile. "It's from the front of *Les Fleurs du mal.*"

"I can recite many of those poems if you like," Martel said.

"That won't be necessary. Three. Name a great French painter who believed Dreyfus was guilty."

"Degas was the most prominent."

"Four. What gland did Descartes designate as the residence of the human soul?"

"The pineal gland." Martel smiled. "That's a rather obscure point, but it happens I read Descartes nearly every day of my life."

"Five. Who was mainly responsible for getting Jean Genet released from prison?"

"Jean-Paul Sartre, I suppose you mean. Cocteau and others also had a hand in the deliverance. Is that all?"

"That's all. You scored a hundred."

"Will you reward me now by disappearing?"

"Answer one more question, since you're so good at answering them. Who are you and what are you doing here?"

He stiffened. "I'm under no obligation to tell you."

"I thought you might want to lay the rumors to rest."

"Rumors don't bother me."

"But you're not the only person involved, now that you've married a local girl."

He saw my point. "Very well. I will tell you why I am here, in return for a *quid pro quo*. Tell me who is the man who tried to take my picture."

"His name is Harry Hendricks. He's a used-car salesman from the San Fernando Valley."

Martel's eyes were puzzled. "I never heard of him. Why did he try to photograph me?"

"Apparently someone paid him. He didn't say who."

"I can guess," Martel said darkly. "He was undoubtedly paid by the agents of *le grand Charles*."

"Who?"

"President de Gaulle, my enemy. He drove me out of my *patrie*— my native land. But my exile is not enough to satisfy him. He wants my life."

His voice was low and thrilling. Ginny shuddered. Even Peter looked impressed.

I said: "What has de Gaulle got against you?"

"I am a threat to his power."

"Are you one of the *Algérie-Française* gang?"

"We are not a gang," he retorted hotly. "We are a—how shall I say it?—a band of patriots. It is *le grand Charles* who is the enemy of his country. But I have said enough. Too much. If his agents have followed me here, as I believe, I must move on again."

He shrugged fatalistically, and looked around at the dark slopes and up at the star-pierced sky. It was a farewell look, consciously dramatic, as if the stars were part of his audience.

Ginny moved into the circle of his arm. "I'm going with you."

"Of course. I knew I would not be permitted to stay in Montevista. It is too beautiful. But I shall be taking a part of its beauty with me."

He kissed her hair. It hung sleek on her skull like a pale silk headcloth. She leaned against him. His hands went to her waist. Peter groaned and turned away toward my car.

"If you will excuse us now," Martel said to me, "we have plans to make. I've answered all your questions, have I not?"

"Just to nail it down, you could show me your passport."

He spread out his hands on either side of Ginny. "I wish I could, but I can't. I left France unofficially, shall we say?"

"How did you get your money out?"

"I had to leave much of it behind. But my family has holdings in other parts of the world."

"Is Martel your family name?"

He raised his hands, palms outward, like a man being held up. "My wife and I have been very patient with you. You don't want me to become impatient. Goodnight." He spoke quietly, with all his force poised behind the words.

They went into the house, closing the heavy front door. On the way to my car I glanced into the front of the Bentley. There was no registration card visible. The things which Martel had taken from his cabana were piled helter-skelter on the back seat. This suggested that he was planning to leave very soon.

There was nothing I could do about it. I got in beside Peter, and turned down the driveway. He rode with his head down, saying nothing. When I stopped at the mailbox, he turned to me in a sort of violent lunge:

"Do you believe him?"

"I don't know. Do you?"

"Ginny does," he said thoughtfully. "She knows him better than we do. He's very convincing."

"Too convincing. He has an answer for everything."

"Doesn't that mean that he's telling the truth?"

"He tells too much of it. A man in his position, wanted by the French government for plotting against de Gaulle, wouldn't spill his secrets to us. He wouldn't even tell his wife if he was smart. And Martel is smart."

"I can see that, the way he answered the professor's questions. What's the explanation, if he's lying? Who is he trying to fool?"

"Ginny, maybe. She married him."

Peter sighed. "I'm starved. I haven't really eaten since breakfast."

He climbed out of my car and started across the road to his Corvette. His foot kicked something which made a muted metallic noise. I peered out into the dark. It was the camera that Martel had smashed. I got out and picked it up and put it in my jacket pocket.

"What are you doing?" Peter said.

"Nothing. Poking around."

"I was just thinking, they're serving dinner at the club tonight. If you'll have dinner with me, we can discuss what to do."

I was getting a little tired of his mournful company. But I was hungry, too. "I'll meet you there."

9
· · ·

I WAS delayed on the way. A quarter of a mile down the road from Martel's driveway, a car was parked in the darkness under a live oak. Its lines resembled Harry Hendricks's Cadillac, and when I got out for a closer look with my flashlight, I saw that it was.

There was nobody in the decayed Cadillac, no registration on the steering post, and nothing in the dash compartment but a Los Angeles freeway map which was several years old and as obsolete as the Cadillac. Harry had probably borrowed the car from the used-car lot where he worked.

I lifted the hood and felt the engine. It was warm. I could imagine Harry skulking around in the brush near Martel's house. I thought of waiting for him, but my stomach decided against it. I could check on him later at the Breakwater Hotel.

I did call on Mrs. Bagshaw before dinner. I parked beside the deserted tennis courts and made my way through the dense gloom under the eucalyptus trees to her cottage. She appeared at the door in a stiff, rustling gown, with a rope of pearls lying cold on her crepe bosom.

"I was just about to go out. But I did make the call you suggested." It seemed to have upset her. Under her rouge, or because of it, she looked years older. She said without quite meeting my eyes, "My friends in Georgetown don't know Francis Martel, at least under that name. I can't understand it. He spoke of them with such zest and familiarity. He knew all about their house."

"He could have got that information from a servant."

"But he knows Washington," she said. "I couldn't be mistaken about that. And I'm still personally convinced he knows or knew the Plimsolls —my friends in Georgetown. Perhaps he knew them under another name than Francis Martel."

"That's possible, too. Did you describe him to them?"

"It was Colonel Plimsoll I talked to, and I did make some attempt to describe him, yes. But it's very difficult to describe someone, particularly these Latin types—they all look alike to me. The Colonel said if I could send him a picture of Martel—?"

"I'm sorry, I have no picture."

"Then I don't know what I can do." Her voice was apologetic, but there was an undertone of unwanted guilt which made it almost accusing: "I can't assume the responsibility for him, or for Miss Fablon. People have to look out for themselves in this world."

"The older ones try to look out for the younger ones, though."

"I brought up my own family," she said sharply, "sometimes under conditions which I would hesitate to describe. If Virginia made an unfortunate choice in men, it's hardly surprising. Her father did what he did when she was at a most vulnerable age. And even in life Roy Fablon was no great bargain." She shook her curls. "I'm expected for dinner now. You really must excuse me." The word had a double meaning. Excuse. Forgive.

I walked around the pool enclosure to the main clubhouse. A bevy of expensive-looking people went in ahead of me. From behind the front desk Ella Strome greeted each of them by name. But she seemed a little remote, consciously out of things.

"You look like a vestal virgin."

"I've been married twice," she said dryly. "Mr. Jamieson is expecting you in the dining room."

"Let him wait. I've only been married once."

"You're not doing your duty by American womanhood," she said with a smile which failed to touch her eyes.

"You sound as if you didn't enjoy being married."

"Being married was all right, it was the men I was married *to*. Do I project a maternal image or something?"

"No."

"I must. I seem to attract very peculiar types. Both of my husbands were peculiar types. It couldn't be pure chance. There aren't that many peculiar types."

"Yes, there are. Speaking of peculiar types, what's your opinion of Mr. Martel?"

"I have no particular opinion. He always treated me politely." Her hands came together on the polished black desk and pushed against each other, fingertip to fingertip. "Why don't you ask Mr. Stoll about him? He had a run-in with him, I believe."

"Who's Mr. Stoll?"

"The manager of the club."

I found him in the office behind the reception desk. The walnut-paneled walls were hung with photographs of parties and tennis matches and other sporting events. Stoll looked like a non-participant. He was a handsome cold-eyed man of forty, overdressed, with the little graces of a pleaser and a pleaser's lack of resonance. The nameplate on his desk said: "Reto Stoll, Manager."

He became quite cordial when I told him I was working for the Jamiesons. "Sit down, Mr. Archer." He had a faint German accent. "What can I do for you?"

I sat facing him across his desk. "Mrs. Strome said you had some trouble with Martel."

"A little, yes. But it's in the past. Let bygones be bygones, particularly since Mr. Martel is leaving us."

"Is he leaving because of the trouble with you?"

"Partly, I suppose. I didn't ask him to leave on account of it. On the other hand I didn't urge him to stay when he finally announced his intention of leaving. I breathed a sigh of relief when he turned in his keys today and paid his bill." Stoll spread his manicured hand on the front of his double-breasted waistcoat.

"Why?"

"The man was a volcano. He could erupt at any moment. We like a quiet friendly atmosphere in our club."

"Tell me about the trouble you had with him. It may be important. What did he do?"

"He offered to kill me. Do you want the whole story from the beginning?"

"Please."

"It happened several weeks ago. Mr. Martel ordered a drink brought up to his cabana. Absinthe. The bar-boy was busy so I took it up myself. I sometimes do that as a special courtesy. Miss Fablon was with him. They were talking in French. Since French is one of my native

languages I hesitated behind the screen and listened. I wasn't consciously eavesdropping." Stoll raised his eyes to the ceiling, virtuously.
"But he appeared to think that I was spying on him. He jumped up and
attacked me."

"With his fists?"

"With a sword." His hand went down his body to his stomach. "He
had a sword concealed in a bamboo cane."

"I've seen the cane. Did he actually stick you?"

"He held the point of it to my body." Stoll fondled the precious curve
of his belly through his striped pants. "Fortunately Miss Fablon got him
calmed down, and he apologized. But I was never at ease with him in
the club again."

"What were they talking about when you overheard them?"

"He was doing all the talking. It sounded to me like some kind of
mysticism. He was saying how this philosopher believed that thinking
was the basis of everything—*la source de tout.*" His mind moved back
and forth between the two languages. "But Mr. Martel said the
philosophe was wrong. *Réalité* didn't come into being until two people
thought together. So the basis of everything was *l'amour.*" The corners
of Stoll's mouth turned down. "It didn't make much sense to me."

"Did it to her?"

"Naturally. He was making love to her. That was the point. He was
angry because I interrupted him in the middle of his pitch. When I
think back over the episode, I'm convinced the man is psychopathologi-
cal. Ordinary men don't get so excited over such a little thing." He
clenched his fist, not very tight. "I should have asked him to give up
his guest privileges then and there."

"I'm surprised you didn't."

He colored faintly. "Well, you know, he is—or was—Mrs. Bagshaw's
protégé. She's one of our oldest members, and now she's moved into
the cottage next to mine—I hated to upset her. I feel my essential role
is that of a—a buffer." He raised his eyes to the ceiling again, as if the
god of innkeepers resided just over his head. "I try to stand between our
members and the unpleasantnesses of life."

"You're very good at it, I'm sure."

He accepted the compliment formally with a bow. "Thank you, Mr.
Archer. The Tennis Club is known in the trade as one of the better-
run clubs. I've given it ten years of my life, and I was trained in the
hotel schools of Zurich and Lausanne."

"What did you mean when you said that French was one of your native languages?"

He smiled. "I have four native languages, French and German and Italian and Romansch. I was born in the Romansch section of Switzerland, in Silvaplana." His tongue caressed the name.

"Where was Martel born, Mr. Stoll?"

"I have asked myself that question. He claims to be Parisian, Mrs. Bagshaw tells me. But from what little I heard of it, his French is not Paris French. It is too provincial, too formal. Perhaps it is Canadian, or South American. I don't know. I am not a linguistic scientist."

"You're the next thing to it," I said encouragingly. "So you think he might be Canadian or South American?"

"That's just a guess. I'm not really familiar with Canadian or South American French. But I'm quite sure Martel is not Parisian."

I thanked Stoll. He bowed me out.

I had noticed a bulletin board on the wall outside his office. Pinned to its cork surface were some blownup candid pictures of people dancing at a party. Below them, like a reminder of purgatory at the gates of paradise, was a typed list of seven members who were behind in their dues. Mrs. Roy Fablon was one of them.

I mentioned this to Ella.

"Yes, Mrs. Fablon's been having a hard time recently. She told me some of her investments went sour. I hated to post her name, but those are the rules."

"It raises an interesting question. Do you think Virginia Fablon is after Martel's money?"

She shook her head. "It wouldn't make sense. She was going to marry Peter Jamieson. The Jamiesons have ten times as much money as Mr. Martel ever dreamed of."

"Do you know that?"

"I can tell people with money from people without, and people who have had it for a while from people who haven't. If you want my opinion, Mr. Martel is *nouveau riche*, and more *nouveau* than *riche*. He's felt out of place here, and he's been spending his money like a drunken sailor, and it hasn't helped much."

"Except that it's got him Ginny. They were married over the weekend."

"Poor girl."

"Why do you say that?"

"On general principles. Mr. Jamieson is having a long wait. Is he the one you're working for?"

"Yes."

"And you're a private detective, aren't you?"

"I am. What do you think of my client?"

"He reminds me of something I read once, that inside every fat man is a thin man crying to get out. Only Peter's just a boy, and that makes it worse." She added meditatively: "I suppose he has the makings of a man."

"We'll see." I jerked a thumb toward the bulletin board. "You have some pictures on the board. Does this club have a regular photographer?"

"A part time one. Why?"

"I was wondering if he took a picture of Martel."

"I doubt it. I could check with the photographer. Eric isn't on tonight, though."

"Get him on. Tell him I'll pay for his time."

"I'll try."

"You can do better than try," I said. "There's a question about Martel's identity, and we need a picture if there is one."

"I said I'd try."

She directed me to the dining room. It was actually two adjoining rooms, one of which had a polished dance floor. A small orchestra was on the stand, momentarily silent. The other room contained about thirty tables, brilliant with flowers and silver. Peter was sitting at a table by the windows, staring out gloomily at the dark beach.

He got up eagerly when he saw me, but his eagerness had more to do with dinner than with me. It was served buffet style by men in white hats. At the sight of the food Peter underwent a transformation, as if his melancholy passion for Ginny had been switched to another channel. He loaded two plates for himself, one with five kinds of salad, cold ham, shrimp, crabmeat; the other with roast beef and potatoes and gravy and small green peas.

He gobbled the food with such eager straining gluttony that he made me feel like a *voyeur*. His eyes were fixed and mindless as he chewed. Sweat stood out on his forehead.

He wiped his plate with a piece of bread, which he ate. Then he went into contemplation, leaning his chin on his hand. "I can't decide what to have for dessert."

"You don't need dessert."

He looked at me as if I'd threatened to put him on bread and water for a month. I felt like telling him to go to hell. Watching him eat, I'd asked myself if I'd be doing Ginny a favor by bringing her back to my client. Martel at least was a man. Maybe Peter had the makings of a man, as Ella said, but when he sat down at the table he turned into something less, an appetite that only walked like a man.

"I don't know whether to have a chocolate eclair or a hot fudge sundae," he said seriously.

"Have both."

"That isn't funny. My body needs fuel."

"You've already stoked it with enough fuel to run a Matson liner to Honolulu."

He flushed. "You seem to forget that I'm your employer, and you're my guest here."

"I do, don't I? But let's get off the subject of personalities and food, and talk about something real. Tell me about Ginny."

"After I get my dessert."

"Before. Before you eat yourself stupid."

"You can't talk like that to me."

"Somebody should. But we won't argue about it. I want to know if Ginny is the kind of girl who goes off half-cocked about men."

"She never did before."

"Has she had much to do with men?"

"Very little," he said. "Mainly me, in fact." He flushed again, avoiding my eyes. "I wasn't always so fat, if you want to know. Ginny and I sort of went steady in high school. But after that for a long time she wasn't interested in—well, sex, necking and stuff. We were still friends, and I used to take her places sometimes, but we weren't going steady in the true sense anymore."

"What changed her?"

"She was hitting the books, for one thing. She did well at college. I didn't." The fact seemed to nag him. "But it was mainly what happened to her father."

"His suicide?"

Peter nodded. "Ginny was very much attached to her father. Actually it took her until just about now to get over his death."

"How long ago did it happen?"

"Nearly seven years. Seven years this fall. He came down to the beach one night and walked into the water with all his clothes on."

"This beach?" I gestured towards the window. The tide was out: the surf was far down the beach and visible only as a recurring whiteness.

"Not right here, no. He went in about half a mile from here." Peter pointed towards a headland which loomed dark against the more distant harbor lights. "But there's a current in this direction and when his body came up it was right offshore here. I didn't go in the ocean for quite a while. I don't think Ginny ever went in again. She uses—she used the pool."

He sat hunched over in silence for a moment. "Mr. Archer, can't we do something about Martel? Find out if they're married legally or something?"

"I'm sure they are. Ginny would have no reason to lie, would she?"

"No. But she's very much under his spell. You could see for yourself that it isn't a natural situation."

"She seems to be in love with him."

"She can't be! We've got to prevent him from taking her away."

"With what? It's still a free country."

Peter leaned across the table. "Have you considered the possibility that he's in this country illegally? He admitted he had no passport."

"It might be worth looking into. But the worst they'd do is deport him. And Ginny would probably go along."

"I see what you mean. It would only make matters worse."

He lowered his cushioned chin onto his fist and became thoughtful. Our side of the dining room was filling up as people came in from outside or from the bar. A few of them wore dress clothes, and occasional diamonds and rubies sparkled on hands and throats like drippings from the past. The low sound of the ocean was lost in the rise and fall of conversation and music.

The people seemed to be talking against the darkness that pressed at the window. Fablon and his death were still on my mind. "You say that Ginny was very fond of her father?"

Peter came out of his thoughts with a start. "Yes. She was."

"What sort of a man was he?"

"He was what they call a sportsman, I guess. He went in for big-game hunting and fishing and yachting and polo and sports cars and planes."

"All those?"

"At various times. He'd lose interest in one sport and try another. He couldn't seem to find the one thing that would absorb his mind. For a while, when I was a kid in high school, he let me follow him around. He even used to take me up in his plane." Peter's eyes blurred reminiscently. "He was in the Air Force at one time, until they invalided him out."

"What was the matter with him?"

"I don't know exactly. He crashed his plane in a training flight and so he never got into the war. That was a big disappointment to him. He walked with a bit of a limp. Which is one reason I think he went in for all those sports."

"What did he look like?"

"I suppose you'd say that he was good-looking. He was dark-haired and dark-eyed, and he always had a deep tan. Ginny got her coloring from her mother. But I don't know why you're so interested in her family. What's the point?"

"I'm trying to understand her, and understand why she fell so hard and suddenly for Martel. Does he resemble her father?"

"Some," he admitted reluctantly. "But Mr. Fablon was better-looking."

"You said he was partly French. Did he speak French?"

"I guess he could when he wanted to. He lived in France at one time, he told me."

"Where?"

"Paris. That was when he was studying painting."

I was beginning to get some idea of Fablon. In these circles he was a fairly common type: the man who tried everything and succeeded at nothing.

"Where did he get the money for all his hobbies? Was he in business?"

"He tried various businesses. Right after the war he started an air-freight business. The trouble was, he was in competition with airlines like the Flying Tiger. He told me once he lost fifty thousand dollars in six months. But he had a lot of fun with it, he said." Peter's tone was elegiac, nostalgic. At another time, in another body, he might have liked to live as the dead man had.

"Who paid for the fun?"

"Mrs. Fablon did, I guess. She was a Proctor." He paused, frowning slightly. "I just remembered something. It's nothing to do with anything, but it's interesting." He turned to the window, indicating the dark headland again. "That beach where Mr. Fablon walked into the water used to belong to the Proctors. It was part of their estate. Ginny's mother had to sell the estate about ten years ago."

"Three years before Fablon died."

"That's right. If she could have waited until now, she'd have got at least a million. But I heard it went for peanuts, to pay Mr. Fablon's debts."

"Who bought it?"

"A cemetery company. They haven't put in the cemetery yet."

"I can hardly wait," I said.

Peter frowned at my levity. A minute later he left the table and ducked out of the room. I saw him a few minutes after that talking at the entrance with a tall man in a tuxedo. The tall man moved his head, and I noticed the hard line of his jaw. It was Dr. Sylvester, whose lunch with Mrs. Fablon I had interrupted.

He went into the bar. Peter trudged to the end of the line that had formed at the dessert table. He stood like an earnest communicant, his eyes dreaming over the pies and cakes and pastries.

10
• • •

I FOLLOWED Dr. Sylvester into the bar. A bartender whose eyes moved like black quicksilver poured him a double scotch without being asked to. Sylvester called the bartender Marco. Marco wore a red waistcoat, a white shirt with long collar-points, and a flowing black silk tie.

I waited until the doctor had knocked back about half of his drink. Then I sat on the bar stool beside him and watched Marco making a daiquiri.

Sylvester's square hairy-backed hands fiddled with his low-ball glass. The hairs were slightly grizzled, like the hair on his head. The bones of his face were prominent, and accentuated by harsh lines running from the base of his nose to his mouth. He didn't look like an easy man to strike up a conversation with.

To have something to do with my hands, I ordered a bar bourbon. The bartender wouldn't accept my dollar.

"Sorry, no cash. Are you a member, sir?"

"I'm Peter Jamieson's guest."

"I'll put it on his bill, sir."

Dr. Sylvester turned and raised his black eyebrows at me. He used them so conspicuously that they seemed to be his main sense organs, distracting attention from his hard bright eyes.

"Jamieson senior or junior?"

"I know them both. I noticed you were talking to the young one."

"Yes?"

I told him my name and trade. "Peter hired me to look into this business of his ex-fiancée."

"I was wondering how you got in here." He wasn't trying to insult me, exactly, just letting me know my place in his scheme of things. "Didn't I see you at the Fablon house this noon?"

"Yes. I understand you were Virginia Fablon's employer at one time."

"That's true."

"What do you think about her marriage?"

I had succeeded in interesting him. "Good Lord, did she marry the fellow?"

"So she told me. They were married on Saturday."

"You've talked to her?"

"An hour or so ago. I couldn't figure out what was going on in her mind. Of course the circumstances weren't normal, either. But she seemed to be living out some kind of romantic dream."

"Most women are," he said dryly. "Did you see him?"

"I talked to them together at his house."

"I've never met him myself," Sylvester said. "I've seen him around here, of course, at a distance. What did you make of him?"

"He's a very intelligent man, highly educated, with a good deal of force. He seems to have Virginia pretty well dominated."

"It won't last," Sylvester said. "You don't know the young lady. She has a lot of personal force of her own." He added wryly: "I've served *in loco parentis* to her since her father died, and it hasn't always been easy. Virginia likes to make up her own mind."

"About men?"

"There haven't been any men in her life, not lately. That's one of the problems she's had. Ever since her father's death she's done nothing but work and study French. You'd think her life was nothing but a memorial to Roy. Then a few weeks ago, as you might expect, the whole thing broke down. She dropped her studies, when she was within easy shooting distance of her degree, and went hog-wild for this Martel." He sipped his drink. "It's a disturbing picture."

"Are you her doctor?"

"I was until quite recently. Frankly, we had a disagreement about the —the wisdom of her course. I thought it best to refer her to another doctor. Why do you ask?"

"I don't like the emotional risk she's taking. She's managed to convince herself that she's crazy about Martel, and she's perched way out on a limb. It could be brutal for her if the limb gets sawed off."

"I tried to tell her that," Sylvester said. "You think he's a phony, eh?"

"He has to be at least partly phony. I've had one Washington reference checked, and it didn't pan out. There were other things I won't go into." The rat, the blood on his heel, the gun peering out of his hand at Harry Hendricks.

"What can I do about it? She's got the bit in her teeth, and she's running with it." Sylvester paused, and finished his drink.

"You want another, doctor?" the bartender asked.

"No thanks, Marco. One thing I've learned in twenty years of practicing medicine," he said to me: "you have to let people make their own mistakes. Sooner or later they come around to reason. The men with emphysema will eventually give up smoking. The women with chronic alcoholism will go on the wagon. And the girls with bad cases of romanticism turn into realists. Like my dear wife here."

A big woman in a kind of mantilla had come up behind us. Her chest gleamed like mother-of-pearl through black lace. She had bouffant yellow hair which made her as tall as I was when I stood up. Her mouth was discontented.

"What *about* me?" she said. "I love to be talked about by men."

"I was saying that you were a realist, Audrey. That women start out being romantic and end up realistic every time."

"Men force us into it," she said. "Is this my daiquiri?"

"Yes, and this is Mr. Archer. He's a detective."

"How fascinating," she said. "You must tell me the story of your life."

"I started out as a romantic and ended up as a realist."

She laughed and drank her drink, and they went in to dinner. Some other people followed them.

For the moment I was the only one at the bar. Marco asked me if I wanted another drink. He was staring at me intensely as if he had something on his mind. His mouth was sort of wreathed with unspoken language. I said that I would like another drink.

"On me," he said as he rapped it down, and poured himself a Cola to take with me. "I couldn't help hearing, you said you were a detective. And some of the things you said about Miss Fablon."

"You know her?"

"Seen her around. She don't drink. I've been here for over twelve years, I knew her father. He drank, but he could carry it. Mr. Fablon was a man. He had *machismo*." Marco's red lips protruded, savoring the word.

"I heard he committed suicide," I said without emphasis.

"Maybe. I never believed it." He shook his bushy black head.

"You think he drowned accidentally?"

"I didn't say that."

"The other alternative is murder."

"I didn't say that, either." Without moving from his position behind the bar, he seemed to back away from me. Then he crossed himself. "Murder is a big ugly word."

"It's an uglier fact. Was Mr. Fablon murdered?"

"Some people thought so."

"Who?"

"His wife, for instance. After he disappeared she was yelling bloody murder around the club here. Then suddenly she quit, and all you could hear from her was a loud silence."

"Did she accuse anyone?"

"Not that I heard. She didn't name any names."

"Why would she change her story?"

"Your guess is as good as mine, mister. Probably better." The subject seemed to make him nervous. He changed it: "But it wasn't that I wanted to talk about. This other guy—calls himself Martel—the big-shot Frenchman?"

"What about him?"

"I got a funny feeling I've seen him before someplace." He spread his fingers. "Anyway, I'm sure he ain't no Frenchie."

"What is he?"

"Same like me, maybe." He made a stupid face, deliberately humbling himself in order to make what he said more insulting to Martel. "Just another *paisano*. He never came in here only the once, and then he took one look at me and never came back."

The orchestra had started up. Some people drifted in from the dining room and ordered brandy. Dodging a few dancing couples, I went back to Peter's table. The dessert plate in front of him was empty except for a few faint smears of chocolate. He looked smug and guilty.

"I thought you'd left," he said.

"I was in the bar talking to some friends of the Fablons."

"Dr. Sylvester."

"He was one of them," I said.

"I had a word with him, too. He puts on that hard front of his, but he's worried about Ginny, I can tell."

"We all are."

"Do you think we better go back to Martel's house?" Peter made a move to get up.

"Not until we have something substantial to hit him with."

"Like what?"

"Some actual proof that he isn't what he claims to be. I'm trying to develop something now."

"And what am I supposed to do?"

Go and take another run on the beach, I almost said. I said: "You have to wait. And I think you better get used to the idea that this may not turn out the way you want it to."

"You've found out something?"

"Nothing definite, but I have a feeling. This one didn't start out happily and it may not end happily. I think it goes back at least as far as Roy Fablon's alleged suicide."

"Alleged?"

"At least one man who knew him doesn't believe he killed himself. Which implies that somebody else did."

"Whoever told you that is making it up."

"Perhaps. He's a Roman Catholic, and he admired Roy Fablon, and he wouldn't want to think that he was a suicide. Your father told me an interesting thing, though."

"I didn't know you ever talked to my father." Peter's tone was formal and suspicious, as if I had gone over to the enemy.

"I went to your house to find you this afternoon. Your father told me among other things that Roy Fablon's body was so chewed up by sharks it could hardly be identified. Just what was the condition of his face?"

"I didn't see it myself. My father did. All they showed me was his overcoat."

"He went into the water wearing an overcoat?"

"It was more of a waterproof." He heard the word, and grimaced at the irony.

It caught in my own mind like a fishhook. It was hard to imagine a sportsman and athlete walking into the ocean in a waterproof coat, from a beach estate which his ways with money had forced his wife to sell, unless he meant to leave her and his daughter a legacy of malice.

"How do you know exactly where he went into the water?"

"He left his wallet and wristwatch on the beach. There wasn't anything in the wallet, except identification, but the watch was a very good one that Mrs. Fablon had given him. It had their initials on the back, and something engraved in Latin on the case."

"No suicide note?"

"If there was one, I never heard of it. That doesn't necessarily prove anything. The local police don't always release notes."

"Do you have a lot of suicides in Montevista?"

"We have our share. You know, when you have money to live on, and a nice house, and good weather most of the time, and *still* your life goes wrong—well, who can you blame?" Peter seemed to be talking about himself.

"Is that how it was with Roy Fablon?"

"Not exactly. He had his troubles. I was a guest in their house, and I shouldn't talk about them, but I suppose it doesn't matter now." He breathed in. "I heard him tell Mrs. Fablon he would kill himself."

"That same night?"

"A night or two before. I was there for dinner, and they were arguing about money. She said she couldn't give him any more money because there wasn't any more money."

"What did he want the money for?"

"Gambling losses. He called it a debt of honor. He said if he couldn't pay it he'd have to kill himself."

"Was Ginny there?"

"Yes. She heard everything. We both did. Mr. and Mrs. Fablon had reached the point where they weren't trying to hide anything. Each of them was trying to win us over."

"Who won?"

"Nobody won," he said. "Everybody lost."

The orchestra was playing again, and through the archway I could see people dancing in the adjoining room. Most of the tunes, and most of the dancers, had been new in the twenties and thirties. Together they gave the impression of a party that had been going on too long, till the music and the dancers were worn as thin as the husks of insects after spiders had eaten them.

11
...

ELLA STROME crossed the corner of the dance floor and came to our table. "I got hold of the photographer for you, Mr. Archer. He's waiting in the office."

He was a thin man in a rumpled dark business suit. He had a lot of brown hair, a lumpy Slavic jaw, and sensitive-looking eyes protected by horn-rimmed glasses. Ella introduced him as Eric Malkovsky.

"I'm glad to meet you," he said, but he wasn't. He glanced restlessly past me toward the door of the office. "I promised my wife to take her to the Film Society tonight. We have season tickets."

"I'll reimburse you."

"That's not the point. I hate to disappoint her."

"This may be more important."

"Not to me it isn't." He was speaking to me, but his real complaint was directed toward Ella. I gathered she had used pressure to get him here. "Anyway, as I told Mrs. Strome, I have no pictures of Mr. Martel. I offered to take some, the way I do with any other guest, but he said no. He was pretty emphatic about it."

"Unpleasant?"

"I wouldn't say that. But he certainly didn't want his picture taken. What is he, a celebrity or something?"

"Something."

My reticence irritated him, and he colored slightly. "The only reason I asked, another person was after me for a picture of him."

Ella said: "You didn't tell me that."

"I didn't have a chance to. The woman came to my studio in the Village just before I went home for dinner. When I told her I didn't have a picture of him, she offered me money to go to his house and take one. I told her I couldn't do that without Mr. Martel's permission. At which she got mad and stomped out."

"I don't suppose she gave you her name?"

"No, but I can describe her. She's a redhead, tall, with a gorgeous figure. Age about thirty. As a matter of fact, I had a feeling that I've seen her before."

"Where?"

"Right here in the club."

"I don't remember any such woman," Ella said.

"It was before your time, at least five years ago." Malkovsky screwed up one side of his face as if he was squinting through a view finder. "I think I took a picture or two of the woman. In fact I'm pretty sure I did."

"Would you still have those pictures?" I said.

"Maybe, but it would be a terrible job to find them. I don't keep files except for the current year and the year before. All the old stuff is stored away in cartons in the back room." He looked at his wristwatch, dramatically. "I really have to go now. The wife will kill me if she misses the Bunuel. And the club doesn't pay me overtime for this kind of a deal." He tossed a sour look in the direction of Ella, who had gone back to the reception desk.

"I'll pay you double time for as long as it takes."

"That would be seven dollars an hour. It could take all night."

"I know."

"And there's no guarantee that I'll come up with anything. It may be an entirely different woman. If it's the same woman, she's changed the color of her hair. The woman I remember was a blonde."

"Blondes turn into redheads all the time. Tell me about the woman you remember."

"She was younger then, of course, with the dew still on her. A lovely thing. I remember now, I did take some pictures of her. Her husband wasn't too crazy about the idea but she wanted it done."

"Who was her husband?"

"An older guy," he said. "They stayed in one of the cottages for a couple of weeks."

"What year were they here?"

"I couldn't nail it down—maybe six or seven years ago. But if I find those pictures I can tell you. I generally make a note of the date on the back."

By this time Malkovsky was eager to get to work. Before leaving for the Village, he gave me the address and telephone number of his studio. I said I would check with him there in an hour or so.

I thanked Ella, and went to the parking lot to get my car. An unsteady wind carrying a gritty taste of desert was blowing down from the direction of the mountains. The eucalyptus trees swayed and bowed and waved in the gusts like long-haired madwomen racked by impulse. The night which loomed above the trees and dwarfed them seemed threatening.

I had been concerned about Harry Hendricks ever since I found his car at the roadside near Martel's house. Harry had no more earned my concern than the alleged rat which Martel said he had killed. Still I had a foolish yen to see Harry alive.

The road to the harbor cut across the base of the headland where Fablon had taken his final swim, and back to the ocean. As I drove along the windswept boulevard, my mind was so fixed on Harry that when I saw the Cadillac parked at the curb I thought I was dreaming. I braked and backed and parked directly behind it, and got out. It was Harry's old Caddie, all right, standing there with a cold engine, empty and innocent, as if it had driven itself down from the foothills. The key was in the ignition. It hadn't been before.

I looked around me. It was a lonely place, especially at this time, with a wind blowing. There was no other car in sight, and nothing across the street but rattling palms and the sighing sea.

On the inland side a tall cypress hedge shielded the boulevard from a view of the railroad tracks and the hobo jungles. Through a hole in the hedge I could see the dark shapes of men crouched around a bonfire which flared and veered.

I went through the hole and approached them. There were three of them drinking dark red wine out of a half-gallon jug which was nearly empty. Their faces all turned toward me in the firelight: the seamed and gap-toothed face of an aging white man; the flat stubborn planes of a young Negro's head; a boy with Indian features and an Indian's stolid apathetic eyes. He wore nothing above the waist but an open black vest.

The Negro got up with five or six feet of two-by-four in his hands. He staggered toward me on the uneven ground.

"Amscray, 'bo. This a private party."

"You can answer a civil question. I'm looking for a friend of mine."

"I don't know nothin' about no friends of yours." Big and drunk, he leaned on his two-by-four like a warrior on his spear. His tripod shadow wavered on the hedge.

"That's his car there," I said quickly. "The Cadillac. He's a medium-sized man in a checkered jacket. Have you seen him?"

"Naw."

"Just a minute." The white man rose unsteadily. "Maybe I seen him, maybe not. What's it worth to you?"

He came up close to me so that I could smell his fiery breath and look deep into the glaring hollows of his eyes. They had a feverish brainwashed wino emptiness. He was so far gone that he would never come back.

"It isn't worth anything to me, old-timer. You're trying to promote the price of another jug."

"I seen him, honest I seen him. Little man in a checkered jacket. He gave me four bits, I thanked him very kindly. You don't forget a citizen like that." The breath whistled through the gaps in his teeth.

"Let's see the four bits."

He searched elaborately through his jeans. "I must have lost it."

I turned away. He followed me all the way to the car. His gnarled fists drummed on the window.

"Have a heart, for Christ's sake. Gimme four bits. I told you about your friend."

"No money for wine," I said.

"It's for food. I'm starving. I came down here to pick oranges and they fired me, said I couldn't do the work."

"They'll feed you at the Salvation Army."

He puckered up his mouth and spat on the window. His saliva ran down the glass between him and me. I started the motor.

"Get away, you might get hurt."

"I'm hurt already," he said with his life in his voice.

He staggered back to the hedge, disappearing suddenly through the hole like a man swallowed up by darkness.

12
...

THE BREAKWATER HOTEL was only a few blocks from the place where Harry's Cadillac was parked. It was possible, though hardly likely, that he'd left it there, for reasons of his own, and gone the rest of the way on foot.

The lobby of the hotel was the mouth of a tourist trap which had lost its bite. There were scuff-marks on the furniture, dust on the phil- odendrons. The bellhop wore an old blue uniform which looked as if he had fought through the Civil War in it.

There was no one at the desk, but the register was lying open on it. I found Harry Hendricks's name on the previous page. He had room 27. I looked at the half-wall of pigeonholes behind the desk, and couldn't see any key in 27.

"Is Mr. Hendricks in?" I asked the bellhop.

He stroked the growth of beard on his chin. It looked like moth- eaten gray plush, but it rasped like sandpaper. "I wouldn't know about that. They come and go. I'm not paid to keep track."

"Where's the manager?"

"In there."

He jerked a thumb toward a curtained doorway with an electric sign above it: Samoa Room. The name meant that it would have bam- boo furniture and a fishnet ceiling: it had: and would serve rum drinks containing canned pineapple juice and floating fruit.

Three rather wilted-looking sharpies were rolling dice on the bar. The fat bartender watched them over his belly. A tired-looking hostess offered me the temporary use of her smile. I told her that I wanted to ask the manager a question.

"Mr. Smythe is the assistant manager. Mr. Smythe!"

Mr. Smythe was the sharpest-looking of the sharpies. He tore himself away from the dice for a moment. If they were his dice, they were probably gaffed. His true-blue All-American look was warped like peeling veneer around the edges.

"You wish accommodations, sir?"

"Later, perhaps. I wanted to ask you if Mr. Hendricks is in."

"Not unless he came in in the last few minutes. His wife is waiting in his room for him."

"I didn't know he was married."

"He's married all right. Very married. I'd give up the joys of bachelorhood myself if I could latch onto a dish like that." His hands made an hourglass figure in the smoky air.

"Maybe she can tell me where he is."

"She doesn't know. She asked *me*. I haven't seen him since this afternoon. Is he in some kind of a jam?"

"Could be."

"You a cop?"

"An investigator," I answered vaguely. "What makes you think that Hendricks is in trouble?"

"He asked me where he could buy a cheap hand gun."

"Today?"

"This aft, like I said. I told him to try the pawnshops. Did I do wrong? He didn't shoot somebody?"

"Not that I know of."

"That's good." But he was subtly disappointed. "If you want to talk to Mrs. Hendricks, there's a room phone beside the desk."

I thanked him, and he returned to the joys of bachelorhood. I didn't bother with the room phone, or with the elevator. I found the fire stairs at the back of the lobby and went up the redlit stairwell to the second floor.

Room 27 was at the end of the hall. I listened at the door. There was faint music behind it, a country blues. I knocked. The music was shut off abruptly.

"Who is it?" a woman said.

"Harry."

"It's about time!"

She unlatched the door and pulled it open. I walked in on her and took the doorknob out of her hand and swung the door shut behind me, in case the screaming expression on her face changed into sudden noise.

It didn't. The fixed lopsided rigor of her face didn't change. Her right fist rose of its own accord to the level of her eyes. She looked at me around it.

"Take it easy, Mrs. Hendricks. I won't hurt you."

"I hear you telling me." But she relaxed enough to unclench her fist and use it to smoothe her red hair. Her lopsided mouth straightened itself. "Who are you?"

"A friend of Harry's. I said I'd look him up here."

She didn't believe me. She looked like a woman who had stopped believing almost everything except the numbers on bills, the price tags on clothes and people. She was dressed with style, in a brown loose kind of half-sleeved something which showed her figure without over-emphasizing it. Her forearms and legs were beautifully made and deeply tanned.

But her face was made up as if she had begun to doubt her looks, or wished to hide them. From under eyelids greener than her eyes, through eyelashes that groped like furred antennae in the air, she peered at me distrustfully.

"What's your name?" she said.

"It doesn't matter."

"Then get out of my room." But she didn't really expect me to. If she had any expectations left, they had to do with possible disasters.

"It isn't your room. It's Harry's. He said he'd meet me."

She looked around the room, at the worn carpet, the faded flowers in the wallpaper, the bedside lamp with its scorched paper shade, as if she was considering her relationship to it. Externally she didn't belong here at all. She had the kind of syle that could be bought, but not suddenly, at Bullocks and I. Magnin's; the brown pouch on the bed with its gold tassels looked like Paris. But she belonged internally to the room, the way a prisoner belongs to his cell. She had done time in rooms like this, and it was setting in again.

"It's my room too," she said. To prove it, and to cheer things up a little, she went to the bedside table and turned up her portable radio. The country blues hadn't ended yet. It had been a long two minutes.

"What—?" Her voice screeked on the word. She was still so full of tension that she was hardly breathing. She tried to swallow the tension;

I watched the marvelous mechanism of her throat. "What kind of business do you have with Harry?" she finally managed to say.

"We were going to compare notes on Francis Martel."

She flapped her eyelashes. "Who?"

"Martel. The man you want a picture of."

"You must be thinking of two other people."

"Come on now, Mrs. Hendricks. I've just been talking to the photographer Malkovsky. You wanted him to take a picture of Martel. Your husband risked his neck trying to get one this morning."

"Are you a cop?"

"Not exactly."

"How do you know so much about me?"

"That's all I know about you, unfortunately. Tell me more."

Laboriously, with hands that jerked a little, she got a gold cigarette case out of her brown pouch, opened it, took out a cigarette and put it between her lips. I lit it for her. She sat on the bed and leaned back on her arm, blowing smoke hard at the ceiling as if to conceal its dinginess.

"Don't stand over me like that. You look as though you're going to jump down my throat."

"I was admiring your throat." I pulled up the only chair in the room and sat on it.

"Swingin'." Her voice was sardonic. She covered her neck with the collar of her fingers, and studied me. "I can't figure you out, unless you're trying to soften me up with the sweet-and-sour treatment. Which will get you nowhere."

"Are you really Harry's wife?"

"Yes. I am." She sounded a little surprised herself. "I'd show you my marriage license but I don't seem to have it with me at the moment."

"How can he afford you?"

"He can't. We haven't been working at it lately. But we're still friends." She added with a kind of rough nostalgia: "Harry wasn't always on the skids. He used to be more fun than a barrel of monkeys."

"And you weren't always in the chips."

"Who told you that?"

"Nobody had to tell me." Your voice told me, doll, and the way you have to keep using your body in little conspicuous ways as if you were treading water. The way you looked at the room told me, and the way the room looked back.

"Are you from Vegas?" she said.

"People are supposed to smile when they say that."

"Are you?"

"I'm from Hollywood."

"What do you do for a living, Hollywood? If anything."

"Private investigations."

"And you're doing a job on me?"

Her look was fearful again. At the same time she signaled for the ashtray from the bedside table and butted her cigarette in it while I held it. She shifted her position, leaning heavily sideways with half-deliberate clumsiness to show how helpless her fine big body was. It needed no help from me, though: it was perfectly at home on a hotel bed.

"You've got things twisted around," I said. "I was hired to do a job on Martel."

"Who by?" She corrected herself: "By whom?"

"A local man. His identity doesn't matter. Martel stole his girl."

"It figures. He's a thief."

"What did he steal from you, Mrs. Hendricks?"

"That's a good question. The real question, though, is whether he's the guy I think he is. Have you seen him?"

"Several times."

"Describe him for me, will you? We may be able to get together on this."

"He's a medium-sized man, about five foot nine, not heavy, but compactly built, and quick in his movements. Age about thirty. He has black hair, jet black, growing fairly low on his forehead. He wears it combed straight back. His complexion is dark, almost Indian dark. He has a long nose with noticeably flaring nostrils. He speaks with a French accent, uses a lot of French, and claims to be a French political refugee."

She had been listening and nodding in confirmation, but my last sentence confused her. "What was that?"

"He says he's a Frenchman who can't live in France because he doesn't get along with de Gaulle."

"Oh." But she still didn't understand.

"De Gaulle is the President of France."

"I know that, stupid. You think I don't listen to the news?" She glanced at the radio, which was playing rock.

"Do you mind if I turn that thing off?" I said.

"You can turn it down a little, but leave it on. I hate the sound of the wind."

I turned the music not too far down. Based on such minor co-operations an intimacy was growing between us, as if the room had provided us with built-in roles. But it was a chancy intimacy, whose rhythm was an alternating current of fear and doubt. She asked me sensible questions and seemed to believe my answers. But her eyes weren't certain that I wouldn't kill her.

"Do you know who he is?" I said.

"I think so, and he isn't any Frenchman."

"What is he?"

"I'll tell you," she said crisply, as if she had decided on her story. "I happen to be the confidential secretary to a very important businessman in the Southland. This man who calls himself Martel wormed his way into my employer's good graces and wound up as his executive assistant."

"Where does he come from?"

"I wouldn't know that," she said. "He's some kind of South American, I think. My employer made the mistake of giving him the combination to the safe. I warned him not to. So what happens? Mr. so-called Martel takes off with a fortune in bearer bonds, which Harry and me—and I are trying to get back."

"Why not the police?"

She was ready with an answer. "My employer has a soft spot in his head for Mr. Martel. Also our business is highly confidential."

"What is your business?"

"I'm not in a position to reveal that," she said carefully. She shifted the position of her body, as if its substantiality and symmetry might divert my attention from the jerry-built flimsiness of her story. "My employer has sworn me to secrecy."

"What's his name?"

"You'd know his name if I could tell it to you. He's a very important and well-heeled man in certain circles."

"The lower circles of hell?"

"What?" But I think she heard me.

She pouted, and frowned a little with her thin painted-on eyebrows. She didn't frown very hard because that gave girls wrinkles and besides I might kill her and she didn't want to die with a frown on her lovely face.

"If you'd take me seriously and help to get that money back, etcetera, I'm sure my employer would reward you handsomely. I'd be grateful, too."

"I'd have to know more about it," such as what she meant by "etcetera."

"Sure," she said. "Naturally. Are you going to help me?"

"We'll see. Have you given up on Harry?"

"I didn't say that."

But her green eyes were surprised. I think in her concentration on me and on her story—her late late movie story—she had forgotten Harry. The room provided roles for only two people. I guessed what mine would be if we stayed in it much longer. Her body was purring at me like a tiger, the proverbial kind of tiger which is dangerous to mount and even more dangerous to dismount.

"I'm worried about Harry," I said. "Have you seen him today?"

She shook her head. Her hair flared out like fire. The wind, momentarily louder than the music, was whining at the window.

"He was talking about buying a gun this afternoon."

"What for?" Gun talk seemed to frighten her basically.

"To use on Martel, I think. Martel gave him a bad time today. He ran him off with a gun and smashed his camera." I produced the flattened camera from my pocket.

She brooded over it. "That camera cost me a hundred and fifty bucks. I ought to've known better than to trust Harry."

"Maybe the picture bit wasn't a good idea. Martel is allergic to cameras. What's his real name, by the way?"

"I don't know. He keeps using different names." She changed the subject back to Harry: "You think Harry got hurt or something?"

"It's possible. His car is parked on the boulevard about half a mile from here, with the key in it."

She jerked herself upright. "Why didn't you say so?"

"I just did."

"Show it to me."

She picked up her radio and bag, got her coat out of the closet, and put it on while we were waiting for the elevator. It may have been the noise of the elevator, or the radio, or some perpetual signal which her body sent out, but when she crossed the lobby with me all three of the sharpies were watching from the curtained doorway of the Samoa Room.

We drove along the boulevard. The rising wind buffeted the car. Out to sea I could make out occasional whitecaps. Faintly phosphorescent, they rose up like ghosts which were quickly swept backward into darkness. The woman peered out along the empty beaches. She turned up the window on the ocean side.

"Are you okay, Mrs. Hendricks?"

"I'm okay, but please don't call me that." She sounded younger and less sure of herself. "It makes me feel like a phony. Call me Kitty if you like."

"You're not Mrs. Hendricks?"

"Legally I am, but we haven't been living together. Harry would have divorced me long ago, only he's a practicing Catholic. And he has this crazy hope that I'll come back to him." She leaned forward to peer out of my side. "We've gone a half a mile. Where is his car?"

I couldn't find it. She began to get nervous. I turned my car and found the hole in the hedge and the fire behind it, which had burned down rapidly to a few breathing coals among the ashes. The three wine-drinkers had blown, leaving their empty jug and the smell of spilled wine.

Kitty Hendricks called to me: "What are you doing? Is Harry there?"

"No."

She came through the hedge. She still had her bag and radio looped over her wrist, and the radio was singing like a semi-detached personality. She looked around her, hugging her coat to her body. There was nothing to see but the dying fire, the railroad tracks gleaming dully in the starlight, the trampled unlovely earth.

"Holy Mother," Kitty said, "it hasn't changed in twenty years."

"You know this place?"

"I ought to. I was born about two blocks from here. On the other side of the tracks." She added wryly: "*Both* sides of the tracks are the wrong side if you live close enough to them. The trains used to rattle the dishes in my mother's kitchen." She peered across the dark railroad yard. "For all I know my mother is still living there."

"We could go and see."

"No! I don't have enough left to put up a front for her, too. I mean, let bygones be bygones."

She made an unsettled movement toward the cypress hedge, as if the place might betray her into further candor. She could handle the dangers of a hotel room, but not the demands of the wild outer night.

Her feeling turned against me. "Why did you bring me here?"

"It was your idea."

"But you said that Harry's car—"

"Apparently it's been stolen."

She backed away from me, stumbling on her heels, into the ragged black branches of the cypress. All I could see was the pale shape of her face and the glints of her eyes and mouth.

"There never was any car. What kind of a car was it?"

"A Cadillac."

"Now I know you're lying. Where would Harry get a Cadillac?"

"He probably took it off the lot. It's an old one."

She didn't seem to be following me. I heard her breath coming more rapidly.

"There never was any car," she whispered. "You're from Vegas, aren't you? And you brought me here to kill me."

"That's silly talk, Kitty."

"Don't you call me Kitty." Her voice was taking on more childish cadences. Perhaps her mind was tracking on something that had happened years ago, between the trains rattling her mother's dishes. "You conned me into coming to this place, and now you won't let me go."

"Go ahead. Go. Go-go."

She only backed deeper into the cypress, like a nocturnal animal. Her radio was trilling from the darkness. A gust of her perfume reached me, mixed with the smells of diesel oil and wine and fire.

I saw in a red flash of insight how two people and a set of circumstances might collaborate in an unpredictable murder. Almost, I thought, she wanted to be murdered. She huddled among the shadows, whimpering:

"You stay away from me, I'll tell my old man."

"Get out of there, stupid."

The scream for which she'd been tuning up came out. I reached for her blindly and got her by the waist and pulled her toward me. She gasped, and swung the radio at my head. It struck me a glancing blow and fell silent, as if the musical side of Kitty's personality had died a violent death.

I let her go. She ran away gawkily on her high heels, across the multiple tracks, until she was no more than a scrambling shadow, a hurrying sound in the night.

13
. . .

ERIC MALKOVSKY'S studio in the Village was on the direct route to Martel's house. I stopped to see how he was getting on with his search. He had dust on his hands and fingerprints on his forehead, like a human clue.

"I almost gave up on you," he said.

"I almost gave up on myself. Did you find any pictures of her?"

"Five. I may have more."

He took me into the back of the shop and laid them out on a table like a poker hand. Four of them were pictures of Kitty, in a plain white bathing suit, taken at the Tennis Club pool. She stood and gazed romantically out to sea. She reclined erotically on a chaise longue. She posed dry on the diving board. Kitty had been a beautiful girl, but all four pictures were spoiled by her awkward staginess.

The fifth picture was different. Unposed and fully clothed in a sleeveless summer dress and a wide hat, she sat at a table with a drink at her elbow. A man's hand with a square-cut diamond on it lay on the table beside her arm. The rest of him was cut off, but Kitty seemed to be smiling in his direction. Behind her I could see the patio wall of one of the Tennis Club cottages overgrown with bougainvillea.

"This is the one she liked." Malkovsky showed me the notation on the back: six 4 × 6 copies @ 5.00—30.00. Pd. September 27, 1959. "She bought six copies, or her husband did. He was in the picture, too, but he made me crop it."

"Why?"

"I remember he said something about beauty and the beast. He wasn't that bad-looking but he was older, like I told you. And he'd taken some punishment in his time."

"What was his name?"

"I don't remember. I suppose I could check it out in the club records."

"Tonight?"

"If Mrs. Strome lets me. But it's getting awful late."

"Don't forget you're on double time."

He scratched at his hairline, and colored slightly. "Could I see a little of the money please?"

I looked at my watch. I had hired him roughly two hours ago. "How about fourteen dollars?"

"Fine. Incidentally," he said with further scratching of his head, "if you want any of these pictures it's only fair that you should pay me for them. Five dollars apiece."

I gave him a twenty-dollar bill. "I'll take the one she liked. I don't suppose there's any chance you could find the rest of it, the part you cropped off?"

"I might be able to find the negative."

"For that I'll pay higher."

"How much higher?"

"It depends on what's on it. Twenty dollars anyway."

I left him rooting enthusiastically among the dusty cartons on his shelves, and drove back into the foothills. This was the direction the wind was coming from. It rushed down the canyons like a hot torrent, and roared in the brush around the Bagshaw house. I had to brace myself against it when I got out of the car.

The Bentley was gone from the courtyard. I tried the front door of the house. It was locked.

There was no light in the house, and no response of any kind to my repeated knocking. I went back into the studio in the Village. With a twenty-dollar glint in each eye Malkovsky showed me the negative of the picture of Kitty.

Beside her sat a man in a striped suit, which was wrinkled by his heavy shoulders and heavy thighs. He was almost bald, but compensating curly hair, white in the negative, sprouted up through his open shirt collar. His black smile had a loose, bland empty cheerfulness which his narrow white eyes annulled.

Behind him near the patio wall, and out of focus, was a mustached young man in a busboy's jacket, holding a tray in his hands. He looked vaguely familiar: perhaps he was one of the servants I've seen around the club.

"I should have a name for these people," Eric said. "Actually it's just good luck that I found the negative."

"We can check them out at the club, as you suggested. Do you remember anything more about the man? Were he and the woman married?"

"They certainly acted that way. She did, that is. He was in poor health, and she fussed over him quite a bit."

"What was the matter with him?"

"I don't know. He couldn't move around much. He spent most of his time in his cottage or in the patio, playing cards."

"Who did he play with?"

"Various people. Don't get the idea that I saw much of the guy. The fact is, I avoided him."

"Why?"

"He was a rough customer, sick or not. I didn't like the way he talked to me, as if I was some kind of a flunky. I'm a professional man," he asserted.

I knew how Eric felt. I was a semi-professional man myself. I gave him another twenty dollars, and we drove in separate cars to the club.

Ella opened up the records room behind the manager's office, and Eric plunged in among the filing cabinets. He had a date to work from: Kitty's pictures had been paid for on September 27, 1959.

I went back to the pavilion. The music was still going on, but the party had narrowed down to its hard core and shifted its main focus to the bar. It wasn't late, as parties go, but in my absence most of the people had deteriorated, as if a sudden illness had fallen on them: manic-depressive psychosis, or a mild cerebral hemorrhage.

Only the bartender hadn't changed at all. He made the drinks and served them and stood back from the party, watching it with his tarnished quicksilver eyes. I showed him the picture of Kitty, and the negative.

He held it up to the fluorescent light at the back of the bar. "Yeah, I remember the man and the girl. She came in here with him one night and tried to get tight on B and B—that's all she knew about drinking—and she had a coughing fit. She had about four or five recruits patting her on the back at once and her husband started pushing them around. Me and Mr. Fablon got him calmed down, though."

"How did Mr. Fablon get into the act?"

"He was with them."

"They were friends of his?"

"I wouldn't want to say that, exactly. He was just with them. They drifted in together. Maybe he liked the woman. She was a knockout, I'll give her that."

"Was Fablon a woman chaser?"

"You're putting words into my mouth. He liked women. He didn't chase 'em. Some of them chased him. But he'd have more sense than mess with that dame. Her husband was bad news."

"Who is he, Marco?"

He shrugged. "I never saw him before or since, and I haven't been sitting around waiting to hear from him. He was bad news, a blowtop, a muscle."

"How did he get in?"

"He was staying here. Some of our members can't say no when they get asked for a guest card. It would save me a lot of trouble if they could learn to say no." He looked around the room with a kind of contemptuous tolerance. "Make you a drink?"

"No thanks."

Marco leaned toward me across the bar. "Maybe I shouldn't tell you this, but Mrs. Fablon was in here a little while ago."

"So?"

"She asked the same question you did, whether I thought her husband committed suicide. She knew him and I were friends, like. I told her no, I didn't think so."

"What did she say?"

"She didn't have a chance to say anything. Dr. Sylvester came into the bar and took her over. She wasn't looking too good."

"What do you mean?"

He moved his head in a quick negative gesture.

A woman came up and asked for a double scotch. She was behind me, and I didn't recognize her changed voice until she spoke.

"My husband's been drinking double scotches and I say what's sauce for the goose is sauce for the gander and vice versa."

"Okay, Mrs. Sylvester, if you say so."

Marco laid down the photograph and the negative on the bartop and poured her a very meager double scotch. She reached past me with both hands and picked up both the drink and the picture of Kitty. "What's this? I love to look at pictures."

"That's mine," I said.

Her whisky-stunned eyes didn't seem to recognize me. "But you don't mind if I look at it?" she said argumentatively. "That's Mrs. Ketchel, isn't it?"

"Who?"

"Mrs. Ketchel," she said.

"A friend of yours?"

"Hardly." She drew herself erect. Her bouffant hair was slipping down her forehead like a wig. "Her husband was one of my husband's patients at one time. A doctor can't pick and choose his patients, you know."

"I share the problem."

"Of course," she said. "You're the detective, aren't you? What are you doing with a picture of Mrs. Ketchel?"

She waved it in my face. For a moment all the people at the bar were looking in our direction. I took the picture out of her hand and put it and the negative back in my pocket.

"You can trust me with your deep dark secrets," she said. "I'm a doctor's wife."

I slid off my stool and drew her away from the bar to an empty table. "Where is Dr. Sylvester?"

"He drove Marietta Fablon home. She's—she was not in a good way. But he'll be back."

"What's the matter with Mrs. Fablon?"

"What isn't?" she said lightly. "Marietta's a friend of mine, one of the oldest friends I have in this town, but she's certainly let herself go to pieces lately, physically *and* morally. I have no objection to people getting plastered—I'm slightly plastered myself, as a matter of fact, Mr. Arch—"

"Archer," I said.

She went right on: "But Marietta came here really looped tonight. She walked in, if walking is the word, literally rubber-legged. George had to gather up the pieces and take her home. She's getting to be more and more of a burden to George."

"In what respect?"

"Morally *and* financially. She hasn't paid her bill, of course, within living memory, and that's all right, I suppose. She's a friend, live and let live. But when it comes to scrounging more money from him, that's too much."

"Has she been doing that?"

"Has she? Today she invited him for lunch—I happened to be at the

BLACK MONEY • • • 499

hairdresser's—and made a sudden pitch for five thousand dollars. We don't have that kind of ready money in the bank, which is the only way I know about it—he tried to get my signature on the loan. But I said nix." She paused, and her alcohol-angered face grew suddenly quiet with anxiety. I think her mind was playing back what she had said. "I've been telling you my deep dark secrets, haven't I?"

"It's all right."

"It isn't all right if you tell George what I said. You won't tell George what I said?" She had unloaded her malice but she didn't want to take the responsibility for it.

"All right," I said.

"You're nice." She reached for my hand on the tabletop and pressed it rather hard. She was more worried now than she was drunk, trying to think of something to make herself feel better. "Do you like dancing, Mr. Arch?"

"Archer," I said.

"I love to dance myself."

Still holding on to my hand she rose and towed me out onto the dance floor. Round and round we went, with her hair slipping down into both our eyes and her breasts jouncing against me like the special organs of her enthusiasm.

"My first name is Audrey," she confided. "What's your first name, Mr. Arch?"

"Fallen."

Her laughter blasted my right ear-drum. When the music stopped I took her back to the table, and went out to the front office. Ella was still at her post, looking rather wan.

"Are you tired?" I asked her.

She glanced at herself in the wall mirror facing her desk. "Not so very. It's the music. It gets on my nerves when I'm not allowed to dance to it." She passed her hand over her forehead. "I don't know how much longer I can hold this job."

"How long have you been in it?"

"Just two years."

"What did you do before that?"

"I was a housewife. Actually I didn't do much of anything." She changed the subject: "I saw you dancing with Mrs. Sylvester."

"Legwork."

"I don't mean that," she said, not explaining what 'that' was. "Be careful of Audrey Sylvester. She isn't a drunk exactly, but when she drinks she gets drunk."

"What does she do then?"

"Anything that enters her head. Midnight swim in the ocean. Midnight roll in the hay."

"Same midnight?"

"I wouldn't be surprised."

"Can she be believed?"

"Depends on who and what she's talking about."

"Her." I got out my picture of Kitty. "She says her name is Ketchel, and her husband was one of Dr. Sylvester's patients."

"I presume she'd know."

"Speaking of Dr. Sylvester's patients, I understand he took Mrs. Fablon home."

Ella nodded soberly. "I helped her out to his car. It took two of us."

"Was she plastered?"

"I doubt it. She hardly drinks at all."

"Mrs. Sylvester says she was."

"Mrs. Sylvester isn't a reliable witness, especially when she's drunk herself. Marietta—Mrs. Fablon was more sick than anything else, and upset. She's much more upset about Ginny than she lets on."

"Did she say so?"

"Not in so many words. But she came down here for reassurance. She wanted someone to tell her that she had done the right thing in encouraging Ginny's elopement."

"She knows about it then?"

Ella nodded. "Ginny came home tonight. She wanted to pick up a few things and say goodbye. She didn't stay more than about five minutes. Which is what upset her mother, basically, I think."

"When was this?"

"In the last hour or so."

"You're a good witness. How would you like to join my staff permanently?"

"It would depend on what I had to witness."

We smiled at each other, warily. We had both had unsuccessful marriages.

I retreated into the records room. Malkovsky was bent over the pulled-out drawer of a cabinet, riffling through file cards.

"I'm making some progress, I hope. As far as I can see there were seven outside guests, individuals and couples, in September of 1959. I've ruled out four of them—people I remember personally, mostly repeaters. That leaves three: the Sandersons, and the de Houvenels, and the Berglunds. But none of the names rings a bell."

"Try Ketchel."

"Ketchel!" He blinked and smiled. "I believe that's the name. I couldn't find it among the guest cards, though."

"It could have been taken out."

"Or lost," he said. "These older files are in pretty poor shape. But I'm morally certain Ketchel is the name. Where did you pick it up?"

"From one of the members." I got out the negative. "Can you make me some copies of this?"

"I don't see why not."

"How long would it take you?"

"I guess I could have some by tomorrow."

"Tomorrow morning at eight?"

After a moment's hesitation, he said: "I can try."

I gave him the negative, with a lecture about not losing it, and said goodnight to him at the front door. When he was out of hearing, Ella said dryly:

"I hope you're paying him decently. All he makes out of his photography is a bare living. And he has a wife and children."

"I'm paying him decently. There's no record in the files of the Ketchels being guests here."

"Mrs. Sylvester could have given you the wrong name."

"I doubt it. Eric recognized it. More likely someone took the record out of the files. Are they easily accessible?"

"I'm afraid they are. People are in and out of the office, and the records room is open a good deal of the time. Is it very important?"

"It may be. I want to know who sponsored the Ketchels as guests."

"Mr. Stoll might remember. But he's gone off for the night."

She directed me to the manager's cottage. It was closed and dark. The wind whimpered like a lost dog in the shrubbery.

I went back to the main entrance of the club. Dr. Sylvester still hadn't returned. I looked in at the bar, saw Mrs. Sylvester slouched over a drink, and retreated before she saw me.

Ella told me more about her second marriage. Her husband Strome was an attorney in the city, an older man, a widower when she married him. She had been his secretary originally, but being his wife was much more demanding, in subtle ways. Her first husband had been too young; her second was too old. An older man was deeply set in his habits, including his sexual habits.

I let the conversation go on. Such desultory continuing conversations were one of my best sources of information. Besides I liked the woman, and I was interested in her marriage.

The story of it blended with the long rough night we were having. She'd stayed with Strome for six years but in the end she couldn't stick it out. She hadn't even asked for alimony.

Some people left the party, and Ella said goodnight to them by name. Others were staying on. Our conversation, or Ella's monologue, was punctuated by gusts of music, laughter, wind.

Dr. Sylvester's arrival brought it to a full stop. He pushed through the door with angry force.

"Is my wife still here?" he asked Ella.

"I think so, doctor."

"What kind of shape is she in?"

"She's still upright," I said.

He turned a stony eye on me. "Nobody asked you." He started off toward the bar, hesitated, and turned back to Ella: "Would you get her for me, Mrs. Strome? I don't feel like facing that mob again tonight."

"I'll be glad to. How is Mrs. Fablon?"

"She'll be all right. I got her calmed down. She's upset about her daughter, and it was complicated by barbiturates."

"She didn't try to take too many?"

"Nothing like that. She took her regular sleeping pills and then decided to come down here to see her friends. Add one drink, and the result was predictable." He paused, and dropped his professional tone: "Go and get Audrey, will you?"

Ella hurried away down the lighted corridor. I leaned on the reception desk and watched Dr. Sylvester in the mirror. He lit a cigarette and pretended to forget me, but my presence seemed to make him uncomfortable. He coughed smoke, and said:

"Look here, what gives you the right to stand there watching me? Are you the new doorman or something?"

"I'm bucking for the job. The wages are poor but think of the fringe benefits, like getting to know all the best people."

"You're bucking to get thrown out on your ear." His jaw had converted itself into a blunt instrument. His hands were shaking.

He was big enough to hit, and unpleasant enough, but everything else about the occasion was wrong. Besides, he was in transit from one troubled woman to another, and it gave him a certain license.

"Take it easy, doctor. We're on the same side."

"Are we?" He looked at me over his cigarette, smoke crawling on his face. Then, as if its burning tip had touched off his outburst, he threw it down on the marble floor and scotched it under his heel. "I don't even know what the game is," he said in a friendlier tone.

"It's a new kind of game." I didn't have the negative of Kitty and Ketchel, so I described it to him. "The man in the picture, the one with the diamond ring, do you know who he'd be?"

It was an honesty test, but I didn't know whose honesty was being tested, his or his wife's.

He hedged: "It's difficult to tell from a verbal description. Does he have a name?"

"It may be Ketchel. I heard he was your patient."

"Ketchel." He stroked his jaw as if to massage it back into human shape. "I believe I did have a patient of that name once."

"In 1959?"

"It might have been. It might well have been."

"Did he stay here?"

"I believe he did."

I showed him Kitty's picture.

He nodded. "That's Mrs. Ketchel. I couldn't be mistaken about her. She came to my office once, before they left, to get instructions about a salt-free diet. I treated her husband for hypertension. His blood pressure was way up, but I managed to bring it down within the normal range."

"Who is he?"

Sylvester's face went through the motions of remembering. "A retired man from New York. He told me he got in at the start of the bull market, lucky stiff. He owned a cattle spread somewhere in the Southwest."

"In California?"

"I don't remember, at this late date."

"Nevada?"

"I doubt it. I'm hardly famous enough to attract out-of-state patients." The remark seemed forced.

"Would Ketchel's address be in the clinic records?"

"It might, at that. But why are you so interested in Mr. Ketchel?"

"I don't know yet. I just am." I threw him a question from far left field: "Wasn't it just about then that Roy Fablon committed suicide?"

The question took him by surprise. For a moment his face was trying on attitudes. It settled on a kind of false boredom behind which his intelligence sat and watched me.

"Just about when?"

"The picture of the Ketchels was taken in September 1959. When did Fablon die?"

"I'm afraid I don't remember exactly."

"Wasn't he your patient?"

"I have a number of patients and, frankly, my chronological memory isn't so good. I suppose it was around about that time but if you're suggesting any connection—"

"I'm asking, not suggesting."

"Just what are you asking, again?"

"Did Ketchel have anything to do with Fablon's suicide?"

"I have no reason to think so. Anyway, how would I know?"

"They were both friends of yours. In a sense you may have been the connection between them."

"I was?" But he didn't argue the point. He didn't want to go into it at all.

"I've heard it suggested that Fablon didn't commit suicide. His widow raised the question again tonight. Did she raise it with you?"

"She did not," he said without looking at me. "You mean he was drowned by accident?"

"Or murdered."

"Don't believe everything you hear. This place is a hotbed of rumors. People don't have enough to do, so they make up rumors about their friends and neighbors."

"This wasn't exactly a rumor, Dr. Sylvester. It was an opinion. A friend of Fablon's told me he wasn't the sort of man to commit suicide. What's your opinion?"

"I have none."

"That's strange."

"I don't think so. Any man is capable of suicide, given sufficient pressure of circumstances."

"What were the special circumstances of Fablon's suicide?"

"He was at the end of his rope."

"Financially, you mean?"

"And every other way."

He didn't have to explain what he meant. Towed by Ella, his wife hove into view. She had slipped another mental disc and was in a further stage of drunkenness. Her mouth was set in grooves of dull belligerence. Her eyes were fixed.

"I know where you've been. You've been in bed with her, haven't you?"

"You're talking nonsense." He fended her off with his hands. "There's nothing between me and Marietta. There never has been, Aud."

"Except five thousand dollars' worth of something."

"It was supposed to be a loan. I still don't know why you wouldn't co-operate."

"Because we'd never get it back, any more than the other money you've thrown away. It's my money just as much as yours, remember. I worked for seven years so that you could get your degree. And what did I ever get out of it? The money comes in and the money goes out but I never see any of it."

"You get your share."

"Marietta gets *more* than her share."

"That's nonsense. Do you want her to go under?" He looked from me to Ella. Throughout the interchange with his wife, he had been talking to all three of us. Now that his wife was thoroughly discredited, he said: "Don't you think you better come home? You've made enough of a spectacle of yourself for one night."

He reached for her arm. She backed away from him grimacing, trying to recover the feel of her anger. But she was entering a fourth, lugubrious stage.

Still backing away, she bumped into the mirror. She turned around and looked at herself in it. From where I stood I could see her reflected face, swollen with drink and malice, surmounted by a loosened sheaf of hair, with a little trickle of terror in the eyes.

"I'm getting old and heavy," she said. "I can't even afford to take a week in residence at the health farm. But you can afford to gamble our money away."

"I haven't gambled in seven years, and you know it."

Roughly he put his arm around her and walked her out. She was tangle-footed, like a heavyweight fighter at the end of a bad round.

14
. . .

THERE WERE lights in the Jamieson house as I passed, and a single light in Marietta Fablon's. It was after midnight, a poor time for visiting. I went to see Marietta anyway. Her husband's drowned body seemed to be floating just below the surface of the night.

She took a long time to answer my knock. When she did, she opened a Judas window set in the door, and peered at me through the grille. She said above the sound of the wind:

"What do you want?"

"My name is Archer—"

She cut in on me sharply: "I remember you. What do you want?"

"A chance to talk seriously with you."

"I couldn't possibly talk tonight. Come back in the morning."

"I think we should talk now. You're worried about Ginny. So am I."

"Who said I was worried?"

"Dr. Sylvester."

"What else did he say about me?"

"I could tell you better inside."

"Very well. This *is* rather Pyramus and Thisbe, isn't it?"

It was a gallant effort to recover her style. I saw when she let me in to the lighted hallway that she was having a bad night. The barbiturates were still playing tricks with her eyes. Her body, uncorseted under a pink quilted robe, seemed to have slumped down on its fine bones. She had a pink silk cap on her head, and under it her face seemed thinner and older.

"Don't look at me please. I'm not lookable tonight."

She took me into her sitting room. Though she only turned on one lamp I could see that everything in the room, the print-covered chairs and settee and the gay rug and the drapes, was faintly shabby. The only new thing in the room was the pink telephone.

I started to sit on one of the fragile chairs. She made me sit on another, and took a third herself, by the telephone.

"Why did you suddenly get concerned about Ginny?" I said.

"She came home tonight. He was with her. I'm close to my daughter —at least I used to be—and I could sense that she didn't want to go with him. But she was going anyway."

"Why?"

"I don't understand it." Her hands fluttered in her lap, like birds, and one of them pecked at the other. "She seems afraid to go, and afraid *not* to go with him."

"Go where?"

"They wouldn't say. Ginny promised to get in touch with me eventually."

"What was his attitude?"

"Martel? He was very formal and distant. Aggressively polite. He regretted disturbing me at the late hour, but they'd made a sudden decision to leave." She paused, and turned her narrow probing face toward me. "Do you really think the French government is after him?"

"Somebody is."

"But you don't know who."

"Not yet. I want to try a name on you, Mrs. Fablon. Ketchel."

I spelled it. Her queer eyes widened. Her hands clenched knuckle to knuckle.

"Who gave you that name?"

"No one person. The name came up. I take it it's familiar to you."

"My husband knew a man named Ketchel," she said. "He was a gambler." She leaned toward me. "Did Dr. Sylvester give you the name?"

"No, but I understand that Ketchel was one of Dr. Sylvester's patients."

"Yes. He was. He was more than that."

I waited for her to explain what she meant. Finally I said: "Was Ketchel the gambler who took your husband's money?"

"Yes, he was. He took everything we had left, and wanted more. When Roy couldn't pay him—" She paused, as if she sensed that melodrama didn't go with her style. "We won't discuss it any more, Mr. Archer. I'm not at my best tonight. I should never have agreed to talk to you, under these conditions."

"What was the date of your husband's suicide?"

She rose, swaying a little, and moved towards me. I could smell her fatigue.

"You've really been digging into our lives, haven't you? The date, if you must know, was September 29, 1959."

Two days after Malkovsky was paid for his pictures. The coincidence underlined my feeling that Fablon's death was part of the present case.

Mrs. Fablon peered up at me. "That date seems to mean a great deal to you."

"It suggests some possibilities. It must mean a great deal more to you."

"It was the end of my life." She took an unsteady step backwards and sat down again, as if she were falling back into the past, helplessly but not unwillingly. "Everything since has been going through the motions. It's a strange thing, Roy and I fought like animals throughout our marriage. But we loved each other. At least I was in love with him, no matter what he did."

"What did he do?"

"Everything a man can think of. Most of it cost money. My money." She hesitated. "I'm not a money-oriented person, really. That was one of the troubles. In every marriage there should be one partner who cares about money more than other things. Neither of us cared. In the eighteen years of our marriage we went through nearly a million dollars. Please notice the first person plural pronoun. I share the blame. I didn't learn to care about money until it was too late." She stirred, and jerked her shoulders as if the thought of money was a palpable weight on them. "You said the date of my husband's death suggested possibilities. What do you mean?"

"I'm wondering if he really killed himself."

"Of course he did." The statement sounded perfunctory, empty of feeling.

"Did he leave a suicide note?"

"He didn't have to. He announced his intention to me and Ginny a day or two before. God knows what it's done to my daughter's emotional life. I encouraged this Martel business because he was the only real man she's shown any interest in. If I've made a dreadful mistake—"

She dropped the end of the sentence, and returned to her first subject. Her mind was running in swift repetitious circles like a squirrel in a cage. "Can you imagine a man saying such a thing to his wife and his seventeen-year-old daughter? And then doing it? He was angry with me, of course, for running out of money. He didn't believe it could happen. There had always been another bequest coming in from some relative, or another house or piece of land we could sell. But we were down to a rented house and there were no more relatives to die. Roy died instead, by his own hand."

She kept insisting on this, almost as if she was trying to convince me, or persuade herself. I suspected that she was a little out of control, and I had no desire to ask her any more questions. But she went on answering unspoken questions, painfully and obsessively, as if the past had stirred and was talking through her in its sleep:

"That doesn't cover the situation, of course. There are always secret motivations in life—urges and revenges and desires that people don't admit even to themselves. I discovered the real source of my husband's death, quite by accident, just the other day. I'm planning to give up this house and I've been going through my things, sorting and throwing away. I came across a batch of old papers in Roy's desk, and among them was a letter to Roy from—a woman. It absolutely astonished me. It had never occurred to me that, in addition to all his other failings as a husband and father, Roy had been unfaithful. But the letter went into explicit detail on that point."

"May I see it?"

"No. You may not. It was humiliating enough for me to read it by myself."

"Who wrote it?"

"Audrey Sylvester. She didn't sign it but I happen to know her hand-writing."

"Was it still in its envelope?"

"Yes, and the postmark was clear. It was postmarked June 30, 1959, three months before Roy died. After seven years I understood why George Sylvester introduced Ketchel to Roy and stood by smiling while Ketchel cheated Roy out of thirty thousand dollars which he didn't have." She struck herself with her fist on her quilted thigh: "He may even have planned it all. He was Roy's doctor. He may have sensed that Roy was close to suicide, and conspired with Ketchel to push him over the edge."

"Isn't that stretching it a bit, Mrs. Fablon?"

"You don't know George Sylvester. He's a ruthless man. And you don't know Mr. Ketchel. I met him once at the club."

"I'd like to meet him myself. You don't know where he is, do you?"

"No, I do not. Ketchel left Montevista a day or so after Roy disap-peared—long before his body was found."

"Are you implying he knew your husband was dead?"

She bit her mouth, as if to punish it for saying too much. From her eyes I got the swift impression that my guess was accurate, and she knew it, but for some obscure reason she was covering it up.

"Did Ketchel murder your husband?"

"No," she said. "I don't suggest that. But he and George Sylvester were responsible for Roy's death." In the midst of her old grief and rage, she looked at me cautiously. I had the strange feeling that she was sitting apart from herself, playing on her own emotions the way another woman might play on an organ, but leaving one end of the keyboard wholly untouched. "It's indiscreet of me to tell you all this. I'll ask you not to pass it on to anyone, including—*especially* including—Peter and his father."

I was weary of her elaborate reconstructions and evasions. I said bluntly: "I won't pass your story on, and I'll tell you why, Mrs. Fablon. I don't entirely believe it. I don't think you believe it yourself."

She rose shakily. "How dare you speak to me in that way?"

"Because I'm concerned about your daughter's safety. Aren't you?"

"You know I am. I'm terribly concerned."

"Then why won't you tell me the truth as you see it? Was your husband murdered?"

"I don't know. I don't know anything any more. I had a real earthquake shock tonight. The ground was jerked right out from under me. It still isn't holding still."

"What happened?"

"Nothing *happened*. Something was said."

"By your daughter?"

"If I told you any more," she said, "I'd be telling you too much. I'm going to have to get more information before I speak out."

"Getting information is my business."

"I appreciate the offer, but I have to handle this my own way."

Another one of her silences began. She sat perfectly still with her opposing fists pressed fiercely against each other, her eyes absorbing light.

Under the sound of the wind I heard a noise like rats chewing in the wall. I didn't connect it right away with Marietta Fablon. Then I realized that she was grinding her teeth.

It was time I left her in peace. I got my car out from under her groaning oak tree and drove next door to the Jamieson house. The lights were still on there.

15

...

PETER'S FATHER answered the door. He had on pajamas and a bath-robe, and he looked even more transparent and withdrawn than he had in the morning.

"Come in, Mr. Archer, won't you? My housekeeper has gone to bed but I can offer you a drink. I was rather hoping you'd drop by, I have some information for you."

Talking as if it was the middle of the day, he led me along the hall to his library. His movements were uncertain but he managed to steer himself through the door and into his chair. There was a drink beside it. Jamieson seemed to be one of those drinkers who held themselves at a certain level of sobriety all day and all night.

"I'll let you make your own drink. My hands are a little unsteady." He raised his hands and examined their tremor with clinical interest. "I should be in bed, I suppose, but I've almost lost the ability to sleep. These night watches are the hardest. The image of my poor dead wife comes back most vividly. I feel my loss like a vast yawning emptiness, in me as well as the external universe. I forget whether I've shown you a picture of my dead wife?"

Reluctantly I admitted that he hadn't. I had no desire to sit up all night with Jamieson and his irrigated memories. The drink I poured for myself from his fresh bottle was a careful ounce.

Jamieson groped in a leather box and produced a silver-framed photograph of a young woman. She wasn't especially pretty. There had to be other reasons for her husband's extended mourning. Maybe, I thought, grief was the only feeling he was capable of; or maybe it was just an excuse for drinking. I handed the photograph back to him.

"How long ago did she die?"

"Twenty-four years. My poor son killed her in being born. I try not to blame poor Peter, but it's hard sometimes, when I think of all I lost."

"You still have a son."

Jamieson's free hand made a small gesture, nervous and irritable. It said a good deal about his feelings for Peter, or his lack of them.

"Where is Peter, by the way?"

"He went out to the kitchen for a snack. He was on his way to bed. If you'd like to see him—?"

"Later, perhaps. You said you had some information for me."

He nodded. "I talked to one of my friends at the bank. Martel's hundred thousand—actually it was closer to a hundred and twenty thousand—was deposited in the form of a draft on the *Banco de Nueva Granada*—the Bank of New Granada."

"I never heard of it."

"Neither had I, though I've been to Panama City. The New Granada has its headquarters in Panama City."

"Did Martel leave his hundred grand in the local bank?"

"He did not. I was coming to that. He withdrew every cent of it. In cash. The bank offered him a guard but he couldn't be bothered. He packed the money into a briefcase and tossed it into the back of his car."

"When did this happen?"

"Today at five minutes to three, just before the bank closed. He'd phoned first thing in the morning to make sure that they'd have the cash on hand."

"So he was already planning to leave this morning. I wonder where he went."

"Panama, perhaps. That seems to be the source of his money."

"I should report to your son. How do I find the kitchen?"

"It's at the other end of the hallway. You'll see the light. Come back and have another short one with me, won't you, afterwards?"

"It's getting late."

"I'll be glad to give you a bed."

"Thanks, I work better out of a hotel."

I made my way along the passageway toward the kitchen light. Peter was sitting at a table under a hanging lamp. Most of a roast goose lay on a wooden platter in front of him, and he was eating it.

I hadn't tried to soften the sound of my footsteps, but he hadn't heard me coming. I stood in the doorway and watched him. He was eating as I had never seen anyone eat.

With both hands he tore chunks of flesh from the goose's breast and forced them into his mouth, the way you pack meat into a grinder. His face was distorted, his eyes almost invisible.

He tore off a drumstick and bit into its thick end. I crossed the kitchen toward him. The room was large and white and bleak. It reminded me of a disused handball court.

Peter looked up and saw me. He dropped the bird's leg guiltily as if it was a part of a human body. His face was swollen tight and mottled, like a sausage.

"What do you think you're doing?"

"I'm hungry." His voice was fogged with grease.

"Still hungry?"

He nodded, with his dull eyes on the half-demolished bird. It lay in front of him like the carcass of his hopes.

I felt like getting out of there and sending him back the balance of his money. But I've always had trouble walking out on bad luck. I pulled up a chair and sat down across the table from him and talked him out of his stupor.

I don't remember everything I said. Mostly I tried to persuade the boy that he was within the human range. I do remember that my broken monologue was punctuated by a banging noise which came from the general direction of Marietta Fablon's house.

The first time I heard the noise, I thought it might be gunfire. I discounted this when it was repeated over and over at irregular intervals. More likely it was a shutter or an outside door banging in the wind.

Eventually Peter said in a clogged voice: "I apologize."

"Apologize to yourself."

"I beg your pardon?"

"Apologize to yourself. You're the one you're doing it to."

His face was like kneaded dough in the harsh light. "I don't know what gets into me."

"You should take it up with a doctor. It's a disease."

"You think I need a psychiatrist?"

"Most people do at one time or another. You're lucky you can afford one."

"I can't, though. Not really. I won't come into my real money for another year."

"Use your credit. You can afford a psychiatrist if you can afford me."

"You really think there's something the matter with my head?"

"Your heart," I said. "You have a hungry heart. You better find something to feed it with besides food."

"I know. It's why I have to get Ginny back."

"You need to do more than that. If she ever saw you on an eating binge—" It was a cruel sentence. I didn't finish it.

"She has," he said. "That's the trouble. As soon as people find out they turn against me. I suppose you'll be quitting, too."

"No. I'd like to see things get straightened out for you."

"They'll never get straightened out. I'm hopeless."

He was trying to lean his full moral weight on me. I didn't want any more of it than I had, and I tried to objectify the situation a little:

"My grandmother who lived in Martinez was a religious woman. She always said it was sinful to despair."

He shook his head slowly. His eyes seemed to swing with the movement. A minute later he dashed for the kitchen sink and vomited.

While I was trying to clean it and him up, his father appeared in the doorway. He spoke across Peter as if he was deaf or moronic:

"Has my poor boy been eating again?"

"Lay off, Mr. Jamieson."

"I don't know what you mean." He raised his pale hands as if to show what a gentle father he had been. "I've been both father and mother to my son. I've had to be."

Peter stood at the sink with his back to his father, unwilling to show his face. After a while his father drifted away again.

Attached to the great main kitchen, with its tiled counters and sinks and ovens, was a smaller outer kitchen like a glassed-in porch. I became aware of this outer kitchen because there was a noise at the door, a scrabbling and a snuffling which was nearer and more insistent than the banging noise.

"Do you have a dog out there?"

Peter shook his head. "It may be a stray. Let it in. We'll give it a piece of goose."

I turned on the light in the outer kitchen and opened the door. Marietta Fablon crawled in over the threshold. She rose to her knees. Her hands groped up my legs to my waist. There was blood like a dyer's error on her pink quilted breast. Her eyes were as wide and blind as silver coins.

"Shot me."

I got down and held her. "Who, Marietta?"

Her mouth worked. "Lover-boy." The residue of her life came out with the words. I could feel it leave her body.

16
...

PETER APPEARED in the kitchen doorway. He didn't come into the outer kitchen. Death took up all the room.

"What did she say?"

"She said lover-boy shot her. Who would she mean by that?"

"Martel." It was an automatic response. "Is she dead?"

I looked down at her. Death had made her small and dim, like something seen through the wrong end of a telescope.

"I'm afraid she is. You better call the county sheriff's office. Then tell your father."

"Do I have to tell him? He'll find a way to blame me."

"I'll tell him if you like."

"No. I will." He crossed the kitchen purposefully.

I went out into the blowing dark and got the flashlight out of my car. A well-defined path led from the Jamieson garden to the Fablon house. I wondered if Peter's childish feet had worn it.

There were evidences that Marietta had crawled along the path all the way from her house: spots of blood and knee-marks in the dirt. Her pink silk cap had fallen off where the path went through a gap in the boundary hedge. I left it.

Her front door was banging. I went in and found the study. It was dominated by an ornate nineteenth-century desk. I went through the drawers. There was no sign of Audrey Sylvester's love-letter to Fablon, but I found a letter that interested me just as much. It had been written to Mrs. Fablon by Ricardo Rosales, a Vice-President of the Bank of New Granada, Panama City, on March 18 of this year. It said in rather stilted English that the special account from which the Bank had paid her periodic sums of money had been exhausted, and no further instructions had been received concerning it. Under the rules and regulations of the bank it was regrettably not possible for them to name their principal.

In a bottom drawer I came across a framed photograph of a young Air Force second lieutenant who was almost certainly Roy Fablon. The glass was missing from the frame, and small half-moon-shaped pieces of the photograph had been clumsily punched out. It took me a minute to come to the conclusion that it had been pierced repeatedly by the sharp heel of a woman's shoe. I wondered if Marietta had stamped on her husband's picture recently.

In the same drawer I found a man's thin wristwatch with four Latin words engraved on the back: *Mutuis animis amant amantur.* I didn't know Latin, but 'amant' meant something about love.

I looked at Fablon's picture again. To my instructed eyes his head was a cruel hollow-looking bronze. He had been dark and dashing, the kind of man a daughter could fall in love with. Though he had been handsome and Martel wasn't, I imagined I could see some resemblance between them, enough perhaps to account for Ginny's infatuation with Martel. I put the picture and the watch back in the drawer.

A light was burning in the sitting room where I had talked to Marietta, and listened to the grinding of her teeth. The cord of the pink telephone had been ripped out of the wall. There were spots of blood on the worn carpet. This was where her crawl had started.

I could hear a wailing in the distance now, louder than the wind and drearier. It was the sound of a siren, which nearly always came too late. I went outside, leaving the light burning and the door banging behind me.

The sheriff's men were in the Jamieson house before I got back to it. I had to explain who I was and show them my photostat and get Peter to vouch for me before they would let me into the house. They refused to let me go back into the kitchen.

Their failure to co-operate suited me reasonably well. I felt justified in holding back some of the results of my own investigation. But I turned them loose on Martel. By two o'clock the officer in charge, Inspector Harold Olsen, came into the drawing room where I was waiting and told me he'd put out an all-points alarm for Martel. He added:

"You can go home now, Mr. Archer."

"I thought I'd stick around and talk to the coroner."

"I'm the coroner," Olsen said. "I told my deputy, Dr. Wills, not to bother coming out here tonight. He needs his rest. Why don't you go and get some rest, Mr. Archer?" He moved ponderously toward me, a big slow stubborn Swede who liked his suggestions to be taken as orders. "Relax and take it easy. We won't be getting autopsy results for a couple of days at least."

"Why not?" I said without getting up from my chair.

"We never do, that's why." He was in charge here, and his slightly bulging eyes were watching me for any questioning of his power. He gave the impression that if he had to choose, he would rather own a case than solve it. "There's no hurry. She was shot in the chest, we know that now, probably through the lung. She bled to death internally."

"I'm interested in how her husband died."

"He was a suicide. You don't need Dr. Wills to tell you that. I handled the case myself." Olsen was watching me more closely. He was sensitive to the possibility that I might question his findings, and already quivering in advance with a faint sense of outrage. "It's a closed case."

"Doesn't this kind of reopen it?"

"No. It don't." He was retreating angrily into bad grammar. "Fablon committed suicide. He told his wife he was gonna, and he did it. There was no evidence of foul play."

"I thought he was badly bunged up."

"By sharks, and by the rocks. There's a lot of wave motion off of there, and it rolled him around on the bottom for ten days." Olsen made it sound a little like a threat. "But all the damage was done after he drowned. He died of drowning in salt water. Dr. Wills will tell you the same thing."

"Where can I find Wills tomorrow?"

"He's got an office in the basement of Mercy Hospital. But he can't tell you any more than I can."

Olsen left the room, wrapped in the brooding pride of a master craftsman whose handiwork has been criticized by a journeyman. I waited until I couldn't hear his footsteps, then made my way to the library. The door was locked, but there was light under it.

"Who is it?" the housekeeper Vera said through the door.

"Archer."

She let me in. She had on a rayon sunburst kimono. When she sat down on the hassock at Jamieson's feet, I could see the two black braids hanging down her back like severed cables.

"It's a dreadful thing," he said weakly. "What do you make of it, Archer?"

"It's too soon to ask me that. Marietta said that lover-boy shot her. Does that have any special meaning to you?"

"No."

"Did she have a lover?"

"Certainly not to my knowledge."

"If she did have a lover, who would it be?"

"I have no idea. Frankly, I haven't had too much to do with the Fablons since Roy died, even before that. It's true we were close friends in college, and for a few years after, but our lives took different turnings. About Marietta's private life I'm completely ignorant. It does occur to me, though, that she may have meant somebody else's lover-boy."

"Martel, you mean?"

"It's the obvious thought, isn't it?"

"It's so obvious I'm afraid of it. But I did come across a peculiar connection between him and Marietta. She's been drawing some kind of an income from the Bank of New Granada."

"Marietta has?"

"That's right. It was cut off within the last couple of months."

"Who was the source of the income?"

"That isn't clear. It may have been Martel, and if it was it suggests a wild possibility. Marietta may have sold her daughter to him."

"She wouldn't do that!" Jamieson was as shocked as his anaesthetized condition would permit.

"Plenty of other mothers do. They don't call it selling, but that's what it boils down to. A debutante ball is the closest thing we have to the Sudanese slave markets."

Vera let out a ribald mirthless laugh. Her employer frowned severely at her, and said as if in rebuke:

"But Marietta is—was devoted to Ginny."

"She also knows how important money is. She told me so herself."

"Really? She used to throw her money around as if her resources were inexhaustible. I've had to bail her—"

Vera glanced up sharply, and Jamieson decided not to finish the sentence. I said:

"Maybe her daughter was the only resource she had left."

I was trying out the idea, and Jamieson sensed my purpose. "Possibly you could be right. Marietta's hardened in these last few years, since Roy died. But even assuming that you are right, why would she marry Virginia off to a dubious foreigner? She had my poor son Peter ready and willing."

"I don't know. The marriage may have been Ginny's idea after all. And the fact that Marietta and Martel got money from the same Panama bank may be pure coincidence."

"You don't believe it is, though?"

"No. I've lost my faith in pure coincidence. Everything in life tends to hang together in a pattern. Of course the clearest pattern so far in this case is death repeating itself. The fact that Mrs. Fablon was murdered brings up the question of her husband's death again."

"But wasn't it established that Roy killed himself?"

Vera frowned, as if he had said something obscene. Unobtrusively she crossed herself.

"That's the official story, anyway," I said. "It's open to question now. Everything is. I understand you identified his body."

"I was one of those who did."

"Are you certain it was Roy Fablon?"

He hesitated, and stirred in his chair uncomfortably. "I was certain at the time. That means I have to be certain now, doesn't it? It's not a memory I care to dwell on, frankly. His face was swollen, and terribly cut up."

Jamieson closed his eyes tight. Vera reached for his hand and held it.

"So you couldn't be certain it was him?"

"Not just by looking at him. He'd gone through quite a sea-change. But I had no reason to doubt it was Roy, either. The doctor at the inquest, Dr. Wills, said he had irrefus—" He stumbled over the word— "irrefutable evidence that it was Roy."

"Do you recall what it was?"

"It had to do with X rays of the old fractures in his legs."

"That ought to take care of that, then."

"Of what?" he said rather irritably.

"The possibility that it was a faked suicide and that somebody else wore Fablon's overcoat into the ocean. It's a possibility worth considering when a man is deep in debt. But what you've just told me rules it out."

"I should think so."

"A minute ago," I said, "you started to tell me about bailing out Mrs. Fablon."

"That was in the distant past. I helped out both of them on occasion. In a way I felt responsible for Roy."

Vera stirred angrily. "You gave her the house."

"What house?"

Jamieson answered me: "The one she's living in—was living in. I didn't exactly give it to her. She had the use of it. After all, she was kind to my poor son. And so was Roy in his time."

"Did he hit you for much?"

"A few thousand. It would have been more, but most of my capital was tied up in trust funds. Roy was desperate for money in his last days. He was gambling, with money that he didn't have."

"Gambling with a man named Ketchel?"

"Yes, that was his name."

"Did you know Ketchel?"

"I never met him, no. I heard about him."

"From whom?"

"From Marietta. During the ten or eleven days that Roy was missing, before his body came up, Marietta did quite a lot of talking about Ketchel. She seemed to suspect him of murdering Roy. But she had no evidence, and I dissuaded her from going to the police. After the fact of suicide was established, she dropped the idea."

Vera moved uneasily and tugged at Jamieson's hand, as if the dead woman was her subtle rival. "Come to bed, you're a crazy man sitting up all night."

The special proprieties of the house seemed to have broken down. I rose to go. Vera looked up with relief.

Jamieson said past her: "I assumed at the time that Marietta was fantasying about murder, simply because it was hard for her to face the fact of suicide. You don't suppose she had something after all?"

"Perhaps she did. Inspector Olsen tells me that Fablon definitely died by drowning in salt water. It could be a method of committing murder, though in this case it isn't a likely one. But I'd still like to talk to Ketchel. I don't suppose you know where I can find him?"

"I haven't the faintest idea. He's just a name to me."

Vera's eyes were on me, pushing me out.

The cops were still in the kitchen. Marietta wasn't. Neither was Peter. The big room had taken on an air of grimy official desolation which was familiar to me. I had once been a cop myself, on the Long Beach force, hardly more than a howitzer-throw from here.

17

• • •

I DROVE BACK toward the harbor by way of the ocean boulevard, to spend what was left of the night at the Breakwater Hotel. One or both of the Hendrickses might turn up there, though I didn't expect them to.

I found myself slowing down as I came near the hobo jungle. It was just as well I did, or I might not have noticed Harry's Cadillac. It was on the strip of grass on the ocean side, nosed into the trunk of a palm tree.

There had been a violent impact. The base of the tree was gashed. The Cadillac's heavy bumper had been forced back into the radiator. The shatterproof windshield was blurred in one place by a head mark. I found some spatterings of blood on the front seat.

Whoever had taken and wrecked the car had left the keys in the ignition. I did what I should have done before: used them to open the trunk.

Harry lay there with his back to me. I put my hand under his head and turned up his face. He had been badly beaten. Until he moaned I thought he might be dead.

I got my arms under his shoulders and legs and lifted him out. It was like delivering a big inert baby from an iron womb. I laid him out on the grass and looked around for help.

The wind hissed in the dry palm fronds overhead. There was nothing human in sight. But I didn't want to leave Harry. Somebody might steal him again.

I walked across the beach to wet my handkerchief in the water and got one of my feet wet, to no avail. Harry moaned when I wiped his face with the wet cloth, but he didn't come to. When I lifted one of his eyelids, all I could see was white.

I calculated that he had been unconscious in the trunk for six or seven hours: there wasn't much doubt in my mind that the blood on Martel's heel was Harry's blood: and I decided to get him to a hospital. I heaved him up in my arms again.

I was halfway to my car when a city patrol car with a red light on the roof drifted into sight. It stopped and an officer got out.

"What do you think you're doing?"

"This man was in an accident. I'm taking him to a hospital."

"We'll do that."

He was a young officer, with a keen edge on his voice. He lifted Harry out of my clutches and deposited him on the back seat of the patrol car. Then he turned back to me with his hands on his gun butt.

"Looks to me like he was beaten."

"Yeah."

"Let's see your hands. Come around in the headlights."

I showed him my hands under the white beam. A second officer got out of the driver's seat and came up behind me.

"I didn't beat him. You can see for yourself."

"Who did?"

"I wouldn't know." I didn't feel like going into the subject of Martel. "I saw the wrecked car and opened up the trunk and he was in it. It's his car. I think it was stolen."

"You know him?"

"Slightly. His name is Harry Hendricks. We're both staying at the Breakwater Hotel. You can reach me there later if you want to." I told them who I was. "Right now you better get him to a hospital."

"Don't worry. We will."

"Which hospital?"

"It'll be County, unless you want to pay for him. Mercy asks for a one-day deposit."

"How much?"

"Twenty bucks, on the ward."

I gave him twenty of Peter's dollars. The officer said his name was Ward Rasmussen, and he would bring me a receipt from the hospital.

The lobby of the Breakwater Hotel was empty except for the ancient bellhop asleep on a settee. I touched him. He started and called out:

"Martha?"

"Who's Martha?"

He rubbed his bleared eyes. "I knew a girl Martha. Did I say Martha?"

"Yep."

"Must have been dreaming about her. I knew her in Red Bluff. Martha Truitt. I was born and raised in Red Bluff. That was a long time ago."

Eye-deep in time he trudged around behind the desk and let me register and gave me the key to room 28, which I asked for. The electric clock over his head said it was five minutes past three.

I asked the old man if the red-headed woman, Mrs. Hendricks, had come back to the hotel. He didn't remember. I left him shaking his head over Martha Truitt.

I fell into bed and dreamed about nothing at all. The wind died just before dawn. I heard the quiet and woke up wondering what was missing. Gray light fogged the window. I could hear the sea thumping like a beggar at the bottom of the town. I turned over and dropped back to sleep.

The telephone woke me. The desk said a policeman wanted to see me. It was full morning, a quarter to eight by my watch.

While I thought of it, I phoned Eric Malkovsky's studio. He was there.

"Have you been up all night, Eric?"

"I get up early. I made some enlargements of that negative. Something came out on them that I want to show you."

"What is it?"

"I'd rather you saw them for yourself and drew your own conclusions."

"Can you bring them to the Breakwater Hotel?"

He said he could.

"I'll either be in room 28 or in the coffee shop."

I pulled on my clothes and went down to the lobby. The young officer, Rasmussen, was carrying Harry's pearl-gray hat. He handed me a receipt for twenty dollars.

"I hate to get you up so early," he said, "but I'm going off duty."

"It's time I was up. How's Harry?"

"He's coming out of it. They'll be shunting him off to County unless you deposit more money today."

"Does that make sense?"

"It's the way the hospital runs its business. I've seen people die on the way between Mercy and County. I don't mean that your friend is liable to die," he added carefully. "The doctor says he'll be okay."

"He isn't my friend, exactly."

"He must be twenty dollars' worth of a friend. Incidentally, if you're going out to the hospital you can give him his hat. I took it out of his car before the wreckers towed it away. It's a good hat, and he'll want it back."

He gave me the hat. I didn't bother pointing out that it had the wrong name in it. I was wondering who L. Spillman was, and how Harry got his hat.

"The car's totaled out," Rasmussen said. "It wasn't worth much, but auto theft is auto theft. We picked up three suspects, by the way. They made it easy for us. One of them got a cut head in the accident, and his buddies brought him to the emergency ward."

"The orange-pickers?"

"Pardon?"

"A white man and a couple of darker brothers?"

"You saw them, did you?" Rasmussen said.

"I saw them. What are you going to do with them?"

"It depends on what they did. I haven't figured it out yet. If they locked your friend in the trunk and drove him someplace, it's technically kidnapping."

"I don't think they knew he was in the trunk."

"Then who beat him up? The doctor said he took quite a clobbering, that he was beaten and kicked."

"I'm not surprised."

"Do you have any thoughts on who did it to him?"

"Yes, but it will take time."

He said he had plenty of time, all day in fact. I bought him breakfast, over his objections, and with his ham and eggs and coffee I made him the dubious gift of a piece of the Martel case.

Rasmussen listened intently. "You think Martel beat up Hendricks?"

"I'm morally certain he did—caught him spying on his house and let him have it. But there's not much point in speculating. Hendricks can tell us about it when he's able to talk."

Rasmussen sipped his coffee and made a bitter face. "How did Hendricks's car get down on the boulevard?"

"I think Martel drove it there, with Hendricks in the trunk, and left it where it would be liable to be stolen."

Ward Rasmussen looked at me sharply over his coffee cup. His eyes had the blue intensity of Bunsen flames. With his square jaw and disciplined young mouth it gave him a slightly fanatical look. "Who is this Martel? And why would Virginia Fablon marry him?"

"That's the question I'm working on. He claims to be a wealthy Frenchman who's in trouble with the French government. Hendricks says he's a cheap crook. Martel may be a crook, and I suspect he is, but he isn't a cheap one. He's traveling with a hundred grand in cash, in a Bentley, with the prettiest girl in town."

"I knew Virginia in high school," Rasmussen said. "She *was* a beautiful girl. And she had a lot on the ball. She made it to college when she was sixteen years old. She graduated from high school a whole semester ahead of the class."

"You seem to remember quite a lot about her."

"I used to follow her down the street," he said. "Just once I got up the nerve to ask her to go to a dance with me. That was when I was captain of the football team. But she was going with Peter Jamieson." A shadow of envy moved across his eyes. He lifted his crewcut head as if to shake it off. "It's funny she'd turn around and marry this Martel. You think he came to town to marry her?"

"That's what happened, anyway. I don't know what his original plans were."

"Where did he get the hundred thousand?"

"He deposited it in the form of a draft on a bank in Panama City, the Bank of New Granada. It fits in with his claim that his family has holdings in various foreign countries."

Rasmussen leaned across the table, elbowing his empty cup to one side. "It fits in equally well with the fact—the idea that he's a crook. A lot of criminal money gravitates to Panama, on account of their banking laws."

"I know. That's why I mentioned it. There's another thing. The woman who was shot last night, Virginia Fablon's mother, had an income from the same bank."

"How much of an income?"

"I don't know. You may be able to get the details from her local bank, the National."

"I'll give it a whirl." He took out a new-looking notebook.

While he was making some shorthand notes, Eric Malkovsky arrived, carrying a manila envelope. I introduced the two men. Then

Eric got his enlargements out of the envelope and spread them on the table.

They were about six-by-eight inches, fresh and clear as though they had been taken the day before. I could see every line on Ketchel's face. Though he was smiling, sickness lurked behind his smile. The lines around his mouth might just as well have meant dismay. He had the look of a man who had fought his way to the top, or what he considered the top, but took no pleasure in that or anything else.

In the enlargement, the meaning of Kitty's face had changed a little. Her eyes seemed to hold a faint suspicion that she was a woman who could do something better than just wear clothes. But in the Kitty I had met last night, here in the Breakwater Hotel, the suspicion seemed to have died and left no trace.

"You did a good job, Eric. These pictures will be a big help."

"Thanks." But he was impatient with me. He reached across me and stabbed at the top picture with his forefinger. "Take a good look at the man in the background, the one holding the tray."

Almost immediately I saw what he meant. Behind the busboy's wide black mustache I recognized a younger version of Martel.

"He was nothing but a waiter at the club," Malkovsky said. "Not even a waiter. A busboy. And I let him walk all over me."

Rasmussen said politely: "May I see one of those?"

I handed him the top picture, and he studied it. The waitress came to the table with a pot of coffee and a breakfast menu spotted with samples of past breakfasts. The waitress herself wore visible clues to her history, in her generous mouth and disappointed eyes, her never-say-die blonde hair, her bunion limp.

"You want to order?" she said to Eric.

"I've already eaten breakfast. I'll have some coffee."

I said that I would, too. The waitress noticed the picture in front of me when she was pouring it.

"I know that girl," she said. "She was in here last night. She changed the color of her hair, didn't she?"

"What time last night?"

"It must have been before seven. I went off at seven. She ordered a chicken sandwich, all white meat." She leaned above me confidentially. "Is she a movie star or something?"

"What makes you think she's a movie star?"

"I dunno. The way she was dressed, the way she looked. She's a very

BLACK MONEY • • • 527

lovely girl." She heard her own voice, raised in enthusiasm, and lowered it. "Excuse me, I didn't mean to be nosey."

"That's all right."

She limped away, looking slightly more disappointed than she had. Rasmussen said when she was out of hearing:

"It's a funny thing, but I think I know her, too."

"You may at that. She says she was raised here in town, somewhere in the neighborhood of the railroad tracks."

Ward Rasmussen scratched his crewcut. "I'm pretty sure I've seen her. What's her name?"

"Kitty Hendricks. She is, or was, Harry Hendricks's wife. According to her, she's still married to Hendricks, but they haven't been living together. Seven years ago she was living with the man in the picture there —his name is Ketchel—and she probably still is. She fed me an elaborate story about being private secretary to a tycoon that Martel stole some securities from. But I don't put much stock in that."

Ward took some notes. "Where do we go from here?"

"You're in this, are you?"

He smiled. "It beats citing people for jaywalking. My ambition is to do detective work. Incidentally, may I keep a copy of this picture?"

"I want you to. Remember she's seven years older now, and red-headed. See if you can track down her family and get a line on her whereabouts. She probably knows a lot more than she told me. Also, she'll lead us to Ketchel, I hope."

He folded the picture into his notebook. "I'll get right on it."

Before he left, Ward wrote his address and telephone number on a page of his notebook. He was still living with his father, he said, though he hoped to get married soon. He handed me the tornout page, and strode out of the coffee shop, eager even on his own time.

My heart went out to the boy. More than twenty years ago, when I was a rookie on the Long Beach force, I had felt very much as he did. He was new to the harness, and I hoped it wouldn't cut too deep into his willing spirit.

18

. . .

THE TENNIS CLUB didn't open till ten o'clock, Eric told me. I found Reto Stoll, the manager, in his cottage next door to Mrs. Bagshaw's. He was wearing a blue blazer with gilt buttons which went strangely with the heavy somber furniture in his living room. There was nothing personal in the room except the faint stale odor of burnt incense.

Stoll greeted me with anxious courtesy. He made me sit down in the armchair where he had obviously been reading the morning paper. He fidgeted and wrung his hands.

"This is terrible about Mrs. Fablon."

"It couldn't be in the paper yet."

"No. Mrs. Bagshaw told me. The old ladies of Montevista have a grapevine," he added parenthetically. "This news comes as a terrible shock to all of us. Mrs. Fablon was one of our most delightful members. Who would want to kill such a charming woman?" No doubt he was sincere, but he didn't have the knack of sounding that way about women.

"You may be able to help me answer that question, Mr. Stoll." I showed him one of the enlargements. "Do you recognize these people?"

He carried the picture to the sliding glass door which opened onto his patio. His gray eyes narrowed. His mouth pursed in distaste.

"They stayed here as guests a number of years ago. Frankly, I didn't want to admit them. They weren't our type. But Dr. Sylvester made an issue of it."

"Why?"

"The man was his patient, apparently a very important patient."

"Did he tell you anything else about him?"

"He didn't have to. I recognized the type. It belongs in Palm Springs or Las Vegas, not here." He screwed up his face painfully, and slapped his forehead. "I should be able to remember his name."

"Ketchel."

"That's it. Ketchel. I put him and the woman in the cottage next to me"—he gestured toward Mrs. Bagshaw's cottage—"where I could keep an eye on them."

"What did you see?"

"They behaved better than I expected. There were no wild drinking parties, nothing like that."

"I understand they played a lot of cards."

"Oh?"

"And that Roy Fablon took part."

Stoll looked past me. He could see the threat of scandal a long way off. "Where did you hear that?"

"From Mrs. Fablon."

"Then I suppose it must be true. I don't remember, myself."

"Come off it, Reto. You're plugged in to the Montevista grapevine, you must have heard that Fablon lost a lot of money to Ketchel. Mrs. Fablon blamed him for her husband's death."

The threat of scandal darkened on his face. "The Tennis Club is not responsible."

"Were you here the night Fablon disappeared?"

"No. I was not. I can't stay on duty twenty-four hours a day." He looked at his watch. It was nearly ten o'clock. He was getting ready to terminate the interview.

"I want you to take another look at the picture. Do you recognize the young man in the white jacket?"

He held the picture up to the light. "Vaguely I remember him. I think he only lasted a few weeks." He sucked in his breath abruptly. "This looks like Martel. Is it?"

"I'm pretty sure it is. What was he doing working for you as a bus-boy?"

His hands made a helpless outward gesture encompassing the past and the present and a fairly dubious future. He sat down. "I have no idea. As I recall he was only part-time help, doing mostly cleanup work. At the height of the season I sometimes use the cleanup boys to serve the cottages."

"Where do you recruit the boys?"

"At the State Employment office. They're unskilled labor, we train them. Some we get from the placement bureau at the state college. I don't remember where we recruited this one." He looked at the picture again, then fanned himself with it. "I could look it up in the records."

"Please do. It could be the most important thing you do this year."

He locked the door of his cottage and took me through the gate into the pool enclosure. Undisturbed by swimmers, the water lay like a slab of green glass in the sun. We walked around it to Stoll's office. He left me sitting at his desk, and disappeared into the records room.

He emerged in about five minutes with a filing card. "I'm pretty sure this is the one we want, if I can trust my memory. But the name is not Martel."

The name was Feliz Cervantes. He had been recruited through the state college and employed on a part-time basis, afternoons and evenings, at $1.25 an hour. His period of employment had been brief, extending from September 14 to September 30, 1959.

"Was he fired?"

"He quit," Stoll said. "According to the record he left on September 30, without collecting his last two days' pay."

"That's interesting. Roy Fablon disappeared on September 29. Feliz Cervantes quit September 30. Ketchel left October 1."

"And you connect those three happenings?" he said.

"It's hard not to."

I used Stoll's telephone to make an eleven o'clock appointment with the head of the placement bureau at the college, a man named Martin. I gave him the name Feliz Cervantes to check out.

While I was still at the club I paid a visit to Mrs. Bagshaw. Reluctantly she gave me the address of her friends in Georgetown, the Plimsolls, whom Martel had claimed to know.

I sent the address Airmail Special, along with Martel's picture, to a man named Ralph Christman who ran a detective agency in Washington. I asked Christman to interview the Plimsolls personally, and to phone the results to my answering service in Hollywood. I should get them some time tomorrow, if everything clicked.

19
...

THE COLLEGE was in what had recently been the country. On the scalped hills around it were a few remnants of the orange groves which had once furred them with green. The trees on the campus itself were mostly palms, and looked as if they had been brought in and planted full grown. The students gave a similar impression.

One of them, a youth with a beard which made him look like a tall Toulouse-Lautrec, told me how to find Mr. Martin's office. Its entrance was behind a pierced concrete screen at the side of the administration building, which was one of a Stonehenge oval of buildings surrounding the open center of the campus.

I stepped out of the sunlight into the cold glare of flourescent lights. A young woman came up to the counter and informed me that Mr. Martin was expecting me.

He was a bald man in shirtsleeves with a salesman's forceful stare. The paneled walls of his office were cool and impersonal, and made him look out of place.

"Nice office," I said when we had shaken hands.

"I can't get used to it. It's a funny thing. I'll be here five years in August, but I'm still nostalgic for the quonset hut we started in. But you're not interested in past history."

"I am in Feliz Cervantes's past history."

"Right. That's quite a name. Feliz means 'happy,' you know. Happy Cervantes. Well, let's hope he is. I don't remember him personally— he didn't stay with us long—but I had his records pulled." He opened a manila folder on his desk. "What do you want to know about Happy Cervantes?"

"Everything you have."

"That isn't much, I'm afraid. Just why is Mr. Stoll interested in him?"

"He came back to town a couple of months ago, under an assumed name."

"Has he done something wrong?"

"He's wanted on suspicion of assault," I said, toning it down. "We're trying to establish his identity."

"I'm glad to co-operate with Mr. Stoll—he uses a lot of our boys—but I may not be too much help. Cervantes could be an assumed name, too."

"But don't your students have to present records, of birth and education and so on, before you let them in?"

"They're supposed to. But Cervantes didn't." Martin peered down at the contents of the folder. "There's a note here to the effect that he claimed to be a transfer student from L.A. State. We admitted him provisionally on the understanding that his transcripts would reach us by the first of October. By that time he'd already left us, and if the transcripts ever arrived we sent them back."

"Where did he go?"

He shrugged, retracting his bald head tortoiselike between his shoulders. "We don't keep track of our dropouts. Actually he never *was* our student." He had no transcript, Martin seemed to be saying, therefore he didn't exist. "You might try his old address here, in case he left a forwarding address. It's care of Mrs. Grantham, on Shore Drive, number 148. She has quite a few apartments which she rents to students."

I made a note of the address. "What courses was Cervantes taking?"

"I don't have a record of that. He didn't stay long enough to have his grades posted, and that's all we're interested in. I suppose you could try the Dean's office, if it's important. He's in this building."

I walked around the outside of the building to the Dean's office. His secretary was a large-busted brunette of uncertain age who handled herself with a kind of stylized precision. She typed Cervantes's name on a piece of paper and took it into a filing room, emerging with the written information that he had registered in French Language and Literature, on the senior level, and upper-division Modern European History.

I was certain for the first time that Feliz Cervantes and Francis Martel were the same man. I felt a certain humiliation for him. He had taken a big leap and found a toehold. Now he was falling.

"Who taught him French Language and Literature?"

"Professor Tappinger. He's still teaching the course."

"I was hoping it would be Professor Tappinger."

"Oh? Do you know him?"

"Slightly. Is he on campus now?"

"He is, yes, but I'm afraid he's in class." The woman glanced at the electric clock on the wall. "It's twenty minutes to twelve. He'll finish his lecture at twelve exactly. He always does." She seemed to take a certain pride in this.

"Do you know where everybody on campus is all the time?"

"Just some of them," she said. "Professor Tappinger is one of our institutions."

"He doesn't look much like an institution."

"He is, though. He's one of our most brilliant scholars." As if she was an institution herself, she added: "We consider ourselves very fortunate to have attracted him and kept him. I was worried he'd leave when he didn't get his promotion."

"Why didn't he?"

"You want the truth?"

"I couldn't live without it."

She leaned toward me and lowered her voice, as if the Dean might have the place bugged. "Professor Tappinger is too dedicated to his work. He can't be bothered with departmental politics. And frankly his wife is no help."

"I thought she was cute."

"I suppose she's cute enough. But she's a flibbertigibbet. If Professor Tappinger had a mature partner—" The sentence faded out. For a moment her efficient eyes were fixed on dreamland. It wasn't hard to guess the identity of the mature partner she had in mind for Tappinger.

She directed me in a rather proprietary way to his office in the Arts Building and assured me he always returned there with his lecture notes before he went home for lunch. She wasn't wrong. At one minute after twelve, the professor came marching down the corridor, flushed and bright-eyed, as if he had had a good class.

He did a double take when he saw me. "Why, it's Mr. Archer. I'm always surprised when I see somebody from the real world in these purlieus."

"This isn't real?"

"Not really real. It hasn't been here long enough, for one thing."

"I have."

Tappinger laughed. Away from his wife and family, he seemed to be much more cheerful. "We've both been around long enough to know who we are. But don't let me keep you standing out here." He unlocked the door of his office and urged me inside. Two walls of shelves were filled with books, many of them unbound French volumes and sets. "I suppose you've come to report the results of the test?"

"Partly. It was a success, from Martel's point of view. He answered every question correctly."

"Even the pineal gland?"

"Even that."

"I'm amazed, frankly amazed."

"It may be a sort of compliment to you. Martel seems to be a former student of yours. You had him for a week or two, anyway, seven years ago."

He gave me a startled look. "How can that be?"

"I don't know. But it can't be pure coincidence."

I got out Martel's picture and handed it to him. He nodded his head over it. "I remember the boy. He was a brilliant student, one of the most brilliant I've ever had. Unaccountably he dropped out, without a word to me." His cheerfulness had evaporated. Now he was shaking his head from side to side. "What happened to him?"

"I don't know. Except that he turned up here seven years later with a wad of money and a new identity. Do you recall the name he used in your class?"

"You don't forget a student like that. He called himself Feliz Cervantes." He looked down at the picture again. "Who are these other people?"

"Guests at the Tennis Club. Cervantes held a job there for a couple of weeks in September of '59. He was part-time cleanup help."

Tappinger made a clucking sound. "I remember he seemed to be in need of money. The one time I entertained him in my house, he ate up virtually everything in sight. But you say he has money now?"

"At least a hundred thousand dollars. In cash."

He whistled. "That's just about ten years' salary for me. Where did he get it?"

"He says it's family money, but I'm pretty sure he's lying."

He studied the picture some more, as if he was still a little confused by Martel's double identity. "I'm sure he had no family background to speak of."

"Do you have any idea where he came from?"

"I assumed he was a Spanish-American, probably a first-generation

Mexican. He spoke with quite an accent. As a matter of fact, his French was better than his English."

"Perhaps he is a Frenchman after all."

"With a name like Feliz Cervantes?"

"We don't know that that's his real name, either."

"His transcripts would show his real name," Tappinger said.

"But they're not on file here. He was supposed to have gone to L.A. State College before he came here. Maybe they can help us."

"I'll query L.A. State. A former student of mine is teaching in the French department there."

"I can get in touch with him. What's his name?"

"Allan Bosch." He spelled the surname for me. "But I think it would be better if I made the contact. We university teachers have certain—ah—inhibitions about talking about our students."

"When can I check back with you?"

"Tomorrow morning, I should think. Right at the moment I'm on a very tight schedule. My wife is expecting me for lunch and I have to get back here in time to look over my notes for a two o'clock class." I must have showed my disappointment because he added: "Look here, old chap, come home with me for lunch."

"I can't do that."

"But I insist. Bess would insist, too. She took quite a liking to you. Besides, she may recall something about Cervantes that I don't. I remember she was impressed with him when he came to our party. And people, frankly, are not my *métier*."

I said I would meet him at his house. On the way there I bought a bottle of pink champagne. My case was starting to break.

Bess Tappinger had on a good-looking blue dress, fresh lipstick, and too much perfume. I didn't like the purposeful look in her eye, and I began to regret the pink champagne. She took it from my hands as if she planned to break it over the prow of an affair.

She had covered the dinette table with a fresh linen cloth cross-hatched with fold marks. "I hope you like ham, Mr. Archer. All I have is cold ham and potato salad." She turned to her husband. "Daddy, what do the wine books say about ham and pink champagne?"

"I'm sure they go together very well," he said remotely.

Tappinger had lost his effervescence. A glass of champagne failed to restore it. He chewed fitfully at a ham sandwich and asked me questions about Cervantes-Martel. I had to admit his former student was wanted on suspicion of murder. Tappinger shook his head over the young man's broken promise.

Bess Tappinger was excited by the champagne. She wanted our attention. "Who are we talking about?"

"Feliz Cervantes. You remember him, Bess."

"Am I supposed to?"

"I'm sure you remember him—the Spanish young man. He came to our *Cercle Français* icebreaker seven years ago. Show her the picture of him, will you, Archer?"

I put it down on the linen cloth beside her plate. She recognized the busboy right away. "Of course I remember him."

"I thought you would," her husband said meaningfully. "You talked about him afterwards."

"What impressed you, Mrs. Tappinger?"

"I thought he was good-looking, in a strong masculine way." There was bright malice in her eyes. "We faculty wives get tired of pale scholarly types."

Tappinger countered obliquely: "He was an excellent student. He had a passion for French civilization, which is the greatest since the Athenian, and a wonderfully good ear for French poetry, considering his lack of background."

His wife was working on another glass of champagne. "You're a genius, Daddy. You can make a sentence sound like a fifty-minute lecture."

Perhaps she meant it lightly, as her consciously pretty smile seemed to insist, but it fell with a dull thud.

"Please don't keep calling me Daddy."

"But you don't like me to call you Taps any more. And you are the father of my children."

"The children are not here and I'm most definitely not *your* father. I'm only forty-one."

"I'm only twenty-nine," she said to both of us.

"Twelve years is no great difference." He closed the subject abruptly as if it was a kind of Pandora's box. "Where is Teddy, by the way, since he's not here?"

"At the co-operative nursery. They'll keep him till after his nap."

"Good."

"I'm going to the Plaza and do a little shopping after lunch."

BLACK MONEY • • • 537

The conflict between them, which had been submerged for a moment, flared up again. "You can't." He had turned quite pale.

"Why can't I?"

"I'm using the Fiat. I have a two o'clock class." He looked at his watch. "As a matter of fact I should be starting back now. I have some preparation to do."

"I haven't had much of a chance to talk to your wife—"

"I realize that. I'm sorry, Mr. Archer. The fact is I have to punch a time clock, almost literally, just like any assembly-line worker. And the students are more and more like assembly-line products, acquiring a thin veneer of education as they glide by us. They learn their irregular verbs, but they don't know how to use them in a sentence. In fact very few of them are capable of composing a decent sentence in English, let alone in French, which is the language of the sentence *par excellence*."

He seemed to be converting his anger with his wife into anger with his job, and the whole thing into a lecture. She looked at me with a faint smile, as if she had tuned him out:

"Why don't *you* drive me to the Plaza, Mr. Archer? It will give us a chance to finish our talk."

"I'll be glad to."

Tappinger made no objection. He completed another paragraph about the occupational sorrows of teaching in a second-rate college, then retreated from the shambles of the lunch. I heard his Fiat put-put away. His wife and I sat in the dinette and finished the champagne.

"Well," she said, "here we are."

"Just as you planned."

"I didn't plan it. You did. You bought the champagne, and I can't handle champagne." She gave me a dizzy look.

"I can."

"What are you," she said, "another cold fish?"

She was rough. They get that way, sometimes, when they marry too young and trap themselves in a kitchen and wake up ten years later wondering where the world is. As if she could read my thought, she said:

"I know, I'm a bee-eye-tee-see-aitch. But I have some reason. He sits out in his study every night till past midnight. Is my life supposed to be over because all he cares about is Flaubert and Baudelaire and those awful students of his? They make me sick, the way they crowd around and tell him how wonderful he is. All they really want is a passing grade."

She took a deep breath and continued: "He isn't so wonderful, I ought to know. I've lived with him for twelve years and put up with his temperament and his tantrums. You'd think he was Baudelaire himself, or Van Gogh, the way he carries on sometimes. And I kept hoping it would lead to something, but it never has. It never will. We're stuck in a lousy state college and he hasn't even got the manhood to engineer a promotion for himself."

The shabby little cubicle, or maybe the champagne that had been drunk in it, seemed to generate lectures. I made an observation of my own:

"You're being pretty hard on your husband. He has to go out and cut it. For that he needs support."

She hung her head. Her hair swung forward like a flexible ball. "I know. I try to give it to him, honestly."

She had reverted to her little-girl voice. It didn't suit her mood, though, and she dropped it. She said in the clear sharp voice she had used with her son the day before:

"We never should have married, Taps and I. He shouldn't have married at all. Sometimes he reminds me of a medieval priest. The two best years of his life came before our marriage. He often tells me this. He spent them in the *Bibliothèque Nationale* in Paris, not long after the war. I knew this, of course, but I was just a kid and he was the white hope of the French department at Illinois and all the other sophomores said how wonderful it would be to be married to him, with his Scott Fitzgerald good looks, and I thought I could finish my education at home." She looked over the partition at the kitchen sink. "That, I certainly have."

"You married very young."

"Seventeen," she said. "The terrible thing is, I still feel seventeen inside." She touched herself between her breasts. "With everything ahead, you know? But nothing is." For the first time the woman was coming through to me.

"You have your children."

"Sure, I have my children. And don't think I don't do my best for them and always will. Is that all there is, though?"

"It's more than some people have."

"I want more." Her pretty red mouth looked pathetically greedy. "I've wanted more for a long time, but I've never had the nerve to take it."

"You have to wait for it to be given," I said.

"You're full of sententious remarks, aren't you? You're fuller than La Rochefoucauld, or my husband. But you can't solve actual problems with words, as Taps thinks you can. He doesn't understand life. He's nothing but a talking machine, with a computer instead of a heart and a central nervous system."

The thought of her husband seemed to nag her continually. It was almost making her eloquent, but I was growing weary of her boxed-in tension. Perhaps I had brought it on, but basically it had nothing to do with me. I said:

"This is all very interesting, but you were going to talk about Feliz Cervantes."

"I was, wasn't I." Her look became meditative. "He was a very interesting young man. A hot-blooded type, aggressive, the kind of man you imagine a bullfighter might be. He was only twenty-two or three— so was I for that matter—but he was a man. You know?"

"Did you talk to him?"

"A little."

"What about?"

"Our pictures, mostly. He was very keen on French art. He said he was determined to visit Paris some day."

"He said that?"

"Yes. It's not surprising. Every student of French wants to go to Paris. I used to want to go myself."

"What else did he say?"

"That was about all. Some other students turned up, and he shied away from me. Taps said afterwards—we had a quarrel after the party —he said that I had been obvious with the young man. I think Taps brought you here to have me confess. My husband is a very subtle punisher."

"You're both too subtle for me. Confess what?"

"That I was—interested in Feliz Cervantes. But he wasn't interested in me. I wasn't even in the room as far as he was concerned."

"That's hard to believe."

"Is it? There was a young blonde girl from one of Taps's freshman courses at the party. He followed her with his eyes the way I imagine Dante followed Beatrice." Her voice was cold with envy.

"What was her name?"

"Virginia Fablon. I think she's still at the college."

"She quit to get married."

"Really? Who was the lucky man?"

"Feliz Cervantes." I told her how this could be. She listened raptly.

While Bess got ready to go shopping I moved around the living room looking at the reproductions of a world that had never quite dared to exist. The house had taken on an intense interest for me, like a historical monument or the birthplace of a famous man. Cervantes-Martel and Ginny had met in this house; which made it the birthplace of my case.

Bess came out of her room. She had changed into a dress which had to be hooked up the back and I was elected to hook it up. Though she had a strokeable-looking back, my hands were careful not to wander. The easy ones were nearly always trouble: frigid or nympho, schizy or commercial or alcoholic, sometimes all five at once. Their nicely wrapped gifts of themselves often turned out to be homemade bombs, or fudge with arsenic in it.

We drove to the Plaza in ticking silence. It was a large new shopping center, like a campus with asphalt instead of lawns where nothing could be learned. I gave her money, which she accepted, to take a taxi home. It was a friendly gesture, too friendly under the circumstances. But she looked at me as if I was abandoning her to a fate worse than life.

20

SHORE DRIVE ran along the sea below the college in an area of explosive growth and feeble zoning. It was a jumble of apartment buildings, private houses, and fraternity houses with Greek letters over the door.

Behind the stucco house numbered 148 a half-dozen semi-detached cottages were huddled on a small lot. A stout woman opened the door of the house before I reached it.

"I'm full up till June."

"I don't need lodging, thanks. Are you Mrs. Grantham?"

"I never buy door-to-door, if that's what's on your mind."

"All I want is a little information." I told her my name and occupation. "Mr. Martin at the college gave me your name."

"Why didn't you say so? Come in."

The door opened into a small, densely furnished living room. We sat down facing each other, knees almost touching. "I hope it isn't a complaint about one of my boys. They're like sons to me," she said with a professionally maternal smile.

She made an expansive gesture toward the fireplace. The mantel and the wall above it were completely taken up with graduation pictures of young men.

"Not one of your recent boys, anyway. This one goes back seven years. Do you remember Feliz Cervantes?" I showed her the picture with Martel-Cervantes in the background, Ketchel and Kitty in the foreground. She put on glasses to study it.

"I remember all three of them. The big man and the blondie, they came by and picked up his stuff when he left. The three of them rode away together."

"Are you sure of that, Mrs. Grantham?"

"I'm sure. My late husband always said I've got a memory like an elephant. Even if I hadn't, I wouldn't forget that trio. They rode away in a Rolls Royce car, and I wondered what a Mexican boy was doing in that kind of company."

"Cervantes was Mexican?"

"Sure he was, in spite of all his stories. I didn't want to take him in at first. I never had a Mexican roomer before. But the college says you have to or lose your listing, so I rented him a room. He didn't last long, though."

"What stories did he tell?"

"He was full of stories," she said. "When I asked him if he was a Mex, he said he wasn't. I've lived in California all my life, and I can tell a Mex when I see one. He even had an accent, which he claimed was a Spanish accent. He said he was a pure-blooded Spaniard, from Spain.

"So I said, show me your passport. He didn't have one. He said he was a fugitive from his country, that General Franco was after him for fighting the government. He didn't take me in, though. I know a Mex when I see one. If you ask me he was probably a wetback, and that's why he lied. He didn't want the Immigration to put him on a bus and send him home."

"Did he tell any other lies?"

"You bet he did, right up to the day he left. He said when he left he was on his way to Paris, that he was going to the University there. He said the Spanish government had released some of his family money, and he could afford to go to a better school than ours. Good riddance of bad rubbish is what I said."

"You didn't like Cervantes, did you?"

"He was all right, in his place. But he was too uppity. Besides, here he was leaving me on the first of October, leaving me stuck with an empty room for the rest of the semester. It made me sorry I took him in in the first place."

"How was he uppity, Mrs. Grantham?"

"Lots of ways. Do you have a cigarette by any chance?" I gave her one and lit it for her. She blew smoke in my face. "Why are you so interested in him? Is he back in town?"

"He has been."

"What do you know. He told me he was going to come back. Come back in a Rolls Royce with a million dollars and marry a girl from Montevista. *That* was uppity. I told him he should stick to his own kind. But he said she was the only girl for him."

"Did he name her?"

"Virginia Fablon. I knew who she was. My own daughter went to high school with her. She was a beautiful girl, I imagine she still is."

"Cervantes thinks so. He just married her."

"You're kidding."

"I wish I were. He came back a couple of months ago. In a Bentley, not a Rolls, with a hundred and twenty thousand instead of a million. But he married her."

"Well, I'll be." Mrs. Grantham drew deep on her cigarette as if she was sucking the juice from the situation. "Wait until I tell my daughter."

"I wouldn't tell anyone for a day or two. Cervantes and Virginia have dropped out of sight. She may be in danger."

"From him?" she said with avidity.

"Could be." I didn't know what he wanted from Virginia: it was probably something that didn't exist: and I didn't know what he'd do when he found out that it didn't exist.

Mrs. Grantham put out her cigarette in a Breakwater Hotel ashtray and dropped the butt into a handleless teacup which contained other butts. She leaned toward me confidentially, heartily:

"Anything else you want to know?"

"Yes. Did Cervantes give you any explanation about the people who took him away?"

"This pair?" She laid a finger on the picture in her lap. "I forget what he said exactly. I think he said they were friends of his, coming to pick him up."

"He didn't say who they were?"

"No, but they looked like they were loaded. I think he said that they were Hollywood people, and they were going to put him on the plane."

"What plane?"

"The plane to France. I thought at the time it was a lot of malarkey. But now I don't know. Did he ever make it to France?"

"I think he did."

"Where did he get the money? You think his family really has money in Spain?"

"Castles in Spain, anyway."

I thought as I drove away that Martel was one of those dangerous dreamers who acted out his dreams, a liar who forced his lies to become true. His world was highly colored and man-made, like the pictures on the Tappingers' walls which might have been his first vision of France.

21
•••

THE CASHIER of Mercy Hospital had eyes like calculators. She peered at me through the bars of her cage as if she was estimating my income, subtracting my expenses, and coming up with a balance in the red.

"How much am I worth?" I said cheerfully.

"Dead or alive?"

That stopped me. "I want to pay for Mr. Harry Hendricks for another day."

"It isn't necessary," she said. "His wife took care of it."

"The redhead? Was she here?"

"She came in and visited him for a few minutes this morning."

"Can I see him?"

"You'll have to ask the head nurse on the third floor."

The head nurse was a starched, thin-mouthed woman who kept me waiting while she brought her records up to date. Eventually she let me tell her that I was a detective working with the police. She got quite friendly then.

"I don't see any reason why you shouldn't ask him some questions. But don't tire him, and don't say anything to upset him."

Harry was in a private room with windows which overlooked the city. With the bandages on his head and face he looked like an unfinished mummy.

I was carrying the pearl-gray hat, and his eyes focused on it. "Is that my hat?"

"It's the one you were wearing yesterday. The name inside is Spillman, though. Who's he?"

"I wouldn't know."

"You were wearing his hat."

"Was I?" He lay and thought about it. "I got it at a rummage sale."

I didn't believe him, but there was no point in saying so. I tossed the hat onto the chest of drawers. "Who clobbered you, Harry?"

"I don't know for sure. I didn't see him. It was dark, and he knocked me out from behind. Then he stomped on my face, the doctor says."

"Nice guy. Was it Martel?"

"Yeah. It happened up at his place. I was poking around the back of his house. The wind was making so much noise I didn't hear him come up behind me." His fingers crawled over the sheet which covered his body. "He must of given me quite a going over. I'm sore all over."

"You were in an auto accident."

"I was?"

"Martel put you in the trunk of your car and parked it on the waterfront. Some winoes stole it and wrecked it."

He groaned. "It isn't mine. My own clunk died on me, and I borrowed the Caddie off the lot. No insurance, no nothing. Is she a total goner?"

"It wouldn't be worth the price of the body work."

"Wouldn't you know it. There goes another job." He lay silent for a minute, looking out at the sky. "I've been thinking about myself this aft. I bet—no, I won't bet, I'll just say it: I'm the biggest failure west of the Mississippi. I don't even deserve to live."

"Everybody deserves that."

"It's nice of you to say so. Incidentally, they told me a Mr. Archer made the down payment on this pad. Was that you?"

"I chipped in twenty."

"Thanks muchly. You're a real pal."

"Forget it. I'm on an expense account."

But he was touched. "I guess I'm lucky—lucky to be alive, for one thing. Then my wife came to see me, which makes it old home week."

"Is Kitty still in town?"

"I doubt it. She said she was leaving." His head lay inert on the pillow for a moment. "I didn't know you knew her."

"We had a talk last night. She's a beautiful woman."

"Don't I know it. When I lost her it was like losing the moon and stars, boy."

"Did Ketchel take her away from you?"

Another silence. "You know *him,* too?"

"I know something about him. What I know I don't like."

"The more you learn the less you'll like it," he said. "The one great foolish mistake of my life was getting caught in his meathooks. It lost me Kitty."

"How so?"

"I'm a gambler," he said. "I don't know why. I just am. I love to gamble. It makes me feel alive. I must be nuts." His eyes seemed to be looking down a hole. "So one hot morning about dawn I walked out of the Scorpion Club onto Fremont Street with nothing, no wife, nothing. How do you like that? I lost my wife in a crap game. She was so disgusted with me she went with him and stayed."

"With Ketchel?"

Harry lay looking at the hat on the bureau. "His real name is Leo Spillman. Ketchel is just a name he uses. It's an old-time boxing name. Kayo Ketchel, he called himself. He was a pretty good light-heavy before he went into the rackets full-time."

"What rackets is he in, Harry?"

"Name it and he has a piece of it, or used to have. He started in slot machines in the Middle West and got fat off of army bases. You might say that he's still in slot machines. He's majority owner of the Scorpion Club in Vegas."

"Funny I never heard his name."

"He's a concealed owner, I think they call it. He learned to keep his name quiet, like traveling under the name of Ketchel. Leo Spillman is a name with a bad smell. Of course he's semi-retired now. I haven't seen him for years."

"How did you get hold of his hat?"

"Kitty gave it to me when she came to see me last week. Leo's a much bigger man than I am but we have the same size head, seven-and-a-quarter. And I needed a hat to go up against the people in Montevista."

"Where can I find Leo?"

"I guess you could try the Scorpion Club. He used to have a suite there next to his office. I know him and Kitty have a hideout someplace in Southern Cal, but she never gave me a hint of where it is."

"What about his cattle ranch?"

"He sold that long ago. Kitty didn't like to see them branding the calves."

"You've kept in pretty close touch with her."

"Not really. But I've seen her over the years. When she gets in a real jam, or has a real need, she comes to old Harry." He raised his head a few inches from the pillow and looked at me. "I'm leveling with you, Archer, and you know why? I need a cohort, a partner."

"So you said yesterday."

"I need one worse today." With a slow sweep of his chin he called attention to his helplessness, and let his head fall back on the pillow. "And you've been a real pal. I'm going to offer you an equal share of a really big deal."

"Like a concussion?"

"I'm serious. There may be more than a hundred grand up for grabs. Is that laughable?"

"You mean the money Martel-Cervantes stole?"

"Martel-who-did-you-say?"

"Cervantes. That's another name Martel used."

"Then he's the man!" Harry sat up in his excitement. "We've got him!"

"Unfortunately we haven't got him. He's on the run, with a hundred grand in cash. Even if we do get hold of it, won't Leo Spillman want it back?"

"Naw." His hand slid up in steep gesture. "A hundred grand or two hundred is just peanuts to Leo. He'll let us keep it, Kitty said he would. The money they're really after, Kitty and him, is up in the millions." His hand went up to the full length of his arm and stayed there for a second in a kind of salute. He fell back onto the pillow.

"Martel stole millions from him?"

"So Kitty said."

"She must be stringing you. There's no way to steal a million dollars, unless you rob a Brink's truck."

"Yes, there is. And she isn't lying, she never has to me. You got to understand that this is the chance of a lifetime."

"The chance of a deathtime, Harry."

The thought sobered him. "Yeah. That, too."

"Why would Leo Spillman put it in your hands?"

"Kitty did. I'm the only one she trusts." He must have noticed my dubious look because he added: "That may sound funny to you, but it's a fact. I love Kitty, and she knows it. She says if I can pull this out she might even come back to me." His voice rose, trying to make it truer.

I could hear soft rapid nurse-footsteps approaching in the hall.

"Kitty told me she used to live here in town."

"That's right, Kitty was a local girl. Matter of fact, we had our first honeymoon in the Breakwater Hotel." His eyes rolled under his bandages.

"What was her maiden name?"

"Sekjar," he said. "Her old man was some kind of Polack. So's her mother. She hated my guts for robbing the cradle, she called it."

The head nurse opened the door and stuck her head in. "That's enough now. You said you'd keep it quiet."

"Harry got a little excited."

"We can't have that." She opened the door wide. "Out now."

"Are you with me, Archer?" Harry said from the bed. "You know what I mean."

I wasn't with him and I wasn't against him. I made a circle with my thumb and forefinger and showed it to him in a gesture of encouragement.

22

...

IN THE NEIGHBORHOOD of Mercy Hospital there were several satellite treatment centers and clinics, and Dr. Sylvester's clinic was one of them. It was smaller and less prosperous-looking than most of its neighbors. A visibly threadbare path crossed the rug in the lobby from the front door to the reception desk. Several doctors and their specialties, headed by George Sylvester, Internal Medicine, were listed on a board beside the door.

The girl behind the desk told me that Dr. Sylvester was still out to lunch. He had a free half-hour scheduled, if I cared to wait.

I gave her my name and sat down among the waiting patients. After a while I began to feel like one of them. The pink champagne, or the lady I had drunk it with, had left me with a dull headache. Other parts of my anatomy began to nag. By the time Dr. Sylvester appeared, I was just about ready to break down and tell him my symptoms.

He looked as though he had symptoms of his own, probably hangover symptoms. He was clearly not glad to see me. But he gave me his hand and a professional smile, and escorted me past his formidable-looking secretary into his consulting room.

He changed into a white coat. I glanced at the diplomas and certificates on the paneled walls. Sylvester had trained in good schools and hospitals, and passed his Boards. He had at least the background of a responsible doctor. It was the foreground that worried me.

"What can I do for you, Archer? You look tired, by the way."

"That's because I am tired."

"Then take the weight off your feet." He indicated a chair at the end of his desk, and sat down himself. "I only have a few minutes, so let's get with it, boy." The sudden camaraderie was forced. Behind it he was watching me like a poker player.

"I found out who your patient Ketchel is."

He raised his eyebrows but said nothing.

"He's a Vegas casino owner," I said, "with a very extensive background in the rackets. His actual name is Leo Spillman."

Sylvester was not surprised. He said smoothly: "It fits in with our records. I checked them this morning. He gave his address as the Scorpion Club in Las Vegas."

"It's too bad you couldn't remember that last night when I could have used it."

"I can't remember everything."

"Try your memory on this one. Did you introduce Leo Spillman to Roy Fablon?"

"I don't remember."

"You know whether you did or not, doctor."

"You can't talk to me like that."

"Answer my question," I said. "If you won't, I'll find somebody who will."

His face slanted forward in thought. It looked both precarious and threatening, like a piece of rock poised on the edge of a cliff.

"Why would Marietta Fablon apply to you for money?" I said.

"I'm an old friend. Who else should she go to?"

"Are you sure she wasn't trying to blackmail you, old friend?"

He looked around his office as though it was a kind of public cage. The lines bracketing his mouth were deep and cruel, like self-inflicted scars.

"What are you trying to cover up, doctor?"

After a thinking pause, he said: "The fact that I'm a goddam fool." He glanced sharply into my eyes. "Can you keep a secret?"

"Not if it involves a crime."

"What crime?" He spread out his large hands palms up on the desk. "There hasn't *been* any crime."

"Then why are you so worried?"

"This town is a hotbed of rumors, as I told you last night. If the word gets out about Leo Spillman and me, I'm dead." His hands curled up very slowly, like two starfish. "I'm moribund now, if you want the truth. There are too damn many doctors in this town. And I've had financial losses."

"Gambling losses?"

He was startled. "Where did you dig that up?" He pounded the desk with his curled hands, not threateningly, more like someone trying to get out. He wasn't a subtle man, and his anxiety had blunted him even more. "What are you trying to do to me?"

"You know what I'm trying to do—get at the facts about this man Martel, and incidentally clear up any doubts about what happened to Fablon. The two things are connected by way of Spillman, possibly in other ways. When Spillman left town, two days after Fablon's death, he took Martel with him. Did you know that?"

He looked at me in a confused way. "Are we talking about seven years ago?"

"That's right. You're involved in all this because you brought Spillman here."

"I didn't *bring* him. He invited himself. As a matter of fact it was his woman's—his wife's idea. Her idea of heaven was two weeks at the Tennis Club." His mouth lifted on one side, showing the edges of his teeth.

"Did you owe Spillman money?"

"Did I not." His eyes were bleak, looking past me at his life. "If I give you straight answers to some of these questions, what use do you intend to make of them?"

"I'll keep the facts to myself, so far as I can. A client once told me he could drop a secret into me and never hear it hit bottom. You're not my client, but I'll do what I can to protect your *bella figura.*"

"I'll take you at your word," he said. "Don't get the idea that I'm one of these compulsive gamblers. It's true I'm in the market, it's the only way to outwit these confiscatory taxes nowadays—but I'm not the Vegas type of gambler. I stay away from Vegas."

"And that's why you never met Leo Spillman."

"I admit I went there in the past. The last time I went to Vegas I was in a bad mood, a destructive mood. I didn't care what happened. My wife—" He compressed his lips.

"Go on."

He said haltingly: "I was just going to say my wife wasn't with me."

"I thought you were going to say that she was having an affair with another man."

His face twisted in pain. "Good Lord, did *she* tell you that?"

"No. It doesn't matter how I found out."

"Do you know who the other man was?" he said.

"Roy Fablon. It gave you a reason for wanting him dead."

"Is that an accusation?"

"I just thought I'd mention it, doctor."

"Thanks very much. You throw some wicked curves."

"Life does, anyway. What happened your last time in Vegas?"

"Plenty. First I lost a few hundred on the tables. Instead of cutting my losses, I got mad and plunged. Before I was through I'd exhausted my credit—it still hasn't recovered completely—and I owed Leo Spillman nearly twenty thousand.

"He called me into the office to talk about it. I told him I could raise ten at most, he'd have to wait for the rest. He blew a gasket and called me a cheat and a fourflusher, and a good many other names. He would have attacked me physically, I think, if the woman hadn't restrained him."

"Was Kitty there?"

"Yes. She was interested in me because she'd found out that I came from here. She reminded Spillman that it was a felony for him to use his fists. Apparently he was an ex-professional boxer. But he was in terrible shape, and I think I could have taken him." Sylvester caressed his fist. "I did some boxing in college."

"It's just as well you didn't try. Very few amateurs ever take a pro."

"But he was a sick man, physically and emotionally sick."

"What was the matter with him?"

"I could see that one of his optic nerves was jumping. After he calmed down a bit, I persuaded him to let me look into his eyes and take his blood pressure. I had the equipment in my car. That may seem like a strange thing to do, under the circumstances, but I was concerned about him as a doctor. With good reason. He had a bad case of hypertension, and his blood pressure was up in the danger zone. It turned out that he'd never been to a doctor, never had a checkup. He thought all that was for sissies.

"At first he thought I was trying to frighten him. But with the woman's help I got the fact across to him, that he was in danger of a stroke. So he suggested a deal. I was to rake up ten thousand in cash, treat his hypertension, and get the two of them a cottage at the Tennis Club. I imagine it was the weirdest deal in history."

"I don't know. Spillman once won a man's wife in a crap game."

"So he told me. He's full of little anecdotes. You can imagine how I felt injecting a man like that into my club. But I had no choice, and he was willing to pay nearly ten thousand dollars."

"It didn't cost him anything."

"It cost him ten thousand less the value of my services."

"Not if you paid him the other ten thousand in cash. He'd save more than enough in taxes to make up the difference."

"You think he was dodging taxes?"

"I'm sure of it. They're doing it all the time in Vegas. The money they hold back is known as 'black money,' and that's a good name for it. It runs into the millions, and it's used to finance about half of the illegal enterprises in the country, from Cosa Nostra on down."

Sylvester said in a chilly voice: "I couldn't be held responsible, could I?"

"Morally, you could. Legally, I don't know. If everybody who collaborated with organized crime was held responsible, half the boobs in the country would be in jail. Unfortunately that won't happen. We treat the crime capital of the United States as if it was a second Disneyland, smelling like roses, a great place to take the family or hold a convention."

I stopped myself. I was slightly hipped on the subject of Vegas, partly because the criminal cases I handled in California so often led there. As this one was doing, now. I said:

"Did you know that Martel left town with Spillman seven years ago?"

"I heard you tell me. I didn't understand what you meant."

"He was a student at the local college, working part-time as a flunky at the Tennis Club."

"Martel was?"

"In those days he called himself Feliz Cervantes. He met Ginny Fablon, or at least saw her, at a gathering of French students, and fell for her. He may have taken the job at the club so he could see her more often. He ran into Spillman there."

Sylvester was listening closely. He was quiet and subdued, as if the building might collapse in ruins around him if he moved. "How do you know all this?"

"Part of it's speculation. Most of it isn't. But I've got to talk to Leo Spillman, and I want your help in reaching him. Have you seen him recently?"

"Not in seven years. He never came back here. I didn't urge him to, either. Apart from my professional contact with him, I did my best to avoid him. I never invited him to my house, for instance."

Sylvester was trying to rescue his pride. But I suspected it had been permanently lost, within the past half-hour, in this room.

23
...

THROUGH the door behind me I heard the telephone ring in Sylvester's outer office. About twenty seconds later the telephone on his desk gave out a subdued echo of the ring. He picked it up and said impatiently:

"What is it, Mrs. Loftin?"

The secretary's voice came to me in stereo, partly through the telephone and partly through the door. It was just loud enough for me to hear what she said:

"Virginia Fablon wants to talk to you. She's in a state. Shall I put her on?"

"Hold it," Sylvester said. "I'll come out there."

He excused himself and went out, shutting the door emphatically behind him. Refusing to take the hint, I followed him into the outer office. He was standing over the secretary's desk, pressing her telephone to the side of his head like a surgical device which held his face together.

"Where are you?" he was saying. He interrupted himself to bark at me: "Give me some privacy, can't you?"

"Please step out into the hall," Mrs. Loftin said. "The doctor is advising an emergency patient."

"What's the emergency?"

"I can't discuss it. Please step outside, won't you?"

Mrs. Loftin was a large woman with a square determined face. She advanced on me, ready to use physical force.

I retreated into the hallway. She closed the door. I leaned my ear against it and heard Sylvester say:

"What makes you think he's dying?" Then: "I see . . . Yes, I'll come right away. Don't panic."

A few seconds later Sylvester emerged from the office in such a blind rush that he almost knocked me over. He was carrying a medical bag and still wearing his white coat. The prosthetic telephone was no longer holding his face together.

I walked beside him toward the front door of the clinic. "Let me drive you."

"No."

"Has Martel been hurt?"

"I prefer not to discuss it. He insists on privacy."

"I'm private. Let me drive you."

Sylvester shook his head. But he paused on the terrace above the parking lot and stood blinking in the sun for a moment.

"What's the matter with him?" I said.

"He was shot."

"That puts him in the public domain, and you know it. My car's over here."

I took him by the elbow and propelled him toward the curb. He offered no resistance to me. His movements were slightly mechanical.

I said as I started the car: "Where are they, doctor?"

"In Los Angeles. If you can get onto the San Diego Freeway—they have a house in Brentwood."

"They have another house?"

"Apparently. I took down the address."

It was on Sabado Avenue, a tree-lined street of large Spanish houses built some time in the twenties. It was one of those disappearing enclaves where, in a different mood from mine, you could feel the sunlit peace of prewar Los Angeles. Sabado Avenue had a Not a Through Street sign at its entrance.

The house we were looking for was the largest and most elaborate on the long block. Its walled and fountained grounds reminded me a little of Forest Lawn. So did the girl who answered the front door. I would hardly have recognized Ginny, she was so drawn around the mouth and swollen around the eyes.

She started to cry again into the front of Sylvester's white coat. He patted her shuddering back with his free hand.

"Where is he, Virginia?"

"He went away. I had to go next door to phone you. Our phone isn't connected yet." Her sentences were broken up by hiccuping sobs. "He took the car and drove away."

"How long ago?"

"I don't know. I've lost track of time. It was right after I phoned you."

"That makes it less than an hour," I said. "Is your husband badly hurt?"

She nodded, still clinging to Sylvester. "I'm afraid he's bleeding internally. He was shot in the stomach."

"When?"

"An hour or so ago. I don't know exactly what time. The people who rented the house to us didn't leave any clocks. I was taking a siesta— we were up most of the night—and somebody rang the doorbell. My husband answered it. I heard the shot, and I ran down here and found him sitting on the floor."

She looked down at her feet. Around them on the parquetry were rusty spots that looked like drying blood.

"Did you see who fired the shot?"

"I didn't actually see him. I heard the car drive away. My husband—" She kept repeating the phrase as if it might help him and her marriage to survive.

Sylvester broke in: "We can't keep her standing here while we cross-question her. One of us ought to call the police."

"You should have called them before you left your office."

Ginny seemed to think I was blaming her. "My husband wouldn't let me. He said it would mean the end of everything." Her heavy look swung from side to side, as if the end of everything was upon her.

Sylvester quieted her against his shoulder. Slowly and gently he walked her into the house. I went next door. A stout executive type in a black alpaca sweater was standing outside on his front lawn, looking helpless and resentful. He owned a house on Sabado Avenue, and this was supposed to guarantee a quiet life.

"What do you want?"

"The use of your phone. There's been a shooting."

"Is that what the noise was?"

"You heard the gun?"

"I thought it was a backfire at the time."

"Did you see the car?"

"I saw a black Rolls drive away. Or maybe it was a Bentley. But that was some time later."

This wasn't much help. I asked him to show me a telephone. He took me in through the back door to the kitchen. It was one of those space age kitchens, all gleaming metal and control panels, ready to go into lunar orbit. The man handed me a telephone and left the room, as if to avoid finding out something that might disturb him.

Within a few minutes a squad car arrived, followed closely by a Homicide Captain named Perlberg. Not long after that we located Martel's Bentley. It hadn't gone far.

Its gleaming nose was jammed against the metal safety barrier at the dead end of Sabado Avenue. Beyond the barrier the loose ground sloped away to the edge of a bluff which overlooked the Pacific.

The Bentley's engine was still running. Martel's chin rested on the steering wheel. The dead eyes in his yellow face were peering out into the blue ocean of air.

Perlberg and I knew each other, and I gave him a quick rundown on the case. He and his men made a search for Martel's hundred thousand, but found no trace of it in the car or at the house. The gunman who took Martel had taken the money too.

Ginny was in slightly better shape by this time, and Sylvester gave Perlberg permission to question her briefly. He and I sat in the living room with them and monitored the interview. Ginny and Martel had been married by a judge in Beverly Hills the previous Saturday. The same day he had rented this house, completely furnished, through an agent. She didn't know who the legal owner was.

No, she didn't know who had shot her husband. She had been asleep when it happened. It was all over when she came downstairs.

"But your husband was still alive," Perlberg said. "What did he say?"

"Nothing."

"He must have said something."

"Just that I wasn't to call anyone," she said. "He said he wasn't badly hurt. I didn't realize he was until later."

"How much later?"

"I don't know. I was so upset, and we have no clocks. I sat and watched the life draining out of his face. He wouldn't speak to me. He seemed to be profoundly—humiliated. When I finally realized how badly off he was, I went next door and called Dr. Sylvester." She nodded toward the doctor, who was sitting near her.

"Why didn't you call a local doctor?"

"I didn't know any."

"Why didn't you call us?" Perlberg said.

"I was afraid to. My husband said it would be the end of him."

"What did he mean by that?"

"I don't know, but I was afraid. When I finally did make a call, he went away."

She covered her face with her hands. Sylvester persuaded the Captain to cut the questioning short. Perlberg's men took pictures, and shavings of the blood-spotted parquetry, and left us alone with Ginny in the big echoing house.

She said she wanted to go home to her mother. Sylvester told her that her mother was dead. She didn't seem to take it in.

I volunteered to get some of her things together. While Sylvester stayed with her in the living room, I went up to the master bedroom on the second floor. The bed, which was its central feature, was circular, about nine feet in diameter. I was beginning to see a good many of these king-sized beds, like hopeful altars to old gods. The bed had been left unmade, and the tangled sheets suggested lovemaking.

The suitcases were on the floor of the closet under a row of empty hangers. They had been left unpacked except for a few overnight things: Ginny's nightgown and hairbrush and toothbrush and cosmetics, Martel's pajamas and safety razor. I went through his suitcases quickly. Most of his clothes were new and of fine quality, some with Bond Street labels. Apart from a book by Descartes, *Méditations*, in French, I could find nothing personal, and even this book had no name on the flyleaf.

Later, as we drove through the endless suburbs to Montevista, I asked Ginny if she knew who her husband was. Sylvester had given her a sedative, and she rode between us with her head on his extended arm. The shock of Martel's death had pushed her back toward childishness. Her voice sounded just a little like a sleep-talker's:

"He's Francis Martel, from Paris. You know that."

"I thought I did, Ginny. But just today another name came up. Feliz Cervantes."

"I never heard of any such person."

"You met him, or at least he met you, at a *Cercle Français* meeting at Professor Tappinger's house."

"When? I've been to dozens of *Cercle Français* meetings."

"This one was seven years ago, in September. Francis Martel was there under the name Cervantes. Mrs. Tappinger identified a photograph of him."

"Can I see the photograph?"

I moved over into the slow lane and worked the picture out of my jacket pocket. She took it from me. Then for some time she was silent. The afternoon traffic fled by us on the left. The drivers looked apprehensive, as if they had been kidnapped by their cars.

"Is this really Francis standing by the wall?"

"I'm almost certain that it is. Didn't you know him in those days?"

"No. Was I supposed to have?"

"He knew you. He told his landlady that he was going to get rich some day and come back and marry you."

"But that's ridiculous."

"Not so very. It happened."

Sylvester, who had been quiet until now, growled something at me about shutting up.

Ginny hung her head in thought over the picture. "If this *is* Francis, what's he doing with Mr. and Mrs. Ketchel?"

"You know the Ketchels?"

"I met them once."

"When?"

"September seven years ago. My father took me to lunch with them. It was just before he died."

Sylvester scowled across her at me. "This is enough of this, Archer. It's no time to poke around in explosive material."

"It's the only time I have." I said to the girl: "Do you mind talking to me about these things?"

"Not if it will help." She managed a wan smile.

"Okay. What happened at this lunch with the Ketchels?"

"Nothing, really. We had something to eat in the patio of his cottage. I tried to make conversation with Mrs. Ketchel. She was a local girl, she said, but that was the only thing we had in common. She hated me."

"Why?"

"Because Mr. Ketchel liked me. He wanted to do things for me, help me with my education and so on." Her voice was toneless.

"Did your father know about this?"

"Yes. It was the purpose of the lunch. Roy was very naïve about

BLACK MONEY • • • 559

exploiting people. He thought he could use a man like Mr. Ketchel without being used."

"Use him for what?" I said.

"Roy owed him money. Roy was a nice man, but by that time he owed everybody money. I couldn't help him. It wouldn't have done any good to go along with Mr. Ketchel's plan. Mr. Ketchel is the kind of man who takes everything and gives nothing. I told Roy that."

"Just what was the plan?"

"It was rather vague, but Mr. Ketchel offered to send me to school in Europe."

"And your father went for this?"

"Not really. He just wanted me to butter up Mr. Ketchel a little bit. But Mr. Ketchel wanted everything. Men get that way when they're afraid they're dying."

The girl surprised me. I reminded myself that she wasn't a girl, but a woman with a brief tragic marriage already behind her. And what sounded like a long tragic childhood. Her voice had changed perceptibly, almost as though she had skipped from youth to middle age, when she began to call her father "Roy."

"How often did you see Ketchel?"

"I talked to him just the once. He had noticed me at the club."

"You say the lunch with him occurred shortly before your father died. Do you mean the same week?"

"The same day," she said. "It was the last day I ever saw Roy alive. Mother sent me to look for him that night."

"Where?"

"Down at the beach, and at the club. Peter Jamieson was with me part of the time. He went to the Ketchel's cottage—I didn't want to—but they weren't there. At least they didn't answer."

"Do you think Ketchel and your father quarreled over you?"

"I don't know. It's possible." She went on in the same flat voice: "I wish I had been born without a nose, or only one eye."

I didn't have to ask Ginny what she meant. I had known a number of girls for whom men insisted on doing things.

"Did Ketchel murder your father, Ginny?"

"I don't know. Mother thought so, at the time."

Sylvester groaned. "I don't see the point in raking it over."

"The point is that it's connected with the present situation, doctor.

You don't want to see the connection because you're part of the chain of cause and effect."

"Do we have to go into that again?"

"Please." Ginny screwed up her face and rolled her head from side to side. "Please don't argue across me. They always used to argue across me."

We both said we were sorry. After a while she asked me in a soft voice: "Do you think Mr. Ketchel killed my husband?"

"He's the leading suspect. I don't think he'd do it personally. He'd more likely use a hired gunman."

"But why?"

"I can't go into all the circumstances. Seven years ago your husband left Montevista with Ketchel. Apparently Ketchel sent him to school in France."

"As a substitute for me?"

"That hardly seems likely. But I'm sure Ketchel had his uses for your husband."

She was offended. "Francis wasn't like that at all."

"I don't mean sex. I believe he used Francis in his business."

"What business?"

"He's a big-time gambling operator. Didn't Francis ever mention Ketchel?"

"No. He never did."

"Or Leo Spillman, which was Ketchel's real name?"

"No."

"What did you and Francis talk about, Ginny?"

"Poetry and philosophy, mostly. I had so much to learn from Francis."

"Never real things?"

She said in an anguished voice: "Why do real things always have to be ugly and horrible?"

She was feeling the pain now, I thought, the cruel pain of coming home widowed after a three-day marriage.

It was time to leave the freeway. I could see Montevista in the distance: its trees were like a green forest on the horizon. The access road straightened out toward the sea.

My mind was on Francis Martel, or whoever he was. He had driven his Bentley down this road a couple of months ago, on the track of a seven-year dream. The energy that had conceived the dream, and forced it briefly into reality, had all run out now. Even the girl beside me was lax as a doll, as if a part of her had died with the dreamer. She didn't speak again until we reached her mother's house.

The front door was locked. Ginny turned from it with a rejected air. "It's her bridge day. I should have remembered." She found the key in her bag, and opened the door. "You don't mind bringing my suitcases in? I'm feeling a little weak."

"You have reason to," Sylvester said.

"Actually I'm relieved that Mother isn't here. What could I say to her?"

Sylvester and I looked at each other. I got the suitcases out of the trunk of my car and carried them into the front hall. Ginny said from the sitting room:

"What happened to the phone?"

"There was trouble here last night," I said.

She leaned in the doorway. "Trouble?"

Sylvester went to her and put his hands on her shoulders. "I'm sorry I have to tell you this, Ginny. Your mother was shot last night."

She slipped from his hands onto the floor. Her skin was gray and her eyes indigo, but she didn't faint. She sat with her back against the wall.

"Is Marietta dead?"

"I'm afraid she is, Ginny."

I squatted beside her. "Do you know who shot your mother?"

She shook her head so hard that her hair fell like a blonde screen across her face.

"Your mother was deeply upset last night. Was something said to her, by you or Martel?"

"We said goodbye." She gasped over the finality of the word. "That was about all, except that she didn't want me to go. She said she'd get money some other way."

"What did she mean?"

"That I had married Francis for his money, I suppose. She didn't understand."

I said: "She told me before she died that lover-boy shot her. Who would lover-boy be?"

"Francis, maybe. But he was with me all the time." Her head fell back against the wall with a thud. "I don't know what she could have meant."

"Lay off her," Sylvester said. "I'm speaking as a friend and as a doctor."

He was right. I felt like a tormenting devil squatting beside her. I got to my feet, and helped Ginny to hers. "She ought to have protection. Will you stay with her, doctor?"

"I can't possibly. I must have a dozen patients stacked up waiting for me." He glanced at his wristwatch. "Why don't you stay with her yourself? I can call a cab."

"I have things to do in town." I turned to Ginny: "Could you stand having Peter around?"

"I guess so," she said with her head down, "so long as I don't have to talk any more to anyone."

I found Peter at home and explained the circumstances. He said he knew how to use a gun—trapshooting was one of his sports—and he'd be glad to stand guard.

He loaded a shotgun and brought it along, carrying it with a slightly military air. The news of Martel's death seemed to have lifted his spirits.

Ginny greeted him quietly in the hall. "This is nice of you, Peter. But we won't talk about anything. Okay?"

"Okay. I'm sorry, though."

They shook hands like brother and sister. But I saw his eyes take possession of her injured beauty. It came to me with a jolt that for Peter the case had just ended. I left before he realized it himself.

24
•••

I DROVE slowly up the pass road which was the shortest route between Montevista and the city. Sylvester kept looking back into the valley where we had left Ginny. The rooftops were half submerged among the trees like flotsam in a turbulent green flood. I said:

"Shouldn't she be in the hospital, or at least have a nurse?"

"I'll see about that later, when I've cleaned up my work at the clinic."

"Do you think she'll be all right?"

Sylvester was slow in answering. "She's a durable girl. Of course she's had lousy luck, compounded by bad judgment. She should have married Peter as she was supposed to. She would have been safe with him, at least. Maybe now she will."

"Maybe. You seem fond of the girl."

"As fond as I dare to be."

"What does that mean, doctor?"

"Just what I said. She's a beautiful kid and she trusts me. You make everything sound like an accusation."

"I don't think so."

"Then listen to yourself. You'll see what I mean."

"You may be right." I wanted him to keep talking. After a moment, I said: "You knew Roy Fablon. Was he the kind of a man who would try to use his daughter to pay off gambling losses?"

"Why ask me?"

"Ginny seems to think he was."

"I didn't gather that from the conversation. At worst, Roy may have been using her, or trying to, to make Spillman more lenient. You don't know how desperate a man can get when a gorilla like Spillman has you by the—" He suppressed the end of the sentence. "I do."

"What you say adds up to an affirmative answer. Fablon was the kind of man who would try to use his daughter."

"He may have toyed around with the idea. But he'd never have gone through with it."

"He didn't, anyway. He didn't have a chance to. Say he made an offer to Spillman and then withdrew it. A blowtop like Spillman might very easily have killed him."

"It works just as well the other way," Sylvester said. "Better, if you know the background situation. Put a man like Roy in a moral vise like that, and he's liable to kill himself. Which is what happened. I checked back with Dr. Wills this morning, incidentally—he's the deputy coroner who performed the autopsy on Roy. He found definite evidence, *chemical* evidence, that Roy drowned himself in the ocean."

"Or was drowned."

"There are cases of murder by drowning," Sylvester said. "But I never heard of one committed by a sick man in the sea at night."

"Spillman was and is in a position to have these things done for him."

"He had no motive."

"We've just been talking about one possible motive. A more obvious one was that Fablon owed him thirty thousand dollars and he couldn't pay. Spillman wouldn't take it lightly. You're a witness to that."

Sylvester moved restlessly in the seat. "Marietta really put a bee in your bonnet. She was cracked on the subject of Spillman."

"Did she talk to you about him recently?"

"Yesterday at lunch, when you barged in."

"You must take her seriously or you wouldn't have checked with Dr. Wills today."

"Check with Wills yourself. He'll tell you the same thing."

We had reached the low summit of the pass. In a sloping field to my left an old palomino stallion wandered in the sunlight, white-maned, like a survivor.

I adjusted my windshield visor against the light as we started down the hill. The city below resembled a maze, put together by an inspired child: it looked both intricate and homemade. Beyond it lay the changing blue mystery of the sea.

I dropped Sylvester off in front of his clinic and crossed the street to Mercy Hospital. The deputy coroner had his office and laboratory in the basement, next to the hospital morgue.

Dr. Wills was a small thin man with a dedicated-scientist look, intensified by steel-rimmed glasses. He handled himself as if his hands, his fingers, even his eyes and mouth were technical instruments, useful but not alive; and the real Dr. Wills sat hidden in his skull directing their external operations.

He didn't even blink when I told him that there had been another killing.

"It's getting a little thick," was all he said.

"Have you done your p.m. on Mrs. Fablon?"

"Not a complete one. It hardly seemed necessary. The bullet nicked her aorta, and that was it." He gestured toward an inner door.

"What kind of a bullet?"

"It looks like a .38. It came through in fair condition, and should be good for comparison if we ever find the gun."

"May I see it?"

"I've already turned it over to Inspector Olsen."

"Tell him it should be compared with the slug that killed Martel."

Wills gave me a quizzical look. "Why don't you tell him yourself?"

"He'll like it better if he hears it from you. I also think he should re-open the Roy Fablon case."

"I disagree about that," Wills said crisply. "A murder, or two mur-ders, in the present, don't change a suicide in the past."

"Are you certain it was a suicide?"

"Quite. I had occasion to look over my notes only this morning. There's no question that Fablon committed suicide by drowning. The external contusions were almost certainly inflicted after death. In any case they wouldn't have been sufficient to cause death."

"I gather he took quite a beating."

"Bodies do in these waters. But there's no doubt he was a suicide. In addition to the physical evidence, he threatened suicide in the presence of his wife and daughter."

"So I've been told."

The thought of it, coming on top of my talks with Sylvester and Ginny, was depressing. The present couldn't alter the past, as Wills had said, but it could make you painfully aware of its mysteries and meanings.

Wills misinterpreted my silence: "If you doubt my word, you can look up the record of the coroner's inquest."

"I don't doubt you're giving me an accurate report, doctor. Who gave the testimony about the suicide threat?"

"Fablon's wife. You can't question that."

"You can question anything human." The ambiguities of last night's conversation with Marietta still teetered in my mind. "I understand that before the inquest she claimed her husband was murdered."

"Perhaps she did. The physical evidence must have persuaded her otherwise. At the inquest she came out strongly for the idea of suicide."

"What was the physical evidence you referred to?"

"The chemical content of the blood taken from the heart. It proved conclusively that he was drowned."

"He could have been knocked out and drowned in a bathtub. It's been done."

"Not in this case." Dr. Wills answered smoothly and rapidly, like a well-programmed computer. "The chloride content of the blood in the left ventricle was over twenty-five percent above normal. The magnesium content was greatly increased, as compared with the right ventricle. Those two indicators taken together prove that Fablon drowned in ocean water."

"And there's no doubt that the body *was* Fablon's?"

"None whatever. His wife identified it, in my presence." Wills adjusted his glasses and looked at me through them diagnostically, as if he suspected that I had an obsession. "Frankly I think you're making a mistake in trying to connect what happened to him with—this." He gestured again toward the wall on the other side of which Marietta lay in her refrigerated drawer.

Perhaps I should have stayed and argued with Wills. He was an honest man. But the place and its basement chill were getting me down. The cement walls and high small windows made it resemble a cell in an old-fashioned jail.

I got out of there. Before I left the hospital I found a telephone booth and made a long-distance call to Professor Allan Bosch of Los Angeles State College. He was in his office and answered the phone himself.

"This is Lew Archer. You don't know my name—"

He cut in: "On the contrary, Mr. Archer, your name was mentioned to me within the past hour."

"You've heard from Tappinger then."

"He just left here. I gave him as full a report as I could on Pedro Domingo."

"Pedro Domingo?"

"That's the name Cervantes used when he was my student. I believe it's his true name, and I know for a fact that he's a native of Panama. Those are the points at issue, aren't they?"

"There are others. If I could talk to you in person—"

His rapid young voice cut in on me again. "I'm jammed at the moment—Professor Tappinger's visit did nothing for my schedule. Why don't you get the facts from him and if there's anything else you need to know you can get in touch with me later?"

"I'll do that. In the meantime there's something you ought to know, Professor. Your former student was shot dead in Brentwood this afternoon."

"Pedro was shot?"

"He was murdered. Which means that his identity is something more than an academic question. You better get in touch with Captain Perlberg of Homicide."

"Perhaps I had better," he said slowly, and hung up.

I checked in with my answering service in Hollywood. Ralph Christman had phoned from Washington and dictated a message. The operator read it to me over the line:

"Colonel Plimsoll identifies mustached waiter in photograph as South or Central American diplomat named Domingo, he thinks. Do I query the embassies?"

I asked the operator to call Christman for me and tell him to try the embassies, especially the Panamanian one.

Past and present were coming together. I had a moment of claustrophobia in the phone booth, as if I was caught between converging walls.

25
• • •

SEKJAR, KITTY's maiden name, wasn't in the telephone book. I went to the public library and looked it up in a city directory. A Mrs. Maria Sekjar, hospital employee, was listed at 137 Juniper Street. I found the poor little street backed up against the railway yards. The first person I saw on Juniper Street was the young policeman, Ward Rasmussen, marching toward me along the dirt path which served as a sidewalk.

I got out of my car and hailed him. He looked a little disappointed to see me. You feel that way, sometimes, when you're out bird-dogging and another man crosses your path.

"I found Kitty's mother," he said. "I went to the high school and dug up a girls' counselor who remembered Kitty."

"That was resourceful."

"I wouldn't say that." But he was soberly pleased. "I didn't have much luck with the mother, though. Maybe she'll say more to you. She seems to think her daughter's in serious trouble. She's been in trouble since she was in her teens, the counselor told me."

"Boy trouble?"

"What else?"

I changed the subject. "Did you have a chance to get to the bank, Ward?"

"Yessir, I had better luck there." He got his notebook out of his pocket and flipped the pages. "Mrs. Fablon has been getting a regular income from that bank in Panama, the New Granada. They sent her a draft every month until last February, when it stopped."

"How much every month?"

"A thousand. This went on for six or seven years. It added up to around eighty thousand."

"Was there any indication of its source?"

"Not according to the local people. It came from a numbered account, apparently. The whole transaction was untouched by the human hand."

"And then it stopped."

"That's correct. What do you make of it, Mr. Archer?"

"I wouldn't want to jump to any conclusions."

"No, of course not. But it could be underworld money. You remember that thought came up at breakfast this morning."

"I'm pretty sure it is. But we're going to have a hell of a time proving it."

"I know that. I talked to the foreign-exchange man at the National. The Panama banks are like the Swiss banks. They don't have to reveal the source of their deposits, which makes them a natural for mobsters. What do you think we should do about it?"

I was anxious to talk to Mrs. Sekjar, and I said: "Get the law changed. Do you want to wait for me in my car?"

He got in. I approached the Sekjar house on foot. It was a small frame dwelling which looked as if the passing trains had shaken off most of its paint.

I knocked on the rusty screen door. A woman with dyed black hair appeared behind it. She was large and heavy, aged about fifty, though the dyed hair made her look older. Handsome, but not as handsome as her daughter. Her cheap dye job was iridescent in the late afternoon sun.

"What do you want?"

"I'd like to talk to you—"

"About Kitty again?"

"More or less."

"I don't know anything about her. That's what I told the other ones and that's what I'm telling you. I've worked hard all my life so I could hold my head up in this town." She lifted her chin. "It wasn't easy, and Kitty was no help. She has nothing to do with me now."

"She's your daughter, isn't she?"

"Yeah, I guess she is." Her voice was rough. "She don't act like a daughter. I'm not responsible for what she does. I used to beat her until she was bloody, it did no good. She was as wild as ever, making mock of the teachings of the Lord." She looked up through the rusty screen. Her own eyes were rebellious.

"May I come in, Mrs. Sekjar? My name is Archer, I'm a private detective." Her face was unyielding, and I went on rapidly: "I've got nothing against your daughter but I'm trying to locate her. She may be able to give me some information about a murder."

"Murder?" She was appalled. "The other one didn't say nothing about a murder. This is a decent home, mister," she said, with the tense precarious respectability of the poor. "It's the first time since Kitty left me that a policeman came to this door." She glanced up and down the street, as if her neighbors were spying on us now. "I guess you better come on in."

She unhooked the screen door and opened it for me. Her living room was small and threadbare. It contained a daybed and two chairs, a faded rag rug, a television set tuned in on a daytime serial which said, in the snatch I heard of it, that things were rough all over.

Mrs. Sekjar switched it off. On top of the television set were a large Bible and one of those glass balls that you shake to make a snowstorm. The pictures on the walls were all religious, and there were so many of them that they suggested a line of defense against the world.

I sat on the daybed. It smelled of Kitty, faintly but distinctly. The odor of her perfume seemed strange in these surroundings. It wasn't the odor of sanctity.

"Kitty was here last night, wasn't she?"

Mrs. Sekjar nodded, standing over me. "She came over the fence from the tracks. I couldn't turn her away. She was scared."

"Did she say what of?"

"It's her life. It's catching up with her. The kind of men she runs with, punks and hoodlums—" She spat dry. "We won't discuss it."

"I think we should, Mrs. Sekjar. Did Kitty do any talking to you last night?"

"Not much. She did some crying. I thought I had my own girl back for a while. She stayed all night. But in the morning she was as hard as ever."

"She isn't that hard."

"She didn't start out to be, maybe. She was a nice enough girl when her father was with us. But Sekjar got himself sick and spent his last two years in the County Hospital. After that Kitty got hard as nails. She blamed me and the other adults for putting him in the County Hospital. As if I had any choice.

"When she was a sixteen-year-old girl she went for my eyes with her thumb nails. I chopped them off for her. If I hadn't been stronger than her, she'd of blinded me. After that I couldn't do anything with her. She ran wild with the boys. I tried to stop her. I know what comes of running wild with boys. So just to spite me she turned around and married the first man that asked her." She paused glaring among her angry memories. "Is Harry Hendricks the one that died?"

"No, but he was injured."

"So I heard at the hospital. I'm a nurse's aid," she explained with some pride. "Who got murdered?"

"A woman named Marietta Fablon, and a man who called himself Francis Martel."

"I never heard of either one of them."

I showed her the picture of Martel, with Kitty and Leo Spillman in the foreground. She exploded:

"That's him! That's the man, the one who took her away from her lawful husband." She jabbed her forefinger at Spillman's head. "I'd like to kill that man for what he did to my daughter. He took her and rolled her in the mud. And there she sits with her legs crossed, smiling like a cat."

"Do you know Leo Spillman?"

"That wasn't his name."

"Ketchel?"

"Yeah. She brought him here to the house, it must have been six or seven years ago. She said he wanted to do something for me. That kind always want to do something for you, and then before you know it they own you. Like he owns Kitty. He said he owned an apartment in L.A. and I could move in rent-free and retire from hospital work. I told him I would rather go on working than take his money. So they left. I didn't see her again until last night."

"Do you know where they live?"

"They used to live in Las Vegas. Kitty sent me a couple of Christmas cards from there. I don't know where they live now. She hasn't sent me any mail for years. And last night when I asked her she wouldn't tell me where she lived."

"So you don't have any idea where I can find her?"

"No sir. If I did I wouldn't tell you. I'm not going to help you send my daughter to the pen."

"I'm not trying to put her in jail. I just want information—"

"You don't fool me, mister. They're wanted for income tax, ain't they?"

"Who told you that?"

"A man from the government told me. He was sitting where you are sitting, within the last two weeks. He said I'd be doing my daughter a favor if I could talk her into coming forth, that her and me could even get a percentage of the money because they're not lawful man and wife. I said it was Judas money. I said I'd be a fine mother, wouldn't I, if I spread my daughter's shame in all the papers. He said it was my duty as a citizen. I said there was duty and duty."

"Did you talk to Kitty about it?"

"I tried to this morning. That's when she left. We never could get along. But that's a far cry from turning her in to the government. I said it to the other one and I'm saying it to you. You can go back and tell the government I don't know where she is and I wouldn't tell you if I did know."

She sat there breathing defiance. A train whistled from the direction of Los Angeles. It was a long freight train, moving slowly. Somehow it reminded me of the government.

Before it had finished rattling the dishes in the kitchen, I said goodbye to Mrs. Sekjar and left. I dropped Ward off at his father's house, which was just about one grade better than Mrs. Sekjar's, and advised him to get some sleep. Then I drove to International Airport and bought a return ticket to Las Vegas.

26
· · ·

IT WAS still day, with a searchlight sun glinting along the sea, when the plane took off for Las Vegas. We flew away from the sun and came down into sudden purple dusk.

I took a cab to Fremont Street. The jostling neon colors of its signs made the few stars in the narrow sky look pale and embarrassed. The Scorpion Club was one of the larger casinos on the street, a two-story building with a three-story sign on which an electric scorpion twitched its tail.

The people at the slot machines inside seemed to work by similar mechanisms. They fed in their quarters and dollars with their left hands and pulled the levers with their right like assembly-line workers in a money factory. There were smudge-eyed boys so young that they hadn't begun to shave yet, and women with workmen's gloves on their lever hands, some of them so old and weary that they leaned on the machines to stay upright. The money factory was a hard place to work.

I worked my way through the early-evening crowd, past blackjack and roulette tables, and found a pit boss watching the crap tables at the rear of the big room. He was a quick-eyed man in an undertaker's suit. I told him I wanted to see the boss.

"I'm the boss."

"Don't kid me."

His glance darted up to the ceiling. "If you want to see Mr. Davis, you got to have a good reason. What's your reason?"

"I'll tell him."

"Tell me."

"Mr. Davis might not want me to."

His gaze came to rest on my face. I could feel his dislike. "You want to see Mr. Davis, you got to tell me the nature of your business."

I told him my name and occupation, and the fact that I was investigating two murders.

He didn't change expression. "You think Mr. Davis can help you out?"

"I'd like a chance to ask him."

"Wait here."

He disappeared behind a curtain. I heard him going upstairs. I stood by one of the green tables and watched a girl in a low-backed gown fling herself and the dice around. This was the creative end of the money factory, where you got a chance to finger the dice, and talk to them.

"They're getting hot for me," she said.

She was a nice-looking girl with a cultivated voice, and she reminded me of Ginny. The man who stood beside her and provided her with money wore furry black sideburns and dude clothes, including high-heeled boots. From time to time, when the girl won, he let out a synthetic vaquero whoop. His hand kept slipping lower on her back.

The pit boss came downstairs and jerked a thumb at me from the edge of the curtain. I followed him behind it. A second man loomed up behind the arras and went over me for iron. His head looked like a minor accident on top of his huge neck and shoulders.

"You can go on up." He followed me.

Mr. Davis was waiting at the head of the stairs. He was a smiling man with a politician's malleable face and a lot of wavy gray hair. He wore a pin-striped gray suit with slanting pockets and pleated shoulders, for action. Mr. Davis hadn't had much action lately. Even the careful tailoring of his suit couldn't harden or conceal the huge soft egg of his belly.

"Mr. Archer?"

"Mr. Davis."

He didn't offer me his hand, which was just as well. I don't like shaking hands with men wearing rings with stones in them.

"What can I do for you, Mr. Archer?"

"Give me a few minutes. We may be able to do something for each other."

He looked dubiously at my plain old California suit, and at my shoes which needed polishing. "That I doubt. You mentioned murder downstairs. Anyone I know?"

"I think so. Francis Martel."

He didn't react to the name. I showed him the picture. He reacted to it. He snatched it out of my hand and hustled me into his office and closed the door.

"Where did you get hold of this?"

"In Montevista."

"Was Leo there?"

"Not recently. This isn't a recent picture."

He took it to his desk to study it under the light. "No, I see it isn't recent. Leo will never be that young again. Neither will Kitty." He seemed to take pleasure in this fact, as if it made him younger by comparison. "Who's the character with the tray?"

"I was hoping you could tell me."

He looked up at me. "It wouldn't be Cervantes?"

"Feliz Cervantes, alias Francis Martel." Alias Pedro Domingo. "He was shot today, on Sabado Avenue in Brentwood."

Davis's eyes went dead. I noticed that this kept happening. They would show a flicker of interest or curiosity, or even malice, then sink back into lifelessness.

"You want to tell me about the shooting?" he said.

"Not keenly, but I will." I gave him a short account of Martel's death and what led up to it. "You can read the rest of it in the early-morning papers."

"And the killer got the money, is that right?"

"Evidently. Whose money is it?"

"I wouldn't know," he said with sudden vagueness.

He got up and walked away from me the length of the long office, surveying the desert photomurals on the walls. His footsteps were silent on the desert-colored rug. There was something a little female about his movements, and more than a little ominous, as if his huge belly was pregnant with death.

"It wouldn't be your money, would it, Mr. Davis?"

He turned and opened his mouth as if to yell, but produced no sound. Soundlessly he walked toward me, making a little sideways dance-step as he passed the horseshoe desk.

"No," he whispered into my face. "It wouldn't be my money and I had nothing to do with knocking him off." He smiled and nudged me as if he was going to tell me a joke, but there was no humor in his smile. "In fact I don't know why you come to me with this spiel of yours."

"You're Leo's partner, aren't you?"

"Am I?"

"And Cervantes was his boy."

"How do you mean, his boy?" Davis nudged me again. His pleated shoulders opened and closed with the gesture, making it obscene.

"I thought you'd be able to tell me, Mr. Davis."

"Think again. I only saw Cervantes once in my life, and that was last year when he came here with Leo. I don't know what the deal was. Whatever it was, I don't want any part of it. I'm a legitimate businessman conducting a legal business, and incidentally Leo is not my partner. There's nothing on the record that says he owns any part of this casino. As for me, I want no part of him."

It was a bold statement. Davis didn't strike me as a bold man. I was beginning to wonder if Leo Spillman was dead, too.

"Where can I find Leo?"

"I wouldn't know."

"You send him money, don't you?"

"He should send *me* money."

"How so?"

"You ask too many questions. Beat it now, before you make me nervous."

"I think I'll stick around. I need help with an income tax problem. Not mine. Leo's. And maybe yours."

Davis leaned on the wall, sighing. "Why didn't you tell me you were Internal Revenue?"

"I'm not."

"Then you misrepresented yourself just now."

"The hell I did. You can talk about income tax without working for the federal government."

"Not to me you can't. You can't con your way into my office masquerading as a federal agent."

He knew I hadn't, but he needed some point of focus for his anger. He seemed to have no continuous focal point in himself. I'd known other front men like him in Vegas and Reno: barroom gladhanders who had lost their gladness, smilers who gradually realized that they were fronting for death and belonged to it.

"The feds are looking for Leo. I guess you know that," I said.

"I guess I do."

"Why can't they find him? Is he dead?"

"I wish he was." He snickered.

"Did you have Cervantes shot?"

"Me? I'm a legitimate businessman."

"So you were telling me. It doesn't answer the question."

"It wasn't a good question."

"I'll see if I can frame a better one—the hypothetical kind they ask the experts in court."

"I'm no expert, and we're not in court."

"Just in case you ever are, it will be good practice for you." He didn't feel the needle, which probably meant he was feeling deeper pains. "How much black money did Leo siphon out of your counting room?"

He answered blandly: "I don't know anything about it."

"Naturally you wouldn't know about it. You're too legitimate."

"Watch it," he said. "I've taken as much from you as I've ever taken from anybody."

"Did he make discount deals with the big losers and use Cervantes to collect and stash the money?"

Davis looked at me carefully. His eyes were dead but unquiet. "You ask the kind of questions that answer themselves. You don't need me."

"We need each other," I said. "I want Leo Spillman, and you want the money he milked out of the business."

"If you're talking about that money in L.A., it's gone. There's no way for me to get it back. Anyway, it's nickles and dimes. Our counting room handles more than that every day of the year."

"So you have no problem."

"None that you can help me with."

Davis took another of his walks to the end of the room and back. He moved warily, with a kind of female stealth, as if his desert-colored office was actual desert, with rattlesnakes under the rug.

"If you do catch up with Leo," he said, "you might let me know. I'm willing to pay you for the information. Say five grand, if it's exclusive."

"I wasn't planning to hire myself out as a finger."

"Weren't you?" He took another good long look at my suit. "Anyway, the offer stands, bud."

He opened the door for me. The man with the wide shoulders and narrow head was waiting to accompany me downstairs. The girl who reminded me of Ginny was at one of the crap tables with a different escort. Everything that happened in Vegas seemed to be a repetition of something that had happened before.

I caught a plane back to Los Angeles and slept in my own bed.

27
...

A JAY who lived in my neighborhood woke me up in the morning. He was perched on a high limb outside my second-story apartment window, and he was yelling his head off for salted peanuts.

I looked in the cupboard: no salted peanuts. I scattered some wilted cornflakes on the windowsill. The jay didn't even bother to come down from his perch. He cocked his head on one side and looked sardonically at the last of the big spenders. Then he dove off the limb and flew away.

The milk in the refrigerator was sour. I shaved and put on clean linen and my other suit and went out for breakfast. I read the morning paper over my bacon and eggs. The killing of Martel was on the second page, and it was handled as a gang killing. The killing of Marietta Fablon was buried back in the Southland News. No connection was drawn between the two crimes.

On the way to my office on Sunset Boulevard I took a long detour to the Hall of Justice. Captain Perlberg had a preliminary report from the Crime Laboratory. The slug which Dr. Wills had removed from Marietta Fablon's chest had almost certainly come from the same gun as the slug that killed Martel. The gun itself, which was probably an old .38-caliber revolver, had not been found, and neither had the person who fired it.

"Got any ideas on the subject?" Perlberg asked me.

"I know a fact. Martel worked for a Vegas casino owner named Leo Spillman."

"Doing what?"

"I think he was Spillman's courier. Recently he went into business for himself."

Perlberg gave me a melancholy look. He lit a cigarette and blew smoke at me across his cluttered desk. He wasn't hostile or aggressive, but he had a kind of enveloping Jewish force.

"Why didn't you mention this yesterday, Archer?"

"I went to Vegas last night and asked some questions. I didn't get very good answers, but I got enough to suggest that Martel was co-operating with Spillman in a tax-evasion dodge. Then he stopped co-operating. He wanted the cash for himself."

"And Spillman gunned him?"

"Or had him gunned."

Perlberg puffed on his cigarette, filling the small office with the fumes, as if smog was the native element in which his brain worked best.

"How does Mrs. Fablon fit into this hypothesis?"

"I don't know. I have a theory that Spillman killed her husband and she knew it."

"Her husband was a suicide, according to the Montevista people."

"So they keep telling me. But it isn't proven. Say he wasn't."

"Then we have three unsolved killings instead of two. I need an extra killing like an extra hole in my head." He stubbed out his cigarette violently. It was the only show of impatience he permitted himself. "Thanks for the information, though, and the ideas. They may be helpful."

"I was hoping for a little assistance myself."

"Anything, if it don't cost the taxpayers money."

"I'm trying to find Leo Spillman—"

"Don't worry, I'll be on it soon as you leave this office."

It was an invitation to depart. I lingered in the doorway. "Will you let me know when you locate him? I'd give a lot for a chance to talk to him."

Perlberg said he would.

I drove across town to my own office. There was a sheaf of mail in the letterbox, but nothing that looked interesting. I carried it into the inner office and filed it on top of my desk. A thin film of dust on the desk reminded me that I hadn't been there since Friday. I dusted it with a piece of Kleenex and called my answering service.

"A Dr. Sylvester has been trying to get you," the girl on the switchboard said.

"Did he leave a number?"

"No, he said he had to make some hospital calls. He'll be in his office after one o'clock."

"What did he want, do you know?"

"He didn't say. He sounded as if it was important, though. And last night you had a call from a Professor Tappinger. He did leave his number."

She recited it, and I dialed Tappinger's house direct. Bess Tappinger answered.

"This is Lew Archer."

"How lovely," she said in her little-girl voice, her statutory-rape voice. "And what a coincidence. I was just thinking about you."

I didn't ask her what she had been thinking. I didn't want to know. "Is your husband there?"

"Taps is teaching all morning. Why don't you come over for a cup of coffee? I make very good Italian coffee."

"Thanks, but I'm not in town."

"Oh. Where are you?"

"In Hollywood."

"That's only fifty miles. You could still get here before Taps comes home for lunch. I want to speak to you, Lew."

"What about?"

"Us. Everything. I was up most of the night thinking about it—about the change in my life—and you're a part of it, I mean it, Lew."

I cut her short: "I'm sorry, Mrs. Tappinger. I've got a job to do. Counseling discontented housewives isn't my line."

"Don't you like me at all?"

"Sure I like you." I was the last of the big spenders, I couldn't refuse her that.

"I knew you did. I could tell. When I was sixteen I went to a gypsy fortune-teller. She said there'd be a change in my life in a year, that I'd meet a handsome clever man and he would marry me. And that's the way it worked out. I married Taps. But the fortune-teller said there'd be another change when I was thirty. I can feel it coming. It's almost like being pregnant again, I mean it. I thought my life was over and done with—"

"All this is very interesting," I said. "We'll go into it another time."

"But it won't wait."

"It will have to."

"You said you liked me."

"I like a lot of women."

It was an oafish remark.

"I don't like many men. You're the first since I—"

The sentence died unfinished. I didn't encourage her to resurrect it. I didn't say a word.

She burst into tears, and hung up on me.

Bess was probably schitzy, I told myself, or addled on bedroom novels, suffering from cabin fever or faculty-wife neurosis or the first untimely hint of middle age, like frost on the Fourth of July. Clearly she had troubles, and a wise man I knew in Chicago had said once and for all: "Never sleep with anyone whose troubles are worse than your own."

But Bess was hard to put out of my mind. When I got my car out of the parking lot and headed south on the San Diego Freeway, she was the one I felt I was driving toward, even though it was her husband I was going to see.

At noon I was waiting outside his office in the Arts Building. At one minute after twelve he came down the corridor.

"I could set my watch by you, professor."

He winced. "You make me feel like a mechanical man. Actually I hate being on this rigid schedule." He unlocked the office door and flung it open. "Come in."

"I understand you found out something more about Cervantes."

He didn't answer me until we were sitting facing each other across his desk. "I did indeed. After I left you yesterday I decided to throw the schedule overboard for once. I canceled my afternoon class and drove up to Los Angeles State with that picture you gave me of him." He patted his breast pocket. "His name is Pedro Domingo. At least he was registered at L.A. State under that name. Professor Bosch thinks it's his true name."

"I know. I talked to Bosch yesterday."

Tappinger looked displeased, as if I'd gone over his head. "Allan didn't tell *me* that."

"I called him after you left. He was busy, and I got very little from him. He did say that Domingo was a native of Panama."

Tappinger nodded. "That was one of the things that got him into trouble. He'd jumped ship and was in this country illegally. It's why he changed his name when he came here to us. The Immigration officials were after him."

"When and where did he jump ship?"

"It was some time in 1956, according to Allan, when Pedro was twenty. He came ashore at San Pedro. Perhaps he thought the place would be lucky for him. Anyway, he practically stepped off the boat into a classroom. He attended Long Beach State for a year—I don't know how he got the college to accept him—and then he shifted to Los Angeles State.

"He was there for two years, and Allan Bosch got to know him fairly well. He struck Allan in very much the same way he struck me —as a highly intelligent young man with problems."

"What kind of problems?"

"Social and cultural problems. Historical problems. Allan described him as a kind of tropical Hamlet trying to cope with contemporary reality. Actually that description applies to most of the Central and South American cultures. Domingo's problems weren't just personal, they belonged to his time and place. But he yearned for the luminous city."

Professor Tappinger seemed to be on the brink of a lecture. I said: "The what?"

"The luminous city. It's a phrase I use for the world of spirit and intellect, the distillation of the great minds of past and present." He tapped the side of his head, as though to claim membership in the group. "It takes in everything from Plato's Forms and Augustine's *Civitas Dei* to Joyce's epiphanies."

"Could you take it a little slower, professor?"

"Forgive me." He seemed confused by my interruption. "Was I talking academic jargon? Actually Pedro's dilemma can be stated quite simply: he was a poor Panamanian with all the hopes and troubles and frustrations of his country. He came out of the Santa Ana slums. His mother was a Blue Moon girl in the Panama City cabarets, and Pedro himself was probably illegitimate. But he had too much gumption to accept his condition or remain in it.

"I know something of what he must have felt. I wasn't a bastard, exactly, but I worked my way up out of a Chicago slum, and I knew what it was to go hungry in the Depression. I'd never have made it through university without the G.I. bill. So you see, I can sympathize with Pedro Domingo. I hope they won't punish him too severely when they catch him."

"They won't."

He noticed the finality of my tone. Slowly his eyes came up to mine. They were sensitive, rather feminine eyes, which had probably been fine-looking before strain reddened the whites. "Has something happened to him?"

"He's dead. A gunman shot him yesterday. Don't you read the papers?"

"I have to confess that I very seldom look at them. But this is dreadful news." He paused, his sensitive mouth pulled out of shape. "Do you have any notion who killed him?"

"The prime suspect is a gambler named Leo Spillman. He's the other man in the picture I gave you."

Tappinger got it out of his pocket and studied it. "He *looks* dangerous."

"Domingo was dangerous, too. It's fortunate for Ginny that she got out of this alive."

"Is Miss Fablon all right?"

"She's as well as can be expected, after losing her mother and her husband in the same week."

"Poor child. I'd like to see her, and comfort her if I could."

"You better check with Dr. Sylvester. He's looking after her. I'm on my way to see him now."

I rose to go. Tappinger came around the desk. "I'm sorry I can't invite you for lunch today," he said with a kind of aggressive fussiness. "There isn't time."

"I don't have time, either. Give my regards to your wife."

"I'm sure she'll be glad to have them. She's quite an admirer of yours."

"That's because she doesn't know me very well."

My attempt to treat it lightly didn't come off. The little man looked up at me with strained and anxious eyes.

"I'm concerned about Bess. She's such a dreamer, so addicted to *Bovarysme*. And I don't think you're good for her."

"Neither do I."

"You won't take it personally, Mr. Archer, if I suggest that perhaps you'd better not see her again?"

"I wasn't planning to."

Tappinger seemed relieved.

28

...

On my way into town I stopped at a gas station with an outside telephone booth and called Christman in Washington. He was still out to lunch. The operator transferred my call to the restaurant where he ate, and eventually I heard him say:

"Christman here. I've been trying to get you, Lew. You're never in your office."

"I haven't been in the last few days. Do you have anything more on our friend?"

"A little. Until a few months ago he was a second secretary at the Panamanian Embassy. He was fairly young for the job, but apparently he's very highly qualified. He has an advanced degree from the University of Paris. Before they transferred him to Washington he held the post of third secretary in Paris."

"Why did he leave the diplomatic service?"

"I don't know. The man I talked to said he resigned for personal reasons. He didn't explain what he meant by personal reasons. But Domingo didn't leave under a cloud, so far as I could ascertain. Do you want me to dig some more?"

"There wouldn't be much point," I said. "You might tell whoever you talked to in the Embassy that their boy was shot in Los Angeles yesterday."

"Dead?"

"Very. They'll probably want to do something about the body, when the police release it. Captain Perlberg is in charge of the case."

I was a few minutes late for my appointment with Sylvester, but he was later. He arrived at the clinic about half-past one, looking harried, and took me into his consultation room.

"I'm sorry to keep you waiting, Archer. I thought I'd better drop in on Ginny Fablon."

"How is she?"

"I believe she'll be all right. Of course she's woozy from shock, and I have her under fairly heavy sedation. But she's accepted the fact of her mother's death, as well as her husband's, and she can see beyond them to some kind of future."

"I still don't think she should be left by herself."

"She isn't by herself. The Jamiesons have given her a guest cottage. They're providing her meals, and Peter is there to wait on her, of course, which is all he ever wanted. She may have a happy ending yet."

"With Peter?"

"I wouldn't be surprised." He added with a sidewise cheerless grin: "You understand my idea of a happy marriage is essentially anything that works."

"How's your own marriage working?"

"Audrey and I will muddle through. We've both had a lot to forgive. But I didn't ask you here as a marriage counselor. I have some information for you." He brought a manila folder out of a drawer of his desk. "You're still looking for Leo Spillman, aren't you?"

"I am. So are the police."

"What if I told you where and how to find him? Could I count on a certain amount of tolerance from you?"

"You'd better explain what you mean by that."

He bit his thumb and studied the dent his teeth made. "I let down my back hair yesterday. Frankly I was rattled. The fact is, you know more about me than anyone else in town. It's beginning to look as if everything connected with this mess is going to be spread out in the public prints. All I'm asking from you is a certain amount of decent reticence about my part in it. I have a great deal to lose."

"What do you want suppressed?"

"Well, I wouldn't want the details of my co-operation with Spillman —Couldn't we keep it a doctor-patient relationship? That's what it was essentially."

"That's what it became, anyway. I'll hold back the rest of it if I possibly can."

"Then the thing that Audrey and Fablon had—does it have to come out?"

"I don't see why it should have to. Anything else?"

"I won't try to press this too far," he said, with a wary eye on my face, "but that money Marietta tried to borrow from me Monday—could we keep it confidential?"

"I doubt it. Mrs. Strome at the club knows about it."

"I've already talked to her. She's safe."

"I'm not."

Sylvester's eyes became shallow and hard.

"Why are you balking at that? It's the least embarrassing thing, really."

"Not if Marietta was trying to blackmail you."

"For what? The Spillman-Fablon business? I thought that was settled."

"It isn't settled to my satisfaction."

"But you can't accuse Marietta of being a blackmailer. It was just a friendly loan she asked me for. Naturally I was hoping she'd keep quiet about the Spillman bit, and Audrey's mixup with her husband."

"Naturally. Was there anything else you wanted kept quiet?"

"By you?"

"By anybody. I've been wondering, for instance, why and how Ginny came to work for you. I understand she was a receptionist here for a couple of years."

"That's right, until two years ago this summer. Then she went back to school."

"Why did she leave school to go to work?"

"She'd been overstudying."

"Was that your opinion?"

"I agreed with Marietta about it. The girl needed a change."

"She didn't come to work here for personal reasons, then?"

"I wasn't her lover," he said in a grating voice, "if that's what you're getting at. I've done some lousy things in my life but I don't mess with young girls."

He glanced up at his framed diplomas on the wall. There was a puzzled expression in his eyes, as if he couldn't remember how he had acquired them. His expression turned faraway, further and further away, as if his mind was climbing back over the curve of time to the source of his life.

I brought him back to the present. "You were going to tell me how to find Spillman."

"So I was."

586 · Archer AT LARGE

"If you'd given me the information yesterday, you'd have saved trouble, possibly a life."

"I didn't have the information yesterday. That is, I didn't know I had it. I stumbled across it early this morning when I was going over Spillman's medical records." He opened the folder in front of him. "About three months ago, on February 20, we had a request for a copy of the records from a Dr. Charles Park, in Santa Teresa. I didn't fill the request myself—Mrs. Loftin's initials are on the notation—and she neglected to mention it to me. Anyway, as I said, I came across it."

"What were you looking for?"

"I wanted to check on how sick Spillman really was. He was sick, all right. Apparently he still is. I called Dr. Park's office as soon as I found the notation. He wasn't in yet himself, but his girl confirmed that Ketchel was still his patient. Apparently Spillman is using the name Ketchel in Santa Teresa."

"Did you get his address there?"

"Yes, I did. It's 1427 Padre Ridge Road."

I thanked him.

"Don't thank me. You and I have an agreement, for what it's worth. I want to add one other small item to it. You mustn't tell Leo Spillman I sicked you on to him."

He was afraid of Spillman. The fear hissed like escaping gas in his voice, and lingered like an odor in my mind. On my way north to Santa Teresa I stopped at my apartment to pick up a hand gun.

29
...

THE CITY of Santa Teresa is built on a slope which begins at the edge of the sea and rises more and more steeply toward the coastal mountains in a series of ascending ridges. Padre Ridge is the first and lowest of these, and the only one inside the city limits.

It was fairly expensive territory, an established neighborhood of well-maintained older houses, many of them with brilliant hanging gardens. The grounds of 1427 were the only ones in the block that looked unkempt. The privet hedge needed clipping. Crabgrass was running rampant in the steep lawn.

Even the house, pink stucco under red tile, had a disused air about it. The drapes were drawn across the front windows. The only sign of life was a house wren which contested my approach to the veranda.

I lifted the lion's-head knocker and let it drop, hardly expecting an answer. But after a while soft footsteps came from the back of the house. The door was opened, minimally, by a hefty middle-aged woman in a wet blue cotton bathing suit.

"My name is Archer. Is Mrs. Ketchel home?"

"I'll see."

The woman stepped out of the puddle that had formed on the tile around her bare feet, and disappeared into the back of the house. I pushed the front door wide open and walked in, conscious of the gun bulging like a benign tumor in my armpit.

There were several closed doors in the hallway, and an open door at the end. Through it I could see across a room, through sliding glass, to the dappled blue water of a swimming pool.

Kitty came out of the water dripping. She crossed the room, leaving wasp-waisted footprints on the rug, and faced me in the doorway. She had on a white elastic bathing suit, and a white rubber cap shaped like a helmet which made her look like an Amazon sentinel.

"You get out of here. I'll call the cops."

"Sure you will. They're combing the state for Leo as it is."

"He hasn't done anything wrong." She hedged: "Not recently."

"I want to hear him tell me that myself."

"No. You can't talk to him."

She stepped forward, pulling the door shut behind her, moving so abruptly that she blundered into me. She put her hands on my shoulders to regain her balance, and recoiled as if I was very hot or cold.

She must have felt the holster under my jacket. Her fear came back. It made her face work as if she had swallowed poison.

"You came here to kill us, didn't you?"

"You and I have been through all this before. You seem to have killing on your mind."

"I've seen too many—" She caught herself.

"Seen too many people die?"

"Yeah. In traffic accidents and stuff like that." She tried to put on an innocent expression. With her paint removed, and her garish hair covered, she looked younger and realer. But not innocent. "What do you want from us? Money? We have no money."

"Don't try to snow me, Kitty. This is the head office of the money factory."

"It's true what I tell you. That cat who calls himself Martel eloped with our ready cash, and we can't realize on our investments."

"How did he get his hands on the cash?"

"He was supposed to be bringing it to Leo. Leo trusted him. I didn't, but Leo did."

"Martel was shot to death in Los Angeles yesterday. Another accident for your memory book. He had a hundred thousand dollars in cash with him."

"Where is it?"

"I thought it might be here. It was black money, wasn't it, Kitty?"

She flung up her arms in a jagged movement, bringing her fists to her shoulders, then flung them down again. "I'm not admitting anything."

"It's time you did some talking, don't you think? There's such a thing as buying immunity with information, especially on an income tax rap."

Though it wasn't cold in the hall, she had begun to shiver.

"On a murder rap," I said, "it isn't so easy. But you can't afford to hold back. Did Leo or one of his boys knock off Martel?"

"Leo had nothing to do with it."

"If he did, and you know he did, you better tell me. Unless you want to go on trial with him."

"I know he didn't. He hasn't left this house."

"You have."

She was shivering violently. "Listen, mister, I don't know what you're trying to do to us—"

"You've done it to yourselves. What you do to other people you do to yourself—that's the converse of the Golden Rule, Kitty."

"I don't know what you're talking about."

"Three murders. Martel yesterday. Marietta Fablon the night before, when incidentally you were in Montevista. And Roy Fablon seven years before that. Remember him?"

She nodded jerkily.

"Tell me what happened to Fablon. You were there."

"Let me get some clothes on first. I'm freezing. I've been in with Leo for about an hour."

"Is he out by the pool?"

"Yes, he's working with his physiotherapist. Don't say anything in front of her, will you? She's a square."

Kitty peeled off her rubber cap. Her red hair blossomed out. When she opened one of the closed doors, I caught a glimpse of a tousled pink female bedroom with a mirror in the ceiling over the king-sized bed, alas.

I went outside. A wheelchair stood among the poolside furniture. The woman in the blue bathing suit was standing breast-deep in the water with a man in her arms. His face was moon-shaped and flaccid, his body loose. Only his black eyes held some measure of controlled adult life.

"Hello, Mr. Ketchel."

"I'll say hello for him," the woman said. "Mr. Ketchel had a little cerebral accident about three months ago and he hasn't said a word since. Have you, honey?"

His sad black eyes answered her. Then they shifted apprehensively to me. He smiled placatingly. Saliva dripped from one corner of his mouth.

Kitty appeared at the sliding glass doors and beckoned me inside. She had put on sequined slacks which winked suggestively, a high-necked angora sweater, a hasty paint job which reduced her face to meaninglessness. It was hard to tell what she had in mind for me.

She took me into a small front room, out of sight of the swimming pool, and opened the drapes. She stood at the window competing with the view. Beside the bulbs and hollows of her body, the sails on the sea looked dinky and remote, like cocked white napkins on a faded blue tablecloth.

"You see what I've got on my hands?" she said with her hands out. "A poor little sick old man. He can't walk, he can't talk, he can't even write his name. He can't tell me where anything is. He can't protect me."

"Who do you need protection from?"

"Leo made a lifetime of enemies. If they knew he was helpless, his life wouldn't be worth that." She snapped her fingers. "Neither would mine. Why do you think we're hiding out in the tules here?"

To her, I thought, the tules meant any place that wasn't on the Chicago-Vegas-Hollywood axis. I said: "Is Leo's partner Davis one of the threats?"

"He's the main one. If Leo dies or gets knocked off, Davis has the most to gain."

"The Scorpion Club."

"He already owns it on paper: the Tax Commission made Leo give it up. And he has a beef against Leo."

"I talked to Davis last night. He offered me money to tell him where Leo is."

"So that's why you're here."

"Stop jumping to conclusions. I turned him down."

"Really?"

"Really. What's his beef against Leo?"

She shook her head. Her hair flared out in the sunlight. Oddly it reminded me of the orange-pickers' fire in the railroad yards. The queer forced intimacy of that night still hung as a possibility between me and Kitty.

"I can't tell you that," she said.

"Then I'll tell you. Internal Revenue is after Leo for the money he took off the top. If they can't find him and the money, maybe even if they can, they'll pin the rap on Davis. At the very least he'll lose his license for fronting for a concealed interest. At worst he'll go to the federal pen for the rest of his life."

"He isn't the only one."

"If you mean Leo, the rest of his life isn't worth much."

"What about the rest of my life?" She touched her furred angora breast. "I'm not even thirty yet. I don't want to go to prison."

"Then you better make a deal."

"And turn Leo in? I will not."

"They won't do anything to him, in his condition."

"They'll lock him up. He won't get his therapy. He'll never learn to talk or write or—" She stopped herself in mid-sentence.

"Or tell you where the money is."

She hesitated. "What money? You said the money was gone."

"The hundred grand is. But my information is that Leo took millions off the top. Where is it?"

"I wish I knew, mister." Through her composed mask I could see the calculation going on behind her eyes. "What did you say your name was?"

"Archer. Does Leo know where the money is?"

"I think so. He still has some of his brain left. But it's hard to tell how much he understands. He always pretends to understand everything I say. So the other day I tried him on some gibberish. He smiled and nodded just the same."

"What did you say?"

"I wouldn't want to repeat it. It was just a lot of dirty words about what I'd do for him if he'd learn to talk. Or even write." Tensely, she clasped her arms across her chest. "It drives me crazy when I think of what I went through in the hopes of a little peace and security. The beatings he handed out, and the other stuff. Don't think I didn't have other chances. But I stuck with Leo. Stuck is the word. Now I'm stuck with a cripple and it's costing us two grand a month to live—six hundred a month just for doctors and therapy—and I don't know where next month's money is coming from." Her voice rose. "I'd be a millionaire if I had my rights."

"Or your wrongs."

She tossed her head. "I earned that money, I ground it out like coffee over the years. Don't tell me I've got no right to it. I've got a right to a decent living."

"Who told you that?"

"Nobody had to tell me. A woman with my looks—I can pick and choose." It was childish talk, self-hypnotic and pathetic. It gave me a hint of the self-enclosed fantasy that had paired her off with Leo Spillman and kept her with him, insulated from life by his larger fantasy.

"You mean you get picked and chosen. Why don't you go out and hustle? You're a big strong girl."

She was still on her adolescent high horse. "How dare you? I'm not a prostitute."

"I don't mean that kind of hustle. Get a job."

"I've never had to work for a living, thank you."

"It's time you did. If you keep dreaming about those vanished millions you'll dream yourself into Camarillo or Corona."

"Don't you dare make threats to me!"

"It isn't me threatening you. It's your dreams. If you won't lift a finger to help yourself, go back to Harry."

"That feeb? He couldn't even stay out of the hospital."

"He gave everything he had."

She was silent. Her face was like a colored picture straining in agony to come to life. Life glittered first in her eyes. A tear made a track down her cheek. I found myself standing beside her comforting her. Then her head was like an artificial dahlia on my shoulder, and I could feel the sorrowful little movements of her body becoming less sorrowful.

The therapist tapped on the door and opened it. She had changed into street clothes. "I'm leaving, Mrs. Ketchel. Mr. Ketchel is safe and snug in his wheelchair." She looked at us severely: "But don't leave him out too long now."

"I won't," Kitty said. "Thank you."

The woman didn't move. "I was wondering if you can pay me something on last week, and for staying Monday night. I have bills to meet, too."

Kitty went to her bedroom and came back with a twenty-dollar bill. She thrust it at the woman. "Will this take care of it for now?"

"I guess it will have to. I don't begrudge my services, understand, but a woman has a right to honest pay for honest work."

"Don't worry, you'll get your money. Our dividend checks are slow in arriving this month."

The woman gave her a disbelieving look, and left the house. Kitty was rigid with anger. She rapped her fists together in the air.

"The old bag! She humiliated me."

"Are there any dividends coming?"

"There's nothing coming. I'm having to sell my jewels. And I was saving them for a rainy day."

"It looks like a wet summer."

"What are you, a rainmaker?"

She moved toward me, humming an old song about what we'd do on a rain-rain-rainy day. Her breast nudged me gently. "I'd do a lot for any man who would help me find Leo's money."

She was being deliberately provocative now, but our moment had passed.

"Would you tell me the truth, for instance?"

"What about?"

"Roy Fablon. Did Leo kill him?"

After a long thinking pause, she said: "He didn't mean to. It was an accident. They had a fight about—something."

"Something?"

"If you have to know, it was Roy Fablon's daughter. The older Leo got, the more he went for the young chicks. It was embarrassing. Maybe I shouldn't have done what I did, but I passed the word to Mrs. Fablon about Leo making a deal for the girl with Fablon."

"You told Mrs. Fablon?"

"That's correct. I was acting in self-defense. Also I was doing the girl a favor. Mrs. Fablon straightened her husband out, and he said nix to Leo."

"I can't understand why he didn't say nix in the first place."

"He owed Leo a lot of money, and that was all the leverage Leo ever needed. Also Fablon pretended not to know what the deal meant. You know what I mean?"

"I know what you mean."

"Like Leo was a philanthropist or something. He'd sell his sick mother's blood for ten dollars a pint and take a deposit on the bottle, Leo would. But he was going to send the girl to school in Switzerland, to improve her mind. And Fablon thought that would be great, until his wife got wind of it. Frankly I think that Fablon hated the girl."

"I thought he was crazy about her."

"Sometimes there isn't much difference between the two. Ask me, I'm an expert. Fablon turned against her when she got pregnant by some fellow, apparently, and Fablon would go to any lengths to get her away from him."

"Who was he?"

"I don't know. Mrs. Fablon didn't know, either, or else she didn't want to tell me. Anyway, Fablon came to the cottage that night and called the whole deal off. Leo and him had a fight, and Fablon took quite a beating. Leo used to be terrible with his fists, even when he was sick. Fablon stumbled out of the cottage in bad shape. He lost his way in the dark and fell in the pool and drowned."

"Did you see him?"

"Cervantes did."

"He must have been lying. According to the chemical evidence, Fablon drowned in salt water. The pool is fresh."

"Maybe it is now. It was salt in those days. I ought to know. I swam in it every day for two weeks."

Her voice lingered on the memory. Maybe she was running into rainy days, and having to sell her jewelry. But she had spent two weeks in the Tennis Club sun.

"What did Cervantes have to say about it, Kitty?"

"He found Roy Fablon in the pool, and came and told Leo. It was a bad scene. Leo was committing a felony just by using his fists. When Fablon drowned it was technically murder. Cervantes suggested he could chuck the body in the sea and fake a suicide. He'd been sucking around Leo before, and this was his chance for an in. When we left town the next day or so, we took him along. Instead of sending the Fablon girl to school in Switzerland, Leo sent the Cervantes boy to college in Paris, France.

"I told Leo he was nuts. He said the reason he was a success was because he looked years ahead. He had a use for Cervantes, he said, and he knew he could trust him, after the Fablon business. That was one time he was wrong. As soon as Leo got sick this last time, Cervantes turned on him." Her voice deepened. "It's funny about Leo. Everybody was afraid of him, including me. He was the big shot. But as soon as he got really sick, he was just a nothing man. A flunky like Cervantes could take him for everything he had."

"At least it was a switch. How did Cervantes get hold of the money?"

"Leo turned it over to him, a piece at a time, over the last three-four years. Cervantes got some kind of a government job, and he could cross the border without being searched. He stashed the money some-place out of the country, maybe in Switzerland, in one of those num-bered bank accounts they have."

I didn't think the money was in Switzerland. There were numbered bank accounts in Panama, too.

"What are you thinking?"

"I was wondering," I said, "if Mrs. Fablon was blackmailing Leo for killing her husband."

"She was. She came to see him in Vegas after the body was found. She told him she protected him at the inquest, and the least he could do was help her out a little. He hated like hell to do it, but I think he sent her payments from then on." She paused, and looked at me sharply. "I've told you everything I know about the Fablons. Are you going to try and trace that money for me?"

"I'm not saying no. Right now I have another client, and two other murders to work on."

"There's no money in that, is there?"

"Money isn't the only thing in life."

"That's what I used to think, until this. What are you, a do-gooder or something?"

"I wouldn't say so. I'm working at not being a do-badder."

She gave me a puzzled look. "I don't get you, Archer. What's your angle?"

"I like people, and I try to be of some service."

"And that adds up to a life?"

"It makes life possible, anyway. Try it some time."

"I did," she said, "with Harry. But he didn't have what it takes. I always get stuck with feebs and cripples." She shrugged. "I better see how Leo is doing."

He was waiting patiently in the cross-hatched shadow of a lattice-work screen. His shirt and trousers were loose on his shrunken body. He blinked up at me when we approached him, as if I planned to hit him.

"Cowardy custard," Kitty said cheerfully. "This is my new boyfriend. He's going to find the money and take me on a trip around the world. And you want to know what's going to happen to you, you poor old clown? We'll put you in a ward in the county hospital. And nobody will ever come to see you."

I walked out.

30
• • •

I DROVE BACK to Los Angeles, stopped there for dinner during the twilight hour, and finished the trip to Montevista in the dark.

Vera answered the door of the Jamieson house. She was wearing her sunburst kimono, and her black hair was loose on her shoulders.

It wasn't that late. The household seemed to be going to pieces in a quiet way.

"He's out in the guest house," she said, "with her." Vera seemed to resent another woman on the premises.

The guest house was a white frame cottage at the rear of the garden. Light spilled from its half-shuttered windows, reviving the daytime colors of the flower beds around it. Sweet unidentifiable odors drifted in the air.

It seemed like a place for an idyll, instead of the sequel to a tragedy. Life was short and sweet, I thought, sweet and short.

Peter called out: "Who is it?"

I told him, and he opened the door. He had on a bulky gray sweater and an open-collared white shirt which revealed the flabby thickness of his neck. There was a rather peculiar gleam in his eye. It could have been pure innocent happiness; it could have been euphoria.

I had similar doubts about the girl in the bright chintz room behind him. She sat under a lamp with a book on her knee, perfectly calm and still in a black dress. She nodded to me, and that was all.

"Come in, won't you?" he said.

"You come out."

He stepped outside, leaving the door partly open. It was a warm night for May, and windless.

"What is it, Mr. Archer? I hate to leave her."

"Even for a minute?"

"Even for a minute," he said with a kind of pride.

"I have some findings to report, about her father's death. I doubt that she'll want to hear what I have to say. He wasn't a suicide. He may have died by accident."

"I think Ginny will want to hear about it."

Reluctantly I went in and told my story, slightly bowdlerized. Ginny took it more calmly than Peter. His foot kept thumping to a nervous rhythm, as if an uncontrolled part of him wanted to run away, even from a room with Ginny in it.

I said to her: "I'm sorry to have to dig this up and throw it in your lap. You've had quite a lot thrown in your lap recently."

"It's all right. It's over now."

I hoped it was over. Her serenity bothered me. It was like the lifeless serenity of a statue.

"Do you want me to do anything about Mr. Ketchel?"

Peter waited for her to answer. She lifted her hands a few inches and dropped them on her book. "What would be the point? You say he's a sick old man, hardly more than a vegetable. It's like one of the condign punishments in Dante. A big violent man turns into a helpless cripple." She hesitated. "Were he and my father fighting about me?"

"That was the general idea."

"I don't understand," Peter said.

She turned to him. "Mr. Ketchel made a rough pass at me."

"And you still don't want him punished?"

"Why should I? That was years ago. I'm not even the same person," she added unsmilingly. "Did you know we change completely, chemically speaking, every seven years?" She seemed to take comfort in the thought.

"You're an angel," he said. But he didn't go near her or touch her.

"There's a further possibility," I said. "Ketchel-Spillman may not have been responsible for your father's death after all. Somebody else may have found him wandering around the club grounds in a daze, and deliberately drowned him in the swimming pool."

"Who would do that?" she said.

"Your late husband himself is the best bet. I've got some further information on him, by the way. He was a Panamanian who came out of a fairly hard school—"

She interrupted me: "I know that. Professor Tappinger paid me a visit this afternoon. He told me all about Francis. Poor Francis," she said remotely. "I see now that he wasn't entirely sane, and neither was I, to be taken in by him. But what conceivable reason could he have for hurting Roy? I didn't even know him in those days."

"He may have drowned him to get a hold on Ketchel. Or he may have seen someone else drown him, and convinced Ketchel that it was Ketchel's fault."

"You have a horrible imagination, Mr. Archer."

"So had your late husband."

"No. You're mistaken about him. Francis wasn't like that."

"You only knew one side of him, I'm afraid. Francis Martel was a made-up character. Did Professor Tappinger tell you his real name was Pedro Domingo, and he was a bastard by-product of the slums of Panama City? That's all we know about the real man, the real life that forced him into the fantasy life with you."

"I don't want to talk about that." She hugged herself as if she could feel a faint chill of reality through her widow's black. "Please let's not talk about Francis."

Peter rose from his chair. "I quite agree. All that is in the past now. And we've had enough talk for one night, Mr. Archer."

He went to the door and opened it. The sweet night air flooded into the room. I sat where I was.

"May I ask you a question in private, Miss Fablon? Are you calling yourself Miss Fablon?"

"I suppose so. I hadn't thought of it."

"It won't be 'Miss Fablon' for long," Peter said with foolish blandness. "One of these fine days it's going to be 'Mrs. Jamieson,' the way it was always meant to be."

Ginny looked resigned, and very tired. "What do you wish to ask me?" she said softly.

"It's a private question. Tell Peter to go away for a minute."

"Peter, you heard the man."

He frowned and went out, leaving the door wide open. I heard him bulling around in the garden.

"Poor old Peter," she said. "I don't know what I'd do without him now. I don't know just what I'm going to do with him, either."

"Marry him?"

"I don't seem to have any other choice. That sounds cynical, doesn't it? I didn't mean it that way. But nothing seems terribly worthwhile right now."

"It wouldn't be fair to marry Peter unless you cared about him."

"Oh, I care for him, more than for anyone. I always have. Francis was just an episode in my life." Behind her world-weary pose, I caught a hint of her immaturity. I wondered if she had grown emotionally at all since her father died.

And I thought that Ginny and Kitty, girls from opposite ends of the same town, had quite a lot in common after all. Neither one had quite survived the accident of beauty. It had made them into things, zombies in a dead desert world, as painful to contemplate as meaningless crucifixions.

"You and Peter used to go together, he told me."

"That's true. Through most of high school. He wasn't fat in those days," she added in an explanatory way.

"Were you lovers?"

Her eyes darkened, the way the ocean darkens under moving clouds.

For the first time I seemed to have touched her sense of her own life. She turned away so that I couldn't look into her eyes.

"I don't see that it matters." That meant yes.

"Did you become pregnant by Peter?"

"If I answer you," she said with her face averted, "will you promise never to repeat my answer? To anyone, even Peter?"

"All right."

"Then I can tell you. We were going to have a baby when I was a freshman in college. I didn't tell Peter. He was so young, and so young for his age. I didn't want to frighten him. I didn't tell anyone, except Roy, and eventually Mother. But even them I didn't tell who the father was. I had no desire to be taken out of school and forced into one of those horrible teenage marriages. Roy was pretty let-down with me, on account of the baby, but he borrowed a thousand dollars and took me to Tijuana. He treated me to the de luxe abortion, complete with doctor and nurse and hygienic atmosphere. But after that he seemed to feel I owed him money."

Her voice was toneless. She might have been talking about a shopping trip. But her very flatness of feeling suggested the trauma that kept her emotions fixed. She said without much curiosity:

"How did you find out about my pregnancy? I thought nobody knew."

"It doesn't matter how I found out."

"But I only told Roy and Mother."

"And they're dead."

A barely visible tremor went through her. Slowly, as if against physical resistance, she turned her head and looked into my face.

"You think they were killed because they knew about my pregnancy?"

"It's possible."

"What about Francis's death?"

"I have no theory, Miss Fablon. I'm still groping in the dark. Do you have any ideas?"

She shook her head. Her bright hair swung, touching her cold pale cheeks with a narcissistic caress.

Peter said impatiently from the doorway: "May I come in now?"

"No, you may not. Go away and leave me alone." She stood up, including me in the invitation to leave.

"But you're not supposed to be alone," Peter said. "Dr. Sylvester told me—"

"Dr. Sylvester is an old woman and you're another. Go away. If you don't, I'll move out. Tonight."

Peter backed out, and I followed him. She closed and bolted the door after us. When we were out of hearing of the cottage, Peter turned on me:

"What did you say to her?"

"Nothing, really."

"You must have said something to bring on a reaction like that."

"I asked her a question or two."

"What about?"

"She asked me not to tell you."

"*She* asked *you* not to tell *me?*" His face leaned close to mine. I couldn't see it too well. He sounded wildly angry and belligerent. "You've got things turned around, haven't you? You're my employee. Ginny is my fiancée."

"She's kind of an instant fiancée, isn't she?"

Perhaps I shouldn't have said it. Peter called me a filthy crud and swung on me. I saw his fist arriving out of the darkness too late to duck it cleanly. I rolled my head away from the blow, diminishing its sting.

I didn't hit him back, but I put up my hands to catch a second punch in case he threw one. He didn't, at least not physically.

"Go away," he said in a sobbing voice. "You and I are finished. You're finished here."

31
• • •

It was a moral hardship for me to walk away from an unclosed case. I went back to my apartment in West Los Angeles and drank myself into a moderate stupor.

Even so I didn't sleep too well. I woke up in the middle of the night. A spatter of rain was rustling like cellophane at the window. The whisky was wearing off and I saw myself in a flicker of panic: a middle-aging man lying alone in darkness while life fled by like traffic on the freeway.

I got up late and went out for breakfast. The morning papers reported no new developments. I went to my office and waited for Peter to change his mind and phone me.

I didn't really need him, I told myself. I still had some of his money. Even without it, and even without his backing in Montevista, I could go out and work with Perlberg on the Martel killing. But for some important reason I wanted him to rehire me. I think in my nighttime loneliness I'd fathered an imaginary son, a poor fat foolish son who ate his sorrow instead of drinking it.

The sun burned off the morning fog and dried the pavements. My depression lifted more slowly. I went through my mail in search of hopeful omens.

An interesting-looking envelope from Spain had pictures of General Franco on the stamps and was addressed to Señor Lew Archer. The letter inside said: "Cordiales Saludos: This comes to you from far-off Spain to call your attention to our new Fiesta line of furniture with its authentically Spanish motif as exciting as a *corrida,* as colorful as a *flamenco* dance. Come see it at any one of our Greater Los Angeles stores."

The piece of junk mail I liked best was a folder from the Las Vegas Chamber of Commerce. Among the attractions of the city it mentioned swimming, golf, tennis, bowling, waterskiing, eating, going to shows, and going to church, but not a word about gambling.

It was an omen. While I was still smiling over the folder, Captain Perlberg phoned me.

"You busy, Archer?"

"Not so very. My client lost interest."

"Too bad," he said cheerfully. "You could do us both a favor. How would you like to talk to Martel's old lady?"

"His mother?"

"That's what I said. She jetted in from Panama this morning and she's screaming for us to release her son's body, also for information. You know more about the background of the case than I do, and I thought if you were willing to talk it over with her, you could save us an international incident."

"Where is she now?"

"She took a suite in the Beverly Hills Hotel. Right at the moment she's sleeping, but she'll be expecting you early this afternoon, say around two-fifteen? She'd make a nice client for you."

"Who would pay me?"

"She would. The woman is loaded."

"I thought she was from hunger."

"You thought wrong," Perlberg said. "The consul general told me she's married to the vice-president of a bank in Panama City."

"What's his name?"

"Rosales. Ricardo Rosales."

It was the name of the vice-president of the Bank of New Granada who had written the letter to Marietta telling her that there would be no more money.

"I'll be glad to pay a visit to Mrs. Rosales."

I called Professor Allan Bosch at Los Angeles State College. Bosch said he'd be happy to have lunch with me and brief me on Pedro Domingo, but he still had a time problem.

"I can drive out there, professor. Do you have a restaurant on the L.A. State campus?"

"We have three eating places," he said. "The Cafeteria, the Inferno, and the Top of the North. Incidentally our name's been changed to Cal State L.A."

"The Inferno sounds interesting."

"It's less interesting than it sounds. Actually it's just an automat. Why don't we meet at the Top of the North? That's on top of North Hall."

The college is on the eastern border of the city. I took the Hollywood Freeway to the San Bernardino Freeway, which I left at the Eastern Avenue turnoff. The campus was a sort of chopped-off hill crowded with buildings. Parking spaces were scarce. Eventually I parked in a faculty slot, and rode the elevator six stories up to the Top of the North.

Professor Bosch was a youthful-looking man in his middle thirties, tall enough to play center on a basketball team. He had a big man's slouch, and a bright disenchanted eye. His speech was staccato, with a Middle Western accent.

"I'm surprised you made it on time. It's quite a drive. I saved us a place by the window."

He led me to a table on the east side of the large buzzing room. Through the window I could see out toward Pasadena and the mountains.

"You want me to tell you what I know about Pedro Domingo," Bosch said over our onion soup.

"Yes. I'm interested in him and his relatives. Professor Tappinger said his mother was a Blue Moon girl. That's the Panamanian equivalent of a B-girl, isn't it?"

"I guess it is." Bosch shifted his bulk in the chair and looked at me sideways across the table. "Before we go any further, why wasn't Pedro's murder reported in the papers?"

"It was. Didn't Tappinger mention that he was using an alias?"

"Taps may have, I don't remember. We both got excited, and we went round in circles for a while." His gaze narrowed on my face. "What alias was he using?"

"Francis Martel."

"That's interesting." Bosch didn't tell me why. "I did see the report of that shooting. Wasn't it supposed to be a gangster killing?"

"It was supposed to be."

"You sound dubious."

"I'm getting more and more that way."

Bosch had stopped eating. He showed no further interest in his soup. When his minute steak arrived he cut it meticulously into small pieces which he failed to eat.

"I seem to be asking most of the questions," he said. "I was interested in Pedro Domingo. He had a good mind, rather disordered but definitely brilliant. Also he had a lot of life."

"It's all run out now."

"Why was he using an alias?"

"He stole a pile of money and didn't want to be caught. Also he wanted to impress a girl who was hipped on French. He represented himself as a French aristocrat named Francis Martel. It sounds better than Pedro Domingo, especially in Southern California."

"It's almost authentic, too," Bosch said quietly.

"Authentic?"

"At least as authentic as most genealogical claims. Pedro's grandfather, his mother's father, was named Martel. He may not have been an aristocrat, exactly, but he was an educated Parisian. He came over from France as a young engineer with *La Compagnie Universelle*."

"I don't know French, professor."

"*La Compagnie Universelle du Canal Interocéanique de Panama* is the name de Lesseps gave to his canal-building company—a big name for an enormous flop. It went broke somewhere before 1890, and Grandpère Martel lost his money. He decided to stay on in Panama. He was an amateur ornithologist, and the flora and fauna intrigued him.

"Eventually he went more or less native, and spent his declining years with a girl in one of the villages. Pedro said she was descended from the first Cimarrones, the escaped slaves who fought with Francis Drake against the Spaniards. He claimed to be a direct descendant of Drake through her—that would explain the name Francis—but I think this time he was spinning a pure genealogical fantasy. Pedro went in rather heavily for fantasy."

"It's dangerous," I said, "when you start to act it out."

"I suppose it is. Anyway, that village girl was Pedro's maternal grandmother. His mother and Pedro both took the name Domingo from her."

"Who was Pedro's father?"

"He didn't know. I gathered that his mother didn't, either. She lived a disorganized life, to put it mildly. But she did keep alive the grandfather's tradition, even long after the old man died.

"There's a French tradition in Panama, anyway. Pedro's mother taught him French along with Spanish. They read together out of *Grandpère's* books. The old man had been fairly literate—his library ranged from La Fontaine and Descartes to Baudelaire—and Pedro got quite a decent education in French. You can understand why the language obsessed him. He was a slum boy, with Indian and slave blood in his veins as well as French. His Frenchness was his only distinction, his only hope of distinction."

"How can you possibly know all this, professor?"

"I spent some time with the boy. I thought he had promise, perhaps very brilliant promise, and he was keen to talk with someone who knew France. I spent a year there on a traveling fellowship," Bosch added in a depreciatory tone. "Also, in my advanced French composition courses I use a device—which incidentally I borrowed from Taps —the device of having my students write an essay, in French, explaining why they're studying the language. Pedro came up with a stunning piece about his grandfather and *la gloire*—the glory of France. I gave him an A-plus on it, my first in several years. It's the source of most of what I've been telling you."

"I don't know the language," I said, "but I'd certainly like to see that document."

"I gave it back to Pedro. He told me he sent it home to his mother."

"What was her name, do you know?"

"Secundina Domingo. She must have been *her* mother's second daughter."

"Judging by her last name, she never married."

"Apparently she didn't. But there were men in her life," Bosch said dryly. "One night I gave Pedro too much wine and he told me about the American sailors who used to come home with her. This was during the war, when he was still quite young. He and his mother had only the one room, and only one bed in the room. He had to wait on the landing when she had visitors. Sometimes he waited out there all night.

"He was devoted to his mother, and I think that experience pushed him a little over the edge. The night I'm talking about, when he got high on my *vin ordinaire*, he went into a wild oration about his country being the trampled crossroads of the world and he himself the essence of its mud, Caucasian, Indian, Negro. He seemed to identify himself with the Black Christ of Nombre de Dios, which is a famous Panamanian religious statue."

"He had Messianic delusions?"

"If he had, I wouldn't know. I'm not a psychiatrist. I think Pedro really was a ruined poet, a symbolizing idealizing soul who inherited too many problems. I admit he had some pretty weird ideas, but even the weird ones made a kind of sense. Panama was more than a country to him, more than a geographical link between North and South America. He thought it represented a basic connection between the soul and the body, the head and the heart—and that the North Americans broke the connection." He added: "And now we've killed him."

"We?"

"We North Americans."

He toyed with the dark meat congealing on his plate. I looked out toward the mountains. Above them a jet had cut a white wound in the sky.

I was getting a picture of Allan Bosch which I liked. He differed from an older type like Tappinger, who was so wrapped up in himself and his work that it made him a social eccentric. Bosch seemed genuinely concerned with his students. I said something to this effect.

He shrugged off his pleasure in the compliment. "I'm a teacher. I wouldn't want to be anything else." After a pause, which was filled with the interwoven noise of the students around us, he said: "I took it hard when Pedro had to leave here. He was just about the most interesting student I ever had, here or at Illinois. I've only taught the two places."

"Your friend Tappinger says the Justice Department was after him."

"Yes. Pedro entered the country illegally. He had to leave Long Beach and then he had to leave here, one jump ahead of the Immigration men. As a matter of fact, I tipped him that they were making inquiries about him. I'm not ashamed of it, either," he said with a half-smile.

"I won't turn you in, Dr. Bosch."

His smile became wry and defensive. "I'm afraid I'm not a Ph.D. I failed my comprehensives at Illinois. I could have tried them again, I suppose, but there wasn't much point in it."

"Why not?"

"Taps had already left. I was one of his special protégés, and I inherited a certain amount of ill will. What happened to him did nothing for my morale, either. I thought if it could happen to one of the most promising scholars in my field, it could happen to anybody."

"What happened to him at Illinois?"

Bosch went into a tight-lipped silence. I waited, and changed my angle of approach:

"Is he still a leading scholar in your field?"

"He would be if he had a decent chance. But he gets no time for his work, and it's driving him crazy. When the grants are handed out, they pass him over. He can't even get a promotion in a bush league school like Montevista."

"Why not?"

"They don't like the way he combs his hair, I guess."

"Or the way his wife combs hers?"

"I suppose she has something to do with it. But frankly I'm not interested in retailing faculty gossip. We were supposed to be talking about Pedro Domingo, alias Cervantes. If you have any more questions about him, I'll be glad to oblige. Otherwise—"

"Where did he get the name Cervantes?"

"I suggested it the night he left. He always struck me as a quixotic type."

I thought, but did not say, that the word applied more exactly to Bosch himself. "And did you send him to study under Tappinger?"

"No. I may have mentioned Taps to him at one time or another. But Pedro went to Montevista on account of a girl. She was a freshman, apparently quite gifted in languages—"

"Who said so?"

"Taps said so himself, and as a matter of fact I talked to her, too. He brought her up for our spring arts festival. We were putting on Sartre's *No Exit,* and she'd never seen a contemporary play in French before. Pedro was there, and he fell in love with her literally on sight."

"How do you know?"

"He told me. In fact he showed me some sonnets he wrote about her and her ideal beauty. She *was* a lovely thing, one of those pure pale blondes, and very young, no more than sixteen or seventeen."

"She isn't so young and she isn't so pure, but she's still a lovely thing."

He dropped his fork with a noise which merged with the continuous clatter of the room. "Don't tell me you know her."

"She's Pedro's widow. They were married last Saturday."

"I don't understand."

"If I told you all about it, it would only make you feel worse. He made up his mind to marry her seven years ago—perhaps the night he saw her here at the play. Do you know if he made any approach to her that night, or afterwards?"

Bosch considered the question. "I'm pretty sure he didn't. Morally certain, in fact. It was one of those secret passions the Latins seem to go in for."

"Like Dante and Beatrice."

He looked at me in some surprise. "You've read Dante, have you?"

"I've read at him. But I have to admit I was quoting another witness. She said Pedro followed the girl with his eyes the way Dante followed Beatrice."

"Who on earth said that?"

"Bess Tappinger. Do you know her?"

"Naturally I know her. You might say she's an authority on Dante and Beatrice."

"Really?"

"I don't mean that quite seriously, Mr. Archer. But Bess and Taps played comparable roles in their time: the intellectual and the girl ideal. They had a very beautiful Platonic thing going before they had—before real life caught up with them."

"Could you be a little clearer? I'm interested in the woman."

"In Bess?"

"In both of the Tappingers. What do you mean when you say real life caught up with them?"

He studied my face, as if to read my intentions. "There's no harm in telling you, I suppose. Practically everybody in the Modern Language Association knows the story. Bess was a sophomore studying French at Illinois and Taps was the rising young man in the department. The two of them had this Platonic thing going. They were like Adam and Eve before the Fall. Or Héloïse and Abélard. That may sound like romantic exaggeration, but it isn't. I was there.

"Then real life reared its ugly head, as I said. Bess got pregnant. Taps married her, of course, but the thing was messily handled. The Illinois campus was quite puritanical in those days. What made it worse, the Assistant Dean of Women had a crush on Taps herself, and she really hounded him. So did Bess's parents; they were a couple of bourgeois types from Oak Park. The upshot of it was, the administration fired him for moral turpitude and sent him off to the boondocks."

"And he's been there ever since?"

Bosch nodded. "Twelve years. It's a long time to go on paying for a minor mistake, which incidentally is a very common one. Teachers are marrying their students all the time, with or without shotgun accompaniment. Taps got a very raw deal, in my opinion, and it just about ruined his life. But we're wandering far afield, Mr. Archer." The young man glanced at his wristwatch. "It's half-past one, and I have an appointment with a student."

"Cancel it and come along with me. I have a more interesting appointment."

"Oh? With whom?"

"Pedro's mother."

"You're kidding."

"I almost wish I were. She flew here from Panama this morning, and she's staying at the Beverly Hills Hotel. I may need a translator. How about it?"

"Sure. We'd better go in two cars so you won't have to drive me back."

32
...

BOSCH AND I met at the desk of the hotel. I was a few minutes late for my appointment, and the clerk told us to go right up.

The woman who let us into the sitting room of the suite was fifty or so, still handsome in spite of her gold teeth and the craterlike circles under her eyes. She was dressed entirely in black. A trace of musky perfume hung around her like the smell of fire, giving her an aura of burnt-out sex.

"Señora Rosales?"

"Yes."

"I'm the private detective Lew Archer. My Spanish is not too good. I hope you speak English."

"Yes. I speak English." She looked up inquiringly at the young man beside me.

"This is Professor Bosch," I said. "He was a friend of your son's."

In an unexpected gesture of emotion, more hungry than hospitable, she gave us each a hand and drew us across the room to sit on either side of her. Her hands were those of a working woman, rough and etched with ineradicable grime. Her English was good but stiff, as if it had been worked over.

"Pedro has told me about you, Professor Bosch. You were very kind to him, and I am grateful."

"He was the best student I ever had. I'm sorry about his death."

"Yes, it is a great loss. He would have been one of our great men." She turned to me. "When will they release his body for burial?"

"Within a day or two. Your consul will arrange to ship it home. You really needn't have come here."

"So my husband said. He said I should stay out of this country, that you would arrest me and take away my money. But how can you do that? I am a Panamanian citizen, and so was my son. The money Pedro gave me belongs to me." She spoke with a kind of questioning defiance.

"To you and your husband."

"Yes, of course."

"Have you been married long?"

"Two months. A little longer than two months. Pedro was content with my marriage. He gave us as a wedding gift a villa in La Cresta. Pedro and Señor Rosales, my husband, were good friends."

She seemed to be trying to justify her marriage, as if she suspected a connection between it and her son's death. I had no doubt it was a marriage of convenience. When the vice-president of a bank in any country marries a middle-aged woman of uncertain background, there has to be a sound business reason.

"Were they business associates?"

"Pedro and Señor Rosales?" She put on a stupid mask and lifted her hands and shoulders in a shrug that half-resembled a bargaining gesture. "I know nothing of business. It is all the more remarkable that my son was so successful in business, *n'est-ce pas?* He understood the workings of the *Bourse*—you call it Wall Street, do you not? He saved his money and invested cleverly," she said in a kind of rhythmical self-hypnosis.

She must have suspected the truth, though, because she added: "It isn't true, is it, that Pedro was killed by gangsters?"

"I don't know whether it's true or not, señora. The killer hasn't been run down."

Bosch put in: "You said you doubted that it was a gangster shooting."

The woman took comfort from this. "Of course, my son had nothing to do with gangsters. He was a fine man, a great man. If he had lived, he would have become our foreign minister, perhaps our president."

She was spinning a web of fantasy to veil any possible truth that might emerge. I didn't feel like arguing with her grief, but I said:

"Did you know Leo Spillman?"

"Who?"

"Leo Spillman."

"No. Who is Leo Spillman?"

"A Las Vegas gambler. Your son was an associate of his. Didn't he ever mention Spillman to you?"

She shook her head. I could see no indication that she was lying. But there were sorrowful depths in her black eyes, depths below depths, like strata of history older than the Incas.

"You believe that Leo Spillman killed my son, is that it?"

"I thought so until yesterday. Pedro embezzled a lot of money from Spillman."

"Embezzled?" She appealed to Bosch. "*¿Que está diciendo?*"

He answered her reluctantly: "Mr. Archer thinks your son stole some money from Mr. Spillman. I don't know anything about it."

Her breath hissed through her gold teeth: "*Está diciendo mentiras. Pedro hizo su fortuna en* Wall Street."

"She says you're a liar," Bosch told me with polite pleasure.

"Thanks, I got the message." I said to her: "I'm not bringing up these matters for fun, señora. If we want to find out what happened to your son, we have to go into the question of his money. I think he was killed for his money."

"By his new wife?" she said on a rising note.

"That's a good question. The answer has to be no, but I'm interested in your reasons for asking it."

"I know women, and I know my son. He was capable of a grand— a great love. Such men are always deluded by their women."

"Do you know that Pedro was?"

"He suspected it himself. He wrote me about his fear that the woman he wished to marry did not love him. I intend to speak to the woman."

"It wouldn't be a good idea," I said. "Within the last four days she's lost both her mother and her husband. Let her be, señora."

She persisted stolidly. "I have lost more than her—than she. I wish to speak to her. I will pay you well to take me to her."

"Sorry. I can't do it."

She rose abruptly. "Then you are wasting my time."

She moved to the door and held it open for us. I was just as glad to go. I'd found out all I was likely to, really all I needed, and I wanted no part of her black money or the black mourning that went with it.

"You were pretty rough on her," Bosch said in the elevator. "She seemed quite innocent and naïve to me."

"She can afford to be. It's pretty clear her husband's the wheeler-dealer. He's latched onto her and her money, and the U.S. government will never see a penny of it."

"I don't understand. What did you mean when you said Pedro was killed for his money? His mother certainly didn't kill him."

"No, and whoever did was probably unaware that the money had passed to her."

"That leaves the field wide open, doesn't it?"

But Allan Bosch was a sensitive man, and he may have intuited the direction my mind was moving in. When we stepped out of the elevator he said goodbye and started away like a sprinter.

"I haven't finished with you, Allan."

"Oh? I wasn't much help, I'm afraid. I thought we'd have a chance to talk to the woman."

"We had our chance. She gave out more than I thought she would. Now I want another chance to talk to you."

I steered him into the bar and maneuvered him into the inside seat in a padded booth. He'd have to climb over me to get away.

I ordered a couple of gin-and-tonics. Bosch insisted on paying for his own.

"What is there left for us to talk about?" he said rather morosely.

"Love and money. And Professor Tappinger and his big mistake at Illinois. Why do you suppose he goes on paying for it twelve years after the event?"

"I have no idea."

"He wouldn't be repeating it, would he?"

"I don't quite know what you're getting at." Bosch began to scratch the back of his head. "Taps is happily married. He has three children."

"Children aren't always a deterrent. In fact I've known men who turned against their children because the kids reminded them that they weren't young themselves. As for the Tappingers' marriage, it's close to the breaking point. She's a desperate woman."

"Nonsense. Bess is a darling."

"But not his darling," I said. "I wonder if he's found another darling among his students."

"Of course not. He doesn't fool around with students."

"He did once, you tell me—"

"I shouldn't have."

"And it's a pattern of behavior that tends to repeat itself. I've had some experience in my work with men and women who can't grow up, and can't bear to grow old. They keep trying to renew themselves with younger and younger partners."

The young man's face puckered in distaste. "All that may be true. It has nothing to do with Taps, and frankly I find the topic slightly disgusting."

"It isn't pleasant for me, either. I like Tappinger, and he's treated me well. But sometimes we have to face up to unpleasant facts, even about people we like."

"You're not dealing in facts. You're simply speculating on the basis of something that happened twelve years ago."

"Are you sure it isn't still going on? Seven years ago, you tell me, Tappinger brought a girl freshman here to see a play. Were there other students in the party?"

"I don't believe so."

"Is it common practice for a professor to bring a girl student, a freshman, sixty or seventy miles to see a play?"

"It could be. I don't know. Anyway, Bess was with them."

"Why didn't you tell me that before?"

"I didn't realize it was an issue," he said with a trace of irony. "Professor Tappinger is not a sexual psychopath, you know. He doesn't require twenty-four-hour-a-day chaperonage."

"I hope he doesn't. You say you talked to the girl. Did she have anything to say about Tappinger?"

"I don't remember. It was a long time ago."

"Did you see them together?"

"Yes. In fact the three of them came to my place for dinner and then we all went to the play."

"How did Tappinger and the girl act toward each other?"

"They seemed to be fond of each other." For a moment his face opened wide—he'd remembered something—and then it closed up tight. He half rose out of his chair. "Look here, I don't know what you're getting at—"

"Of course you know what I'm getting at. Did they behave like lovers?"

Bosch answered slowly and carefully: "I don't quite get the implications of that question, Mr. Archer. And I don't see its relevance to the present. After all, we're talking about seven years ago."

"There have been three murders in those seven years, all of them connected with Ginny Fablon. Her father and mother and husband have all been killed."

"Good Lord, you're not blaming Taps?"

"It's too early to say. But you can be sure these questions are relevant. Were they lovers?"

"Bess seemed to believe they were. I thought she was imagining things at the time. Maybe she wasn't, though."

"Tell me what happened."

"It didn't amount to much. She got up and walked out in the middle of the play. We were all sitting together: Bess was between me and Taps and the girl was on his far side: and Bess suddenly got up and blundered out in the dark. I followed her. I thought she might be sick, and in fact she did lose her dinner in the parking lot. But it was more of a moral sickness than a physical one. She poured out a lot of stuff about Taps and the Fablon girl and how she was corrupting him—"

"*She* was corrupting *him?*"

"So Bess claimed. It's one reason I didn't take her too seriously. She was obviously pregnant at the time, and you know how women in that condition are sometimes crazily jealous. But possibly there was something in what she said. After all, Taps did fall for Bess when she was no older than the girl." Bosch flushed darkly, like a man being choked. "I feel like a Judas, telling you all this."

"What would that make Tappinger?"

Bosch sipped at his drink. "I see what you mean. He's not exactly a Christ-figure. Still, it's a long step from playing around with a pretty girl to murdering her parents. That's unimaginable."

"Murder usually is. Even murderers can't imagine it, or they wouldn't do it. What time did Tappinger visit you the other afternoon, Tuesday afternoon?"

"Four o'clock. He made an appointment, and he arrived on the button."

"When did he make the appointment with you?"

"Less than an hour before he arrived. He phoned and asked me when I'd be available."

"Where did he phone from?"

"He didn't say."

"What was his state of mind when he arrived?"

"You sound like a prosecuting attorney, Mr. Archer. But you're not, and I don't think I'll answer that question, or any others."

"Your friend Pedro was shot in Brentwood Tuesday afternoon. Your other friend, Tappinger, left Montevista around one. Between one and four he had time and opportunity to do the shooting, and come over to cover himself with you."

"Cover himself?"

"He used his visit to you to explain why he canceled his Tuesday afternoon classes and made the trip to Los Angeles. Can he handle a gun?"

Bosch wouldn't answer me.

"He mentioned going to school under the G.I. Bill," I said, "which means that he was in some branch of the service. Can Tappinger use a gun?"

"He was in the infantry." Bosch hung his head, as if the mounting evidence was tending to prove his own guilt. "When Taps was a boy of nineteen or twenty, he participated in the Liberation of Paris. He wasn't—he isn't a negligible man."

"I never said he was. What was his mental state when he came to you Tuesday?"

"I'm no authority on mental states. He did seem very taut, and sort of embarrassed. Of course we hadn't seen each other for years. And he'd just got off the freeway. That San Berdoo Freeway is really tough—" He cut himself short. "Taps seemed badly shaken, I can't deny that. He practically went into hysterics when I identified Pedro Domingo from the picture, and told him the basic facts about the boy."

"What did he say?"

"He didn't say much of anything. He had what you might call a laughing fit. He seemed to think it was all a tremendous joke."

33
...

Bess Tappinger came to the door with the three-year-old boy holding onto her skirt. She had on a torn and faded sleeveless cotton dress, as if she was dressing the part of an abandoned wife. Sweat ran down her face from under the cloth she had tied around her head. When she wiped her face with her forearm, I could see sweat glistening in her shaven armpit.

"Why didn't you tell me you were coming? I've been cleaning the house."

"So I see."

"Will you give me time to take a shower? I must look hideous."

"As a matter of fact you look fine. But I didn't come for the view. Is your husband at home?"

"No. He isn't." Her voice was subdued.

"Is he at the college?"

"I don't know. Won't you come in? I'll make some coffee. And I'll get rid of little one. He hasn't had his nap."

She led the protesting child away. When she came back, a long quarter of an hour later, she had bathed, changed her dress, and brushed her dark thick hair.

"I'm sorry to keep you waiting. I *had* to get cleaned up. Whenever I feel really bad, I get this passion for cleaning." She sat on the chesterfield beside me and let me smell how clean she was.

"What do you feel bad about?"

Suddenly, she thrust out her red lower lip. "I don't feel like talking about it. I felt like talking yesterday, but you didn't." Abruptly she got to her feet and stood above me, handsome and still trembling with expectancy, as if the body that had got her into her marriage might somehow get her out of it. "You don't want to be bothered with me at all."

"On the contrary, I'd like to go to bed with you right now."

"Why don't you then?" She didn't move, but her body seemed to be more massively there.

"There's a child in the house, and a husband in the wings."

"Taps wouldn't care. In fact I think he was trying to promote it."

"Why would he do that?"

"He'd like to see me fall in love with another man—somebody to take me off his hands. He's in love with another girl. He has been for years."

"Ginny Fablon."

As if the name had loosened her knees, she sat down beside me again. "You know about her then. How long have you known?"

"Just today."

"I've known about it from the beginning."

"So I've been told."

She gave me a quick sidewise look. "Have you discussed this with Taps?"

"Not yet. I just had lunch with Allan Bosch. He told me about a certain night seven years ago when he and you and your husband and Ginny went to a play together."

She nodded. "It was Sartre's *No Exit.* Did he tell you what I saw?"

"No. I don't believe he knew."

"That's right, I didn't tell him. I couldn't bring myself to tell him, or anyone. And after a while the thing I saw didn't seem real anymore. It sort of merged with my memory of the play, which is about three people living in a kind of timeless psychological hell.

"I was sitting next to Taps in the near-dark and I heard him let out a little grunt, or sigh, almost as if he'd been hurt. I looked. She had her hand on his—on his upper leg. He was sighing with pleasure.

"I couldn't believe it, even though I saw it. It made me so sick I had to get out of the place. Allan Bosch came out after me. I don't remember exactly what I said to him. I've deliberately avoided seeing him since, for fear that he might ask me questions about Taps."

"What were you afraid of?"

"I don't know. Yes, I do know, really. I was afraid if people found that Taps had corrupted the girl, or been corrupted—I was afraid that he'd lose his job and any chance of a job. I'd seen what happened at Illinois, when Taps and I—" She caught herself. "But you don't know about that."

"Allan Bosch told me."

"Allan is a terrible tattletale." But she seemed relieved not to have to tell me herself. "I suppose I had some guilt left over from that. I almost felt as if Ginny Fablon was re-enacting *me.* It didn't make me hate her any less, but it tied my tongue. I seemed to have spent the last seven years concealing my husband's love affair, even from myself. But I'm not going to do it after today."

"What happened today?"

"Actually it happened early this morning, before dawn. She telephoned him here. He was sleeping in the study, as he has for years, and he took the call on the extension there. I listened in on the other phone. She was in a panic—a cold panic. She said that you were hounding her, and she couldn't keep up a front any longer, especially since she didn't know what had happened. Then she asked him if he killed her father and mother. He said of course not: the question was ridiculous: what motive would he have? She said because they knew about her baby, that he was the father."

Bess had been speaking very rapidly. She paused now with her fingers at her lips, listening to what she'd said.

"Who told them, Bess?"

"I did. I held my tongue until September of that first year. That summer, when my own baby was born, the girl dropped out of sight. I thought we were rid of her. But then she turned up again at the *Cercle Français* icebreaker. Taps took her home that night—I think he was trying to keep her away from Cervantes. When he came back to the house we had a quarrel, as I told you. He had the gall to say I was interested in Cervantes in the same way he was interested in the girl. Then he told me about the abortion the girl had had to have. I was to blame, just because I existed. I was supposed to get down on my knees and weep for the girl, I suppose.

"I did weep, off and on for a couple of weeks. Then I couldn't stand it any longer. I called the girl's father and told him about Taps. He disappeared within a day or two, and I blamed myself for his suicide. I decided I would never speak out about anything." Again she seemed to be listening to her own words. Their meaning seeped into her eyes and spread like darkness. "Do *you* think my husband killed Mr. Fablon and Mrs. Fablon?"

"We'll have to ask him, Bess."

"You think he did, don't you?" Even as she asked the question, she was nodding dolefully. "Her mother phoned here the other night."

"Which night?"

"Monday. Wasn't that the night she was shot?"

"You know it was. What did she say?"

"She asked for Taps, and he took the call in the house. I didn't have a chance to listen in. Anyway, it didn't amount to anything. He said he'd talk to her, and went out."

"He left the house?"

"Yes."

"What time?"

"It must have been quite late. I was on my way to bed. I was asleep when he came in."

"Why didn't you tell me this before?"

"I wanted to, yesterday morning. You didn't give me a chance." Her eyes were wide and blind, like a statue's.

"Was anything else said on the phone this morning?"

"He said he loved her, that he had always loved her and always would. I said something into the phone then. It was a dirty word: it just came out. It seemed so terrible to me that he could speak like that to another woman with our three children sleeping in the house.

"I went out to the study in my nightgown. It was the first time I'd gone to him since little one was conceived—our last happy time." She paused, listening, as if the three-year-old had cried out in his sleep. But the house was so quiet I could hear water dripping in the kitchen sink. "Since then our life has been like camping on ice, on lake ice. I did that once with Daddy in Wisconsin. You find yourself thinking of the ice as solid ground, though you know there's deep dark water underneath." She looked down at the worn rug under her feet, as if there were monsters swimming just below it. "I suppose in a way I was collaborating with them, wasn't I? I don't know why I did it, or why I felt as I did. It was *my* marriage, and she was breaking it up, but somehow I felt out of it. I was just a member of the wedding. I felt as if it wasn't my life. My life hasn't even started."

We sat and listened to the dripping silence. "You were going to tell me what happened when you went out to the study early this morning."

She shrugged. "I hate to think about it. Taps was sitting at his desk with the gun in his hand. He looked so thin and sharp-nosed, the way people look when they're going to die. I was afraid he was going to shoot himself, and I went to him and asked him for the gun. It was almost an exact reversal of what happened the night that little one was conceived. And it was the same gun."

"I don't understand."

She said: "I bought that gun to kill myself with four years ago. It was a secondhand revolver I found in a pawnshop. Taps had been out night after night with the girl, pretending to be tutoring, and I just couldn't stand it any longer. I decided to destroy all three of us."

"With the gun?"

"The gun was just for myself. Before I used it I called Mrs. Fablon and told her what I was going to do and why. She'd known of the affair, of course, but she didn't know who the man was. She'd assumed that Taps was merely Ginny's tutor, a kind of fatherly figure in the background.

"Anyway, she got in touch with Taps wherever he was and he rushed home and took the gun away from me. I was glad. I didn't want to use it. I even managed to convince myself that Taps loved me. But all he had in mind was avoiding a scandal—another scandal.

"Mrs. Fablon didn't want one, either. She made Ginny drop out of college and go to work for some clinic near the hospital. For a while I thought that the affair was over. I was pregnant again, with our third child, and Taps would never leave me, he promised he wouldn't. He said he threw my suicide gun in the ocean.

"But he was lying. He'd kept it all these years. When I tried to take it away from him this morning, he turned it on me. He said I deserved to die for using a filthy word in Ginny's hearing. She was absolutely pure and beautiful, he said. But I was a filthy toad.

"I took off my nightgown, I don't know why exactly, I just wanted him to see me. He said my body looked like a man's face, a long lugubrious face with pink accusing eyes and a noseless nose like a congenital syphilitic and a silly little beard." Her hands moved from her breast to the region of her navel, then lower to the center of her body.

"He ordered me out and said he'd shoot me if I ever showed myself in his private room again. I went back into the house. The children were still sleeping. It wasn't light yet. I sat and watched it grow light. Some time after dawn I heard him go out and drive away in the Fiat. I got the children off to school and then I started cleaning. I've been cleaning ever since."

"You say he isn't at the college?"

"No. The Dean's office called this morning to see if he was ill. I said he was."

"Did he take the revolver with him?"

"I don't know. I haven't been in the study, and I don't intend to go in. It will have to stay dirty."

I made a quick search of the study. No gun. I did find in a desk drawer about twenty versions of the opening page of Tappinger's "book" about French influences on Stephen Crane. The most recent version, which Tappinger had been working on when I first came here Monday, was lying on top of the desk.

"Stephen Crane," it began, "lived like a god in the adamantine city of his mind. Where did he find the prototype of that city? In Athens the marmoreal exemplar of the West, or in the supernal blueprint which Augustine bequeathed to us in his *Civitas Dei*? Or was it in Paris the City of Art? Perchance he looked on his whore's body with the massive cold pity of Manet's *Olympe*. Perchance the luminous city of his mind was delved from the mud of Cora's loins."

It sounded like gibberish to me. And it suggested that Tappinger was breaking up, had been breaking up when I first walked in on him.

Beside the hopeless manuscript lay a rough draft of the five questions he had devised for Martel:

"1. Who responsible for *Les Liaisons* old and new?
"2. 'Hypocrite lecteur'
"3. Who believed Dreyfus guilty?
"4. Where Descartes put soul? (pineal gland)
"5. Who got Jean Genet out of jail?"

Seeing the questions as they had occurred to Tappinger, I realized their personal significance. He had used them, perhaps unconsciously, to speak of the things that were driving him close to the edge: a dangerous sexual liaison, hypocrisy, guilt and imprisonment, the human soul trapped in a gland.

If the questions had seemed oddly one-sided to me, it was because they were answers, too, forced out in a kind of code by Tappinger's moral and emotional conflict. I recalled with a slight shock that the answer to the fifth question had been Sartre, and wondered if, in Tappinger's queer complex academic code, it referred to the night at the play seven years before.

34
· · ·

THE ABSENCE of the gun probably meant that Tappinger was carrying it. I went outside and got my own gun and harness out of the trunk of my car. Because there were children in the street, I retreated into the house to put the harness on.

"You're going to kill him," Bess said. She looked widowed already.

"I won't use this unless he forces me to. I have to protect myself."

"What will become of the children?"

"That will be pretty much up to you."

"Why should it be up to me?" she said in her little-girl voice. "Why did this have to happen to me?"

You married the wrong man at the wrong time for the wrong reasons, I told her silently. But there was no use saying it out loud. She already knew it. In fact she had been telling me about it, in her own queer inarticulate little way, ever since I met her.

"At least you've survived. That's something to be thankful for, Bess."

She raised her fist in an impatient, almost threatening, gesture. "I don't want to survive, not this way."

"You might as well. The life you live may be your own."

The prospect frightened her. "Don't leave me by myself."

"I have to. Why don't you call one of your friends?"

"We don't have any. They dropped away long ago."

She seemed to be lost in her own house. I tried to kiss her goodbye. It wasn't a good idea. Her mouth was unresponsive, her body as stiff as a board.

The thought of her stayed with me, poignant and unsatisfying, as I drove across town toward the Fablon house. Perhaps below the level of consciousness, down where the luminous monsters swam in the cold darkness, Bess was in love with her husband's love affair.

Ginny was at home, and he was with her. His gray Fiat stood under the oak tree. When I knocked on the front door, they answered it together. He was red-eyed and sallow. She was shivering.

"Maybe you can make him stop talking," she said. "He's been talking for hours and hours."

"What about?"

"I forbid you to say." Tappinger's voice was hoarse and unnatural. "Go away," he said to me.

"Please don't," she said. "I'm afraid of him. He killed Roy and the others. That's what he's been talking about all day—all the reasons why he had to kill Roy. And he keeps giving different reasons, like he saw Roy kneeling by the pool trying to wash his bloody face and he felt so sorry for him that he pushed him in. That's the euthanasia reason. Then there's the St.-George-and-the-dragon reason: Roy was delivering me into the hands of Mr. Ketchel and something had to be done to stop it."

Her voice was savage and scornful. Tappinger winced under it. "You mustn't make fun of me."

"This is making fun?" She turned to me. "The real reason was very simple. You guessed it last night. I'd been pregnant by him, and Roy found out somehow that Taps was the father."

"You let me think it was Peter."

"I know I did. But I'm not covering up for Taps any longer."

He gasped as if he had been holding his breath. "You mustn't talk like that. Someone might hear you. Why don't we go inside?"

"I like it here."

She planted herself more firmly in the doorway. He was afraid to leave her. He had to hear what she might say.

"What were you doing at the Tennis Club that night, professor?"

His eyes veered and then held steady. "I went there for purely professional reasons. Miss Fablon had been my student since February. I counseled her, and she confided in me."

"Did I not," she said.

He went on spinning out his string of words as if it was his only support in a void: "She confided that her father, with the aid of a scholarship from a Mr. Ketchel, was going to send her to a school in Switzerland. I felt that my advice as an educator would be useful to them, and I went to the club to offer it.

"I got there rather too late to be of use. I saw Mr. Fablon staggering across the lawn, and when I spoke to him he didn't know me. He stumbled into the pool enclosure, apparently with some idea of washing his face, which was bleeding, and before I knew it he had fallen in. I'm not a swimmer myself, but I tried to fish him out with a pole they keep for that purpose, with a padded hook on the end—"

"You mean," she said, "you used it to hold him under water."

"That's a ridiculous accusation. Why do you keep repeating it?"

"Francis gave me an eyewitness account the other night. I didn't believe him then—I thought he was making it up out of jealousy. But I believe him now. He saw you push Roy in and hold him under with the pole."

"Why didn't he interfere if he was there?" Tappinger said pedantically. "Why didn't he report it?"

"I don't know." She peered up past me at the declining sun, as if it might abandon her, leave her in cold darkness. "There are a lot of things I don't understand."

"Did you take them up with your mother Monday night?" I said.

"Some of them. I asked her if it could be true that Taps drowned Roy in the swimming pool. I shouldn't have, I suppose. The idea seemed to throw her."

"I know it did. I talked to her after you left. And after that she talked to Tappinger on the phone. That was her last talk. He came here and shot her."

He said without conviction: "I did not."

"Yes you did, Taps." Her voice was grave. "You killed her, and then the next day you came to Brentwood and killed Francis."

"But I had no reason to kill either of them." There was a questioning note in his denial.

"You had plenty of reasons."

"What were they?" I said to both of them.

They turned and looked at each other as if each felt the other possessed the answer, the multiple answer. I was struck by the curious resemblance between them, in spite of their differences in sex and age. They were very nearly the same height and weight, and they had the same fine regular features. They could have been brother and sister. I wished they had been.

"What were the reasons for killing Martel?" I said.

They went on looking into each other's faces, as if each were a dream figure in the other's dream which had to be interpreted.

"You were jealous of Francis, weren't you?" Ginny finally said.

"That's nonsensical."

"Then you're nonsensical, because you're the one who said it in the first place. You wanted me to call the whole thing off."

I said: "What whole thing was that?"

Neither of them spoke. They looked at me with a kind of dimly comprehended shame, like children caught in forbidden play. I said:

"You were going to kill him and inherit his money, weren't you? But it's always the con artist who gets conned. You were so full of your own wild dreams that you believed his stories. You didn't know or care that his money was embezzled from an income-tax evader."

"That's not true," Ginny said. "Francis told me the whole story of his life last weekend. It's true he started out as a poor boy in Panama. But he was a direct descendant of Sir Francis Drake through his mother, and he had a parchment map which was handed down in the family, showing the location of Drake's buried treasure. Francis found the treasure, over a million dollars' worth of Peruvian gold, on the coast of Panama near Nombre de Dios."

I didn't argue with her. It no longer mattered what she believed, or said that she believed.

"And it isn't true," she went on, "that we planned to kill him, or anybody. The original plan was for me to marry Peter. I was simply to divorce him and get a settlement, so that Taps and I could go away—"

He shook his head at her in quick short arcs. His hair frizzed out like a woman's.

"Go away and study in Europe?" I said.

"Yes. Taps thought if he could get back to France that he could write his book. He'd been trying to get it started for years. I was getting desperate, too. It got so shabby, making love in the backs of cars, or in his office, or in a public motel. Sometimes I felt as if everyone on the campus, everyone in town, must know about us. But nobody ever said a word."

"You mustn't tell him all this," Tappinger said. "Don't admit anything."

She shrugged. "What difference does it make now?"

I said: "You originally planned to marry Peter and divorce him, is that right?"

"Yes, but I hated to do it to him. I only agreed because we were desperate for money. I've always liked Peter. When Francis came here and asked me to marry him, I switched the plan. I didn't owe Francis anything."

"You were attracted to him." The words seemed to come out of Tappinger's mouth involuntarily, as if a ventriloquist was using him as a dummy.

"I said you were jealous of him, didn't I?"

He sputtered. "Jealous? How could I be jealous? I never even saw the man, until—" He shut his mouth, biting back the words.

"Until you shot him," she said.

"I tell you I didn't shoot him. How would I know where to find him?"

"I gave you the address. I shouldn't have. Francis told me after you shot him that it was you. He said it was the same man who killed Roy."

"He said that because he hated me."

"Why would that be?" I said.

"Because Ginny and I were lovers."

"You admit it, do you?"

His mouth worked, trying to produce the words that would support him over the void. "We were lovers in the Platonic sense, I mean to say."

She looked at him scornfully. "You're not even a man. I'm sorry I ever let you touch me."

He was trembling, as if her shivering chill had infected him. "You mustn't talk to me like that, Ginny."

"Because you're so *sensitif?* You're about as sensitive as a mad dog. I doubt that you know any more about what you're doing than a mad dog does."

He cried out: "How dare you treat me with disrespect? You were an ignorant girl. I made a woman of you. I admitted you to the intimacy of my mind—"

"I know, the luminous city. Only it isn't so luminous. The last dim little light went out Monday night, when you shot Marietta."

His whole body leaned toward her suddenly, as if he was going to attack her. But the movement was inhibited. I was there.

"I can't stand this." He turned away abruptly and almost ran into the sitting room.

"Be careful of him," Ginny said. "He has a gun in there. He was trying to talk me into a suicide pact."

The gun coughed apologetically. We found Tappinger lying on the floor of the room where he had shot Marietta. The revolver he had used on her and Martel had left a dark hole in his own temple. The briefcase of money stood behind the door, as if he hadn't dared to let it out of his sight.

I took the revolver, which still had three rounds in the chambers, and went next door to telephone the county police. Peter became very excited. He wanted to come back to the Fablon house and look after Ginny. He was the one who needed looking after. I ordered him to stay home.

It was just as well I did. She was lying on the sitting room floor face to face with Tappinger, their profiles interlocking like complementary shapes cut from a single piece of metal. She lay there with him, silent and unmoving, until the noise of sirens was heard along the road. Then she got up and washed her face and composed herself.

A NOTE ON THE TYPE

THE TEXT of this book was set on the Linotype in Fairfield, a type face designed by the distinguished American artist and engraver Rudolph Ruzicka. This type displays the sober and sane qualities of a master craftsman whose talent has long been dedicated to clarity. Rudolph Ruzicka was born in Bohemia in 1883 and came to America in 1894. He has designed and illustrated many books and has created a considerable list of individual prints in a variety of techniques.

A NOTE ABOUT THE AUTHOR

Ross MacDonald was born near San Francisco in 1915. He was educated in Canadian schools, traveled widely in Europe, and acquired advanced degrees and a Phi Beta Kappa key at the University of Michigan. In 1938 he married a Canadian girl who is now well known as the novelist Margaret Millar. Mr. Macdonald (Kenneth Millar in private life) taught school and later college, and served as Communications Officer aboard an escort carrier in the Pacific. For over twenty years he has lived in Santa Barbara and written mystery novels about the fascinating and changing society of his native state. Among his leading interests are conservation and politics. He is a past president of Mystery Writers of America. In 1964 his novel *The Chill* was given a Silver Dagger award by the Crime Writers' Association of Great Britain. His *The Far Side of the Dollar* was named the best crime novel of 1965 by the same organization. And *The Moving Target* was made into the highly successful movie, *Harper*, 1966.